the company of the dead

the company of the dead

david j. kowalski

TITAN BOOKS

The Company of the Dead

Print edition ISBN: 9780857686664
E-book ISBN: 9780857686671

Published by Titan Books
A division of Titan Publishing Group Ltd
144 Southwark St, London SE1 0UP

First edition: March 2012
10 9 8 7 6 5 4 3 2 1

This is a work of fiction. Names, characters, places, and incidents either are the product of the author's imagination or are used fictitiously, and any resemblance to actual persons, living or dead, business establishments, events, or locales is entirely coincidental. The publisher does not have any control over and does not assume any responsibility for author or third-party websites or their content.

Visit our website: **www.titanbooks.com**

What did you think of this book? We love to hear from our readers. Please email us at: readerfeedback@titanemail.com, or write to us at the above address.

To receive advance information, news, competitions, and exclusive offers online, please sign up for the Titan newsletter on our website: www.titanbooks.com

A CIP catalogue record for this title is available from the British Library.

Printed and bound in the USA.

For Lisa

OVERTURE

Phlebas the Phoenician, a fortnight dead,
Forgot the cry of gulls, and the deep sea swell
And the profit and loss.
A current under sea
Picked his bones in whispers. As he rose and fell
He passed the stages of his age and youth
Entering the whirlpool.
Gentile or Jew
O you who turn the wheel and look to windward,
Consider Phlebas, who was once handsome and tall as you.

I

April 14, 1912
North Atlantic

Jonathan Wells stood by the starboard railing, a gaunt figure in a dinner jacket. His coat billowed gently, borne by the ocean liner's rapid passage. His hair, thick and black, lay damp against his brow. His eyes blinked and watered in the frigid air. The strFJains of a Strauss waltz rose from somewhere behind him, a low, soft melody that was swiftly surrendered to the night.

I've entered uncharted waters, he thought. *Hic sunt dracones. Here there be dragons.*

The magnitude of his undertaking began to dawn upon him. Tentatively he placed both hands on the ship's rail. It was one final test of reality, one final test of faith. Cold steel retaliated with teeth of ice. He held his grip till the burn of it receded to numbness.

Two hours earlier he'd found one of the lookouts, alone on the forecastle deck.

"A cold night, isn't it, Mr Fleet."

"Aye, sir," the man had responded with steady deference. "And it's going to get colder."

"I believe it's your watch."

Fleet nursed a steaming mug of coffee. He nodded between mouthfuls.

Wells withdrew a package from under his coat. "I've been asked by Mr Andrews to supply you with these."

Fleet's eyes widened at the shipbuilder's name. Since leaving Southampton four days ago, Thomas Andrews had busied himself about the vessel, attending to minor design flaws and overseeing last-minute repairs. Wells hoped that the delivery of these binoculars would be seen as merely another example of Andrews' attention to detail.

The crewman turned them over in his hands, studying them in admiration. The binoculars were remarkably compact and extremely light by comparison with the standard issue.

Drop them, Wells thought, *and it simply wasn't meant to be.* His pulse was racing now. He realised he was holding his breath. He exhaled slowly. "They're German," he said. "The latest design."

"Bugger me if I can't see all the way to Dover," Fleet marvelled. He reddened at the sudden outburst and doffed his cap, apologising.

Wells, concerned with other white cliffs, offered a polite smile. He'd seen this night play itself out a thousand times in his dreams. He fought the urge to tell the lookout everything he knew. "Just keep a sharp watch, Mr Fleet," he murmured. "Good night."

He walked away briskly, mute fears clawing at his resolve. He had two hours to kill.

Seeking distraction he toured the Café Parisien and the first-class lounge. He tried to appear relaxed. In the mahogany-panelled smoking room he bought a round of drinks and spoke with a number of its regulars. Even to the last he maintained his one strict, if morbid, rule. His one pessimistic precaution. Captain Smith, Thomas Andrews, Harry Widener, Isidor Straus, Benjamin Guggenheim, John Jacob Astor: he only kept company with the dead. There'd be time enough to forge new acquaintances when the deed was done.

He returned to the boat deck, his agitation mounting. He could feel the bourbon's warmth slowly leaking from his bones. He glanced towards the ship's stern and watched as a young couple emerged from the aft stairwell, their burst of laughter cut short by the sudden cold. They huddled together and after a brief exchange returned to the warmth within.

Wells allowed himself a moment's pride. They'd never know how cold this night could get.

Resuming his vigil he was startled by the brittle clang of the ship's bell. Three sharp reports issued from the darkness above. The final peal still rang over the waters as he reached for his watch.

Half eleven. Nodding slowly to himself, he replaced the timepiece. His hands shook violently.

"Steady," he murmured.

He was almost certain that he could feel the ship altering course beneath his feet. Somewhere, orders were being given and received, calloused hands were straining against levers. Fleet must have accomplished his task, for slowly but inexorably their course was shifting.

"Steady..."

He could feel it. The flutter of butterfly wings that would herald a brighter, better world. He looked out to the flat, calm ocean, the moonless night. Beyond the ship's illumination the dark waters rose up so that he felt as if he and the ship lay at the centre of a vast opaque bowl. Then, at a distance, under the starlight's dim flicker, he saw it. First, a jagged edge, then two irregular peaks, riding black against the black night sky.

Long minutes passed as the iceberg faded from view. A new melody coursed up from behind him: ragtime. He found himself tapping his foot to the muted rhythm. He turned so that his back now rested against the railing and his face basked in the reflected light of a multitude of windows.

Towards the ship's bow two crewmen shared a cigarette. They stamped their feet while talking, the cigarette smoke mingling with their fogged exhalations. He approached the entrance to the Grand Staircase, a smile slowly forming on his lips. By the time he reached the crewmen he was laughing openly. They glanced in his direction, nodded respectfully, and returned to their conversation, hushed and conspiratorial in the cathedral night.

Entering the Grand Staircase he peered upwards. The glass dome filtered out the night sky. A chandelier illuminated the room, its own constellation. One of the stewards silently appeared at his side. "Up late, sir?" he said.

"Just taking a turn on the deck. It's a beautiful night. Almost perfect."

The steward nodded doubtfully and vanished into the first-class lounge.

Wells descended the stairwell two steps at a time. Down three flights and he was on C deck. The door to the purser's office was ajar, the elevator unattended. Here, apart from the soft footfall of other passengers and crewmen down other corridors, and the low steady thrum of the engines, all was silent. He walked down the hallway, withdrew a key from his coat pocket and entered his cabin.

The room was cool and dark. He lit the lamp. He crossed to the porthole, placed an outstretched palm against the wall and opened the window, taking in a lungful of cold, crisp air before closing it. Removing his scarf, he drew an ornate chair up to a table that was bare apart from a dog-eared journal. He took a pen from his breast pocket, inspected its nib, and turning to a blank page began to write.

II

April 14, 2012
North Atlantic

The night had passed without incident.

Lightholler decided to take advantage of the forenoon watch's arrival to spend a few moments on deck. His mug of coffee sat on a window ledge near the ship's wheel, a film of condensation blooming on the thick pane above it. Picking up the mug, he ran a fingernail in lazy swirls on the misted glass. He gazed seawards and spied the bridge's reflection: his spectral crew superimposed upon the Atlantic dawn. He focused on the image. Men stood gesturing animatedly against a tableau of gauges and switches; Johnson was handing the ship's wheel over to the first officer. He caught a glimpse of himself and examined the square-jawed, sloe-eyed face that belonged more to a prize fighter than a ship's officer.

He moved away from the window and stepped out onto the deck. He walked over to the first of the lifeboat davits and glanced back over his shoulder at the squat tower of the bridge. The sun crept weakly across the officers' promenade. Lightholler let its warmth seep into his bones and looked out to sea. The tapered ribbon of land that had drawn his eyes at first light was now a thickened crust on the horizon. Above it the threat of thin dark cloud mirrored the image below.

He stood for a while, taking occasional sips from his coffee. He didn't hear the approach of footsteps behind him until he saw a taller shadow engulf his own.

"Almost there, sir," came a familiar voice. Lightholler turned and had to raise an arm to shield his eyes against the morning sun.

"Not long at all now, Mr Johnson," he replied to his second officer. "We should make harbour by noon."

"We're still riding low in the water, sir."

"I know," Lightholler replied carefully.

The two stood in silence for a few moments.

"Aren't you even curious, sir?" Johnson ventured finally.

"We're ferrying eight of the world's most important political figures across the Atlantic, Mr Johnson. Curiosity is a luxury we can hardly afford."

"Sir, we're riding low in the water, and I can't account for it in our cargo manifest. We're carrying something we don't know about."

Lightholler remained silent.

"I'm talking about E deck, sir," Johnson pressed, his voice low.

"E deck has been sealed off for repairs, Mister Johnson, and we have our orders."

"I'm an officer of the White Star Line, sir, so why do I feel like a smuggler?"

Lightholler turned again to survey the darkening shore and frowned. "Smugglers usually know what they're carrying."

Johnson excused himself and left. Lightholler listened as the footsteps faded away behind him and took another mouthful of coffee. It was cold.

Seabirds could be seen wheeling and hovering over the ship's prow. As she drew nearer to shore, their numbers swelled, driven by the oncoming storm. The morning's breeze rose to a brisk wind that raced along the decks and howled through the maze of her superstructure.

The sun was lost within a fold of heavy cloud, turning the ocean blue-black. Waves beat and broke against the ship's hull in sprays of white froth, the water parting unwillingly before her steady advance. Along the foredeck, men scurried back and forth between the wireless room and the bridge, heads down, scraps of paper clutched to chests or beneath jacket folds, bearing a stream of radio traffic.

Lightholler returned to the darkened wheelhouse and turned his attention to the amassed correspondence that awaited him there: confirmations of arrival times, changes in docking procedures, and offers of congratulations that seemed premature in the face of the approaching squall.

He examined the close-circuit screens, the only anachronism permitted aboard his floating memorial. A light rain from the west drizzled against freshly scrubbed decks, driving most of the passengers indoors. On the poop deck some people stubbornly remained standing by the ship's rail or seated on benches out of the wind's path. He cued the audio. The occasional shouts of children merged with the squawks and cries of circling gulls. At the ship's stern a flag—white star on red—slapped against its pole with every sudden gust.

Passengers sat in the Palm Court drinking tea and coffee, listening to a string quartet play Mozart. In the smoking room they stood in small clusters discussing the recent events in Europe and Asia; the talk mostly of war. The majority, though, would be in their cabins and staterooms, packing away the last of their belongings. The ship sailed on, buffeted by rough wind and water, but in the lounges and dining rooms the only reflection of the turbulence was the gentle swish of liquid in crystal decanters. In fully laden cargo holds, naked light bulbs swung pendulously, marking the ship's passage in wide arcs.

By the time lunch was announced, the rain had passed and the wind had dropped to a caress. A wall of grey fog greeted passengers who had been summoned on deck by the knock of a steward at the door or the trumpet call of young boys in brass-buttoned jackets. The ship lay swathed in a blanket of cloud, occasional beams of sunlight shining through gaps in the haze like the face of God.

Lightholler sent word to the wireless room, giving instructions to alert the harbourmaster. They would be arriving at dock shortly. He requested that a pilot be standing by to guide the ship up the Hudson to the newly constructed pier on Manhattan's lower west side. Then, for the first time in days, he allowed himself to relax. The politics and the ice floes lay well behind them. Staring out of the bridge window into the swirling haze, he allowed a smile to form on his face and contemplated his evening ashore.

III

Manhattan lay crouched in the fog.

The ferries to Liberty Island had ceased running at eleven o'clock due to overcrowding. Later estimates suggested that there were twelve thousand people in Battery Park that day, but no one could say how many people swarmed around the terminal and streets surrounding piers nineteen and twenty. From the pebble-strewn beaches of Brooklyn, on past Governors and Ellis islands to the Jersey shore, a flotilla of small boats and yachts rose and fell among the waves. Every now and then a shout would rise from somewhere in the multitude, swell to a roar and fade away in false alarm.

Finally, wreathed in the last of the fog, she appeared on the horizon. At first, in the distance, it appeared as though a small part of the city, its prodigal, was returning home. The great ship grew from the armada's midst, billows of smoke rising from her funnels and swirling into the clouds above. The small fleet scampered and parted before her prow. The liner's promenades brimmed with passengers, shouting and waving. All along the boat deck the ship's officers stood at rigid attention as she steamed past Liberty Island.

A small group of tugboats detached themselves from the piers off Battery Park and slalomed a path through the wall of pleasure crafts to the approaching leviathan.

Lightholler, standing at the ship's wheel, turned to the first officer and gave the order. Blast after blast emerged from the ship's foghorn. Johnson, at his station on the forecastle deck, signalled the release of the rockets and one by one they screamed, piercing the dense veil above to explode in flares of blue and white.

New York replied with a series of fireworks that erupted into the grey skies from countless barges. Fire ships in the bay shot jets of steaming water hundreds of feet into the air, turning the heavens into a deluge of rainbows where the sun caught the spray. A cacophony of horns and trumpets bellowed from red-faced men lining the shores and crowding the bobbing boats.

Lightholler and the first officer stood in the wheelhouse watching the spectacle that played out before them.

"Well, sir, we did it," the first officer said.

"Better late than never, Mr Fordham." Lightholler smiled.

Giant airships slowly descended from the heavens. German Zeppelins competed with Chinese Skyjunks and Confederate dirigibles, bearing messages of greeting in a host of languages. A century overdue, but heartily welcome, the *Titanic* nudged her way into New York Harbor.

THE BURIAL OF THE DEAD

I

April 21, 2012
New York City, Eastern Shogunate

Captain John Jacob Lightholler woke with a start. Having spent the better part of a fortnight aboard the *Titanic*, he was pleasantly reassured to find himself in his hotel suite at the Waldorf-Astoria.

Nightmares had plagued him through the restless nights at sea. Never an easy sleeper, he'd attributed them to fatigue, yet still they persisted. By daylight they would slip from his mind, leaving a filmy residue that often darkened his mood. Nightly, he would find himself back aboard the ship, not as its captain but as a fixture of the vessel. A figurehead like those that had adorned the ships of old, pinned to the prow as it ploughed forwards into a shelf of ice that stretched out, vast as a continent, before him.

The last few days were a blur. Speeches, luncheons, keys to the city. He'd been hounded by the media, who delighted in reporting the fact that he was a direct descendant of two of the original *Titanic*'s most notable voyagers: Charles Lightholler, the ship's second officer; and John Jacob Astor, the first-class passenger who had gone on to become the Union's third president. It served to distract the public from the darker aspects of the voyage.

The last-minute inclusion of the Russo-Japanese peace talks aboard ship had proved a disappointment. Under the supervision of the supposedly neutral German diplomats, no satisfactory conclusion had been reached. What had begun as a skirmish between Russian and Japanese soldiers over a border town in Manchuria held the threat of becoming a full-scale war. Newspapers carried accounts of mounting violence in Asia and the eastern provinces of Russia as the Japanese Imperial forces held to their westwards advance.

Both the Russians and the Japanese on board had maintained a veneer of civility, despite the inconclusive nature of the peace talks. Over the past week, under the pretence of social gatherings, Lightholler had been closely questioned by Russian and Japanese envoys alike; both parties displaying a surprising interest in his take on the conference. The Germans, who had up till now remained out of the escalating conflict in Asia, seemed particularly intrigued by his opinions on the subject.

He licked parchment-dry lips. His head throbbed.

He gingerly picked up the phone at his bedside and ordered breakfast and the morning paper. He was told that a stack of messages awaited him at the lobby desk. He replaced the phone and lay back on the bed, gazing dreamily at the ceiling, lulled sleepwards by the faint sounds of the New York morning that drifted through his hotel window.

He was jolted out of his reverie by a knock at the door. He eased himself out of the bed and grabbed a dressing gown that lay draped over his bedside chair. He padded down the short hallway to the door and opened it. Three men stood there, decked out in grey suits. They shared the haggard appearance of journalists chasing an elusive story.

"I'm not doing any interviews today," he said.

"We're not reporters, Captain," the tallest of them said with a ready smile. "We're here on government business." His voice, rich in timbre, held the slightest tremor.

Lightholler couldn't place the accent. He arched an eyebrow, saying, "Which government?"

"We're from Houston." The smile faded as the man drew a wallet out of his coat jacket and flashed his identification.

Lightholler peered forwards to examine the card. It identified the man as Joseph Kennedy, an agent of the Confederate Bureau of Intelligence. He scrutinised his visitor.

"Captain, if we could have a few moments of your time."

"Not today," Lightholler replied curtly. "You can contact me via the offices of the White Star Line on Monday if you wish." He began to close the door.

One of the other men wedged his foot into the gap and placed a wide hand on the door's frame. He was stocky, his red hair cut close to his scalp. He raised his glance leisurely to meet Lightholler's.

Lightholler sighed. "You're Confederates. You have no jurisdiction here."

"We're well aware of that, Captain. However, we have a delicate matter we need to discuss with you," Kennedy said. "A matter of some urgency."

Lightholler wondered at the delicacy involved in having three Confederates barge into his hotel suite at this early hour. Relations between the Union and Confederate states remained cool at best, even though the Second Secession had occurred eighty years ago. That the separation of the southern states hadn't led to outright civil war *that* time did little to alleviate the ill feelings that remained between the two neighbours.

Kennedy now appeared more familiar to Lightholler as he swept the years away from his visage. The red-haired man was unknown. The third man, however, had been aboard the *Titanic*. He'd claimed to be an historian.

Kennedy glanced over his shoulder, bared a toothy grin, and added, "Besides, you don't want your breakfast to get cold."

They stood aside to reveal a thin negro dressed in the white livery of the Waldorf's staff. He was carrying a silver dining tray. "Excuse me, Captain," he said, smiling. "Eggs Benedict, toast, Virgin Mary and coffee?"

Lightholler stepped back, nodding. "Yes, yes, I suppose so. Thank you." He motioned the man towards the drawing room.

Kennedy waited for the attendant's departure before speaking again. "This is Commander David Hardas." He waved expansively towards the red-haired man, who nodded in acknowledgment. "You've met Darren Morgan," Kennedy added.

Lightholler nodded. "Yes, on my ship." He tightened the sash around his dressing gown. "So you're Joseph Kennedy."

"Yes."

"*The* Joseph Kennedy."

Kennedy smiled.

Lightholler reappraised the situation.

Major Joseph Robard Kennedy, the great-grandson of Joseph Kennedy I; Joseph the Patriarch. *This* Kennedy had enjoyed a brief but distinguished career in the Second Ranger War, back in the 1990s. Leading the shattered remains of a Confederate division through the San Juan Mountains and across the Rio Grande, he'd cut the supply lines of the invading Mexican army. The subsequent arrival of the German Atlantic fleet in the Gulf of Mexico had led to the hasty withdrawal of Mexican troops.

For the Texans, it was the third war they had fought with the Mexicans in a hundred years. The first was in 1920, when the Mexicans invaded the former United States of America. They were only beaten after a protracted two-year conflict that bled both countries dry. Soon after, America had endured the secession of the Southern States, while Mexico had experienced its last great revolution. The second time the Mexicans went to war with America, in the late 1940s, it was as the newly established Mexican Empire. Having absorbed its neighbours to the south, and following the occupation of Cuba, Mexico had returned its attention to the North. The Texas Rangers, forming the bulwark of the Confederate defence, had narrowly defeated them, thereby lending their name to the conflict.

Barely fifty years later, the Second Ranger War had been another close call for the South. Though it could be argued that it was German intervention that halted the conflict, it was Joseph Robard Kennedy who had been the man of the moment. Riding high on his popularity, Kennedy had run for president of the Confederacy in 1998, but without success. His ingenuous policies were attributed to youth, but it was the stigma of his name that haunted him throughout his fleeting political career. Even then, Lightholler supposed, over thirty years after the event, Southerners recalled the blood spilled at Dealey Plaza.

There had been little news about Joseph Kennedy since his departure from politics. Now, it appeared, he was working with Confederate intelligence. A curious form of backsliding to say the least. The easy grin that had adorned the television broadcasts of the time was barely altered by the passage of time. He still looked like he was in his early forties, at most.

"Just what is it you want, Mr Kennedy?" Lightholler asked.

Hardas coughed quietly and reached into his coat pocket. Lightholler stepped back abruptly.

Kennedy let loose a good-natured laugh. "Captain, please, it's not like that." He nodded towards Hardas. "Here. This might help clear things up."

Hardas drew a slender cream envelope from his pocket and handed it to Lightholler. The thick red wax bore the seal of King Edward IX. Lightholler slit the envelope with a thumbnail. The letter within was brief and to the point. He shook his head slowly. Without looking up he turned and made his way back down the short corridor. His visitors followed him into the drawing room.

Hardas walked over to a window and rested a hand on the sill. He whistled softly to himself as his gaze took in the room's opulence. "Hell,

Major," he said, "I think I might just have to sign up with White Star."

Kennedy gave him a half-smile, then turned to Lightholler. "Captain, I take it the letter's contents are clear to you?"

"They're clear alright, Major. They just don't make any sense."

Lightholler dragged a chair over to the dining table. Absently, he waved the others to find seats. They took up positions on the various plush chairs that lined the room.

The letter was dated April 19, written soon after his arrival in New York. The message was terse, the orders precise. He was instructed to offer the CBI his services until further notice. He folded the document carefully and placed it in one of his pockets.

"There must be some mistake."

"Why is that, Captain?" Kennedy enquired.

"Because I resigned my commission in the Royal Navy prior to leaving Southampton. I'm a civilian. These orders are from the War Ministry."

"If I'm not mistaken, they're from the King himself," Kennedy replied.

Lightholler swore softly to himself. He'd seen it before. Associates who'd been demobbed, then shifted from military to civilian posts, usually high-profile occupations. Within a few months their names would turn up in the local papers, brief obituaries marking their passing. It was a recognised variation in recruitment for intelligence work. American officers, both Union and Confederate, called it "sheep-dipping". But if that was the case here, why did London want him to work directly with the Confederacy rather than MI5? And why hadn't London informed him directly, instead of using agents from a nation that was at best, the ally of an ally.

"Your director must be well connected," Lightholler observed carefully.

Kennedy grinned wolfishly. "Let's just say that some people owe me a favour or two."

A scowl swept Morgan's features. Hardas remained impassive.

Lightholler's initial shock was fading to be replaced by anger. "Mind if I smoke?" he asked.

"Your room, your lungs," Kennedy said, smiling. He glanced at Hardas. "I'm used to it."

Lightholler retrieved a packet of Silk Cut from the window sill.

Hardas rose from his seat and removed a butane lighter from his pocket. He lit Lightholler's cigarette. "Mind if I join you, Captain?" He lit one of his own and returned to his chair, where he sat hunched forwards, his cigarette cupped in both hands. He smoked rapidly.

Navy, Lightholler thought, *with too many years on deck*. Hardas's hair was cut short, little more than a red tinge on his broad scalp. A scar, barely visible, ran from his hairline across the right temple.

Morgan was eyeing the breakfast. Lightholler took another drag of his cigarette. Of the three, the historian looked the worse for wear. His face was pallid, accentuating the bags under his eyes. His forehead gleamed with a thin layer of drying perspiration, the kind that accompanied sleepless nights rather than any exertion.

"You make an unusual group," Lightholler said finally. He tapped the ash from his cigarette. "I'm surprised you were allowed past the hotel foyer. In fact, considering the recent events in Russia, I'm surprised you were allowed across the Mason-Dixon Line at all."

"Well, Captain, these are strange times. And as I said earlier, people owe me favours."

"So what do you want from me?"

Kennedy turned to Hardas with a gesture. Hardas lifted himself from his seat with a grunt. He mashed his cigarette into an adjacent ashtray, then pulled a small rectangular object from one of his coat pockets.

Lightholler gave Kennedy a puzzled look.

Kennedy was examining his fingernails.

The object in Hardas's hand emitted a low whine. He held it before him, sweeping it in broad strokes from side to side as he walked the extent of the room. Kennedy started whistling tunelessly through his teeth.

"We're clear, Major," Hardas said, returning to his seat.

Kennedy's whistle faded away.

"Just a formality?" Lightholler asked. It seemed a little late in the conversation to be checking for surveillance devices.

"A precaution," Kennedy replied. "We need to talk to you about the *Titanic*."

"I thought I made it clear that I'm not doing any more interviews." Lightholler forced his expression to appear amiable, keeping it light.

"Not your *Titanic*," said Kennedy. "I'm talking about the original ship."

This was becoming ludicrous, Lightholler thought. Confederate security agents in his hotel room, with a letter of authority from the palace demanding his assistance, here to discuss a matter that was the focus of every magazine and news programme across the planet.

He forced a laugh. “Surely you didn’t cross half the continent to listen to stories about the original ship.”

“No, Captain.” Morgan spoke up. “We crossed half the continent to *tell* you one.”

Lightholler let his gaze fall on each of the men in turn. “Must be one hell of a story.”

“It has its moments.” Kennedy rose out of his chair. He straightened his jacket. “But this isn’t the place to discuss it.”

“Where did you have in mind?” Lightholler took a bite from a slice of toast.

“Dallas suits our purpose.”

He almost choked. “*Texas?*”

“You have three days. I’ve arranged a flight for Tuesday.”

“That’s impossible,” Lightholler spluttered. “The *Titanic* is due to sail this Friday, after the Berlin peace talks have concluded.”

“She’ll sail without you,” Kennedy said. “You’ll have plenty of opportunities to return to the ship later.”

Lightholler stood quickly and walked over to Kennedy. “I’m going to contact my embassy, Major. Perhaps I should have a chat with the local authorities too. They might be interested to hear about your little invitation, not to mention your presence here in the Union.”

“That wouldn’t be very wise, Captain. I’d hate to think of the complications that might cause you.” There didn’t seem to be any threat in Kennedy’s voice. If anything there was a touch of sadness. “You have three days,” he repeated. “Contact your superiors at the White Star Line. Get in touch with the Foreign Office in London if you need to confirm the letter’s authenticity, but be discreet.”

Lightholler felt light-headed. It was all happening too fast.

“Meet me here, Tuesday, two o’clock,” Kennedy concluded, handing Lightholler a card.

Lightholler examined the piece of paper. The words “Lone Star Cafe” were pencilled in broad strokes. The address was in Osakatown, in the East Village.

Three days would be more than enough time to extricate himself from this predicament. He said, “I’ll consider it.”

“Come alone. Don’t worry about your belongings—they’ll be taken care of.”

"I'll consider it."

Hardas and Morgan rose from their seats. They moved towards the hallway entrance.

Kennedy nodded at the letter in Lightholler's pocket. "I'm afraid it's out of your hands, Captain." He pressed his lips together in a tight smile. "We'll see ourselves out."

In the hour that followed, Lightholler checked his hotel suite door twice, making sure it was locked. He paced the floor and slammed his fist into the wall of his bedroom, leaving a faint impression in the plaster. He smoked seven cigarettes, lighting one from the other.

He stood in the bathroom before the full-length mirror. He ran the palm of his aching hand over a stubbled chin, teeth clenched. Snatches of the conversation repeated themselves in his mind, the words playing over and over till their meaning was lost.

White noise.

You have three days...

He went over to the shower, a glass-walled cubicle that took up nearly half the room. He ran the water cold at first, sending a shock through his frame, then slowly increased the heat. He looked up at the showerhead and screwed his eyes up tightly, letting the furious stream blast into his face.

He stood there, eyes closed, hands braced against the wall, and pictured the great ship as his great-grandfather had described her, all those years ago.

II

April 15, 1912

RMS Titanic, North Atlantic

Wells sprawled over the cabin's table, one hand outstretched on the journal, the other cradling his head. A tumbler lay on its side. An amber slick traced a pathway across the creased paper. At the table's edge an empty bottle rolled precariously.

He woke to an explosion of sound at the door. Muffled shouts came from without. Unsteadily he rose and eyed the clock on the mantle: three o'clock, and still dark outside.

He leaned heavily against the door as he opened it. Crawford, his steward, framed the doorway. Behind him, Wells could see passengers in various states of undress moving hurriedly back and forth.

"I'm terribly sorry to disturb you at this time, Mr Wells," the steward said.

Wells swayed at the cabin's entrance, rubbing his eyes. "What's happening?" he slurred.

Crawford glanced nervously over his shoulder. "We are experiencing a small difficulty. No need for alarm, sir; however, Captain Smith has asked that all passengers make their way to the boat deck till matters are sorted out."

"You're kidding me."

"I'm afraid not, sir." His smile was strained and unconvincing.

Wells noticed the thin line of perspiration moistening the elderly man's moustache. Slowly his back straightened, his mind cleared. Despite the noise of scurrying passengers, he realised that the ship's engines had fallen silent.

The air was pierced by a sudden shriek that filled their ears.

"They're venting the steam," Wells said. "We're not moving. Why have they stopped the ship?"

"I'm not sure, sir," Crawford replied hurriedly. "However, if you would please make your way topside, I'm certain we will be under way again in no time."

The ship was *not* moving. Wells had an unpleasant sensation of *déjà vu*. "Crawford, have we struck something?" His voice was almost lost in the din.

A look of surprise flickered over the steward's face. He lowered his eyes. "I believe we may have grazed an iceberg, Mr Wells."

"*Grazed?*"

"That is my understanding."

"*Motherfucker*," Wells hissed to himself.

Crawford's face registered shock. Only his unfamiliarity with the term seemed to hold him in place. Wells realised another slip like that would not be tolerated. "How long do we have?" he asked.

"I'm sure I don't know what you mean, sir." Crawford's curt reply spoke of more than just dismay. He departed quickly and silently.

Wells stared for a moment at the open doorway. Turning back into the cabin, he glanced at the journal and swallowed a harsh laugh. He went to the cabinet and removed a fresh bottle. He righted the fallen tumbler, placed it on the table's edge and poured himself a measure.

Staring at the glass, he noticed a slight tilt in the fluid level.

"I'll be damned…"

He folded the journal under his arm. Taking his scarf and coat from where they lay on the bed, he strode out into the vacant hallway.

I have to assess the damage, he thought. *Just keep calm.* Yet it beggared belief. He'd stood on the boat deck at eleven-forty, and watched the iceberg slip past with hundreds of feet to spare. There'd been no collision. Surely they couldn't have struck a different iceberg, later in the night? The possibility was outrageous.

He had to speak to Andrews, Captain Smith, Officer Lightholler… someone. But first he had to deal with the journal. It was his only link to the world he'd known. The thought of losing it was unbearable. He had to place it where he could reclaim it later, when he had used his knowledge of the ship to save it.

He entered the C deck stairwell to find a small queue forming outside the purser's office: mainly servants and maids along with the occasional bewildered first-class passenger. Glancing at his watch he saw that it was ten past three.

A woman's voice, sharp and penetrating, issued from the office. Wells tapped his foot, muttering to himself, "No good, this is no good." He shouldered past the crowd and moved towards the entrance, ignoring the disgruntled mutterings behind him.

Within, a middle-aged woman in a nightdress leaned over the purser's desk. Behind the glass the purser's face was a glazed veneer of sweat.

"Madam, may I be of assistance?" Wells interrupted.

"This... *fellow*," she indicated the purser with long, outstretched fingers, "cannot find my jewellery box."

The purser began to splutter a response. Wells raised a hand to stop him. "Why on Earth would you want your jewellery box at this hour, madam?" he asked gently.

"Because I am *not* leaving this ship without it." She spat the words out with venom.

"No one is leaving the ship."

"Have you been on deck, sir? They are uncovering the lifeboats as we speak."

"I'm sure it's just a precaution, madam," he replied, echoing the steward's lie.

The woman paused to examine Wells' calm mask. He held it together. *They might still be saved. All of them.*

She turned to toss the purser a final scowl and swept out of the small office.

"Thank you, sir. It's been like that ever since they started waking the passengers."

Wells nodded absently. He reached under his jacket and withdrew the crumpled journal. "I represent Mr Ismay. This contains all my notes, ship modifications, everything. It must be secured in the ship's safe. I must find Andrews and I don't want the damn thing lost in all the confusion. Is that clear?"

"Crystal, sir," the purser replied, accepting the book carefully.

Relieved, Wells slipped from the room.

III

Wells pushed past the growing queue. The banshee's cry of venting steam struck his ears again, louder now, rattling the teeth in his jaw.

It was less crowded on A deck. A few people wore dressing gowns. The majority were still in evening wear. Colonel John Jacob Astor stood by his wife, Madeleine, outside the entrance to the first-class lounge. A young couple, clutching each other like honeymooners, were comparing notes with one of the stewards. The man was describing how he'd been woken by an unusual scraping sound at around half past two.

"It sounded like a huge nail being scratched down her side," he said, demonstrating with an outstretched hand.

Some of the passengers were dismayed at the delay. Others looked excited by the prospect of an adventure at sea. Wells smiled at those who smiled at him, hoping fervently that he, too, would have stories to tell when they arrived in New York.

If they arrived in New York.

He tried to cast the bitter thoughts from his mind as he climbed to the top of the stairs and stepped onto the boat deck. The evening had grown colder. Earlier, the deck had been desolate and silent as he watched the iceberg drift by. Now, crowds thronged the open promenades. Children clung sleepily to their mothers' coats, or ran about the boat deck laughing, pursued by their nannies. Men in dinner jackets stood quietly in small gatherings, smoking and peering out to sea.

He approached the port-side railing as if in a dream. Noise swelled up from below as the passengers lined the walkways and gazed up at the lifeboats. He could hear music: Wallace Hartley had assembled his fellow musicians by the gymnasium and they were playing "Oh, You Beautiful Doll".

He could sense the slight list of the floorboards beneath his feet and it was almost too much for him. He'd wanted to prevent all of this; had come aboard specifically to stop this from taking place. He felt dizzy, nauseated. A tide of fear rose in him.

He'd seen the iceberg with his own eyes. What could possibly have gone wrong?

He peered out over the still waters. They were drifting in a field of ice. He stared at the small icebergs, the growlers, the field ice that dotted the flat, coal-dark sea. To the north and west an unbroken field stretched out to the horizon. He tore himself away from the railing and worked his way along the promenade towards the second-class stairs.

"Jonathan," a voice cried out. "Thank God it's you."

He turned and saw her standing a small distance from the crowd. A slender woman with an oval face. A white shawl was wrapped tightly around her head and neck; fugitive wisps of auburn hair trailed her lined brow.

"Virginia, what are you doing here? Why aren't you on one of the lifeboats?"

He'd met her in the Café Parisien on their first night aboard. Unsure of her place on the list of the damned, he'd pursued a cautiously detached flirtation.

"I was about to climb into one when I saw you rush past."

He grabbed her by the shoulders. "Are you insane? Why did you follow me?"

She drew back from him, stunned. "I couldn't find you earlier this evening. You disappeared straight after dinner." She made a vain attempt at a smile. "I thought you might have resumed your mysterious little exile."

"You must get off this ship."

"What is the urgency? Mr Murdoch told us that everything would be alright." She stared up into his eyes. "Everything is going to be alright, isn't it?"

"I don't know," he replied. She was trembling with the cold and new fear. "Take this." He removed his heavy coat and threw it over her quivering shoulders. He turned to leave.

She took a step to follow him. "Jonathan? Won't you need it? Where are you going?"

His shoulders slackened but he didn't look back. "Get into one of the boats, Virginia."

He approached a group of passengers trying to return to their rooms. Two crewmen barred their way.

"Has Mr Andrews been here?" he asked.

"Went below not ten minutes ago, him and the carpenter," the taller man replied.

"Where were they going?"

"I heard them say something about the boiler rooms," the smaller one piped up.

"Then I have to join them immediately," Wells said firmly.

"No one's allowed below decks."

"Do you know who I am?"

"I don't care if you're Mr Bruce Ismay himself. I have my orders."

Wells' voice dropped to a hiss. "And who do you think *gave* those orders?"

The two men glanced at each other in confusion and parted sheepishly. Wells turned to face the crowd. "You there," he said, raising his voice. The din subsided for a moment. "All of you, please assemble by the lifeboats. You'll all be able to return to your cabins shortly."

The passengers remained there for a moment, muttering and grumbling. They eyed one another with suspicion and slowly thinned out towards the lifeboat davits. The taller of the two crewmen raised a hand to his cap.

Wells passed carefully between them and into the stairwell. Bright light assailed his eyes. He raced to the staircase and descended rapidly, his feet beating a staccato on the wooden stairs. This part of the ship appeared deserted.

He encountered a group of crewmen on the D deck landing. "Andrews," he gasped. "Where is he? I must find him."

"Follow me, sir," a crewman responded.

Glancing over their shoulders, he could see the steerage passengers standing quietly behind a single velvet rope. He stood transfixed by the vision.

"Sir?" the crewman said.

"Sorry. Thank you. Lead the way."

The crewman winked at one of his fellows and guided Wells down the stairs to E deck. "We can't go via F on account of all the riff-raff down there. This way then." He led Wells to Scotland Road—the crew's nickname for the passageway that ran the *Titanic*'s length, permitting crew and staff to traverse the ship out of the passengers' sight.

"Down here, sir." The crewman pointed to an unmarked iron doorway in the wall. "This will take you through to the engine room. Mr Andrews should be there." The young man chuckled, "Be glad when you gents have the ship running again."

Wells let himself through the iron door. It clanged behind him, ringing in his ears. He found himself in darkness. A wave of heat swept over him. Crewmen's voices wafted up from below. He stamped down a thin metal stair onto a narrow walkway, then wound his way into the depths of the ship, keeping one arm on the banister for guidance. He crossed the metal causeway that led to the first of the boiler rooms.

Andrews was there, hunched in conversation with an older frosty-haired man in a crumpled brown suit. He glanced up at Wells' approach, rolled up the set of blueprints he had been studying and tucked them under an arm. "What brings you down here, Wells?" he asked. He looked appalling. His brown hair hung in thin damp clumps, his shirt was stained with perspiration and oil.

Wells was now more thankful than ever that he'd made the man's acquaintance earlier in Belfast. "I came to see you," he said. "To see if I could help. The steward said we've struck an iceberg."

Andrews sighed heavily. "And so we have. Short of manning the pumps, however, I don't think there's much you can do down here." He turned and said something quietly to the older man, who made a small bow and disappeared down the walkway. "Ship's carpenter," he explained, and headed towards the forwards boiler rooms.

Wells dogged his heels.

The elevated walkway was dimly lit by the occasional lantern. Most of the light came from below. He followed Andrews from boiler room to boiler room, glancing down at the piles of black coal, the shadowy black-masked faces of men under-lit by the red stage lights of the furnaces. Their inarticulate shouts merged with the rising shrieks of the boilers. He looked to his guide and thought of other guides and infernos. Recalling that Dante's vision of Hell ended in a lake of ice made him shudder.

They stopped in the fourth boiler room. Charles Lightholler, the ship's second officer, stood in the middle of the passageway, his eyes fixed on the scene below. Engineers struggled to repair the frothing mouth of a wound that coursed along the visible length of the bulkhead. Firemen manned the pumps. Inches away from the tumult, sweat-soaked boiler men continued shovelling coal into the furnace's gaping mouths.

"It's the same in boiler room five," Andrews said. "Number one hold, number two hold, boiler room six, the mailroom..." His voice trailed away.

Wells looked into Andrews' face. "How long until we have matters in hand?"

"Matters in hand? She's been gutted along the greater part of her length. The lower decks forwards to F deck are awash. The squash court is flooded, and the water is rising too damn fast."

Wells made a quick calculation in his head. The iceberg had struck the ship on her port side. Historically, the *Titanic* had been snagged to starboard, receiving a glancing blow along the first three-hundred feet of her hull. The first four compartments and forwards boiler room had been damaged and in less than ten minutes the ship had flooded to fifteen feet.

This time it appeared that more than four-hundred-and-fifty feet of hull had been torn along the port side. The consequences would be the same. It didn't matter if it was the port or starboard side. It didn't matter if the tear was an inch wide or a jagged gash. If more than five of the *Titanic*'s sixteen watertight compartments flooded, the ship could not remain afloat. And according to Andrews' description, at least seven watertight compartments had been compromised.

She was going to sink. *Again.*

Wells cast about furiously in his mind. There was one possibility... something he'd read, something that might at least buy them time.

Clouds of steam billowed up from below. The air was moist and thick in their lungs. Lightholler turned to his companions, suppressing a cough.

"Any word from the wireless room, Charles?" Andrews asked.

"None as yet. So far we've only been able to raise the *Olympic*. Everyone else appears to have switched off for the night."

"What about the *Carpathia*?" Wells urged. "Or the *Californian*?"

Lightholler seemed to notice him for the first time. "What are you talking about?"

The *Californian* was a tramp steamer that had been locked in a field of ice, allegedly in full view of the sinking *Titanic*. It had been the *Carpathia* that had rushed to the *Titanic*'s rescue. Captain Rostron had given the order to 'go north like hell'. The *Carpathia* had arrived too late to save the ship, but had taken all seven-hundred-and-five of the survivors on board.

Wells asked again, "Have we heard from the *Carpathia*? Is she coming?"

"The only ship we have heard from is our sister ship and she is five-hundred miles away. Cape Race is attempting to contact other vessels," Lightholler replied. He glanced at Andrews. "I had best be returning to the bridge. Is there anything I can tell Captain Smith?"

"I have told him everything," Andrews said softly.

Lightholler nodded.

Wells cleared his throat. It was worth a shot. "Perhaps if we kept moving?"

"I beg your pardon?" Lightholler said.

"Perhaps if we kept the ship moving. We might take on less water."

Lightholler stared at him blankly.

Andrews shook his head. "I don't know, Jonathan," he said. "I don't know. It is impossible to say."

Wells continued hopefully. "Back in New York, we conducted a study on ship collisions. Projections suggested that ships with tears along their bow would ride higher, take on less water, if they kept in motion."

Lightholler shook his head. "I'm not familiar with that article."

Wells persisted. "The passengers might find it reassuring as well, if we were under steam."

He turned to look at Andrews. Suffused in the red reflection of the furnaces, the man's face shone wetly. Condensed steam—or tears—streamed down his cheeks.

"In the face of the damage we have sustained, I cannot be certain whether it will help or hinder our situation," Andrews replied.

They all fell silent.

"I shall run it past Captain Smith," Lightholler offered finally. He gave a brisk nod. "See you up top then," he said, and he strode back the way they'd come.

Water was coursing through the lower portion of the bulkhead, swirling at the feet of the engineers and boiler men.

"What are you going to do now?" Wells asked Andrews.

"I have to remain down here for the moment. There still may be a way we can purchase some time."

Wells left him in the boiler room.

IV

Scotland Road was empty.

Wells imagined a low tide at its bow end, inexorably working its way up in frigid ripples to swallow them all. He spun around in the empty passage, aimless, and his eyes fell upon an axe cradled within a sealed glass cabinet. Above it a sign read “In case of Emergency, smash glass”. He lashed out with a booted heel. The glass cracked. He kicked again and it shattered, spraying his leg and chest. A shard stung his face. He stood breathing raggedly, staring at the broken cabinet, the axe that hung within.

He leaned back against the wall and slowly sank to the floor. His hands were splayed out on the cold steel floor. Flecks of drying blood peppered his knuckles.

Did I do all that I did just to end up here?

A faint vibration teased his fingertips. He felt it through the heels of his boots. He spread his palms wide, confirming the fact. They were moving again.

He raised himself off the floor uncertainly. “Well, what do you know?” he murmured. He brushed the flakes of broken glass from his coat and trousers. He looked up and down the corridor. Ahead lay the stairs to second class that he had descended. He started up the inclined passageway.

On the D deck stairwell, crewmen stood shouting at a small crowd that had formed behind the flimsy barricade. The steerage passengers were calling back in their native tongues. Other members of the crew were erecting a small metal gate of trellised iron. One of them turned to see Wells on the staircase, surveying the scene. “Back in business?” he shouted.

Wells shrugged and continued up the staircase. On C deck he glanced down the corridor that led to his cabin. Two men had a steward penned up against a wall. He couldn't hear their words. The steward broke away from their rough embrace and continued walking up the passage, checking the cabins. The men, clad in a blend of dinner wear and nightshirts, observed the steward's retreat. Dogs, lost in the rain.

Approaching the boat deck, Wells could hear the rising clamour. More crewmen stood at the entrance to the second-class stairs and were arrayed further down the stairs. They blocked the passage of third-class passengers from below and first-class passengers from above. Pandemonium reigned. He broke through the assembly and dashed over to the starboard railing.

Far below he could see a lifeboat in tow near the ship's stern. Another drifted into view, caught in the froth of the ship's wake. Its passengers were shouting at the crewmen who stood by the tiller, at the people at the ship's railing.

The ship was moving slowly. Five, ten knots per hour. He couldn't be sure.

An officer stood nearby at an empty lifeboat cradle. It was William Murdoch, the ship's first officer. He was calling out to the crewman in the first lifeboat Wells had seen. Another officer ran up to join him, his uniform in disarray, his hat crushed under one arm.

"Mr Murdoch," he panted, "what should I do? I was asked to lower the lifeboats not ten minutes ago. Now we are making headway again."

"Lower your voice, man. Compose yourself." Murdoch scowled. "Ensure that the lifeboats are ably manned. We can always return, or send another ship to retrieve them."

The dishevelled officer nodded frantically.

"For the moment, though, keep the remaining lifeboats uncovered."

Wells made his way towards the stern. He descended the narrow stair to the poop deck. A few of the steerage passengers were already gathered there. He followed their gaze.

The two lifeboats had both been drawn into the ship's wake. The ropes securing them to the liner hung taut. The tiny craft rolled and swayed in white foam. They could not have been more than one-third full; all of the passengers were women, who sat gripping the gunnels. Each small crash of the lifeboats in the ship's spume was punctuated by their cries.

The officer appeared at Wells' side and called out to the crew manning the ropes. Two of them grabbed lengths of chain from piles of twisted cable at their feet. They threw the chains over the straining ropes and wrapped the metal links about their wrists. As one they stepped over the rail and balanced precariously there. They launched themselves from the ship's stern, sliding down the ropes into the darkness. When it seemed as though they would crash into the small boats, they released the chains and dropped into the seething water. In a tangled flurry of arms and legs they were dragged into the boats.

A cheer rose from the passengers on the poop and upper decks. Wells was surprised to find himself joining in.

Crewmen were working on the secured portion of the ropes at the flagpole's base, preparing to cast off. Wells stared down at the two small boats. They seemed so fragile in the wake of the mighty liner. In moments they would be released.

His gaze shifted, up past the red flag that hung limply from the flagpole. The ship seemed to rise to the heavens. It stretched out before his tired eyes towards the horizon. Invulnerable. Indestructible. Unsinkable. For the first time he truly understood why the lifeboats had been undermanned. Who could leave this vast city of a ship for the insecurity of the small, frail craft that creaked and swung in the lifeboat davits? Even with everything he knew, the choice seemed unclear.

Should he jump now and risk the cold waters? Try to make his way to one of the boats? He looked down at the water's surface, trying to judge the distance in the gloom. His head swung crazily back and forth, from the ship to the lifeboats and back again.

Beside him, two passengers rushed the railing. One swung himself over the top and stood there, facing the crowd. He met Wells' eyes with a brief look of comprehension. A crewman swung a swarthy arm to grab at the passenger's worn coat sleeve.

There was a sharp twang as both ropes snapped free from their restraints, whistling through the icy air. The passenger's face tore open in an ugly red weal. Its flayed remnant managed to convey his astonishment before he dropped into the ocean.

There was a groan of dismay from the assembled crowd. Wells backed away from the railing, shaking his head. In the distance he could see the two small boats recede, lanterns swinging from their prows like fireflies courting in the gathering dark.

V

Most of the lifeboats on the port side had been lowered to the level of the boat deck. No more would be released until the ship was once again still. Passengers stood close by the cabin entrances, as far back from the railings as possible. In the cold, black night it seemed as though the amply lit bulkheads were their only sanctuary. The ship's railing had become a border between the safety of the ship and the ocean's abyss.

Wells couldn't remain still. A cacophony rang dully in his ears. The voices of the passengers and crew, mingled with the music of the band and the churn of the ship's mighty propellers, formed a continuous howl that penetrated his brain. With every step, his perceptions jarred and staggered so that it appeared as though the ship was populated by drunkards or marionettes. He clenched and unclenched his fists by his sides as he walked, dazedly, towards the first-class promenade.

Here, the crowds had thinned. He saw Aida and Isidor Straus standing in earnest conversation with a young woman. Aida was offering her a fur-lined coat. Further back, Archie Butt stood sharing a joke with Colonel Gracie. Widener stood alone. He was reading from an ancient cloth-bound book that fluttered in his small white hands. Wells knew the book's title without a further glance. It was the only existing 1597 edition of Bacon's *Essays*. He recalled the story of how Widener had purchased the volume. He'd joked with the bookseller, saying that should he ever be lost at sea the Bacon would go down with him, clasped to his heart. He'd been seated in a lifeboat when a companion reminded him of his oath. Widener had then returned to the sinking ship to find the precious work, never to be seen again.

Wells weaved through the small groups without purpose and found himself standing outside the wireless room. He arrived just in time to see Captain Smith stoop through the small doorway. The captain was ashen-faced, staring vacantly ahead, seeing nothing. Wells approached hesitantly. What was there to say?

I came back to save you all. With a pair of binoculars.

Smith's face told the entire dismal story. His hollow eyes held no hope, his mouth hung slack. A young officer in a torn jacket stepped out of the night, cutting between Wells and the captain. Words spilled out of his mouth in a tripping rush. "Andrews... E deck... flooding..."

Smith motioned for the young man to follow him and stumbled back towards the bridge. The officer gave Wells a despairing look before trailing after the captain.

A little way ahead he made out the silhouette of John Jacob Astor, standing near an empty davit, smoking. His valet stood to one side, gloved hands folded behind his back. According to the varying accounts of survivors, Astor's last moments had been heroic. Astor had assisted his wife, Madeleine, onto lifeboat four. He asked the officer loading the boat, Charles Lightholler, if he might accompany his wife, as she was in a delicate condition. Lightholler refused, stating that at present it was women and children only. Astor hadn't mentioned that his wife was pregnant. Had he told Lightholler, he might have been allowed on board. He might have survived along with her.

Wells remembered the first time he had read the story, sitting in an operating theatre's tearoom, killing time between cases. It had been a thin *Reader's Digest* history of the sinking of the *Titanic*, found among a pile of old magazines.

Colonel John Jacob Astor IV, merchant prince and heir to millions, had stood there and accepted the judgment of the ship's second officer with quiet acquiescence, as if it had come from the Lord on high. And then he had descended to F deck and released all the dogs from their kennels.

What would I do?

What will *I do?*

Wells approached the railing, and realised he was standing in almost the same place he'd occupied during last night's vigil. It felt as though long ages had passed.

Astor was speaking to his valet. He fell silent at Wells' arrival.

"May I have a cigarette?" Wells asked through chattering teeth.

"Good God, man, you must be freezing," Astor said, reaching into a coat pocket. He withdrew a thin lacquered case and thumbed open the latch.

Wells accepted with trembling fingers. "I gave someone my coat," he muttered.

Astor's valet produced a lit match and ignited the tip of the cigarette.

Wells thanked him and turned back to face Astor. He inhaled a lungful of rich Moroccan tobacco. "Where's Mrs Astor?"

"Lifeboat two," Astor said quietly. He leaned over the railing.

Wells peered down over his shoulder. A lifeboat hung just feet above the water, fully laden with first-class passengers. All women and children. Crewmen had secured the boat snugly against the *Titanic*'s hull where it scraped gently against her side with every tempered wave.

She's supposed to be in lifeboat four.

Astor was speaking to him but the words didn't penetrate. He felt a numbness spreading within.

Port side, even numbers. Starboard side, odd.

He sucked at the cigarette as if it might combat the cancerous ice at his core with its fragile flame. He felt a firm hand on his arm. The valet said something. Was trying to lead him towards the bulkhead. He resisted.

Small changes, rippling...

What have I done?

The valet became more insistent. Wells finally allowed himself to be taken to the Grand Staircase. On the landing, a stewardess was attending to a young boy's lifebelt. She cooed like a dove, murmuring softly in reassuring tones as she fastened the last buckle. The boy examined her clear face with wonder throughout the entire procedure. Behind him, a man in a tuxedo stood with a long, thin hand outstretched on the boy's head, tousling his hair casually. A woman was talking urgently into his ear. The man nodded slowly in reply.

Wells inched past them and followed his companions down the staircase to the smoking room. It was decorated in Edwardian splendour, and resonated the sum and substance of an age unknowingly on the verge of extinction. Here, the spirit of empire reigned undisputed, from the elaborate mahogany furniture, inlaid with mother-of-pearl, to the lavish Axminster carpeting.

There were a few men leaning awkwardly against the unattended bar. Four more sat around a low table, playing a round of bridge. A cloud of blue cigar smoke swirled above their heads.

Wells shambled towards the fireplace, where he fell into a semi-crouch, rubbing his hands, falling into the meticulous rhythm he'd adopted when scrubbing for surgery. He felt his face begin to flush, his hands smart in the crackling heat.

After a few moments he rose and approached the bar. A silver-haired man absently waved at some bottles that sat opened near several upturned glasses. Wells grabbed a bottle without reading the label and poured a measure into a crystal glass. The alcohol seared its way down his throat in long gulps.

A sudden high-pitched scream tore the air, followed by the muffled crump of an explosion. He recognised it immediately. Turning to the silver-haired man he said, "They're launching the rockets."

The man stared back at him warily.

"See," Wells continued, "they're going to launch them, one by one, every five minutes. And the thing is, if anyone sees them, they're going to think that we're having a celebration on board."

The silver-haired man turned away.

"And then," Wells said, louder now, "they're going to launch them all, and that fucking band is going to keep playing, and this ship is going to *sink like a fucking stone*."

The man shot him a dark look, picked up his glass and stormed away.

"This filthy fucking ship is going to sink, and I'm going to drown."

Fifty years before I'm even born.

He refilled his glass unsteadily. He felt a light tap at his shoulder.

"Very eloquent, Mr Wells. Exceedingly so. Now, may I have a brief word with you?"

It was William Stead. A self-styled mystic, Stead was travelling to the United States at the request of President Taft. In his capacity as journalist, he was to attend a series of peace talks. In his role as medium, he was to give lectures on spiritualism and its relevance in the modern world. He was a slightly built man with light brown hair. A thick beard and narrow oval glasses adorned an otherwise unremarkable face. The dismal fact that he'd gone down with the ship had facilitated their acquaintance.

Wells looked up at him and said nothing.

"We'll talk, because we always talk, but all in good time."

Stead made his way to a plush chair by the fireplace. He sat staring into the fire, sipping from a wine glass.

Wells topped up his own glass and moved, falteringly, to sit in a nearby chair.

Stead's smile was half-formed. Enigmatic. "Shall we begin?"

"I don't understand," Wells said. "Begin what?"

"The same dreary subject we always discuss, I'm afraid. Not that it ever comes to much."

"I think you've mistaken me for someone else."

Stead shook his head morosely. "There's no mistaking the likes of you." His tone was strangely weary.

A new dread took Wells. This was no insult, nor a threat. This was something more sinister. The implication of the statement awoke old fears, but he remained fixed in his chair. "The likes of me?"

"Yes. This is how it always begins."

Wells leaned in close. "Who the fuck are you?"

"Are expletives so common in your era?" Stead asked quietly. "Or was it lack of polite society that urged you back here in the first place?"

Wells' glass slipped to the floor with a soft thud. A small puddle formed on the carpet.

"I wouldn't worry," Stead said. "This carpet will be damper yet. Would you care for another?"

"Who *are* you?"

"A man not unlike yourself. In the wrong place, at the wrong time."

"Who sent you?" The accusation was a whisper.

Stead shook his head meaningfully. "No one sent me anywhere, Mr Wells." His face took on a sanguine appearance, reflecting the flame. "I'm sorry," he continued after a few moments, "I share your evident dismay at this meeting. I'm a frank man by nature, so believe me when I tell you that I find all of this as uncomfortable as you do. The fact remains, however, that you need to know certain things, and I would have some answers myself." He swirled the near empty glass in his hand, looking past Wells into the blaze. "All I seek is understanding, and in return I offer wisdom. Alas, how terrible is wisdom when it brings no profit to the man who is wise." He smiled sadly. "The role of Tiresias ill suits me. Cassandra less so, but why else would I be here? The absence of Greeks makes this no less a tragedy." He removed his glasses and began to polish them. "So tell me, young man, what is it exactly that you have done?"

"Are you from the future?" Wells breathed the question.

"Good Lord, no." Stead gave a low chuckle. "And neither, may I add, are you. Not any longer, that is." He paused. "I have always enjoyed a small aptitude in matters of the spiritual world; a prescience, if you will. Nothing that has ever approached this magnitude, however."

"You're trying to tell me you *foresaw* all this?" Wells demanded. He struggled to keep his voice low.

"Not entirely. I have had glimpses here and there. More comes to me with each passing moment, unfortunately."

"Glimpses?" Wells snorted. "Then tell me why on Earth would you be here? On *this* ship, of all places?"

"I was about to ask you the very same question." Stead took a sip of his wine. "You see, Mr Wells, it is my affliction to see portions of the future. I am, however, quite incapable of altering it. You, on the other hand..."

Wells' reply was curtailed by a sudden mild lurch beneath them. He hooked both hands under the chair's armrests. There was no further movement. He tried to compose himself, brushing a lock of hair from his eyes, some ash from his trousers.

"What do you mean, I'm not from the future?" he asked after a moment.

"What did you do last night?"

"I gave a man a pair of binoculars," he said hesitantly. "They had certain... properties."

"Such as?"

"Radar enhancement, night vision."

Stead looked back uncomprehendingly.

Wells avoided his eyes. "I was hoping to make a change."

The two men studied each other.

"You've succeeded," Stead said finally. "How long have you been here?"

"I boarded ship at Queenstown."

"How long have you *been* here?"

"A year."

"You've been among us for more than a year?" Stead asked, his eyebrows raised.

Wells said, "I thought you knew it all."

"Please, Mr Wells. I know that at around nine-forty last night, you did something that has thrown an entire world off balance. Your future, as you recall it, no longer exists." Stead drained his glass. "You are, in fact, quite literally a man out of time."

The air was pierced by another screaming explosion.

"How can that be? I failed. What have I changed?"

"Even the smallest twist in the kaleidoscope may produce chaos."

"What happens in the future then?"

"That is closed to me. All I know is that it provides for your return."

"My return?" Wells pushed his face forwards, until he was inches away from Stead. "What happens to me?"

"The same thing that always happens to you, Mr Wells." Stead spoke softly again. "You die with this ship." He closed his eyes as Wells sat back in his chair. "Your passing goes unrecorded and unmourned. Despite all of the subtle changes you effect in the flimsy repetitive cycle of your lives, you always return to this ship and you always die here. Death by water."

"Always?" Wells felt his anger slip away. "How many times have I done this?"

"Many, many times. I would suggest you get used to it."

Wells rose shakily out of his chair. "You're wrong," he said in a thin voice. "You're wrong," he shouted as he staggered to the lounge's exit, all eyes turned towards him.

Stead did not look after him. He just stared into the flames. "Not this time I'm afraid," he murmured.

VI

Wells ran down the Grand Staircase, taking the stairs two and three at a time. Gaining C deck, he raced down the vacant corridor. His cabin door had been forced. His trunk lay to one side, its contents scattered. His lifebelt was gone. He grabbed a blue woollen coat from the wardrobe and stepped back into the room.

"I'll be damned if I'm going to let everyone die on this godforsaken ship."

He strode out of the cabin without looking back and began walking towards the bow end of the hallway. He had to place an even pressure on the balls of his feet to keep them steady on the slanting floor.

The Grand Staircase landing was deserted. Passengers were either lining up outside or crowding the various lounges that offered easy access to the decks.

The purser's office was unattended. He was stunned to find his journal beneath a pile of papers scattered on the desk. It appeared undisturbed. The safe, embedded in the wall behind the desk, was partially open. Only a few items remained on its bare shelves.

He examined the manuscript for long moments before turning to the last page. He took a pen from the drawer and wrote a single word in the margin. He waited for the ink to dry, blowing gently against the fresh markings. His exhalation was a fine mist. He closed the journal and slid it onto a shelf and sealed the safe, before returning to the first-class promenade.

The ship was motionless. He approached the rail to see how low in the water they rode, but he was forced back by one of the crew. The great ship not only tilted forwards but was now listing obviously to port. He felt the dark, cold waters calling to him.

Was he finished? Was there anything left for him to do? Stead's dire prophecy echoed in his mind. Had he truly done this before? If someone had told him eighteen months ago that he was destined to travel back in time, he'd have laughed in their face. Yet he was here now, wasn't he?

Was it possible that his fate was somehow entwined with that of the *Titanic*? That he was cursed to wander back and forth through the twentieth century, each time to die with the ship?

Or could he break the chains that bound his destiny? Perhaps board one of the lifeboats now? If he could find one with few women around, he could no doubt escape, but what then? He'd read accounts of passengers who had disguised themselves until the lifeboats had been well away from disaster. Those men had been vilified, branded as cowards.

It wasn't so much a question of whether he could live. More a question of whether he could live with himself.

He looked around.

Ben Guggenheim, in full evening dress, stood by his equally attired valet, prepared to go down like a gentleman. Would he press that top hat firmly to his head as the water flowed over him? Would he cry out for his mother, or clamp that stiff upper lip against his chinless jaw?

John Thayer, his young son by his side, was arguing vehemently with Officer Lightholler. The Strauses, locked in a firm embrace, were already heading back to their stateroom.

Now, more than ever, Wells felt as though he was observing a play, part melodrama, part tragedy. All farce. Some vast performance for the amusement of dispassionate gods. What was his part? Was he the fool, forever spouting nonsense yet unable to reveal the truth?

Trapped in this era, this time, for just over a year, he'd set his mind on this course months ago and what had he achieved?

He'd ingratiated himself with Thomas Andrews, architect and designer of the three Olympic-class vessels. He'd had ample time to suggest appropriate design changes, roofing the watertight compartments, increasing the number of lifeboats. Had he set his mind to it, he might have surely found a way to delay the sailing of the ship, thus avoiding this calamity. He could have done anything he wanted, and instead he had given a man a pair of binoculars from the future.

A pair of binoculars. He began to laugh. A thick belly laugh, tinged with tears.

As if that could change everything. As if that could change anything.

He'd ignored the fact that the ship had been travelling at excessive speeds in ice-dense waters. Ignored the lack of safety precautions for passengers and crew alike. Instead, his own hubris mirrored that of an entire generation. He was no better than any of the others involved in the tragedy. He'd desired to be the author, but his own role in this play was now starkly evident. He was the leading man. It was time to act accordingly.

Another lifeboat began its descent into the calm frozen waters. Three remained. Astor was standing alone now, near the ship's railing. Wells thrust his hands into his coat pockets and walked up to him.

"Are you feeling better?" Astor enquired politely.

"Yes and no," Wells replied.

"Well, and what now, I wonder?" Astor reached into his coat pocket and withdrew a cigarette case. The match trembled in his hand.

"Colonel, I have to tell you something." Wells leaned forwards to cup the wavering flame. Their faces arched in the creviced shadows thrown by the sudden burst of light. "Everything I know tells me that we are going to sink before any help can arrive."

Astor lit up and dropped the match over the side. "Nonsense. The captain himself assured me that the *Olympic* is already steaming towards us."

"Did he bother to tell you that she's currently five-hundred miles away?"

"There are other ships in the vicinity." Astor sounded less sure of himself.

"No one's answering our distress signals, Colonel. No one else knows what's happening here tonight."

Astor turned his attention to the dark waters.

"There are people below deck, hundreds of them, who are little wiser," Wells pressed.

"They'll be taken care of."

"By whom?"

Astor resumed his silence.

"Who's taking care of *you*, Colonel? Where's your valet?"

"I dismissed him from my service."

"Now why would you go and do a thing like that?"

Astor studied him for long moments before asking, "What exactly do you have in mind, Mr Wells?"

VII

Wells had gathered as many of them together as he could. Men of wealth, men of influence and power. With Astor as his lodestone they had flocked to his side. Guggenheim, Thayer, Hays, Widener, Ryerson: the company of the dead.

He assigned them their tasks. Besides the two collapsibles lashed to the roof of the officers' house, there were five remaining lifeboats suspended in the davits. The remainder of the complement bobbed on the still waters by the *Titanic*'s pitched bow.

He sent Guggenheim and Hays to the starboard side to brace Murdoch and Chief Officer Wilde. The lifeboats had been lowered with only a portion of their seats taken. They would have to be recalled. The others, swinging in their davits, had to be filled. All told, there were enough seats for twelve-hundred people. With the *Titanic* carrying twenty-two-hundred souls Wells worked the odds. An even chance at a lifeboat berth was a better prospect than anyone had entertained the last time the ship had gone down.

He sent Thayer and Widener below; Ryerson was dispatched to locate Andrews. There was a surplus of lifejackets in storage. If a sufficient number were fastened together, makeshift rafts could be fashioned, durable enough to last till any help came.

He kept Astor by his side.

They found Lightholler by one of the swaying lifeboats. A few women sat huddled within. A circle of men were gathered by the davits. Crewmen prepared to lower away.

Spying their approach, Lightholler called out, "Women and children only." His voice was hoarse from the litany.

"First. Not only," Astor said, firmly.

Lightholler stared at him. "No one else will board."

Wells surveyed the barren boat deck. Clots of men stood by the railing, cowed by their sense of duty. "There are women and children below," he said. "Hundreds of them."

"We can't have that lot up here," a crewman muttered. "It'll be bedlam if we do."

"It's murder if you don't," Wells replied coolly. His eyes were on Lightholler.

"I have my orders," Lightholler murmured.

"Who do you answer to at a time like this?"

Lightholler cast a glance at his men. He shrugged. "Get them," he growled. His hand slipped to his side where the butt of a large Webley pistol protruded. "But only the women and children."

They strode back towards the stairway and descended. Each stage in their journey took them to a lesser world. Spacious landings were replaced by more confined areas, less ornate. Pine substituted for mahogany, gold alchemised into bronze. The stairs narrowed. On D deck, the Grand Staircase ended, opening into a wide lounge occupied by wicker chairs and small oval tables that stretched into the darkness.

Every now and then Wells heard a noise at the periphery. A rending, tearing sound. He tried to cast away the image of buckling walls and rising waters.

They ranged through the lower decks. Astor cajoled crewmen and stewards alike; Wells directed them to set up pathways to the boat deck above. Lured with Astor's promise of a year's wages and more, crewmen took down hastily assembled barricades. They set up perimeters, guiding the bewildered passengers through the warren of the third-class corridors. Everyone was issued a lifejacket.

There were Bostwick gates, required by immigration laws, closing off portions of E deck and below, but the barriers impeding the passage of those in steerage were more than mechanical. Many spoke no English; the majority of those who could had trouble reading the signs that led up to the waiting lifeboats. Stewards and maids cleaved their way among the thronging masses. Families refused to separate. Knots of men forced their way past protesting crewmen. The occasional pistol was brandished but the tide of terrified humanity swept away all in its path. They flooded the stairways. The crewmen fled their posts. The hallways emptied.

Astor turned to Wells and said, "I think we've done all that we can."

Wells considered the vision that would greet them at the lifeboats. "I think we've done too much," he replied. "Let's go."

Astor eyed him strangely but did not move.

"We have to leave now, Colonel."

"My dog is still somewhere down here, in the kennels. I need to find her."

Astor had done this before, in a previous existence. Wells wondered what drove him now.

"Best she stays down there, Colonel," he said. "It will be swift. Merciful."

"Nothing about tonight will be merciful," Astor murmured.

"Good night, Colonel. Good luck." Wells turned to leave.

Astor grabbed his arm. "I don't know where they are. I don't know how to get there from here."

The walls and floor were still dry, yet already they radiated an icy cold. There wasn't much time left.

Wells gazed at the man. Astor was spent. Ruined.

Don't you know you're already dead to me?

"The kennels are on F deck," he said, finally. "Follow me."

VIII

Cutting back across Scotland Road, they traversed the abandoned crew's quarters. Wells led Astor down a metal stairway and beyond. Their serpentine trail opened into a dimly lit passage. The kennels lay ahead. Wells felt the carpet squelch underfoot with every step. He'd advanced halfway along the corridor when there was an insistent tap on his shoulder. Astor was pointing up.

He looked up to see a stain spread across the ceiling. Here and there, thick drops of black water spilled onto the carpet. He held out a hand, palm open. A large globule fell heavily onto his fingertips.

"The compartments above us must have flooded."

Astor was wide-eyed as they reached the cargo-hold entrance. The door was secured by a heavy lock. They prised it open and stepped into an expansive, high-roofed compartment, illuminated by a series of bare light bulbs that dangled forwards like magnets drawn to a pole.

There was an intense stench, a riot of noise. Cries of distress echoed within the four walls as the assorted animals noted their arrival. They were packed into cramped pens that were lined with fouled newspaper. Bowls of food lay upturned, their contents spilt onto the grimy floor.

Astor made his way to a larger stall at the far end of the cargo hold, calling out for his dog in reassuring tones. A sharp yapping reply was chorused by the other animals. Within moments he returned, smiling triumphantly. Behind him padded a small wiry dog, its coat dappled in gold and black.

Wells began working on the other cages. Most of them were sealed with makeshift catches that opened easily. Soon the cargo hold was transformed into a menagerie: animals ran furiously around the room, snatching at portions of food and menacing each other.

The two men made for the doorway with some difficulty, trying to avoid the animals underfoot. Astor had his dog tucked up under an arm. Wells held open the door while Astor scurried past, pursued by a small horde that raced, barking, into the damp passageway.

Wells looked down to see rivulets of water escaping from the mottled carpet onto the metal floor. He heard a faint mewling sound. A scrawny ginger cat crouched behind him, backing away from the advancing puddle.

"Swift and merciful," he murmured to himself.

He scooped it up in a single fluid motion. He considered breaking its neck.

"Hurry up," Astor shouted from up the hallway.

The cat settled in his arms. He tucked it into one of his coat pockets. The door slammed behind him as he dashed up the corridor. Astor was waiting below the winding stair, his dog clasped firmly to his breast. Water spiralled down in a fountain of icy spray. Some of the dogs were milling around Astor's feet; the rest had raced up the darkened corridor.

"Let's go," he cried and began climbing the stairs.

Wells followed at his heels, the dogs chasing them up the watery stair. At the top he saw Astor staring past him. Wells clambered up and turned to follow his gaze.

The crew's quarters were awash. A dark tide ebbed and flowed at the stair landing. The water stretched out to the corridor's ceiling in the distance, the roof lights casting an eerie illumination at their depths.

Wells clasped Astor's shoulder and they turned to face the iron portal that opened onto Scotland Road. The dogs stood at the gate barking frantically. Astor got there first and held the gate wide open till the procession had passed through.

Wells ran up the hall, catching Astor at the foot of the stairway to D deck.

"After you," Astor said.

"Do you know the way from here?"

Astor frowned. "Surely. But aren't you coming?"

"I'll see you on the boat deck."

"If we miss each other tonight, we must catch up in New York."

Wells was unable to match the man's bravado. "That's not going to happen, Colonel."

Astor forced a smile. "Come, come. Things aren't as dark as all that."

They stood facing each other, the ship creaking and groaning about them.

"I'm afraid they are, Colonel," Wells said. "You're on my list. You don't get to New York."

Astor paled.

Wells reached out awkwardly with a free hand and grabbed Astor's palm. "Goodbye."

Astor stood momentarily, the dogs swarming about his heels. Finally he began to ascend the narrow stairs. The howling pack was his sombre entourage.

Wells started up Scotland Road towards the ship's stern. He patted the warm bundle under his coat pocket, seeking reassurance. The axe was where he'd left it, cradled in the wooden case. He reached out to seize it by the shaft. Holding it in both hands, he gave it a few gentle swings. He walked up to the stairs to D deck, whistling a tune yet to be composed. At the foot of the stairs he heard a wailing marriage of screams and shouts. He concealed the axe along his flank and ascended.

The crewmen were gone. His arrival on the landing was greeted by a sudden upsurge in the clamour. The steerage passengers were crushing themselves against the newly constructed barricade. Men gripped the metal bars in blanched fists but the partition refused to separate from its solid frame.

Wells removed his coat and hung it on the banister. The crowds behind the barricade stared and fell quiet. The men at the front tried to force themselves backwards, only to be pushed forwards again by the agitated crowds.

"Please," he said softly. "Everyone stand back."

A small space opened up.

He raised the axe above his shoulder and swung it down in a mighty arc against one of the hinges. It buckled but held fast. The passengers renewed their anguished cries.

He lifted the axe a second time. It fell with a sharp crash, the hinge splintering wildly.

Before he could begin working on the other hinge, the passengers resumed rattling the metal bars. The barricade creaked forwards under the pressure. He stepped back, letting the axe fall to his side, and reached out to retrieve his coat.

The final hinge sundered with a heavy crack and the barricade slammed down onto the thinly carpeted floor. The steerage passengers surged through the doorway and up onto the second-class staircase. He leaned against the opposite wall and took his cigarettes from a coat pocket. He lit one and watched the corridor empty. When he'd smoked the cigarette to his fingertips he let it fall to the floor. Wearily he began to ascend the second-class stairs for the last time.

IX

Though he could hear the sounds of passengers in flight, the upturning of tables, the slamming of doors, Wells saw no one till he reached the aft boat deck entrance. He leaned out of the doorway, holding it for support. From where he stood he could see two lifeboats. With the ship's pronounced tilt they hung well over the water. Thick ropes, stretched tight, secured them.

Crewmen at the railing were still attempting to load the boats. Others had formed a barricade against the newly arrived steerage passengers. Women and children were ushered through. The men were held back at gunpoint.

There was the sharp crack of pistol fire. Chief Officer Wilde stood on the railing by a lifeboat davit, one arm entwined around the braided cord, the other brandishing a long, thick weapon. A small cloud of smoke hung thinly in the air above him, slowly dispersing. He was shouting, his words lost amongst the hoarse cries of the passengers.

Wells edged out of the doorway. Looking down to the ship's bow, he could see no other lifeboats. Swarms of passengers were making their way towards the stern, which now drew high above the waters. He began to follow when a second shot rang out. He looked back.

Wilde's face was aghast. Wrapped around his feet, at the ship's rail, a young man lay in a spreading pool of blood. The chief officer was screaming at the crowds, his voice shrill. He waved the gun wildly. Still the passengers threw themselves against the human rampart.

A third shot and Wells saw Wilde falter. For a moment he swung with his arm caught in the rope, the corpse of the man he'd slain seeming to grip him. He was reaching out to disengage himself when a second man fell upon him. All three dropped into the ocean in a twisting heap.

Passengers clambered across the securing ropes towards the fully laden lifeboats. Those within were shouting at the approaching men. Imploring them to turn back.

A number of the scrambling passengers managed to climb aboard before one of the ropes snapped. The lifeboat's prow fell free, spilling its occupants into the icy waters below. It swung wildly before crashing into the side of the other boat, which splintered at the sudden impact. Both boats tore away from the remaining ropes to plunge below.

The *Titanic* gave another sickening lurch. It seemed to twist as it rose into the night sky. Passengers tore past him, streaming towards the stairs that led to the poop deck, now level with the ship's second funnel. From his vantage point he could see the starboard side. All the lifeboats were gone. The ship spread out beneath him. To either side, passengers were attempting to gain the poop deck. Some stood poised at various points along the railings. A few had already plunged into the polar depths in the desperate hope of gaining a lifeboat.

The ship's funnels were arrayed before him, angled rakishly towards the approaching waters, which washed the foredeck and swirled over the officers' promenade. Crewmen were working on releasing the last of the collapsibles. A horde of passengers fell upon them and a frenzied mêlée broke out. The gunfire sounded like crackers. The bodies slipped in water and blood and were swept away with a final dismissive slap by the ocean.

Wells looked away. He wrapped an arm about the stern rail and reached into his coat pocket. The cat clambered up his arm, seeking shelter in the folds of his coat near his collar.

He glanced up at the clear black skies and the constellations winked back at him knowingly. All he'd managed to do was compound this night's terrors and there were no more bargains to be made.

Out to sea he saw a number of lifeboats scattered across the ocean's expanse. Lanterns flickered, a mundane reflection of the panoply above. The ship's stern twisted again and began to rise heavenwards. Wells grabbed the protesting cat and replaced it in his coat pocket. He took a firmer grip on the railing that seared his flesh with ice.

A terrible grinding sound ensued from below. He could see it in his mind's eye. Every unfixed object crashing forwards. Grand pianos tearing through elegantly papered walls. Plates, tables, chairs—people—

hurtling into the chasm. The boilers would be shearing themselves from their fixtures, dropping through bulkhead after bulkhead till they finally ripped through the bow to pepper the ocean floor.

The waters seethed as the great ship slowly began her corkscrew descent. He pressed himself into a tight ball, locking his legs under and around the railing. The world began to spin. The first of the ship's funnels slapped into the roiling waters with a furious thunderclap. Two huge waves shot away from the descending funnel to sweep into the enlarging circle of waters and dissipate.

Wells looked on in horror as he saw first one and then another of the lifeboats drift towards the forming maelstrom. The air was filled with one long scream. It was as if a new voice joined in as the previous one faltered, to continue the hellish, unbroken chorus of misery. His own throat felt hoarse and dry. He bit down hard on his lower lip. The taste of blood was bitter and thick in his mouth.

The ship began to revolve faster, the ocean rising in great gulps to meet him. The second funnel snapped as it slammed into the water, sending a towering spume into the air. The two lifeboats began to circle rapidly in the spiralling ocean.

The airborne mass of the great ship was now almost perpendicular with the boiling surface of the ocean. He swung himself back over the railing and gripped the ship's metal floor, now almost upright. A deluge of passengers fell from the decks above, crashing into portions of the superstructure or plunging straight into the unforgiving waters.

The *Titanic* began her final ear-splitting descent into the vortex she had created. She sliced into the heart of the whirlpool.

As the last of the funnels smashed into the ocean he felt himself cast from the railing. Unsure if he jumped or fell, he tumbled through the air and landed in an icy explosion of pain. All was black. A million frozen needles speared him.

He clawed at the razor-cold water, a seizure of blind movement that brought him spluttering to the surface. His coat billowed around him, dragging him down. He flailed wildly, finding purchase on a jagged piece of wood, a fragment from one of the shattered lifeboats. He scratched his way up the sodden flotsam and threw himself onto its widest portion, laid outstretched on the wooden shell, his feet dangling in the burning cold waters.

He reached to his coat pocket and undid the flap. The cat's waterlogged mass lay unstirring beneath his probing fingers. He raised his eyes to observe the *Titanic*'s stark silhouette, now entirely unlit, standing black against the cimmerian night.

With a last protracted groan, she vanished into the churning waters.

He felt the deathly cold rising to envelop him. It stole its way up nerve endings, through the hollow stems of his bones. The air was filled with a low keening sound. Around him, bodies bobbed and jerked in the ocean's eddy amid the detritus of man's boldest creation.

His makeshift raft was moving faster now, caught up in the inexorable swirl of the mighty ship's departure. His eyes stung with salt, his breaths were a concertina of stabbing gasps and wrenching hacks.

He cleared the crest of the whirlpool's eye and stared down into the abyss, his face frozen in a bare-toothed snarl. The black ocean's wall broke down upon him. Thoughts were starbursts and he experienced them all in an engulfing whorl. That first night in the desert, his rude arrival in this era, and for the first time in memory he was no longer afraid. He thought of the mystic, Stead, and wondered what would happen next. But only briefly.

X

Dawn broke over the North Atlantic, transforming her still waters into a carpet of diamonds.

Throughout the early hours of the morning, a few of the lifeboat passengers, communicating by shouts, cries and whistles, managed to locate one another. Their boats lay drifting, moored together by frail ice-encrusted ropes. Further out, rippled by the *Titanic*'s departure, other lifeboats lay scattered amid wide sheets of field ice and the flotsam of the great ship.

The survivors spoke quietly amongst themselves, conversations punctuated by sobbing and soft moans of realisation. When not looking at one another, they cast their gaze at sodden feet on the damp lifeboat decks or out towards the glowing horizon. No one could bear to look at the bodies that bobbed to all sides in the gentle ocean's swell.

At around six-thirty that morning ship's time, Wireless Operator Evans of the *Californian* finally received the news that had already raced around the world. The White Star liner *Titanic*, out of Southampton on her maiden voyage to New York, had struck an iceberg and foundered in the North Atlantic off the Grand Banks of Newfoundland. The coordinates marking her last known position put the ship less than thirty miles from the *Californian*'s current location.

Evans rushed to the bridge to find Captain Stanley Lord, first officer Stewart, and second officer Stone in earnest conversation. He caught snatches of their words concerning the rockets that had been seen the previous night, before blurting out his own news.

Captain Lord, eyes widening in horror, asked him to repeat the message. He then turned to his second officer.

"Captain, they were white rockets. Not red. We thought there was some kind of party going on."

"At four o'clock in the morning?" Lord shook his head in disbelief. "Mr Evans,see if you can find out anything more. Mr Stewart, set a course for the *Titanic*'s last known position."

"What about the ice, sir?" Stewart stammered.

"Set a sharp lookout and damn the ice, Mr Stewart." White-faced, Lord continued barking commands as Stewart relayed the orders to the wheelhouse and engine room. "Summon the surgeon, the nursing staff, we'll need plenty of blankets..."

Throughout the ship, men ran to their posts as the *Californian* slowly inched its way out of the ice field and swung north. She caught up with two lifeboats within the first hour. Lord was on hand to greet the survivors. Apart from three of the *Titanic*'s crew, both lifeboats were occupied entirely by women. It took little over half an hour to secure the passengers.

By the time they had resumed their course, Evans had brought the captain further news. The *Mount Temple* and *La Provence* had found more lifeboats to the north. Captain Rostron of the *Carpathia* had telegraphed that his vessel, was on its way.

Lord stood at the bow railing, binoculars pressed firmly to his eyes. As the morning's mist thinned, burnt away by the encroaching sunlight, he saw first one and then another of the rescuing ships take form in the distance. As the *Californian* closed the gap between the vessels, evidence of the disaster became more apparent. Deckchairs and parasols, fragments of wood and children's toys littered the surface of the ocean. After the first body was sighted, floating serenely face down among the wreckage, Lord ordered that all passengers be taken below decks.

By early afternoon, the last of the lifeboats had been recovered. Captains Rostron and Lord stood on the forwards deck of the *Carpathia.* All up they had located eleven of the *Titanic*'s original sixteen lifeboats and two of the four collapsibles. The five remaining lifeboats appeared to have been lost with the wreck. Of the two-thousand-two-hundred-and-twenty people thought to have been aboard the *Titanic* only five-hundred-and-twenty-four had been rescued. Search parties from the *Carpathia* and

Californian had sifted among the bodies that rose and fell in the frozen waters. The crews of the rowboats returned, ashen and pale. Not one of the bodies they had recovered had shown any sign of life.

"And what did Ismay have to say?" Lord asked.

Bruce Ismay, president of the White Star Line, had been brought aboard the *Carpathia* in one of the last lifeboats to be found.

"Not much, actually. Asked me to contact the White Star offices in New York. Arrange matters with them. Hasn't spoken to anyone since. Says he would like to be left alone, if possible. He's currently in my stateroom with the doctor."

Lord nodded in response.

"By the time I contacted the New York office they had already spoken to my superiors at Cunard," Rostron continued. "They have come to some arrangement. I've been asked to bring the survivors back to New York."

"Cunard wishes to be magnanimous in its support, I suppose," Lord said.

"Precisely."

"Sirs?" They were interrupted by Bisset, the *Carpathia*'s second officer, who'd arrived unnoticed on the boat deck. "We've found five more survivors on one of the collapsibles."

The two captains turned to face him.

"It was floating, capsized, three miles from here; fourteen men secured to its keel. Apart from the five we retrieved the rest were all dead. Astor looked in poor shape for a while, but he perked up after we gave him some brandy."

"Astor's alive?" Lord exclaimed.

"Yes, sir. Officer Lightholler will tell you the entire story. Apparently they were both thrown clear from the *Titanic* just before she went under. They were both in the water when Mr Lightholler spied the collapsible. Astor was unconscious but Mr Lightholler towed him to the boat."

"Good man," Rostron said. "What of Astor's bride?"

"We've identified all the first-class passengers among the survivors, Captain. She didn't make it."

"Does Astor know?"

"I don't believe so, sir. He is still recuperating below decks with the others. He kept ranting about some list, sir. I believe he may have lost some important document with the ship."

"He's lost a damn sight more than that. Thank you, Mr Bisset." Rostron turned to face Lord. "Stanley, are you happy to transfer your survivors to the *Carpathia*?"

"Certainly," Lord replied.

"I'll wire New York. The sooner we get these people home, the better." Rostron paused. "Look, Stanley, the *Mount Temple* and *La Provence* have already sent their survivors across. They're all set to depart."

"What is it, Arthur?"

"The New York office enquired as to whether you might organise the recovery of the *other* passengers."

Lord lifted his gaze to the surrounding waters. The congregation of the dead, dispersed around the still vessel. He sighed heavily.

"I think we're going to need a larger boat."

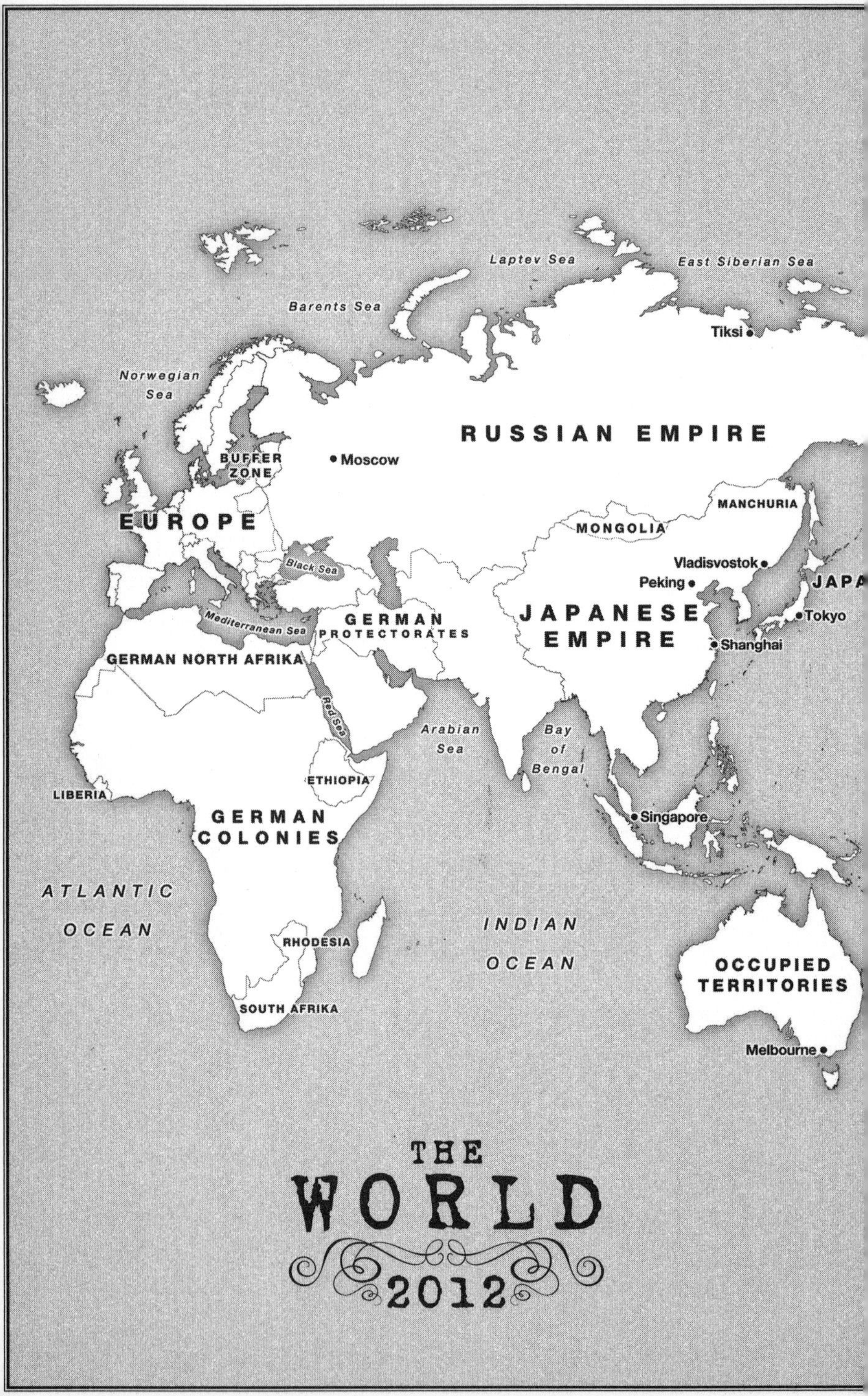
Laptev Sea
East Siberian Sea
Barents Sea
Tiksi
Norwegian Sea
RUSSIAN EMPIRE
BUFFER ZONE
Moscow
MANCHURIA
EUROPE
MONGOLIA
Vladisvostok
Black Sea
Peking
JAPA
JAPANESE EMPIRE
Tokyo
Mediterranean Sea
GERMAN PROTECTORATES
Shanghai
GERMAN NORTH AFRIKA
Red Sea
Arabian Sea
Bay of Bengal
ETHIOPIA
LIBERIA
GERMAN COLONIES
Singapore
ATLANTIC OCEAN
INDIAN OCEAN
RHODESIA
OCCUPIED TERRITORIES
SOUTH AFRIKA
Melbourne
THE WORLD 2012

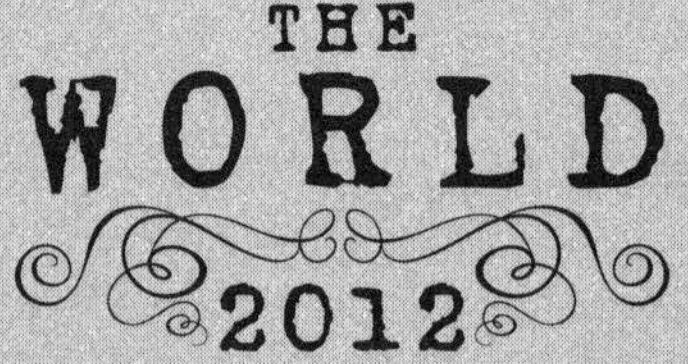

ARCTIC OCEAN

Beaufort Sea

Baffin Bay

OCCUPIED TERRITORIES

CANADA
ALLIED WITH
GREAT BRITAIN
AND
GERMANY

Hudson Bay

Baring Sea

Gulf of Alaska

FREE QUEBEC

WEST COAST
DEMILITARISED
ZONE
(OCCUPIED BY JAPAN)

Seattle

THE UNION

PREFECTURE
OF NEW YORK
(OCCUPIED BY JAPAN)

New York City

Chicago

Washington, D.C.

NORTH PACIFIC OCEAN

Los Angeles

Dallas

SECOND CONFEDERACY
(ALLIED WITH GREATER GERMANY)

Gulf of Mexico

ATLANTIC OCEAN

HAWAII
(OCCUPIED BY JAPAN)

Mexico City

Caribbean Sea

MEXICAN
EMPIRE

SOUTH PACIFIC OCEAN

COUNTRIES
ALLIED WITH
JAPAN

COUNTRIES
ALLIED WITH
JAPAN

EUROPE
2012
Norwegian
Sea
ICELAND
SWEDEN
NORWAY
ESTONIA
BUFFER
ZONE
LATVIA
LITHUANIA
RUSSIAN
EMPIRE
DENMARK
GREAT
BRITAIN
London
HOLLAND
Berlin
DUCHY
OF
POLAND
BELGIUM
GREATER
GERMANY
Paris
KINGDOM
OF
FRANCE
SWITZERLAND
ROMANIA
Black
Sea
SERBIA
BULGARIA
KINGDOM
OF
PORTUGAL
KINGDOM
OF
SPAIN
KINGDOM
OF
ITALY
ALBANIA
TURKEY
GREECE
Mediterranean Sea
GERMAN
PROTECTORATES

A GAME OF CHESS I

Opening Moves

I

April 21, 2012
New York City, Eastern Shogunate

Showered and dressed, John Jacob Lightholler sat at the dining room table of his hotel suite. He wore a dark blue woollen suit. A crumpled plain burgundy tie hung from his neck like an afterthought. He worried its frayed edge between his fingers.

Before him, smoothed out and spread across the table, lay the letter. A cigarette burned in an ashtray near one of its edges. He found himself staring at the glowing tip.

It had been over two hours since Kennedy and his men had left, yet little had changed—the breakfast tray remained, its contents long cold, and the newspaper lay unopened on one of the cushioned chairs.

A question formed in his mind. Reverberated through his thoughts to be borne out in a single word.

Why?

He said it softly, as if questioning the meaning of the word itself. He said it and wondered how his life could unravel so quickly. From ship's captain to Confederate lackey in the space of a morning.

Why would the King of England parcel me off to work for the Confederate Bureau of Intelligence?

He had served with the Royal Navy for ten solid years, and in that time he'd never been approached for intelligence work, never been assigned any post that suggested he was being groomed for anything covert.

True, in the last few days, he'd been approached by a number of foreign dignitaries. He'd sat with the Russian ambassador. He'd been invited to an audience with Hideyoshi, titular governor of the Prefecture of New York, Shogun of the Japanese Empire's eastern dominions and twin brother to

Emperor Ryuichi. Finally, he'd been asked to attend a short-lived meeting with the German foreign minister, whom he'd met on the voyage. The minister had been preparing to leave for Berlin to resume the Russo–Japanese peace talks, scheduled to be held at the Reichstag.

For some reason each group had queried his opinion on how the peace talks had gone. Lightholler had dismissed the Japanese incursion into Russian Manchuria as just another manifestation of the half-century old Cold War between the empires of Japan and Germany. In the fifty years since Germany had secured the domination of western Europe and northern Afrika, and Japan had extended itself from the borders of China to the American West Coast and New York, both empires had bickered constantly.

But the King's letter pre-dated those meetings.

Could it have something to do with the centennial voyage itself?

He thought back to the crossing, trying to summon up something, anything, that would be of value to the Confederates. He recalled a brief encounter with Morgan, the historian who'd accompanied Kennedy that morning.

It had been halfway through the Atlantic passage, on April 15. They had held a memorial service for those lost on the maiden voyage of 1912. The crowds were filtering out of the first-class lounge at its conclusion; Lightholler had been one of the last to leave. Wishing to avoid the other passengers, he'd made his way to the ship's stern, where he spied another man by the railing: Darren Morgan. He remembered those pale blue eyes as the historian had caught his glance and turned quickly away—a clumsy movement that failed to conceal what he'd been doing.

Morgan had been casting breadcrumbs into the ship's wake.

Lightholler had walked up to him and nodded in greeting and Morgan responded with an embarrassed shrug.

"It's just in case," Morgan said. "Just in case we lose the way home."

Only then had Lightholler perceived the alcohol on the man's breath. They parted, and he had all but forgotten the incident.

Little else had happened that was out of the ordinary. E deck had been sealed off due to fire damage, prior to the ship leaving dry dock in Bremen. No one in, no one out. There were Johnson's concerns about the displacement of the *Titanic*, but Kennedy had said it was the *original* ship that they were interested in. It made no sense.

Kennedy had issued a challenge, almost daring him to confirm the validity of the letter. *Contact the White Star Line*, he'd said. *Contact the Foreign Office in London*. It was as good a start as any.

Still, Lightholler sat by the telephone for long minutes before dialling the first number.

The Foreign Office in London confirmed that his assignment had indeed come directly from the Palace. No one he spoke to, however, could supply any details.

He contacted the London branch of the White Star Line only to be told that he'd been placed on leave of absence. Indefinitely. If he would be so kind as to come down to the Manhattan offices, there was some paperwork to be taken care of.

Lightholler slammed down the phone. So the letter was authentic, and the *Titanic* had been taken away from him, placed under the care of Fordham, his first officer.

He could only think of one man to turn to: Rear-Admiral Lloyd. The officer who had organised his honourable discharge from the Royal Navy and facilitated his assignment to the *Titanic* late last year.

He smoked another cigarette to calm his nerves before dialling the number that would connect him to the offices of the Admiralty. Discretion could go fuck itself.

II

Joseph Kennedy stood before an open window, hands clasped behind his back. He considered the message he'd just received, trying to make sense of it in the hidden augury of the street. His glance rose to the houses opposite, bland replicas of the brownstone he'd leased a month ago. He turned and his eyes fell on the sparse decoration of the room. An oval kitchen table occupied one corner. Three folding chairs, now collapsed, were arranged against the chipped surface. A pre-Secession flag, the stars and stripes, hung on otherwise bare walls. Its worn material, seemingly cut from the same cloth as the curtain, held his gaze.

The news was from Saffel, a freelance operative assigned to the German embassy at Project Camelot's inception. Having no direct affiliation with the CBI, he provided Kennedy with intelligence that was free of Bureau censorship; he provided the means of keeping watch on the watchmen. Usually, his monthly reports were read and dismissed over a quick coffee. This morning's report had been read twice and slowly. It had been shredded to fine strips of paper and torched, the burnt remains now smouldering on the kitchen table.

Project Camelot was the reconciliation of the Confederate and Union states by covert means. It was a long shot; its chances of success slim, its price incalculable. Kennedy had come to understand that even before he'd met Hardas and learnt the truth in Red Rock. Yet for a brief time it had borne a promise that he'd clung to with the faith of an agnostic who secretly desires the Kingdom of Heaven. Pipe dream though it was, however, its sheer audacity held an appeal that had enamoured the leaders of three nations: Germany, the Union and the Confederacy.

Yet if Saffel's report was in any way accurate, Camelot was doomed. Its veil of lies would be torn away, leaving Kennedy's true agenda exposed.

Martin Shine entered the room. He'd changed out of the staff uniform he'd worn earlier to deliver Lightholler's breakfast at the Waldorf. He sniffed at the air and gave the table a swift glance before fixing on Kennedy with a perplexed look. After a moment, he spoke up.

"Major, Commander Hardas is calling in. I'm scrambling the line."

"I'll take it next door," Kennedy said, dismissing him with a nod.

He reached for Lightholler's dossier and considered adding it to the ashed residue on the kitchen table. Instead, he thumbed through the document. The text blurred before his eyes. All he saw were the white bones and coiling black smoke of the vision bequeathed to him at Red Rock, Nevada.

"You played me for a fool, Captain," he murmured.

III

Lightholler was treated to an earful of static as Admiral Lloyd obtained a secure phone line.

"Ah, that's better. Now, you were saying, John?"

"I was saying, Admiral, that I've just been informed that I'm now on leave from the White Star Line." Lightholler had difficulty suppressing his anger.

"It doesn't sound as if it was handled very well, and I can imagine how you must feel, John. My understanding is that the *Titanic* may now be required for other duties."

"Duties that don't include me, it would seem."

"True. As far as the White Star Line is concerned, you've been recalled to active service in the Royal Navy."

"But why am I only hearing this now, sir? Why was I not consulted?"

"We couldn't tell you anything ourselves until we were certain that you had been properly contacted."

"That is another of my concerns, sir. Though it was issued by the crown, the commission I received this morning was given to me by agents of the CBI."

"I can imagine you found that somewhat surprising," the admiral conceded.

"One of them was Joseph Kennedy."

Lloyd fell silent for a moment. "We've had dealings with the Confederates before," he said, finally.

"True enough, Admiral, but considering the fact that one of the goals of the cruise was to cement ties between Britain and the *Union*,

I'm surprised we're negotiating with the Confederates at all."

"These are dark days, John, and we have to take what's offered us. What did Kennedy tell you?"

"Nothing as yet, sir. He expects me to accompany his team to Dallas."

"I see..."

"There's another thing. Part of the arrangement that allowed me to take command of the *Titanic* was an honourable discharge from the Navy, as you yourself organised. Now that I've been "reinstated" am I to understand that I once again represent the Admiralty in my dealings with the Confederates?"

"No, not exactly. All I said is that as far as the *White Star Line* is concerned, you've been returned to active duty."

"Then on whose behalf am I acting, sir, if not the Admiralty's?"

"The order comes from the Palace." The admiral spoke slowly, in measured tones. "If you want to know more, perhaps you should take the matter up with your new associates."

So that's how it was. He was being disowned. Cut loose from the White Star Line and denied by the Navy, with no one to answer to save some shady characters representing the Confederacy.

"John? Are you still there?"

"Yes, sir. I was just... thinking."

"I'm afraid there isn't much I can tell you, and believe me, it's more from ignorance than subtlety." Lloyd gave an unconvincing laugh that faded into nothing. "But what would you say if I told you that it was on request from the Reichstag, from the Kaiser himself, that you were appointed to the *Titanic* in the first place?"

"The Kaiser?" Lightholler had been as surprised as anyone that his transfer had been approved, even *with* the admiral's assistance. Up till now he had never been given a satisfactory reason for the move. He said, "The centennial cruise was supposed to be a joint British–Union venture; I had no idea that there was any German involvement. Certainly not back then, before the addition of the peace talks."

"Is there *any* British venture the Germans don't have their paws in these days?"

If nothing else, that proved their line was secure. Rear-admiral or not, Lloyd's comment could get him in a lot of hot water if the Abwehr, the German intelligence agency, was listening in.

"Still, it was supposed to be a milk run," the admiral continued. "You were more than qualified for the job: ferrying a bunch of ageing politicos, journalists and what-not across the Atlantic. The peace talks were a last-minute addition—I scarcely believe they could have had anything to do with your selection."

"So why were the Germans so interested in me?"

"I can't be certain. Perhaps it has something to do with your family's history. Not only are you related to the senior-most surviving officer of the *Titanic*—"

"I'm also the great-grandson of the man who single-handedly kept America out of the Great War," Lightholler finished.

"You sound bitter, John. Astor was a good man, and a fine president."

Lightholler could just imagine the old admiral shaking his head. "He was a good friend to Germany, if that's what you mean." The words came to him with difficulty. "It's just that sometimes I think he kept the United States out of the wrong war."

"You're entitled to your own opinion, son. Astor's actions as a private citizen during the *Titanic* hearings certainly contributed to the ill will between England and America at the time. But he was just one man, John. One man may start a war; it takes a few good men to stop one. As for his conduct during the presidency, you have to consider that the Supreme Court was still sorting out the formation of the Confederacy. There was a lot of resentment between the North and the South at the time, and barely a generation had passed since the Civil War.

"When the South turned to Japan for trade, it left the North isolated both politically *and* economically. And when the Mexicans invaded the South during the First Ranger War, Astor had to convince all of Congress in order to send military aid to the Confederates. By the time the Japanese seized Pearl Harbor, though, he was left with no options."

Lightholler remained silent, allowing the admiral to continue.

"It was a testimony to Astor's ability as a statesman that he was able to achieve the peace terms he did with Japan."

"The Japanese ended up annexing the majority of the Union's West Coast and Alaska, as well as occupying New York," Lightholler said. "That had to be a bitter pill to swallow."

"It certainly was a better deal than the Chinese got."

True enough. Even today, more than half a century after the Pacific

War, stories of the atrocities still circulated.

"And what do you think would have happened if the Americans had entered the Great War, John?" the admiral asked.

"Well, sir, the Russians were out of the picture, and the French were on the verge of mutiny. But the Germans were exhausted too—they had been fighting a two-front war for three years. With fresh troops, such as the Americans would have supplied, the Allies might have won."

"Do you really think the Americans might have swung the balance?"

"Looking at them now, sir, I don't know." Lightholler paused, collecting his thoughts. "But at the very least, entering the Great War would have prevented the Secession."

"Perhaps, John, but who could have known what was to come? If you ask me, the Great War had no victors. In fact, to my way of thinking, the damn thing isn't even over yet. There's just been a slight rearrangement in the sides since 1917. Since then, we've all been taking a bit of a breather," he added. "Mustering our strength in readiness for the final round."

Lightholler mulled over the admiral's words, his original question almost forgotten. "The Germans aren't exactly famous for their sentimentality, Admiral; there must have been some other reason I was selected as captain for the *Titanic*."

"I'd be surprised if there wasn't. Particularly in light of your new assignment." Lloyd fell silent.

"So that's all you can tell me, sir?"

"I'm afraid so, John. Good luck to you. And remember what I said to you the day you left Southampton." Lloyd's voice had resumed its grandfatherly tone.

"You told me to stay away from icebergs, sir."

Lightholler said his goodbyes and hung up, little wiser by the end of the call. If anything he had more questions.

What in the world did the wreck of a hundred-year-old ocean liner have to do with Confederate security? Or the Germans, for that matter?

On being informed of his appointment to the new *Titanic*, he'd assumed that genealogy had played a role in the decision. His mother's grandfather had been the original ship's second officer. No surviving crewman from the disaster ever rose to the rank of captain in the White Star Line—or any other shipping line for that matter. Association with the wreck had tainted them all. Yet one hundred years later, he had brought the *Titanic* into New York Harbor. And now, out of the blue, she was being taken away from him.

There was one thing he knew for certain. He would attempt to do whatever was asked of him—it appeared as though he had little choice in that regard. But when it was over, he would return to England. He would return to his ship.

Lightholler emerged from the hotel lobby at twelve-thirty. He needed fresh air and time to collect his thoughts. Despite the early spring sunshine, chill gusts of wind raced down Park Avenue. He flipped up his collar and wrapped his coat tightly around himself. He tucked his fedora under his arm. The avenue was teeming with people. Businessmen on lunch breaks, children capering from storefront to storefront, tourists in town to see the *Titanic*. Some samurai slouched against a phone booth, smoking. They gave him a quick once-over and resumed their conversation, eyeing the crowds with the detachment of zookeepers long since weary of their charges.

Since his arrival Lightholler had noticed a steady increase in the military presence. Not for the first time he yearned to be back in London. At least there the soldiers spoke English. New York enfolded him with the insincere embrace that most newcomers fell for. Before the navy and fresh out of the academy, he'd come to New York to celebrate the turn of the millennium. He'd visited Astor Place and taken coffee with distant cousins and listened as they reiterated the stories he'd been raised upon. John Jacob Astor and Charles Lightholler, clinging to the remains of a broken lifeboat, forging covenants that would be borne out in ways they could never have imagined.

Astor and Lightholler, New York and London. The two worlds that bound him.

A doorman approached him. "Call you a cab, Captain?"

"Thank you."

The doorman gave an ear-splitting whistle and threw an arm up in the air. In moments a dilapidated yellow taxi pulled up to the kerb. Lightholler ducked into the back after handing the doorman a thousand-yen note.

The driver glanced at him in the rear-view mirror. He asked for Lightholler's destination in broken English. A thin pale scar ran from his left temple to just above his lip—probably a refugee from one of the Occupied Territories.

"St Marks Place," Lightholler replied, and sank back into the worn leather seat.

Despite the chill, he wound down the grime-stained window as they proceeded east on 50th Street, then downtown on Second Avenue. On his right, the scarlet towers of the Summer Palace soared into the smog-ridden heights. To the left, through narrow intersections, he caught glimpses of the East River. The Brooklyn shore, grey and broken, stretched out along the waterway. As they crossed 14th Street, the spires and skyscrapers of Midtown grudgingly gave way to the tenements and brownstones of the Lower East Side. If you closed your eyes, he thought, just slightly, made the street signs a blur so that the names were illegible, you could almost believe the Japanese had never been here at all.

Almost.

The taxi pulled up at the Second Avenue corner of St Marks Place in a garland of brown exhaust. Lightholler paid the fare, just managing to escape the cab before it rushed back into the seethe of morning traffic.

IV

Kennedy took the call in what passed for the brownstone's office. David Hardas's voice sounded strained on the other end of the line.

"What have you got?" Kennedy asked, trying to keep his darker thoughts at bay. "Lightholler spent most of the morning on the phone. He's just left the Waldorf."

Kennedy checked his Einstein watch. It was twelve-forty. "Did he check out?"

"He wasn't carrying any suitcases."

"He won't run. Who's watching him?"

"Good question," Hardas replied. "I saw the doorman put a tail on him."

That was pretty fast. Not surprising, but fast. Playing host to the Russo-Japanese peace talks would attract some attention; involvement in the operation outlined by Saffel would garner a lot more. Kennedy had allowed the surveillance devices in Lightholler's suite to operate just long enough to verify the identity of his visitors. His association with Project Camelot would confer immunity within the higher echelons of the intelligence communities. The question was: who had placed Lightholler under surveillance—the Germans or the Japanese?

"Abwehr or Kempei-Tai?" he asked.

"You won't believe this, Major. They're Bureau."

"You sure?"

"Positive. I made the doorman. He's one of ours."

Kennedy considered the possibilities for a moment. The Bureau's mandate didn't extend beyond the Confederacy's borders. Camelot, by its very nature, was the exception. So what the hell was going on here?

"Then he's double-dealing," Kennedy said. "Has to be."

"I doubt it. I caught the last part of his transmission, Major. Got zip on the standard Jap and Kraut bandwidths so I put it through one of our decoders for the hell of it. He was using a Bureau frequency."

"Anything tricky?" Kennedy asked.

"No, Major. Routine settings. Way I see it, they don't know we're after him, or they simply don't give a shit."

"Neither option's appealing."

Kennedy tried putting it all together. First Saffel, now this. Was the CBI watching Lightholler independently, or keeping tabs on Camelot itself?

"Any mention of our visit to the captain?" he asked.

"None, but I only heard a snatch before he broke off."

"What've you done about it?"

"I've got Collins and Shaw following the tail."

Collins and Shaw: two CBI operatives who'd accompanied Kennedy here from Nevada. They'd been with him since Camelot's inception.

"Do they know they're following CBI agents?" Kennedy asked.

"It won't take them long to figure it out. Is that a problem?"

"Could be. We'll see how it plays out. Have them report back to you on one of *our* frequencies and get back down here. I need you here straightaway."

Kennedy ended the call.

So another player had entered the game. Someone within the Bureau was offering new pieces and changing the rules, advancing pawns of a different colour. Behind them, emerging from the void, would come the knights, the castles and finally the sovereign.

But who was moving them?

V

It took Hardas twenty minutes to cross town. Shine handed him a glass of rye as he entered the suite. Kennedy ushered him towards a chair. He drained the glass and poured himself another, anticipating the worst.

Kennedy told him about Saffel's report.

He listened, asking the occasional question and nodding his head gravely at each reply. It was bold and it was insane, but it was possible. Nevada had taught him that *anything* was possible. He smudged a finger through the pile of cold ashes on the table and spoke up.

"Why would the Germans pull a stunt like this now? As far as anyone knows, Camelot is ready to roll."

"This stunt was years in the making. Maybe they were using Camelot as a smokescreen."

"They wouldn't be the first."

Kennedy offered a cool smile. "It may amount to nothing. We need to know for sure before we start changing our own plans."

"You think Lightholler is involved?"

"I have to assume the worst. I want you to prove me wrong."

"And the Bureau knows what's going on?"

"Like I said..." Kennedy's voice trailed away.

"Do you think they know we're here?" Shine asked. "The CBI?"

Hardas started at the sound of the man's voice. Shine made a habit of slipping into the background.

"They will soon enough," Kennedy said. "I'm going to call in."

"You sure that's a good idea?" Hardas said. "Director Webster thinks we're in Louisiana, Major."

"If Webster has a watch team on Lightholler, it won't take him long to connect the dots. We don't want to be tarred with the same brush. Besides, we don't have any choice. Camelot has been in the works for the past three years and in all that time we've had free rein in its operation. Now that it's on the boil, the Bureau sends another team across the border. I need to know why."

"Why take the chance?" Hardas asked. "We're about done here anyway. All we have to do is grab Lightholler and run. Hit Nevada and then…" he snapped his fingers, "we're gone."

"It's not that simple. If Lightholler is part of the German plot, he's a liability. We may have to forget about him."

"Forget about him… how?" Shine asked.

Kennedy cast him a glance. "Just forget about him." He paused a moment. "Thing is, we lose Lightholler and we lose our contingency plan."

"We don't need a contingency plan, Major," Shine said softly.

"Everyone needs a contingency plan." He shoved his hands into his pockets and walked over to the window. He stood before it with his face twisted into a scowl, then turned his gaze towards the old flag and murmured, "I've got a bad feeling that this is where it all starts."

"It's too early," Hardas said.

"We don't know that. We don't know *how* it begins, just how it ends."

Hardas suppressed a shudder. It was time to ask the question no one wanted to hear.

"Do you think Webster knows?" he asked. "Do you think he has any idea about what we're really up to?"

"I can't see how," Kennedy replied after a long silence. "He'd be doing a lot more than watching us if he even suspected such a thing." When he spoke again it was with a measure of renewed vigour. "Morgan will be back around five, right?"

Hardas and Shine both nodded.

"Get going then, David. We need to know what we need to know. Martin, I need you to stay here. I have no idea how Webster's going to react once I blow our cover. With a second CBI task force in New York—one that's potentially hostile—we'll have to move fast. I need us ready to ship out at a moment's notice. Can you take care of that?"

"Sure thing, Major," Shine replied.

"If Morgan gets back before we do, keep him in the dark. We need him clear and focused."

"We need him like a hole in the head," Hardas muttered.

Kennedy cut him off. "Keep a sharp eye out, Martin."

Hardas rose to join Kennedy as he made for the doorway.

"If things go our way, we're going to need somewhere close by to complete Lightholler's recruitment," Kennedy said, closing the door behind them. "Somewhere the CBI doesn't know about."

"I can think of a place," Hardas said as they descended the stairs.

Outside the building, the afternoon sun assailed their eyes. Hardas lit up, then turned his face away to exhale before speaking. "Maybe we make for Neverland."

"I thought that was what you had in mind."

"It's underneath the radar, Major, and it's a day away from Red Rock. We fly in, turn Lightholler, fly out."

Kennedy, silent, seemed lost in thought.

"A ranch in Arkansas is the last place anyone will be looking for us." Hardas sensed Kennedy's uncertainty and added, "If you think we can take Lightholler straight to Nevada, that's what we'll do—you're the boss. But if you think we need a place to sort him out, where else did you have in mind?"

"Neverland," Kennedy said after a moment. "Where else would lost boys go?"

Hardas had only visited the ranch once. He tried to picture a younger version of Kennedy playing pirate around the coves and thickets of Lake Hamilton.

"We're not lost, Major. Just a little shook up is all." Hardas tried to muster a smile. He took a drag on his cigarette and waited for a reply.

"Go down to the pier. Find out what the hell is going on. I've got a call to make." Kennedy checked his Einstein. "We'll meet back here at four."

Hardas watched Kennedy leave. He thought about what he had to do and where he had to go. He thought about what he'd set in motion, all those years ago. He frowned and tossed his cigarette onto the pavement and made for the pier.

VI

The twin towers of the Krupp Corporation rose above the plaza where Fifth Avenue ended at Waverly Place, casting lengthy shadows across Wilhelm Square.

Standing at the entrance to the park, Kennedy caught a glimpse of the statue that had fascinated him in his youth. Age-worn and mistreated, the Kaiser's effigy still held on to his stallion's bridle with a firm grip. Under an Uhlan's helmet, his fiercely moustached face glared down at the communist hordes who cowered beneath his mount. Streaks of rust smeared the high cheekbones of his grim visage with bloody tears. The plaque at the pedestal's base, commemorating the Kaiser's victory over the Soviets and the reinstatement of the Tsar in 1945, was barely decipherable.

The monument's condition was symptomatic. "Little Prussia" was finally falling apart. In the brief interim between the Great War and the Second Secession there'd been a vast migration of war-weary Germans to the East Coast. The majority had settled around this neighbourhood, but what had been a thriving community nearly a century ago had been reduced to a few streets around the square. The ink had scarcely dried on MacArthur's offer of unconditional surrender in 1948 before the first wave of Japanese settlers had arrived, and they'd been coming ever since.

All that remained were the Krupp towers and the park. Despite growing anti-German sentiment during the Cold War, the city's new masters had thought it imprudent to change the square's name. It remained an enclave to those Germans who were too old or too poor to leave.

Kennedy shook his head and strode past the statue across the park, to the southwest corner. He was greeted by a familiar sight beneath the spread of wide-branched trees. Men sitting on benches, hunched over the chessboards that had been carved into the tables. The youngest of them had to be at least sixty. They wore a variety of shabby greatcoats; the litany of a dozen German campaigns documented on the faded crests of their lapels.

Of all the places I could have chosen, he wondered, *why come here*?

In 1947, just prior to the Japanese Occupation, Joseph Patrick Kennedy I, his great-grandfather, had moved the clan south. The Secession may have been ratified in '32, but for many Americans the country's fracture was an ongoing process. A considerable number of New England families had gone on to form a Union enclave in New Orleans. While the Rothschilds and the Roosevelts maintained a ghetto-like existence in the fledgling nation, the Kennedys, with their new money and political connections, were readily assimilated into the burgeoning Confederate "aristocracy". At least until 1963 and the bloodshed of Dealey Plaza.

Kennedy's grandfather, Joseph Patrick II, was appointed the Confederate ambassador to the Union. He returned to the North in the late fifties with his youngest brother, Edward, while his brothers John and Robert stayed to pursue their interests in the South. Kennedy's grandfather relinquished his post in '63, when the circumstances of his brothers' deaths laid to rest any desire he might have had for a future in politics. He'd stayed in the North, however, maintaining a residence on Fifth Avenue.

Nearly every winter up until the age of thirteen, Kennedy could recall accompanying his father to New York. His earliest memories were the journeys through old battlefields and towns, little more than smudges along the railway tracks. The sweet musk of the rocking carriages, the vacant stares of the border guards as they changed trains prior to entering the Prefecture of New York. Once he'd even made the long journey by airship.

Between visits to museums and galleries and quiet evenings at the mansion, his father would take him to the park. They would bring sandwiches wrapped in waxed paper. They would stand and watch the men play chess in silence. Occasionally his father would lean down, whispering a soft explanation of the intricacies being played out before them, and Kennedy would nod between bites of his sandwich in what he hoped passed for understanding. Despite many offers, Kennedy's father had always refused to play with the old soldiers.

One time, however, Kennedy himself had been asked. An elderly man with wild white hair had offered him a game. Gaining his father's approval, he'd clambered up to the high table. He had to squat on the bench to gain a good vantage of the board.

The man placed two different pawns, one in each hand, behind his back. Kennedy had stared at the man as if his gaze could burn through his skin, as if he could see the very pieces themselves. The man had laughed when Kennedy sat unmoving as the bronze and orange leaves spiralled onto the untouched board. Eventually he shrugged his left shoulder.

"That one," Kennedy had called out. "The left."

"Not all choices will come to you so easily," the man had said, smiling. "No matter how long you deliberate." He opened his hand to reveal the black pawn rolling in his palm. "Chess is not a game of trust."

Kennedy had frowned and turned to his father, who said nothing. The man set the board up with a briskness that belied his age, his elbows sweeping away the accumulated leaves, his fingers darting over the pieces as he positioned them.

"We start," he said, advancing his king's pawn with a flourish.

Kennedy responded by mirroring the move.

The man brought forwards a knight to threaten the pawn.

Kennedy advanced his own to offer protection.

The man advanced his bishop to threaten the exposed knight. He pointed a wavering finger at Kennedy's pawn. "I think you like this piece too much."

Kennedy had leaned back on his haunches, examining the board.

The man sat watching Kennedy's face with a thin smile. "What to do? Threaten my bishop, thus imperilling your defences? Retreat your knight ignominiously and lose your much-loved pawn?"

Kennedy felt a firm hand on his shoulder.

"Either way, Joe," his father said, "you have to lose something." He knelt down and added, "Eventually you have to lose a piece. Just make it worthwhile."

Kennedy had gone on to lose piece by piece, the man drawing him out in exchange after exchange until the board was sparsely populated by isolated pawns and other lower pieces. The two kings stood warily at opposite sides of the board.

"Remember, young man, you start the game with all of your pieces. An infinite number of possibilities await your decision, await the revision of a thousand decisions. But at the end of the day, and at the end of the game, it all comes down to this." He gestured absently with an arthritic hand.

"I don't understand," Kennedy had said.

The man nodded at him solemnly. "But one day you will." He placed his finger on a bishop and slid it down the length of the board. "Check..."

Kennedy studied the barren board.

"...and mate in two."

Kennedy sullenly flicked over his king and glanced up at his father, who gave a gentle shake of his head. Kennedy remembered his manners and thanked the old man for the game.

"The pleasure was mine," the man had said. "You show promise. Perhaps, next time, victory shall be yours."

There had never been a next time. Although he'd visited the park several more times that winter, Kennedy never saw the elderly man again. Soon afterwards, his grandfather had travelled to the German Mideast on family business. When he failed to return following the Sinai Crisis, the rest of the family had returned to the South for good.

Thirty years, Dad. It's been thirty years.

Kennedy thrust his hands into his coat pockets and walked up to the chess players. He stayed to watch a few games. Standard openings gave way to combinations that varied from the familiar to the bizarre. Slashing attacks and fierce sorties triumphed in sudden raids or ended in futile sacrifice. The boards emptied. Robbed of vicious queens and unpredictable knights and surrounded by a lean detail of pawns, the kings moved ponderously and grandly across desolate battlefields.

He sauntered from table to table, looking for some portent to guide his way.

An infinite number of possibilities.

He left the park by the corner entrance and wandered a block over to Sixth Avenue, then turned downtown. The late morning traffic was swarming downtown in tides that broke at each traffic light, swelling and reforming to thunder down to the next intersection. He found a phone booth outside a tavern on Bleecker and punched in a number. He triggered the stopwatch on his Einstein and said, "Director Webster, please."

"Identification?"

"201166; watchword, Pendragon."

"Confirmed. One minute, sir. You're calling unsecured—I'll put you through the scrambler."

There was a dial tone, the click of a recording device, and then, "Well, well, well. Speak of the devil. Good afternoon, Joseph."

"Good afternoon, sir."

"How's the weather treating you up there? I find that New York is always lovely in April."

"The weather's fine, sir," Kennedy replied, cursing inwardly.

"So you've been in touch with our Mr Lightholler? He strikes me as a practical sort of fellow. Granted he sounded a little anxious on the phone tap this morning, but that's understandable, isn't it? How did you find him, Joseph? More to the point, *why* did you go looking for him?"

"The same reason I look for anyone, sir. Information."

"I'm feeling a little inquisitive myself, so indulge me," Webster replied. "Why are you in New York trawling for information from the captain of an ocean liner? Are you considering a new occupation for yourself?"

"No, sir. I'm just—"

Webster cut him short. "Well, perhaps you should. The role of delivery boy seems to suit you well, and bearing a letter from the palace at that. And, as you seem fond of saying, you are 'owed some favours'. But for what services, I wonder?"

Kennedy offered no reply. Clearly Webster was well aware of his earlier conversation with Lightholler. Shine had confirmed that the captain's phone line wasn't tapped, but that didn't account for anyone he might have spoken to after they had left.

Who the *hell* had Lightholler called in the Admiralty?

He pictured Webster hunched at his long, wide oak desk. Would he be wearing the eye patch or had he taken it off for the call?

"Yes..." Webster stretched the word out painfully. "Let's see now. Information. Tell me, Joseph, why were you in contact with Captain Lightholler?"

"I thought we'd benefit from his take on the peace talks." He decided to keep it simple. "Their failure affects our timetable."

"Since he arrived in New York, Lightholler's sat with representatives of the Shogun, the Tsar and the Kaiser," Webster purred. "I suppose you felt esteemed enough to join their ranks."

Kennedy didn't bite. "I valued his point of view, sir."

"Valued it enough to recruit the man."

"Yes, sir."

"For my Bureau."

"Yes, sir."

"But why do so via British intelligence? If indeed there is such a thing. And while we're at it, remind me, just when did I authorise this?"

"I approached him via the British in order to secure his full and rapid cooperation. As for your authority, with all due respect, I thought I had a sanction to deputise for the project."

"Subject to my final approval, you do. And I don't recall giving you that."

"That's why I'm calling in. I wanted to have his answer before bringing you into the picture."

Webster's silence was an accusation. Kennedy found he was gripping the handpiece knuckle-white. Drawing a deep breath, he decided to play it through.

"Frankly, I have some questions of my own. I'm wondering where all this is going. I'm wondering why the Bureau has him under surveillance. Why have you sent *another* team across the border?"

"All good questions, Joseph," Webster answered calmly. "What was Lightholler's answer?"

Kennedy wished he knew.

"He said yes."

"Did he now. You must be as pleased as punch, Joseph." Webster said the name like he was sucking on a lemon. "I don't know what exactly went on in that hotel room, since for *some* reason our recording equipment malfunctioned during your interview. Given that fact, I want a complete record of your conversation."

"I'll send it down today."

"I want it hand delivered. After all, that seems to be your forte. My office. Tomorrow. 0800 hours."

"Tomorrow?"

"You planned on flying Lightholler to Dallas on Tuesday. I want you and your crew here in Houston tonight. I'm calling you in for debriefing."

Kennedy felt swept up in some tide. A current held him back with landfall a hand's breadth out of reach. He said, "I have a meeting scheduled in Washington tomorrow afternoon. I'll send Hardas." He checked his watch. Two and a half minutes gone. In ninety seconds they'd complete the trace.

"You'll rain check it. If you hadn't phoned I'd be contacting you myself. I'm calling you in. Project Camelot—and your role in it—are up for reassessment."

"My role?"

"Your recent activities have attracted more attention than I would have liked. Too much, considering our goals and your name."

Anger and indignation swelled to replace fear. "My recent activities are project related and as such they are subject only to the President's scrutiny."

"Yet here I am, scrutinising you. Up until today President Clancy was unaware of your separate dealings with British royalty and German intelligence—he's less than pleased. You'll have the opportunity to explain your position to both of us tomorrow morning, and it had better be good. This isn't a request, Joseph, this is a chance for you to place all your cards on the table; convince us that our concerns are … unfounded."

Sixty seconds left…

"I'll contact the President myself if need be," Kennedy said. "I'm up here to finalise the Union targets for Camelot and I'm in the middle of negotiations."

"My office. 0800 hours, with your report and a detailed list of all Camelot operatives. If everything checks out you'll be in Washington by tomorrow night."

Anger, indignation, and now an element of curiosity. Why bring him down, just to send him back? Why send him back, if he was up for re-evaluation?

"And it's come to my attention that the men in your training camps are ready to ship out," Webster continued. "I want them on ice until we've sorted this out."

Thirty seconds…

"The camps have been mobilised since the centennial voyage, sir. They won't stand down without a direct order from me."

"Then give the order, Joseph. Meanwhile, I'll arrange four tickets for you on a red-eye. Lightholler, Morgan, Hardas and yourself. Call back in an hour. Susan will have the details ready for you by then."

"Yes, sir," Kennedy replied.

Ten seconds…

"And, Joseph, have a safe flight."

Kennedy cut the connection. He let the phone slip from his hand and stared at the tavern, thinking it through. Webster was suspicious alright but that was all. If the director had any inkling of what was really going on, he'd be on a slab by now. It was that simple.

Kennedy's secret was known to a chosen few. He'd intended Lightholler to be the last. Months had gone into cultivating him as the final member of the team. Weeks still might be required to secure his willing support. Understanding would come later, as it had to the rest of the men.

For the moment, it looked like CBI knew nothing about Red Rock.

Yet he'd counted on weeks to put his plan into action, and now he had days. Perhaps hours. His options were steadily dwindling and this game had barely begun.

He needed to put through a call to Red Rock.

VII

April 21, 2012
Houston, Texas

Patricia Malcolm watched the proceedings with mounting apprehension. Seated towards the back of the room, avoiding the curious gaze of the agents, she fought every urge to run to the door.

Webster knew. He *had* to know. Why else would she be here?

The director's office was spartan in its decor. The only illumination spilled from a lamp perched at the edge of his desk, an oval of orange-tinged light. She hoped she wasn't expected to take notes.

Webster hung up the phone and turned to an agent waiting by the door. "Did you get a trace?"

"He's at a pay phone in Greenwich Village; corner of Bleecker and Thompson. The number's engaged again."

"Have Close Watch send in a team."

She had never seen the director up close before now. Never seen him without the eye patch. He turned his gaze to take in the rest of the room. The puckered scar that had once been an eye swept over her. It fixed on the agent he'd been addressing.

"Why are you still here?"

"Director Webster, I thought you needed—"

"Don't think, Robbins. *Do*."

The agent exited the office.

Webster pressed a switch on his intercom. "Susan, in the unlikely event that Assistant Director Kennedy calls back, please arrange four seats on a plane from Idlewild for tonight. Use a Confederate airline, and get them on a direct flight." He released the switch without waiting for a reply and turned his attention back across the desk. "Agent Williams?"

"Sir," replied a balding man wearing horn-rimmed glasses.

"Should they board that flight, I want a squad of tactical agents waiting for them at the airport, your best men."

"Yes, sir."

"And what about Saffel?"

"He's being brought across this evening."

"Has he said anything to your men?"

"Not as yet, Director."

"Perhaps he'll be more forthcoming once you've outlined to him what comes of treason against our fair state."

Williams' face contorted. "I'll make it clear to him, sir."

Webster favoured him with a smile before shifting his attention to Malcolm. She felt the fear rising within her. It looked like all of Joseph's contacts were being run to ground. She hadn't spoken to the bastard for almost two years but she was going to be dragged down with him.

"Miss Malcolm, you're presently assigned to..." Webster glanced down at a notebook on his desk, "Lab Division."

"Yes, sir. Evidence Response." The reply was almost lost in her throat.

"You worked Maritime with Kennedy."

"Yes, sir. In 2006."

"You're the only person I have on active duty who worked with Kennedy prior to his current project. The only one he didn't take with him, that is."

He paused, and she waited for the axe to fall.

"I'm shifting you to OPR, effective immediately."

"*OPR?*" She could barely contain her surprise.

He ignored her interruption. "You will have full access to data concerning Assistant Director Kennedy, Agent Malcolm. I want you to build a case. I want you to sift through everything there is to know about him, from his shit-heel of a great-grandfather to that joke of an election campaign. I want a list of *all* his affiliates, including those of colour. I want a list of every contact he has made in the last three months. And I want to know why he has become so interested in the *Titanic*."

"Yes, Director."

Shock mingled with amazement. She'd expected to end the day in a prison cell at best. Instead, she was receiving an unprecedented promotion. The murmurs sweeping the room confirmed that the move had taken all the agents by surprise. She felt every eye upon her.

The Office of Professional Responsibility was the Bureau's division that investigated any and all allegations of criminal misconduct by CBI employees, from the smallest infraction to outright treason.

What has Joseph gotten himself into?

She was assailed by a mixture of emotions. This transfer meant elevating her to a department that had previously been closed to women. She was going to be the first female agent in the Bureau's history.

"If he's truly gone rogue, I want to know who he's working for—the Germans, the japs, or our Union brothers. I want to know what makes him run." Webster's eyes flicked away from her as if he'd just completed an unsavoury task. "Agent Cooper?"

"Sir," the man seated next to Malcolm replied. He'd been gazing at her disapprovingly.

"Right now Kennedy is somewhere in Greenwich Village. The last Close Watch has on him are the transcripts we lifted from MI5." Webster tapped his pencil against the ornate base of the lamp. "Coordinate with Robbins. Your boys are in charge now. I want a tail on him ASAP. If he doesn't go to Idlewild, I want to know where he is and where he goes at all times. I want to know who he talks to and what he says. If he defecates, I want to know what he's had for lunch."

"Do you want me to split teams or transfer Close Watch to Kennedy?"

"Our observation of Lightholler has been compromised," Webster said pointedly. "Use your own men. I suspect that one will almost certainly lead to the other."

Cooper smiled.

"This is a dry operation, Agent Cooper," Webster continued.

"Of course, sir, it's just that my department ain't exactly known for its surveillance." Cooper sounded mildly disappointed.

"I know what Wetworks does, Agent Cooper. You'll get the chance to do what you do best."

"Yes, sir."

"On my sanction."

"Yes, sir."

Malcolm squirmed in her seat, unconsciously shifting away from the man. There was a whispered exchange among the agents behind her that she didn't catch. She wondered why the director had asked her to build a case, when the verdict appeared all but decided.

"As for you, Agents Reid, Carter."

She heard the two men behind her shift in their chairs.

"I'll give you the precise location of Alpha and Bravo camps. Kennedy says they're mobilised. That could mean anything. Take four squads each. I want all of his senior staff replaced with our men. You'll be given a list of all the veteran officers who've served under his command. They're to be culled from the ranks. I want the rest left unarmed. Arrest them, ship them to New Mexico, I don't care. I just want them under wraps. The last thing we need is Kennedy's private army running wild."

"Do you really think that'll happen, sir?" Carter ventured. It was clear from his tone that by the end of the sentence he was sorry he'd asked it.

"Agent Carter, I've no idea what sort of stunt the major has up his sleeve." Webster's good eye bore down on the man mercilessly. "But while a man can scarcely carve out an empire for himself with four thousand men, he can certainly bring one down. I appreciate that all of you have had to assimilate a great deal in a small space of time. Up until this meeting, most of you had never even heard of Camelot. By the time this whole thing is over, you'll likely wish you'd remained ignorant.

"For the past three years we've trained men at two facilities: one in Nevada, the other in Louisiana," he continued. "At a designated time, and coincident with a number of other planned events, these men will cross the northern border. They're highly skilled in sabotage, demolition, force multiplication, insurgency and a number of other unpleasantries. In *no* way can they be linked with our government. Their targets include major Japanese industrial centres in the Union and the Demilitarised Zone. Their aim is to bring about the paced destruction of key facilities. This will precipitate a buildup of Japanese soldiers in the North. Timed correctly—shall we say at a time when Japanese soldiers are needed elsewhere—it will lead to a substantial consumption of manpower.

"Agents of the CBI and Union intelligence have been placed in military and judicial posts throughout the North and South. Both the Confederate and Union provisional governments will respond to the disturbance with a declaration of martial law. The Union will mobilise, and offer assistance to the japs. We'll mass our troops on the border in friendly support during this time of crisis."

Webster rose from his seat and placed both hands wide on the desk.

"They can keep Alaska, and good luck to them, but finding themselves outnumbered and outgunned, thousands of miles from home, a firm diplomatic shove will push them out of New York and back onto the West Coast, and they'll *thank* us for it."

He paced slowly back and forth behind the desk.

"There'll be a continent-wide call for intervention, and that's what both our governments will provide. A show will be made of bringing the vandals to justice. German sponsorship will be slight but apparent. Having accomplished its objectives, Camelot will result in something that should have occurred well over a century ago: a confederation of united states stretching from Canada to the Mexican border, under *Southern* leadership."

He picked up his eye patch and turned it over in his hands.

"The men at Kennedy's two camps were drawn primarily from indian and negro stock; a considerable number came from his old command in the last Ranger War. They were trained by and remain utterly loyal to him. This loyalty may extend beyond patriotism and it may not. But you all know what a capable few were able to do at Mazatlan. What do you think an army of such men, scattered throughout the Union and Confederacy, would be capable of accomplishing?"

There was a murmur of discontent.

"Understand that you're all suspended from your current duties till this matter has been dealt with." He stared at them intently. "I want Camelot contained before any of our associates in the Abwehr or Kempei-Tai start looking for someone to blame. Make it happen, gentlemen."

One by one they left their seats and exited the room.

"*Agent* Malcolm."

She stood at the office entrance, one hand resting on the door's frame.

"There's one more thing…"

VIII

April 21, 2012

New York City, Eastern Shogunate

Fighting through the lunchtime crowds, Morgan made his way south in the direction of Canal Street, with brief detours to the various book stores that punctuated Broadway.

He was held up by a traffic jam near Union Square that had spilled onto the sidewalk. Two carriages had collided. Following what could only be described as a breach of etiquette, the streets were full of samurai. One group wore the royal blue sashimono and scarves of the Emperor's Imperial Watch; the other was decked out in the crimson body armour of the Shogun's Guard.

As a result of the Japanese expansion, the four main islands of the Homeland constituted less than two per cent of the empire's land mass. So before his death, Emperor Hirohito, Ryuichi's father, had reinstated the office of Shogun. Handing Ryuichi the central reins of power, he'd apportioned the east and west to his younger sons Hideyoshi—Ryuichi's younger twin— and Tsunetomo. The Western Shogunate supervised China, Korea and Manchuria; the Eastern covered the Pacific conquests, occupied North America and the satellite nation of Union states. In each place, however, Emperor Ryuichi maintained his own significant forces.

Hirohito had left three sons to rule the Eastern World. To Morgan, the potential fracas that brewed here was indicative of mounting tension between those three factions. Hadn't Hirohito read *King Lear*?

The horned-devil faces of the samurai's helmets clashed oddly with the machine pistols that hung from their shoulders. Angered shouts gave way to bows and apologies as the representatives of Emperor Ryuichi and his brother Hideyoshi swiftly made their peace.

Morgan crossed to Fourth Avenue, avoiding the scrutiny of soldiers who now turned their attention upon the gathering crowd. Encountering Lightholler again had been a disappointment. Time and circumstance had prevented asking the questions that burned inside him—the same questions he had wanted to ask on the centennial voyage. As far as Morgan was concerned, Lightholler was the mother lode. He carried the genetic distillation of three generations of the two families that had fuelled Morgan's interest throughout years of historical research. In truth, he'd never imagined he would meet the man—especially under these circumstances.

But then again, who could have imagined such circumstances?

Morgan found what he was looking for in the fifth book store he visited. He emerged with his prize bundled carefully in a plastic bag under his arm.

He reached Canal Street, where the midday crowds were particularly thick, and stopped at a street corner to buy some sushi. A few businessmen stood nearby, eating their meals. He was surprised to note that a couple of them were Japanese. Try doing that on the streets of Hiroshima and you would be politely cautioned, if you were lucky. As with all empires, here at the outskirts things had grown lax.

Many of the stores were closed but the tourist trade had offered the tired street a boom. Hawkers plied their trade from makeshift booths. Spying a vacant step leading up to an abandoned shopfront, Morgan sat down heavily. He opened his own bag and slipped one of the sushi rolls into his mouth. Savouring the taste, he pulled out the book. It was a cheap paperback edition, the embossed title reading *Titanic: Calamity and Consequences*. Beneath the bold lettering was the illustration of an iceberg, its crystal facets reflecting the ill-fated ship's approach. At the bottom of the cover was the name Darren Daniel Morgan.

He'd never liked that tawdry cover.

On the back, beneath a blurb oozing praise, was a black and white photo. The eyes the same, the hair a little longer, perhaps a little thicker. His cheeks were sallow. He'd been hungrier then. And there had been a wedding band on his curled finger.

He examined the bare fingers of his left hand. With a sigh he opened the book, turned past the acknowledgments and dedications—which he knew by heart—to the foreword. Reading his own words, he found himself mouthing the syllables, and slowly disdain crept across his face.

The book had first been published in 1999, just weeks before the discovery of the wreck. He'd thanked good fortune back then that the fruit of so many years' labour had received such a timely release. The fact that his research had concentrated more on the far-reaching repercussions of the sinking, rather than on the event itself, did little to turn away its avid readers. The book had brought him money, a modicum of fame and—much later—the attention of Major Joseph Kennedy.

He set aside the remainder of his meal and began to read.

FOREWORD

As the second millennium hastens toward its close, our urge to find meaning in its bloodshed and its discoveries, its dreams and disappointments, becomes all the more apparent. Everywhere one looks, from the cinema to the novel, from advertising to architecture, there is the attempt to transmute the lessons we *think* we have learnt into what we imagine is to come. The majority of these visions portray a bright future. The novels of Anne Frank, despite their evident propaganda, show a new Germany. Echoed by the provocative art of Hitler and the stirring symphonies of Karajan, they embrace the transformation of the cold Teutonic lands into a fertile expanse, from whose fecund soil will emerge a guiding light to the future.

Across the oceans, Mishima's novels, and the films of Takeshi and Sato, mirror these sentiments. However, from their point of view it is obvious that the only joy and prosperity offered by the twenty-first century lie within the boundaries of the Greater Empire of Nippon.

While these promising futures are mutually exclusive, they reveal each culture's preoccupation with examining the roots of its recent past before embracing the promises of a new millennium. Of more interest are those visions of a more dystopian nature. Employing the same sources and examining the same events that shaped this century, the works of Vonnegut, Barnes, Murasaki and Moore, as well as the films of Welles and Kurosawa—particularly those made after the latter's self-imposed exile—display a startling similarity. With a vast difference in cultural ancestry, and hailing from disparate backgrounds, they portray a bleak world of discontented colonials, and empires on the point of dissolution. They suggest that all we have learnt from this century's warfare is a better way to fight.

The dystopian view is a contemporary one, and in no small measure has the recent invention of atomics contributed to its rise. The fact that now we have the ability to cause destruction on an unforeseen and apocalyptic scale has made the world a smaller, more fragile place.

There were undercurrents of doubt as far back as 1920, however, when the world's nations were rising from the ashes of the greatest conflict humanity has ever fought. In the shadow of the German victory and hot on the heels of the formation of the Soviet Union, Sir Wilfred Owen wrote his epic *Wasted Lands*. An elegy to the senseless loss of the world's youth, from the fields of Flanders to the steppes of Russia, it arrived on the scene to receive scorn and vilification both sides of the ocean.

It is of interest to note that, in retrospect, *Wasted Land*s may be read as a template for the subsequent affairs of Europe and indeed the world at large. Even in the twenties, there existed a vision of the world separating itself into two armed camps, each eyeing the other across the ocean with increasing fear and hatred.

On April 15, 1912, the *Titanic*, sailing on her maiden voyage from Southampton to New York, struck an iceberg and sank. On July 3, 1999, the wreck of the *Titanic* was discovered, lying in 10,000 feet of water, south of the Grand Banks of Newfoundland.

The loss and subsequent rediscovery of the ship may be seen to form a framework for our century. And notwithstanding the passing of the years, interest in the ship has never been greater. For, then as now, the loss of the *Titanic* has become a modern-day myth to rival the Greek legends of old.[1]Mankind's boldest creation, setting out on her first voyage from the Old World to the New, doomed never to arrive.

The sinking of the great liner on her maiden voyage became symbolic of the struggle of minorities, ranging from the short-lived Suffragette Movement to the negroes. Religious groups used the event to respond

1. A comparison of the war between the gods of the Greek Pantheon, wherein Zeus and the Olympians overthrew the Titans, to the sinking of the *Titanic*, has not been lost among the more sensationalist accounts of the disaster. However, it is interesting to note that following the loss of the *Titanic*, the directors of the White Star Line chose to rename the third of its superliners *Britannic*, rather than the now auspicious title of *Gigantic*. Perhaps a further perusal of Greek mythology informed them that while the Olympians conquered the Titans, it was the Titans who conquered the Earth's first inhabitants, the Giants.

to the claim that *Titanic* was "the ship God himself could not sink".[2] For political groups, be they Democratic or Republican, Tory or Whig, "rearranging the deckchairs on the *Titanic*" has become common parlance for any delaying tactics that appear to serve no purpose.

Over the years the iceberg has come to represent fate, destiny, God's will, and the evils of technology. The *Titanic* has been used to describe arrogance and foolishness, but also bravery and courage. The purpose of this work, however, is not to examine why this single event has so captured the public's eye for almost a hundred years. That may be left for psychologists and sociologists to debate. The main goal here is to reveal how the events of the morning of April 15, 1912 may have influenced the early course of the century.

Looking back, it remains difficult to depict the magnitude of the event from our present perspective. We have since experienced the Great War, the European War, the division of France, and the numerous Wars of Japanese Expansion, including the conquest of the American Union and China. Even if we ignore other squabbles, such as the numerous battles fought between the Confederate States of America and the Mexican Empire, we confront the loss of tens of millions of lives. Thus the loss of two thousand souls on an ocean liner may seem insignificant.

Yet tales of the disaster dominated the newspapers for years. Up until the actual outbreak of hostilities in Europe, the sinking of the *Titanic* and the tribunals in America and England were the leading stories in nearly seventy per cent of the existing periodicals on both sides of the Atlantic.[3]

The conflicts arising from the differing opinions held by the British and American investigations make for interesting reading today. On close examination, they bear the seeds of discontent that were to flower into the American Isolation Policy that prevented the former United States from entering the Great War on the side of the Allies.

One cannot contemplate these events clearly without considering the singular role played by Colonel John Jacob Astor during the American Tribunals. That he, as a survivor himself, might show undue bias in the proceedings was ignored at the time. It was an amazing oversight,

2. The *London Times*: April 17 and 21, 1912

3. Statistically, the *Titanic* is the fourth most popular topic in Western literature, following Jesus, the American Civil War, and the Southern Secession. Some authors, however, choose to regard the last two subjects as a single topic.

considering that his young pregnant bride, Madeleine, was among the small number of first-class passengers lost that night. Perhaps the fact that the investigation was being held in the Astoria Lounge of the Waldorf Hotel, as well as Astor's substantial contribution of monies to the Titanic Relief Fund, went some small way to alleviate the consciences of the senators making up the tribunal.

Before we can look to the future, we must re-evaluate our past. Our governments dream of raising rotting hulks from the ocean's depths. They dream of sending men into space. Meanwhile, they test their weapons of mass destruction in the vast rice fields of occupied China and on the Pacific atolls of Colonial Germany.

The historian is a detective of sorts, investigating a sublime mystery. There is the Event, and the historian must sort through its causes and after-effects. He must question the motives of all the parties involved. Who has gained and who has lost? Any alibi must be thoroughly tested out. And at the end, rarely, the truth may be found.

However, by then it is invariably too late to punish the criminals.

Morgan looked up from the book to see that the crowd had thinned out. He glanced back at the pages wistfully.

"All wrong," he said to himself. "All wrong."

He rose from the steps.

Major Kennedy, he thought, *I forgive you your arrogance. It has some basis. I forgive you your callousness, the choices you have to make time and again. It goes with the territory, goes with the job. It's in your blood, for God's sake.*

He picked up the sushi's remains and tossed them into the bag with his book. Sealing the bag in a tight knot, he cast it into an adjacent bin.

I just can't forgive you for showing me that everything I ever knew or held dear is a lie.

IX

Down at the pier, a cool breeze sauntered along the Hudson's sluggish current. It hinted at the oil of machinery, yearned for the briny taste of ocean. Standing near the bow of the new *Titanic*, Hardas felt almost relaxed. Looking out past the massive pontoon that served as a pier for the ship and averting his eyes from the opposite shoreline, he could just about imagine he was there. Aboard the *Titanic*. The original ship.

His hands were still clammy but his breathing had settled down. Back at the brownstone, the major had said, "Locate the first officer. He's an Abwehr operative. Fordham's the name he goes by. Ask him if he likes Wagner."

"The composer?"

"The composer."

"Who the fuck likes Wagner?"

"Mention his name and our association and Fordham should start talking. We need to know how much time we have before this whole thing blows up in our faces."

Hardas had gone straight to the Lower West Side of Manhattan. Flashing identification that confirmed him as a member of the International Maritime Commission, he'd had no trouble boarding the massive ship. One of the crewmen swiftly brought him to the first officer, hardly giving him the opportunity to take in the extravagant surroundings.

Fordham was in the gymnasium, just aft of the bridge. Here, as elsewhere aboard ship, no effort had been spared in replicating the splendour of the original *Titanic*. The walls were decorated with illuminated pictures of the ship. The various apparatus spread throughout the large room were of a bygone age. Fordham stood between a rowing machine and a complicated series of pulleys and weights, gazing at a framed map of the world. It was a map from 1912 stained heavily with the crimson of the British Empire's holdings; criss-crossed with a network of lines showing the White Star Line's steamship routes.

The first officer had his back to them, but turned as the crewman announced his arrival. Hardas was puzzled to note that Fordham had nothing of the sea in him. His skin was sallow. Thin wispy hair swiped across a narrow brow. His eyes were too pale a shade of blue, as if covered by a thin film.

Hardas waited till the crewman departed, then flashed his Bureau identification. Fordham appeared bemused when Hardas told him that he worked with Major Kennedy, and nodded politely. Then Hardas mentioned the composer. Fordham eyed him appraisingly and said, "I've never met the major but I'm hardly surprised that he enjoys the works of Wagner."

He turned abruptly, indicating that Hardas should follow. He led him past the Grand Staircase to the elevator, allowed Hardas to enter first, and withdrew a small key from one of his pockets. As the lift doors hissed shut, he placed the key in a narrow slit beneath the control panel and gave it a sharp twist.

"Now I remember," Fordham said. "You commanded the *Schlieffen*."

Hardas nodded. "Briefly, yes."

"That was done well." Fordham leaned against the elevator wall, appraising him. "But tell me, when did the CBI start enlisting submarine commanders to do their dirty work?"

"Maybe around the same time the Germans began placing agents in the White Star Line."

"I am no spy," Fordham said with distaste. "I'm a military man, like yourself. It just so happens, however, that Wagner is my favourite composer."

Hardas said nothing. He counted the levels of their descent, marking the floors through the frosted window of the elevator door.

"E deck," Fordham announced. "Here, let me show you something." The doors slid open to reveal a narrow corridor. There was no sign of any fire damage, recent or otherwise. "On the original ship, Thomas Andrews designed a single passageway that ran the length of the vessel to accommodate the movement of crewmen and certain passengers. Those in first class referred to it as Park Lane; the crew called it Scotland Road."

Hardas nodded.

Fordham guided him to a rectangular door at the corridor's end. He opened it to reveal a wide, brightly lit avenue that vanished into the distance.

"Below decks, we have rechristened this pathway *Wilhelmstrasse*." Fordham continued. "We like to think of it as the Kaiser's variation on a theme."

The *Wilhelmstrasse* cut through the heart of Berlin. Hardas had seen it back in 2002, whilst on furlough. Every year, on the anniversary of Armistice, the German army paraded down its length as part of the victory commemoration.

Hardas stood watching doorways open and shut. He caught brief glimpses of the contents of the vast chambers that lay to either side of the passageway. He felt the blood draining from his face.

"When is it going to happen?" he asked.

"Maybe tonight, maybe never," Fordham said, his palms in the air. "It all depends on what the Japanese do next."

"It's going to happen," Hardas said. "This cost you too much for it all to be thrown away."

"It was far less expensive than waiting for Camelot to produce any results."

"We just needed more time," Hardas murmured. With Saffel's report confirmed, there was just one more detail he required. "Does Captain Lightholler know anything about this?" he asked.

"Why should he?" Fordham gave him a meaningful look. "The Kaiser did not want any interference with the peace process."

Hardas could think of a few choice replies but chose to remain silent.

Back in the gymnasium, Fordham led him to an antique exercise device. "Recognise this, Commander?"

"I've seen the original."

The machine had been hazy in the diluted beams of the submarine's floodlights, lying on its side and adorned with the rust of eighty years' exposure to the Atlantic's icy grasp. His memory of the drowned ship merged with his presence in the reconstructed room. Briefly, Hardas felt the unsettling experience of standing upon the wreck itself.

"Of course you have, and what a sight she must have been."

"She was," Hardas replied.

"Astounding, isn't it?" Fordham continued. "I come here and look at it often. A riding machine made up to look like a camel. So exotic, so unnecessary. What *were* they thinking?"

"Who?" Hardas was still caught in his reverie.

"The British. What dreams were they dreaming when they conceived of this monstrosity?"

Hardas placed a hand on the warm leather of the machine's saddle. "Dreaming of an empire. One on which the sun was never supposed to set. It was a different time, I guess."

"Yes, it was. 1912. A twilight dream to enjoy, with a terrible war on the horizon. Look around you, Commander. Look and think of it as it must have been. An unsinkable ship for an unconquerable nation." Fordham raised an eyebrow, awaiting a response that wasn't forthcoming. After a moment, he sighed. "And now a century has passed and all that was Britain's belongs to us. All that was Alexander's, Caesar's, and Bonaparte's. Sometimes I wonder if we shall fare any better. The fall of Troy only foreshadowed the rise of Rome, and she too fell. That brings me little comfort. Tell the major what you have seen; that his work and career have enjoyed my sympathies." Fordham was looking again at the map he'd been examining when Hardas arrived. "If you or your companions should encounter any of my men, name the crowning achievement of dear Wagner's work, *Twilight of the Gods*, for it is surely what you will witness."

Hardas took a deck of cigarettes from his shirt pocket and lit up. His hands, almost dry now, cupped the glowing tip. *Twilight of the Gods*, alright. A lightning strike from Germany into the heart of the Japanese Occupation. It was bold and it was insane, but it was *possible.*

He finished his cigarette and tossed it into the swirling brown waters. He made his way to the gangway and stomped down the irregular wooden planks to the pontoon. As he looked up at the immense ship from the gently swaying platform, it seemed like the only solid object in the world. He turned away without another glance and strode the long expanse of the pier to the shore.

He walked along 23rd Street till it intersected Broadway, then turned downtown, contemplating the journey to come. He recalled the many hours he'd spent with Kennedy and the others, the seeds of their wild speculations evolving into a complex plan. A plan that relied more on hope than strategy, more on mania than method.

He walked the streets with his face set in a hard grimace that parted the scanty crowds before him.

X

Shine reassessed his orders. Kennedy had said, *Keep a sharp eye out.* Nothing more.

The two agents had burst through the door to find Shine standing in the hallway, an empty suitcase in his hands. They'd gone through the motions, searching the rooms of the brownstone and finding it otherwise empty. One of them caught a glimpse of the pre-Secession flag furled in the corner of the room. He snorted and said, "Where's your boss, nigger?", lowering his gun.

The other was reaching for his two-way radio. "Where's Kennedy?"

"Can't say where he is, sir," Shine said, adopting a slight curve to his back and staring at the floor. "He just told me to pack his bags, like he always does. I don't ask questions—none of my business."

Shine approached the gunman deferentially, as custom required. Letting the suitcase drop to his side, he reached for the sheath by his bootstrap. They ignored him as expected. He slipped the blade between the agent's ribs, slicing upwards, then back out. Nothing fancy. A quick pirouette and he triggered the knife's grip. The blade shot across the room, embedded itself in the other agent's throat.

Clawing at his lapels, the second man collapsed back. Shine crossed the room, knelt beside him and withdrew the splattered blade. The agent tried to say something. Shine replaced the blade in its grip and severed the arteries that coursed along his torn throat. He leaned over the body as the spray of blood slowly diminished. He turned off the two-way, rifled through the agent's wallet, and produced a handful of false IDs, a CBI badge and a much-folded photograph of Lightholler. Shine pocketed them all, as well as the small Colt automatic tucked beneath the dead man's armpit.

He looked up to find Kennedy and Hardas standing in the doorway.

"Just two of them?" Kennedy asked, surveying the carnage.

"Looks like two is all they sent, Major," Shine replied. He realised his breath was coming in ragged gasps and stilled himself.

Kennedy inspected the bodies. "Reilly," he said, looking at the dead gunman. "And that one's Birmingham. What happened?"

Shine told him.

"Webster's concerns must have gotten the better of him," Kennedy said, finally. "They're Wetworks."

"They weren't very good."

"You surprised them." Kennedy's look was indecipherable. "I shouldn't have called in."

"They had to have tracked Commander Hardas here from the Waldorf, sir. It wouldn't have made a difference."

Hardas scowled.

Shine shrugged.

"Maybe," Kennedy said. "Let's clean up. If Morgan sees this, he'll have a seizure."

They dragged the bodies into one of the bedrooms and stowed them in an empty wardrobe. They worked on the carpet, scrubbing away at the stains. They ended up throwing a rug over the mess.

"What happens now, Major?"

"Tell him, David."

"I've been down to the ship. Saffel's story checks out. We're screwed."

"So Captain Lightholler's part of it," Shine mused.

"Guy doesn't have a clue. But I figure even if he is clean, he ain't going to be much use to us if he doesn't know the layout of his own ship."

"Lightholler has more to offer than just giving us directions," Kennedy said, firmly. "If push comes to shove he can command the ship, and it may come down to that."

Coming down to that implied a slip-up on Shine's part. It was his turn to scowl.

"We have to move out," Kennedy continued. "Webster's shutting Camelot down. And if today's disturbance is anything to go by, he'll have the Bureau swarming all over our camps before the day is out."

"All of them?" Shine asked.

"The ones he knows about," Kennedy replied. "But that still puts him too close to where we need to be."

"What's our move then?"

"I put a call through to Nevada and ordered a fade-out. The only thing he's going to find at Alpha and Bravo are empty shacks and tumbleweeds."

"The director will think you've turned."

Kennedy was staring at a streak of black blood that braided the carpet. "It's too late to worry about that. Besides, judging from what David tells me, the director's going to have bigger fish to fry. We move out tonight."

Shine felt something shift within him. He interpreted it as anticipation. With or without Lightholler, they were going to make a run for Nevada. They were going straight to Red Rock.

XI

April 22, 2012
New York City, Eastern Shogunate

Lightholler stirred to the sound of birdsong. He yawned and blinked at his surroundings. A field of green stretched out before him towards the low stone fence that separated Battery Park from the lapping waters of New York Harbor. Morning light dappled the waves. The Statue of Liberty stood ironically in her tarnished mantle, a jade glint in the distance.

More than a week had passed since he'd sailed into New York but the park still bore the signs of the thousands who had stood there in anticipation. Lightholler turned away, his recollection of the previous day returning with unpleasant clarity.

He'd gone from St Marks Place to wandering downtown Manhattan in a daze. His journey took him past the Lone Star Cafe, where he was to meet with Kennedy in two days' time. He walked aimlessly, circumnavigating the narrow streets that bound Osakatown and the Chinese Ghetto till he found himself outside Astor Place in the early evening. St Marks was a street away and he had come almost full circle.

A cinema nearby had been playing a double feature: *Touch of Evil* and *Citizen Kurtz*. The first film was almost over. Lightholler, having no desire to return to his hotel, accepted the ticket stub from a surly woman and shuffled into the theatrette. Four or five other people were already seated in the dusty room. The proprietor was taking a small risk in showing the feature. Orson Welles' portrayal of the Vietnam War hardly cast the Japanese in a favourable light, nor did it make any attempt to smooth over the difficulties that the Germans and Japanese had endured during the conflict. Welles had taken Conrad's *Heart of Darkness* and reset it in the jungles of Indochina. Kurtz had become a German military adviser gone rogue; Marlowe was now a Union officer, dispatched by his Japanese masters to subdue him. All the characters were daubed in shades of grey. Flawed men reduced by circumstance to blind savagery.

By the time Lightholler had left the cinema the street had gone dark. Lamps flickered along the avenues to either side, but the street itself was a shadow bridging glittering shores. He'd made his way back to the Waldorf slowly, watching his own shadow lengthen and diminish in the pools of light of solitary streetlamps. He'd clambered into bed, hoping that his wanderings would confer the reward of a dreamless night. Instead, he'd tossed and turned, until finally throwing off his sheets.

Before he was even aware of it, he was dressed and walking back down the corridor of the hotel, past the Astoria Lounge where a century earlier his great-grandfather had stood proclaiming the incompetence of the *Titanic*'s owners. Out on the street, a thin mist was dissipating, the eastern sky hinting at dawn. A Japanese soldier approached him, pointed to his watch and back to the hotel, mouthing one word: curfew.

Lightholler, thankful that he had remembered to bring his wallet, produced the necessary papers. The soldier gave a small bow and Lightholler set out again. Apart from the odd sentry post, where soldiers lolled and spat on the cool pavement, he saw no one. Once on Broadway he followed its long course down to Battery Park, and by the time he arrived so had the morning light. He had sat on the splintered park bench, looking out to sea, till sleep had finally taken him.

Standing and stretching, he pulled at the cuffs of his shirt and straightened the hem of his jacket as he turned to face the gate that opened out of the park and back onto Broadway.

XII

Shine, in his guise as hotel staff, returned to the Waldorf. Hardas was watching the pier; Shaw and Collins were trawling the downtown bars. It looked like Lightholler was long gone.

Kennedy, informed by Saffel's missive, had thought that Lightholler wouldn't run. Now he knew the truth of it: Lightholler was merely a pawn in the Germans' game. Alarmed by Kennedy's visit and discarded by his superiors, he could be anywhere.

Abandoning the brownstone, Kennedy had spent the night on the streets, Morgan contritely by his side as he issued orders from his two-way. By the time Shaw called in, announcing that their quarry had been sighted on Fourth Avenue, Kennedy knew exactly what to do. With a man like Lightholler, honesty would yield the best results.

Kennedy recalled Shine. Two kills and no sleep made him a liability.

He spoke to Shaw and arranged for Lightholler to be brought over to Kobe's joint on 12th Street. As neither Shaw nor Collins could be privy to the recruitment, Hardas would have to escort Lightholler on to the Lone Star. Shine would be held on tap.

There was no way of knowing how Lightholler would handle the revelation at hand.

XIII

It was Lightholler's third shower in less than twenty-four hours. It restored much of his vigour, but a seedy aftertaste of the night lingered.

He'd entered the suite's lounge, still feeling somewhat at a loss, when he heard a knock at the door. He started at the sound. Kennedy had said that they'd meet up again on Tuesday, and he wasn't expecting any visitors today. Reluctantly he opened the door. Two strangers framed the entrance.

"Captain Lightholler," one of them said. "Major Kennedy sent us. I'm Collins. This is Shaw." They flashed their badges. "Would you please accompany us?"

They wore the drab grey suits that seemed to be *de rigueur* for Confederate operatives. Both men were heavy-set, their square heads squatting on thick necks that threatened to burst through their shirt collars.

"What happened to Tuesday?" Lightholler asked warily.

"The major needs to see you now, Captain," Collins said. "I'm afraid we don't have any time to waste."

"Could you give me a moment?"

Motioning the men to step into the inner hallway, Lightholler walked back into his bedroom, surprised to find that he was experiencing some sense of relief, some purpose to this strange day. He grabbed a jacket and smoothed out the lapels, slipping it on as he emerged from the room. The two men were still standing in the hallway. They stepped to either side as he passed through the doorway.

They rode the lift in silence and led him out of the lobby. A white Hotspur was idling in the valet parking area. The agents directed him into the back seat and positioned themselves to either side. A third man drove. A light drizzle of rain sprinkled against the windshield.

"Isn't the Lone Star downtown?" Lightholler asked.

Shaw laughed.

The driver picked up his radio and said, "Tell Mr Cooper to send his team to cover the Lone Star."

The reply was too garbled for Lightholler to understand.

The driver glanced up at the rear-view, appraising him, and added, "No. We're fine. We'll see you at Kobe's after we make the pickup in Queens. Hardas will wait. He wants this package."

Collins turned to stare at Lightholler, giving him a long, hard look. Lightholler returned the gaze. Slate-grey eyes blinked back at him slowly. The agent appeared to come to some conclusion. His face relaxed into a confident smile as he turned away.

These agents were a different cut from Kennedy's men. They seemed as resolute as the others had seemed desperate. They were certainly more consistent with Lightholler's expectation of intelligence men. Yet there was something wrong here.

The Hotspur made a right-hand turn onto 42nd Street. Rain slashed the asphalt. Up ahead, the entrance to the Queens Midtown Tunnel appeared.

Lightholler considered his options.

XIV

Kobe's sushi bar sat on the corner of Third Avenue and 12th Street. Wide awned windows received a spatter of rain while permitting a clear view of the narrow street. From where he sat, Hardas could observe anyone who approached.

Through the bar's open door wafted the sounds of distant traffic. Car horns, the occasional whinny of a carriage horse, fragments of conversation from passers-by, all borne on the swell of auto fumes. He glanced at his watch, not even bothering to check the time but going through the same motions he'd repeated since his arrival. He glared at the phone booth, three feet away on the pavement's edge, willing it to ring.

He'd spoken with Shaw almost an hour ago. They should have been here by now.

He lit up a Texas Tea and thought about it.

Kennedy was convinced the Bureau was shutting them down. It all fell in to place. Webster, as director of the CBI, was aware that Kennedy had recruited Morgan, an expert on the *Titanic*. He'd also discovered that Kennedy was trying to recruit Lightholler, the man who'd brought the new *Titanic* to New York. And, somehow, he must have gotten wind of what she carried in her hold. That, along with Hardas's own involvement with the wreck of the original ship, presented a compelling body of evidence. Webster had added one plus one and got three. Odds were that he thought Kennedy and his crew had thrown in with the Kaiser.

For all Hardas knew, the Bureau could have been monitoring Shaw's phone line as well, which meant they knew about Kobe's place. He had to get out of there.

Rising from his chair, he pinched the remains of his cigarette between yellow fingertips. The Lone Star was five minutes away at a run. He made his way to the back of the bar and found Kobe sitting staring at a small television.

Kobe's face was a sickly hue in the reflected light of the screen. But his eyes shone with a contained energy. He was slight and seemed lost in the folds of a leather kimono. When he raised a hand to wipe away a tear of laughter, Hardas glimpsed the tattooed tail that flicked about his wrist to envelop his arm in a red-green dragon. A potent reminder that this man was yakuza.

"One minute, Commander, this is the best part."

Hardas glanced at the screen. The picture quality was grainy black and white. A fat man in a tight suit stood beside a ridiculously thin man who was scratching his head in confusion to the accompaniment of a tinny piano.

"That's another fine mess, no," Kobe mimicked, before muting the television.

"I have to leave," Hardas said. "I was expecting someone, though. If he arrives, could you make certain he remains here till I return?" He pulled out a photograph of Lightholler, the one Shine had lifted from the Bureau assassin. He passed it to the gangster, who rotated it a full three-hundred-and-sixty degrees before passing it back. "And keep him out of sight."

"I don't know. You all look the same to me, Mr Hardas." Kobe rolled his eyes.

Hardas reached back into his pocket and withdrew a wad of ten-thousand-yen notes. He peeled a number of bills off the top of the roll and handed them over.

"I feel a sudden improvement in my vision," Kobe said with a smile.

"I bet you do." Hardas smiled back through his teeth. "If I'm not back in the hour, could you send him on to the Lone Star?"

Kobe's eyes returned to Hardas's billfold.

Hardas took some more notes from the roll and handed them over. "Is there a way out back?" he asked.

"Always."

Kobe took the rest of the bills from Hardas's hand unceremoniously. Slipping them somewhere within his kimono, he replied, "If I see this man, I will take care of it. Consider your contribution an insurance payment."

He patted his kimono. “That’s the best deal you’ll get in Osakatown.”

Hardas watched the red-green dragon writhe on gold hairless skin and said, “I know it.”

Kobe led him out of the bar.

XV

The Hotspur was perched at the lip of the tunnel entrance, waiting for the traffic to pass. The driver snapped on his lights and a single beam illuminated the car ahead.

"You ought to get that fixed," Lightholler said, addressing the back of the driver's head. "A sentry might pull you over."

The two agents traded a look. Collins withdrew a gun from his shoulder holster and let it rest in his lap. A Dillinger parabellum with a customised leather grip.

"What tipped you off?" Collins asked carelessly.

"You had no idea about the Lone Star."

"We do now, Captain. Thank you."

Lightholler felt the panic seep. Cold fear worked its way from the nape of his neck to his fingertips. There was a lurch as the Hotspur waded into the tunnel's traffic.

"Who are you?"

"CBI, Captain, like we said," Shaw replied. "Kennedy sold us out. *You've* sold us out. Keep your nose clean and you just might have an exciting story to tell your grandchildren."

Lightholler felt the muzzle of another gun poke up against his right flank. There'd been no telltale click of the safety's release but that meant little. Familiar enough with small arms, he entertained no confidence in snatching the other agent's weapon in time to gain any advantage. Besides, he'd done nothing wrong.

They were only a few car lengths into the tunnel when the traffic started to pile up. The far left lane, usually reserved for the aristocracy, was empty.

Amazingly, the driver veered into it. Clearly, he was new to New York. Lightholler felt a faint swell of hope.

"Hey, what are you doing?" Collins called out.

The driver opened up the throttle and the Hotspur coughed into fourth gear. "I'm making time," he replied.

A red light began to flash at the tunnel's far end, above their lane.

"Fuck," Shaw said.

"What's going on?" The driver spoke out of the corner of his mouth.

"What are you? An idiot?" Shaw snarled. "Never touch the left lane unless you're on horseback or dragging a shitload of rich nips in the back of a limo. Jesus, just pull over. I'll deal with this."

"You'd better let Cooper know," Collins said. There might have been the slightest edge of alarm in his voice.

Lightholler felt the gun's muzzle slip away as Shaw reached for the radio. Collins placed his own weapon beneath the flap of his jacket, his hand still firmly on its grip. From another pocket he withdrew a thick roll of yen notes, saying, "This ought to take care of it."

"Behave nice, Captain," Shaw growled. "We don't want to spark off an international incident now, do we?"

The others seemed to find this comment amusing and were still chuckling as the car rolled to a halt. Lightholler peered into the tunnel.

Ahead, into the single beam of the Hotspur's headlight, stepped a solitary figure.

XVI

Kennedy had selected the Lone Star Cafe for a number of reasons. Its owner, Friedman, was an old friend—a veteran who'd served under his command in the Second Ranger War. It was situated in a busy neighbourhood. It had three exits. As one of the last outposts of Southern culture remaining in the Union, its sheer obviousness made it ideal. The perfect place to hide a Confederate conspiracy was among a group of bitter Southern sympathisers who spent their afternoons exchanging tales of the glory days between mouthfuls of whiskey and cheap Texan beer.

The café's door was tattooed with the mandatory faded yellow rose that grew from the sawdust-paved floorboards. Dim light filtered through bronze-tinted windows in a permanent sunset. The walls were adorned with flags, including the old Texas State banner and a tattered Confederate battle standard. Between them hung the flag of the Second Confederacy: a blue star ringed by eleven smaller stars, surmounted on a concessionary field of red and white stripes. Beneath the flags hung maps marking out the territories that had rushed to join the new Texan Republic following its secession from the Union in 1930: Florida, Georgia, Tennessee, Alabama, Oklahoma, Mississippi, Arkansas, Louisiana, New Mexico, Arizona and Nevada.

There was an eclectic assortment of photographs that ran the gamut from Hank Williams to President Patton, all arranged around a centrepiece depicting the last meeting between Lee and Jackson. To one side, a more recent portrait of Thomas Clancy—incumbent president of the Confederacy—had been defaced. Someone had added a monocle and spiked German helmet to his photo. Friedman had left it hanging with no attempt at removing the crude alterations. For all Kennedy knew, he might have made the "improvements" himself.

Kennedy and Morgan sat at a wooden table in the back. Kennedy had his back to the wall. He let his hand slip down the side of the chair leg to feel the reassuring presence of the leather satchel beneath his feet.

"Another drink?" Morgan ventured, breaking the silence.

"Coffee, thanks," Kennedy replied. "You could probably do with one yourself."

Morgan eyed him sourly and made a beeline for the bar.

Kennedy's glance swept across the mixed crowd of Confederate wannabes. He felt displeasure rise within him at the young Union business types and tourists who thought that wearing a string tie or a faded grey shirt conferred upon them the immediate status of Johnny Rebel. Then again, hadn't an affinity between South and North been one of the more peaceful precepts of Camelot?

Perhaps, but the South was a nation. North was just another direction on the map.

It was almost midday and still no word from Hardas. Kennedy's forces were scattered, spread wide across the board and largely unsupported. He needed to regain some semblance of control.

The saloon doors swung open. Kennedy rose from his chair at the sight of Hardas's silhouette. He was alone. He caught sight of Morgan at the bar and followed him back to the table.

"Anyone see you come in?" Kennedy asked.

"No."

"Sit down. Talk to me."

"Shaw and Collins didn't show." Struggling with the words, Hardas stared at the floor.

"If they had him, they would have brought him in by now," Kennedy said.

"I left a snapshot of Lightholler with Kobe," Hardas offered.

"We're not waiting. Whoever neutralised Shaw and Collins is going to come after us."

"Kobe took my money. He won't talk," Hardas said.

The yakuza held little love for any authority, East or West, that was true enough. Currency was their creed. Under reasonable circumstances

Hardas's words might have been a guarantee. But Kennedy was familiar enough with Bureau extraction procedures. He felt a stab of remorse. He said, "Whoever's on our tail will make Kobe talk. We have to cut our losses. Our flight is booked for 2100 hours."

XVII

The sentry stood at a distance, his dark coat haloed cherry-red in the strobe's flicker. He seemed to be waiting for something. In the other lanes the traffic proceeded at a crawl.

Over the years, certain laws might have been observed with increasing laxity but one held firm. In a world where the stultifying progress of technology was an affront to those who held power, the older ways were held in high regard. The roadways reserved for the passage of the aristocracy were sacrosanct. You could only travel in the left lane in a horse-drawn vehicle or rickshaw, and you could only occupy such a conveyance if you held the title of *daimyo* or greater.

Lightholler eyed the agent's bankroll. Money could buy you out of a lot of trouble in New York City, but not under the watchful lenses of the traffic cameras. The drivers and passengers in the other cars kept their eyes straight ahead, in careful control of their curiosity.

The sentry finally approached the Hotspur, his coat straining slightly against his stocky frame with each step. He placed a hand against the driver's door and waited as the man wound the window down. His head was shaved to a raw stubble. He wore his collar raised. His face, shrouded in shadow, was concealed behind a filter mask.

"Officer, I can explain everything," Shaw began, leaning towards the open window with a cheek-wide grin. His voice was infused with warmth.

There was a blinding flash of light. Lightholler heard the sound of bone shattering even before the ear-splitting blast of gunfire registered. Shaw's body jerked and his head snapped back in a shower of blood. Lightholler's face tingled with sticky warmth.

With ridiculous slowness the sentry brought his firearm back across Lightholler's line of sight. A part of him noted the weapon's singular design, the long thick bulk of the magazine clip in front of the trigger guard, the dark aperture of the Mauser meeting his own eyes briefly as it swung towards Collins, who was now fumbling for his Dillinger.

Both guns discharged simultaneously.

The Dillinger barked twice within the fold of the agent's coat, punching small holes in the driver's seat. Collins rolled forwards onto his weapon with a groan.

The windshield behind them was a mosaic of bone and brain. The driver was twitching spasmodically in his seat, his hands clasping his abdomen where Collins' stray rounds had emerged. His face twisted in the rear-view mirror, then exploded with the sentry's third bullet.

It all happened in less than a minute.

The sentry turned his gun back towards Lightholler, who was bound in a struggle with the two fresh corpses. He had one foot on a bloodied skull, slipping against the slick car door seeking purchase, squeezing behind the other's body towards the other locked door. Warmth spread in his groin and a small part of him regarded the moisture, hoping for piss rather than blood.

"Captain," the sentry said in English.

Lightholler threw his arms up in front of his face, biting blood out of his lower lip in expectation. His eyes screwed shut as moments stretched towards eternity.

"Captain…"

Captain?

Lightholler froze, then slowly lowered his arms.

"Get out of the car." The sentry's voice, filtered by the mask, was laboured.

Lightholler's legs were water as he shifted across one of the bodies and made his way out the passenger door.

"Please…" he started to say.

"Walk." The sentry motioned towards the road divider with his gun barrel. "Climb across."

Lightholler clambered over the divider. Unable to ignore him now, drivers began staring at the Hotspur's blood-curtained windows. He weaved through the cars, the sentry at his heels.

Sirens began to sound in the distance.

A cab pulled up, slowly.

"Wait here." The sentry approached the vehicle. He hunched over for a few moments and then turned back to Lightholler. "Where were you supposed to meet Kennedy?"

"You're out of your mind if you think I'm going anywhere with you."

"Believe me when I tell you, you've nowhere else to turn." The sentry indicated the Hotspur with a nod. "You're a marked man." His distorted voice sounded almost compassionate.

The sirens were closer. The whole tunnel was lit with flashing red lights. Crazy shadows began to leap the walls.

"Get in. *Go.*" The sentry gestured towards the waiting vehicle.

Lightholler didn't need to be told twice.

XVIII

Hardas was gazing past Kennedy's shoulder. Kennedy turned to see Friedman appear at his side.

Friedman said, "There's someone here to see you, Major."

For a fleeting moment Kennedy didn't recognise the man Friedman escorted to the table.

Lightholler's eyes flicked from Hardas to Morgan before finally settling on Kennedy. His shirt was unbuttoned, damp with sweat and stained with wide splashes of dark brown. He held his jacket crumpled and wound around one arm like a bandage or a falconer's glove. His face was concrete-grey except for the harsh red-etched lines of his mouth. He swayed slightly where he stood.

"You fucking bastard." His voice was low, his eyes centred on Kennedy.

Kennedy stared at his shirt. "You've been shot."

"As it turns out," Lightholler snarled, "I'm the only one who wasn't."

"What the hell happened?"

"I've lost my career, my ship, and I've been abducted." His face flushed scarlet with anger. "I've just come from a fucking firefight. What the *fuck* have you gotten me into?"

Kennedy glanced at Friedman, who responded with a nod before heading to the front of the café. He'd noted the unhealthy attention of some of the café's occupants. A few men near the bar were already staring with something like anticipation, perhaps in the hope of a brawl to break the monotony of their afternoon.

"Please, Captain, sit down." Kennedy hadn't counted on this godsend. Somehow, Lightholler was back in the picture.

Lightholler appeared to appreciate the fact that they'd gained an audience. Kennedy watched the emotions play across his face: a struggle taking place between a desire to satisfy the forming crowd and some decidedly English form of discretion. Hardas caught Kennedy's eye, waiting for a signal. Kennedy didn't respond. There was no need for a show of strength. Better to allow him the illusion of alternatives.

"If I don't like what I hear, I'm leaving." Lightholler lowered himself slowly into a chair. "Marked man or not, I'm going to the nearest police station. I'm going to the embassy. If I *really* don't like what I hear, I'm going straight to the fucking Shogun. Is that clear?"

"Are you hurt?"

"It's not my blood."

"Who took you?"

"They said they were CBI. They said that you'd sent them."

"I sent two men for you. Agents Shaw and Collins."

"That's them. They had a driver." Lightholler's anger gave way to a calmness that was all the more disturbing.

"A driver?"

Morgan said something under his breath. Hardas chewed at his lower lip in silence.

"Where are they now?" Kennedy asked.

"They're dead," Lightholler replied. "Why don't you know that?"

The alternatives raced through Kennedy's mind. Lightholler's bloodstained shirt. Webster's words. The CBI assassins that Shine had removed. Wetworks were in town and someone had put another three men in the ground.

Why don't you know that?

"Who killed my men?" Kennedy's question was a whisper.

"They weren't your men." There was a note of satisfaction in Lightholler's tone.

"Explain yourself."

"Shaw said you were a sell-out, he had no idea where you…" Lightholler's satisfaction faded into horror. "They're coming here."

"Who's coming? You said they were dead."

"Someone called Cooper. His team, whatever that means."

"Christ," Hardas said. "We're screwed."

"He won't try anything here," Kennedy said.

"It's Cooper, damn it," Hardas replied. "There's going to be a fucking bloodbath."

"Call Shine. Have him set up a corridor to the other place. Tell Friedman what's going on."

Hardas left the table to make the call.

"Major?" Morgan's voice was barely a croak. "I can't do this."

Kennedy turned on him. "You got back late last night. You dealt us this hand. Not another word from you. Understand?"

Morgan fell silent.

Hardas returned to the table. "It's done," he said.

Kennedy turned to Lightholler and said, "Captain, who killed my men?"

"A tunnel sentry," Lightholler replied, more cooperative now. "He took out all three of them. He put me in a cab and sent me here."

Kennedy tried to process the information. "A Japanese sentry?"

"He was wearing a filter mask but he sounded Caucasian. He called me Captain," Lightholler replied. "He knew who I was."

"It's the Germans," Hardas said. "Has to be. You may not have been working for them as we first suspected, Captain, but that doesn't mean they don't need you."

"Need me for *what*? I don't understand."

"It seems as if everyone wants a piece of you, Captain Lightholler," Kennedy said. "And you're the only one who doesn't know why." He softened his tone, lowered his voice. "I can help you. I'm going to start by filling you in on some of what's happening here."

It's not going to be easy, though, Kennedy mused silently. The only means of convincing Lightholler lay buried under a rock in Nevada. Lying to him now might poison any chance of cooperation when it was needed. Telling the truth would render him an unwilling companion. Kennedy had to take that chance.

He added, "When I'm finished, you won't believe a word of it, but I assure you, that will change."

"What the hell do you *want* from me?"

"There's a war coming, and it will defy anyone's previous understanding of the word, Captain. A war with no victors. Maybe even no survivors," Kennedy said. "All I want is for you to help us prevent that from ever happening."

XIX

Kennedy rose from his seat and gestured towards a door at the rear of the café, an unspoken invitation to the point of no return. The others scraped back their chairs and stood to join him.

Leave or stay? Lightholler's alternatives were a twirling rondo in his mind.

Three men were dead in the Queens Midtown Tunnel. The tally would rise—of that he was certain. As far as he could tell, there were no options. He rose to follow them.

They reached the door and Kennedy unlocked it. It opened onto the street. Lightholler followed him outside, Morgan close behind, Hardas bringing up the rear.

The rain had cleared. They wound through the streets of Greenwich Village to enter a small, unassuming building on Downing Street. The "other place" turned out to be a shabby echo of the Lone Star. Kennedy nodded to the bartender and hustled Lightholler into a darkened alcove near the back of the bar. The others followed him in and Kennedy closed the door.

A sink rested against the opposite wall. A round table stood in the room's centre, bearing a stack of crystal glasses, a bottle of rye, a pitcher of iced water and a star-shaped ashtray already littered with half a dozen stale cigarette and cigar butts. Four uncomfortable-looking folding metal chairs were arrayed around the table.

Kennedy said, "Make sure he's clean."

Hardas produced the same device he'd used back at the Waldorf. He scanned Lightholler and said, "All clear, Major."

Lightholler sat down. He bunched his jacket on his lap and stared at the water rings that marked the table. He patted his pockets, then rummaged through his jacket with more purpose.

Hardas reached into his shirt pocket and withdrew a pack of Texas Tea. He gave it a shake and slipped one of the cigarettes into his mouth before offering one to Lightholler, who accepted it. He lit it.

The others dropped into their chairs.

"It's time I got some answers," Lightholler said. "If my life is in danger, and my own country has kicked me loose, I think I have the right to know why."

"Let me tell you what you won't be reading in the papers," Kennedy began. "Japanese forces have engaged Russian units all along the Siberian border."

"There's a ceasefire in place."

"It's not holding," Kennedy replied. "The German–Confed war games finished last month, but the German 5th Fleet is still squatting in the North Atlantic. There are eighteen divisions of German infantry stationed in Arkansas, maybe more. At least one of them are Brandenburgs."

"Brandenburg divisions have been banned from operating outside of German territories since the Vietnam pact."

"Yet they're here," Kennedy said. "I saw them."

"They're here, alright," Hardas muttered.

"What about the peace talks?" Lightholler asked.

"That media circus they held aboard your ship was a sham, Captain," Hardas said. "Nothing more than a publicity stunt."

"They've been rescheduled to continue in Germany," Lightholler said, with more assurance. "The Japanese Imperial airship is moored over Berlin, and the Emperor's son himself is part of the delegation. Surely Ryuichi wouldn't send one of his own sons as ambassador into hostile territory if he didn't intend to pursue peace."

"Smoke and mirrors, Captain," Morgan said glumly.

"Still, what you're implying makes no sense," Lightholler said, "Japan can't *afford* a prolonged war with Russia."

"What if they expect it to be brief?" Morgan countered. "They don't want peace with the Russians—they just want to keep Germany out of the picture long enough to secure their own conquests. They know that sooner or later the Germans are going to have to come to Russia's aid, and they want to put that off as long as they can."

"Look," Lightholler said doggedly, "this happens every few years. A skirmish takes place in some godforsaken hole, the Japanese and Germans rattle their sabres at each other across the oceans, and that's that. The Tsar has problems enough as it is. He *has* to back down. The Germans are unlikely to come to their aid, treaty or no treaty. Hell, they just dismantled the Paris Wall last year. They aren't looking for trouble. Emperor Ryuichi knows that, and that's why he sent his son to Berlin."

"No matter what you believe, what's happening in Russia right now is no simple skirmish," Kennedy said. "And there's more at stake here than deciding who owns a couple of ports in the East China Sea, or helping the Tsar save face. What if the next border war occurs in *this* godforsaken hole?"

Lightholler shook his head in disbelief. "The last thing the Americans want is another war on their own soil."

"It's not about what the Union and the Confederacy want," Kennedy said. "You know that as well as I do. For the last eighty years, it's been about what the *empires* want."

Lightholler stubbed out his cigarette and stared at the table. "For the last two thousand years, it's always been about what empires want. Okay, say you're right. If the next border war happens here, I intend to be as far away as possible."

"We figure on being able to accommodate you," Hardas said.

Lightholler didn't bother to look up. "What in God's name does this have to do with the *Titanic*?"

"Everything, it seems," Morgan muttered into his coffee. "That's why you're here."

Kennedy placed a satchel on the table's surface. The jug tottered, ice clinking, crushed lemon releasing a golden sunrise swirl. Ice on summer seas.

"What do you know about the CBI, Captain?"

"You're a domestic intelligence bureau, formed soon after the First Ranger War and loosely based on the German Abwehr. You have ties with German, British and Canadian intelligence services."

"Near enough," Kennedy said. "As you've said, the CBI is restricted to working within the borders of the Confederacy. Three years ago the Bureau was approached by representatives of the Abwehr. A clandestine meeting was held, a meeting that I, as director of anti-terrorist activities, was asked to attend. It was to be an exchange of ideas and methods. Information. This meeting started off as a routine discussion about establishing more formal associations with German intelligence. It ended as an outline for a project allocated the code name of Camelot."

"Camelot?" Lightholler sounded the word.

"Round table, one land, one king," Morgan intoned.

"Camelot," Kennedy repeated. "A three-year plan, with the ultimate goal of reuniting the Confederate and Union states."

"Of course," Lightholler said. "Right after you pull the sword out of the stone, I suppose."

Kennedy pressed on. "A reunion brought about under the auspices and umbrella of German authority. I was assigned to organise the military wing of the project."

Lightholler couldn't believe his ears. They actually seemed to be *serious* about it. Another Kennedy, trying to reunite the states?

He thought about it for a moment and when he spoke he did so slowly and carefully. "Astor tried to do that." He said the name without relish. "So did Vidal. Look where it got them."

And John and Robert, your uncles. The names he didn't mention, couldn't bring himself to say to this man. This Kennedy, scion of an infamous family that had tried to pull this trick off once before and had failed miserably.

Instead, he said, "You were running the military wing of an attempt at a peaceful reunion? You're sounding more like a soldier than a spy."

"An *ultimately* peaceful process, Captain. An iron fist can be maintained within a velvet glove."

"No. I don't buy it." Lightholler shook his head emphatically. "Even if the Americans wanted such a thing—which is pretty bloody unlikely—the Eastern Shogunate would *never* give up control over the North, and certainly not to a German-backed United States of America."

Yet saying those words, *United States*, he was stirred by them.

"Nothing's impossible, Captain. It's all a matter of resources, and a question of perspective," Morgan said. "In December of 1860 the First Secession took place. Eleven states broke from the Union. The bloody war that followed lasted four years and left the South devastated. *Ruined.* That War of Northern Aggression supposedly settled the question of the permanence of the Union, and yet seventy years later Texas broke away in a *clearly* unconstitutional act and no war ensued. Why was that, Captain?"

He continued without waiting for a reply. "There's no simple answer, but in a nutshell, no nation willingly embarks upon a war unless it's somehow convinced that it may win. The belief may be short-lived and naive, it may be based on misinformation or arrogance, but it's shared by *all* participants, and is a constant in military history.

"Prior to the War of Northern Aggression, the First Confederacy expected military support from Europe, certainly from Britain and France. Both countries relied heavily on Southern exports of cotton for their textiles industry. Did you know that seventy-five per cent of all British cotton came from the South? Yet that military support never came, and the rest is history. Bottom line is that both the Union and the Confederacy went to war because both sides thought that they would win. They *didn't* go to war in '32 for the same reason."

"And you believe," Lightholler said, "that the North and the South can be reunited through peaceful means because neither the Japanese nor the Germans would go to war over such a matter?"

"I never said that," Morgan replied. "The War of Northern Aggression, the Mexican invasion of 1920 and the Great Depression left the South virtually bankrupt. Texas backed out of the Union when it couldn't—and wouldn't—meet its share of the national debt. No one believed it would last, but when the Kaiser offered finance, munitions and armed support, in exchange for oil there was nothing the North could do about it. It was only a matter of time before the rest of the South followed suit. After all, America had narrowly driven off the Mexicans, while the Germans were the newly declared masters of Europe."

"Not *all* the rest," Hardas murmured.

Lightholler knew where that came from. That Virginia and the Carolinas never joined the Second Confederacy remained a sore point among many people both North and South. While the governments of those states had argued back and forth about using terms like Confederacy, and disputing the purity of Texan motives for secession, the population of Virginia and the Carolinas had made a point of dividing itself. A series of migrations went north and south, until the new Mason-Dixon Line was established at the Georgian border and a new capital was raised in Houston.

"Still, it was a war the Union could not hope to win, Captain." Morgan narrowed his eyes. "You claim the Americans would never want to be reunited. Yet Union and Confederate soldiers marched together only a few years after tearing at each others throats. People remember what they choose to and even old wounds heal eventually. Had it not been for what happened next, the Secession would not have lasted." A strange look entered his eyes. "Wasn't even supposed to have happened, goddamn it."

"All in good time, Darren," Kennedy said softly.

Morgan drew in a deep breath. "The only reason it *did* last was that the North couldn't afford to aid the South during the First Ranger War. Had they intervened, the Mexicans would have been swiftly defeated and the two nations reunited."

"Now you're just speculating," Lightholler interrupted.

"Perhaps, but if the North had supported the South, if they'd displayed some unity, the Japanese might have been more hesitant in attacking Pearl Harbor in '46."

"Of course," Lightholler said, enjoying the man's discomfort. "They might have attacked in '47 instead."

"If Astor had sent help to the South," Morgan said, with some exasperation, "then Patton might have felt obliged to aid the North after the Japanese attacked. Instead of the Confederacy battling the Mexicans while the Union was fighting the Japanese, it might have been a United States of America—"

"Fighting a two-front war," Lightholler interrupted again. "Against two powerful enemies."

"A *winnable* two-front war," Morgan replied. "The Germans managed it, for God's sake."

"That was a long time ago."

"Gentlemen," Kennedy said, "we're getting off track here. To answer your question, Captain, no, we don't actually believe that the North and the South can be reunited by any means. Not any longer. As a matter of fact, recent developments suggest that this solution is going to be *anything* but peaceful. What our historian is trying to say, though, is that, for a time, both the Confederate and German governments thought it was a possibility. There was also some serious support from elements in the current Union administration. My task force was created to make that possibility a reality."

"What happened?"

"The project was up and running within three months of the meeting. You can imagine its initial appeal. A United States of America, with a centralised government based in Houston and complete German support, as opposed to Japanese control. The japs would be left with Alaska and the Occupied Territories on the West Coast, *possibly* New York; the rest would fall under German influence. The Germans saw it as a way to destabilise the Japanese bases on the occupied West Coast, believing that a unified America would not tolerate such a Japanese military presence for long."

"The Japanese have occupied the West Coast since 1948," Lightholler said. "They're not likely to pull out now. Emperor Ryuichi is no fool."

"No, and neither is his brother, though something might be said about his loyalty. You see, last year Japanese agents in Richmond got wind of Camelot."

"So you were shut down?"

Kennedy smiled. "You know how it goes. Anything's fair game, but once you get caught, there's the slap on the wrist, an informal apology, and we all pretend that nothing ever happened. Right? The agents reported their findings to Hideyoshi, the Eastern Shogun."

"And *he* shut you down." Lightholler recalled his own meeting with the man just over a week ago.

"Last November, his men met with us in West Virginia. They knew all about Camelot—the names of our agents, our sponsors in the Union. Everything."

"And?"

"He made us a proposal. Gave us three options. Certain targets had been selected in the Union: pipelines, power stations, heavy industry—Japanese targets. The project involves their timed destruction, demanding an increased Japanese commitment to holding power in the North. A commitment they would find untenable in the long run. So … three options: firstly, that we shut it down, just like you said."

"Go on."

"Secondly, that we proceed, but on a different schedule. Cause less damage. Slow things down a little." Kennedy watched Lightholler closely, as if to gauge his response.

"Why the hell would he let you destroy Japanese targets?"

Hardas lit another cigarette. He rested an elbow on the table and blew a thin stream of smoke towards the ceiling. Lightholler glanced at him. He tossed over a cigarette and slid his lighter across the table.

Lightholler lit up, and when Kennedy didn't reply immediately he followed his own thoughts. "That would give the Japanese more time to mobilise their troops in the Union."

"Exactly." Hardas held his eyes.

"Leaving them with a firmer grip on the Union."

"Yes."

"That's crazy." Lightholler's head was spinning. "Crazy that he'd even think you'd go through with that."

No one replied.

The only sound was Hardas tapping away the ash.

Lightholler let his cigarette burn slow to his fingertips; he followed the glow's spread along the rolled paper. "What was the third option?" he asked finally.

Kennedy spoke softly. "We change the targets."

"Union targets?"

Kennedy shook his head.

"Confederate targets? He actually expected you to say yes to destroying your own? What on earth did he offer you?"

"In exchange for uniting the states under Japanese hegemony—his hegemony..." Kennedy gave a miserable laugh that rang hollow in the small room, "he offered me the presidency."

It was beyond comprehension, all of it. What had Admiral Lloyd gotten him into?

"Listen," Kennedy said, "by virtue of being born nine minutes before him, Hideyoshi's twin brother gets to rule the entire Japanese Empire, while he's left governing the East. A United States, under his control, would become an excellent bargaining chip. It would give him the opportunity to extend Japanese influence as far south as the Panama Canal. If he controls the Canal, he controls the movement of all trade between the Atlantic and Pacific. Think of the support that might gain him in the Home Islands, if he ever chose to make an attempt on his brother's crown."

"Insane," Lightholler said. "Completely. You of all people..."

"What?"

"You took the third option, didn't you?" Lightholler moved as if to rise from the table. Hardas was already standing by his side, a hand firmly on his shoulder.

Lightholler shook him off, but remained in his seat. "You make them look good, you know, JFK and RFK. They were just doing it for the money. But you?"

Kennedy reddened. "They had no idea about the money. The worst crime they committed was naivety."

"And it ended on a bloody afternoon in Dealey Plaza. You won't be so lucky. They're going to hang you, Major Kennedy. Benedict Arnold's going to be remembered as a saint next to you."

Morgan was talking, his words soft but rising. "Captain, you've got it all wrong. This is different."

"He's playing both sides against each other," Lightholler continued. "He's selling you out for something he couldn't get any other way. How the hell is that different?"

"There's more you have to hear, much more. This is just the tip of the iceberg."

"Why the hell am I here?" Lightholler asked, his voice almost cracking. "What the hell does this have to do with me?"

"We're at an impasse," Kennedy said. "The japs have us, and we have them. They let Houston know what's going on and we hang. We contact Tokyo and Hideyoshi is commanded to commit suicide on the steps of the Summer Palace. But while we're at this standoff, we buy the time to finish what we started."

"And what's that?" Lightholler said bitterly. "The Mexicans still control the Canal. They'll be no friendlier to the japs than they've been to the Confederates, especially with you as president. Not to mention the fact that Ryuichi would never allow a Shogun to wield that much power, particularly his own brother."

"Absolutely," Kennedy replied. "Both empires think they have everything to gain by a reunited America. Both are probably wrong."

"So who wins?" Lightholler asked. "Conspiracies have a habit of being brought to light. There's no way this is going to work."

A melancholy smile flickered across Morgan's face.

"No one wins," Kennedy said. "Not in the long run."

Lightholler shivered. Someone walking over his grave. He craved another of Hardas's sour cigarettes.

Kennedy continued. "A large portion of the Bureau has been operating independently from the Confederate states for the last three years in pursuit of Camelot. My team has been operating independently from the CBI for the last two. We've met with surprising success in negotiating a reconciliation considering it was the last thing on our minds. Financial backing from the Germans *and* the Japanese didn't hurt either."

Lightholler surveyed the men sitting around the small table. This changed everything. Rendered the letter useless. Unless, of course, the Palace supported Kennedy. That might explain Admiral Lloyd's ignorance. It would explain a number of things.

He said, "Back in my hotel room, you only checked for surveillance devices after you introduced yourself. And *well* after you had told me that you were from the South."

"We checked your room the night before you arrived," Kennedy said. "We knew where the bugs were."

"Aside from that, you didn't mind if someone knew you'd been there. You weren't checking for surveillance devices, you were neutralising them. And whoever was observing your progress now believes that I'm involved."

"They were watching you, not me," Kennedy said. "You're implicated in far more than Camelot now."

"What you've done is commit treason and draw me into the process. Thanks to you, they were ready to imprison me."

"Your abduction would have ended in your death. The men who took you were assassins."

"They only took me because they thought I was part of your crew, damn it."

"They would have taken you anyway," Kennedy said.

"When did you discover that I was under surveillance by the CBI?"

"Yesterday."

"So now your boss knows you've been double-dealing."

"He knows, but for all of the wrong reasons," Kennedy said.

Lightholler sighed. There was more to this. Layers of deception and confusion. And still, *Why neutralise the bugs at all?*

"Ultimately, we don't care about the Confederacy—or the Union," Kennedy said. "Not in their present form. We don't care about the Germans or the Japanese. The concept of treason here is irrelevant. We're looking at a bigger picture—much bigger."

"The big picture," Lightholler said deliberately. "Something bigger than you becoming president of the USA? Something bigger than rearranging the borders of the two empires?"

The Palace had offered his assistance to the CBI under the assumption that they were doing work that would benefit England. Whatever the "big picture" was, it went far beyond anything the Foreign Office had imagined. And it was only after Hardas had neutralised the bugs in his hotel suite, that Kennedy had mentioned the ship.

"And still you claim all this has something to do with the *Titanic*?"

"That's where it all starts," said Morgan. "That's where it ends."

XX

Kennedy reached for the satchel and withdrew a number of photographs. He handed them to Lightholler.

"What do you make of these?" he asked.

Lightholler placed them before him carefully. After a moment, he asked, "Where did you get them?"

"They're from a recent expedition," Hardas answered.

"I didn't know they'd scheduled any dives recently," Lightholler said, his eyes fixed upon the images spread out on the table.

Three of the photographs showed the wreck of the *Titanic* seen from various angles. Its massive hull stretched out, intact and rising from the floors of the Grand Banks as though cresting one last muddy wave. Two of the great funnels were visible. She seemed remarkably well preserved. The images were the clearest Lightholler had ever seen.

He'd participated in one of the later dives, following the failure to raise the wreck in 2007. It had been part of the media lead-up to the centennial cruise. The trip had been made in an over-crowded bathyscaphe, brimming with journalists and retired naval officers. They'd hovered for half an hour, approximately fifty feet above the wreck. Despite the powerful beams of light that bathed the ship, all detail had been lost within those seemingly impenetrable depths. He thought he'd seen all of the available footage, but the details of these photos astounded him.

"You must have gotten pretty close. What kind of submersible did you use?"

"A special one," Hardas said, smiling for the first time.

"What about these?" The last two photographs were the only ones he couldn't make out distinctly.

"Sorry about those two," Hardas said. "I took them myself."

Lightholler stared at him.

"By remote camera, of course. They're from inside the ship."

Lightholler observed the faces around him. There was no hint of amusement among them. As far as they were concerned, this was no joke.

"These photos are from the purser's office on C deck." Hardas leaned forwards, pointing with a stubby finger. "And this here's the purser's safe."

Lightholler peered at the grainy images. The flash from the camera was reflected a hundred times in a cloud of floating debris. He could make out a wall only with difficulty. It was lined with shelving, streamered by seaweed. A barnacle-crusted shape squatted beneath it.

"Now you see it," Hardas indicated one of the images, "and now you don't." He pointed at the last photograph.

Lightholler leaned back in his chair. "Why the secrecy about the dive?"

"Dives," Hardas corrected, smiling again.

Kennedy turned his attention back to Lightholler. "The dives weren't supposed to be a secret. At least not initially," he said. "Hardas is ex-navy. He was part of a team appointed to put a new series of German submarines through their paces."

"In Japanese waters?" Lightholler asked.

"Part of the tests were to see if we would be detected by any of the new Japanese destroyers," Hardas said, warming to the subject. "If we were detected, we could always say we were mounting an independent dive to the *Titanic*."

"Without a surface vessel to support you, that would be a pretty weak excuse," Lightholler replied.

"With the current fervor for the *Titanic* sweeping the world, and considering the recent Japanese infringements of German territorial waters, it was hoped that such an expedition would be … overlooked," Kennedy said.

"Besides," Hardas added, "we weren't detected."

"So why were you testing submersibles for the Germans?" Lightholler asked.

"It was a fringe benefit of the Camelot project," Hardas replied. "We give them some of our submersible technology, they let us in on stratolite construction."

"I always wondered how you guys got strat technology before we did," Lightholler said. He'd never seen a stratolite. Not outside of newsreel footage, anyway. The first one, the *Kaiser Wilhelm I*, had been launched back in '99, amid much fanfare. The first permanent high-atmosphere dwelling. It was still up there. Somewhere over the South Pole as he recalled. The cynics had said that if the Germans couldn't make it to the Moon, they would settle on building one for themselves. With a radius of just under a mile, it was, at the time, the largest vessel ever built. The Germans conceded to having seven in operation, the Japanese, five, but back in the navy he'd been told to double those figures. And three years ago the Confederacy had commissioned its first one, the CSS *Patton*. The *Times* had done a write-up on it, reporting that its construction had sent their national budget skyrocketing.

Lightholler lit another cigarette, his eyes again falling to the last two photographs. "So what was in the safe?"

Kennedy pressed forwards in his chair, waiting for Lightholler to meet his eyes. "Some gold, some jewellery, stocks, bonds, and this." He reached into the satchel and withdrew a book.

Morgan pulled his chair closer, staring at the object as though it were some holy relic. Kennedy slid it across the table to Lightholler. Its front cover was thick cardboard, water damaged and stamped with a splash of rust-coloured material. He could make nothing of the smudged writing that appeared there. There seemed to be someone's name, handwritten, on the top right corner. Its binding and the roughly cut edges of its pages were encrusted with a thin layer of green mould. The pages themselves were curled back, coated with a slender sheet of plastic. Probably some form of preservative.

Lightholler studied the book, but didn't touch it. What could it possibly contain that would be of any significance now?

"Are these Archibald Butt's private papers?" he asked. He recalled that Butt, adviser to President Taft, had been aboard the *Titanic*. It had been speculated that he'd carried some important documents meant for the president, yet lost at sea.

"Morgan?" Kennedy cued, settling back into his chair.

"What shapes history, Captain?" The historian leaned forwards. "Events or personalities?"

Lightholler, struck by the non sequitur, made no reply.

"Are you familiar with your great-grandfather's memoirs?"

Lightholler tendered a tight-lipped smile. "It was required reading in my home. Yes, I know them. A long list of rantings and justifications by an inept fool." It felt good to say it aloud.

"A list, you say." Morgan's expression turned contemplative. "How much do you recall from his chapter on the sinking of the ship?"

"Just scraps. I always thought his view of the event was somewhat jaundiced. Where are you going with this?" Lightholler glanced again at the book. "Are those Astor's papers?"

"No," Kennedy replied. "But he does rate a mention," he added darkly.

Morgan pressed on. "Astor only devotes a small portion of his memoirs to his actual rescue. He dwells quite a bit on Charles Lightholler, of course."

"Of course." Lightholler suppressed a frown. Through that one pivotal event, an unholy dynasty had been born.

"In his writings, Astor's distraught, bereaved," Morgan continued. "Taken aboard the *Carpathia*, still damp from the Atlantic, he's told that his wife and their unborn child were lost at sea. So of course he fails to make mention of any list."

"List?"

"According to the *Carpathia*'s log, Astor was somewhat preoccupied with a list when he was first brought aboard. The captain also noted that Astor mentioned a strange encounter in the cargo hold, just before the *Titanic* foundered. He'd been told by someone that he was on some list. Told that he wouldn't see New York."

"I've never heard this," Lightholler said. "But what of it? The man was clearly raving, and with damn good reason."

"That's what it was put down to, and Astor never mentioned it again. It was left as a minor footnote to a terrible catastrophe." With that, Morgan reached for the journal. He handled it gingerly, opening it to a pre-selected page. "Until now."

He slid it over to Lightholler.

The names were handwritten. It appeared to be a register of some kind. He scanned down the page. *Smith, John: Captain. Murdoch, William: first officer. Andrews, Thomas: Ship's builder. Astor, Colonel J.J. Butt, Major*

Archibald. Guggenheim, Benjamin. Rothschild, M. Stead, William T. Thayer, J.B. Widener, Harry.

"What is this?"

"A who's who of some very powerful, very wealthy, very influential people," Morgan said. "All of them sailed on the *Titanic*, and all—with a singular exception—were lost at sea."

"This could be about anything. A lot of people died that night."

"True enough," Kennedy said. "But that's not the only list in the book."

Lightholler leafed through a few pages. The next sheet that caught his attention had been divided into two columns. The left bore another series of names. He recognised most of them. *Picasso, Kandinsky, Duchamp, Chagall*; artists who'd left their mark on the twentieth century. The names on the right were a different breed. *Stalin, Sorel, Mussolini*—tyrants and murderers all. There were more names he didn't recognise.

"Who are Mengele and Eichmann?" he asked.

Morgan shrugged.

"And you've got Hitler on the wrong side of the ledger. Why isn't he with the artists?"

Morgan shrugged again.

He turned over and read on. *American Telephone and Telegraph. General Motors. Krupp. Lockheed Aircraft. October 1929. Wall Street.*

"A projected investment portfolio, we believe," Morgan said. "As for the date and location, I'm thinking it's close enough to the Great Depression."

A fragment at the bottom of the page caught his eye. *Sarajevo: Princip. Archduke Franz Ferdinand and wife. June 28, 1914.*

"And you found this intact, in the purser's safe."

Morgan nodded.

"This last line describes the assassination that sparked off the Great War."

"That's correct."

"The ship went down almost two years prior to that."

"Also correct."

"It's a hoax," Lightholler said. "What else could it be?"

Hardas shook his head.

"You retrieved this document from the *Titanic*, right?"

Hardas nodded.

"So why couldn't someone else have left it there, to be found?"

Kennedy placed his fingertips on the manuscript's edge. "Considering the expense involved in the dives, that would be a fairly costly deception. Having said that, we considered the possibility. We considered *every* possibility. This manuscript also contains a diary. It outlines a series of events that happened long after the sinking. Some are accurate, and some quite bizarre. There's an agenda that involves making timely purchases in some very lucrative industries. There's also what appears to be a hit list: select individuals the author may have targeted for assassination. Sarajevo may be a case in point. Certain passengers on the *Titanic*, another. This manuscript is many things, but I assure you it's no hoax," he said, his eyes steady.

"You're trying to tell me that some madman ran around killing all those people while the ship was sinking?"

"No," Morgan cut in. "At the time, the *Titanic* was considered man's greatest creation. It was built to be *virtually* unsinkable. I stress the word 'virtually' because clearly, in retrospect, she demonstrated some obvious design flaws. But tell me, who could have appreciated that at the time?" He gave Lightholler a pointed look. "We believe she may have been deliberately sunk, in order to remove those men."

"She hit a fucking *iceberg*."

"The question that intrigues us, Captain," Kennedy said, "is *why* did she hit that iceberg?"

"I could give you five reasons right now," Lightholler replied hotly.

Kennedy said, "The death of all those men created a powerful vacuum in turn-of-the-century America. A vacuum that could be exploited by someone privy to the knowledge contained in this journal. The author of this text had enough information at his fingertips to engineer any number of events. He also clearly documented his intention to intervene on the ship. We don't know the details of what happened on the night of the sinking. We don't know how he figures into what happened at Sarajevo, or the years that followed. We just know where it starts."

Lightholler was in a daze. Three men were dead in the Midtown Tunnel—for this? He shook his head, aghast. "How could you possibly believe what you're saying? Your sordid tale about reuniting America was preposterous enough. Camelot..." He spat out the word. "How could anyone come to possess this knowledge in the first place?"

Kennedy remained calm. He nudged the manuscript across the table again and said, "The man your great-grandfather spoke to in the cargo hold of the *Titanic* wrote this journal. His name was Jonathan Wells. As to how he came about this knowledge, it's all here."

Lightholler reached out for the journal and was surprised to find that his hand was shaking. His fingers left small rings of moisture on the cover. "What is this?"

"The memoirs of a time traveller, Captain," Hardas replied.

Lightholler sat back in his chair. How could these madmen have influenced people at such a high level? Who, outside of this room, knew what they were up to? Kennedy and his cronies had misled the intelligence agencies of at least four countries, all for the sake of what lay on the table before him.

"You were right," he said to Kennedy, rising from his seat. "I don't believe a fucking word of it."

"We'll discuss it further after you've read it. And don't worry, I don't expect you to cover all of it in one sitting."

"Not interested. You've got me here under false pretences, and I have no intention of staying."

"You don't really have much choice. You're wanted by the CBI. You're integral to our plan, and you're not moving from this room until I say so. So you might as well settle back and read, Captain."

The three Confederates left the room. He heard the tumble of a key in the lock.

Lightholler sat there for a few minutes, the anger welling up inside him. He kicked over the chairs and gave the ashtray a backhand that swept its contents across the floor. He went to the door and kicked it. No one responded.

He returned to the table.

Despite all his fury he opened the journal with care. It was handwritten throughout, with bold cursive strokes. Compared to the cover, the writing within was quite clear. The first page contained a list of names. It was smudged. A thumbprint here, an ink-stained impression there. The next few pages contained widely spaced paragraphs that had been crossed out roughly. In places, the nib of the pen had torn through the coarse-cut paper, indicating the writer's dissatisfaction.

He sat amongst the scattered furniture, the cups and glasses and the spilt ash, and began to read.

XXI

March 20, 1911

March is reasonable.

It's been March for the last three weeks. And before that came February.

But the year? What the hell can I add after writing that?

I'm beginning to forget things, important things, and memories are all I've left to me.

I want to break something, but I'm haunted by the image of a spider gnawing through the scaffolding of its own web.

March 21, 1911

If you are reading this journal and your name is not Jonathan Wells, then one of two things has happened. Either I've finally forgotten. Forgotten that I was even trying to remember anything at all. Or I'm dead.

You found this in some abandoned room or on a park bench. It might have been clutched to my chest. Either way, my recommendation is the same. Take a match and burn this fucker before you read another line.

March 22, 1911

Not today.

But every word and thought that comes until you're right again.

It happened. It really happened.

So deal with it, you sad, miserable little shit.

May 24, 1911

I've written journal articles in the past. (If I press the pen any harder on the paper, will it lend any greater significance to that word?) Prepared papers for various medical meetings. And in my teens I kept a diary of sorts, though it was really just a chronicle of gropings. A paper belt notched by my pen so I wouldn't forget anyone's name.

The diary is long gone and the names are half-recalled, but to no purpose I can think of. I've been here for just on two months and already I feel my past slipping away.

Writing down words like "past" and "time", I think I need to devise a new lexicon because the old words have lost their meaning.

It's as if I'd lived my entire existence as a speck, a single dot on a page full of single dots, blindfolded, and then all of a sudden the blindfold was torn away and I found myself extending both forward and back, unfolding as a line beyond the confines of any diagram.

And if two lines, end to end, were to look at each other, what would they see? A point of existence, a fraction of their being. That is the ignorance in which we live, in which I have lived till now.

For some reason I don't fully grasp, I'm beginning to forget things. My memory was never a problem before, but here, in the backwoods of a small Nevada town, I feel it all slipping away. The line behind me being slowly, inexorably erased.

Since I am the only time traveler I've ever met—the only conscious one, that is—I've got no one to compare my experiences with. Nowhere in my years of medical experience have I encountered a syndrome that behaves similarly. Prolonged thiamine deficiency will produce extreme memory loss, and Korsakoff's syndrome will inhibit the formation of new memories. But to have the memories slip away?

There's a pattern to it. My early memories are fine: childhood, school, college, all intact. But my recent memories—the seminar, the Waste Land, Gershon—are all fading away. My working theory is that it's a psychological process rather than physiological. Regardless, I'm unfolding.

I suppose that since I've been torn from everything I ever knew, I've lost the cues that we as human beings unconsciously rely upon. There are no planes in the sky. The cars that trundle through this small town so infrequently are rudimentary at best. There's no television, of course. No radio. There are telephones, but I won't be able to make a long-distance call for a while. After all, the loading coil won't be invented until next year.

The list could probably go on for pages, this catalogue of unmade things.

There's no safe harbor for my memories, so I feel compelled to moor them here. No one has ever needed a confidant as I need one now.

My name was Jonathan Wells. I was a neurosurgeon. I have taken to calling myself Herbert since I arrived—a private joke few here would appreciate. I found a copy of *The Time Machine* in a dime store in Las Vegas and I keep it by the bed. I'm taking it with me when I leave town. Taking the book and leaving that name, once I've decided what the hell I'm going to do about all this.

I'll be born in New York on October 20, 1964, which makes me minus fifty-three years old. Black hair, thick and in dire need of a cut, blue eyes, bloodshot, and pale, pale skin. My reflection in the warped glass above the table might be trying on Dorian Gray for size. It neither contradicts nor supports the above statement but wavers in an approximation of my state of mind, and it isn't pretty.

I'd been a neurosurgeon for about two years before I started to subspecialize. I ended up doing purely vascular work: aneurysms, vascular malformations, and of course the operation that got me here in the first place, the external-carotid to internal-carotid bypass. EC-IC for short.

But it wasn't always vascular. In my second year as a consultant I got into a little difficulty while operating on a lumbar spine. The dura was torn, the nerve roots obscured in the sludge of welling blood. I couldn't see a damn thing through the operating microscope. So I made a bargain with God. I promised that if He got me out of that situation, if the patient could be spared paraplegia, I would never touch another spine again. Not as long as I lived.

Promises, promises.

I finished the operation. The patient eventually walked, and so did I—straight from the patient's room to my office. I phoned the Mayo Clinic. Two months later and I was on their advanced program, and it was vascular all the way.

I'm tired. I'm not used to writing with a nib and I can't hang around waiting for someone to invent the ballpoint pen. Jesus, my hand is aching and I'm thinking strange thoughts.

May 27, 1911

I'm so fucking scared.

I was re-reading my last entry, thinking about the surgery I used to perform, and I picked up a knife. A dirty, tetanized knife. I was wondering if I still remembered what to do with it.

Before I knew it, I was drawing the blade across my wrist. A shallow diagonal that would divide the radial artery at an angle, and prevent the arterial spasm that God has designed to stop us from bleeding.

Shallow cut, little droplets of blood. But after I stopped shaking, even while I was shaking, I started to laugh. I mean, at least I remembered my anatomy. Specifically *my* anatomy.

But no more knives.

It was early February, 1999, and I'd been invited to attend a conference in Las Vegas, a seminar on cerebral ischaemia. An opportunity to get out of Boston for a while. It suited the hospital and it suited me. And hell, it was Vegas.

I was supposed to present our unit's experience with the EC-IC bypass. The topic was chosen as a response to recent undercurrents of doubt in the procedure's validity. These doubts weren't based upon the operation's results, which were largely dependent on the experience of the unit and its surgeons, but rather in the actual indications for the operation.

Originally the op had been designed to treat patients who'd suffered damage to the brain's circulation. The neurological equivalent of a cardiac bypass. Conceptually quite simple. Take the blood supply of the face, head and neck, and re-route a portion of it to supply the brain directly. Technically, it was demanding. Aesthetically, it was beautiful. You marshal the body's defences. You utilize the patient's own "spare" tissues to aid in their reconstruction.

Unfortunately, studies suggested that the absolute indications for the operation were diminishing. The only valid ones remaining involved the treatment of rare tumors and trauma. The operation I'd trained in, that I believed would be a staple in the management of neurological patients, was to be relegated to obscurity. And so was I. With the radiologists shoving their tubes and pipes into sealed vessels and the physicians dissolving blockages with their snake oil, my work was disappearing.

Our paper proposed that EC-IC bypass was a *significant* component in the management of arterial disease in the brain. A controversial statement, and quite possibly a false one.

I should know. I wrote it. That's how I got to be in Vegas, and that's why *they* picked me. The right person, in the wrong place, at the wrong time.

June 1, 1911

Strange week, skulking around town, trying to keep a low profile. It's a smaller world I've stumbled across. No one travels and no one trusts travelers and no one here could conceive of the miles behind me.

I mustered the courage to sell some of the gold today. Enough to ensure that I had better think about moving on soon. The ingots they'd provided were small enough to be carried on my belt and had been molded to resemble freshly mined gold. The impurities might have been added, as well as the fine dust that silted the belt's many pouches.

I wonder if they had to erase any serial numbers in their twisted alchemy. I wonder why I'm thinking about serial numbers at all, and then of course I remember all too clearly and wonder at my wondering.

Enough. I need to be out of here by the end of the week. I'm going to head north. I have a dead man's promise to keep and it starts with this. Getting it all down on paper. I need to get it right too, so I can make sense of how I came to be in this place and time. A combination of my experiences, along with the things Gershon told me. Some of it's speculation. And I suppose a bunch of it's a crock, but it's as close to the truth as I will ever get.

It was late February and I'd been in Vegas two days before I got the call.

The conference didn't start till the next morning so I'd gone to the Flamingo. I was playing blackjack, chipping up, and the cash was flowing my way for a change. Then my cell phone began to ring. I had to leave the table to take the call, which bugged the hell out of me. No matter what the interruption is, whether they change the dealer, refill the float, or some clown spills his drink, by the time you place that next bet your luck has gone stone cold. You might as well throw your chips in a wishing well. Having said that, I can't think of a time I ever chipped down. Always hoping to break that streak.

I took the call.

The speaker's voice sounded very crisp for a cell phone; he could have been standing next to me. He introduced himself as Captain Burns and told me that I was required for an urgent consultation.

I told him I wasn't on call. I told him I was nowhere near Boston. But I kept it nice. I didn't know who the guy was, and if my ex-wife's lawyer taught me one thing it's that it pays to know who you're offending.

"We know exactly where you are, Doctor," he replied. "You're standing approximately five feet away from pit seven, table three. Your last hand was a pair of aces. You won on the split; not bad but not wise against a picture. Incidentally," he informed me, "your drink has just arrived."

I remember feeling the hairs on the back of my neck rise. I remember asking, "What's wrong with splitting aces?" I turned to see that a cocktail waitress had brought my bourbon to the table. The dealer was pointing me out to her.

Burns said, "Take one card instead, you might get a seven, eight or nine. That's a safe hand."

"I might get a ten and then I'm screwed." I scanned the room. I couldn't see anyone making a call. "Split them and I might get a picture and cover my loss. Besides, he busted."

"Dangerous play, relying on the other guy to fold."

"That's why it's called gambling..." I glanced up. There were cameras everywhere. It had to be a practical joke. But why? My anxiety was rapidly turning to exasperation. "Who is this?"

"I told you who I am. We need you to help us with an injury. Our MD thinks he's had an internal carotid artery dissection."

"Who gave you my number? Where are you?"

"I'm in a car just outside the hotel lobby."

"*What* the hell are you?"

I heard a muffled voice. Someone talking to Burns.

"Sir, I'm Air Force, out of Nellis." He paused. "The car is a black Oldsmobile just behind the taxis." He hung up.

I went back to the table and took my chips. Didn't touch the bourbon. I was in a daze as I walked to the cashier and cashed my chips.

I was starting to hope it was a joke.

It was about four o'clock in the afternoon. I knew that because I was wearing a watch. No decent casino allows natural light in the place and no clocks. Ever. Time can only be measured in an exchange of plastic across green felt, the accumulation of butts in an ashtray. And if they're real good, you won't even notice that.

Walking out of the hotel lobby, I looked around, hoping for a friendly face, but there, parked a little distance away from the taxi line, was the Olds. As I approached, the black-tinted driver's window slowly slid down. A pale hand in a black sleeve emerged from the darkness.

A voice called out to me. Burns's. "Thank you for your cooperation."

The hand disappeared, then returned, and a wallet emerged and flipped open to reveal a badge. I didn't recognize the insignia. It was nice and shiny.

I said, "The pleasure is all yours," or something equally stupid.

The rear door swung open.

"Time is of the essence, Doctor. Please get inside."

At this point the edge of the map began to blur. I was entering uncharted waters. *Hic sunt dracones.*

I asked, "How do I know you're who you say you are?"

His face was gaunt and pale. "Who else would we be?"

There was a hollow chuckle from inside the car.

Blindly, I got in.

I'm certain that if I hadn't done so, I would have been kidnapped. I'd like to think I never had a choice.

The back seat was empty. The car smelled new. Burns was sitting next to the driver, and they both had the same close-cropped haircut. I was being abducted by the Bobbsey twins. The Olds pulled away.

I told him that I had to attend a conference the next morning, that I was giving a talk. He told me that there had been a change in arrangements. Someone else was flying out from Boston to speak on my behalf. Apologies had been made to the seminar's organizers.

Perhaps I was relieved. After all, the paper was a form of professional suicide. So I settled back into the seat and watched the backs of the casinos go by, with an occasional glimpse of the monorail overhead. It looked like we were heading for the airport.

"Are we going to Nellis?" I asked.

"Somewhere close by," Burns replied.

I remember thinking that they'd better hurry up if this really was an arterial dissection.

"So what's going on?" I asked, after we had left the outskirts of the city.

"Doctor, I've told you, one of our staff has sustained a head injury that requires your expertise."

"What was he doing?" I asked, surveying the flat desert around us.

"Water skiing?"

At the airport we were rushed through a side door, down a long hallway and into a small office. Above the desk, written in red crayon on the wall, was the phrase "Janet Airlines. Have a nice day." I showed them my driver's license, signed a non-disclosure form, and had my photograph taken. I was led through another doorway, which opened onto the tarmac. I asked about my gear and Burns told me it was being brought from the hotel.

We climbed into a small plane on the edge of the tarmac. It looked like a Gulfstream. It probably took less than ten minutes from our arrival at the airport to lift-off. I was seated between Burns and his companion in an uncomfortable chair in a blackened-out cabin. All that was missing was a briefcase cuffed to my wrist. Nothing felt right.

"So where are we really going?" I asked as we taxied.

Burns glanced over me to his companion. "Pete?" he said.

The other guy just shrugged.

"We're taking you out to the Lake," Burns said.

"The lake?"

They looked at each other, then back at me.

"Place has got many names," Pete said. He looked like he was enjoying the expression on my face. "Just sit back and enjoy the ride, Doctor Wells."

At six p.m., February 26, 1999, I arrived at Groom Lake. A final blast from the jet's engines sent a wave of pebbles skimming across the tarmac. The sun was just settling upon a low ridge on the horizon as we walked the short distance to a chain of bunkers. A lone black Chinook squatted nearby.

Beyond, past the bunkers and the slowly lumbering gas tankers that rumbled from hangar to hangar in swirls of orange dust, was Groom Lake itself. It stretched out toward a shallow range of mountains that encompassed the entire complex. Further south were a series of lakebeds that had run dry long ages before the arrival of man.

Maybe I'm getting better. Sure beats slashing my wrists. I remember the scent of the air out there. It tasted good. Maybe I'm getting better. I'm smiling. Hell, maybe I've just lost it. I remember reading somewhere that if you are wondering if you are insane, you still have a shred of sanity. Alternatively, those whom the gods would destroy, they first drive mad.

* * *

It had rained recently. A thin smear of water shimmered across the surface of the lake. In the distance, huddled together, were more buildings in groups of four or five, connected by gravel roads that ran up into the hills. It was getting chilly and I was only wearing a thin jacket. I was directed toward the closest building, where I was greeted by three men at the door: a tall gray-haired man, Gregory Jenkins, who was base director; an air force officer whose name I forget; and Dean Gershon, their MD. He had a medium build, thick, close-cropped curly black hair, and an easy smile. He shook my hand for about five minutes.

"I expect you want to see our patient," Jenkins said in a gravelly voice.

"I want to see his scans."

He nodded, and led the way down a low-ceilinged corridor. The staff we encountered avoided my gaze. There were no patients anywhere. It was a bureaucrat's dream.

Some men fell into step behind us. Jenkins made a brief apology about calling me away from the conference and Gershon began filling me in on the case. One of the pilots had lost consciousness in a flight simulator. Gershon had seen him and found the man unresponsive. On examination the patient had a Glasgow Coma Scale of 6. He'd ordered a CT and an MRA. The findings were consistent with left-sided cerebral ischaemia. It looked like the internal carotid artery had torn so that the blood had seeped within the artery's walls, blocking the flow.

He handed me a file and I thumbed through photostats of the scans. The affected portions of the brain were dead or dying. I read on and saw my name listed with those of other vascular neurosurgeons.

Gershon told me that he'd tracked down one of my recent articles on Medline. He told me how thrilled he was to find that I was actually in Nevada.

I tried to restrain my own joy at being pulled from the conference.

I wonder. Can I blame him for what was to happen if he did it to save my life?

They had the patient in an isolation room. He was intubated, hooked up to a ventilator. Two armed guards stood by the door. A third flanked a nurse who was changing the fluid bag on his IV pole. He was taped up to an EEG. The display showed near complete flatline. Minimal brain activity.

"Why the guards?" I asked without thinking.

I was cautioned to keep my questions pertinent to the case.

I checked the IV flask. Thiopentone had been added to the solution. "You've got him on full burst suppression," I said.

"He's hibernating. Just the way you like them, pre-op," Gershon replied.

There wasn't much to find on examination. His pupils were fixed and dilated. He had retinal hemorrhages, as I would have expected from an acceleration-deceleration injury. Basically, he looked like shit.

Time travel will do that to you, I guess.

We operated on the patient that night. The case went well. Gershon was competent and fine company to boot. That's crucial during a long case. I could almost forgive him for being the reason I was there. He compared favorably to the dull, black-suited officials who watched my every move.

Apart from Gershon and myself there was an anesthetist, a scrub-sister and a scout nurse. At the door stood two security agents, clearly uncomfortable in their scrubs. We operated well into the night, Tom Waits' voice emerging from the small CD player on one of the Mayo tables, telling it like it is.

We finished closing up at about 1 a.m. Gershon came over to shake my hand like we'd just played a tennis match. I looked up at the observation gallery. If any of the guards had changed shifts, I wouldn't have been able to tell. Jenkins was still sitting there, his chin resting on his palm. Relaxed, surprisingly indifferent. He met me at the scrub basin. He asked me how I thought it went.

I told him that the procedure had gone well enough. Whether or not it was successful would be a matter of time. The patient would need to be transferred to a neurological intensive care unit. Long-term rehab options would have to be considered.

Jenkins shook his head slowly. He told me they had a high dependency unit, well-trained nursing staff. The patient wasn't going anywhere.

"He could bleed again," I said.

"I know that, Doctor. I read your article. He needs expert supervision."

He was courteous about it. He let it look like it was my decision. I might have been exhausted but I had a fair idea of what was going on. I asked him how long he wanted me to stay.

Jenkins smiled. "Until his condition stabilizes, one way or another."

"But I get to leave eventually?" I asked. I don't think there was any tremor in my voice.

"Of course," he replied. The smile broadened, bordered on warmth. "These things happen all the time. You'll be compensated for your services, Doctor, but you'll be obliged to remain silent about your time here. I'm sure you're familiar with confidentiality in your line of work."

"I'm sure."

"And when you return to Boston, your difficulties with the hospital will be sorted out. It's also most unlikely that you'll be hearing again from your ex-wife's attorneys either."

That took me by surprise. "I see."

"And you'll be compensated for your services, Doctor. The funds will be placed in your Swiss bank account."

"I don't have a Swiss bank account," I said, carefully.

His thin lips parted to reveal those even white teeth. "You do now, Doctor."

He knew too much about me, but then again I suspect he knew too much about a lot of people. It was at that time that I made a conscious decision. Up until then my curiosity had been aroused. There was so much I wanted to ask Gershon, but he was here for keeps. For all I knew, he may have been recruited in a similar manner to me. I'd asked him how he'd ended up here, earlier in the operation, and he'd replied, "The same as everybody else. Bad directions."

I was in uncharted territory alright. There were no maps for this region, and there was only one way out. So I resolved not to ask any questions. I resolved to perform my job to the best of my abilities. It was a windfall, really. The cash, and the chance of seeing my life fall back into order.

I had to wonder what Jenkins might have offered had my marriage been happy and my finances secure, but I wasn't foolish enough to believe that I'd like the answer.

The next few days were as indistinct as the desert horizon. I made daily rounds to see the patient, and as he became more coherent his armed escort grew.

Perhaps they thought he might give away state secrets while I was examining him. I mean, the guy couldn't scratch his ass, he couldn't string more than three words together in a sentence. He was improving though, and certainly, in the fullness of time, would regain most of his faculties.

But by the time he would be capable of telling me who killed John F Kennedy, I would hopefully be long gone.

Having only one patient to care for left me with too much free time, and the devil loves idle hands. I exercised. I read. I swam in the pool. Jenkins maintained a significant presence. I wondered what he used to do for kicks before I came along.

Gershon's company provided a thankful distraction. His library, dog-eared and sun-bleached, was composed of crime novels. He told he used to read sci-fi novels, until they had become irrelevant. I understand now what he meant.

We'd smoke, watch videos, play cards and shoot the shit. I let him do most of the talking and I never asked him any questions about the base. Toward the end of my stay, however, when he and I were sitting in his quarters, overlooking the sand and rocks, he volunteered the following.

"The locals call this place the Ranch or the Box. I'm talking about the boys up at the Skunk Works, the flyboys down here on assignment from Nellis. Others call it Dreamland. You know the types—plane-spotters, UFO buffs nuts for their first close encounter. They sit out on Freedom Ridge with their deckchairs and JC Penny telescopes, staring up into the desert skies…"

He looked over at me from where he lay sprawled on the unmade bed. "I've been here for longer than I care to remember, and I've got a better name for the place."

"What's that?" I asked.

"Waste Land," he said. "I call it the Waste Land."

I nodded. It seemed appropriate.

But he looked a little disappointed. "Like the poem. *Where the sun beats*," he began to recite, "*and the dead tree gives no shelter, the cricket no relief, and the dry stone no sound of water.*"

Sitting in his room, desiccating slowly in the fetid air-conditioning, I had to agree with him.

It was early March and I was due to go home. My bags were packed. Money had been wired to my new account. I could scarcely believe it. I'd almost gotten used to the little shit-hole. I say little but I've no idea how large the damn installation was. I'd been confined to the medical wing. In all my time at the facility I never saw a fence or signpost. I guess once you get as far into the place as I did, there really was no way out.

There was a knock on my door. I opened it thinking it was Gershon, here for my farewell. It was Burns. He didn't look too happy. "You're needed right away," he told me. "Medical emergency."

I had images of the patient re-bleeding. But it was way too late for a secondary hemorrhage.

Burns must have read my confusion. "This is a new patient," he told me. "In our other facility."

Other facility? That set off alarms in my head.

The fact that he was wearing a side arm didn't help any.

They were going to kill me. I knew jack shit, but they were going to kill me anyway.

He whisked me into a dusty black jeep and we passed the brief journey in silence. In five minutes we'd crossed a small tundra of dark sand and scrub to reach an arched entrance. It stood alone, embedded within a three-sided structure that was all curves. There were no angles, no sharp edges. Beyond, an isolated crag of red rock kept watch. Burns said nothing as I clambered out of the jeep. He gave me a long look.

"I thought you were going to shoot me."

"No such luck, Doctor Wells."

He put the jeep into gear and disappeared into the dusk.

A shadow detached itself from the shadow of the arch. It formed into a man wearing a single-piece black jumpsuit. He had no insignia or rank displayed on his uniform. My mind was racing but my body froze. He took a step toward me. He grasped my arm and drew me forwards.

There were two men in similar garb on the other side of the arch. The shallow depression of a doorway slid open at my approach. I was shown into the narrow capsule of an elevator and launched into the depths of the desert.

I wish I'd taken the time to catch one last glimpse of the sand and stars. Granted Burns's reprieve, it never occurred to me that they would be the last familiar sight I'd ever encounter.

When the lift stopped, I swallowed my stomach and groggily stepped into another world.

June 7, 1911

I'm sick. I'm taking time out.

Last night, after dark, I wandered the streets. I looked up at the lit windows of shabby houses and watched the couples on their porches observing my shaky path. A dog, hollow-chested and ragged, followed me down the road. I stopped to pet it, calling to it, but each time it settled on its haunches and growled a low, miserable lament.

I haven't been able to keep any food down. I've been unable to take any steps from my bed that didn't lead to the toilet. I'd like to think it's a virus.

I've been here almost three months and my memories appear to have stabilized. This was to be my archive. Now I don't know what it is, but if I'm to have any success in exorcising this ill feeling I have to finish what I started. And I've got things to do. But not today.

June 8, 1911

I was in a bunker beneath the desert, as exhausted as I'd ever been. Gershon was there, wearing scrubs. He was unshaven, his theatre hat askew. The expression on his face, usually so frank and open, was unreadable. There was misery there but its source was beyond me.

"I'm sorry," he said. "It seemed like the right thing to do at the time."

"What have you done?" I asked. There was no blood on his gown or shoes. He hadn't been operating.

"I called you down here," he replied.

I looked from him to the three black-suited men. One of them shook his head slowly in Gershon's direction. He put a hand to an earpiece and said, "You can take him through."

It was Gershon's turn to lead me, and he brought me into the heart of the Waste Land.

We entered a chamber that was huge and white and brightly lit. Rows of fluorescent lights lined a ceiling that stood at least two storeys high. Two figures stood by the entrance. They wore white environment suits with narrow white globular helmets that concealed their features behind a distorted reflection of my own.

A nurse stood beside a gurney. Upon it lay a man in a similar environment suit that had been sliced open to the waist. He emitted a series of low moans and while his arms writhed, fingers grasping at nothing, his face twisted in pain. His trunk and legs were dead things on the trolley.

Jenkins stepped forwards. His arms were held before him, fingers steepled. He wore a look of deep displeasure on his face. Behind him was the machine. Glimpsing it, I felt a lurch of dizziness that I attributed to fatigue. I had to look away. I caught Jenkins eyeing me with curious intent, gauging my response to the thing. I'd become a peripheral yet valid part of his experiment.

The machine… Christ. It was a black and silver orb supported by twelve thick, stubby legs. It had a baroque quality to it. Ornate engraved paneling bisected it horizontally. It could have been reproduced from one of Da Vinci's nightmares; the spawn of a vulgar, ostentatious genius. There was a small aperture in its underbelly. Coiled tubing, wide as tree trunks, connected it to roof and floor. It shimmered, as though vibrating at a very high frequency, like a drawn sword, but made no sound. There was an icy coldness emanating from its core and the tart stench of ozone in the air.

I wanted to vomit.

Behind the machine was a similar object, identical in shape and size. Its surface was scorched black in places. One third of it was missing, as if sheared off by a single stroke. It squatted, partially suspended by heavy chains that hung taut from the ceiling.

Two more uniformed men stood between the objects. Machine-guns, stark and black, hung from thick shoulder straps.

I turned back to the patient.

I knew what the machine was in the same way that I knew the sun was the sun or that water was wet. It was a form of preconscious knowledge that I'd acquired in some dark recess of my mind. The insanity of its existing at all fueled my attempts at denial.

"What happened here?" The words were dead leaves in my mouth.

"Spinal cord compression," Gershon told me. "L 3. He's got ascending paralysis and he's too unstable to be moved to the main hospital." He looked at me pleadingly.

"How did it happen? Another acceleration injury?"

"Not this time," Jenkins replied.

"You're a dangerous man to work for," I murmured.

"I have my finer points. I'm just here to help. Can you do anything for him?"

"I need more information."

Gershon glared at me, Jenkins shrugged, and I, seemingly bent on suicide, persisted.

"I can't operate if I don't know what's happening."

Gershon's face seethed with quiet desperation.

For some reason, that was when it dawned on me. Jenkins manufactured that cold, thin-lipped excuse of a smile and I realized that I'd sold my soul. I may have had no choice at the start of all this, but I'd been offered money and security and an alimony-free life and I had accepted it all with both hands.

I'd said I'd never operate on a spine again. I'd made a promise to God that I was going to break for the devil. How's that for damnation? I didn't trust my hands and I didn't trust my nerve and I sure as hell didn't trust Jenkins.

A small alcove opened halfway along the room's wall. I followed Gershon as he pushed the trolley toward it, the squeak of its wheels echoing loudly. Numbly, I followed him inside.

There were two nurses setting up the necessary equipment. I gave the tools a cursory inspection. They passed muster. My side of the table offered a partial view of the machine. I found myself peering at it while the anesthetist went to work putting lines into the patient.

"For fuck's sake," Gershon muttered under his breath at my side. "Will you stop looking at it?"

The room had been designed for first aid rather than surgery. A tight squeeze for a mobile ventilator and the five of us. They intubated the patient while he was on the gurney. Gershon had located two thick foam rests and placed them on the operating table. We carefully rolled the patient onto his stomach and placed him on the supports.

A CT scan was pinned up to a lightbox. The blood clot was a pulpy opacity over and interlacing the second and third lumbar vertebrae. The spine itself had an unusual translucency that I put down to artefact. I wasn't thinking clearly.

Jenkins was standing just beyond the doorframe. Gershon led me to the cramped basin and began washing his hands. The sister next to us had finished her scrub and was now gowning up.

"Want to tell me what's going on?" I asked.

Gershon kept washing his hands.

"You've seen the guy's back. He's had previous spinal surgery, but I don't see any sign of fusion on the scan."

Gershon looked up at me. "It's still not too late for you, Jon. Just wash your hands and let's do this and get you home. Wouldn't you like to go home?"

I nodded dumbly.

“Don’t look at the machine. Don’t ask any questions.”

Home sounded sweet but nothing about this night was part of the bargain. I placed my hands under the stream of water. I moved in the sluggish wash of a trance. Gershon nudged me toward the waiting nurse who handed me my gown.

After the patient was prepped and draped, reduced to a portion of exposed anatomy for us to work on, I made a linear incision across the previous scar. The wound practically slipped open. It was recent work. I couldn’t see any trace of suture material. I wondered how this wound had been closed. I was looking at the para-spinal muscles. They should have been scarred—knotted and fibrous and bound together by thick non-absorbable sutures—but they were pristine.

Gershon’s theatre cap was soaked with perspiration. Jenkins was watching us as close as ever.

The para-spinals slid easily away from the lumbar pedicles and so far there were no large clots or bone fragments, no telltale signs of any injury. Blood, bone and meat reminded me how much I despised the gross carpentry of spinal work. We spent a few more moments ligating some small bleeders that were quietly seeping into the wound. When I next glanced up, Jenkins was gone, the doorway empty. He was probably having a cigarette or starting World War Three.

“I’ve done a bad thing,” Gershon said quietly. He put a hand over mine in the wound, pressing a large sponge over the vertebrae I’d been trying to expose.

“Your opening could have been neater.”

“I’ve done a real bad thing.” He tightened his grip on me.

“How bad?”

“Sometimes in this place…” Gershon’s frown creased his mask. “I wasn’t thinking it through. I’ll take it from here,” he offered weakly. “Go. Unscrub.”

“You’d be lost.”

I shifted his hand and saw what he’d been trying to conceal. I looked back at him, incredulous.

“Having problems, Doctor Wells?” Suddenly Jenkins was standing by my side. He peered into the wound. “Interesting. Much more advanced than we anticipated.” The look he gave me now was sly, conspiratorial.

The exposed vertebrae were translucent. I could see the layers of muscle beneath them clearly. My first thought, as I tried to rationalize my vision, was that the bone had been treated with something. But nothing made bone see-through. My mind fought for clarity.

This was some form of prosthesis. It had been fashioned around the entire spinal cord, as if somehow grown. No wonder the scan appeared so strange. Fine wiring laced between the artificial bones. There were no signs of tissue reaction.

No one, anywhere, had a product like this.

I leaned closer. Each vertebra was imprinted with a number. A thick wad of blood sat between the middle vertebrae and the spinal cord. I looked at the cord itself. A string of numbers and letters ran its length. The spinal cord was prosthetic. An outright impossibility.

"What do you make of it, Doctor Wells?"

I was light-headed. Dazed. I glanced out the doorway at the machine and returned my gaze to its pilot's wound. "There's been some secondary hemorrhage," I said. "The initial surgery might be about two weeks old."

I asked for a sucker and removed the clot. An arteriole was pumping away steadily, forming a new pool of blood where the clot had been. I asked for a diathermy wand and coagulated the vessel. Gershon dabbed the wound. There was no fresh bleeding. He wouldn't meet my eyes.

"Nice work, Doctor Wells." Jenkins was still by my side. "You will need to be debriefed, of course."

"I'm fine," I replied. "I'm okay. I just need to go. I need to go home now."

"Of course, Doctor. Everything has been organized for your departure."

Gershon was pale. He looked at me now and the meaning was clear. I'd seen something I wasn't supposed to see and my ongoing silence had to be ensured. I wasn't going anywhere.

I had to do something.

"Knife."

The nurse handed me the scalpel with a curious look. I moved fast.

Jenkins said, "What do you think you're doing?"

"You've seen me use one of these." I had the blade up against his throat. Ran it shakily along the side of his neck, opening the skin. "With my next cut you bleed out. I get it wrong and you drown in your own blood."

The nurse stepped back from the table, knocking a tray of instruments to the floor. The anesthetist and the other nurse had their backs up against a wall, as far away from me as possible.

"Doctor Wells," Jenkins rasped, "such melodrama."

"Jonathan?" Gershon was staring at me, dumbfounded.

"Doctor Wells, what happens after you kill me?"

"That won't be your problem." The four guards were framing the doorway; they leveled their weapons in my direction. "I mean it, they shoot and I take you with me."

"I believe you," he said. "Guards."

Keeping the blade close to the skin I looked in their direction.

"If he does anything to me, shoot Gershon—kneecaps, balls, then abdomen. Then do the same for our guest."

"Greg?" Gershon said.

The guards swung their weapons toward Gershon, who edged back toward the ventilator.

Jenkins said, "Your move."

"Greg, please," Gershon was saying. He collided with one of the oxygen cylinders, then put his hand on it to support himself.

"Clock's ticking, Doctor. I thought you were a gambling man."

I was about to drop the knife when Gershon spoke.

"Greg." His voice sounded different. There was the hiss of escaping gas coming from one of the oxygen cylinders. "Anyone shoots, and we all die," he said.

The guards looked at each other and lowered their weapons.

"You heard the man, Jonathan," Gershon said. "Your move."

He nodded toward the doorway. I shoved Jenkins over to the exit.

"Get out of the way," Jenkins snarled at the guards. The veneer of his composure slipped away.

Gershon elbowed his way past the guards to join me in the main chamber.

"Director," someone said. It was the fucking anesthetist.

I twisted around and shoved Jenkins away from me, back into the room. I should have cut him while I had the chance.

"Director, they're bluffing."

I threw the scalpel wildly in Jenkins' direction. The blunt end caught him in the eye. He reeled backwards, both hands clasped to his face.

Gershon sprinted toward the machine.

I didn't know where else to go.

"Shoot them," I heard Jenkins cry. "Shoot the fuckers."

Two more men stepped out from behind the machine. Flashes leapt from their guns. The room filled with thunder.

"Not the carapace," Jenkins yelled from behind me. "Don't fire at the carapace."

There was the sudden screech of an alarm. Clouds of pale green gas wafted from unseen vents. I'd somehow fallen near one of the machine's supports. Gershon, hunched over, was by my side. The firing stopped. The air was burning in my lungs.

Jenkins' voice crackled from inside a mask. "Let the gas do its work." He was crouched by the entrance to the operating room. Behind him, the anesthetist and nurses were writhing on the floor. I felt an arm grab me as gray film seeped over my vision. I felt myself being dragged. It was cold. Intensely cold. I was being lifted, hauled into the belly of the machine. And that's the last thing I recall.

I woke in the desert.

I was lying on my back, in shadow. It hurt to raise my head, but looking past my feet I could see the furrow my body had made in the sand. The trail was laced with streaks of drying blood. I patted myself down; it wasn't mine.

Above me towered a huge rock formation, tinged red in the last of the sun's rays. It looked familiar. My head throbbed with a dull, heavy ache.

Gershon was sitting next to me, propped up against an abutting shelf of the rock. He said, "You owe me one." His eyes had a partially glazed look.

I asked him where he was hit. He spread his fingers slightly. His gown had an ugly tear across the mid-section. Near its hem were speckles of blood and bone from the operation, but above was a slowly spreading stain.

"I think they nicked one of my renals," he said. "I'll be pissing blood for a month." He smiled wanly. Unconvincingly. He wasn't going to survive the night outside of a hospital.

"Where are we?" I asked.

"The Waste Land," he said, looking around.

The desert was ochre-red in the last of the light. Long shadows stretched across its undulating expanse. I could now make out the enclosing perimeter of low mountains to all sides. I scanned out toward the horizon, past the long, flat surface of the lakebed. No buildings, no hangars, no runway.

"Where's the base?"

"It'll be here in, say, another forty years."

"I really have to get you to a hospital."

Gershon laughed. The laugh turned into a cough that racked his body. The spittle on his lips was flecked with blood. "No hospital here can help me," he said. "Listen carefully, there's a few things you need to know."

Despite my protests, he spoke, and I finally gave in and listened. He continued talking as dusk turned to night, and the desert sands cooled, and I learnt many things.

"The base will be constructed in 1955," he said. "Eight years after Roswell."

"Roswell?" I rolled my eyes and ignored Gershon's use of tense for the moment. Soon I would learn a new way of thinking about time. About cause and effect.

"You must know the story. In July 1947 something crashed in Roswell, New Mexico."

I nodded, though it hurt like hell.

"Roswell is the only documented case where the government ever claimed to have found a flying saucer." He caught the frank disbelief in my expression but pressed on. "An intel officer from the 509th, one of the first on the scene, said that an object had crashed onto a farm, that it had been recovered and shipped away. It made the front page of the *New York Times* but the headlines didn't last too long. The 509th was a special unit. Heard of it?"

"Can't say that I have," I replied.

"They saw some interesting action in the war. I'm talking about Hiroshima, Nagasaki. They were the only unit in the world capable of delivering an A-bomb. And then this thing crashed in their backyard. Anyway, the official story was revised to state that it had been a weather balloon, of all things, that had crashed."

"Was it?" I asked.

"You saw what it was."

"The machine? The thing Jenkins called the carapace?"

"No." Gershon coughed. "It was the thing you saw behind the carapace."

The partially dismantled object, seared and sliced.

"That's what they found?"

He paused, wiped phlegm from his lips, and tried to find a more comfortable position. I took off my gown and wrapped it around him.

"What was it?" I asked.

He looked at me wide-eyed. I supposed then that I could admit what it was. I just couldn't say the words.

"It was a time machine, Jon," he said.

While he spoke I fashioned a dressing from strips of his torn theater gown, which he pressed firmly against his abdomen. "Where, *when* did it come from?"

"No one was sure. One of the project's top consultants said that though most of the working parts could be assembled with current technology, it's impossible to imagine how such a design might have been conceived in the first place." Gershon shrugged. "As to where it was from, all I can say is that the operating interface communicates in English."

"How do you know all this?"

"I was base doctor for ten years. These guys had to talk to someone or go insane. Before I did med I was a physics and math major, so I could relate to some of the shit. And I wasn't going anywhere." He smiled. "The way I see it, it was one of ours, from the future."

"So there was no crash?"

"There was a crash alright. I guess you could call it that. The machine partially materialized inside one of the ranch's stables. There was some kind of explosion. Only one body was recovered from the wreckage. Quite dead."

I looked at him meaningfully.

He smiled again. "The body was human, Jon. I don't know anything more about him than that."

"So why the stories about the flying saucer and the weather balloon?" I asked.

"What would *you* tell the public?"

"I don't know."

"You'd lie, that's what you'd do," he said. "And you'd lie like a mother fucker. 1947—World War Two barely finished, and the Cold War just brewing up. What are you going to tell the people? That we found a time machine? What the hell are they going to think?"

"They're not going to think it was a weather balloon."

"Damn straight, they're not," Gershon said. "Government couldn't keep the crash a secret. So they had to construct a lie and then wrap it within a more elaborate one."

"And then spend the next fifty years denying the existence of flying saucers," I said. "And no one bothers to guess what else it might have been."

"Uh-huh."

"Why flying saucers?"

"Flavor of the month, I guess. The term 'flying saucer' had only been coined a few weeks earlier. Some pilot had been flying around the Cascade Mountains in Washington and described seeing nine objects moving at nearly fifteen-hundred miles an hour. He said that they seemed to skip across the clouds like a saucer skipping on a pond. The idea of flying saucers can be frightening—forces beyond our understanding and the like—but the idea of contact with aliens has an optimistic side too. Significantly, any threat that contact with extraterrestrials poses is only a threat to the future."

I saw where he was headed. I said, "A time machine, however, poses an entirely different threat to humanity. It doesn't just affect the future—it threatens the past and present as well. It threatens our very existence."

"Better to keep it a secret," he said, and he began coughing again.

Gershon went silent. I did what I could to keep him warm.

Nightfall had transformed the desert. Stars, familiar yet strange, shone above us, yet they seemed slightly askew. Was the passage of little more than eighty years reflected in the movements of the galaxies beyond? I didn't think so. Perhaps it was my imagination, some after-effect of the journey, or some residual disorientation from the machine itself?

I don't know, but I never experienced that phenomenon again. I did not realize it but even then I was being synchronized, adjusted, slotted into the time I'd been transported to.

The moon had yet to rise and there were no discriminating shades. All was black. Gone were the shales and shelves of rock, the yucca and sagebrush that dotted the otherwise desolate perspective. The surrounding landscape appeared as though it had been carved from one single fragment. But not only that: the history, the ongoing narrative of our existence, that is revealed in every leaf and tree, every pebble and grain of sand, was concealed in that complete darkness. Time was held captive.

It felt as if the universe had in that moment been created.

When Gershon spoke again, we talked in hushed tones.

"Did they ever explain why the machine crashed in the first place? And why Roswell?"

"I don't think they ever recovered anything like a 'black box', that they could identify or recognize, so they never learned what happened during its last moments. As for why Roswell, no one was sure. But the timing may have been important. That was the year that the armed forces were separated into army, navy and air force. It was the year the CIA was formed and Chuck Yeager broke the sound barrier. Who knows how significant these events might appear to the future? And less than an hour away from Roswell sat the repository of America's first atomic weapons."

"So are there UFOs?" I asked.

"I've seen plenty of things flying around that I couldn't identify," Gershon replied, "but they weren't piloted by Little Green Men."

I asked him what had happened after I'd passed out, back in that room.

The gas was everywhere, he said. He'd dragged me up a gangway and into the machine itself, shutting the hatch.

Within the carapace was a chamber. Six seats arranged in two tiers. The console was a low, narrow shelf that took up a third of the cabin. Above it, undetectable from without, was a window or viewscreen. There, concave screens that resembled a computer monitor, a keyboard that could be accessed easily from either forwards chair.

A single thick lever was set astride the central keyboard. To either side of it, beneath a sheet of rippled clear glass or plastic, were two palm-sized disks. The left one was bright green, the right one, a dull red color. User friendly.

Gershon could see what was happening in the room.

Jenkins was gesturing wildly. More men entered. The gas started to dissipate. There was a loud hammering from outside the capsule. Someone was working on the door.

Gershon thought he saw some of the men attempt to disengage one of the coils from the carapace, and that's when he did the only thing he could think of. He shifted the lever. The transparent covers slid back and he slammed his fist onto the left switch, which was pulsing with green light.

"What happened then?" I asked.

Gershon was pale. He had the two gowns bundled around him and was lying down. I'd elevated his legs on a mound of sand.

"The screen went black for a moment. I felt this weird rocking sensation, so I climbed into one of the chairs next to yours. A message flashed on the HUD, and there was this sound, like an eggshell cracking, but loud. The hammering stopped. I looked out the viewscreen and saw Jenkins' men, caught in freeze-frame." He seemed to be looking past me as he recalled the events. "That silence was so total, so complete. It was as if I'd gone deaf. It's…" He was shaking his head, confounded.

"I'm not sure how much time passed. That rocking sensation returned a couple of times and that cracking, two, maybe three times. Like we were passing through a series of barriers. Barriers that should never be crossed, yet the machine went through them like tissue paper. That was when I realized I'd been hit. You were out but you were breathing. The red disk on your armrest was glowing. On the screen there was a new message: "COMPLETE INSERTION IN PROGRESS: STAGING COMPLETE: QUERY ABORT?" There was that rocking feeling again and suddenly a new image appeared on the screen."

He leaned his head forwards. He was unable to move his arm. "And this is what I saw. All of this."

A thought struck me. "Where's the carapace now?"

He said that as soon as the carapace had settled, a new series of messages rapidly scrolled up the screen. One message repeated itself, to the accompaniment of a faint beeping noise: "AUTO-RECALL IMMINENT: STAGING CONFIRMED: QUERY ABORT?"

Gershon told me a countdown began flashing along the HUD. He pushed the lever forwards to its original position and the plastic sheaths slipped back over the disks. He dragged me from my seat, opened the hatch and pushed me out into the desert. When we were about ten feet from the vehicle, he turned to look back at it.

"It was the most amazing thing I've ever seen." His eyes blazed momentarily with the fervor of an ecstatic.

"When I was learning my bar mitzvah they had this book there, a kid's version of the Bible. There was this picture of Abraham on the cover and…" He smiled. "Anyway, *Exodus* was my favorite. Plagues, rivers of blood, the departure from Egypt. There was this bit about how they followed a pillar of fire by night and a pillar of cloud by day, through the desert. That's what it looked like."

"Which one?"

"Both. The body of the carapace was barely visible, but I couldn't make out the legs. It seemed to just float on this cushion of fire and cloud. The air crackled and that portal I'd dragged you out of, it blinked at me once, like God's great eye, and the carapace sank into the cloud.

"All at once there was a tremendous rush of wind, and the whole thing, the clouds, the flame, all seemed to fall in on itself. It was like watching an explosion played backwards. And then it vanished."

I felt a sudden surge of new panic.

"How long have we been here? Aren't they going to come after us?"

"Relax." Gershon coughed. "No one's coming after us. If they had any means of following us, they would have been here by now. Hell, they would have been waiting for us."

Gershon said again that the base wouldn't be built for forty years. He knew that because a digital readout had displayed the date: March 10, 1911.

We had been here, in 1911, for about two hours already. I had been unconscious for little over an hour.

Gershon believed that, somehow, our very presence in this time negated the possibility of pursuit. Perhaps the future was already being altered in some way. The flutter that had been created by our arrival evolving into a hurricane of change over the years.

We remained undisturbed that night and nothing has happened since then to suggest that we were ever followed. Perhaps it is something I have already done, or something I am going to do. I plan on keeping my eyes open.

I wonder what I'm going to do.

What do I ever do?

Gershon was dying. Shutting down. His hands were cold and pale. His pulse, thready beneath my fingertips.

I got up to stretch my legs and followed the trail that marked where I'd been dragged from the carapace. It led to a flat, hard-packed layer of ground. Starlight reflected dimly from thin patches of glass that had been burnt into the sand by the vehicle's passage. Shards of frozen time.

Lying on its side was a pack of some sort. Gershon hadn't mentioned it. I rushed to it, hoping it might contain some medical supplies.

Something I could use to help him. I spilled its contents onto the ground. There was a torch, a knife, a compass, chocolate, a ground sheet, a packet of cigarettes, and a pair of binoculars. Within the pack's lining was a thick belt with numerous pockets, each of which held a slender, malformed ingot of solid gold. I replaced the bag's contents and walked back over to Gershon.

"Good, you found it." He gave a weak laugh. "Wouldn't you know it, I grabbed the wrong pack. Medical supplies went back with the carapace, I guess."

"Tell me, how the hell did you manage to avoid the gas?"

He looked at me, sighed, then grinned. "You know that swimming pool near the rec room?"

I nodded.

"I used to dive in that pool and sink to the bottom. Pretend I was anywhere but here, and see how long I could hold my breath. My record was three minutes."

He was slipping in and out of consciousness. We lay close together and I did my best to keep the both of us warm. Whenever he woke, he wanted to talk. He talked about women. He talked about God.

"What happens now?" he asked at one point. "Have we put God on rewind? Taken him back eighty years? Sent him spinning? Was He expecting this? Is it part of the Grand Plan?"

I asked if he was religious. His pale, drawn face locked in a grimace.

He talked about the people who'd lived here and passed on. The Shoshone and the Paiute, the Bannock and the Washoe. He talked about the ocean, about how much he missed the open water. He asked me what I was going to do. Where I was planning on going. As if we were just separating for a while.

I was already surveying the packed sands for a place to bury him.

"I'd be heading to New York," he said.

"Why New York?"

"Why not?" He smiled as if he'd made a wonderful joke. "Do me a favor, Jon. Next time you see the open sea, wade on in a few steps and spare me a thought."

He seemed so calm and serene and I asked him that most meaningless of questions.

"Are you okay?"

"I'm okay." And then, somehow reading my thoughts, he added, "I'm not scared.

"When you had Jenkins by the balls and those goons had lowered their guns, I thought I had a chance of surviving and I was as scared as I have ever been." He shrugged. "Now I know I'm going to die."

I told him how sorry I was and he shrugged it off.

"Hell," he replied, "I was dead these last ten years. Just didn't know it."

June 18, 1911

It was deathly cold that night. The sweat froze on my back as I dug his grave. I don't plan on being that cold again.

I've resolved to head north. Back to New York. Back to my home and Gershon's destination. I'll go to Coney Island and wade on in. Sparing him a thought won't be an issue. I'm hoping it might make it a little easier for me to think less often of him, actually.

It's easier to recall things now: dates and times and facts I'd read in that world I've left behind. I plan on putting the knowledge to good use, a little bit at a time.

There's an archduke in Europe who could do with living beyond 1914, and an Austrian painter with nasty ideas who could do with a more valid, if brief, reason for hating Jews. I'll be dealing with him shortly.

There's no rush.

Jenkins showed me what I'm capable of. There are investments to be made and interventions to consider.

But first I have a boat to catch. "Change or die" is my new creed. "What if" becomes "why not", and everything old is new again.

A GAME OF CHESS II

En Passant

I

April 22, 2012

New York City, Eastern Shogunate

Morgan spied their car a block down from the bar. A Yamamoto Kobe had procured for them earlier in the week. The plates identified it as a medical officer's transport—ideal for parking, unlikely to be pulled over for a random search. There were two suitcases in the boot. Shine had packed light. He'd also found time to go clean out Lightholler's suite. Everything they needed was crammed into the back.

Morgan climbed in, squeezing his legs beneath the dash. The car's narrow confines made him feel oafish. He leaned back in his seat and waited. Kennedy had said that the flight wouldn't be leaving for another few hours.

Something had gone seriously wrong. Morgan was certain of it. Why else would the major have started Lightholler's re-education so prematurely? The arrangement had been to take him south first. Tell him what they knew a little at a time and then finish the job in Nevada. That was the way they'd recruited Doc.

That was the way they'd recruited him.

He let his mind replay those events. The things he'd said, the things he should have said. But he couldn't dwell on it for long—not if he wanted to retain any vestige of his sanity. He found it easier to dwell on his companions.

He thought about Shine and wondered how the role of lackey sat with him. Kennedy had needed someone undercover in the Waldorf, and where else was a negro going to hide in New York City, much less the Union?

The reservations were all in the Midwest and they were full. The only negroes permitted in the North were in major cities, and they had to be registered in the employ of a landowner or some company. Ironically, things weren't as bad in the South. You could be self-employed if you were black, perhaps even run your own business, thanks to the major. But the best prospects, for both negroes and indians, remained in the army.

Shine's father had served in Kennedy's unit. Had fought with him at the Battle of San Juan. He was among the soldiers Kennedy had petitioned to receive land rights after the last Ranger War. Soldiers who'd sworn to follow Kennedy into hell itself, and then did so at Mazatlan.

Land rights for the disenfranchised. There was a precedent for Kennedy's actions, but you had to look back. To Rome. To Marius, Sulla and, of course, Julius Caesar. Men who had inspired armies to follow them rather than the state. Men who had brought down a republic.

Hot on the heels of his military victories and backed by the fervent support of key public figures, Kennedy's proposals had been tolerated as one would endure the wishes of a favoured child. Once he ran for public office, however, turning his own indulgences into party politics, he encountered an immovable wall of resistance. Suggestions of a secret agenda. That he wanted civil rights extended to *all* blacks in the South, and indians too. What had been perceived as eccentricity began being interpreted as folly by his supporters and rabble-rousing by his opponents. The election results shouldn't have surprised anyone.

The men and families of Kennedy's unit, the 4th Mech-Cavalry Division, got their land and Kennedy was parcelled laterally into the CBI. A polite shift out of the political arena.

Considering it now, Morgan had to wonder. For a brief moment Kennedy had enjoyed the support of the people and the army. What had held him back, stopped him from seizing what he might have considered his birthright? Was it the same thing that appeared to drive him now?

Joseph Patrick Kennedy I, the patriarch of the Kennedy clan and the major's great-grandfather, had started off as a bootlegger during Prohibition and ended up as Union ambassador to the German Empire after the Secession. Old Joseph had four sons: Joseph Junior, John, Robert and Edward.

Reconciliation. It could have happened. It almost did happen. But at what price?

In 1963, the Kennedys were well established in the North and the South. They had money. They had power. But of course there had always been the rumours. Rumours that old Pat the Patriarch had never quite broken his ties with organised crime, that he in fact merely represented its legitimate face to the watching world. Nothing was ever proved, but somewhere along the line Pat must have let some of his colleagues down. He was given a reprimand that neither he nor America would soon forget.

November 22, the last leg of the fundraiser for the United America Project. The crowd had greeted John and Bobbie with flag-waving enthusiasm as the brothers received recognition for their contributions to the city, their motorcade winding through downtown Dallas.

The Warren Commission never found a specific motive linking the assassins, though suspects ranged from Southern separatists to Mediterranean-based cartels. They never determined why Oswald, Ellroy and Stone, three senior members of a Dallas crime outfit, had decided to spend that day catching up on their reading in the book depository.

Zapruder had captured it all, his camera panning across Dealey Plaza. John, with his arm around Norma Jean. Robert's dazzling smile. Spouts of asphalt. John's head snapping back and forth as the Continental screeched to a halt. The street full of the dead and dying. Final tally: eleven dead and twenty-three wounded. Amongst the dead, the Kennedy boys and their spouses, an assortment of bodyguards and local count-sheet thugs. The remainder, a bunch of tourists and well-wishers.

Major Joseph Robard Kennedy had inherited a name forever linked with infamy and violence. Initially, he'd shunned the path chosen for him. He took the low road and joined the Confederate Army. Assigned to a third-rate unit of Buffalo soldiers and reservation rejects, he turned them into a force that had helped save Texas.

They gave him a shot at public office, and when he came close to success they smeared him with the detritus of his family history. They gave him a shitty little portfolio in the back office of the Bureau and he dished them back Camelot. What might he craft from the red sands of Nevada? What could he do about something he actually *believed* in?

Morgan surveyed the quiet street, and felt the fear steal upon him. He'd known it all of his life: the suspicion that the pieces of his world did not quite mesh. The feeling that a swift sideways glance at the occasional flicker that danced on the periphery, once pinioned and held in freeze-frame, might reveal the world as it truly was—or as it truly should be. The only difference was that now he knew why.

He closed his eyes and tried to slow the whirr of rushing thoughts.

Something had gone wrong.

II

Hardas did his best not to draw too much attention to himself. He held a cigarette in one hand and a glass in the other and watched the women who came and went across the shell-strewn floor of the bar.

He'd always considered himself a pragmatic man. Presented with a problem, he'd find the solution. That was his speciality. Tactics. Leave the strategy to others. Let them concentrate on the forest, while he dealt with the trees.

But this was getting to be too big for him. And all because of the *Titanic*. Both *Titanics*, in fact.

He'd been happy in the Navy, working his way up the ranks, making commander in almost record time. His unblemished record earned him the new Confed-designed, *Kaiser*-class German submarines. It never occurred to him to question why the Confederate Navy was working so closely with the Germans.

In early April 2010, he found himself aboard the *Schlieffen*, scuttling across the floor of the North Atlantic. They'd remained undetected in Japanese waters for more than a month before the recall order had arrived. Then one of the chiefs of staff in Berlin got the bright idea of bringing back a trophy. "A gift for the Kaiser's fiftieth birthday."

They arrived at the wreck on the fifteenth; ninety-eight years to the day after the *Titanic* had sunk. A small memorial service was held in the mess. Hardas, leading the service, was amused at the hypocrisy. There they were, praying for the lost souls while planning to plunder their last resting place.

The bathyscaphe was cradled in a small hold towards the rear of the submarine, resembling an egg, clasped by a nest of iron twigs. Studded with lights and antennae in an array that seemed haphazard, it was designed for submersed repairs, clearing mines and deep-sea reconnaissance.

Hardas, his second officer and two engineers sat crowded inside the claustrophobic vessel as it spiralled its way down. Their two-hour journey was made in silence, each man lost in his thoughts. The North Atlantic lay heavily upon them. At these depths, the smallest leak in the hull could produce a razor-edged jet of water. Cut a man in two before he could blink.

At first, ghost-like, she appeared as a faint green glow on the ultrasound screen. One of the crewmen activated the cameras. Lights blazed into the Stygian depths. The bathyscaphe's propellers coughed to life, a dull constant thud that vibrated through the vessel and its occupants.

On the centre screen an image congealed out of the darkness. Hazy at first, it took on a grainy semblance that gained form, particulated, to reveal the ocean floor. Before them, basking in light for the first time in almost a century, a bronze deck bench sat perched upon the seabed.

"We're in the debris field. She lies due north, Commander," one of the engineers whispered.

With a sigh, the bathyscaphe wafted over the sand-swept plains of the North Atlantic. Bed springs and baroque oddities littered their path. Wine bottles, their corks firmly ground into their necks, lay spread out between shards of pottery and the rusted plates of boiler casings.

The ultrasound monitor pulsed with a green luminescence that bathed their faces with a sickly glow. The video screen flickered momentarily, white noise resolving into black shadow as, before them, the hull of the wreck rose out of the eternal night.

At first glance, she resembled an ancient creature from mythology. The husk of the Leviathan. Hardas could make out her bow. The encrusted shell was torn in many places, huge ragged gaps where the boilers had torn their way through the dying ship.

They took a slow run over her decks. There was the ominous creak of the turbines rotating on their axles. The screen misted over with churning sand and the bathyscaphe began its ascent up the sheer face of the *Titanic*'s prow.

Hardas ignored the perplexed looks exchanged among his crew. He'd been asked to bring back a trifle, some small object of note to adorn the mantlepiece of the leader of the Western world. But Hardas wanted to do something more, something that might make all of his accomplishments to date pale into insignificance. This was a unique opportunity, and he was, after all, a pragmatic man.

Earlier expeditions had returned with samples from the debris field, the odd ornament prised loose from the ship's superstructure. The greatest prize, to date, had been the recovery of the ship's bell. Hardas had set his sights much higher. He was determined to retrieve the contents of the *Titanic*'s safe and let the Kaiser take his pick.

As they pulled up just below the level of the boat deck, he took a few moments to explain his scheme to the crew, who murmured their approval. The bathyscaphe hovered in the murky darkness; her targeting lights splayed against the hull of the ruin while her acetylene torches punched holes in the rusted metal.

In less than two hours they had gained C Deck. Another two hours and the ship's safe lay secure in the mechanical grip of the bathyscaphe's grappling arms.

Back aboard the *Schlieffen*, there'd been some discussion as to what to do with the safe. Open it now or wait till it was safely on German soil? Hardas gave the order to make for New Orleans while he awaited further orders from Berlin.

Six days later, they encountered the *Bremen* in the Gulf of Mexico. The cruiser's captain told Hardas that both the Confederacy and Germany were exceedingly pleased with the mission's success. However, the Kaiser remained unaware of the gift they were bearing. Rather than risk staining the sumptuous carpets of the palace, it was decided that they would open the safe aboard the *Bremen*. Admiral Merkur, flown out from Berlin, was present to supervise.

So much for Hardas's golden opportunity.

Film crews were on hand to document the historic event. The Germans liked to film everything. A torch was employed to burn open the outer door. It clanged onto the *Bremen*'s deck, releasing a small torrent of rank seawater that sprayed the uniforms of the closely observing crew.

Hardas hung back, behind the cameramen and journalists, an unlit Texas Tea dangling from his lips. After the men had dispersed, and the contents of the safe were inventoried, he was approached by the *Bremen*'s captain.

"Herr Kommandant," the man had said, "a small token of esteem from Admiral Merkur. We were unable to find Captain Smith's logbook. He must have taken it with him to the bottom of the ocean, *nicht wahr*? However, we have found this journal. It is in English, and appears to be of a personal nature." He handed the book to Hardas. "Please accept this with the admiral's best wishes."

And what would the captain be taking, and Merkur himself, Hardas wondered. He suspected that by the time the safe's contents reached Berlin, the Kaiser would be lucky to find a paper clip.

He took the journal with a nod of thanks.

He doubted that the officers of the *Bremen* would even remember his name, much less mention it to the Kaiser. What the hell, he reasoned as he returned to the *Schlieffen*. He'd be back in New Orleans in no time. And from now on, he would leave the games to the politicians.

It took two more days to reach harbour. The pace was leisurely, and once they arrived Hardas decided the crew could do with a rest after a month spent in the ocean's depths.

He started to read the journal the night before they reached New Orleans. He'd planned on skimming it briefly before handing it over to one of the senior officers at the base. It took him six hours to complete the manuscript from cover to worn cover. Much of it was damaged beyond recognition by nearly one hundred years of exposure to the icy depths. What he could decipher was clear enough. He could not give this journal to his commanding officers.

He made a few phone calls. He smoked too many cigarettes.

He was contacted by Maritime Surveillance.

Within a week he was summoned to the CBI complex in Dallas.

Kennedy was tall and smiling and looked like a publicity photo of himself. He said, "Commander, I think we need to talk."

Maybe I did the right thing, Hardas thought, slouching outside the locked door. *Ever since Red Rock, it's too much for me to grasp. I don't want to think about it any more.*

His eyes found Kennedy.

The major, meeting his glance, gave him a smile he couldn't return.

III

Kennedy sat at the back of the bar nursing his third cup of coffee.

According to Shine, Japanese detectives had sealed off the Queens Midtown Tunnel. Three bodies had been recovered from the crime scene. They had yet to be identified.

And there'd been a shooting in Osakatown. Perhaps Cooper was chasing the Germans who'd gunned down his men. Perhaps he was planning on coming downtown in force. It didn't matter. Shine was watching the perimeter.

Kennedy checked his Einstein. Two hours and they'd be gone. Dawn would find them in New Orleans. They'd make Red Rock by dusk. And Lightholler, primed by today's induction, would see the carapace. He would believe.

But they were cutting it close.

Kennedy had known for more than a year that war was coming, had known ever since he and Hardas had taken the carapace on its first test run at Red Rock. He'd always allowed for the fact that Lightholler's instruction might take some time. He just hadn't counted on the world starting to fall apart in the interim. The failure of the peace talks, the Japanese offensive in Russia, the German subterfuge closer to home—all pointed to the future he'd glimpsed in Nevada.

For nearly a century the empires of Germany and Japan had spread across the surface of the planet. There was no place on Earth where the influence of one of these great powers wasn't felt. And now they were in deadlock. Each had a vision of the future that held no place for the other.

This wouldn't be a war of punitive expeditions into disputed territories.

Men wouldn't lie in trenches staring down the barrels of rifles into a fog of barbed wire and mud. The new weapons would change all that.

Kennedy looked up to find Hardas standing by his table.

"Has Lightholler tried to leave the room?" Kennedy asked.

Hardas shook his head.

"We've got an hour till we have to move."

Hardas pulled up a chair. "I don't like the captain's story, Major."

"It's a little far-fetched, isn't it?"

"So why are we moving ahead?"

"We don't have any choice. And we need him."

"We've got Shine," Hardas countered.

"Shine isn't allowed on the boat."

Hardas lit a cigarette. His forehead creased in deliberation. "It shouldn't have to come to that."

"Shouldn't doesn't mean won't," Kennedy replied.

"If Lightholler's working for the Bureau..."

"Let's just say for the moment that he is," Kennedy said. "Let's say Webster was using him as bait."

"Then he has to know what we're up to."

"Webster recalls me after our meeting with Lightholler, then sends Wetworks scurrying after us the very same day. That's clumsy."

"Or desperate," Hardas said.

"The way I figure it, if Webster thought we had a device like the carapace, we'd be down in Houston right now, at Intel Extraction," Kennedy said. "That, or dead. No, this is all tied up with the German thing."

"I hope you're right," Hardas murmured.

"Two days from now and we're gone," Kennedy said.

"I hope to God you're right."

IV

Lightholler rose from the table as Kennedy and Hardas entered the room, "It's a fake," he began.

"It's no fake, Captain," Kennedy said. "We can be certain of that."

Hardas offered Lightholler a cigarette. He lit up with trembling hands.

"But it's absurd. I never heard of any crash at Roswell, any flying saucers," he said. "Las Vegas is just a wide spot in the road. And as for this secret installation..."

Kennedy and Hardas remained silent. It was exasperating.

Lightholler pointed at the journal. "This guy is talking about someone starting World War Three." His eyes were glistening. "What the hell is a world war?"

"We don't plan on finding out," Hardas said quietly.

"What's the *matter* with you people? Why would you believe any of this... this bullshit?"

Kennedy let the question hang in the air for a moment before replying. "We went to Nevada, Captain. We found the carapace."

Lightholler started to laugh. "You found the carapace…" He drew back deeply on the remains of his cigarette and said, "You're lying."

"What you believe at this moment isn't a concern of mine," Kennedy said. "What does concern me is the fact that the people who've been watching you are very good at what they do. There's the risk that you've been working for them, the risk that you've been doing so without even being aware of it. And if that's true, it makes you a serious liability."

Lightholler tried to interrupt. Kennedy motioned him to silence.

"Two of my men are dead. I have your account of the matter, Captain, and

I'm prepared to assume—for the moment—that you are entirely innocent. I also respect the fact that none of this may be your fault, but I must stress to you, right now, that this is *your* problem; not mine. That means that from here to Nevada you never leave my sight. That means that if I have to voice my concerns again, regarding yourself and the Bureau, it will be in the company of an associate of mine. You won't enjoy the experience."

"I don't take kindly to threats, Major."

"I don't make threats, Captain. I outline possibilities."

"You talk out of your arse."

The flicker of a smile crossed Hardas's lips. He turned to Kennedy and said, "I like this guy."

Kennedy ignored him. "Regarding the carapace, Captain, I promise you that you'll believe it when you see it."

"When I see it?"

"You're coming with us," Kennedy said, softly now. "We need you."

"What the *hell* do you need me for?" Lightholler mashed the cigarette onto the table's stained surface. He looked from one man to the other and then back at the journal. "Shit." It was almost a whisper. "You've got to be kidding." His gaze turned towards the ceiling. He focused on a swirl of smoke that spiralled around the naked light bulb. After a moment, he spoke again.

"That's why I was selected for the maiden voyage." He slapped the table with an open palm. "You were *training* me. You actually believe you can go back in time. Back to the *Titanic*..."

"That's right, Captain."

Lightholler was shaking his head. "You're out of your fucking minds." Then another thought occurred to him. "How much pull do you guys have? A letter from the King; you've got the Admiralty in your pocket..." His voice trailed away.

"Things go our way every now and then," Kennedy said.

"For all I know, you organised for the *Titanic*'s replica to be built."

"A little beyond our budget." Kennedy smiled. "We had nothing to do with the new ship's construction, though Morgan was consulted on her design. You were, however, one of a select few that we had wanted for her captain."

"Why me in particular?" Lightholler asked. Despite his scepticism, he found himself curious.

"I guess I'm just sentimental."

Hardas said, "Let's go."

Kennedy gathered up the journal and the photographs and wedged them gently into his satchel.

Lightholler felt a gun's muzzle nudging against the small of his back. He turned to Hardas and said, "You don't need that."

Hardas motioned him towards the door.

"I thought you liked me."

Hardas smiled. "There's like and there's like, Captain. Let's move."

The place had started to fill with the early evening crowd. Lightholler was reeling. He could feel no centre of balance.

"You feel disorientated, don't you, confused?" Hardas said.

Lightholler nodded.

"You'll get used to it."

Kennedy worked a path through the slack knots of drinkers that ebbed and flowed along the bar's edge. Everyone seemed to be moving too slowly. The next time Lightholler heard country music would be too soon.

There was a small sedan parked outside. He was nudged into the back seat, between Kennedy and Hardas. Morgan was seated up front. Lightholler noted, without surprise, that their driver was the same negro who'd been attending him during his stay at the Waldorf.

"Any more details on Osakatown, Martin?" Kennedy asked as they pulled away from the kerb. They headed uptown. Lightholler peered out of the rear window into the forming dusk.

"There was a shooting. Two men. Both dead."

"Kobe's joint?" Kennedy asked.

"Two blocks from Kobe's," Shine replied.

"That's where they were supposed to be going," Lightholler said. "The men who kidnapped me."

Kennedy turned to face him.

"The *other* men who kidnapped me." Lightholler offered a faint smile.

"Thank you for the clarification, Captain."

"This is getting all fucked up, Major," Morgan said.

"Someone gets shot every other day in Osakatown, Darren," Kennedy said. "We're fine."

Hardas was leaning against his window. The gun remained firmly in his grip. Lightholler eyed the pistol, noting the calibre and the thick bulk of the magazine clip in front of the trigger guard. He decided not to say anything.

"Streets are quiet," Kennedy muttered.

"What are you thinking, Major?" Hardas asked.

"I'm thinking this is a good time to be leaving New York."

Shine drove the sedan up Mercer Street and turned onto Bleecker.

"Where are we going?" Lightholler asked.

"Central Park," Kennedy replied.

"Oh, good," Lightholler said wearily. "I love the park."

They ignored him.

"We should check the radio," Hardas said.

Lightholler sensed that something had changed since Kennedy had approached him in the hotel room, only yesterday. The dynamic seemed all wrong. It was time to stir the mix. He cleared his throat.

"When we do get hauled in, I'll be sure to remind them to add abduction to the charges of conspiracy and treason."

"We'll just have to plead insanity," Morgan replied. He left the sentence hanging, as if he expected a reply. When none was forthcoming, he turned his head to view Lightholler with a half-hearted attempt at a smile.

Lightholler shook his head. "Amateurs."

"Of course we're amateurs," Kennedy said softly. "We'll only get one chance at this, and it's not as if there are any precedents."

"Think of us as pioneers," Hardas added.

They travelled in uneasy silence. The radio whined through a chorus of crackle.

"There," Kennedy said. "Hold it."

They listened as a reporter described the shootings in Osakatown and the Midtown Tunnel.

"Jesus," Morgan said. "They happened round the same time."

"Looks like someone's cleaning house," Hardas said.

The reporter's voice trailed into static again. Shine adjusted the frequency. The static roared, then sputtered.

Kennedy asked, "Can you get anything else?"

"Can't get anything at all, Major."

Hardas squinted out the window, scoping the aerial. "We got static and no reason for bad reception."

Kennedy said, "Even if they called a curfew on account of the shootings, they wouldn't shut down the radio stations. Check out the police and army bands."

The static roared again, wearing at Lightholler's frayed nerves.

"I'm getting nothing, Major," Shine said.

Kennedy and Hardas exchanged a look.

"Maybe someone's jamming the transmissions," Lightholler offered.

They both looked at him.

"What do you know about this, Captain?" Hardas growled.

"I know you're shitting yourself," Lightholler said. "You'll get used to it."

"You don't have a fucking clue," Hardas told him. "You brought those fuckers halfway around the world and you don't even know it."

Lost, Lightholler fell silent.

"What do you want me to do, Major?" Shine asked.

"I'm thinking," Kennedy replied.

"We have to avoid the shore," Hardas said. "Head to the East Side, stay well away from the Summer Palace and the barracks at Gramercy Park."

"What's going on, Major?" Morgan asked worriedly.

Kennedy didn't answer him. He said, "Take Second Avenue. Any signs of police or military and we turn right around. We'll cross back to Lexington once we've passed the Hirohito Bridge."

"How about the Holland Tunnel to Jersey? We can double back later." A tone of exasperation crept into Shine's voice. He had been about to turn on to Ninth, now he had to cut across town.

"Please," Lightholler said, "no tunnels."

Hardas glanced at him.

"And for God's sake, point that gun elsewhere unless you plan on using it right now."

Hardas let the gun slip into the folds of his creased overcoat. "No tunnels, Martin." He glanced across at Kennedy with a twisted smile. "Anyway, who the hell would want to go to Jersey?"

Shine swung the sedan onto 13th Street. The last of the sun's rays were setting behind them, but the horizon ahead glowed faintly. They drove through a confluence of shadows, the husks of tenements lining the narrow road to either side.

V

Lightholler had given up trying to process the day's events.

When he'd first encountered Kennedy at the Waldorf, the man had exuded an aura of quiet confidence and control. What had happened between then and the Lone Star?

And when Hardas had drawn his pistol in the back room of the café, it seemed more like an afterthought than any planned action. If they had wanted to abduct him, they'd had ample opportunity at their first meeting. More to the point, his participation in Kennedy's scheme seemed to have been planned for at least a year. That was when he'd been informed that he would captain the new *Titanic*.

So no matter how bizarre their goal was, they hadn't intended to recruit him by violent means. Something must have forced their hand.

There was no point trying anything now, he decided. They were improvising—he was certain of it—and that meant they would eventually slip up. Perhaps in the park, perhaps later. Then he would steal away and contact London. Contact Admiral Lloyd and find out what the hell was going on.

Their sedan encountered little traffic as it barrelled up Second Avenue. They crossed over to Lexington at 57th. A jeep was pulled up on the kerb. Through the fogged window Lightholler made out four soldiers. Two of them were Imperial Watch; the one still seated in the vehicle was shouting, his hands striking the steering wheel repeatedly. The other two men were Union reserves. They stood before the jeep's hood while thick streaks of smoke curled up from the engine block. All four turned to face the passing sedan, their expressions lost between misted windowpane and the escaping fumes.

They entered Central Park via 79th Street. The trees sparkled with fairy lights, their illumination spilling into the dark places beyond the reach of streetlamps. It gave the place an ethereal quality so that Lightholler felt as if by entering the park they were leaving more than the city.

Kennedy leaned forwards to tap Shine on the shoulder.

Shine put the car in neutral and they coasted to a gentle stop near a clump of low bushes. Lightholler asked Hardas for a cigarette as they spilled out of the back seat. Hardas eased the gun into his shoulder holster and handed his packet over.

"When was the last time you were here, Captain?" Kennedy asked.

"At least ten years ago," he replied, lighting up.

"I think you're in for a little surprise."

"More surprises? Be still my heart."

Shine opened the trunk and they removed their belongings.

"Why are we leaving the car here?" Morgan asked, frowning.

"We're going in by the back door. I'd rather we see anyone before they see us," Kennedy said, hefting a bag over one shoulder.

He led them away from the paved road towards a shallow hill. Lightholler could see a bright glow through the trees ahead. Two spotlights were aimed skywards; their beams swung scouring the night, trying to pierce the heavy clouds the evening winds had gathered. As they crested the rise, Lightholler saw her and stopped dead in his tracks.

"She's the *Shenandoah*." Kennedy halted at his side. "What do you think?"

The massive airship lay nestled in a long wooden cradle in the small valley before them. It hadn't been visible from the transverse.

"When did they build the terminus?" Lightholler asked.

"Last year," Morgan replied.

They walked down the grassy knoll, the cigar-shaped dirigible growing before their eyes.

"How big is she?" Lightholler asked.

"Seven-hundred-and-ninety feet long," Kennedy said. "That's just a little shy of the *Titanic*. It's difficult to make out from here, but she carries two gondolas beneath her."

Lightholler thought he could see the living compartments suspended below the airship's massive frame. "I see them, fore and aft," he said finally.

"But what's that between them?"

"She carries a hangar between and below the living quarters," Kennedy said. "It's a special feature of the Cavalier-class dirigibles. She's capable of accommodating up to five aircraft, with cargo. They can be released or taken aboard while in flight."

"But why?" Lightholler asked, astonished.

"I think they use them for supplying the stratolites," Morgan said.

"Impressive," Lightholler murmured. He could now see the details of the terminus that lay spread below the airship. It was surrounded by a high wire fence that enclosed the entire perimeter. The vehicles that raced around the building were playthings next to the *Shenandoah*'s conspicuous bulk.

Lightholler's suitcase was becoming heavy in his arms. They were now about two hundred feet from the wire fence. He said, "There's a lot of traffic down there."

At least seven vehicles were arrayed beside the aft gondola. The soft thrum of the *Shenandoah*'s engines was apparent now, it seemed to come from everywhere. He thought he could feel the vibration in the soles of his tired feet. He heard distant thunder punctuated by the occasional sound of a brittle crack.

"What's that smell?" Morgan asked.

Lightholler sniffed at the air. He watched as a vehicle broke away from the small motorcade and tore through the gates towards them. A small beam wavered in their direction as they stood in the penumbra of the terminal's floodlights. "So much for the back door," he muttered.

Hardas growled, "Get back." He dropped his bag, slipped a hand beneath his jacket flap and planted his feet.

Kennedy assumed a similar stance.

Lightholler glanced at both men, then back at the oncoming vehicle, obscured in the glare from the terminal beyond.

"Oh, shit," Morgan said.

Shine, down on one knee, was reaching into one of the suitcases.

The vehicle skidded to a halt, showering them with tufts of grass and soil. It was black with irregular grey shading on all of its steel-plated surface. Its turret swung lazily towards them, the muzzle of its cannon coming to bear on them. A black iron cross emblazoned the vehicle's side.

A goggled face emerged from the top of the half-track. "*Hände hoch!*"

All five men dropped what they were carrying. A machine-gun clattered at Shine's feet. Morgan looked at his companions, in shock. The others raised their hands slowly.

"Morgan, for God's sake put your hands in the air," Lightholler said under his breath.

"*Sind Sie Amerikaner*?" The soldier removed his goggles in a swift motion and clambered from the vehicle, dropping to the up-turned soil with a heavy thud.

Kennedy took a slight step forwards, peering at the insignia on the man's uniform. He said, "*Jawohl, Herr Leutnant. Wir sind Amerikaner. Aus dem Suden.*"

What the hell was German armour doing in Central Park?

"*Konföderierte?*" the German officer asked. "Confederates?"

"*Jawohl, Herr Leutnant, wir sind Konföderierte.*"

More soldiers were approaching from the terminal at a fast trot. The scene fell into focus. Distant thunder became the continuous low rumble of explosions, those brittle cracks, gunfire that had all but faded away.

The German stepped up to Kennedy. "*Haben Sie papieren?*"

"*Jawohl, Herr Leutnant,*" Kennedy replied.

"Would someone mind telling me what the hell is going on?" Morgan whispered. Beads of sweat streamed down his face.

"Shut up," Hardas whispered back. "It'll be alright." He didn't sound convinced.

Black-garbed soldiers formed a semicircle around them. They held their weapons at waist level, machine-guns and rifles trained on the smaller group.

"*Herr Leutnant,*" Kennedy said. "*Götterdämmerung.*"

The officer narrowed his eyes.

Kennedy repeated the word: *Götterdämmerung*, Wagner's *Twilight of the Gods*.

Shaking his head slowly, the officer began to laugh. A slow, harsh, guttural sound. He turned then and spoke rapidly to the other soldiers before returning his gaze. "You are Joseph Kennedy, of course."

"*Jawohl, Herr Leutnant,*" Kennedy replied. "*Sprechen Sie Englisch?*"

The officer nodded.

"May we put our arms down?" Kennedy asked.

"Certainly, *Herr Major.*"

The German officer saluted Kennedy and then extended a gloved hand. "Tobias Freilich, Third Brandenburg Regiment."

Kennedy shook his hand.

"You were anticipated, *Herr Major*, however not so soon and not here."

"What's happening?" Morgan said.

"Many things," the German replied brusquely. He turned to include the others in his gaze. Ignoring Shine, he gave small nods of acknowledgment to Hardas and Morgan in turn. On reaching Lightholler he gave a slight bow. "Captain Lightholler. Thank you for ensuring our safe, if uncomfortable, passage."

"I beg your pardon?" Lightholler responded.

"Granted," the German replied.

"I don't understand." Lightholler became aware that his heart was beating, as the adrenaline rush subsided. His shirt clung to his arms and chest, damp beneath his creased suit jacket. He gave the officer a furtive once-over. He noted the windproof jacket, the respirator pouch, the crest at his collar: a wolf's head surmounting a jagged bolt of lightning.

You brought those fuckers halfway around the world and you didn't even know it.

"We have been advised to offer you and your men transportation, *Herr Major*," Freilich continued. "Retrieve your weapons, please. You must leave now though, if that is your wish."

"Now is fine," Morgan said. "Fine with me."

A soldier approached Freilich and spoke in his ear. Freilich turned to Kennedy. "The *Japaner* will be returning in force," he said. "There is not much time."

Hardas and Shine grabbed their bags. Morgan was stumbling around, bewildered. Hardas picked up the guns, glinting shards of starlight in the tall grass.

Kennedy faced Morgan and Lightholler. "Now. Come on. We have to go."

"You want to be here when the japs get back?" Hardas added as he pushed past Morgan.

Morgan swore to himself and picked up a suitcase.

Lightholler stumbled after the others. Freilich led them down to the captured terminus. The other soldiers fell in on either side.

Morgan's eyes were focused on the path before him. He said, "You have a lot of explaining to do, Major."

"You were expecting this?" Lightholler asked.

"Not entirely," Kennedy replied.

"But you knew the Germans were here."

"I knew they were in New York."

"You knew they were on my bloody ship," Lightholler snarled.

Kennedy increased his pace to match the officer. Lightholler sped up to join them. He wasn't finished with Kennedy yet. When they reached the wire perimeter fence, Freilich halted them, briefly, to let the armoured vehicle through the gates.

"You said you expected us, *Herr Leutnant*?" Kennedy asked, taking advantage of the moment.

"I was briefed that a party of covert operatives, under your command, was present in New York. We were ordered to offer you aid; transportation if possible." His smile was strained. "It just so happens that we have some transportation available." He gestured grandly at the *Shenandoah*, then ushered them along the vehicle's trail.

"Why now?" Kennedy asked. "Why tonight?"

Freilich stopped in his tracks. He snorted and shook his head. "Four hours ago an atomic device was detonated over Berlin."

"What?" Lightholler said. "How?" The questions were a shout in his mind; he wasn't aware that he'd spoken aloud. His ears were filled with voices.

"The *Divine Wind*," Morgan murmured. "The Japanese Imperial airship."

"That is our belief." Freilich arched an eyebrow appreciatively. "The High Command identified the airship's last known position as the epicentre of the blast. Of course, the *Japaner* deny all knowledge. Who would admit to such an act?" His voice was ground glass.

"Our first strike was directed against the barracks at Battery Park. We caught them in mid-celebration. They had been given the order to invoke martial law. In fact, they had been given a number of orders." His face twisted bitterly. "Now we give them a taste of martial law."

To one side, Lightholler saw fifteen, perhaps twenty men, Japanese soldiers, lined up near the wire fence. Five Germans stood before them, machine-guns raised. A cache of weapons lay in a small pile about twenty feet away. In the shadows near the terminal's entrance he could see three or four bodies splayed on the ground, their limbs at awkward angles.

"The Emperor's son was aboard that ship," Lightholler said. "He was to be the next Western Shogun."

"It would be considered a worthy sacrifice," Kennedy replied. "The Emperor has other sons."

They had reached the entrance to the forwards gondola.

"I still want to know what half the German army is doing in the middle of Central Park." Morgan glared at Kennedy and Hardas.

"Starting what we have to finish," Kennedy replied. "Any more questions?"

Morgan looked away.

Lightholler let his bag drop to his feet. A wave of exhaustion swept over him.

The airship's engines rose to a shrill whine. He was buffeted by occasional blasts of warm air as the turbines were rotated on their axles in preparation for departure.

Freilich addressed them all, his lips compressed in a disconcerting smile.

"The 1st Regiment has secured all of the bridges and tunnels leading out of Manhattan. Elements of the 2nd are now engaging units of the Shogun's Guard at the Summer Palace. The harbour is alight. We control all access in and out of the island. Reinforcements are on their way."

There was the explosive crump of mortar fire. It roared across the valley.

"God speed, *Herr Major*." Freilich turned away from the gondola.

Kennedy led the way up the ramp, Shine and Morgan in tow. Hardas brought up the rear. Lightholler, his foot on the gangway, was struck by a thought. He turned to Morgan.

"You called the Japanese airship the *Divine Wind*."

"That's the English translation of her name. Back in the 1200s, the Mongol hordes dominated Asia. They dominated the known world. They sent an armada to invade Japan but it never arrived. A typhoon laid the entire fleet to waste. The Japanese believed it was a gift from their gods, sent to destroy their enemies. They named it the Divine Wind. The *Kamikaze*."

VI

April 22, 2012

CSS Shenandoah, out of New York

Kennedy and Shine sat at one of the tables in the cabin's lounge by the gondola's bow. Morgan had disappeared below, ostensibly to check out their berths. Three other men sat in the open area of the gondola. Lightholler made them for Confederate airmen, possibly commercial crew, off-duty and slumming it back south.

It was half an hour since the airship had cleared Central Park, since Lightholler had learned about Berlin and what had been unleashed from the cargo holds of his ship. He stood, numbly, waiting for Morgan by the winding stairwell. A few carefully worded questions might clarify any number of things. Hardas, arms folded, the ubiquitous cigarette dangling from his lips, watched him through narrowed eyes from across the cabin.

The only passengers permitted aboard the *Shenandoah* were those with proof of Confederate or German nationality, and only a handful of those had chosen to embark. They sought berths in the aft gondola, beyond the hangar.

The stigma of their association with the Brandenburg Division suggested that there was more to Kennedy and his companions than met the eye. They were left to themselves. The Brandenburgs had cut their teeth defeating the first British tank formations in 1917. They'd accompanied Kaiser Wilhelm's victory march into Paris at the end of that year. During the European War they'd swept behind Soviet lines to crush Stalin's dream of communist expansion.

Over the last fifty years they had been brutally employed in the colonial wars of German North Afrika and the Middle East. It was even rumoured that a division had been sent to Vietnam, thus prolonging

Japan's disastrous campaign in that region. They were the most feared military corps on the planet and Lightholler had brought them to New York. In doing so, he may have ensured the city's destruction.

Berlin, in her death throes, had unleashed her wrath upon the Japanese Empire. New York was only a stone's throw away from German-aligned Canada. An assault force could arrive in the beleaguered city before dawn. Moreover, if Kennedy's sources were correct, there were at least eighteen divisions of German infantry massed beyond the new Mason-Dixon line; there was a German fleet assembled offshore. The Japanese forces, stationed on the West Coast and along the southern border, would have a hard time deploying on all fronts.

There were three regiments of elite German troops deposited in the heart of the Japanese Occupation. If there was anything Lightholler had learned from his time at Sandhurst it was that the primary purpose of inserting troops behind enemy lines was to give your ground forces incentive to get in there and relieve them. That alone was reason enough for Lightholler to go along with Kennedy. Whatever was happening in New York was merely a hint of what was to come. The tip of the iceberg.

Morgan was taking his time downstairs. Kennedy stood, and walked over to one of the gondola's wide curtained windows. Lightholler joined him.

"Enjoying the show?" he asked.

Kennedy shrugged. Behind him, through the thick plated glass, New York was a battlefield.

Lightholler placed a palm against the glass. He thought about Berlin. Below, the remains of the Sinatra Island aerial tramway were already in flames. Only a skeleton, shrouded in thick smoke, remained of the Summer Palace spires that had once gleamed over the city. He paced along the gondola wall from window to window, edging past scattered tables and chairs. Mushrooms of smoke hung over the bridges leading into Manhattan. The barracks at Battery Park were aflame.

"Over here," Hardas called out. "This what you're looking for?"

Lightholler crossed the lounge.

"That ship might just be bad luck after all," Hardas said.

"Why don't you shut your mouth," Lightholler growled.

"See for yourself." Hardas drew a cigarette from his pocket and went over to join the three strangers by the cabin's rear entrance.

Lightholler peered into the darkness below. The *Titanic* lay crooked at her mooring, plumes of smoke rising from her scarred deck. Further out to sea, he made out the silhouette of two Japanese battlecruisers. He watched the silent puffs of smoke bloom from the decks of the two ships. Tracer trails illuminated the paths of their shells as they shattered in scarlet licks on the ocean liner's deck.

Lightholler grabbed the satin sash of the window's curtain in a balled-up fist. He felt a hand on his shoulder.

"There she goes," Kennedy said.

The *Titanic* seemed to leap out of the water. Her centre, rent from topdeck to waterline, rose up, dragging her sagging bow and stern in an eruption of boiling water.

"There must have still been some ammunition stowed aboard her." Lightholler leaned his forehead on the glass.

Thick billows of black cloud obscured their view as the *Shenandoah* continued her ascent.

Lightholler allowed Kennedy to lead him back to their table. Morgan, returned from below, pulled up a chair next to Shine. Hardas had struck up a conversation with the strangers and was seated at their table. Every now and then a burst of laughter emerged from their group, ringing blasphemous in Lightholler's ears.

Morgan offered him a cold glass of water.

"I could do with something stronger," Lightholler murmured.

Morgan withdrew a flask from his coat pocket. If he was aware of Kennedy's stern expression, he chose to ignore it. "Bourbon," he said, gathering empty glasses and pouring out a measure for each of them.

Kennedy slid into a chair. "Captain," he began hesitantly.

Lightholler ignored him. He turned to Morgan and said, "My ship's gone. My command's gone. I've been implicated in the filthiest piece of subterfuge since the Greeks left their horse outside the gates of Troy. And I've nowhere left to turn. So tell me, is that the way Major Kennedy recruits his staff?" He eyed Morgan squarely. "What did he do to *your* life? How long were you researching the *Titanic* before you found out that it was all grist for the mill, something to fuel this fantasy field trip?"

"I'd finished my study on the *Titanic* years before anyone approached me," Morgan replied. "I was on the lecture circuit, rehashing the same material I'd been presenting for as long as I could remember. I was offered a chance to experience that material—that world—first-hand. Unlike you, I jumped at the opportunity, Captain."

"Well, you're a fugitive from your own government now," Lightholler said. "Is that what you had in mind?"

"It's not as simple as you make it out to be." Morgan's voice faltered.

"Preying on people with nothing left to lose doesn't seem very complicated to me," Lightholler said. He cast Shine a glance.

Shine said, "Captain, please don't even *think* about trying that shit on me."

Lightholler, taken aback by the negro's response, fell silent.

"I have a profile on you, Captain," Kennedy said. "I worked for the Bureau as an assistant director. That means I have a profile on everyone. What you have, what you wanted, what you never got … it's all there. If I was looking to recruit people who thought they'd have nothing to lose, I'd have amassed the largest army in human history. That's no way to change the world. That's how you destroy it."

"And you plan on saving the world?"

"I plan on stopping the psychopath who condemned it to its current fate."

"That's right, I almost forgot," Lightholler said. "You have a time machine. Tell me, Major, how does it all end? With a bang, or a whimper?"

"A whimper."

Kennedy's look held such despair that Lightholler could almost believe him.

He downed his drink.

VII

"I wouldn't get too comfortable, gentlemen."

It was Hardas. He'd returned with one of the strangers in tow. As he approached, he nodded his head in the direction of the starboard-side windows. "We've got company."

"Fuck." Instantly Morgan was out of his seat and backing towards the other side of the gondola.

"That was pretty fast." Kennedy approached the window for a closer look.

The others crowded around him.

Lightholler could make out at least three seaplanes. Mitsubishi Fukuryus, Crouching Dragons. The Japanese had first employed them in the aftermath of Pearl Harbor. Squadrons of them would squat in the islets that dotted the archipelagos of the Pacific, awaiting convoys. Their ungainly fuselage and poor manoeuvrability made them easy prey for the Union fighters, earning them the nickname "Fuck Yous". Lightholler had never seen one in flight.

"I make four of 'em," Hardas said.

"I thought the japs put those crates out to pasture a long time ago," his companion drawled.

Lightholler gave the stranger a quick once-over. He was a mess. Unshaven, unkempt. A shock of brown hair. Faded dust jacket, torn jeans. Your average red-neck poster boy. He returned his gaze to the night skies. "Same here," he said. "I didn't think they were using prop planes any more."

"Must've been all they could muster at short notice," Kennedy said.

The aircraft skimmed below the dirigible, ducking out of sight.

"Where are they going?" Morgan asked over their shoulders.

On cue, two of them reappeared. There was a brilliant flash from one of the plane's gun turrets. Morgan gripped Kennedy's shoulder tightly.

Kennedy shrugged him off. "It's just a warning, Darren. They want us to turn back."

"But this is a civilian vessel," Morgan began to protest.

"A *Confederate* civilian vessel, and one that just took off from a captured aerodrome," Hardas responded.

"Jesus," Morgan said. "We have to turn around."

"We're miles out." Kennedy turned to face him. "You want to go back?"

Morgan glared at him, shifted his glance to the stranger and then back. "There are still people we can deal with in New York."

"Not after tonight," Kennedy said firmly. "But we have another option."

The *Shenandoah* was slowing down. The bright lights of Manhattan Island swung back into view, glowing through a cerement of blackened smudge.

"Give me a minute," he said, starting towards the front of the gondola.

"Where are you going?" Lightholler asked.

"I'm hoping the *Shenandoah*'s captain was planning on doing a supply run *en route*." Kennedy disappeared through a door in the front of the cabin.

"I don't get it," Morgan said.

"If the *Shenandoah*'s making a supply run, there ought to be some transport planes in the hangar."

"You're shitting me."

No one answered. They turned back to the window and continued to observe the spectral sight of New York's flames in uneasy silence.

Kennedy returned shortly. "I've requisitioned the *Shenandoah*'s scout planes. The captain says he can spare us one of his crew to act as a pilot. You've flown a scout, haven't you, David?"

Hardas curled up the corner of his mouth. "It's been a while."

"How many hours have you logged?"

"Enough."

Morgan, ashen, spoke up. "Please tell me you're kidding, Major."

The five of them were now assembled near the cockpit's entrance. Hardas's new acquaintance had rejoined his companions and they were standing near the cabin's rear hatchway in earnest conversation.

On both sides of the gondola, their escort was apparent. Three seaplanes to either side, flying in loose formation.

"I want you two to go with the pilot," Kennedy said, addressing Shine and Morgan. "Captain Lightholler and I will go with you, David."

"Wait a minute here," Morgan said. "This is crazy. You want us to take our chances in a couple of scouts against six Jap fighters?"

"I'm willing to cut you loose, Darren." Kennedy's voice was soft and coaxing all of a sudden.

Morgan eyed Shine warily.

"Nothing more than that," Kennedy added briskly. "But this is the only way we're going to get out of New York, and you know what happens next, don't you?"

The edge of Morgan's lips pulled back, baring the tips of even white teeth; his anger was palpable, yet directionless. A moment passed and his shoulders sagged.

And you know what happens next. What did Kennedy have on Morgan, on all of them, Lightholler wondered?

"There are four scout planes in the hangar and five of us. Six including the *Shenandoah*'s pilot," Kennedy continued.

"Eight," a voice said. It was the man who had been talking to Hardas. Lightholler hadn't noticed his return. "There are eight of us. My pals and I don't care to return to New York just to spend the rest of this war in some internment camp."

"Then there may be a problem," Kennedy said. "We're CBI."

Hardas loomed ominously at Kennedy's side. Shine, clearly the major's real threat, hadn't moved a muscle.

"Doesn't mean much to me, apart from the fact that you guys are pretty tight with our Kraut buddies back there. But you've got no problem here." The man nodded to his friends who'd slouched out of their seats to join him. "No problem at all, Mr Kennedy."

A smile formed on Kennedy's face.

"We're pilots," one of the others added. He was short and stocky, more muscle than fat, with strands of wavy blond hair plastered over his balding head. "With the 32nd Squadron. We just got our papers. We're supposed to join up with the 15th at Baton Rouge." He stuck out a burly hand, which Kennedy accepted immediately. "I'm Tucker, this here is Rose." He indicated the man who had remained silent. "You've met Newcombe."

"What are you suggesting?" Kennedy asked.

Lightholler observed the exchange. This was the same Kennedy he had encountered in his hotel. He was back in his element. Skin-of-his-teeth, seat-of-his-pants; but with a plan of sorts, Lightholler suspected.

"My boys and I will fly your men," Newcombe said. "Name your destination and we can settle the price."

"We don't need your help," Hardas sneered. "I can fly."

"Hell, Commander, suit yourself. There are four planes, we just need one. Sure you can fly, but can you take off from an airship at night *and* evade our friends out there?"

"Money isn't going to be an issue. If we're going to do this, we'd better get moving," Kennedy said. "Four planes, eight men."

"There's just one more thing," Newcombe continued. "When I said eight, I was counting the *Shenandoah*'s pilot. That's four planes; four pilots with passengers. The nigger stays."

Hardas muttered something under his breath. Morgan took a step backwards.

"Listen, mister, I didn't vote for you then, and I sure as hell ain't risking my ass for some jungle-bunny butler now."

"Impressive," Shine said. "You know how to vote."

Newcombe's jaw dropped. Sudden silence gripped the gondola, so deep that Lightholler had to wonder if Shine had spoken at all.

Morgan chuckled softly.

"He's CBI?" Newcombe asked Kennedy incredulously.

Kennedy looked to Shine. Lightholler, astonished, realised he was seeking permission to answer on the man's behalf. Kennedy said, "You don't want to know what he is."

"I'll take him, Major." Rose spoke up, an easy smile spreading across his gaunt face. "The airship's crew can't spare a pilot if they're going to drop the hangar for us."

He turned to face Newcombe. "I wasn't old enough to vote, but I reckon a man's politics is his own business. The 4th Mech-Cavalry saved our hides is all I know, and a bunch of those guys were blacker than a coal miner's ass. If we're doing this for cash, you ain't giving the orders."

Newcombe scowled but did not reply.

Rose slapped him on the back. "Hell, Newcombe, just think about the money."

VIII

There were seven men inside the *Shenandoah*'s hangar, a long, high-roofed compartment they'd gained via a slender enclosed gangway. Kennedy was elsewhere with the dirigible's captain, making final arrangements.

For the moment, the airship hovered within a bank of thick cloud just over the southeastern portion of Manhattan. The Japanese aircraft circled nearby.

Newcombe and Tucker paced from plane to plane, four of which were arrayed along a depressed aisle that ran down the middle of the deck. They were biplanes. Red and blue roundels, surmounted with white steer's heads, marked the wing surfaces and tailplanes. The short, stubby fuselages were counterpointed by the broad wings that extended out towards either side of the hangar.

"What are these?" Morgan was on his knees, pointing at the undercarriage of one of the biplanes. Thick cables extended from beneath the aircraft to the deck, ending in sharp twin-bladed hooks that strained against bolts in the hangar's floor.

"Arrester hooks," Hardas replied, "for landing on flight decks. Usually carriers." He turned to the Confederate pilots. "What do you think? They pass inspection?"

Rose slapped a hand against the side of the foremost biplane. "High aspect ratio, extensive de-icers on the wing surfaces. Twin turbocharged, gyratory, Santos-Dumont aerodiesels. I'm familiar with the military's version, but this here's your standard supply-delivery aircraft."

"We've all flown 'em," Newcombe called out. He was inspecting the cargo hold on one of the other planes. "This one's fully loaded."

"Same here." Tucker struck the cargo door on the last of the planes. "They must have been planning on rendezvousing with a stratolite somewhere between here and New Orleans."

"What makes you say that?" Lightholler asked. He was standing with Morgan, watching as the pilots made their quick inspection.

Tucker reached a hand into the cargo hold of his plane and withdrew a roll of toilet paper. "This stuff is gold up there," he said with a laugh.

"Aren't they going to be too heavy, carrying three men apiece and all those supplies?" Morgan asked.

"Won't be a problem," Rose chipped in. "These crates might be relatively slow, but they have to climb to at least fifty-thou to reach the stratolites, and they can stop on a dime. That'll count for something."

But will they be able to get away from our escort, Lightholler wondered. And where the hell was Kennedy? They'd stopped the *Shenandoah* nearly ten minutes ago. Surely the japs would be getting impatient by now.

It was about as uncomfortable as Lightholler had ever felt. The soft sway of the deck beneath his feet was eerily reminiscent of the sea. He kept trying to forget that only a thin strip of metal separated him from a drop of thousands of feet to the ocean below.

Hardas approached one of the planes. "Any weapons?"

"Nothing I can find," Rose replied. "Here's where the rocket-launchers would be." He'd clambered up the side of one of the planes to check out its cockpit. "Used to have a gun mount back here for the co-pilot. It's sealed up now, but I've got me a couple of ideas in case things get hairy out there." He gave Tucker and Newcombe a wink. "Tell me what you think of this," he said, leading them to the front of the hangar.

A few moments later, all three of them climbed into the cargo holds of the planes. There was the sound of things being torn, crates rattling, and raucous laughter from within.

"What gives?" Morgan asked Hardas. "Are they nuts?"

"Damned if I know," Hardas said. "Who can figure out what runs through a flyboy's head?"

Lightholler's face broke into a wry smile. "Anyone who prefers being cooped up in one of these things, when they could be on the solid deck of a ship, has a few screws loose to start with."

Morgan rolled his eyes. "I don't call anything solid unless it's got trees growing out of it."

Kennedy emerged through a hatch near the top of the hangar. "The captain's given us five minutes to get moving. He's stalling the japs right now."

Lightholler caught his eye.

"He's told them he's having engine trouble. He's pouring junk out of the starboard engine nacelle to sell it. When he cuts the running lights, then we roll." Kennedy scrambled down a narrow metal stair that dropped onto the hangar's floor. One of the dirigible's crewmen followed him down.

"What about the Fuck Yous?" Hardas asked.

"Only two of them still out there," Kennedy said. "The others turned back five minutes ago."

"Those odds sound a little better," Newcombe said.

"They're as good as we're going to get," Kennedy replied.

As the *Shenandoah*'s crew entered the hangar and began making preparations for launch, Kennedy and the three Confederate pilots outlined a strategy. They would use three of the biplanes. Kennedy and Lightholler would go in the first scout, with Tucker as their pilot. Morgan and Hardas would take the second with Newcombe. Rose and Shine would bring up the rear. The *Shenandoah*'s captain would give the signal once he had both the remaining Mitsubishis on his starboard side inspecting the "damaged" engine. The entire operation would take place while they were suspended in cloud cover.

The plan called for a rapid launch sequence. No more than forty-five seconds between each scout's departure. Then, close-formation flying, keeping the dirigible's massive frame between them and the Japanese escorts, in an attempt to obstruct any radar. At five minutes out, the *Shenandoah* would release its starboard engine housing. That had been the captain's idea. After that, they would be able to limp back to New York while still rendering the airship unusable by the Japanese for any length of time.

Dumping the engine would be the signal for all three scouts to descend to just above sea level. Any pursuit would assume that the scouts, by virtue of their specifications, were flying high. Keeping radio silence, and maintaining an altitude below radar detection, they'd make for Richmond, Virginia. Kennedy knew of a landing field where they could refuel without undue attention.

It sounded simple enough.

IX

The low rumble of engines echoed through the hangar.

Lightholler was secured in the navigator's seat, with Kennedy pressed tightly against him in the narrow confines of Scout One's cockpit. He struggled to peer over Tucker's hunched shoulders. Crouched in the pilot's seat, Tucker sealed the ungainly bubble of the cockpit's canopy overhead. Through it, Lightholler could see the figure of the *Shenandoah*'s crewman standing by the bay doors.

The air was thick with fumes.

Lightholler did a quick inventory. Radio transceiver. Intercom headphones. Ground proximity warning system. Compass. Altimeter. Tachometer. The canopy provided an almost three-sixty-degree view.

He picked up his pair of phones and placed a hand over the mike.

"You trust him?" he asked under his breath.

"He wants off this airship as much as we do," Kennedy replied. "Besides, I don't think we have much choice."

"I wonder how far we'll get in these rust-buckets?" Lightholler watched as the crewman secured himself to a fixture by the hangar door.

"Rose seems to think as far south as Charlotte. I reckon we'll be lucky enough to make Charlottesville. From there, we make our own way across the border. I know a few bootleg routes."

"I'm sure you do." Lightholler had to smile. "But I thought we were making for New Orleans."

"We were." Kennedy's face creased thoughtfully. "But that could change. We might have more options once we cross the border. It all depends."

"On what?"

"On where we're welcome. That might not be in too many places, North *or* South. But I know a spot where we can hole up till we're ready to head for Nevada."

"Nevada," Lightholler probed. "So that's our final destination?"

Kennedy smiled. "No, Nevada's how we *get* to our final destination."

"I'm sorry I asked."

Three bursts of static rattled the intercom.

"Lights are out. That's the signal," Tucker growled over his shoulder.

Lightholler felt a sudden lurch. The biplane listed on the grooved runway as its retractable arrester hook slid from the hangar deck to snap against the scout's undercarriage. He could feel the hangar's descent in the pit of his stomach.

"Hold on," Kennedy said.

The crewman disappeared from view. The bay doors slid apart fore and aft. Exhaust fumes swirled out, cotton-candy cloud swirled in. Thin beams of light, emanating from somewhere beneath the *Shenandoah,* converged on the grey-white flurry ahead.

The biplane edged forwards as the runway deployed on an ever steeper decline.

"We're clear." Tucker reached for the throttle. The whine of the plane's engines rose to an ear-splitting roar.

"Tally-ho," Lightholler said through gritted teeth. He was thrust back into his seat as the plane surged into the vast emptiness below.

X

Seated in Scout Two, Morgan watched as Tucker's biplane cleared the runway ahead of them.

"Just lean back and shut your eyes." Hardas reached across to tighten Morgan's restraint.

"I'm fine," Morgan murmured.

Their tether snapped loose and the plane began to taxi forwards. Morgan squinted through half-closed eyes, his earphones too tight, his head throbbing. There was the impression of the biplane's wheels bouncing on the deck and then a horrible disconcerting drop. He clutched his armrest in a white-knuckled embrace as he felt the plane plummet.

He could see Tucker's plane below them, skimming in and out of the clouds. The solar cells on its upper wing glinted in the moonlight as it completed its turn to port. He sensed their own wings gripping thin dark air.

Hardas was also looking at Tucker's plane, shaking his head. "He's turning too wide. Cargo must be heavier than he thought."

"I see it," Newcombe said. "Going to try and compensate."

An abrupt twist and the view shifted, the night sky whirling in a kaleidoscope of bright stars. Tucker's plane was five hundred feet ahead and to their right.

"Passive night vision enabled." Newcombe flicked a couple of switches on the instrument panel. "Infrared. Optronics. RWR. *Shit.*"

"RWR?" Morgan stumbled over the letters.

Hardas, eyes straight ahead, spoke out of the corner of his mouth. "Radar warning receiver. They've seen us."

Newcombe scanned the radar and threw a sidelong glance at his port reflector. "I've got a visual." He toggled his radio transceiver. "Bandits, two o'clock. Tucker, Rose, you copy? Over."

The only response was a harsh crackle.

"Hold on, boys, we've got trouble."

The world spun counter-clockwise. Morgan caught a glimpse of one of the Fuck Yous. Then stars, sea, stars. The *Shenandoah* emerged from a cover of cloud, her running lights still down, a vast black shadow against the moonlight. Roiling billows of smoke poured from her starboard engines, obscuring any view of the hangar. Tucker's plane was nowhere in sight.

"Where's Scout Three?" Morgan asked.

Hardas checked the display. "I can't see them. They'd have cleared the *Shenandoah* by now. They must be behind her."

Morgan twisted in his seat, trying to orient himself, his head spinning.

Newcombe growled, "Keep still, you dumb fuck."

Morgan kept still, tasting bile.

The Mitsubishis peeled away from the *Shenandoah*, making a beeline for Scout One.

"Tucker," Newcombe said into the transceiver, "they're coming in right behind you."

Tucker's reply was hoarse. "I know it."

"Coming in *right* behind you."

Morgan could see Tucker's scout well ahead of them. Both of the Mitsubishis were on its tail, weaving across each other's path.

Newcombe made a noise in his throat. "They're toying with him." He scoped the radar. "Where the fuck is Rose?"

"What are they waiting for?" Hardas said.

Tucker's plane began to bank. A sharp, angled turn, trailing twin streams of vapour. The Fuck Yous made to follow, pursuing a wider curve. Still weaving, as if deciding who would take the kill.

"What's he think he's doing?" Newcome hissed. He swung their scout into a spin, bringing them up behind the Mitsubishis. He pushed forwards on the throttle.

Morgan, hand over his mouth, willed a thought to Newcombe. *The fuck you think you're doing?*

Beyond the Mitsubishis and well ahead of Tucker's scout, the darkened outline of the *Shenandoah* swung back into view, backlit by a thousand stars.

"Turn around, damn it," Newcombe hollered into his transceiver. "*Turn.*"

Morgan watched as Tucker's biplane jagged left, then right, sweeping back towards the *Shenandoah*'s hangar. The first Mitsubishi opened fire. Orange-yellow tracer raked the scout's wingtips, a torrent of flame spewed from its port engine. Tucker's biplane skewed crazily.

"Shit." Newcombe spat out the word.

The cabin filled with light. The *Shenandoah* loomed before them, all her lights suddenly ablaze. Newcombe jerked the control column forwards.

A dark shadow whipped overhead in a screaming rush.

"What the hell?" Newcombe threw his body to starboard, leaning hard on the stick.

The bright flash of an explosion seared Morgan's vision. The scout was buffeted by a wave of turbulence, tossing him against his restraint. Before them, outlined in red flame, the fuselage of a plane spiralled downwards in a shower of fragments.

"Newcombe, you okay?" A voice crackled over the radio transceiver.

"Tucker, you *bastard*. I thought you'd bought the farm. What the hell happened?"

"*I* happened, you dumb fucks."

Morgan looked up to see Rose's scout burst through a cloud of smoke and debris. Its arrester cable swung wildly below it, shredded rope where the hook should have been.

Hardas said, "I don't fucking believe it."

Morgan gave him a confused look.

"Rose was in the hangar the whole damn time," Hardas explained. "When the *Shenandoah* hit her lights, he could come out as slow as he liked. The japs couldn't see him for glare."

"Come out with what? He had no weapons."

"He had an arrester hook."

Morgan pictured the hook's blade slicing through the enemy pilot's cockpit. He wanted to throw up.

"Hate to break up the reunion, but my port engine's gone," Tucker's voice announced. "I'm losing juice here by the gallon."

"Copy that," Newcombe replied. He manoeuvred the biplane so they were flying above and to the right of the injured aircraft. "I see it. I'll give you some cover."

"Where's that other jap? My radar's out."

"Looks like he's coming back for seconds," Rose cut in.

"We got to climb, climb, climb. Can you do it, Tucker?"

"Negative. Losing power here."

Newcombe swore. Morgan followed his gaze.

Rose's plane had completed its turn and was dropping down to take up Tucker's other flank. The *Shenandoah* was well behind them now and rising fast. Silhouetted in her light, the remaining Mitsubishi was closing in.

"Think it's time we lightened our load." Tucker's voice, warped by static, almost sounded amused.

"Sounds good to me," Newcombe replied.

Morgan glanced at Hardas who shrugged back at him.

The flames were out on Tucker's scout but thick smoke still surged in its wake. All three biplanes were flying in loose formation.

"Wait for it." The distortion barely hid Tucker's desperation.

The Mitsubishi was slowly gaining on them. Strands of tracer filled the sky as it drew a bead on its prey.

"*Now.*" Tucker's plane dipped and rose in a shower of white. Refuse spun and unravelled in its trail.

Newcombe hit the cargo release and Morgan felt the plane lurch as the cargo doors swung back and snapped away at their hinges. All three of the biplanes began a steady climb. The Mitsubishi was obscured by the expanding cloud of toilet paper that formed behind them.

"Guys, I've got about forty-five minutes usable left." Tucker's voice was strained. "I'm going to have to turn back or ditch."

"Major Kennedy, do you copy? Over." A fresh voice broke into the conversation.

There was a moment's hesitation before Morgan heard the reply.

"*Shenandoah*, this is Scout One. We copy. Over." Kennedy sounded edgy.

"That was one hell of a show, Major. Suggest you make your course northeast to Clark's Harbour and hole up with the Canadians till the smoke clears. Over."

"Sounds swell, *Shenandoah*," Newcombe cut in, "but we still have a bandit on our tail. Over."

For long moments there was no response. There was an explosion of feedback and the transmission resumed. "... those other four Mitsubishis returning, now north and east of your position at fifteen thou. Long range is picking up another flight just out of Paterson, heading due west. They're moving a lot faster than those Fuck Yous. My co-pilot thinks they're Mitsubishi FS-Zs, and I'm inclined to agree."

"Interceptors," Hardas said incredulously. "They're sending interceptors."

Newcombe toggled the instrument panel. "*Shenandoah*, this is Scout Two. Say again. I repeat, say again. Over."

Static, and then: "... bunch of bogeys bearing three-ten degrees, distance twenty-five miles and closing at eight thousand feet. Eagles at ten. Just beyond visual from here. Should make things interesting. Good luck, boys. Over and out."

"Jesus. Where the fuck did they come from?" Newcombe slammed a fist against the canopy. "Those interceptors aren't for us. There's a whole wing of German fighters heading our way. We hold formation and we're caught between them. We break, and Tucker's gone."

Morgan felt faint. The back of Newcombe's head swam in and out of focus. His stomach lurched throatwards as the plane swung a loop.

Tucker's biplane was ahead of them now, its port engine sputtering like a roman candle. Lines of tracer fire hounded their new trajectory like shooting stars. Morgan squinted past them into the glittering night sky. He watched as the trailing Mitsubishi fired a final round and peeled away. Watched as more than a score of lights winked into hazy existence.

Newcombe activated his radio again. "I'm getting multiple signatures here, but I can't get a friend-or-foe ID. I make at least three wings. You see that, Rose?"

"Affirmative. Low and to the west, low observables. No wonder we didn't spot 'em on radar. Friend or foe, my ass, look at that formation. They're Krauts alright. Carrier-based."

"They're coming in low," Newcombe replied. "Making a silent run."

"They're headed for Manhattan," Hardas said.

"Need some quiet here, boys." It was Tucker again. "The major's going to try something."

Kennedy's German was flawless. The response, when it came, was lukewarm by any standard.

Hardas turned to Morgan, peering at him expectantly.

"The major gave them a head's up on the jap interceptors. He told them who we are," Morgan explained. "He asked for sanctuary. They're thinking about it."

The German formation broke. One by one, the lights ahead flickered, then vanished. The Japanese interceptors wouldn't know what hit them.

Newcombe tapped his phones and turned to Hardas, saying, "We've got the green light from the Germans. I've got their coordinates."

"Scout Two, Scout Three, this is Kennedy. We're not going to reach that flotilla, so we're using this cover to head back. We're making for the ranch. You find a faster way to the Rock, you take it. You don't hear from us by the twenty-seventh, you keep on going, and God speed you. Over and out."

Morgan watched as Kennedy's plane began its turn, wondering if he would ever see them again.

"What's the ranch?" Newcombe asked.

"It's a ranch," Hardas replied.

"What's the Rock?"

"It's a goddamned rock."

"How am I supposed to get paid if your boss is hightailing it back to the mainland?"

"I've got your share."

"I didn't count on hooking up with the German fleet."

"I can get you more, once we're down south."

"God bless the CBI," Newcombe said. He leaned back hard on the control column, easing out the throttle. "Let's see what this crate can do."

Morgan turned in his seat to face the rear of the cockpit. There was no sign of the *Shenandoah* now. No sign of the other scouts either. There was a bright flash in the distance. Then another.

"Air-to-air missiles," Hardas said.

Twin pinpricks of bright flame blinked on and off in a rapid sequence across the sky.

"After-burners," Hardas said.

The night exploded in streaks of fire. The clash of distant thunder and cottonwool bursts of yellow hung in the air like newly formed constellations. Ten minutes later, a final broadcast from Kennedy rattled through the transceiver.

"Looks like they're going to make it," Hardas said with a grunt.

It was two hours before Morgan made out the luminescent V of a carrier's wake.

Scout Three had been climbing for ten minutes. Threads of yellow fire cobwebbed across the night sky below.

"We need to turn around," Shine said. "Escort the major back to the mainland."

"One scout might make it in all this heat," Rose replied. "Two is just too damn risky."

Shine considered coercing the pilot. He said, "I need to go south."

"Where's this ranch supposed to be?"

Shine envisioned the lake's edge, the dense forests, the hot springs where the steam rose in a veil of fine mist. "It's in Arkansas," he replied.

"I'll get you there, but for now the safest place is neutral ground."

"What about the carrier group?"

"No arrester hook, no deck landings. I'm thinking of taking the *Shenandoah*'s advice."

"Meaning?"

"Ever been to Quebec?"

They were flying so low that Lightholler could see the whitecaps form and fade on the ocean's surface. A nor'westerly whipped the choppy swell below them. In the distance a lone lighthouse swept the waters with bright glances. Beyond, the coast rose formless and black on the horizon.

No words had been exchanged since they'd sighted land, and that was twenty minutes ago.

"I'm going to find us a nice patch of highway and set us down," Tucker announced. "I don't much like our chances of getting clearance to land on the Jersey turnpike, and I don't know how much further this bird is going to fly."

Lightholler leaned back in his seat. The shore ahead, jagged and glistening, transformed into an icy glacier beckoning them on.

INTERLUDE

Here is Belladonna, the Lady of the Rocks,
The lady of situations.
Here is the man with three staves, and here the Wheel,
And here is the one-eyed merchant, and this card,
Which is blank, is something he carries on his back,
Which I am forbidden to see. I do not find
The Hanged Man. Fear death by water.

I

April 22, 2012
Berlin, Greater Germany

Prince Sada-Omi, Imperial Ambassador to the German Empire and second son of Emperor Ryuichi, sat on a raised platform, a sheet of red felt cloth beneath his crossed legs. He wore a blue *kamishimo* that hung loosely on his thin body. Before him lay the ornamented dagger that had accompanied the Imperial orders.

Morishita, his household administrator, sat directly across from him, freshly tonsured. The thinning remains of his grey hair were tied back in a topknot. That morning Sada-Omi had found the old man's new appearance amusing, the two swords rattling clumsily against his bony waist as he made his way down the aisle of the gondola to present himself to his master. Sada-Omi had managed to restrict his mirth to a thin smile as he had accepted the old man's thanks for this honourable appointment. The promotion to samurai must have come from the Emperor. Sada-Omi would need to have a samurai present in order to fulfil the mission.

Beside Morishita sat Norimitsu, Colonel of the Kempei-Tai, the Special Police. He was looking past the Prince, his stare lost somewhere beyond the confines of the *Kamikaze* and her cabins. The only other occupants of the gondola were two swordsmen of the Imperial Watch, who stood by the entrance to the pilot's cabin, and the German minister for defence.

The minister's mottled face tilted to one side and blankly returned Sada-Omi's stare. As the *Kamikaze* slowly gained altitude, passing through gentle buffets of thermal currents, the minister's head lolled back and forth, accompanied by the clink of the poisoned *cha* glass that sat on its saucer. A trail of spittle had worked its way down from the corner of his mouth to the high lapels of his crumpled dress uniform.

Sada-Omi addressed him in a whisper. "Where you go, I shall follow."

"My Lord?" Morishita enquired, eyes still downcast.

"I find the minister for defence an attentive audience."

The colonel snorted gruffly. "Finally, he accords you honour."

"The first of many," the Prince replied softly.

He returned to the letter. His father's calligraphy stark and heavy on the rice paper that was so light in his hands.

On the tenth day of the tenth month in the twentieth year of Kanei, Master Shinmen Musashi took up his brush and began a work that you will complete. I speak of the Go Rin No Sho, *the Book of Five Rings. I read to you from this book as you lay at your mother's breast, as I did to your brother, the Crown Prince, before you. I never understood the true meaning of Musashi's words, even though the priests now assure me that I must have had some glimpse of them when I named you Sada-Omi, Noble Destiny.*

The Book is of five parts: Ground, Water, Fire, Wind and, finally, Void. It was written as the total distillation of Master Musashi's thoughts on strategy in war. Often it has steered my course. Time and again it has lit a pathway for me through trails of bewilderment and indecision. And now, in this dark time, it brings me some small comfort.

That which I ask you to do, as a Knight of Bushido, and a Prince of the Empire, I do not request. I would not insult you by suggesting that you have a choice in this matter. For I offer you the greatest of gifts. Immortality.

I sent you into the camp of our enemies as an envoy of Peace. In order to make our deception complete I had to deceive you, and for this I am sorry. It was my belief that were you to approach the Kaiser and his men with the full knowledge of Victory, you would have been unable, in your youth, to conceal your pride.

There can be no peace with the Germans, no truce with barbarians.

They looked at our history and attributed our victories to the weakness of our foes. They believed that any success we had was by the grace of our fortune. And now they are wondering, what has happened? These funny yellow people who love to bow and live in houses of paper and wood, how have they become so powerful? So ignorance breeds fear.

They talk of Peace and they summon us to their parleys while their warships plough our waters and their soldiers march towards our borders.

They desire war and they desire it on their own terms.

Let me tell you about war, my son, for though you are to be my instrument and weapon, you have always been the poet rather than the warrior. War is the resolution of confusion and the definition of power. When there is peace it is because nations perceive the strengths of their neighbours. They know when to take what they want and they know when to back down. It is the same when two men encounter each other walking down a street, the weak bowing before the strong.

You have heard the phrase "fog of war", describing the smoke that comes from gunpowder and cannon and obstructs a view of battle. To me, no phrase is more apt. War is two men approaching each other on a narrow mountain path, lost in the mist. To each, the other is obscured. To each, the other looms in shadow. At times they appear larger, then smaller, as the fog swirls in and out. Footsteps ring heavily on stone, then soft on patches of soil and grass. Each must ask himself, do I continue or stand aside? An inner conflict is waged. In some form or another it must be manifested.

So it is with nations.

The Germans ask us to back down because they cannot conceive of us carrying the fight to them. They cannot perceive our strengths and believe that we will quietly return to our "villages" like good little natives. If they knew our strengths, then as brothers we could rule. But how to prove it to them, my son? Only through war. To prove ourselves their equal, we must become their masters.

So why have I sent you?

Though you go resolutely, you do not have to go in ignorance. There will be time enough later for you to understand all, as you sit alongside the throne of Jimmu, our first Emperor, and look down at our victories. But for now, know this. You are my son.

The Germans believe that I value you and your brother beyond all things. They are correct, for it is the greatest gift I bestow on you. You will be permitted where others are banned. You will be courted where others would be despised. For though you are an enemy, you are the son of an Emperor.

I sent you with few men, for I wished your humility to make the Germans haughty. You may go unmolested where others will be carefully searched. You carry with you a vast weapon that is beyond our enemy's conception, and you bring it to their very doorstep.

I have heard of military operations that were clumsy but swift. I have never seen one that was skilful and protracted. A prolonged military action against so strong an enemy can never be beneficial. You shall be as swift as the thunder that peals before you have an opportunity to cover your ears, as fast as the lightning that flashes before you can blink your eyes. You are the final chapter of Musashi's book. You will level the earth and dry the waters. Flames will ride before you and a great blast of wind shall flatten all who remain.

Sada-Omi, you are the bringer of the void to our enemy.

Now that you know what exists, you can know that which does not exist. That is the void. In the void there is virtue, and no evil. Wisdom has existence, principle has existence, the Way has existence. Spirit is nothingness.

Sada-Omi placed the letter on his lap.

"Is it time?"

"Soon, my Prince," the colonel replied. "Your father has planned this to the exact moment."

The Prince turned to look at Morishita, the man who had borne him on his back when he was a child, who had taken him to classes, who had served him and his family faithfully since his grandfather had ruled.

"You are to be my *kaishaku*, my second."

Morishita nodded solemnly.

The Prince repositioned himself for comfort on the thin cloth, closed his eyes and waited. In no time at all an eternity elapsed. It was all so clear to him.

Earth, water, fire, wind.

Void.

"My Lord, it is time."

Sada-Omi opened his eyes.

Morishita nodded almost imperceptibly in the direction of the German minister's corpse. "Shall I have him removed?"

"That won't be necessary." The Prince glanced out of the gondola window. A sliver of moon hung in the distance on a sea of cloud.

"My Prince," the colonel said, "the Germans have been trying to contact us. They want to know why we have ascended. They suggest that we moor the dirigible as a storm is approaching."

"They are correct. What is the time, Colonel?"

"It is nine o'clock."

Sada-Omi turned towards the small altar near the front of the gondola and bowed. Morishita slowly rose to his feet and shuffled towards the Prince. He held a briefcase before him and placed it gently in the Prince's lap. A braid of wiring trailed behind it. The Prince took it up in both hands, raised it to his forehead, then laid it down again upon his knees.

Morishita picked up the dagger from the edge of the red cloth and walked around the small dais to stand behind the Prince's left shoulder. He held the blade close to the Prince's throat.

"What is the time at home, Colonel?" the Prince asked in a soft yet distinct voice.

"It would be five o'clock in the morning, Highness."

Sada-Omi grasped the briefcase clasps and opened the lid. The top of the case was lined with black velvet. At the bottom was a small silver console embedded in similar material. The console was bare, with the exception of two small switches. The Prince flicked the left switch forwards. The console emitted a small high-pitched note.

"*Sonno joi*," the colonel said. *Revere the Emperor, expel the Barbarians.*

The Prince placed his right hand on the second switch. He looked up at the colonel.

"Once," he said, "I went with my father and brother to stay with our cousins in Kyoto. On the last morning of our visit I was awakened by a soft knock at my door. It was Keiko, my oldest cousin. She would have been nineteen at the time. I was sixteen."

Sada-Omi could feel Morishita's breath against his neck. The colonel was gazing at him thoughtfully.

"She led me out of the house and down through the palace gardens to the temple. Are you familiar with the temple in Kyoto?"

"I am," the colonel replied with a little smile.

"She took me to the edge of the lake that lies before the temple's entrance, bade me to sit down on the shore, and, without a word, she dived into the water. She emerged a few moments later and stood upon a small rock a short way out into the lake. The sun was just rising and the water was the lightest shade of blue."

Sada-Omi shook his head slowly, the fingers of his right hand stroking the soft felt around the second switch.

"I looked at her and at her perfect reflection as she stood upon this little rock, and I willed my own likeness, my mirror image, to go out and embrace hers. Recalling that moment, I think the time must have been about five o'clock."

He flicked the second switch.

II

April 22, 2012
Outskirts of Stettin, Greater Germany

The royal train had left the Bismarckplatz at eight o'clock, bound for Danzig. Kaiser Wilhelm Friedrich Ludwig III sat in the rear-most carriage.

He had yet to offer his apologies to Prince Sada-Omi for his absence from the upcoming peace talks. That could wait till morning. He faced the rear of the carriage. By day he enjoyed viewing the countryside, a thin plume of grey smoke marking the train's serpentine trail. By night he took pleasure in watching the city lights recede in a tide of luminescent hillsides and valleys.

The Empress had contacted him two hours earlier to inform him that his youngest son had taken ill. She'd implored him to leave the capital as the royal physician was concerned about the boy's health. He had then spoken to the doctor himself, who had earnestly reassured him that the boy would be well. The truth be told, he was more concerned about his wife's well-being.

These Romanovs have been nothing but trouble for my family, he mused, sighing. *My wife may well be Empress of Prussia but she'll always be the Tsar's daughter.*

He reached out a hand and grasped the gold-braided rope by his side, giving it a gentle tug.

He pondered the events that had led him to this moment. His marriage had been one of convenience, orchestrated by his grandfather whilst he had been studying at Oxford. The royal wedding had been the culmination of an arrangement forged thirty years before his birth to cement the ties between the royal families of Germany and Russia.

Following the Great War and the subsequent revolution in Russia, Tsar

Nicholas II had petitioned all the royal families of Europe for sanctuary. The Windsors had refused. They had enough troubles in the wake of England's defeat without having to care for a royal family that had more legal claim to their throne than they did. In Spain and Austro-Hungary, the Romanovs were again turned away. Finally, the Tsar had been forced to request a meeting with his enemy, Kaiser Wilhelm I of Prussia. The armies of White Russia, by this time exhausted, were on the verge of defeat at the hands of the Bolsheviks. It was exile or death for Tsar Nicholas and his family.

Wilhelm accepted the Romanovs' plea with a single stipulation. He offered the deposed Tsar a palace in Königsberg by the sea. He accorded Nicholas every honour in exchange for one promise: should the Romanov family ever be reinstated to the Russian throne, the Tsar's first-born daughter would be betrothed to the German Prince-Regent. The crown of Russia would then pass to their descendants, linking both nations under one rule. German rule. The empire, thus formed, would extend from the Rhine to the steppes of Asia.

Less than a generation passed before this gentlemen's agreement became a possibility. In February of 1941, following a brief skirmish with the Japanese over Eastern interests, Stalin had turned his attention to the West. The USSR invaded Lithuania, Estonia and Carpathia. The recently formed Duchy of Poland turned to the Germans for assistance, fearful that the Soviets would refuse to halt at their borders. The English, beholden to Germany for its aid during the Irish revolt of 1925, and fearing communist expansion, offered naval support. Then, in a surprising turn of events, the Axis Powers, comprised of the fascist governments in France, Italy and Spain, declared an alliance with the Russians.

Though France and Russia had been allies in the Great War, their unconditional defeat and respective revolutions had led to the formation of regimes that lay at opposite sides of the political spectrum. Yet they shared a common goal: the destruction of the German Empire. Less than twenty-five years after the War to End All Wars, the major nations of Europe were once again embroiled in conflict. The European War had begun.

There was a knock at the carriage door. Wilhelm III glanced up at the rear-carriage window.

"Come."

A servant in a white dress coat entered the cabin. He glided with a steady grace, unmindful of the train's undulation, and placed a metal tray on the Kaiser's lap. He bowed slightly and backed out of the carriage.

Wilhelm III returned to his musings. The European War. A brief but bloody conflict that ended with German victory and the restoration of monarchies to all the nations of Europe. A continent of kings, but with only one Emperor. Wilhelm II, his grandfather.

He sipped slowly at his brandy.

I love my wife, he thought. *A happy accident, all things considered, but she has only brought me liability. The Russian Empire is a toothless lion that I am now obliged to defend. They* chose *to provoke a century-old argument with the Japanese, and look what it has brought them.*

The Japanese now hold a line from Tiksi to Vladivostok. They obviously have had a hand in the uprising in Kazakhstan and there have been rumours of Japanese troops sighted as far west as Omsk. What do they hope to achieve?

It happened with great swiftness.

Wilhelm felt the train lurch forwards.

A wave of pure force swept through the carriage. It crushed him into his chair, forcing it back on straining hinges. Caught in that moment between reflex and reason, he watched as the stained glass windows shattered in rapid sequence. The spinning brandy glass, caught mid-turn, exploded in a shower of glittering motes. And then the wind came.

III

The fires still raged over the horizon yet it was deathly cold. Wilhelm sat in the front seat of a wagon beside an elderly man wearing a worn greatcoat. Behind him, a few of the blast's survivors huddled on the wagon's sawdust-strewn tray. Looking about, he made out various cloaked figures on horseback.

A thin fog had risen, skirting the trees.

His entourage was made up of cavalry officers and cooks, statesmen and servants. After the blast had struck, the train had careened wildly off its tracks. The locomotive and its first four carriages slammed into the side of a station house, bursting into flames. Caught in the winds that accompanied the explosion, they were engulfed by an inferno.

The last three carriages had remained on the rails. Wilhelm, crouched behind his upturned seat, watched in wonder as his carriage traversed the wall of fire to emerge, unscathed, on the other side of the small building.

In moments he'd been dragged from the carriage and into the open air. Slowly he realised what had occurred, even though it was beyond any measure of comprehension.

Berlin was gone. Where the city had once stood, a vast rolling cloud was settling. It pulsed and glowed with unearthly light beneath an expanding mushroom of heated air and flame.

Most of his honour guard lay crushed or burnt inside the wreck. The remainder formed around him, phantoms in their dark cloaks and mud-specked helmets. Behind them, a ragged squad of the other survivors stood in disarray. There were no radios. The torches did not work.

Nothing worked.

His men stood, shoulders slack, faces pale and slick with perspiration. And then the words had issued from his mouth. "Stand firm. We will mourn our city once we have avenged her."

Those who could walk followed their Kaiser along the railway track. Somehow he'd led his men to a derelict farmhouse and enlisted the aid of this elderly man. Sitting now in the wagon, he could not recall a further word he'd said.

There was much to do.

Once he reached a functioning radio, he would need to set up headquarters and assess the extent of the damage to his empire. *How high was the detonation? What was the range of the pulse?*

Even in the unlikely event that this horror was the action of a third party, there was no doubting that the Japanese would capitalise on the situation. They already had large numbers of men committed in East Russia, but there were numerous potential fronts for armed conflict. From the westernmost provinces of Occupied China, they could enter and support the communist rebels in Kazakhstan. They could also, just as easily, swing southwest into India and Pakistan, threatening German interests there as well. And they could always rely on the Mexicans to make trouble in Confederate America should they consider taking on the Southern states.

Of course, the Reich had been mobilised for weeks now. When the *Titanic* had sailed out from the new Harland-Wolff shipyards in Bremen to pick up the delegates at Southampton, she already had a complement of nearly three thousand men on board. Two years of meticulous planning had delivered the cream of Germany's shock troops past all of the Japanese defences. In the unlikely event that ongoing peace talks succeeded, they would be redeployed elsewhere. Perhaps secreted into the soft underbelly of Japan's East Asian holdings where they might play havoc for years, undetected. Moreover, the 5th Fleet remained deployed in the Atlantic, under the pretence of war games. Crack troops in Bavaria, India and the Confederate States of America were available for active duty.

War with Japan.

Wilhelm considered the scenarios, played each of them out in his mind to their violent conclusion.

It starts with an atomic strike. A crippling blow to destroy my government, crushing my people's spirit. They will dig in to their positions in Russia, forcing a stalemate. They mean to dispose of the Confederacy, apportion the Southern Continent to the Mexicans. Canada, cowed by the threat to its borders, will not take action, and we will be compelled into an unacceptable peace, leaving the New World to the Japanese. That is what I would do, were I Ryuichi.

But God in Heaven, they started with an atomic strike. *We have always entertained a contingency plan to* end *any possible conflict with nuclear weapons, but to* commence *one with them? Where will this end?*

No long-range bombers could have reached Berlin, not without raising an alarm. Therefore the device had to have been aboard the *Kamikaze*. So it was unlikely that any other cities had been attacked, as yet. The enemy *had* to be under the assumption that he was dead, that his government was undone. Why else risk the enmity of the world, unless they concluded that this would bring them swift victory? Cut off the head of the empire and leave the carcass floundering while they divided it piecemeal.

They had made their play and it was found wanting.

He would find the place where the electromagnetic pulse of the blast had waned. He would broadcast the orders himself. Coordinate the vast movements linking the Anglo–Canadian forces in the North with the Germano–Confederate forces of the South. He would seize and hold New York—the Shogun would die in his place. The city would burn for Berlin.

Where would this *end*? He'd seen what happened to the survivors of the first atomic tests in North Afrika, and he'd been caught too close to his city to escape that fate. But he would have his revenge. His stratolite fleet would visit such vengeance upon the Japanese Isles. They would make a suitable pyre for his own inevitable funeral. They would sink beneath their own ashes.

He felt his eyelids flutter and grow heavy. His men were singing softly, an ancient song of war and conquest. He fought the urge to sleep. He saw his men through the swirl of the mist. The old horses they rode, ribbed and manged, seemed transformed into mighty steeds. The cooks and train engineers had become his squires and footmen. He dreamt he was a Teutonic Knight, riding eastwards into history.

IV

April 22, 2012
New York City, Eastern Shogunate

Nightfall, and the tanks were rolling down Broadway.

Eight days earlier, the *Titanic* had berthed at the Lower West Side docks of Manhattan. After the fireworks and the speeches, as twilight settled upon the city, the first wave of Brandenburg shock troops moved into position. Once in place, the operatives who'd strolled down the ship's gangway in suits, overalls and crew uniforms met with their various contacts. In bars and cafés, private homes and movie theatres, they went over their various assignments.

Eight days, then the world changed forever.

Protocols had been put into place and they were followed with meticulous fervour. Power lines went down and fuel dumps blazed. Computing systems were disabled and a series of assassinations were carried out throughout the blackened city. Frogmen, emerging from concealed hatches beneath the *Titanic*'s waterline, swam out to attach magnetic mines along the hulls of nearby Japanese warships. They targeted the engine rooms, sonar domes, screws and rudders, and were safely back aboard their ship before the first explosions rocked the harbour.

Reports began to arrive as Fordham led his men down West Street. The docks lining the Lower West Side had been reduced to a cinder-red glow. Sandbagged machine-gun entrenchments would prevent immediate retaliation from across the Hudson. Having demolished the entrance to the Holland Tunnel, they secured their left flank, then advanced uptown block by block. Three files of light armour rolled down the *Titanic*'s gangways: one heading towards Central Park, a second for the Harlem River crossings, while the third smashed its way through a series of hastily assembled roadblocks down West Broadway.

Beyond the Chambers Street police station, freshly ablaze, Fordham made out elements of the third column: four tanks and two personnel carriers rumbling along the Church Street approach to the Summer Palace. A detachment of the Imperial Watch, caught between the tanks and Fordham's advancing troops, lay strewn between the buildings. The street was encrusted with a dazzle of blue armour and blood; lapis lazuli etched upon the rubble. The burnt-out remains of a single Dragon tank crouched in their midst, the snout of its flamethrowers still grunting and smouldering.

The palace itself had dominated the skyline from as far back as Eleventh Avenue, glowing a dusky cherry-red, the harbinger of what was to come. Rising tiers of paper and wood encased an array of concrete redoubts only hinted at by their spies' intelligence.

Black-uniformed Germans leapfrogged across the long green lawn leading up to the palace stairs. The soil erupted in mortar fire as Hideyoshi's Guard descended—row upon row of men in crimson body armour, their devil-grins fixed in a metal grimace, ornate machine-guns slung in place of swords.

The New York bay area had once been inhabited by the native Algonquian and Iroquois nations. Riding to battle, they'd hurtled down the great white swathe between Manhattan's island of hills, forming a trail that would one day be cobblestoned, and later paved. A succession of bright lights now illuminated that ancient warpath and a new army was on the march. New York was about to enter its final stage. Oblivion.

V

April 23, 2012
Houston, Texas

Two days had passed since Patricia Malcolm had been promoted to the highest level a woman had ever achieved in Bureau history, yet Director Webster had dealt her a Pyrrhic victory. In the same breath that gave her the position, he'd stated that it was a consequence of her previous connection to Kennedy. And all he had given her to work with were the standard Bureau files.

Word had spread fast. Her colleagues addressed her as "agent", but with a blend of nuances that suggested anything but respect. In order to demonstrate her abilities, she now had to participate in the destruction of Kennedy's career, possibly his life.

She made sure she was the first to arrive, knocking on the door to the director's outer chamber, then waiting, her heart fluttering in her chest.

Sensation is disorganised stimulus...

As the others filtered in, she sat with her notes on her lap, straightening the pages, thumbing through the leaves and making sure they were in order.

Perception is organised sensation...

She heard the director's voice say, "This meeting was scheduled for ten, let's get started."

Conception is organised perception...

She rose from her seat and crossed to the front of the room. She wore a dark blue skirt and jacket; her hair was tied back as usual. Pumps. No make-up. One of the boys.

And organised perception...?

A blue rectangle formed on the wall behind her. She picked up a pointer from where it sat on the lectern.

"Director Webster, agents." She surveyed the darkened room briefly.

Organised perception is knowledge.

Apart from the director of the Bureau, there were twelve other men in the room. They slowly fell silent under her gaze. Only Williams had been present at the last meeting, the one where she'd been transferred to OPR and asked to give her presentation. Reid and Carter were now at the training camps. Cooper and Robbins had been sent to New York to apprehend Lightholler and bring Joseph back.

Knowledge is power...

Joseph's mantra.

She looked down at her notes: the words were just strokes and marks on the page.

Robbins had been found in the front seat of a Hotspur in the Queens Midtown Tunnel with a bullet in his brain, and no one had heard from Cooper. Nothing made sense any more.

Sensations: An atomic bomb over Berlin; a division of Brandenburg Special Forces now in possession of New York City; air battles over the North Atlantic; British and Canadian troops massing at the northern border; Mexican raiding parties attacking Confederate bases at Laredo and El Paso.

As far as reliable sources were concerned, Union and Confederate soldiers had yet to come into conflict, but it was only a matter of time.

Perceptions: Joseph Kennedy, a decorated war hero, a senior officer of project Camelot, a man entrusted with the most delicate of Confederate state secrets, had gone rogue. This much had been confirmed.

Conceptions? How would they exist, when the organised perceptions refused to make sense? It was the heart versus the mind, as it always had been when it came to Kennedy.

"This is Joseph Robard Kennedy, Assistant Director, New Orleans branch." She said it slowly, as if the name held no meaning for her. An image flickered on the screen, accompanied by murmurs from the audience. She let the pointer thud against it. "Born in Dallas, Texas, 1968, the only child of Richard Fitzgerald Kennedy. He is the great-grandson of Joseph Patrick Kennedy I and Howard Hughes, and a grand-nephew of John Fitzgerald and Robert Francis Kennedy.

"JPK I, as I'm sure most of you know, held the post of Union ambassador to the German Empire soon after the Second Secession."

A series of black-and-whites flashed across the screen. Shots of Joseph senior on a variety of balconies with an assortment of foreign dignitaries.

"The Kennedys came south with the great migration of '47, establishing themselves in New Orleans."

There was a cough from the back of the room that barely concealed the word "carpetbaggers" within its bark. A sprinkle of tense laughter followed. She waited till it died down before continuing.

"JPK had nine children, four sons. Joseph Patrick II, his eldest, served with the air force in the First Ranger War and subsequently followed his father into politics, securing an appointment as Confederate ambassador to the Union in '58. He resigned his post after Dealey. In the early eighties he was part of the Confed–German delegation to the Ottoman Empire Dissolution talks. He disappeared during the Sinai Hostage Crisis of '83, just prior to the German annexation of the Arab Emirates. He had three sons, Richard Fitzgerald Kennedy being the youngest."

A new set of images detailed a fresh brood of Kennedys.

"Richard Fitzgerald kept a remarkably low profile for a Kennedy." Malcolm caught Webster's cold smile and paused while the chuckles faded away. "He studied at Xavier, majored in engineering and worked on the Mississippi-Gulf Outlet Project in the late sixties before moving to Texas. He married Janet Hughes in 1963 and died in '99 of lung cancer. His wife passed away three years ago of heart failure. This left our subject with a sizable portion of the Hughes Tool Company, Hughes Aeronautics, the Summa Corporation, and a number of hotel interests."

She found herself almost smiling at a memory that came unbidden. That weekend at the Desert Inn Hotel. She thought she'd forgotten.

"Assistant Director Kennedy attended Patton High in Houston and college at Southern Methodist where he majored in philosophy and political science, graduating with honours. A chess player since childhood, he devised the line of play known as the Kennedy Defence while in his teens. It enjoyed a brief popularity, I'm told." She glanced at Webster, who responded with a nod.

"After taking a First in philosophy at Yale he returned to the Confederacy in '89. His post-Master's year was spent at the Naval Research Facility, New Orleans, 1989–90. He joined the military the following year. Officers school. Rapid promotion through the ranks. He was approached for recruitment by the CBI initially in November of '93 and again in May of '94, declining on both occasions." Malcolm waited for some comment from the audience that was not forthcoming. "He was attached to the 4th Mechanized-Cavalry Division when the Second Ranger War broke out, and received a field commission to major after the Battle of Mazatlan. He marched into Mexico City with Clancy."

A new image filled the screen. Kennedy: younger, his face full of promise, standing next to General Clancy in front of the Mexican National Palace. It was quickly replaced by another picture: Joseph Kennedy in dress uniform, posing before a billowing Confederate flag. Malcolm thought she could detect smiles in the audience.

"He ran for president in 1998 as an independent candidate," she continued. "Approached again in '00 by the CBI and recruited successfully. Field agent from 2000 to 2003. Attached to National Security, Maritime Surveillance 2004 to 2007, appointed assistant director in 2008. Shifted to Counterterrorism, Covert Action Branch."

She replaced the pointer on the lectern and clasped her hands before her, pale and white against the folds of her suit.

"Last known to be working on Project Camelot."

The room had been quiet before. The occasional rustle of someone moving in his chair, the tap of a pen against a desk. Now there was total silence. The hum of the slide projector filled the air. She could imagine their thoughts.

Camelot.

A phrase that had been repeated in hushed tones in the cafeterias and commissaries, whispered at bars by agents off duty. Just saying it out loud to these men confirmed the fact that the CBI had been operating with the Germans and Union Intelligence Agency, clandestinely and unbeknown to most of their own government's officials. And by saying it, announcing an undeniable association with the terrible events that were now unfolding.

"Thank you, Agent Malcolm, that's enough for now." Webster rose from his chair. "As some of you may have heard, there's been a hiccup with the containment effort in Nevada and Louisiana. We have tactical agents on the ground at both facilities. Show us the updated schematics we got from the *Patton*, Agent Williams. Show us the camps."

VI

April 24, 2012
Red Rock, Nevada

The water was tepid. No longer completely cool from the desert night, yet to be warmed by the hot day the forecast had promised. Doc lay on an inflatable mattress, heels dangling in the water, his damp hair in thick curls against the cushion. Two large palm trees leaned over the pool's shallow end. A phonograph, set on a table beneath the swaying fronds, played the *Goldberg Variations*.

The world was going to hell, yet floating here he could almost imagine himself between two realities and travelling back towards salvation.

"Doc." A cry disturbed his reverie.

"What's going on?"

"Tecumseh wants you in the radio room." It was one of Kennedy's ghost dancers. Decked out in civilian garb he could pass for an average American indian fresh off the reservations.

Doc knew better. In his haste to respond, he almost capsized. "I'm on my way."

"The major's patching through on a secured line."

It had been three days since Doc had heard from the major, calling from a pay phone in Manhattan, of all places. Kennedy had made two requests: prime the carapace; and pass a command on to the Camelot facilities, tell them to fade out. The fade was a vanishing act. The camp pulled a Houdini and two thousand people disappeared into the desert.

The warning had been timely. Bureau tactical agents had swarmed the deserted barracks of Alpha camp just before sundown. Then the shit hit the fan. The war.

What the hell was going on?

The ghost dancer offered him a hand as he clambered out of the water. Dripping, he ran across the grounds to the small bunker that served as the base's communication centre and burst through the door to find Tecumseh crouched over the radio.

The wide bulk of Tecumseh's frame made the transceiver look like a toy. His chair groaned as he swivelled to face Doc.

"Sorry," he said. "The major just cut the call."

"Damn," Doc muttered. "I wanted to tell him about that power surge we had. What did he say?"

"He wanted to make sure we had the camouflage in place."

Red Rock lay near the flight path of the *Patton*. Normally it remained in visual range for a maximum of two days. With the camouflage up, observers wouldn't see shit for sand.

"Anything else?" Doc asked.

"He wanted to know if any of the others had been in touch. They had to split up after New York. The major's alone, except for the package."

They had Lightholler. Good.

"He also mentioned something about a ranch." Tecumseh eyed him curiously. "Said he should be there by Thursday, maybe the day after."

"That means they're still north of the border. We need to send someone out there."

"He wants us to be 'go' within the week. Can you do that?"

"We'll be 'go' in twenty-four hours. We still need to do a power-up this afternoon, though."

"Want to test the auxiliary while we're at it?"

Doc thought about the cable network that snaked under miles of Nevada desert, attaching their generator to the main power array at Alpha. "It's not like we want to attract any attention from the Bureau," he replied. "Go ahead, but let's make it quick."

Before Doc could ask, Tecumseh was already anticipating his next question. "No one's going to see us unless they're coming in through the front door."

The Pacific Ocean was a five-hour drive west; the nearest Japanese military post three hours away. If the japs decided to move on Confederate territory from the Occupied Zone, they had to pass through Nevada. If the Eastern Shogun had survived New York, if he presented the Japanese High Command with working knowledge of Camelot, any advancing troops might take a detour through Alpha base. That was too close.

"How many men do we have?"

"Same as yesterday."

Two hundred ghost dancers, with no possibility of reinforcement. They were good alright, but not *that* good.

"Nearly two thousand more around Alpha," Tecumseh added.

Doc sighed, "Might as well be twenty for all the good it'll do us here."

Returning to the pool, he surveyed the sights he'd grown accustomed to. There on his left was the commissary. When he'd first arrived it had been a small bungalow. Workers, brought in from the Dallas compound, had replaced it last year. A long, low building now stretched out in its place. The entire facility appeared to be an officer training camp. The staff were shipped in and out every two months from somewhere down south; no one who spoke English, no one who saw anything that lay outside the perimeter. Wheels within wheels. Deceptions within deceptions.

Project Camelot had involved setting up two camps for the training of interdiction, sabotage, force multiplication. They were located in Nevada and Louisiana. Alpha camp lay sixty miles to the south, but Red Rock was the business. No one who'd been to Alpha had also been to Red Rock. Anyone who'd been to either believed they'd been to the only camp in Nevada.

Red Rock was hidden in plain sight.

Of the staff who worked here on a day-to-day basis, who cooked and cleaned, repaired the roads and maintained the barracks, only a few were aware of its true purpose. If anyone else was curious enough, if their questions seemed pertinent enough, they soon disappeared. Found themselves working in a Hughes aircraft factory, and were usually glad about the pay rise.

Beyond the compound, stretching away from the collection of small buildings, lay the Timpahute and Pahranagat mountain ranges. Lands where Tecumseh's people once roamed.

Wells' journal had mentioned that the Waste Land lay near Groom Lake. When Kennedy first obtained maps to the region he had found no such place, of course. But he *did* find a Groom mine, situated near the Naquinta Springs. He put Morgan on the case.

Morgan discovered that Groom had been a miner on his way to Oregon to find his fortune. Coming across a passable chunk of ore in 1864, he'd claimed the region and built the mine. When this area was first surveyed by white men, it was described as one of the most desolate regions on the face of the Earth.

Doc returned to the pool, its surface rippled with the glint of late morning sun. He made a final inspection of the horizon.

It was nice to know that some things didn't change.

VII

April 24, 2012
Houston, Texas

Last night she'd dreamt he was cradling her in his arms and she'd woken up in a sweat. She'd wondered if she sought protection for him or from him. She couldn't finish her breakfast, nauseated at the thought she'd contemplated either form of betrayal.

That morning, driving through the rain along silent streets to her office, she tuned in to a Japanese propaganda broadcast. A "good-ol'-boy" was saying that it had been nearly a hundred-and-fifty years since American soldiers had fought brother against brother, father against son. "Is that what you want to happen again?" he asked.

Joseph, you dumb bastard. What have *you done?*

Arriving at Headquarters, she brushed past the security guard and went directly to Archives. As the director had promised, the last of the available files on Joseph Kennedy had been left for her, forming a two foot stack on her desk.

She went through pages and pages of charts and notes, tracing the tentacles of Camelot. The material had been heavily censored. She read between the lines, following where the money went. There were two operational bases, two-thousand trainees per base. For some reason there was a cultural divide within the cadre. While Bravo was composed of a mixed assortment—disenfranchised Texicanos, Mexican exiles, negroes, white trash—Alpha camp appeared to be mostly American indian. All were recruited from Special Forces.

Yet more than five thousand men had been drawn from that reserve.

She did the maths.

Despite the extra recruits, Camelot was running at a profit.

Webster had too many men. Joseph had too much money.

Interesting.

She scanned the documents on Hardas, Morgan, Saffel, Friedman, Kobe, Tecumseh. Scanned the documents and read about agents and gangsters, historians and bartenders, lawyers and holy men. Cowboys and indians.

A slender file on Lightholler yielded little; the odd man out in Joseph's coterie. She cross-referenced Shaw and Collins, the two CBI agents previously affiliated with Alpha and Bravo camps, found dead at the Queens Midtown Tunnel. There was a note in Webster's untidy scrawl, below pages of typed print, that posed the question: *Kennedy wrapping up loose ends?*

There was a list of Kennedy's close associates over the years. Her own absence from the list was an oversight worth noting. Who else might have been omitted? *Who else did you know when you knew me, Joseph?*

There was too much here for a day's work and a day was all she had. She separated the files, arranging them by relevance, and that was how she almost missed it.

Rising from her chair to stretch her legs, she knocked aside a pile of folders she thought had little bearing on her inquiry. A stapled set of papers slipped out of the topmost file, catching her eye. It was a CBI memorandum, marked *Extremely Confidential* and addressed to Director Bush, Webster's immediate predecessor.

There was a list of names and pay-offs; there was a list of meetings, presumably political rallies of some sort. A few of the names were familiar, a couple of them significant; no direct mention of Joseph was necessary.

She read the closing paragraph twice: "The subject in question is a flash in the pan. Excellent for short-term projects, with neither the will nor the stamina for the long haul. He has an unhealthy preoccupation with desegregation that can be used effectively to contain him. If presented with the option of concessions to some of his coloured constituents or the risk of a backlash against all of them, he will accept the former without a fight. Having said that, he may be of some future use to the Bureau. Please extend to the President my warmest regards and best wishes for his second term in office."

It was dated September 14, 1998, placing it two months before Joseph's election bid. It was signed "Assistant Director Glen Webster".

She went over to the typewriter and made a copy of the document on a standard Bureau letterhead. She used a sheet of carbon paper to fashion a reasonable forgery of the signature and replaced the papers in the folder. She took the original and folded it and folded it till it was a thick bulky strip and slipped it beneath the garter of her stockings.

It was four o'clock and she had been in the office seven straight hours. She went to the bathroom and spent a moment trying to catch a thought that lurked behind the reflection of her eyes, before applying a thin smear of pale lipstick.

"It's time," she mouthed quietly to herself. "I think I know your game."

She made her way down the corridor to his office.

Webster must have been expecting her because he'd already removed the eye patch. He'd lost his right eye at Mazatlan, a Bureau tactical agent in the wrong place at the wrong time. He'd had the eye exenterated; a complete orbital clearance from roof to floor. The socket never changed; scar tissue stretched taut across the rigid margins of the orbit. The left eye's condition waxed and waned with its sympathising response to the trauma. Today it was laced with a red nebula of burst capillaries. Neither presented a particularly enticing view; the left spoke of decay, the right of death.

Behind them lay Webster's dark, brooding mind.

Malcolm presented him with an abridgment of her findings. She dwelt at some length on Lightholler and Morgan, two fish out of water. Morgan had involvement with Kennedy prior to the New York trip. She reviewed transcripts of phone calls, the receipt for a round-trip flight to Belfast, a one-way to London, and some hotel bills. Morgan had been in Ireland for two weeks last year. She could establish no association between Morgan and Lightholler prior to the maiden voyage. Before Camelot, Morgan was clean. He'd been giving some lectures at Southern Methodist, the major's *alma mater*. He'd owed a great deal of money to his ex-wife's father; debts that had been promptly dealt with by December 2010. It didn't look like blood money, but it was safe enough to assume Kennedy's involvement from that point on.

No direct links existed between Lightholler and the major. John Lightholler was born John Jacob Astor II. He'd dropped the "II" and taken his mother's maiden name after leaving school. He studied at Sandhurst before transferring to the navy. His areas of interest had been military history and maritime law.

Hardas was ex-navy. Kennedy had been in Maritime Surveillance—perhaps there was a connection there?

The one thing they had in common was the ship. Hardas had been part of the *Titanic* retrieval dive, Morgan was a historian with a special interest in the *Titanic,* and Lightholler had sailed her replica into New York Harbor with a cargo hold full of German soldiers. Strange connection there.

"What else do you have on Lightholler?" Webster asked.

"He spent ten years in the navy and got his first command in 1998: HMS *Jellicoe,* a destroyer. He was transferred to the *Warspite* before receiving an honourable discharge late last year, just in time to be offered the helm of the *Titanic.* Now, despite numerous assurances from the British High Command that Lightholler was unaware of his cargo, his collusion remains suspect."

"It does, doesn't it?"

Malcolm forced a smile. "Anything more I need to know?"

"You're aware we picked up on the Lightholler connection after obtaining transcripts from our friends in MI5. Transcripts of a conversation between the captain and the late Rear-Admiral Peter Lloyd regarding Kennedy."

"Late?"

"Yes," Webster said with a sigh. "Following some rather vigorous questioning, the poor man suffered a heart attack. Anyway, we now know that Lightholler's selection for the maiden voyage came from high up in the food chain."

"The King of England," Malcolm replied.

Webster shook his head slowly. "Think big, Agent."

"I'm sorry, you've lost me."

"Kaiser Wilhelm Friedrich Ludwig III."

"Jesus. Who knows this?"

"Friends of Germany know this, and we're all friends of Germany here, aren't we. Especially now."

"So Lightholler knew," Malcolm said finally.

"Of *course,* he knew. That shit-heel Kennedy knew. Commander Hardas met with a Brandenburg officer the afternoon before they launched the assault on New York."

Webster took a slim cheroot from his breast pocket and lit it. He reached for the eye patch and slipped it into place.

"The smoke, Malcolm," he said. "Doesn't bother my good eye, but plays havoc with the socket."

She just nodded.

He exhaled. "So now you see how everything fits into place."

I think I do, sir, I think I do. You were at Mazatlan, Joseph was at Mazatlan. You lost an eye, he lost an election.

"I wasn't convinced that Lightholler was a willing accomplice, sir," Malcolm said. "I'll have to rethink my theories based on this new information."

"Perhaps I overestimated you, Malcolm," he said. "Do you know what was to be? One America, united and governed by Americans. *Texans*, by God. And what do we have now? Those German war games in Arkansas. They said it was to be the biggest peacetime manoeuvres. They said they had a hundred-thousand troops, including Confederates. I just got off the phone with Clancy. They have thirty-five divisions here, twelve of them armoured and three of them are Brandenburgs. That's *half a million* German soldiers on Confederate soil.

"There are a million Japanese troops along the occupied West Coast. Half of them are massed on the Nevada border alone, and we have two-hundred-thousand of our own men facing them. The Mexicans are building up for a push across the Rio Grande. Meanwhile, the Germans have moved their forces up to the new Mason-Dixon Line. They say we've beaten the Mexicans twice, we'll do it again." Webster mashed the remains of the cigar into his palm. "Know what I say?"

His fury filled the room. Thank God he had replaced the patch.

"I say Kennedy gave the Germans New York, and he plans on serving Dallas to them on a silver platter. Christ knows what they've offered him. He may yet make president."

She had to play it carefully. Webster and Joseph were both holding out on each other. Which was the lesser evil?

She needed more time.

"Sir, Major Kennedy had Hardas waiting for Lightholler at a yakuza joint just hours before the attack. And he's been spending more cash than he's supposed to have, a lot more. I don't think he succeeded in giving the Germans New York; I think he failed in keeping it in Japanese hands."

"Go on, Agent." Webster was smiling.

"Two of our men were killed in the Queens Midtown Tunnel and

Lightholler's nowhere to be found. I think Major Kennedy was trying to doublecross the Germans and it blew up in his face. I think he's on the run."

"Good girl."

"What do you want me to do, Director?" Malcolm asked softly.

"Both Alpha and Bravo camps were finally secured last night. There was some trouble in Louisiana, but the Nevada camp was easily contained." Webster opened a drawer in his desk and withdrew an envelope. He slid it across the desk towards her. "It appears, however, that it was undermanned." He paused, letting the weight of his words sink in. "Eight of my agents are missing or dead, and it looks like some of Kennedy's men may have evaded the lockdown."

Malcolm picked up the envelope. It was an effort to keep her hands from trembling.

"We've had to beef up the security at every major facility west of the Mississippi," Webster continued. "I want you to find Kennedy. He's making his way to Alpha or Bravo camp. He's looking for his men. Find him and bring him to me."

He dismissed her from the office with a wave.

A guard was waiting for her outside the room. Still reeling from the meeting, she allowed herself to be ushered into a waiting elevator.

Webster keyed a switch at his desk console. A portion of the wall behind him slid open.

Agent Williams entered the room. He was holding a transcript of the conversation.

"Did you get everything?"

Williams nodded.

"What do you make of it?"

"Are you testing *me* now, sir?"

Webster examined the tobacco stains on his palm and wiped them off with a cloth. He said, "They expect melodrama and I hate to disappoint. Did she take the memo?"

"Yes, sir. And left a fairly decent facsimile of it behind in case we checked. She must have learned something in Evidence Response."

"I should hope so." Webster eyed the transcript in Williams' hands. "What do you think?"

"She has the makings of a decent analyst, sir, but that's not why you signed her up."

"No, it's not. Make sure it's no secret that she's attached to the case. Let's capitalise on the blunders of New York. I want him to know she's looking for him."

"Yes, sir."

Williams backed out of the office.

Webster lit up another cigar and permitted himself a smile. He was looking forwards to his next meeting with Assistant Director Kennedy.

Malcolm felt the bulk of the envelope clasped between her fingertips and became uncomfortably aware of the memorandum she had taken from Archives, scratching against her thigh.

The guard left her by one of the basement offices. Within, a bored duty officer, seated with his feet crossed on the edge of his desk, glowered at her over the top of scuffed shoes.

She said, "I'm here to sign on."

"I'm just about done here, miss. Can we do this in the morning?"

She held the envelope out.

"Honey, this had better be good." He rose from his desk languidly. "You anxious to get started with your clerical duties?"

He snatched the envelope from her grasp and returned to his station. He leaned back in his chair, eyeing her with irritation as he slit the letter open with a penknife. Scanning the contents, he rose from his chair with a start. "Jesus, ma'am, I mean, sorry, Agent, I mean … *Christ*."

He said "Agent" like he meant it. He walked over to a cabinet that stood against the back wall. He opened it and inserted a key in its rear panel. He slid the panel open and withdrew a copy of the dossier she'd formulated two days earlier. He handed it to her along with another sealed package. He issued her with a standard nine-millimetre Dillinger and two boxes of ammunition. He punched her ID into one of the computer terminals and assigned her a new watchword.

"100364, Guinevere. This gives you Level B clearance. Only the director and the President have higher." There was no mention of Joseph. "Sign here, please."

The names on the register above her own were a who's who of senior Bureau personnel.

"Welcome to the major leagues, Agent Malcolm. Welcome to Project Avalon."

By the time she returned to her own office it was early evening. She cleared out her desk, leaving her open cases heaped in a pile in her out-tray. She drove home in the rain.

Reaching the relative safety of her own kitchen, she made herself a coffee and opened the package, scanning the documents twice before replacing them, along with the memorandum.

Camelot. Stronghold of Arthur Pendragon, where knights inspired by ideals of courage and honour held vigil. Avalon. Arthur's final resting place. Webster's perverse coda to Joseph's schemes.

I thought you were better than this, Joseph.

She packed her bag and waited for the phone to ring.

A GAME OF CHESS III

Gambit

I

April 24, 2012
Quebec City, Free Quebec

Shine and Rose had reached Quebec airspace only to discover that their scout plane had become part of a fleet of aircraft that had been re-routed to Jean Lesage International airport in the wake of the Berlin incident. They'd circled the skies above the city for more than an hour before finally receiving permission to land.

While mechanics scoured their plane, a black sedan swerved off the tarmac and headed directly towards them. The back of the hangar was dark, thrown into deep shadow by the oncoming headlights. Shine didn't think twice.

There was an emergency exit by one of the workbenches. They gained the terminal by a service entry, their flight jackets passing for crew uniform. There they found themselves caught in the squeeze of a shocked and hostile crowd. People swarmed the check-in counter or sat with their faces in their hands while security officials pressed their way back and forth.

Shine nudged Rose and pointed to the flight board, saying, "No one's going anywhere tonight."

Rose hailed a cab. By the time they arrived at the hotel, they resembled any other Confederate travellers. While Rose reached for the first of many beer bottles, Shine turned on the television. He watched Prussian tanks clank across a rubble-strewn Brooklyn Bridge. A woman pressed her charcoal-stained bundle into the camera's lens. New York smouldered.

Rose had apparently made some wordless pact that involved emptying the bar fridges in both their rooms. Each time he appeared he had a fresh glass of liquor in his hand, a divination at his moist lips.

"World's gone to hell," he said. Watching a fly make its way sluggishly across the french windows, he added, "That's us, boy. Nowhere to turn, and nowhere to run."

Shine couldn't muster a single emotion beyond frustration.

Tension manifested itself in the small things. He hungered between meals only to pick at his food, and found it harder and harder to tolerate Rose's banter. He kept to himself, and lost hours trying to book a flight south. He checked the train stations and the bus depots. Nothing was running. The Canadian border was locked down.

With nothing else at hand, he slept.

One minute he was back in the scout plane, roaring out of the Shenandoah's *hangar. The next, he saw Kennedy and Lightholler walking the dust of an untravelled road while behind them the wreckage of a plane glowed. Hardas and Morgan were flying west over the Atlantic towards an ever-receding sanctuary.*

He awoke at dusk, stared at the television, and was stunned when Kennedy's face filled the screen. It gave way to granular pictures of Morgan and Hardas in rapid succession. Then Morgan and Kennedy were on a street near the Lone Star, caught mid-stride, running. The shots were blurred. They were both wearing long grey coats.

Are they back in New York?

Shine upped the volume.

"…wanted in connection with the murder of eight men. They may be associated with radical factions of a German splinter group, though the German embassy offered no comment as to..."

Eight deaths? Shine could only account for five.

"…are believed to have passed through Quebec City within hours of the attack. If you see these men, please notify local authorities immediately. Citizens are urged not to approach…"

There was something about the images that didn't gel. The angles seemed wrong. He'd taken Morgan and the major down to the Lone Star himself that day.

The photos were fakes. They had to be.

Webster.

The door to Rose's suite was unlocked. Shine cracked it open to find him sprawled on his bed, asleep. A bottle lurked near his open palm, yielding a dribble of red on the muslin. Shine placed a stack of thousand-dollar bills carefully on the bedside table.

He took a cab back into town. He returned to the airport. He purchased a brown pinstriped suit and a full-length coat of darker brown that he buttoned to the lapels. He watched the departure times flicker. A clock above the display ticked away the minutes but it might have only been measuring the regular movement of its own hands across its bland white face.

He turned away. A television mounted on the wall flashed its images mutely. Glimpses of a vast cloud, pierced by sprouts of red flame and topped by the shells of burnt-out towers. The image was replaced by earlier footage of the *Kamikaze* floating above a Berlin reborn. A city where countless buildings held countless people. They still lived on the screen; breathed and went about their business. Was it possible that somewhere, even now, caught in time, they were still breathing?

He wondered how many people might be staring at a television screen, thinking the same thought right now. Wishing for the magical words that might send the airship sailing away into some better future, or bring everything back as it was.

He said, "Red Rock."

Nothing happened.

Even though he'd paid off Rose, there was more than enough money in his wallet to pick any destination on the board. There were no flights to the Union, of course. And all Confederate flights had been cancelled or re-routed east via Bermuda. Fly west and all points beyond Vancouver led to Japanese territories. Fly west and keep flying, past Bermuda, and another world lay in wait. A world where Nevada was just a yellow smudge on the map.

That wasn't an option.

He felt the eyes of a security guard wash over him. Shine was black, but he was well dressed. He might have been a thief or he might have been a diplomat. It looked like the guard favoured the latter. There wasn't any trouble.

He gave the board a final glance and walked towards the exit. There was a bench outside, along the road, sheltered by an awning that kept the worst of the wind at bay. It was just shy of ten o'clock. The last flight of the evening departed in ninety minutes.

Bermuda, he decided. Bermuda and then back south.

He heard a cough and someone behind him drawled, "Hey, boy, where you runnin' to?"

II

April 24, 2012

North Atlantic, 35"02' N, 75"03' W

Diamond Shoals Lookout was less than fifteen nautical miles west, by Hardas's reckoning; Cape Hatteras was another fifteen from there. Beyond the sandy islands of the Outer Banks and across the still Palimco Sound lay the breadth of North Carolina.

It was early evening and the boat they sailed was a dim silhouette on darkening seas.

Morgan, near-delirious with exhaustion and morphine, sat hunched by the *Parzifal*'s engines and listened. Hardas and Newcombe were talking, two shadows by the boat's wheel in the burgeoning dusk. Their words were hammered into nothingness by the engine's insistent clamour.

Red sky at night, sailor's delight. Or so they say.

Fingers of the sun's last light smeared the horizon in daubs of burgundy-blue.

The wine-dark sea.

Morgan sat and listened. The ocean, churned and channelled through the ship's propellers, spoke to him. If there were no sea there would be no message, just the dry scream of spinning metal. If there were no boat, there would just be the gentle slap of wave upon wave, as it had been since the Deluge.

And I need to sleep.

He couldn't forget the frenzied escape from the *Shenandoah*, just two days earlier. The setting sun of New York behind them, lost like Atlantis beneath the waves. The dark skies above and the dark seas below, until the first glow of the German flotilla greeted them; a glittering crucifix that resolved into a carrier's flight deck.

They'd arrived aboard the *Prince Bismarck* as refugees. A lengthy interview between the carrier's chief officer and Hardas, coupled with the *Luftwaffe*'s success over Manhattan, elevated them to the status of tentative allies.

The following morning they'd been given a tour of the ship, and watched as a flight of planes catapulted skywards to deliver fresh supplies to New York's new masters. There was a fuzz of cloud on the horizon, and everywhere the security of metal and concrete and men going about their business in disciplined celebration. The battle seemed far behind them, and Berlin's destruction was too terrible to grasp, so they had watched and joked and laughed for no reason Morgan could fathom, save perhaps that they'd spent an evening amongst the dead to wake with the living.

Their scout had been secured in one of the hangars. They were given restricted access to most of the carrier but had no way off-ship. "SentCon Three", Hardas had said. No civilian flights, in or out, until the Germans stood down.

Sentinel Condition Three. Level one was standard for all fleet ships at sea; two was employed in war games and police actions, as when the Germans had dealt with the Haitian revolt in 1997. Four was full-scale war; five was theoretical—the deployment of tactical atomic weapons, which, of course, officially did not exist.

Later that day, heralded by the distant sound of thunder, the morning's fuzz formed a canopy of grey. The last of the supply planes returned and they'd taken a mauling. A fresh squadron of Japanese Zeroes—rerouted from the West Coast—had caught them over Long Island. Despite the setback, however, it appeared as though the gods still smiled upon Germany. Aeolus had thrown up a curtain of cloud, low and thick, over the entire battle group, whilst Poseidon remained at rest, his murky waters surging gently, a mild chop against their hulls.

Hardas suggested that it might be worth checking the scout's cargo hold to see if any of their belongings had survived the flight. He led Morgan below deck, and when they were alone he assessed their situation.

"Clouds won't stop the radar," he said. "But in this soup, no one's going to fly close enough to do us any harm."

The rest of the German battle group was approximately one-hundred-and-fifty nautical miles due south, he said, and steaming towards them. It was commanded by Admiral Merkur, the officer who'd been present at Hardas's *Titanic* salvage. Merkur had at his disposal three troop ships brimming with Confederate marines, along with two carriers of his own. Four carriers would make this fleet the most powerful to sail the Atlantic since the European War. Hardas explained that with eighty-five aircraft and about five thou crew apiece, the carriers were deployed worldwide in support of German interests and commitments from the Mediterranean to the South China Sea.

He was telling Morgan things he already knew, but he listened anyway. In the absence of Major Kennedy, Hardas was opening up just a little, making a pleasant change from their usual interactions.

"Despite stratolite deployment the carrier continues to be the centrepiece of the forces necessary for *forwards presence*."

Morgan nodded.

"And you can bet your boots that, when this shit went down, Emperor Ryuichi was yelling, 'Where the fuck are the German carriers?'"

"Maybe not those exact words."

"Okay, maybe not those exact words." Hardas had chuckled briefly and then his face had gone smooth. Grey smudges remained under the eyes but the lines of laughter faded. "That puts us in either the safest or most dangerous place on the planet right now. But soon as Merkur gets here we should be fine to leave. I have a little leverage with him."

"You think so?" Morgan said.

"If he's the same man I knew three years ago. Either way, he'll take us where we want to be."

"How do you figure that?"

Hardas smiled through his teeth. "Merkur's assuming command when he arrives. The Brandenburgs hold Manhattan. They've got commando units that will disperse across the East Coast. There's a lot of options there: troop movements, fuel dumps, unit headquarters and so on. Multiple targets. Ship's talk is that Merkur's going to make a run south once he's united the battle groups, then link up with the confed fleet off Savannah and return in force."

And if four carriers aren't force, Morgan wondered silently, *what the hell is?*

"What's happening on the mainland?" he asked.

"There's been a skirmish between the Canadians and japs on the northern border, but so far no American troops have been involved.

Merkur's stuck till something happens. He can't deposit three divisions of Confederate troops anywhere till he knows whether they're going to fight or shake hands with our northern cousins."

"They won't fight," Morgan said with little certainty as they entered the hangar.

The scout had been refuelled. Additionally, someone had remounted a twenty-millimetre cannon on the gun rest by the co-pilot's seat.

Hardas examined the cargo hold. "No luck," he said. "When we dumped the cargo on that Fuck You, we lost everything."

They were both still wearing the faded blue coveralls supplied by the German crash and salvage crew who'd welcomed them the previous night. It was all they'd have till they reached Savannah—if that was where they were headed.

A lookout and the boatswain's mate caught them as they emerged from the hangar bay.

"Commander Hardas, the duty officer wishes to ask you again about the two vessels you saw engaging the *Titanic*."

They were led towards the bridge. In the operations room, someone handed Hardas some photographs.

"That's them alright, battle cruisers, Yamamoto class." Hardas handed the photographs back. "Where are they?"

"Close enough."

Two hours later, back on the flight deck, Newcombe rejoined them. They stood by two naval officers who were passing a pair of binoculars back and forth between them.

One said, "I'll wager the one on the right is the *Tokiwa.*"

Two ships had been sighted fifteen minutes earlier, escorting a small flotilla of surface ships.

"Nonsense. It's a destroyer or at best a cruiser," the other replied.

"No," Hardas said quietly. "I've seen them before. They're both battle cruisers."

Morgan had the binoculars. He could see two German dreadnoughts and a destroyer in the distance. The Japanese task force lay further back, receding into the distance.

"They don't like it much when someone's expecting them," Newcombe said. "This ain't Pearl Harbor."

"They were expected at Pearl Harbor," Hardas replied. "Astor just didn't bother letting his troops know."

You're both wrong, Morgan thought, saying nothing.

Hardas took the binoculars. "They're targeting the port-side ship. Here goes."

Morgan saw it before he heard it. Towering spouts of water erupted between the two battle cruisers. Then the muffled sound of cannon fire rolled over them.

"Commander?" It was the boatswain's mate again. "Please return with me to operations."

Morgan didn't know whether to remain by the deck's edge or wait outside the ops centre. Planes were lifting from the other carrier's deck, and soon the decision was made for him in a jostling exchange of piecemeal English. He was led to the bridge, thinking he should have gone below.

"We're in trouble," Hardas said, encountering him on the stairway that led up to ops. He was crammed between two sailors, both of whom were wearing side arms. Their uniforms were a darker shade of grey. Morgan knew a police officer when he saw one.

He pointed out where he'd left Newcombe and the two of them were marched back across the deck.

"It's not as bad as it looks," Hardas said. "We're just confined to quarters for the moment, is all."

Yet police—military or otherwise—brought to mind Camelot and a trail of agents' corpses. The Germans might have put a call through to Houston. The CBI's reach extended pretty far these days.

To sea, Morgan could make out the German dreadnoughts, but the haze near the horizon's edge obscured all sight of the Japanese. There was more smoke than he would have expected.

A cluster of fighters, presumably from the other carrier, was winging away in tight formation; an arrow loosed into the void. Nearby, an elevator was just levelling with the deck, bearing two more fighters that were hastily wheeled towards one of the catapults.

Newcombe seemed to have no trouble reading the situation. He ignored Hardas's attempt to explain the change in circumstances and sang his plea to the Germans. The two naval officers began to distance themselves from what was obviously trouble, but the military police weren't so easily satisfied. When one reached for his holster, Morgan almost wished he'd do something, *anything*, to their fair-weather friend.

A klaxon wailed, interrupting the dispute, and men came running across the deck. Crash and salvage teams, mobilising.

Morgan scanned the skies. A speck in the distance grew fast. One of the police spoke and Morgan translated. "It's German, but not part of the carrier group."

Newcombe ceased resisting, possibly relieved to find a reason to obey the Germans, who were urging them away from the flight deck. The plane was coming in low and fast. Morgan stole quick glances, looking for signs of damage—flames or smoke—and saw nothing.

They'd reached one of the anti-aircraft emplacements when the Germans, pistols drawn, urged them to get under cover.

Morgan looked up. "Isn't that fighter coming in too fast?"

"He has to be at full throttle just before he strikes the arresting cables," Newcombe explained. "In case he misses them and ends up in the drink."

Hardas said, "This guy's been on after-burner since first sighting."

And he *was* coming in fast, through a haze of heated air. And behind that haze Morgan thought he saw something else.

Hardas was a sudden blur. "*Down!*" he screamed in Morgan's ear, bowling him over.

One moment the German fighter appeared to float, suspended in mid-air. The next, a fireball pummelled them in searing waves. There was a shower of fragments that might have been metal and might have been bone.

Morgan's head pounded.

Hardas's mouth moved soundlessly.

There was no sound but the slosh of blood behind Morgan's bruised eardrums. He was shoved up against the thick metal wall as more bodies swept in. He tried to look up, but Hardas forced his head back down. Newcombe's knees were in his face.

The metal point of a booted foot propelled Morgan away as hands clawed for ammunition feeds and someone started swinging the anti-aircraft gun skywards. There was gunpowder, sweat and the reek of gasoline everywhere.

A gunner yelled at one of the policemen, pointing to the emplacement's edge. Morgan felt arms slung beneath his damp armpits and was lifted, thinking *fuck this*, but unable to resist the eviction.

He was back on deck with Hardas and Newcombe and they were running again, side-stepping pilots who were still fastening belts, adjusting helmets, streaming to where others clambered below. The deck shuddered as two fighters catapulted past and screamed into the sky. Towards its edge a gaping fissure exposed the carrier's entrails. Sunlight fell where it shouldn't on the wreckage of craft caught in the hangar below. Morgan thought crazily, *That's a big hole*, then recalled what he'd seen within the hot trail of the crashing plane.

A second plane.

Suddenly he was caught in a swift shadow. Looking up, he saw the plane plummet. Looking side-ways at Hardas and Newcombe running beside him and then leaping sideways, rolling, rolling, with them beneath and above him and then nothing.

When the first waves of narcotic-fuelled dreams parted he'd found himself in the infirmary, Hardas at the foot of his bed.

"Finally," Hardas had said, and smiled.

A dull ache beat its way through the haze. Morgan's eyes shifted to the crude bandage wrapped around his leg.

He spent that afternoon in the infirmary. Hardas explained what had happened. How a second fighter had crashed into the deck. How Morgan had grabbed and hurled both Newcombe and Hardas from its path.

They were fire-planes, Hardas had said. Old German fighters, captured from some other conflict—maybe Suez, maybe Vietnam, he didn't know—but piloted by Japanese warriors strapped in bonds that were never meant to be undone, and bristling with incendiary devices and live ammunition. There'd been fifteen in all. Two had managed to crash into the *Bismarck* before ship's defence had kicked in. Two more had smashed through the hull of one of the dreadnoughts they'd seen earlier. The others had been shot out of the sky.

Then a flight of Japanese FS-Zs had fallen upon the fleet.

It had been a close call until Merkur's planes had arrived and the japs had been beaten back.

"Where's Newcombe?" Morgan asked.

"That shithead's locked up in the admiral's cabin. We'd all be in the brig, but I managed to have a quick word with Admiral Merkur after he arrived."

"You got your leverage?"

"I think so. Our scout's gone but something else came up. We're leaving as soon as you're mobile."

"I'm just going to be a liability now."

"Christ, Morgan, you were always a liability." Hardas fixed him with an appraising eye. "We'll make do."

The painkillers had rendered the rest of Morgan's time with the Germans a muddied void. The fragments of conversation and subsequent events were mercifully unclear. Now sequestered by the smoke of battle and the *Parzifal*'s steady wake, the remnants of the fleet lay beyond the darkened horizon.

Savannah remained a further two days south.

Awake and asleep, Morgan listened.

Thálatta thálatta: a Greek chorus of sound that pummelled his ears and vibrated through his bones, a cry of woe beating out an ancient and indecipherable code. *Thálatta*: Ancient Greek for ocean, for Homer's wine-dark sea. The Atlantic, named for Atlas, world-bearing Titan of Greek mythology.

They had spent two days crossing the Sargasso Sea, while sortie after sortie of Japanese aircraft left indelible marks in twisted metal and blood on the flotilla's decks. Two days crossing the Sargasso, the only sea in the world bordered by ocean currents rather than land. Calm and warm, an ellipsis of water, flowing ever clockwise in an inexorable whirlpool that could sink a continent.

This wide dank sea had spawned so many myths. Here lay Atlantis, bound by the Devil's Triangle, and here lay ships lost or abandoned. Yes, here lay the *Titanic*. Here lay—

"Why don't you go below, grab some shut-eye?"

"What's that?" Morgan's eyes snapped open.

"You almost fell over the side." Hardas had to shout above the engines. "Go below."

Morgan tried to stand, but his leg gave way. Hardas came over and slid an arm beneath his shoulder, taking the weight off his injured limb.

"How you holding up?"

"I'm okay."

Hardas nodded in the direction of the stairs. "Go below. I'll send Newcombe to get you when it's your watch. If you're up to it."

"I'm up to it."

"You've got four hours."

Hardas stayed close by his side as Morgan limped towards the bow of the *Parzifal*.

Up until eight hours ago it had been the property of the German navy; Admiral Merkur's own private barge. A lightly armed runabout, designed for inter-ship transfers, it had been handed over to Hardas with little ceremony; payback for the intelligence Major Kennedy had provided concerning the Japanese fighters. A last gasp of Camelot's ties to the Germans.

Morgan had been unable to assist Hardas and Newcombe in provisioning the vessel. His injury confined him to light tasks. Instead, he'd made his own minor contribution. Settling himself near the bow and using a tin of paint he'd found aboard the vessel, he made the ship their own, working the name *Parzifal* onto the side in a spidery scrawl of red. It was the German name for King Arthur's wise-fool, whose quest had ultimately claimed the Holy Grail and renewed Camelot. A spiritual change that had passed unnoticed in a world reborn.

Newcombe, one hand on the wheel, looked over his shoulder. "How's our hero?"

Morgan smiled weakly by way of reply.

"He's doing fine," Hardas said.

Morgan paused for a moment, resting against the gunnel. The moon had yet to rise; just stars and the play of the *Parzifal*'s lamp on the black waters. *I will be here again*, he thought. *I'm going back.* He glanced at Hardas. We're *going back. I seem to be forever crossing and recrossing these waters, but I'm closing in on you, Doctor Wells.*

"Give me one of your cigarettes," Newcombe said.

Hardas reached for his packet and gave it a shake, yielding three cigarettes. Newcombe leaned across, snaring one of the butts with the side of his mouth. Hardas looked at Morgan.

"Sure, what the hell." Morgan took one and let it dangle between his lips.

"Light?" Hardas asked.

"Eventually. Let me look tough for a while. Coughing tends to detract from the otherwise debonair appearance this lends me."

Hardas smiled.

"What do you think will happen to them?" Morgan asked after a while. "The Germans."

"Even with Merkur at the helm, they're in trouble," Hardas replied. "The japs can pull in planes from any airfield in the Union. It's going to be steady attrition. And they can't afford to lose another carrier."

Morgan nodded. He'd witnessed the fate of two of the massive vessels.

"I can't look at you like that. Makes me think of quitting." Hardas leaned over to light the cigarette.

Morgan pulled away. "I'll have it next watch." He placed the cigarette carefully in his breast pocket, nudging it down with his finger.

"See you in four hours," Hardas said. "I'm going to do some more work on the aft deck. I'll take a break around five. Accounting for drift and course corrections, we should make Cape Fear by sun-up. Another one-sixty'll get us to Savannah."

"After picking up more fuel," Morgan added.

"After picking up more fuel."

"And we're just going to roll up to some mooring and buy us some gasoline in a German utility boat..." Morgan caught himself, then continued, "Hell, we could always tie a piece of wood to my leg and stick a parrot on my shoulder. We'll say it's a pirate raid. After all, my name *is* Morgan."

The flash of a passing thought creased Hardas's brow. He dropped his gaze to the injured leg, saying, "You need something more for the pain?"

"I'll pass. Might help me sleep, but won't be much good when I need to be awake."

Morgan hobbled below decks and dropped heavily on one of the bunks. He stared up at the low ceiling, but sleep would not come. Just the rush of thoughts and a German melody he'd overheard aboard the carrier.

The lights bothered him now so he slipped the thin pillow over his forehead, just shielding his eyes, as he had done as a child. The cotton felt coarse against dry skin. It carried the antiseptic flavour endemic to hospital and military wash, and made him think about Red Rock and wish for home.

He slept, and dreamt he was back in the desert. The campfire's crackle and the buzz from one beer too many and Major Kennedy's voice. He was there with Kennedy, Hardas, Shine and Doc. There was no installation. Red Rock was just a makeshift depot, a tarp thrown over the carapace.

Kennedy had returned like Lazarus, back to tell them all, and he told them all.

And then Morgan realised what that scent was that wasn't the coals or the bark or the leftovers or anything else but the taste of the time machine's ozone afterglow. So it was that, angered and frightened, he asked Kennedy not where, but *when* he had gone to.

And Kennedy told him.

He dreamt he was pressed close to the *Parzifal*'s hull, riding low in the water like some pilot fish, but being guided by rather than guiding this shark of a vessel. It *was* a shark, its teeth twin-barrelled machine-guns concealed beneath a tarpaulin on the bow, and Hardas—no, Newcombe—was its dark brain, and it had to keep moving, moving. The future was a continent, shifting slowly on tectonic plates, waiting for just the right shove. Morgan rode an eternity of Atlantics, rising and falling with the *Parzifal*'s steady motion.

Beneath him, littering the oceans' floors, lay an infinity of *Titanics.*

III

April 24, 2012
Flat Rock, Kentucky

It was early evening and outside the window the street was slowly dying, shopfront by shopfront. Curfew. They'd seen it in all the towns they'd passed through, from Trenton to Louisville.

Lightholler glanced at his watch and then back out the window. "You think you can rely on this man?"

"He's our best bet." Kennedy shrugged. "But if he doesn't show by nine-thirty, we go it alone."

Five past nine on the clock mounted above the bar. Blackout would be in full swing by ten. If they weren't out of town by then, it would be another day lost.

Kennedy was aware that his hold on Lightholler was slipping. The mission was taking on an illusory quality. Reality was outside. It was the sparks thrown by horses' hooves on the cobblestone paths, the trucks full of soldiers that swore and spat their way down the main street of every town they negotiated. The half-cooked meals wolfed down, the boxcars they'd rode, the hay and chaff trapped in every fold of their clothes after a night spent cramped and cold in a stranger's barn. The carapace was beyond Nevada now; it lay in the realm of dream, as far away as yesterday.

He believed he was arriving at some twisted understanding of his quarry. Somewhere across time, Wells had written a journal, making of it an anchor. He'd fashioned a talisman that he'd only parted with at sea.

What evil had followed? Casting away his journal, had Wells cast away his former life and melted into a world of his own making? Had he roamed history's backlot with a nudge here and a push there as planned?

Kennedy felt him everywhere, only finding solace in the fact that, by now, the fucker must be long dead.

I will supplant you and remake the world as it should be. World without end, hallelujah. Amen.

"That your man?" Lightholler spoke as if with the mildest interest.

Kennedy looked up with little expectation. It was the crowd's response that spurred him to wakefulness. Had it been one of those old westerns, the band would have stopped playing mid-note and the cowboys would have slid out of their chairs nice and slow, reaching for their holsters.

The man strode into the bar with as much purpose as the circumstances appeared to demand. He spotted them and smiled broadly; his teeth were gold-capped and filed to a point. His eyes were narrowed slits issuing an age-old challenge that was received with the better part of valour. The barflies and the soldiers and the deadbeats and maybe even the spies turned back to their glasses and their conversations.

"Watanabe," Kennedy said, as the man bowed slightly before them.

"Boss."

The acknowledgment was spoken softly. If there was a touch of sarcasm to the title Kennedy chose to ignore it. He rose and bowed with convincing sincerity, and Lightholler, after a moment's hesitation, followed suit.

"Everything has been prepared for your crossing."

Kennedy reached for the satchel, the talismans within, and tossed a couple of coins on the table. Lightholler stood, a bag containing all his worldly goods tucked under his arm.

"I should drink a toast to the both of you," Watanabe said, inclining his head. "To better days."

"Can't see them getting worse," Lightholler replied without conviction.

The Cadillac's interior was plush. It would take more than a shower and fresh clothes for Kennedy to feel clean again. He planted his feet wide on the expanse before him and reclined, leaning against the door rest.

Watanabe sat opposite him and smiled generously. "I barely recognised you, boss."

Kennedy had dyed his hair black and hadn't shaved in days, but he was sure that Watanabe wasn't talking about his appearance.

"Tell me," Watanabe continued, "which one of you is supposed to be Tom Sawyer, and which one is Huck?"

Kennedy offered a smile. "How's business?"

"I get by." Watanabe's eyes twinkled with contained mirth. "The cross-border express is a recent but lucrative development."

The yakuza voiced little love for authority, East or West, and they made a show of their disdain. That was their history. Tradition. Behind the scenes they dined with princes and invested in big business. They loved the Kennedy legacy: politicians and bootleggers on one side; arms contracts and air fleets on the other. Watanabe's master, Kobe, dealt with Kennedy by virtue of old debts, long outstanding.

The streets were silent save for Union soldiers and cars like the one in which they rode, exempt and abrogated by the contents stored under their hoods. The Japanese may have demilitarised, but their presence was entrenched within the yakuza's hydra-like folds. Even in Kentucky.

Indian summer lay plastered over the town, formed in the smelters and foundries located along this stretch of countryside. Alluvial sands and windswept silts had once provided some of the best agricultural land this side of the Mason-Dixon Line, but there was coal here, it ran thick in the veins of the Appalachian Plateau, and it was pursued ruthlessly. Bluegrass to black soot in the space of fifty years.

"How *is* Kobe?" Kennedy asked after a while.

"He has concern for your well-being."

"How deep does his concern run?"

"You are currently worth a hundred-thousand Confederate dollars. Another fifty for your friend."

"Chump change for a traitor's bounty," Kennedy replied.

"These are hard times, with worse to come, boss. Bad for business, which of course reminds me." Gold flashed between purple-flecked lips.

Kennedy patted his chest. "Fifty now, the rest when we reach Arkansas."

"You get a discount for warning Kobe about New York." Watanabe smiled. He turned his attention to Lightholler. "I am now thinking something completely different," he said. "You know who I am, who I represent?"

Lightholler, nonplussed, replied, "You're yakuza. You're a very scary gangster. You're going to get us to safety."

"Yes, it's true, I am *kobun*, a man to be feared. But I wonder, with all respect to Mr Kennedy, if you both are not, by strict definition, yakuza yourselves."

“How’s that?” Lightholler asked, ignoring or missing Watanabe’s thrust.

“It’s Watanabe’s oldest and only joke, I suspect,” Kennedy said. “We’ve just been insulted.”

“You will land on your feet, boss. You always do.” Watanabe gave his bullion grin. “For this round, however, you have been dealt a losing hand to the tune of a hundred-and-seventy-five-thousand dollars.”

“Ya-ku-za,” Kennedy enunciated for Lightholler’s benefit. “The name comes from a losing hand in a card game you don’t want to play, unless you feel like losing a thumb.” He cracked his knuckles, then splayed his fingers, saying, “Five and five, Watanabe. How’s about you?”

The gangster held up both hands. A tattoo of livid red and green scales ran down one arm, to the amputated stub of an extended finger. The mark of his crime family blending with the mark of a recent defeat. “Swings and roundabouts as they say, boss. Swings and roundabouts.”

IV

April 24, 2012
North Atlantic, 33"27' N, 77"39' W

A clear night and the ocean. Stars in such numbers reminded Hardas that at times imagination was no substitute for reality.

Before they had left the German fleet, Merkur had taken him aside. Perhaps the admiral had felt a need to justify why he was letting them go. He mentioned a sizable bounty on their heads and told him that they had been accused by the Confederacy of some undisclosed and terrible crime. This was the last assistance they could expect. All debts were now paid.

The Germans had been reduced to two carriers and two squadrons of fighters, and were still waiting on a fuel convoy.

Merkur said, “I am going to issue a communication to Danzig and Houston. My report will state that my men were overpowered and three Confederate renegades stole the captain’s boat. Do you understand?” He paused, and when he received no answer, said, “You are now an enemy of the North, the South, and the German Empire. May God have mercy on your soul.”

Boarding the *Parzifal*—aptly named—Hardas had felt as if he was walking out of a Wagner opera mid-act—which was sometimes the wisest choice. They might have been lowering him from the *Flying Dutchman* rather than the *Prince Bismarck*. Merkur wore his doom like a laurel wreath. A dismal chorus of German navvies waved them off in silence.

Hardas was alone on deck now. He’d found a pea jacket in one of the lockers, and wore the collar up and the cuffs low over his wrists so the cold only snapped at his fingers and seared his cheeks. He’d sent Newcombe below but asked him to let Morgan rest a while longer. It looked like Morgan might have a fever. His wound was haloed with a scarlet rim of inflammation. They'd need antibiotics. They'd need fuel sooner.

He returned to the business at hand. Betrayal and treachery. One way or another, Newcombe had to go. He would have sold them to the Germans already, given half a chance. It was a matter of striking first.

I could go below deck now and make it look like self-defence.

Morgan would never buy it. Did that matter?

He lit a cigarette and observed the finer stream of smoke twirl within the release of each fogged breath. He wasn't Shine. There would be other ways to deal with Newcombe before they reached Savannah. Something Morgan said last night had stirred the seed of an idea. A way to get fuel and take care of Newcombe to boot.

Red Rock and beyond. Each destination more distant, more nebulous, and everything else spiralling out of control. He thought about Kennedy, Lightholler and Shine; somewhere under these stars, and making for the carapace.

V

April 24, 2012

New Mason-Dixon Line, Kentucky—Tennessee border

Lightholler retraced his steps as if trying to evoke a lost path. Hansel in the forest; Theseus in the labyrinth; Dante on the road to Hell. There was no trail of breadcrumbs for him though; no trace of Ariadne or her ball of string; and certainly no Virgil to act as his guide.

Kennedy sat by his side, immersed in his own thoughts or maybe just dozing. Watanabe sat with an arm dangling out the window and his eyes propped at half-mast, watching everything.

Lightholler retraced his steps. The stretch of highway leading into Long Branch, where they'd left their pilot, Tucker, a good deal richer than when they'd met him. On to Trenton and a boxcar through the delights of Fairless Hills, Willow Grove, Norris Town, Modena and Gap. A night under the stars before Lancaster and York. A nameless river crossed in a stolen boat to Harrisburg. Talk of heading west to Colorado, but instead they'd kept to the numbered roads through Bedford and Wheeling. Avoiding a chain gang on the outskirts of Columbus, Ohio, then standing in a washroom in Cincinnati, watching Kennedy run black dye through his hair while he examined his own barely recognisable visage in the mirror's peeling face. Then Bowling Green, Memphis Junction… Each mile had drawn him further away from the world he knew.

The road they were on now, leading up to the low wire fence that marked the new Mason–Dixon Line, was lined with vehicles, a log jam caused by at least five lanes of cars massed on a road built for two. There were pack horses and carts too. Children chased each other around parked or abandoned vehicles, racing in and out of the circles thrown by spotlights on the perimeter wire. A trader strolled from car to car offering hot dogs and sandwiches. A woman led an older man through the crush, desperately calling out that her husband was a diabetic.

Japanese border officials worked their way through the crowd. Watanabe beckoned one over and within ten minutes a pathway had been created through the throng as vehicles were towed or driven off the road.

Then a slow crawl to the gates.

The new Mason-Dixon Line ran true here, an old border re-established. With the Second Secession there had been a reshuffling of "North" and "South", as new allegiances were forged in the aftermath of war with Mexico and the Depression. Kentucky had been a part of the Union before, yet her sons had been divided in the Civil War. Here at the crossing, Lightholler could see the consequence of that legacy in the faces of the frontier guards.

They eyed Watanabe with a mixture of fear and disdain. The soldier who'd taken his money stamped their papers in silence. He may have been a veteran or he may have been one of Watanabe's regular customers. Border guard equalled jailor, so despite the transaction it was with some show of reluctance that the car was allowed to pass through the gateway.

There was twenty yards of no-man's-land to cross, a concavity formed where the wire fence had separated into two boundaries. The border's pregnant bulge had birthed a region that was neither North nor South.

They reached the second checkpoint. A week ago there might have been two or three men here who would inspect the vehicle for fresh food or livestock. Now there were two small towers that had been erected in the interim, three guards per post. One with binoculars, another to check the ammo feed, a third hunched over the newly assembled machine-gun emplacement. There was an odd stillness here as well; the hushed expectation that follows a bolt of lightning or precedes the executioner's blade.

Watanabe said, "*Tagitsu se no naka ni mo yodo wa ari cho wo.*"

Kennedy provided a translation. "They say there is a still place even in the heart of the rushing whirlpool."

Watanabe ordered the driver to slow down. He turned back to Kennedy and said, "If you are ready."

It was hard for Lightholler to tell if he felt more frightened or foolish as he followed Kennedy's lead. Kennedy flashed him a thumbs up before allowing the gangster to lower the seat cover over him. Lightholler glanced up at the tinted window before crawling into the smuggler's cache beneath his own seat. His last vision was Watanabe's gleaming smile as the yakuza sealed the crawl space from above.

The metal floor was unprotected. Unintended for human cargo, it made an excellent conduit for the engine's heat. Lightholler felt the sweat bead and roll down his forehead, felt it pooling beneath his shirt and at the back of his legs. The car continued its slow progress and he swore he could feel every speck of gravel as it crunched under wheel. Beneath probing fingertips he felt grooves in the floor, told himself they were made by boxes of contraband that had scraped these floors countless times. By gun muzzles and ammo boxes, paint tins and food crates. He imagined a car jack or an overturned toolbox, its contents scratching and abrading into the floor. Imagined anything that didn't resemble fingernails clawing the hot metal.

He looked up to where the bottom of the seat and the cache's roof met. There was a seam of light and then nothing.

VI

April 24, 2012
Quebec City, Free Quebec

Shine spun around to see Rose standing in the shadows. He scanned the darkness.

Rose said, "I'm alone."

"I know." Shine slid his thumb away from the knife's trigger. He replaced the blade.

Rose missed the manoeuvre. He said, "You left the flight schedule on your dressing table." His glance fell on Shine's suit. He flicked an imaginary mote from his own rumpled jacket.

"You've been paid in full. What more do you want, Mr Rose?"

"That German or jap money you're giving away so freely?"

The pilot's life was as forfeit as anyone else's unfortunate enough to be born in the world Wells had generated. Shine decided to grant him a few more days.

He said, "If I was working for the Germans, I would have stayed in New York. If I was working for the Japanese, I would have stayed on the *Shenandoah*. That's all you need to know. The money's clean. Walk away, and you'll have the chance to spend it."

"Are you threatening me?"

"Look at my face."

Rose fell silent for a moment. Then he said, "They were looking for you, back at the hotel."

Shine made to push past the pilot.

Rose blocked him. "They're looking for you in there too." He indicated the airport. "Looking for both of us."

"What do you want from me?"

"If I'm not in Baton Rouge by Tuesday, I'm AWOL. I'm AWOL, and there's no point being anywheres."

Shine recalled his training. The ghost dancers spoke of spurs and reins along life's journey. This man had aided his escape from New York. What more could he offer? Shine asked him again, "What do you want from me?"

"I know where the scout is. They shipped it to the Three Rivers yesterday. They plan on using it for a paper run to the Union, before sending it back down south."

"I thought there were no flights south," Shine said.

"No *passenger* flights," Rose replied. "This is a paper run."

"Meaning?"

"A lot of foreign companies have offices here. Quebec doesn't share funding codes with Germany or Japan. The only way to move money is on paper." Rose was rubbing his fingers against his thumb. "The big corporations are offering bigger bucks to move their paperwork across the border."

"We get paid to fly out of here?"

"Nope," Rose replied. "All of tonight's flights will have been contracted out. But I know these types. We offer one of these guys more money to stay, take his place, and we're gone. Fifteen thousand francs will get us in the air."

"You have that."

"I may need another pair of hands."

"You get me to Arkansas, I'll foot the entire bill and you can keep your fee."

The money in Shine's bag would be worthless after Red Rock anyway.

They waited thirty minutes for a cab to pull up. The late-night traffic was sparse. They arrived to find Trois-Rivières airport shrouded in darkness. There was the hint of lamplight in the distance.

Rose said, "Anyone here'll be at the operations office or out by the hangars. That runway on the right is the one we'll use. The other one's hooked up to an ARCAL system. Airport activated lighting. We want to avoid that."

As if suddenly evoked, floodlights poured on the field with blinding radiance. Rose grabbed Shine's arm and led him away from the lit area.

"*Damn*. Now we have to wait an hour before we can move." Rose had to raise his voice to be heard above the rising drone of an incoming flight. He pointed to a frail-looking tower visible by the paved airstrip. "When those lights up there start flashing, we've got fifteen minutes to get airborne."

Figures were running across the tarmac in the distance, carrying light sticks.

Rose nodded towards the distant buildings. "Let's go."

They stopped in a clearing beyond the arced perimeter of the floodlights. A hut squatted close by.

Shine said, "I don't recall this part of the plan."

"If we don't pay a cent, we'll be harder to trace."

"You want to steal a plane?"

"I want to steal *our* plane."

Shine emerged from the hut wearing a pair of dusky overalls. Rose smiled at him with satisfaction. Shine swore under his breath.

"The scout's in hangar three," Rose explained. "The pilot hasn't arrived, so they won't have started loading the cargo. We walk in there nice and easy. I'll distract the operations officer, you start removing the caps from the scout's air intakes, like I showed you. There'll be a bunch of containers lying around near the cargo bay. I want you to start loading her up. Soon as I've gotten rid of the ops officer I'll start her up. You climb aboard and we're gone. Simple as can be."

"You keep saying that, but this just keeps getting more complicated," Shine murmured.

"It's not like I do this every day."

"Clearly."

Five planes were lined up along one edge of the field. Several men were sitting by the first plane, caught up in a game of cards. One of them called to Rose, brandishing a bottle in his hand. It felt like a shanty town. Shadows roamed between the buildings, calling to each other in a mixture of grunts and patois.

"It's like catching up with an old friend, isn't it?" Rose said, pointing towards a building. They headed straight for it.

The containers were grouped near the cargo door, as Rose had promised. The scout was the only aircraft in the hangar. The ops officer was examining a manifesto pinned to the door.

"Wonder why this doesn't happen more often," Shine said quietly.

"Easy enough to steal a plane," Rose replied. "Harder to explain how you got it, once you land."

Shine began working on the air intakes while Rose approached the officer. The airfield still basked in the glow of the floodlights. They'd been on for near forty minutes already, and they'd start flashing in five. He hefted up one of the containers and eased it onto the cargo bay's edge. When he turned around, Rose was standing beside a grizzled-looking man in coveralls and a leather smock.

"*Pourquoi il n'est pas avec les autres noirs?*"

"See," Rose was saying. "Just like I told you."

The officer repeated the question.

Rose started walking to the cockpit. The officer dogged his heels, shouting at his back. Rose clambered up the fuselage and began working on the securing latches.

"See," he said, lifting the canopy. "Clean as a whistle."

The officer reached for a radio at his belt and was putting it to his ear by the time Shine reached him. The blow wasn't lethal. The officer slipped to the floor.

Shine gave Rose a dark look. "We're gone."

Rose held the hatch door open for him and gave him a wide berth as he climbed inside. He said, "You've done that before."

"Clearly."

Shine was still adjusting his restraints as Rose sealed the canopy.

Rose flicked a sequence of toggles on the instrument panel. "Lights are flashing. We're set. Hold tight."

The engines built to a roar. Shine felt a slight lurch as the scout edged out of the hangar. The card players had risen from their game and were racing across the connecting track to the paved runway. One sped onto the tarmac ahead. A pair of headlights flicked on, pouring over the ground before them. The scout listed towards the runway. A pick-up truck rumbled beside them. Two men stood bouncing on the tray.

There was the flash of small arms fire. It went wide. Rose let out a loud whoop as the turbines roared to life. The scout leapt skywards. There was a spread of low cloud to the north and the moon was a pale sliver. It gleamed balefully.

VII

April 25, 2012
North Atlantic, 33"24' N, 78"17' W

Morgan said, "You should have woken me."

"I wasn't tired," Hardas replied without looking up.

"Like hell," Morgan muttered. His mouth felt gummy. A cigarette might take that away. "Should I go wake Newcombe?"

"Let him catch a few more Zs. How you doing?"

"Better, I think." Morgan put some weight on the injured leg, felt it give slightly, and flinched.

"I'm going to disable the auto helm. Want to take the wheel while I grab us some chow?"

Morgan inched over to the seat and took the helm. His fingers slotted into the furrows that Hardas had left in the leather grip. Moisture from Hardas's palms on his own grimed hands.

Dawn was a red rim on the aft horizon with the sky growing brighter by the moment; a couple of scattered clouds lay over the west, but otherwise the promise of a clear day.

"Where are we?" Morgan asked.

"I make us about thirty nauts off Myrtle Beach."

"That's a lot of water covered."

"Harder to see our wake by night so I opened her right up. Made some good time. I took a break around three." As an afterthought Hardas added, "We have half a day's fuel left."

Instinctively Morgan eased back on the throttle. "Will that get us to shore?"

"It'll get us somewhere."

Morgan frowned, but Hardas ignored him and disappeared down the cabin stairs. When he returned he was carrying two cans of rations and a bottle.

"Got through to Nevada last night," he said, placing the food on a drop-tray by the wheel.

"And?" Morgan asked eagerly, checking the cabin entrance, making sure there was no sign of Newcombe.

"The major and Captain Lightholler made it to the mainland. Last word is they're at the border."

"Anything on Shine?"

"We won't hear zip."

"Mind if I ask how you plan on getting us to shore?"

Hardas outlined his plan over breakfast. Every protest Morgan could think of was met with the same answer: maybe.

Yes, maybe there would be enough fuel and, yes, maybe jap reconnaissance wouldn't spot them and, yes, maybe it would be safe to sail onto some secluded beach with Newcombe on board. The accumulation of maybes, however, snowballed into the one question Hardas couldn't answer.

"Just how far do you think our luck will take us?"

Providence was not a factor to be relied upon. Cause and effect had become Morgan's new creed. Half-remembered splinters of last night's feverished dream edged their way into his consciousness, and he asked, "Will there be a fight?"

"We shouldn't need to fire a single round."

VIII

April 25, 2012

New Mason-Dixon Line, Tennessee

Kennedy decided that there was trust and there was faith and there was just plain stupidity.

I might only need to squeeze off a shot. Maybe two.

He had his hands clasped together across his chest. The grip of the Beretta carved a tattoo on his palms. He had his back to the cache floor; knees bent against his abdomen, feet close together upon the roof.

Thirteen-round capacity, but only three left in the magazine. Fire, then kick, then fire and roll forwards, and then?

Just a crack of light above his eyes. He focused on it intently, wishing he had matches or a lighter. A torch. Wishing he hadn't left the fucking Mauser in his bag.

Going to be a blinding glare when that door opens. Fire, then kick, then…

He judged that they were back on the road. The going had been smoother for a while now. First the slow procession between the border gates, then the interminable wait at the Confederate post.

If I was Watanabe, I'd wait till we were somewhere quiet.

Fifty grand plus the bounty was a tidy sum, but he would have to run far and fast. Kobe had promised a safe passage. Watanabe would have to make it look good if something nasty happened to his guests.

If I was him I wouldn't do it. Still…

Fire, then kick, then fire and roll forwards…

Smooth asphalt was replaced by a wooden clatter. A bridge. There was a river about five miles from the border. The car rolled to a stop.

Kennedy felt the veins throb at his temples.

Ari cho wo. Easy now.

Someone was unfastening the cache's latch. Kennedy squeezed a finger against the trigger, a slight tremor back and forth across the metal.

"It's me, Major. I'm okay." Lightholler's voice.

Very slick, Watanabe.

Kennedy exhaled, letting his finger slip from the guard, and eased the pistol into the sleeve of his jacket.

"Pleasant Valley's up ahead. That's where we change cars, fix you up with the appropriate papers..." Watanabe made a vague gesture in the air. "Then on to Nashville, another car change. We reach Memphis by nightfall. Tomorrow you see Arkansas."

They were back on the highway. Kennedy and Lightholler were both still kneading the kinks out of their necks.

Watanabe continued, "I'll assume I don't need to ask you if you're carrying any Union papers."

"We don't plan on returning any time soon," Kennedy answered.

Lightholler was examining his fingertips. "That's fine by me." He flicked the nails against the inside of his palm, leaving red flecks in the creases. Looking through Watanabe with dead eyes, he added, "I need a smoke."

IX

April 25, 2012
Scout Three, Ozark Plateau, Arkansas

Rose had said there was barely enough fuel to make Missouri, but fumes had brought them well across the state line. There'd been a flurry of transmissions from the conning tower at Jean Lesage after take-off. Apparently a number of pilots had decided to take unofficial midnight flights. The conning tower could see them on their radar, but without the scout's transponder code for calibration the plane was just a vague blip on the screen. There were no attempts at interception.

Shine dozed while the world below turned.

Morning was a pale gleam. The cloud banks blushed against cobalt sky. They flowed storm-fast towards the heavens, snail-slow where they coated the forest-laden crests of the Boston Mountains.

"Where's this place you're looking for?" Rose probed again.

"Depends on where we are."

"We're just outside of Jacksonville. That puts us fairly close to Little Rock and a lot of radar. I'm thinking of setting her down some place. Got to find me a nice wheat field, is all."

The ranch was at Morning Star, a small township on the outskirts of Hot Springs. There was a pile of maps under the co-pilot's seat, but none showed any more detail than major cities. Hot Springs looked to be about sixty miles from the state capital.

Rose took to humming a tune. The back of his head swayed from side to side in accompaniment. Shine removed his headphones. If Rose wanted his attention, he could always rap on the canopy, as he'd done earlier pointing out the White River.

Looking back towards sunrise, Shine made out a few tardy stars twinkling on the horizon's edge. One appeared slightly brighter at the edge of sunglow.

Make a wish.

Venus, Phosphorus, Lucifer… The Morning Star, winking at him as if in sly acknowledgment. He turned up the collar of his jacket and nestled against the canopy, crossed his arms and let the metronome of Rose's head tick-tock him back to sleep.

X

April 25, 2012
North Atlantic, 32"53' N, 79"24' W

Hardas had laughed at first, protesting that he'd got the idea from Morgan.

Piracy.

Capture a civilian boat, secure her crew, and leave them aboard the *Parzifal*. Siphon the fuel onto the new boat, disable the *Parzifal*'s radio and disarm her guns. When they got to port they could make an anonymous call, giving the authorities the whereabouts of the disabled barge. And the best part—the beautiful part—was that they could leave Newcombe aboard with the others.

Hardas had said a civilian boat, not Union or Confederate; not German or Japanese, for that matter. Hostilities thus far had been confined to the Germans and the Japanese. Seizing a Union ship while sailing under a German flag would be interpreted as an act of war. Taking a Confederate vessel was much worse—the betrayal of a fifty-year alliance.

Twice while Newcombe was still below, and once later on, quietly in Hardas's ear, Morgan had asked, "And no one gets hurt?"

Mantra-like, Hardas had responded, "They won't be armed, we just give them a scare. And no one gets hurt."

They'd sighted the trawler less than an hour ago. That was when Hardas told Newcombe the plan. Newcombe asked for a weapon. Hardas refused. Newcombe demanded more money. Hardas asked how much more, and Newcombe replied, "Enough to make me forget about the bounty on your heads."

They'd locked eyes. A smile formed on Hardas's face. "It's a deal."

Newcombe said, "It's going to cost you."

* * *

Another bullet ricocheted off the flash guard.

"Damn it, they're firing back," Newcombe cried, flattening himself on the deck.

Hardas, at the machine-guns, sent another scatter of bullets across the trawler's bow.

"At least give me your pistol," Newcombe called out, edging back to the safety of the wheelhouse.

"Not on your fucking life. Morgan, hit the throttle."

Morgan leaned forwards on the stick till he felt the joint about to give. Every crash of the *Parzifal*'s hull on the wave-tossed sea jarred his wound. Newcombe clambered to his side, seized a handful of his windbreaker and shouted, "Where's the other gun?"

"Get back up there, make sure the ammo feed is secure."

Something smashed against the windshield, cracking a seam from edge to edge. Morgan felt the spew of glass shards against his face.

"Fuck you." Newcombe spun away, ducking and making for the aft deck.

We shouldn't need to fire a single round...

Morgan needed both hands on the wheel. The vibration made it impossible to focus.

"Don't let them draw a bead on us," Hardas called back from the gun-mount, fragmented through the splintered windshield.

What began as a couple of pot shots from the trawler had evolved into a barrage of gunfire. And she was moving faster than any trawler should be moving. Best guess: smugglers.

Morgan swerved. The compass spun crazily on its gimbals. The *Parzifal* careened, skewing Hardas side to side. His line of fire tracked lower, spraying against the trawler's hull. It burst into flames.

This isn't what we wanted, Morgan thought. Something was unravelling. Playing itself out to an irrevocable conclusion. There was a light, so searing and bright that the air burnt. Hardas, hunched over the machine-gun, wasn't moving. Newcombe was beside him. *How the hell had he found that pistol?*

XI

April 25, 2012
Pleasant Valley, Tennessee

The waitress's eyes were the dishwater colour of the coffee she poured for them. Lightholler followed her hips as she swung away.

The early morning traffic consisted of grey trucks that thundered by or pulled up for gas, seizuring to the mournful accompaniment of their air brakes. Outside the truck stop, the Cadillac was pulling away. Watanabe had promised to return in an hour. There was a problem with the other car, he'd explained apologetically.

"I don't care if I never see him again," Lightholler said.

"You'd better hope we do," Kennedy replied. "We don't hand him the other seventy-five grand, we'll have him coming after us as well."

Lightholler turned his attention to the window, shutting Kennedy out.

The waitress returned, balancing two plates of flapjacks, a newspaper bundled under her arm. Favouring them with what might have been her first smile for the shift, she nodded at the paper and said, "Let me know if you find anything good in there."

Kennedy shifted his satchel to one side.

Lightholler spread the paper out on the table. "They were planning this for a while," he said, after a few minutes of silent reading.

"The japs or the Germans?"

"Both." He pointed to a piece halfway down the second page. "All those German divisions they're referring to, the trains being rerouted in Arkansas and Georgia, the armoured columns in Arizona. There's too many soldiers."

"Could be German propaganda. Disinformation."

"And those planes we encountered? What was a German carrier

group doing so close to New York?"

"Your guess is as good as mine," Kennedy murmured.

"It's safe to assume that the peace conference in Berlin was a set-up. The Japanese can't have wanted the initial talks aboard the *Titanic* to succeed. Both sides must have been planning pre-emptive strikes."

"You don't think the Berlin bombing was a response to fear that the Germans were falling in with Russia?"

"I'm becoming more convinced that's exactly what the Japanese wanted all along. What I want to know is what you think."

Their untouched meals were slowly cooling.

"I think that a couple of days from now none of this will matter."

Lightholler lit a cigarette. "If the japs hoped to disable the German High Command, they've been far from successful. Everything we've seen in the last two days indicates that the German military is intact. There's still someone holding the reins, which means this is far from over."

An image began to coalesce in Kennedy's mind. A desert plain at sunset, low clouds too red in the diminishing light. A crater-ridden plain both recognisable and alien at once. Twisted metal and the remains of tanks ... and something else that had fallen from the heavens. White bones blanched by more than sunlight in the sand's sluggish tide. Waste Land.

"Back in the Lone Star," Lightholler continued, "you asked me, what if the next border war occurs in this godforsaken hole? What would prompt a question like that?"

"This isn't the time or the place to give you an answer."

"Are you behind all of this?"

"No."

"You showed me the writings of a madman, as if that might explain everything. What was it that convinced you, made it so important that you fuck up my life—maybe the entire world—just to complete your mission?"

"I can't afford to tell you. If we get captured..."

Lightholler pointed to another item in the newspaper. "No word on Bureau fugitives wanted in connection with eight murders," he quoted. "It's a little late for caution, isn't it? They'll just put us both in an asylum, if we're not hung for treason." He ashed his cigarette. "I need to know more. I need to know what you did with the time machine."

PRELUDE

I

February 10, 2011
Alpha Base, Nevada

Hardas tossed the last of the bags in the back of the jeep.

"Did you pack the oilskins?" Kennedy asked.

"There ain't a cloud in the sky, Major."

"The weather boys on the *Patton* say we're due."

Hardas directed a glance at clear skies. "All that technology floating up there, and we end up with the most expensive weather balloon in history."

"Your tax dollar at work, Commander."

The stratolite had been operational eight months now. It crossed the Confederacy in unhurried arcs from the Nevada-Occupation Zone to the Atlantic and back in four months. One phone call from the director and it added Alpha and Bravo camps to its sweep as well. Webster's eye in the sky.

Kennedy took in the surroundings; not that there was much to look at. A cluster of prefabs at the east end of the compound, a small airstrip, the motor pool and the armoury. Out on one of the training grounds, a squad of ghost dancers were finishing their manoeuvres. Eastern martial arts were actively discouraged elsewhere in the Confederacy. Here, karate-do and kendo were part of the basic training for men who might one day cause havoc in the Union's streets; a necessary evil of Camelot.

"Let's roll," Kennedy said. "We should make the Rock by nightfall."

Hardas took the wheel and spun onto the dirt track that ran to the camp's gate. Five men crouched in the shade of a spread of palms by the roadside rose to attention as the jeep rolled to a halt. The oldest of the group approached the vehicle slowly.

"Hey, Tom. How you doing?" Kennedy asked.

"Can't complain, Major."

Kennedy's glance encompassed the entire group. Mostly in their late forties, all had served with him in the 4th Mech-Cavalry; all had been with him at Mazatlan.

"Now, none of you get into any mischief while I'm away. I heard a couple of you got as far as Tucson in that last fade-out."

There was a sprinkle of easy laughter among the veterans. One of them said, "Got to go native in a fade, Major Kennedy, sir."

"*No* mischief, gentlemen. You need to set an example for the others." He finished with a grin.

Tom Shine mustered a brittle cough. "My boy taking care of things, Major?"

"Martin's doing a fine job, Tom."

Agent Collins sauntered over to the jeep.

Hardas wiped the sweat away from his brow and muttered, "We're *never* getting out of here."

"When can we expect you back, Major?" Collins asked.

"Not too sure, maybe a week. When does Shaw get here?"

"Friday at the earliest. Some problem with the new recruits at Bravo."

"New recruits are always trouble," Kennedy said. "I'll contact him from Las Vegas in three days. He can make a full report of any teething problems then." He slapped the dashboard, giving the signal to move. Collins's salute turned into an uncomfortable wave as the jeep lurched away and sped through the gates.

They turned off the road thirty miles from the camp and headed north over a plain of sand and parched scrub. Somewhere beneath them, coiled below the loose sand and dense strata, lay Red Rock's lifeline. An umbilical cord capable of diverting all of Alpha's power into Red Rock's quiescent heart. Barely perceptible, a trail was forming here, the product of the infrequent journeys they'd made over this land in the last few months.

Ghost music boomed from the cartridge player jammed between their seats. Kennedy turned down the volume, and when Hardas turned to face him he said, "We're going to have to find another route."

"Was thinking the same thing myself."

The sun was low. Tendrils of heat wafted in the middle distance, rising from the sands. It appeared as though they were driving into a landscape newly formed or slowly dissolving; when Kennedy thought about it, maybe both.

The sky held that impossible blue tincture that heralded twilight in the desert.

"When do the others arrive?" Hardas asked.

"Saturday. Morgan gets back from Belfast tomorrow. He should be here Sunday."

Hardas shook his head. "Why does he have to be here at all?"

"Same reason he's going back with us."

Hardas's face twisted into a scowl.

"Okay, pull over."

If anything the jeep might have sped up. Kennedy turned the player off and wrapped his hand around the handbrake.

"*Pull over.*"

The jeep skidded to a halt in a shower of sand. Kennedy reached for the canteen. He swallowed a mouthful and, dabbing a finger to the cap, ran the moisture under both eyes and across the bridge of his nose where the grit and powder had accumulated.

"Here." He passed the canteen to Hardas. "We've a big day ahead of us, Commander. What exactly is your problem with Mr Morgan?"

"I may not feel too cosy around your ghost dancers, but at least they're pros." Hardas took a couple of swigs before wiping his mouth with the back of his hand. "Morgan's a liability. He's told us what he's got on the ship, and he's checked out Lightholler. What else does he have to offer? Seems to me like he's done."

"You brought me the journal, David. There are times when I can't thank you enough, and there are times when I curse your name to hell. But tell me, what else do *you* have to offer?"

Hardas narrowed his eyes. "Well, I guess when you put it like that, you had to recruit me or kill me, didn't you."

"I always figured that killing the messenger was a waste of resources. I feel the same way about Morgan. Look, Shine's the best hunter-killer I've got, but I have to consider every possibility. Say he fails."

Hardas's look was sceptical.

"Say he does," Kennedy continued. "Then everything comes down to the *Titanic*. We'll need Lightholler in case we have to make a move on the ship. He knows it inside out. We're going to need an expert on the era. So Morgan comes along. As for Doc—"

"I know why we need Doc. *Both* reasons," Hardas said pointedly, "but why do we need me?"

"You know how it is, Commander. Every group needs its malcontent, its card-carrying asshole. I like to have someone around who makes me feel a little better about myself. Plus, there's a spare seat on the carapace."

"And you're calling *me* an asshole?" Hardas shook his head. "Can we go now, Major?"

Kennedy turned the music back on. "Giddy-up."

II

February 11, 2011
Red Rock, Nevada

"Now that we've covered the basics—environment suits and controls, restraints, fire control, user's interface and information acquisition—tell me, are you guys happy with manipulating the partial insertion and extraction devices?"

Doc replaced the pointer on the makeshift lectern and leaned forwards onto his fists, surveying his audience of two. Behind him was a chalkboard bearing the list of topics he'd mentioned, accompanied by a series of timelines. A model of the time machine, constructed from steel and brass, sat in two parts on a table beside him. Afternoon sunlight slanted across the room from a single window in the west wall. Peering through retreating storm clouds, it beat against the clay walls of the adobe so that they shone with sweat, but the air retained the scent of the recent downpour. And outside that window, under a tarpaulin still slick with rainwater, squatted the carapace.

Mission time was less than twenty-four hours away.

Kennedy had constructed the foundations of the Red Rock installation on the ghost of Jenkins' original base; had started to build around the sand-crusted shell of the machine he'd discovered here less than a year ago. In the journal it said that the largest airstrip in the world had been here, along with fifty years of black ops and secret science.

This room was where he felt it most.

There were other places he had visited since discovering the device where the shadows hinted at that other world. Where that true reality was distinctly palpable. In the dusty town of Las Vegas, with its unpaved roads and a solitary truck stop that never closed and a church that hardly ever opened, there were times when he sensed a panoply of bright lights around him, and heard a low hum almost ringing in his ears.

There were places in New York where the Japanese and Germans he encountered seemed to *know* that they didn't belong, and exuded an awkwardness beyond their own comprehension. But Red Rock was the worst. Here was the nexus point. From here, things had travelled from beyond the sight of God and Man. Some rift still remained. Blink, and you might see a row of buildings where nothing stood. Tell yourself it was a trick of light and shimmering sand and heat. Deny the twist and exposure of a deeper architecture of reality. But count the moments till you leave this place.

Mission time was less than twenty-four hours away.

Are you guys happy?

"Maybe we should take a break," Doc said into the silence.

"We're fine," Kennedy said.

"Doc," Hardas said, "when you ask about manipulating the partial insertion and extraction devices, do you mean do we know where the 'on' and 'off' switches are?"

Doc wore a pained expression on his face. "Essentially, yes."

"I'm not trying to be a smartass. It's just that the carapace is preprogrammed. It's only a partial insertion, so the carriage remains here and we travel in the pod. All we do is sit back and enjoy the ride."

"*This* time it's just a partial," Doc said. "It won't be next time. What if you need to use the environment suits?"

"Frankly, Doc, if we need the suits that means the pod has crashed, which means we're pretty much fucked up. We're only going eighteen months into the future, so why should we need the suits at all?"

Kennedy spoke up. "If we knew what to expect, we wouldn't need to go in the first place. Go ahead, Doc."

"Okay, we have limited information. Basically we have the journal. Apart from that, we have experimental data from limited unmanned partials performed on-site. This is as important as it gets, so if you'll indulge me," he peered meaningfully at Hardas, "I'll go over some fundamentals.

"We have no idea why the carapace can act in either partial or complete movements across space–time," he continued. "In partial movements, it works like one of those paddleballs. The paddle is the carriage, the ball is the pod. The carriage provides kinetic and chroncentric energy. Power for launch comes from the generator. Failing that, we can access juice directly from Alpha.

"The carriage slings the pod in either direction across space–time for a limited duration. The further you go, the briefer you stay. Energy released by the return voyage sustains battery power that's used for life support. We assume that a partial insertion is mainly for observation, reconnaissance perhaps, as it seems to place a minimal strain on the carapace. Our simulations confirm that there's only a ten-year radius in either direction.

"A complete insertion, on the other hand, is quite different. Then the carapace is both slingshot and projectile. It appears to drag itself across space–time, pod and carriage. We have only three examples of complete movements. The journey that Wells made back to 1911 from his reality; the return unmanned insertion to here, where you guys found the damn thing; and Roswell."

"And we know that no one walked away from that," Hardas interrupted softly.

Kennedy recalled a passage from the journal: *Some kind of explosion. Only one body was recovered from the wreckage. Quite dead.*

"The crash in Roswell in true 1947," Doc replied, "is difficult to explain."

"Gee, Doc, have you considered hobgoblins?" Hardas said dryly.

"Commander?" Kennedy said.

"We don't know what we don't know. That's all."

"That's right," Doc admitted. "We don't know shit. But one day, the good Lord willing, we'll do a complete insertion. Now, while the partial is a discrete movement back and forth across time, we know that a complete insertion requires staging. Think of it as skimming a stone across the surface of a lake. For a hundred-year journey we're looking at two stages: initially two hours, then approximately two hundred hours into the past. From there, the final movement slings us to the target. All things being equal, the entire carapace will re-establish itself there and then. No returns, and no comebacks, because if all goes well there won't be anything recognisable to return to."

Doc drew a breath, then continued. "I said the crash at Roswell was difficult to explain." He cast his eyes on Hardas. "I think that what happened there was a complete insertion, but an *unstaged* one. We have no idea which era the original time machine came from. We have to assume, however, that the journey it was making was a complete rather than partial. It's hard to imagine that the machine came from anywhere within a ten-year radius of 1947, whichever reality you're considering." Doc sighed. "This is where it gets esoteric."

"That's one word for it," Hardas said.

Doc nodded. "To paraphrase Doctor Wells, we've been in uncharted waters ever since day one, so don't look at me for direction. All I can do is give you what we know, which is precious little."

"Sorry, Doc. Go ahead."

"Tomorrow you're going partial. It's a partial 'cause we can't be sure … we can't be *certain* about a return trip. You go, you activate the information acquisition devices. You capture any radio or television transmissions. You obtain *one* soil sample. *You do not try to leave the carapace.*"

Hardas and Kennedy glanced at each other, each of them trying not to smile.

Kennedy said, "We're not leaving the carapace, Doc."

"Damn straight."

And so it went, each significant comment Doc made being parenthesised by the phrase "we think".

The people of some unimaginable era who had constructed the first carapace were beyond consideration; but Jenkins and the men of that other world, that "True Earth", had been engineering this machine for nearly fifty years. Even working with that time frame, things had gone wrong. At least one test pilot had experienced a significant head injury, as was confirmed by the journal. And this same machine had been in Kennedy's possession for little more than six months…

Everything was, at best, conjecture.

Tomorrow would bring about the confirmation of their dearest hopes, or a swift death. And with that, at least, the end of all desires.

III

February 12, 2011
Red Rock, Nevada

Once upon a time, two men embarked upon a journey.

For the shortest measure of what might be called time, they became the focal point around which all that we know of as reality whirled.

Reality folded.

It twisted upon itself, writhed and unwound.

Reality unfolded.

Smoothed and spread itself out anew. The world worm, Ouroboros, swallowing its own tail.

Chronometers aboard the carapace measured a mission time of thirty minutes. Information acquisition devices were activated. An attempt was made to capture transmissions. A soil sample was obtained.

No one left the vessel.

Revelation, when it came, was the butterfly's broken promise to the chrysalis.

IV

February 13, 2011
Red Rock, Nevada

They sat close by the embers. They might have been mistaken for pagans worshipping in the shadow of a single raised obelisk. The rock towered over the landscape. Night had bled all colour out of the formation.

If anyone noticed anything different about the sand, they weren't talking, but it was there for all to see. The shiny scar of earth around the tarpaulin had widened; shards of time, encroaching upon the adobe wall.

Kennedy had been planning this discussion since the previous night, grasping at each thought, pursuing it to a conclusion that seemed reasonable enough to be said aloud.

"It rained here yesterday," he began. "Check the papers a year from now and it will still have rained. That's a constant truth. That's unchangeable." He paused, thoughtfully. "It's *supposed* to be unchangeable."

No one said a word.

"A ship leaves Southampton dock, bound for New York. She's the most magnificent means of transportation constructed to date. She's supposed to be unsinkable. She had design flaws, but it would have taken a certain perspective to recognise them."

"Cue Doctor Wells," Hardas said.

"She hits an iceberg. She sinks like a stone. And within three years the world is plunged into the worst war it has ever known. We have dates, we have a hit list. We have the agenda of a psychopath." He tossed the journal onto the sand before him. "I thought that was enough."

"Enough for what?" Morgan asked.

"Enough to justify stopping him."

"What *more* do we need?" Shine asked.

Morgan climbed to his feet, sniffing the air. He took a few steps towards the tarpaulin and the time shards cracked like dry twigs beneath his feet. He looked back from the darkness at Kennedy. "Christ. You did it, didn't you?"

"Yesterday," Kennedy replied.

"When?"

"Early afternoon."

"*No*, damn it." Morgan came stamping back to the fire. "When? *When* did you go to?"

"I'm getting there."

"You're taking your sweet fucking time."

"We're not talking about a stroll through the park here." Hardas's voice rumbled menace.

Morgan ignored him. "What did you see?"

Kennedy noted how tired, how worn, Hardas looked. He said, "Seeing isn't always believing." He gestured towards the tarpaulin. "This is beyond our understanding. It was beyond the understanding of the people who built it. This isn't science, Darren. It's magic."

"Bullshit. When did you go? *What did you see?*"

"A year, nearly two," Hardas said, and gazing at Morgan's expression he added, "Into the future."

The fire had died but no one seemed to notice. They might have thought the chill was brought about by Kennedy's words alone.

"We were there for thirty minutes. The transition was smoother than we expected." Kennedy glanced at Hardas, who nodded back stonily. "We went forwards about twenty months. We were aiming for eighteen."

Doc shrugged.

"Has to be more reliable than that," Morgan muttered.

"It will be," Doc replied.

"When the viewscreen activated, it was all just black smoke and dust. Within moments it was caked all over the screen. Something kicked in, a low-level vibration, and the screen cleared itself. The smoke was still there. At first we thought it was an effect of the journey, but it stayed that way the entire time we were there."

"And by *there*," Morgan said quietly, "you mean right here, don't you?"

"That's right. The carapace was programmed to maintain the same location—which, of course, meant it had to move in order to stay in the same place."

"You've lost me," Shine said.

"Doc?"

"The Earth is hurtling through space. We're constantly moving. Fast. If the carapace doesn't compensate for that movement, it inserts itself into empty space. Or worse."

Morgan was looking around into the shadows as if he could already see licks of black smoke in the darkness. Shuddering, he said, "It's getting fucking cold."

"Let's get inside," Kennedy said.

They shuffled into the adobe. A single light shone weakly from a lamp on the table. They huddled around it, scraping their chairs together into a circle.

"We made out some prefabs through the haze," Kennedy continued. "A few of them resembled designs Doc and I have been working on, a couple I didn't recognise, but they were all in ruins. Sand piled up against the walls, broken windows—"

"Maybe you went further ahead than you think?" Morgan prompted.

Doc shook his head.

"I mean, if you jumped further ahead than we expected—"

Hardas gave him a surprisingly compassionate look, actually reached across to squeeze his shoulder. He said, "No, Darren." And just as swiftly, the mask dropped back into place.

Kennedy knew what the look was for. They had made a deal before disembarking from the carapace, on shaking legs. They would tell the others what they'd seen, but they wouldn't tell them everything. And Doc… Doc could make what he wanted from the footage.

"Ruins and black smoke," Morgan said.

"Major," Shine asked hesitantly, "was there anything else? I mean, did you see anybody?"

That was a question of semantics. Did silhouettes etched onto the wall of a burnt-out shack count as "anybody"? How about white bones in the dust?

"We didn't see anyone," Hardas said. "And no one saw us."

"We got a sample of the soil for testing," Kennedy continued after a moment. "It's still in the lab."

"What do preliminaries show?" Morgan's voice held no emotion now.

Doc had been examining the carriage portion of the model, rotating it in his hands. Without looking up he said, "The levels are through the roof. It's hot—real hot."

"Christ," Morgan moaned. "Radioactive ruins. This just gets better and better. When does it happen?"

"We can't possibly know," Kennedy said.

"Sometime late next year, as close as we can estimate," Doc said. "When the base is up and running."

"Who would use atomics to bomb a place like this? I mean, I know this is *big*. The carapace and everything—"

"Calm down," Shine said.

"No. *You* calm down. *Fuck*. Someone is going to destroy this place. Destroy everything."

"We're not going to let that happen, are we?" Kennedy said gently.

He told them all that he could. About the information acquisition devices, about the fact that despite thirty minutes of monitoring all radio and television bands they were unable to detect *any* transmissions. From anywhere on the planet.

A crater-ridden plain both recognisable and alien at once. Twisted metal and the remains of tanks ... and something else that had fallen from the heavens. White bones blanched by more than sunlight in the sand's sluggish tide. Waste Land.

The journal alluded to future technology, to a world that had endured at least two global conflicts but at least endured. Yet all Kennedy had found was death and silence.

They didn't shake hands that night, nor was any pledge sealed in ink or blood. But a pact was made. Silently, nodding to each other as they left the adobe and made their ways to the campsite, each made and confirmed his promise. World without end, hallelujah. Amen.

A GAME OF CHESS IV

Forced Moves

I

April 25, 2012
Pleasant Valley, Tennessee

Kennedy had been talking for more than an hour. He spoke about the expedition to the carapace and beyond with a detachment that belied the fact that he'd kept this secret to himself for so long. It might have been coldness, that presentation of data with order and clarity. It might have been because he admitted to details he'd never revealed to Shine or Morgan or even Doc. More likely it was the sheer corrosive effects of the last few days. Regardless of the cause, the effect was undeniable. Lightholler finally found himself able to consider certain possibilities.

Consider was the key word here. Anything more than that meant stepping beyond the bounds of sanity. It wasn't the road to Damascus, but it was a start. Yet even consideration led to one unavoidable question: *If Kennedy's words were truly gospel, did a world need to be sacrificed in order to be saved?*

"My apologies for the delay," Watanabe said, sliding into the seat next to Kennedy. His glance fell upon the open newspaper. "Is this where you get your information these days?" He traced an article down the page. "How are the mighty fallen."

Kennedy let the comment slide. He said, "I didn't know politics interested you."

"Only when they impinge on my trade. In times of war, people get excited, foolish. Patriotism rears its ugly head and poor Watanabe goes a little hungrier than usual."

"You really look like you're suffering," Lightholler murmured.

"Captain, tell me, are you a patriot?"

"Maybe," Lightholler replied. "The lines have become a little blurred of late."

"You've spent too much time with the major."

"If you feel that way, why are you helping us?" Kennedy asked.

"I help you because you pay Kobe a substantial fee of which I will receive no mean portion. And because I believe that you might find a satisfactory end to all of this, before it has gone too far."

Lightholler's mind flitted back to Kennedy's deal with the Shogunate. He wondered how such an end might look to the gangster, and envisioned an endless tide of rice paper and curlicued red-tiled roofs.

Kennedy spoke again. "The papers are calling me a murderer and a traitor."

"I would be more concerned if they were praising you, boss. Kobe says he knows what you are, and what you might be capable of accomplishing. He is my *Oyabun*, you understand? If he tells me that a crow is white, then as far as I am concerned, it's white." He flashed them both his golden smile. "So far we have made good time, but you must never cease spurring a running horse."

He looked at the tab and peeled some notes from a billfold, which he scattered on the table. "Let's go. It's my treat."

"He's so generous with my money," Kennedy said to Lightholler, but his smile was one of relief.

They followed Watanabe to the door. He ushered them towards a tan Pierce Arrow sedan idling by one of the gas pumps. It had Tennessee plates. Watanabe climbed into the front seat.

Lightholler whistled softly, getting into the passenger seat.

"Nice ride."

"Good enough for Babe Ruth," Watanabe replied.

"Where's your driver?" Kennedy asked, climbing into the back.

"Inconvenienced." Watanabe threw an arm across the seat, turning to face them. "From here, it's just me and you."

II

Morning sunlight stole over the low hillside. To either side of the highway gravel gave way to dark green fields and pastures, the odd farmhouse breaking up an otherwise monotonous landscape. It was a little over an hour to the Nashville city limits. Kennedy saw two police cars on the highway and what may have been a third, unmarked, by the roadside.

Traffic was sparse, mostly heading south. Watanabe made a point of sticking close to a huddle of cars they'd caught up with outside of Lohman.

"I'll be glad when we stop running," Lightholler said, stretching through a yawn.

"That won't be till Arkansas," Kennedy replied. "Which reminds me…" He leaned forwards, tapping Watanabe on the shoulder. "I'm going to need to make a call."

"Looking for more trouble, boss?" Watanabe tried to sound like he was interested, but he was too busy watching the road to muster any real enthusiasm. He strummed his fingers on the dashboard, then flicked on the radio. Hank Williams poured out of the speakers, singing about lost love.

"Torch and twang," he called back. "Just in case you forgot where we are."

They turned off the highway where a faded signpost indicated an older portion of road. Kennedy pointed to a phone booth outside a country store and Watanabe pulled over. Securing a position in the booth where he could view the car and still catch any movement along the road, he started slotting dimes.

The phone rang twice before someone patched him through. Tecumseh took the call. In lieu of updating the codes and acquiring a secure line, it would have to be a brief exchange. Kennedy asked for an update.

Tecumseh told him Morgan and Hardas were moving by sea. They would be in Savannah by nightfall. There was no word from Shine.

Kennedy said, "We've crossed the border. We should make the Rock by the twenty-eighth, sooner if we get a plane. It all depends on how long it takes us to link up with the others."

"You'll want to move fast. It's getting busy out here. The Bureau shut down Alpha two nights ago. They flew in three squads of tactical agents. Trucks have been rolling into the joint ever since."

"How's the fade going?"

"We let them capture two hundred ghost dancers. The *Patton*'s doing fly-bys, but I think it's watching Alpha. I've set watches along the perimeter. No one's taken any interest in us so far."

"What about Louisiana?"

"Same deal. Closed for business."

"I'll call in from Arkansas." Kennedy rang off.

He went over the moves in his head, trying to impose some order on the chaos. Webster had connected him with Lightholler, and by default with the Brandenburgs, but the newspapers were only talking about the murders in New York. Why was Webster holding back on the accusation of treason?

Kennedy put a scenario together. *Webster sends tactical agents to close down the camps. He sends assassins to New York. He has Lightholler abducted. Lightholler is rescued and turns up at the Lone Star.*

The moves were desperate, clumsy, but what if they were *meant* to look that way?

What if the kidnapping had been staged?

Kennedy peered out onto the street. Lightholler was leaning up against the passenger door of the Pierce Arrow, smoking a cigarette. Apart from the time he'd spent reading the journal, and a brief time on the *Shenandoah*, Lightholler hadn't been out of his sight. Could he have been wearing a wire? Could the Lone Star have been bugged?

If Lightholler was working for Webster, he had the makings of a damn fine agent. He'd given nothing away.

But if you can't trust your instinct, Kennedy thought, *and instinct's all you have to go on, then you're finished.*

He caught Lightholler looking up at the phone booth. He returned the captain's vague smile over gritted teeth.

Worse case scenario: Webster gets wind of the deal with the Shogun. He takes over the camps, thinking I may use the men against Confederate targets. He learns that they harbour a band of fanatics practising an outlawed religion. He finds them under-manned and thinks I'm already making my move. He frames me for the death of eight of his men. That way he can come after me with Union as well as Confederate enforcement agencies.

Kennedy put the remaining change in his pocket, opened the door to the phone booth and walked back to the car.

Worst case scenario: Webster knows about the carapace.

III

April 25, 2012
Nashville, Tennessee

It wasn't the Waldorf, but it was the best Lightholler had seen in days.

He ran the water cold. Clenched his jaw and screwed his eyes shut, keeping his face under the icy blast. It was almost a form of chastisement.

Finally, he relinquished. He turned on the heat and sank to the stained tiled floor, letting the water pour over him. His nails were chipped and dirty. Examining them, he recalled the metal floor of the Cadillac and shuddered. His face stung where he'd shaved too close and it felt good. So did the thrum of water on his bare scalp.

"Keep the beard," Kennedy had suggested, emerging from the bathroom with the start of a newly fashioned goatee, dyed black to match his hair. Sunburn lent a swarthiness to his appearance so that he might even pass for a Mexican. Anything but a stately Southern politician.

"Can't do it," Lightholler had replied. "I'll settle for a haircut." He'd taken an electric razor into the bathroom and given himself a crew cut.

Scrubbing at the caked layers of dirt now, he felt he was being shriven. Pared down to an essence that he barely recognised; washing away Lightholler and Astor to leave some new form that could deal with the days ahead.

He left the shower wearing a robe the hotel provided. Coarse, but the abrasion was merely another mode of purification. Only four days had passed but he felt leaner, lighter. Honed.

"You look like a boxer," Kennedy said from his perch by a small window that opened onto the street. He was wearing clothing that Watanabe had provided. Pale olive trousers and a navy blue jacket over a white shirt. A similar uniform was spread out for Lightholler on one of the beds. There was no sign of their old clothes.

"I used to fight," Lightholler replied. "Back in the academy." He lined his fists in front of his face, fixing his glance just above the knuckles. Took a few swings, then let his arms fall.

His eyes wandered the room, taking inventory. There were two single beds, a small table between them with a desk light. The table held a single drawer; there'd be a Bible tucked somewhere within. A dressing table against the opposite wall had a vanity mirror fixed above it that failed to give the room any illusion of extra space. A door in the wall led to Watanabe's room.

"You might have thought he'd spring for a third room," Lightholler said. "Or are you still worried about letting me out of your sight?"

"Should I be?"

Lightholler gave the room a swift reappraisal. "Where are my things?"

"In the drawer."

"Hope you found what you were looking for." Lightholler made himself grin.

"No recording or transmitting devices." Kennedy wasn't smiling. "No wires."

"After all the shit you've put me through, you better be kidding me."

"I'm not." Kennedy's reply was the scrape of a whisper.

"What the hell are you talking about?"

"Webster seems to know more than he should. Much more. Unless the leak is in my organisation, then everything points to you."

Lightholler measured the distance to the door, considering his options. He said, "You've got no right to level accusations. You got me into this."

"A necessary trait for any decent intelligence agent is a special open-mindedness. Perhaps you know that. Nothing is impossible just because it seems improbable. The carapace taught me that, once and for all. I had to convince myself of your innocence."

Lightholler sighed. He almost pitied the man. "Are you satisfied?"

"I won't be satisfied till we've reached Red Rock." Kennedy smiled a bitter smile. "I've decided to go on faith."

He rose from the window ledge slowly with an audible sigh. "I'll be next door. There are things I need to organise. Watanabe's trying to charter a flight to Little Rock from Memphis, which means we'll probably leave here tonight."

"Wasn't that always the plan?"

"It all depends on what Watanabe can arrange. If there aren't any flights, we might be safer here for the moment."

"He's your guy," Lightholler said, probing carefully. Circumstance had prevented any enquiry about the nature of the two men's relationship. Everything he'd seen suggested a connection that extended beyond simple finances. A string of shady deals and honoured debts, the backdrop of their warped brand of mutual respect.

"Memphis is half a day's drive from here, and each step south takes him further away from his circle of influence," Kennedy explained. "I think something happened with his driver. I think he's having a harder time moving us than he expected."

"Like I said, he's your guy." Lightholler's gaze dropped to the satchel that sat by Kennedy's feet. It had gathered quite a few more scrapes and creases since he'd first seen it. "You mind if I read some more of that while we wait?"

"There's some wild stuff in there. Dark," Kennedy replied levelly. "Let me know what you make of it."

Kennedy let himself into the adjoining room. Looking back he said, "Give me a yell if you need anything." He closed the door behind him.

Lightholler stared, waiting for it to re-open. He edged towards it and heard the sounds of Kennedy moving around. He walked to the main door of their room and tried the handle. It swung easily and he almost slammed the door closing it. A broad smile began to form on his face.

Alone.

And with the journal.

He dropped onto one of the beds, arms outstretched. The ceiling was painted off-white. A cheap chandelier dangled, refracting the afternoon light in dirty rainbow hues. A radio was playing somewhere. He heard snatches of a saxophone; alternating piano trills.

He was tired beyond reason but he wanted to get up, explore these streets, follow the music to where it might lead. He wanted a woman beneath him, or his fists in someone's face, knuckles peeling like paint and blood on his hands. He wanted to race through the streets till the air tore ragged in his lungs, the hot pavement scalded his feet.

He had a fleeting image of that girl from the diner as she sashayed towards him. Breasts impossibly firm and hips that flowed from waist to thigh with the promise of desire's satisfaction. A composite of girls from the street, the ship, the parties, all blending into one perfect creature.

He lit a cigarette. He'd taken to Texas Teas, having smoked enough of Hardas's, and Silk Cut was nowhere to be found. No ashtray, so he walked around the room smoking and knocking ashes into his palm; walked to the window and shook his hand out over the street, then wiped it against the sill.

Explore these streets? He felt the contradiction between anonymity and the sensation that every eye was upon him. No, there was nowhere for him to go except west—to Nevada.

Still … a woman beneath him.

He let his thoughts roam where he couldn't. Perhaps Watanabe could organise something. Perhaps a girl could be brought up to the room. The crumple of bed sheets, the cash on the table, the shower and a cigarette. The caustic reappraisal over a glass of whatever was handy.

The satchel lay near the window, where Kennedy had left it. He opened it and found the journal bundled within the folds of a flag. He removed the flag gently and the journal slipped onto the floor. So did Kennedy's gun.

He had a vivid flash of the Midtown Tunnel. The sentry's pistol firing into the agent's head, and then swinging past him to fire again. He picked up the gun gingerly. *Does everyone in New York City carry a Mauser?* He wrapped it in the flag and replaced them both. There was a drawstring pouch at the bottom of the satchel but he didn't touch it. He closed the window and shut the blinds.

He brought the journal to his bed, lay down and leaned on an elbow and read into the late afternoon.

Wild stuff. Lucid accounts fused with paranoid delusions.

He rested his head on folded arms, thinking he might doze for a while. Thinking about what Kennedy had told him earlier, at the truck stop.

When sleep came, he dreamed he was still listening to an exposition that soared and carried him to unmeasured heights, gaining a clarity he would never recollect in waking hours. The quilted landscape of the past, present and future mapped clearly before his sleeping eyes.

IV

April 25, 2012
Savannah, Georgia

Agent Reid was waiting for her on the tarmac. His suit was rumpled and the thick curls of his fringe lay plastered to his forehead. His face, haggard, with grey pouches beneath bloodshot eyes, held the remains of a frown.

"Welcome to the frontier, Agent Malcolm."

She made no protest as he took her bag and led her to the waiting Hotspur. As they walked, he glanced back at the sleek form of the black Raptor, now taxiing towards the runway.

"Didn't know they took such good care of OPR."

Malcolm smiled a weary smile. "You're not under inspection. I'm working Avalon now."

Reid stopped in his tracks. "There is no Avalon."

"Would you like my watchword?"

He scratched the back of his neck, eyeing her thoughtfully. He said, "An operation goes shadow and suddenly everyone's working it." A strange smile crossed his face. "First OPR, now this. The director's sure got you jumping through hoops."

"Why don't you just say what you mean?"

"Goes against all my training, Agent." His face remained deadpan.

Unsure how to respond, Malcolm said, "Well, just don't think too loudly. I've had a long flight."

Reid's look suggested some disappointment. He was nodding slightly, as if in answer to some question posed within. He said, "You really think you're up to this?"

"I'd be insane to say yes."

She held his stare till he shrugged and turned away. He started up again, briskly, for the car.

She matched his stride, saying, "I thought you were at Bravo camp."

He kept his back to her. "I was … till last night. The director wanted someone local up here. This is the biggest break we've had."

She slid some warmth into her voice. "I never figured you for a Georgia boy."

"Savannah born and bred." He placed her bag on the ground and leaned against the Hotspur with his arms crossed. "Look, I've been down at the docks all morning. I've been dealing with National Security all day. Then I get a call to pick you up from the airport. I figure, being with Professional Responsibility, you're here to keep an eye on me and spin the story we're going to run on what happened this morning. Now you tell me you're hunting Kennedy, that you're working Avalon…"

She raised a hand to shield her eyes from the noon sun glare. "What *did* happen this morning?"

He reached into a pocket and pulled out a pack of cigarettes. He offered her one and, when she refused, lit up. "Why are you here?"

"I've worked Evidence Response five years. I'm here to see what your boys come up with."

"Ever been outside a lab?"

Malcolm frowned. "You said it yourself, Agent Reid, Director Webster's got me jumping through hoops. But I promise you I'm not going to interfere with your investigation."

"You're doing that already."

"Listen, Agent Reid, I've seen five cities in the last day or so, and I've dealt with exactly the same crap from all of you, so let me set a few things straight right now. I've been sent here to tag what's been retrieved from the scene, and maybe question the survivor after you've had your fun. So save the tough cop routine for the prisoner."

Reid started to laugh. "Now that's more like it." He paused for a moment, but held her stare. "Hell, I guess I *could* always do with another pair of hands." He picked up her bag and dropped it in the back of the Hotspur, then went around to open the passenger door for her. "So, how does it feel being assigned to a project that doesn't exist?"

"You tell me."

He climbed into the driver's seat, grumbling. "All I know is I didn't get flown up here on no Raptor."

* * *

Less than twenty-four hours had brought Patricia Malcolm halfway across the Confederacy, chasing a comet's tail of faint trails and falsehood. Field offices from Florida to New Mexico had reported numerous sightings of Kennedy. Sometimes he lurked in the shadows of a pool hall and sometimes he was polishing a car fender at a gas station. One report had him at the head of a column of troops wading through a cotton field at dusk. She could picture that.

Malcolm stared out the car window, seeking something that would confirm where she was. The streets, unknown yet familiar, slipped by. *Anytown, CSA*. After a while she said, "Tell me more."

"Huh?" Reid's eyes were fixed on the traffic ahead.

"You said you thought I was here to help with a cover-up."

"The coast guards who found the boat, the wreckage, they're all being sent down to Fort Worth. Same with the naval police that brought him in."

Malcolm had received the call from one of Webster's minions early that morning. Someone had been fished out of the Atlantic by a coastguard vessel following a disturbance on the edge of Union territorial waters. The "disturbance" turned out to be a skirmish between two boats, one of which had been identified as a German captain's barge. There wasn't anything to link it to Kennedy, but it was the closest they'd come since Berlin had gone up in flames. After reading the reports, she had her theories. What she needed was confirmation.

"Any word from our opposite numbers in the Union?" she asked.

"Zip," Reid replied. "It's like the whole thing never happened. That's why I thought you might be working on the story."

Malcolm sighed. "Looks like there is no story. Like I said, I'm here to do a prelim on whatever they brought back from the scene, maybe get flown out there, maybe listen in on your interview. Then I'm back to Houston. I'm just wondering why they bothered sending me up here if they plan on shipping everything back down to Texas."

Reid cast her a sideways glance. "No one's said anything about moving the prisoner."

"He's in a bad way?"

"Word is he's burnt up pretty bad."

The traffic had slowed to a torpid crawl. Reid confined his frustration to a growled murmur. Malcolm unwound her window and leaned out, peering into the distance. The air was warm against her face, a billow of pungent exhaust. She felt momentarily giddy, but couldn't make anything out past the long stretch of vehicles ahead. There was something unusual about the whole scenario, but she couldn't place it.

She said, "I thought it was fifteen minutes from the airport."

"Been like this since I arrived," Reid replied. "I'm going to try and turn off onto Park Avenue and see if it's any faster along Broad. We're not far away now."

That's it, she thought. Apart from the steady rumble of the cars, there was no other sound. Where were the car horns, the shouts of frustrated drivers?

"What's going on? What's causing the backup?"

"It'll be a troop convoy," Reid replied. "They've been shipping army from Louisiana and Florida since this whole thing started. There's a military aerodrome out near Fort Stewart and another by Hunter Field. Everyone seems to think that if push comes to shove, it's going to happen here."

"So no one's complaining."

"Let's just say no one here plans on giving Lincoln another Christmas present."

A gap had opened up and Reid swung the Hotspur onto Park. The surreal experience of the silent street and Reid's strange words set her wondering.

"Christmas present?"

"Back in the Civil War, General Sherman was marching toward the sea. He burnt Atlanta to the ground and everything else that stood in his path. When he seized Fort McAllister, the locals decided to evacuate Savannah. It saved the city. Just before Christmas, Sherman wired Lincoln a telegram offering Savannah as his gift."

Malcolm nodded.

"That's Forsythe Park coming up on the left."

She looked out at the lush green border of the park. The bronze statue of a soldier gazed confidently past her, facing the south.

"Is he from the war?" she asked distantly.

"Spanish–American War. He's post-bellum." Reid shook his head. "Last time North fought South, we had Carolina between us. This time, we're right on the firing line."

"It may not come to that," Malcolm offered.

"I ain't takin' bets."

The field office was on East Bryan Street. The occasional call of a ferry's horn reminded her that only a couple of blocks separated them from the bank of the Savannah River. The local Evidence Response Team was still going through the wreckage. Close proximity to Union waters had prevented any major dives around the site. The team leader told her that they'd just managed to get in and back out with a small amount of material. It might be a while before they had anything for her, he said apologetically.

The prisoner hadn't been brought in yet and, with both of them at a loss, Reid brought her to the roof of the building, at least affording a decent view of the city and the riverfront.

He leaned against the roof's balustrade with a cigarette in the corner of his mouth and told her about the Bravo compound in Louisiana. There'd been a firefight, short and sweet. He described Kennedy's men as being a scary bunch of fuckers and she could tell he was watching her face for a response. He spoke about the weapons they had seized, and how the prisoners had walked onto the trucks wearing the stony expressions of the dead. His cigarette bobbed in animated counterpoint to his cold recollections.

The prisoners were being sent to Alamogordo, New Mexico, as the director had suggested. The border. There they would be issued different weapons and expected to mount an early defence against the inevitable Mexican incursion. First at bat, first to go down.

"What's happening in Nevada?"

"Carter found the place half-empty. I heard his tac squads managed to round up a bunch of them in the desert last night. They're contained. Demobbing them might take a little longer, but they're getting the same deal." He almost sounded sad.

"Some of them fought Mexico before, though," Malcolm ventured. "Some of them were at Mazatlan."

"They had tanks then." A thoughtful pause. "They had Kennedy."

"You make that sound like it's a good thing." A nudge on Malcolm's part.

"Believe me, fuckhead that he's become, all he has to do is raise his standard against the North. God knows how many soldiers would still follow him."

"You served in the army..." It wasn't a question.

"My dad was a Ranger." Reid lit another cigarette. "Those poor fucks. If the Mexicans don't get them, the japs will."

The brief silence that followed might have been shared mourning in advance.

Reid asked, "Come up with anything interesting in your travels?"

It was back to shop talk, born of melancholy and boredom and not really expectant of a meaningful reply.

"Maybe," Malcolm said. She thought about the camps and what she'd found in Archives on the day of her interview with Webster. "Do you have a database here? The only decent one I've seen is back in Houston."

"You can access Houston from here. They'll flash up what you need in a jiffy."

"Any idea when we get to see the prisoner?" Malcolm asked. She felt the haze of the city upon her. She needed a shower.

"They're bringing him over from the infirmary any day now." Reid snorted.

"And he hasn't talked to anyone yet?"

"Hasn't talked, period."

In the distance, heat curled the skyline into a dream of cement and metal. Reid told her that heavy cloud cover and smoke from the smelters working overtime put a lid on the city. She let her thoughts roam in the warmth's narcotic mantle. Half an hour may have passed before Reid reached for the pager at his belt.

"Looks like my guest has arrived." He dealt her a look that was part invitation and part challenge.

"Point me in the right direction and I'll check out the database."

Reid smiled. "No problem."

The database was an ENIAC 12. Being a fairly advanced model, it only took up two rooms rather than the entire floor. She produced her ID and, after receiving the standard double-take, was pointed in the direction of an available terminal. She was told it would be free for the next hour or so.

She opened her bag and placed an envelope on the table before her. Within were a series of notes she'd used to outline her hypothesis—nothing she would dare commit to the database herself. Director

Webster's watchword gave him access to all of Camelot's files, and it was a safe assumption that he could view any information she cared to place on tape.

She'd left a copy of the notes with her sister for safekeeping.

She removed the punch cards she'd brought with her from Houston and looked over them one by one, calculating the algorithm she planned on assigning the ENIAC. Once she was satisfied, she punched the cards into the back of the terminal and waited. The screen flashed a working message. Behind the screen, along the back wall of the room, the tapes spooled on their racks and the ENIAC hummed a new cadence.

She had some time to kill so she picked up the phone and dialled the Houston office. She asked for the evidence lab and was put through to a tech she'd worked with previously. He confirmed that all her open cases had been doled out to the appropriate staff.

It was a secure line and he was in a talkative mood. He told her that the last word they'd received from the Kempei-Tai in New York, prior to the German occupation, was that the ballistics report on the Osakatown murders was on its way south. Forensics, however, already had a match on two sets of prints from the Mauser they'd recovered: Joseph Kennedy and Darren Morgan. A partial print, lifted from the barrel, was pending. The serial numbers on the pistol corresponded to one of the German firearms that Kennedy's men used instead of the standard Bureau Colts and Dillingers. The Kempei-Tai were sending the gun down as well.

Open and shut case.

She asked him why the Japanese Special Police had been so obliging with the evidence and he told her that the Japanese wanted Kennedy as badly as the Confederacy did. It looked as if Kennedy might have soured a deal with the Shogun prior to the fall of New York.

She asked him to flash her a copy of the ballistics report. She replaced the phone with a clatter that drew the eyes of the Bureau staff at the neighbouring terminals. She felt the threat of angry tears and held them off with gritted teeth. She glowered her neighbours down and returned to the computer screen.

Malcolm could buy a conspiracy theory or two, but wholesale murder? It seemed gauche. Just not his style, if such a word could be used to describe the man she once thought she'd known so well. On one hand there was the subtlety of Camelot, and on the other a series of bloody, undisguised slayings. Different departments had been assigned to separate aspects of the case but who was seeking the connection?

The screen flickered and then began to flash up a series of numbers. The funds allocated to Camelot. She went over the figures and checked them against her notes.

The cash discrepancy could be explained away, at least partially, by Japanese pay-offs. She checked out Joseph's business portfolios. Hughes Aeronautics hadn't made any money in two years. At least he wasn't guilty of embezzlement. He'd siphoned off at least two-hundred-thousand Confederate dollars into registered charities and only two of them were Bureau fronts.

She supposed that cash always moved sideways when it came to Bureau activities—par for the course. It was the men she couldn't account for. More than a thousand names, somehow lost within the folds of Camelot, somewhere between the camps that had been designated Alpha and Bravo.

Mindful of the fact that her data time was subject to the director's scrutiny, she pulled up a name. Roberts, G; negro, ex-engineer with the Tulsa Third Air Arm. Two consecutive five-year terms for arson and armed robbery. Sentence suspended 2010.

She picked three more names at random: Barrett, Davis and Stone. Stat rape, homicide, armed robbery. All were black, all had criminal records and all had their sentences suspended sometime in 2010. While they had all previously served under Major Kennedy's command, none had received the specialised training afforded to the men in Nevada or Louisiana. They were cut from a different cloth.

She ran off copies for her files.

If she could put aside all the emotional baggage associated with Joseph, she might be left with a believable theory that tied both of these bastards together. If she could just put it all aside…

She was struck by a thought. She drew a deep breath and called for one of the ENIAC operators.

"Do you have an Atlas program?"

He nodded, and disappeared through a doorway. Moments later he returned with a new set of punch cards, asking, "What can I rack up for you? Need a CSA search?"

"World-wide."

"Agent Malcolm, I'm sorry, but you only have half an hour left on this terminal."

"It shouldn't take that long—I think I know what I'm looking for." She looked at him, capitalising on the lustre anger had left in her eyes, urging him on with the curve of her smile. "I'm sorry to trouble you. I'm not very good at this, you know. My watchword is playing up. Would you mind logging on for me? I promise I won't be more than twenty minutes."

He hesitated for a moment, then leaned over her keyboard. "No problems," he said.

He tapped in his code while Malcolm made a show of looking away. He said, "I've timed you in, so you behave yourself."

"Operator, did you just wink at me?"

"Got something in my eye, is all."

She held the smile till he walked away.

"Let's see now," she murmured to herself. "Lost boys go to Never Never Land."

It had been Joseph's way of sweet-talking her when he had to leave town for a few days, for when he disappeared. Briefly, she'd considered the possibility of another woman. She almost smiled to herself, thinking, *He could barely handle me*. Then she thought, *I could give a damn.*

She tapped an entry on the keyboard. "Never Never Land" produced no results. She thought about it and typed in "Never Land".

Three results. Never in Amur, Siberia; Never Delay, Belize, in Mexico; and the Never Sumner Mountains in Colorado. Siberia was right out. Mexico and Colorado were possibilities, but only if he'd been double-dealing back then, and she found it hard enough to accept that he was double-dealing now.

She searched her memory for the reference. Peter Pan. Never Never Land was supposed to be an island of some sort anyway.

She checked her watch, ten minutes left on the terminal.

"Second star on the right..." Staring at the watch's face till the hands blurred before her eyes. "And straight on till morning."

She typed in another entry and got a Peter Pan Park in Emporia, Kansas.

I'm going insane. Comet tails...

A smile dawned on her face and she typed in one last name.

"Morning Star" yielded nine results: one in Western Cape, South

Afrika; the rest on American soil. There were two Morning Stars in North Carolina and another in Virginia and Mississippi. Four in Arkansas… She did a county search and came up with Garland, Greene, Phillips and Searcy. She wrote the names down in her notes. She looked up to see the operator beaming down at her.

"Found what you were after?"

The interrogation room, aka "the Box", took up a small corner of the floor. The rest of the room was partitioned off with low felt-lined dividers that might occasionally provide an agent with the illusion of privacy. A red light above the Box's door indicated that the room was in use. Malcolm made her way to the observation room next door.

"'Scuse me, sister. You lost?" An agent stepped up and took her arm firmly at the elbow. His jacket was off and his Colt slapped against his shirt within its holster.

She freed her arm with a deft motion and flashed her badge. She gave him her sweetest smile. "Get me a coffee, black and strong. One sugar. If anyone has updates on the wreck, I'll be in the obs room or the Box."

There was a murmur of laughter from the adjacent cubicles and the agent moved off sheepishly.

There were two more agents in the obs room. She showed them her badge before either could open his mouth and waited for them to leave.

On the other side of the two-way mirror, a man sat in the facing chair with his head slumped to the table on folded arms. His head was heavily bandaged. Tufts of singed brown hair protruded from gaps where the dressing had come loose. She watched as one of his hands snaked across the table to a bottle. He poured into a glass with shaking hands, downed the shot, and let his head fall back on his arms.

There was a soft footfall behind her.

Still staring at the glass, she asked, "How much has he had?"

"That'll be his second." Reid had a coffee cup in his hand. "I assume you're the 'witch-queen' that's taken up residence in obs, so I reckon this is for you."

"In the flesh." She accepted the cup with a small bow. "I get coffee and he gets bourbon."

"Whisky, actually. Working the case alone means I get to play good cop and bad cop. What do you think of his story?"

"I just got here," Malcolm replied. "But he's guilty. Has he called for a lawyer yet?"

Reid looked through the two-way and chuckled softly. "Asleep already? Bad for him. What makes you so sure?"

"If the perp's innocent, he's wide awake. He's looking at the doors, the ceiling … the mirror. If he's asleep, he's already given up. He just doesn't know it yet."

"Our guy says he hasn't slept in three nights."

"Me neither." Malcolm gave the Box another glance. "Who is he?"

"Roy Newcombe. Says he's a flier with the 15th Bomber Group."

"Are they a local outfit?"

"Baton Rouge," Reid replied.

"He's a long way from home. What's his story?"

"Short version? He reckons he was on his way to New Orleans via the *Shenandoah*."

"Now where have I heard that name?" Malcolm spoke more to herself than to her colleague.

"That was the airship the japs impounded on its way out of New York City. He says that Kennedy was on board." Reid was smiling like the cat who caught the canary.

"Bingo."

"It gets better. He says he was offered a pay-off to help fly Kennedy's crew off the airship." Reid raised a hand to ward off any interruption. "There were two other confed pilots on board. They flew them off on some supply planes that the *Shenandoah* had in her hangar. They split into three groups. He took two characters named Hardas and Morgan, but doesn't remember the way the others paired off."

"David Hardas and Darren Morgan," Malcolm said softly. Morgan's prints had been lifted from the gun in New York. He certainly got around. Could he have been the shooter? *Let's see now, the mild-mannered historian versus the soldier-king.* She only clutched at the hope for a moment.

"There's this dogfight just off New York City," Reid continued, "japs and huns. The crew split up, and our guy makes for a German carrier group out in the Atlantic somewhere."

"Now think carefully, Agent Reid: did he tell you all this before or after you gave him the bottle?"

"German 5th is operating somewhere off eastern coastal waters." Reid shrugged. "I'm just telling you what he said. They spend two days with the group and then this guy—Hardas, right? He's ex-navy—somehow he steals the captain's gig off a carrier, for Christ's sake, and they head south."

Malcolm whistled through her teeth. "Did he have any of the cash on him?"

"He had nothing. Says he lost everything during the battle."

"Ah, the battle."

"They didn't have enough fuel to get to Savannah so Hardas was all for stealing another boat."

"And our guy?"

"Hell, our guy's a regular hero. He tried to call it off. But…" Reid held his hands out, palms up. "There were two of them. What could he do?"

Malcolm nodded and sipped the coffee.

Reid continued, "Thing is, the boat they tried to take was armed."

"They attacked a navy ship?"

"Uh-uh. Fishing boat. Newcombe reckons they might have been jap smugglers."

Malcolm put down her cup. "Do we have any corroboration from the coastguard?"

"Not yet. I've got some guys checking it out."

"Any other survivors? Any sign of Hardas or Morgan?"

"We've got five bodies in the morgue. Pretty badly burned. ME's working on them."

"What a terrible shame." Malcolm pursed her lips. "The snaps I've seen of their boat show some fairly rudimentary changes to the superstructure, an effort to make her silhouette less recognisable. A one-man job, which supports Hardas's presence on the vessel."

Reid's look was appreciative.

Malcolm turned back to peer through the two-way. Newcombe hadn't moved. "We need a positive ID on this guy."

"His file is being flashed up from Louisiana. It could arrive any time."

"It's good to know that at least *one* of us is having a productive day."

Reid cracked his knuckles. "Hell, I'm just getting started."

"Have you said anything to the director yet?" She made the question sound careless.

"You don't call the director till you have everything, Agent Malcolm. Words to live by."

"I'll keep that in mind, Agent Reid." Malcolm's brow creased momentarily before she continued. "Do you have any OPR up here, working the story?"

"National Security." Reid gave her a look. "And you."

"How does this sound? You said it was a Japanese fishing boat? The smugglers are Union boys, yakuza-linked, and moving weapons north out of Savannah. Hardas and Morgan, seeing the error of their ways, get wind of this somehow and with the help of a brave airman..."

"I like where this is going."

"I like it better than the story your guy is spinning us."

"It plays out. I'll have someone get to work on it."

"Let me know if you need a hand. I'm going to give it another couple of hours or so, but after that I'm moving on."

Reid's eyes flashed. "Got a lead?"

She wondered what to call the idea that was forming in her mind. She said, "I've got something."

"Tell you what, you can join me in the Box while you wait."

She gave him her smile and said, "Agent Reid, I don't want to interfere."

Reid smiled. "Truth of the matter is, I think the other agents might feel safer with you out of the office."

She laughed, saying, "I do hate causing a fuss."

"I'm starting to think that it's one of the things you do best."

She was thinking about Joseph, thinking about Arkansas. She let a slight blush rise to her cheeks and said, "Now who have you been talking to?"

He led her to the prisoner.

V

April 25, 2012
Nashville, Tennessee

There had been fires to the south of the city. The sun was a low, brown smear on the asphalt sky. Rain was predicted, but the heavens offered no intimation of the future. Ash danced slow in the still air and Kennedy kept walking.

He'd spent an hour in Watanabe's room, taking advantage of the gangster's absence to make a thorough inventory of its contents. He'd found a printout of available flights to Memphis on the bedside table by the phone. He'd found the shreds of a hotel stationery envelope on the bed and a loaded Shingen automatic, its safety off, tucked between the mattress and the wall. The creases in the flight list didn't match the envelope.

Watanabe had said he'd be an hour or so, ninety minutes at the most. If he hadn't been late at the border station, Kennedy might have let it go. If he hadn't kept them waiting at the truck stop, Kennedy might not have been so curious about the missing letter. Watanabe had told them, "Wait till I get back," but sitting there in that empty room, watching the empty minutes slip past, Kennedy's wandering mind provided him with too many ways that things might have gone sour.

So he kept walking.

They were half a block behind him, the phone booth was just up ahead. They had to be Watanabe's men. Yakuza. He'd spotted them across the street from the hotel as he was leaving, unable to make any of them for the driver who'd brought him across the border. They followed him with shuffling steps, colliding with each other as they walked, laughing.

They couldn't touch him on the street. Not this far south. They stumbled to a halt as he pushed open the booth's door. He threw them a glance. Their awkward poses suggested a moment's uncertainty, then one of them drew a packet of cigarettes from his leather kimono and they all lit up, crowding around the thin licks of flame.

He picked up the phone and dialled Kobe's New Jersey number. The call timed out. He slotted more coins and dialled Chicago. No answer.

He started walking back to the hotel. Watanabe had chosen a shabby district of town for their sanctuary. There was a bar across the road. A series of dilapidated shopfronts lined the narrow concourse. Notices in faded script advertised businesses long gone. Anything of any value had shifted uptown. Nashville had grown up and away from these worn streets.

Watanabe's men were engaged in a heated discussion as he approached. Startled, they parted swiftly, each taking a sudden absorbed interest in a shop's display or the pattern of cracks in the sidewalk. He stopped and stood among them, letting their discomfort buoy his spirits. He followed the motion of their abruptly upturned faces and his eyes fell on Watanabe, standing before the hotel's façade. His face was a glowering mask.

Kennedy approached him, keeping his pace to a saunter now, his hands in his pockets jangling the remainder of coins and stolen bullets.

"I've heard many things about you of late, boss," Watanabe said, "but no one bothered to tell me that you'd become a fool."

"I don't need someone to tell me you've sold us out."

Watanabe made a complicated gesture with one of his hands. Kennedy heard three guttural replies from behind, but did not turn around.

"Where's the captain?" Watanabe asked.

"In his room, where I left him."

"Good." Watanabe scanned the street. "Shall we continue this inside, or do you want to stay out here in plain sight?"

Kennedy thought about Watanabe's goons. At least Lightholler was upstairs. He said, "After you."

They mounted the staircase in silence. Kennedy had made no attempt to disguise his search and Watanabe acknowledged the room's rearrangement with a grunt. Kennedy leaned against the far wall, his arms crossed loosely under his jacket. He watched as Watanabe picked up a bottle of rice wine from the dressing table and poured the pale liquid into two glasses. He offered one in Kennedy's direction.

"No, thanks."

Watanabe replaced the glass on the dresser. He drank from his own, leaning against the opposite wall in casual mimicry of Kennedy. He said, "So."

"So."

"If you're going to use that gun, you'd best do so now."

Kennedy let the gun slip back into the holster and brought his hands out from under his jacket, palms open.

"What are you packing these days?" Watanabe asked lightly.

"A Mauser, if anything."

Watanabe nodded towards Kennedy's shoulder. "That's no Mauser."

Kennedy pulled out the pistol.

"Ah," Watanabe said, smiling. "A Beretta."

Kennedy nodded. He held the gun lightly now, his hand away from the grip.

"Never use one myself," Watanabe said. "Only really good for close work. And even then…" His voice trailed off.

Kennedy placed the pistol on the window ledge.

"Apologies for my rudeness outside," Watanabe continued, "but that dye job and beard would fool only the most uninterested of observers."

Kennedy stroked the stubble at his chin. "I'm making the best of a bad situation."

"By walking down Main Street? I told you to stay here."

"Where the hell *were* you?"

There was a brief silence, breached only by Watanabe's delicate sips of wine. The sips became mouthfuls. He topped up his glass and said, "I wonder where I should start."

"Your driver," Kennedy said. "Why did you get rid of him?"

"For your protection. Too late, sadly, to be of any benefit."

They were talking quietly. It was unlikely that Lightholler heard anything unless he was pressed up against the door.

"I saw the flight list and the envelope," Kennedy said. "I couldn't find the letter. I've been wondering what changed between Pleasant Valley and here. I'm wondering if you even tried to arrange our flight."

"I think you know the answer to that," Watanabe said softly.

"I'd like to hear your reasons. But for the sake of everything we've been through, tell me, is this something you're going to handle yourself, or are you just keeping me busy till the rest of your boys arrive?"

The Beretta lay on the window's ledge beside him. Good for close work, but even then…

"This is my responsibility and it's a simple matter," Watanabe said. "But not as simple as you might have supposed. Only one of us is going to leave this room alive."

It was hard to believe that this was where it ended. Kennedy recalled the fear he'd experienced at the border crossing, sealed in the Cadillac's cargo hold. Where was that feeling now?

He said, "I'll have some of that wine now."

"My driver had hidden affiliations with Shimamura."

"Shimamura works the southeast coast. I've dealt with his people before."

"He is now aware that I—that Kobe's Family—had you under protection. My driver made the call while we were changing cars." Watanabe took another mouthful of wine and licked his lips. "He told me that before I killed him."

"Cold comfort."

"Shimamura knows that we arranged to get you across the border. As a result of your little adventure just now, he probably knows you're in Nashville."

Kennedy shrugged. "Does that matter now?"

The Beretta might not stop Watanabe, but it could slow him down. How long would it take Lightholler to get into the room? Were Watanabe's men just outside the door?

"Not all the Families are as open-minded as ours about your dealings with the Shogun."

"What dealings?"

"Please," Watanabe said, "the least you can do is speak plainly with me. Not *everything* went up in flames when the Germans took New York."

Kennedy brought the wine to his lips. He nodded, urging Watanabe on.

"You struck a deal with the Shogun, that much is certain." Watanabe shook his head. "The fact that Hideyoshi entertained Imperial aspirations, that he desired the Chrysanthemum Throne, was one of the worst-kept secrets in the Shogunate, but it was a secret. Do you understand this?" Watanabe was keeping his hands visible and low. He'd made no move for the Shingen. "We have suspected your involvement for some time now."

The Shogun's representative had intimated as much at their last meeting: that certain yakuza Families would move with them when Hideyoshi challenged the Emperor. But if Kobe had been involved, why was this such an issue now?

"Has Kobe been called before the Imperial court?" Kennedy asked.

"It's only a matter of time," Watanabe replied. "Hideyoshi's honourable death by *seppuku*..." He gave Kennedy a curious look. "Ah, you didn't know that. His death and this war change everything. I expected you to have a better understanding of the people you'd been dealing with." His voice held a measure of disgust. It was the trace of pity in his demeanour that Kennedy couldn't place. "Let me just say this. Whatever role you played on the Shogun's behalf will enter the realm of mythology."

"Mythology?"

"Hideyoshi and Ryuichi trace their lineage to the first Mikado, to the birth of history ... the Gods themselves." Watanabe poured himself another glass of wine. He swayed slightly before the dressing table. "The Gods themselves. You, me, Kobe—we're mortal. They dice with us, use us as they will. It's always been that way." He waved his hand dismissively and continued. "But a God has fallen. Hideyoshi is dead by his own hand. This means that he now sits by the throne of Jimmu in the Heavens.

"And you? You're in the shit. You've lost your benefactor. You've lost your friends. A single moment has reduced you from Deity's agent to traitor, and how many men have died for the whim of a god?" Watanabe drained the glass with a single, swift toss. "You're in the shit, and I..." He slammed the glass onto the table. "I have come to my decision."

Watanabe was only a few feet away now. He peered at his own reflection in the mirror above the dressing table. He brought a hand up to his face, touching the skin around his eyes. He broke into a dazzling golden smile.

Kennedy inched towards the window, saying, "You believe all this?"

"I do and I don't. It doesn't matter what I believe, so long as I have belief." Watanabe's chuckle issued from the edge of madness. "It's your lack of faith that led you to this place. But here's where we stand. That letter was from Kobe, of course." Watanabe turned to face him. "The money you gave me will be returned to your estate after the other Families have received their cut. I'm to deliver your head to Shimamura by morning."

"What about Lightholler?"

"Nothing was said."

Kennedy had the Beretta angled at the floor between Watanabe's feet.

Watanabe laughed out loud. He raised a hand, gesturing for Kennedy to stop, to wait a moment. With his other hand he held his chest as the laughter faded away.

"You understand," Watanabe said. "Even if you were my brother..."

A sudden deft movement and his left hand snapped back and forth. If it wasn't for the silver blade in his grasp, he might not have appeared to have moved at all.

Kennedy raised the Beretta in a swift arc even as Watanabe dropped to his knees. He'd reversed the blade. Its tip was now pressed between the folds of his kimono.

Kennedy stepped forwards, bringing the gun's barrel to his temple.

"Please," Watanabe said through gritted teeth, "you'll ruin my concentration."

"Put the blade down."

"Is there no end to your ignorance?"

"*Put the blade down.*"

"Your neck or my intestines," Watanabe said. He inched the blade deeper to expose the flat board of his abdomen.

"What the fuck is going on here?" Lightholler stood in the open doorway, blinking.

"There's a gun in my bag," Kennedy said, without looking back. "Bring it."

His entire world was at the end of his Beretta. Each fine strand of Watanabe's hair, each individual pore. An artery pulsed its tortuous course under pale golden skin.

"You're not going to make him—"

"*Get the fucking gun.*"

They sat cross-legged in the centre of the room; Watanabe's blade lay on the carpet between them. Kennedy had the Mauser by his side while Lightholler balanced the Beretta in his hand. He gazed at Kennedy's gun with a look of deliberation before placing his own on the ground.

"It is a peculiar irony when an enemy offers the opportunity for honour." Watanabe's voice was thick, the words came slowly. As if he'd already crossed some threshold.

Kennedy nodded.

"Kobe broke his promise of sanctuary. I won't break mine. Kill myself, and I avoid the task of your disposal." Watanabe paused. "Shimamura's men will be here soon and I don't care to witness their arrival. You should go now."

"Come with us," Lightholler said.

Watanabe's response was a low growl. "They will arrive at dawn, and expect to find you sleeping in your room. Me in mine."

Kennedy told himself he was talking to a dead man. He said, "Car keys."

Watanabe withdrew them from a pocket. He placed them next to the sword. "Change cars as soon as possible."

Lightholler rose from the floor slowly. "I don't want any part of this."

"Those men you had outside," Kennedy said, reaching for the keys.

"One is watching the corridor, the others are with the car. They'll let you pass."

There was the faint rumble of thunder, dim and distant, more felt than heard. Watanabe glanced towards the window.

Kennedy fought the urge to pursue Lightholler's approach, to show further disrespect to the yakuza. "Will it take you long to pack?" he asked Lightholler.

"Done."

He looked back at Watanabe. He couldn't resist a final gesture. He said, "You told me I had no benefactors left, no friends. You were wrong."

"Leaving you to Shimamura is no act of kindness. A better friend might have killed you," Watanabe replied. "I was speaking of something else."

Lightholler said, "Let's go."

Another boom of thunder, louder now. Kennedy walked to the window and sniffed at the air. Ash and the scent of distant fire but nothing more. He said, "Tell me."

"There's not much to say."

"Tell me."

"There was a battle at sea. A German boat engaged a smuggling vessel off the South Carolina coast."

Kennedy felt a sense of dread rising from within.

Lightholler said, "This doesn't involve us."

Kennedy silenced him with an open palm.

"We do business in Savannah," Watanabe continued. "It's close enough to the border, and information is the currency of the day, so..." He sighed heavily. "This I heard in passing. Enemies of the state, previously associated with yourself, died defending the South. Does this mean anything to you?"

"Who?"

"Hardas. Morgan." Watanabe shrugged. His eyes returned to the blade.

Lightholler said, "I'm sorry, Joseph."

Kennedy turned and let himself into his room. Bars of yellow brightness spilled onto the ceiling through half-closed blinds. He felt along the wall for the light switch, flicked it, and observed the chandelier rocking slowly from side to side. He walked over to the window and parted the blinds. The odd star winked back through a pall of low cloud. No rain, but a plume of smoke rising in the distance.

He leaned out the window. Two plumes of smoke.

He heard the thunderous rolling crash again, closer, and the sill trembled beneath his hands. Somewhere, a siren began its plaintive wail.

Hardas. Morgan.

He walked into the bathroom and caught his face in the mirror. His hand scrabbled across the sink, closing on the razor he'd used earlier. He reached for soap and ran the water and scrubbed the soap into his beard. His image shuddered momentarily, then corrected itself.

Lightholler called from the other room.

He ran the blade over the gristle of his beard in long sweeps. Struck the blade sharply against the sink and then ran it back up under the curve of his chin to his lower lip. He splashed cold water over his face. The smile that answered his was thin and cruel.

When he re-entered Watanabe's room he saw Lightholler standing by the exit, holding the Beretta in one hand and the satchel in the other. Watanabe stood in the centre of the room; his sword lay in two pieces on the ground before him.

Lightholler had an unlit cigarette in his mouth. He slid an arm out of his jacket and made a show of slinging the satchel over his shoulder before replacing the sleeve. He said, "Watanabe thinks Shimamura's men are blowing up hotels."

"Crude," Kennedy said. "Definitive. I'm in the mood to deal with it."

"So much for honour." The gangster picked up one of the broken pieces of sword and, examining it, said, "They told me dawn." He went to the table, grabbed the wine bottle and emptied it with a toss of his head. "And this is how they come for you." He spat on the floor.

"I hope the Families will understand," he said, raising the splintered remains of the sword, "why this now goes in Shimamura's heart."

"Your Shingen's where you left it." Kennedy reached into his pockets. "Here are the bullets."

"Give it to the captain." Watanabe stooped to one knee and drew another Shingen from his ankle holster. "He'll need more than a Beretta."

Kennedy removed the pistol from behind the mattress and turned it over in his hands. He loaded it and rocked the grip in the palm of his hand. He handed it to Lightholler.

The next explosion rocked the room.

Kennedy drew his Mauser and released the safety. "Let's go."

"The staircase leads to the lobby and out the main entrance. Another set of stairs takes you down to the garage, otherwise there are three more exits via the kitchen, laundry and staff quarters." Watanabe pointed down the length of the corridor. "Fire escape at the bottom opens out back."

"What about the roof?" Kennedy asked.

"Too far from the other buildings. Too exposed."

"Then we take the stairs." Kennedy scanned the corridor. "Where's your man?"

"If he's not dead, I'll kill him myself." Watanabe led them towards the staircase.

"I smell smoke. Close by," Lightholler said. "Why explosives?"

"They want to be sure," Watanabe said. "It's been done in the past. Nothing on this scale, though."

Voices raised in fright or anger came weakly from behind closed doors. The siren's wail had peaked to a crescendo and now there was the sharp crack of sporadic gunfire that might have been coming from anywhere. Lightholler gave Watanabe an enquiring look.

Watanabe shrugged.

"Unless Shimamura got his hands on a recoilless rifle, or rockets, whatever his men are up to has to be close range," Kennedy said. "Small arms means the police might be involved, maybe even the military. That, or his crew needs to secure a perimeter before planting any more explosives."

"These guys aren't soldiers," Lightholler said.

"Just telling you how I'd go about it."

"What a misfortune to see such terrible times." Watanabe had the broken shard of his sword in one hand and his Shingen in the other.

A door to their left opened and a woman, hair damp in rollers, stared out. Catching a glimpse of Watanabe, she crossed herself furiously and slammed the door shut again.

Watanabe sniggered, securing his blade to the sash of his kimono. "The japs are coming."

"That's what everyone'll think." Kennedy scowled. They'd reached the stairs. It was two flights down to the lobby. Close by, they heard the sound of pounding footsteps, but no one was in sight. "Where's the car?"

"In front of the hotel."

Shattering glass and more screams from below. A door burst open behind them and Kennedy saw a man emerge from one of the rooms. He almost bowled them over before they had a chance to bring up their guns. He was through them and taking the stairs two and three at a time.

Kennedy moved to follow but Watanabe had his sleeve.

"Too late for him," Watanabe said. "He'll draw them out."

Kennedy's attempt to break the gangster's grip was perfunctory.

"Wait," Watanabe said. He caught Kennedy's glance, smiled, and said, "Please."

The man disappeared from view. There was the clatter of desperate feet on tiles, then the sound came back up the staircase. Kennedy shoved Watanabe and Lightholler behind him with an outstretched arm. "Get back."

The man reappeared a flight below, legs spread mid-stride, spine arched back and arms flung wide like a runner at the finish line. He was swept forwards by the salvo of bullets, leaving a smear of blood on the wall as he struck it and crumpled to the floor.

"Such a misfortune."

"Down," Kennedy ordered. He dropped to one knee and Watanabe and Lightholler fell in behind him. All three had their pistols trained above the man's corpse.

The staircase shuddered beneath the rushed scramble of many feet.

"*Now.*"

Heads jerked into view. Four men in black suits, their black hair slick and tied back tight and high. The first volley hit them chest level, an invisible wall that held back their frenzied movements. One fired his automatic repeatedly into his shoes. The second volley dropped them onto the landing.

"There'll be more," Watanabe murmured, surveying the carnage.

"I know."

"Look at their hair, what's left of it. Topknots."

"Shimamura's men," Kennedy said. "How's the corridor?"

Lightholler's head swung back and forth. "It's clear."

"How many more down there, you think?" Kennedy asked.

"Six, maybe seven," Watanabe replied. "A few more watching the back exit. That's if they're taking out all the hotels along the strip."

"They've got explosives, they're in the building, they know they've got us," Lightholler said. "We have to move now."

The muzzle of a machine-pistol poked tentatively into view on the landing, followed by another Topknot. Watanabe put a bullet between his eyes.

"Okay," Kennedy said. "We take the fire escape. John, cover the stairs." Kennedy rose from his crouch, turned to Watanabe. "You take the left, I'll take the right."

He ran to the first door and kicked it open. Empty. Ran to the next and kicked it. It swung on loose hinges to reveal a couple: young, white, arms around each other, cowering on the nearer of two beds. "You, out now. The fire escape. This place is about to blow."

"What the fuck are you doing?" Watanabe shouted at him.

"Take the left side."

"Crazy fucker."

Watanabe ran to the first door on his left and crashed into it. Yelled and crashed it open with the second blow. "Some crazy fuck wants to save your lives," he shouted. "Get out now."

There were more shots from the staircase.

"Captain?"

Lightholler was face down on the landing.

"John?"

"I'm out, throw me your gun."

Kennedy tossed his Mauser down the hallway. He heard more blasts from behind him and didn't look back. There were four more doors between him and the fire escape, seven people were crowded round it.

"Go, go, *go*."

Further encouragement was unnecessary as the dull thud of a detonation swayed the corridor.

"These are empty, you crazy, crazy fuck." Watanabe was laughing.

Kennedy checked the last door. "We're clear."

Down the corridor Lightholler was clicking on empty.

"John, get over here."

Watanabe rammed another clip into his Shingen. The last of the civilians had taken the fire escape.

"John. Over here. *Now.*"

Lightholler was on his feet and running. A hail of bullets smashed the top of the stair where he'd crouched moments ago. He ran low, careening side to side along the hallway. His foot snagged a tear in the carpet and he tumbled forwards, Watanabe firing over his head. The discharge in the narrow passage was deafening.

Two Topknots fell away from the landing in a heap, one crashing through the banister, a blood-chilling scream wrenched from his throat.

Lightholler, back on his feet, was steps away. Kennedy leapt forwards, grabbed his extended arm and yanked him towards the fire escape. Lightholler stumbled down the concrete stairs.

"Too many." Watanabe's tortured exhalation. "Not just Shimamura's crew."

Four Topknots were now on the opposite landing. Kennedy grabbed the back of Watanabe's kimono. The gangster brushed his hand away, thrusting Kennedy backwards.

"Go."

Watanabe twisted and Kennedy saw a dark stain spread where his hand had been. Watanabe was falling back onto the concrete.

Kennedy caught him in one arm and slammed the door of the fire escape shut behind them. He took the gun from Watanabe's wavering grip and fired twice into the lock. Counted to three and emptied the rest of the clip through the door. Lightholler was clambering back up the stairs. He took Watanabe's legs as Kennedy slung his arms under the man's shoulders.

"I'm never wrong." Watanabe was smiling, and the gold of his teeth was ruby-tinted. Spittle of blood marked the corners of his mouth. "You're a crazy fuck."

Lightholler took point and they staggered down the two flights in darkness, Watanabe swaying between them. Kennedy felt the jagged end of the yakuza's blade coursing along the surface of his thigh.

There was a splintering crash from above, then another. The Topknots were almost through.

Below, streetlight cast crazy shadows against the landing. Beams of torchlight probed the stairwell. Kennedy's holstered Shingen slapped uselessly against his chest. Shifting the bulk of Watanabe's weight, he struggled to unsheathe the broken blade. A curtain of sweat filled his eyes.

"Police." A voice cried out from below. "You okay?"

"Above us," Lightholler yelled. "More of them above us."

Men poured into the fire escape from below. Nashville's finest. One joined Kennedy in supporting Watanabe's back. His head lolled under the folds of Kennedy's jacket.

"You okay, bud?" the officer asked.

"Better now," Kennedy replied hoarsely. "The place is mined. Kennedy's holed up there. Jap bodyguards."

"Kennedy?" An anxious expression flickered across the officer's face. "Fall back, for Christ's sake," he shouted to his men. "Fall back. Resume your positions."

A press of bodies hemmed them in a tight crush. Kennedy felt Watanabe being prised away from his grip. The scent of sweat and panic and blood was a tide engulfing him.

A shove and he was out on the street.

Pressure against the back of his legs and he was on the ground.

Someone's knee held him to the pavement, his face rubbing against gravel.

Someone's gun lodged itself firmly at the base of his skull.

VI

April 25, 2012
Morning Star, Arkansas

Shine worked his way down from the roadside to a line of tall trees. He was on the edge of a gentle slope. The woodland fell in a grand sweep towards darkness. He had been here a number of times with the major, but only once at night, and that time they had arrived by light aircraft, skirting the tree tops in moonlight before dropping onto the private airstrip.

Nothing about this place was familiar now.

Twin beams of light swung across the branches of the nearest trees. He crouched down and let his palms rest against the thin topsoil. The truck crunched along the unpaved road behind him; a low rumbled echo of its passing that was swallowed by the night. He rose to his feet slowly. He examined his watch. It was almost three days to the hour, and many miles, since they'd all parted company over the Atlantic.

Behind him, the foothills of the Ouachita Mountains climbed into the black jagged horizon. A road sign informed him that Lake Hamilton lay somewhere past the next turn-off. The ranch would be beyond the next valley. Instinct suggested that the front door might not be the most advisable form of entry.

He spent the next hour working his way steadily through the undergrowth. He crossed wide paddocks, approaching a line of foliage that marked one edge of a wide, flat clearing: the ranch's landing field. Trees stretched out along both sides of the runway. A rustle of unseen leaves carried the breeze, punctuated now and then by the sharp crack of canvas. Shine tracked the sound to the outline of a small crop-duster secured beneath a tarpaulin.

An ethereal glow, distant and dim, swathed the ranch house. The evening had conjured a thin mist. Lamplight poured through it. He strained his ears, catching only the sounds of the night.

Two shadows bounded out of the darkness.

He dropped to the ground.

Growls slashed the dark. If Shine didn't know better, he'd have made them for lions. Rhodesian ridgebacks. It took less than a moment for the dogs to catch his scent. He fought the instinct to scramble into the undergrowth. They would harry him till he dropped.

He didn't bother with his blade. He kept still.

There was a blast of fetid breath. He kept still.

A torch beam swept over him. Cantered. Caught his blinking eyes.

"*Ayusta*." The command issued from the shadows. The dogs drew back.

Shine moved slowly. He rolled up a sleeve to reveal his tattoo. Torchlight played over it.

"*Lechi u wo*."

The dogs vanished.

A ghost dancer slid out of the night. He held the torch in one hand, a pistol, waist high, in the other. "*Nituwe he*?"

Shine said, "I don't speak Lakota."

The ghost dancer examined his tattoo, a splayed red hand, the index finger surmounted with a small triangle. He slid the pistol into a holster. "Come inside."

He led Shine up to the ranch house. The dogs trotted along at his heels.

The doorway opened into a small dining area. A candle flickered on the kitchen bench beside the remains of a meal. An ivory-shaded lantern on a table by the wall offered its own trickle of light.

Shine turned to the ghost dancer and asked, "Where are the others?"

VII

April 25, 2012
Savannah, Georgia

The Box contained a table, three chairs, an ashtray. No windows. The bottle was long gone, along with Newcombe's glass. The two-way mirror ran along a third of the back wall, close to the single doorway that opened into the chamber and as far away from Newcombe's seat as was humanly possible.

She'd heard that the Box was where rookie agents cut their teeth. She'd heard that they ran it three to five degrees warmer in summer and a darn sight colder in winter. Heard that the perp's chair wasn't built for comfort and the phone books weren't there for looking up numbers. Each field office had an interrogation room and each Box held its own share of mythology.

Five years of Evidence Response had brought every possible rumour to Malcolm's notice and from all that time she had been able to glean one truth amongst the chaff. Each Box held one exit, and it wasn't necessarily as obvious as the way in.

Lost in her own thoughts, she found herself missing scraps of the interview. It was a dance of words, and caught in her own suspicions she had difficulty following the twists and turns of Reid's inquiry.

Reid had given her a series of photographs and asked her to work her way through them while making the odd notation on a pad he'd provided for her. He'd asked her to lay them out on the table when she'd finished with them. The photographs were mostly aerial shots, the detail was poor—flotsam around the half-submerged remains of the German vessel—but Newcombe wasn't to know that. Reid had thrown in a couple of photographs of the bodies for good measure. Charred, unrecognisable imitations of human beings that had been taken prior to letting the MEs get down to business.

Newcombe hadn't batted an eyelid, but he was talking now. His bandage had loosened further and seemed to be held to his head by a clot of matted hair and blood. Though one of his arms remained wrapped in gauze, she had the impression that his burn injuries might have been overestimated. He winced as he spoke. She focused in.

"You're calling me an enemy combatant?"

"You were in the company of known conspirators," Reid replied. "What else should we call you?"

"Am I under arrest?"

"Why? Have you committed a crime? Maybe I should get you a lawyer."

Reid pushed himself out of the chair. He glanced at Malcolm and snarled, "Come on, let's see what Morgan's had to say. They should be through with him by now."

Newcombe opened his mouth as if to speak.

Reid waited for a long moment. A cold smile formed on his lips. He gestured towards the door.

She waited till they were clear of the Box to speak, but before she could say anything Reid was talking.

"He doesn't know the others are dead. I thought it was worth a shot."

"The Prisoner's Dilemma?"

"Like he doesn't have enough problems."

Reid's expression was blank and she didn't feel like explaining the reference.

They were back in the observation room. She'd left the photographs on the table and they watched as Newcombe sifted through them. He kept returning to the same shot. It was difficult to say from the angle but Malcolm thought it may have been one of the cadavers. She said, "He's definitely lying."

"Everyone lies," Reid replied. "We just need to know if he's lying more than usual. Four hours in there with him and I've got nothing but a headache. Says he can't remember what happened in New York before boarding the *Shenandoah*, says he has no idea where Morgan and Hardas were headed."

"I checked with 15th Bomber, Baton Rouge," Malcolm offered.

"Neither Tucker nor Rose have signed on yet, but they aren't due in till the twenty-sixth."

Reid nodded distantly.

"Do we know for a fact that these guys weren't working with Kennedy in New York?"

"Nope. Nor can we question any of the pilots' KAs. This has to stay under wraps."

"How long can we hold him?"

"As long as we like," Reid replied. "What are you thinking?"

"You haven't got confirmation on his ID yet, have you?"

"Pending." Reid scowled. "We don't have positives on any of the stiffs either."

She thought about her call to the evidence lab in Houston. "What about prints?"

"You need fingers if you want prints."

Malcolm suppressed a flinch. "I'm talking about our guy."

"*Our* guy isn't under arrest."

"But we can hold him as long as we like?" Malcolm asked incredulously.

"We're investigating treason. We aren't building a case yet, and chances are that when we do, he's going to cut a deal. Besides, he's small potatoes next to Kennedy's crew."

"He may *be* part of Kennedy's crew."

Reid seemed to be thinking. He said, "We could lift one from the bottle, I guess. We can always print him formally later on."

His eyes met hers, and for a moment she felt they shared the same thought. War had come to America. North and South might be hours away from bloodshed. What would "later on" bring?

She said, "My Raptor isn't due till tonight. Provided he's on file, and I get a decent latent, I might have an answer for you in two hours."

The evidence lab had been working in tandem with response all day. Staff from the night shift had stayed on and every station had at least two technicians working on some aspect of analysis. There was a faint stale odour. A nimbus of cigarette smoke writhed beneath the ceiling.

She grabbed some bench space and got to work on the bottle.

It was almost a pleasure to return to lab work. For a short time she could forget the mystery of covert operations and the motives behind bloody slaughter. For now, it was all ridges, curves and imperfections. All her attention was focused on localising the whirling vortex of a brand that would exist only once throughout eternity, as individual as its owner.

She didn't notice the minutes slipping past, didn't notice Reid till he coughed a second time to get her attention.

"I've got three decent prints," she said. "I'll run them by one of the latent examiners and we can scan it against the database."

"I'm hoping we won't need it."

She had her eyes on the last print. There was some puckering on the ridge detail that suggested a recent injury. Perhaps a small cut. She said, "What was that?"

"We won't need it."

Malcolm glanced up. A number of technicians were looking their way. They caught the cold wall of Reid's eyes and returned to their work.

"Where's your Raptor bound for?" he asked softly. He had a stillness about him that implied restraint rather than calm.

"I was supposed to be returning to Houston, but there are some leads I want to follow up out west."

"Think you could provide transport for our prisoner and me?"

She rose from the workbench. "What's happening?"

"German paratroopers have landed at Richmond. They're fighting the japs, maybe even Union regulars. British and Canadian tanks crossed the Union border at Buffalo and Detroit. And the japs have broken through Russian lines along the old Mongolian border."

Malcolm felt light-headed. She realised she'd been holding her breath. She said, "Anything else?"

"Kennedy's attacking Tennessee."

VIII

April 25, 2012
Nashville, Tennessee

Kennedy's eyelids flickered open. There was a dull, boring pressure along his spine and something was on fire.

He was hauled to his feet and thrown forwards. He landed hard on his knees with Lightholler on the ground beside him. His ears rang from the detonation and the air was thick with fumes.

A young police officer crouched close by, his pistol waving uncertainly in their direction, his mouthed words lost in the subsiding roar of the blast. Behind him, the building was mantled in a shroud of ruby smoke. His eyes flickered across to a group of hotel guests swarming across the debris.

Kennedy began to work his way towards Lightholler.

"Stay *down*," the officer yelled. "Hands where I can see them."

Kennedy reached for his back pocket. "The enemy's in there, son."

"*Hands where I can see them*."

Kennedy stood up. He had his badge in his hands. He held his palms upward. "For Christ's sake. Go do something useful."

The officer looked around indecisively. A few police squatted behind the barrier of a nearby patrol car but it looked as if the fighting had shifted further along the street. Kennedy gave a dismissive nod and made a show of turning his back on the officer. He approached Lightholler, his eyes darting everywhere.

The fire escape door hung from a single hinge. Three Topknots lay in a twisted heap before it. The officers who'd climbed the stairs earlier were now standing around a flatbed truck as a squad of soldiers struggled with a tarpaulin. They rolled it back to reveal the harsh outline of a twelve-seven-millimetre machine-gun. Kennedy made them for heavy infantry and watched with wonder as they trained the weapon on the fire escape door.

He motioned Lightholler towards the awning of a bus shelter across the street. He felt the young officer's eyes watching his every step.

Lightholler said, "There's another squad at the end of the street. It looks like they've blocked off the whole area. I don't see our car anywhere."

"Watanabe said it was in front of the hotel."

The twelve-seven jackhammered. It spat flame-sheathed metal at the fire escape. Two more Topknots, almost severed at the waist, toppled to the ground.

"Use your ID," Lightholler said, surprisingly unmoved. "Requisition a patrol car."

"Can't risk flashing my badge again."

Something passed between them.

Lightholler said, "Our problem is that you look too much like Kennedy."

They were standing in the awning's shadow. The officer had disappeared from view.

"You said you used to box."

Lightholler took a step towards him. "How do you want to do this?"

"We've seen two squads of troops. That means at least a company of heavy infantry on deck, with more coming. Add police, militia, firefighters..."

Lightholler nodded grimly. "What do you want?"

"I want to find Watanabe and get the fuck out of here."

Lightholler didn't ask why. He didn't frown or shake his head. There was just the slightest tremor in the folds around his right eye. He said, "I can make you difficult to recognise. You'll be a little groggy."

Kennedy scanned the street. "Take your best shot."

"Give me your badge."

He retrieved it from his pocket and handed it over.

"This will work better." Lightholler had the Mauser in his hands. He held the pistol by its barrel. It sparkled for a moment in the sweep of a passing headlight. Something was making its way down the street towards them. He said, "I'm going to bring this down hard over your eyebrows. It's going to hurt like hell."

Kennedy bared his teeth. "Knock yourself out."

He caught the chill of Lightholler's smile, a flash of sudden movement, and he was on his knees, blind with throbbing pain. Hands under his arms shifted him back onto watery legs. He wobbled, wanting to drop again. He heaved and felt his mouth fill with bile.

Vision returned in the bright halo of a headlight. Lightholler was supporting him with one arm, he was talking with someone. Kennedy squinted through a stream of blood to see two distorted forms converge into a motorcycle and sidecar. The cycle wavered on an unseen tide and he heard voices replying. He opened his mouth to say something, and felt warm fluid pour down his chin. He swayed in Lightholler's unsteady clinch, reached out a hand towards the cycle and felt Lightholler seize it in a grip of iron. The two riders hazed into view. He tried to smile and almost vomited.

"I think he took a round on the fire escape," Lightholler was saying.

It must have been the worst attempt at a Southern accent Kennedy had ever heard. Laughter bubbled behind his lips but it was easier to stand now. The cycle and its riders had stopped their weaving motion.

"An FTMC's been set up north of the combat zone," one of them said. "I can rustle up a wagon if you like."

Combat zone?

FMTC, a Forwards Mobile Triage Center; that meant at least a battalion of Confederate infantry was in the region. Local troops on hand for crowd control, or maybe just passing through Nashville, on to the border.

Kennedy managed to say, "I'm fine."

The rider looked doubtful. He looked like he was about to say more when the sidecar's radio crackled into life. The rider shot them a final glance and the cycle roared off with a snarl.

"Can you walk?" Lightholler asked after a moment. "We need to go up that way."

Gazing at Kennedy's face, his eyes may have held a hint of admiration at his own handiwork. Kennedy grimaced beneath his caul of blood.

"Did you catch any of that?" Lightholler added. "At least five hotels were attacked. Up to sixty japs are thought to be involved, perhaps more."

They kept to the sidewalk and soon fell in with a small number of men: soldiers and police, the walking wounded. They slowed their pace.

"They think you led the japs into Nashville."

"Honestly." Kennedy spat blood onto the roadside. "The things I get up to."

"When I said we were Bureau, they told me a bunch of tactical agents were on the way. They think you're still holed up in the hotel."

Kennedy grunted a reply. Talking hurt. Everything hurt.

They reached the end of the block. The cross street was cordoned off at both ends. Watanabe's car, gutted, rocked where it lay halfway up the pavement in front of the hotel. An arm dangled from a broken window. Three more bodies were strewn before the entrance. Watanabe's boys.

Three trucks and a fire engine were arrayed around the wreckage; police and soldiers were spread out along the length of the street. None of the streetlamps were working. Muted starlight wavered in black pools of water along the gutter while spotlights played against the side of the hotel. Searchlights swept the cloud-laden skies.

The night already held the taste of aftermath. The sound of gunfire, near and far, diminished to the odd isolated exchange. The cries of the wounded issued from a grey thatched marquee, thrown up a few hundred yards north of the hotel. The thready procession of injured soldiers and police made its way towards the tent. The occasional blank stare of a civilian turned to Kennedy. Lightholler drew him to one side of the group and they watched as medics came forwards to make their rapid assessments.

"Amber, green, amber, amber. We've got a red here."

They slapped coloured patches onto the sleeves of the men who shambled by, or fastened them to the metal sides of gurneys as they wheeled past on cracked asphalt.

"Green," the medic told them. He did a double-take. They wore the attire of civilians, bloodstained and torn, but his practised glance had seen more.

"Bureau," Kennedy replied to the unasked question.

"Damn," the medic said. "We got ourselves a regular who's who here tonight." But he'd already lost interest. His eyes were moving to the next man in line.

Kennedy made out another group of wounded towards the rear of the tent. Two were on gurneys while the remainder sat in a circle with their hands clasped behind their topknots. A shallow pool of blood spilled beneath them to slake the dull pavement. A squad of MPs had rifles trained in their direction while a single medic fussed from patient to patient.

"Where you taking them?" Kennedy asked. He'd made one of the gurney patients for Watanabe. The body lay still on the cart. Two paramedics were now easing him into the back of an ambulance.

"Slants are being taken to military hospital," the medic replied gruffly.

After what had happened tonight, Watanabe would be lucky to see a surgeon by dawn, if at all.

"That's no good, we need to question one of them now."

"No can do."

"Do I need to show you my badge?"

"You need to let me get on with my job." The medic was examining a soldier's arm. "Brachial plexus," he said. "Green." He tossed Kennedy a final damning look, then nodded his head towards the back of the tent. "Take it up with the lieutenant."

The lieutenant was talking with one of the MPs. He listened to Kennedy's request and said, "With all due respect, sir, these fuckers go to military."

The paramedics had Watanabe secured in the ambulance bed, straps fastened over his inert body. Scarlet and black slashes spattered across Kennedy's vision. Thoughts of Hardas and Morgan and another cold companion to add to the roster. Watanabe's empty gun was cool against his warm flesh. Kennedy reached for the holster.

Lightholler stepped forwards, placing a firm hand on his shoulder. "Lieutenant, mind if we accompany the slant down to military?"

The lieutenant looked sideways at one of the paramedics, who replied, "Be a bit crowded, but we'll manage."

A staccato of gunfire ripped the night. The lieutenant twisted his head past the tent flap, following a spotlight's beam. Kennedy joined him. A window on the hotel's top floor flared a rapid pulse of tracer. Return fire trailed spurts of masonry up the hotel's façade, ending the exchange.

"This slant's pretty important?"

"Key player," Lightholler replied.

The lieutenant stared at Watanabe's still form. "If you say so."

There were now angry shouts coming from the front of the marquee. Two police officers were muscling their way through the crowd towards them. A detachment of soldiers had made their way around to the back of the tent and were shouting at the ambulance drivers.

"Shit, I told them we were set too far forward," the lieutenant muttered.

One of the paramedics had climbed into the back of the ambulance and was crouching alongside Watanabe. The other was closing the rear hatch.

A quick glance confirmed that one of the advancing police officers was the young rookie who'd released them earlier.

"You mind?" Kennedy asked paramedic.

"Just try not to breathe," he replied as Kennedy squeezed past him. "Ride up front with me," he added to Lightholler.

Kennedy peered out through the tinted casement. The cop approached the lieutenant.

The driver had the engine idling and his window down, calling out to a guard to shift the barricade. The paramedic was readjusting the strap over Watanabe's legs and everything was moving just too fucking slow.

"John?"

The lieutenant was approaching the ambulance with the rookie in tow.

"*Lightholler?*"

No one else in the ambulance registered the name. Maybe they just hadn't read the morning paper. Lightholler caught a glimpse of Kennedy's view and swung back to the driver. "What are you waiting for?"

"I wonder what the hell he wants?" the driver said, glancing up at the rear-view.

The lieutenant was hammering his fist against the hatch.

Lightholler brought his pistol up against the driver's temple. "Hit the siren and roll."

Kennedy tumbled against the rear hatch as the ambulance lurched forward. He felt a spray of powdered glass burst over his face as the hatch window fractured into a spider web. He tried to squat, finding no space to move in the cramped confines of the ambulance.

He saw the paramedic, both arms crossed over his head, curled into a ball. Saw Watanabe, deathly still. Turned and saw, through the shattered window, the lieutenant's receding face, swollen and bloodied, as he pitched forwards.

The marquee had been pierced by a thousand shards of flying metal and glass. Beyond its flapping shreds, Kennedy watched as the hotel tottered on its foundations, engulfed within an expanding fireball. From above, the syncopated throb of approaching helicopters filled the night.

IX

April 25, 2012
Savannah, Georgia

Malcolm was back on the field office roof. A pale radiance suffused the clouds overhead. Moonbeams bathed the night in a soft glow. From beyond, at the edge of hearing, came the mounting drone of an approaching helicopter.

Reid had the prisoner cuffed and blindfolded. He whispered in Newcombe's ear. "We're off to see your pal, Kennedy. It's going to be a sweet, sweet reunion, and the two of you are going to sing me the sweetest little song."

A tactical agent stood close by, geared for urban assault. Below, the streets were at a standstill. Curfew was due within the hour but it looked as if all of Savannah had turned out, determined to drag the last spent butts of the evening to its soiled fingertips before the black patrol vans began their evening round-up of the city. It would be lights out. No landmarks for pilots, no targets for air raids. Dark continent.

The bars and the restaurants were full along the riverfront. News from Nashville, patchy at best, seemed to prompt last-minute excess rather than the austere moderation of impending war. Live broadcasts, shot from rooftops and hovering copters, showed a city besieged from within. A crimson horizon and the slow billow of black smoke spreading an uneven stain over the skies, but also lines of prisoners being marched into the backs of waiting army trucks.

The evening had been proclaimed a small but portentous victory for the South. Incursions had been made and factories might be burning near the border, yet what was claimed to be Kennedy's first assault on his own homeland had been nipped in the bud.

Malcolm could tell the broadcasts had been finessed by deft hands. Smiling soldiers filled every second shot, arms around their companions and an enthusiastic wave to the family back home.

She'd called Houston, of course, and with her new watchword had little difficulty being directed to Webster's private line.

The director was pleased with her handling of the Savannah incident. Making Hardas and Morgan into posthumous heroes had developed into a charming prequel for the events unfolding in Nashville. He'd told her that punishment meted out to the evil was good copy, but a bit of redemption—now and then—was better for the soul. The civilians lapped it up.

Then he'd laughed mirthlessly, saying that her story might have even flushed Kennedy out of whatever godforsaken hole he'd been hiding in, to boot.

She told him that they had a prisoner in custody. That she'd planned on heading west anyway, in her pursuit of Kennedy, and that Reid had requested transport to Nashville along the way.

"I *want* you there, Agent Malcolm," Webster had purred. "I'd pay good money to see the look on his face when he sees you."

The bastard had known all along, of course. Little wonder he so enjoyed her Morgan/Hardas scenario. It looked like betrayal was to be the theme of the day. Would he be so pleased to know, she'd wondered, about the damning evidence that inexorably linked him to the shadows behind Camelot?

Was there anything she could do about it?

Before signing off she'd said, "Director, I don't buy what's happening in Nashville. I think it's a diversion, if it's related at all. Kennedy's associations with the Japanese may run deep, but everything you gave me on the major connects him with black and indian operatives. No formal links exist with Japanese terrorists or Special Forces."

"And yet there he is," Webster had replied. "At the heart of it all. Have a chat with Agent Reid. Ask him about Mazatlan. Then when you hear that Kennedy's stormed the gates of heaven, you'll think twice about doubting it. Happy hunting, Agent Malcolm."

The helicopter dropped out of the night on a squall of churning air. Invisible tendrils lashed at her coat and sent her hair whipping about her face. It balanced above them for a moment before settling onto the roof with surprising grace.

Newcombe cast about wildly, hardly the seasoned aviator. Blindness and restricted mobility had reduced him to animal instincts.

Reid had ordered the helicopter to save them struggling uptown to the airport. He'd ordered the tac agent because he meant business. Maybe because he'd suddenly found himself holding a ticket to the hottest game in town—a showdown with Kennedy on the streets of Nashville. That was how he was playing it anyhow, wasting little time hustling the group onto the helicopter. She may have provided the Raptor, but Reid was determined to make it his show.

Malcolm was directed to a small seat behind the pilot. The prisoner sat resignedly in his own seat while Reid fastened his cuffs to an adjacent handrail. Reid caught her eye, mouthed "Hold tight", and they were snatched into the air. The city below them, a circuitboard of flickering lights, faded in the thickening wisps of low cloud.

Her few attempts to speak with Reid during the flight were rendered futile by the rotor's engine. Mazatlan would have to wait. She contended with the shudder and shake of the helicopter, thankful that the airport was a blissfully short distance away.

On the ground, there was barely a moment to grasp her bag before they were whisked to a runway at the edge of the complex. Fatigue had thrown her orientation, casting her adrift. She felt lost on the dark expanse of tarmac. The Raptor, a glitter-edged shadow against the blacktop, seemed familiar, but had she really stood here this morning, debating her worth with Reid? That moment felt like years ago.

Reid had a cigarette in his mouth. He'd shoved Newcombe into a crouch on the runway's pitch, and stood by him like a hunter celebrating fallen prey.

"Where was it?" he asked her. He was puffing at the cigarette hurriedly, drawing a long bright glow from its wandering tip.

"Where was what?" Malcolm replied.

"You said you had some leads to follow out west." He had his eyes on the ground crew, as if the strength of his will, powered by nicotine and adrenaline, might drive them faster at their appointed tasks.

She thought about it carefully before replying. "Arkansas."

There was a flicker of movement in the corner of her eye—one of the prisoner's little paroxysms. He'd made the occasional outburst a few times since having the blindfold applied.

"Arkansas, huh?" Reid said absently.

"Yes."

Reid was inspecting the Raptor now. He had his mind on other matters, talking to hear the sound of his own voice. Talking to kill time. He probably wouldn't even remember her reply.

Her eyes were on the prisoner. She said, "Morning Star, Arkansas."

Newcombe's head cocked itself in her direction for a moment too long.

Earlier, waiting on the roof for the copter, Reid had been talking for the prisoner's benefit. He'd been discussing a German interrogation technique, acquired from their Afrikan holdings. It had been inspired by the native account that inserting a red hot poker in a canary's eye prompted it to sing so much sweeter. He'd then adjusted the bandages and fastened the blindfold over the man's pale blue eyes, saying, "I guess cultural exchange is one of the boons of an effective colonial system."

She'd shuddered then, but now, looking down at the unseeing face, she couldn't help but experience a moment of satisfaction. Newcombe had sung his song.

The Raptor growled to life.

It was time to bring Major Joseph Kennedy out of the cold.

X

April 25, 2012
Nashville, Tennessee

Lightholler fumbled at his feet for the Mauser. Kennedy had his Shingen trained on the paramedic's chest. Both pistols were empty.

What had been a barricade five seconds ago now adorned the ambulance's grille. What had been a hotel ten seconds ago was a flaming shell.

Kennedy said, "Don't slow down."

The driver shifted up a gear and they resumed their wild pace. Lightholler, pistol back in his hand, kept him covered. The wind shrieked past the cracked window. Other sirens joined their own in a rising wail. Red and yellow glowed against the wall as a convoy of ambulances screamed past in the opposite direction. There was a sputter from the radio.

"Unit five, what is your condition?"

Watanabe was moving. His hands clasped his abdomen, fingers clutching where the bullet had entered. He was covered in a mantle of broken glass. A flask of saline slapped against its drip stand, whipping the IV back and forth.

"Repeat—unit five, what is your condition?"

Shards of glass bristled between Kennedy's collar and neck. His mouth was dry, his head throbbed with dull exhaustion and pain. "Can you help him?" he asked the paramedic.

The paramedic's face was pale. Blood trickled from a ragged cut just above his left eyebrow. He checked the monitor array and looked back up at the flask. He eyed Kennedy with contempt.

Kennedy holstered the Shingen.

The paramedic adjusted a valve on the IV and passed the chamber over to Kennedy. “Keep squeezing this,” he said.

Kennedy squeezed. Fluid filled the chamber and coursed down the tubing into Watanabe’s arm.

“Unit five, current location?”

“Tell them you’re headed to military,” Kennedy said.

The driver reached for the mike. “This is five, copy. We’re on Franklin and making for military. Over.”

“Roger that, five.”

“Cross the river,” Kennedy said. “Get us on the interstate.”

“Don’t cross the river.” Watanabe’s voice was the scrape of a blade against concrete. “Where are we?”

“Franklin Street.” Kennedy looked up at the paramedic for confirmation.

“Franklin, turning onto First,” the paramedic muttered.

“There’s a place … on Deaderick … near the museum. Take me there.”

“That’s close,” the paramedic said, relieved. “Mike, we’re going to Deaderick. Take a left at Confederate, and then turn into Sixth.”

“We can take you to a hospital,” Kennedy said.

“That’s no good for either of us. At Deaderick they can fix me, or fix it so I don’t feel this.”

“Okay. Take it easy—you’re going to be alright.”

A blur of cafés and boutiques flashed by. Beyond, the Cumberland River flowed darkly.

Kennedy listened in on the radio reports. Three hotels on Fourth had been attacked; the Japanese embassy on McGavock was in flames. All city hospitals were on disaster alert. Two infantry battalions were being diverted from their march to the border and were making camp at the city limits. There was talk of a Japanese guerrilla attack, talk of a traitor’s secret army. It sounded like a twisted version of Camelot. Strange ideas presented themselves at the edge of Kennedy’s thoughts.

“Where on Deaderick?” the driver called back.

“Across from the museum, two storeys, red brick,” Watanabe gasped. Kennedy repeated it to the driver.

A few moments later they pulled up outside the building, siren still wailing.

The windows lit up on the second floor.

“Leave me here.” Watanabe’s voice was a frothing whisper.

The siren withered to nothing, leaving a low buzz in Kennedy's ears. The engine idled, the IV pump ticked a low, rapid staccato. The paramedic stared at him apprehensively.

"Leave me here and go," Watanabe said again.

Kennedy ignored him. He asked the paramedic, "You know who I am?"

The paramedic nodded. His jaw jutted forwards, the muscles of his face working to maintain an element of self-control. Kennedy looked over at the driver. Lightholler had the gun at his chest.

Kennedy examined the paramedic's name tag. "You both get to go home tonight, Nick. Everything will be okay. Help me get him out of here."

Lightholler followed the driver onto the street and helped him work the hatch open. Kennedy unlatched the gurney lock while the paramedic adjusted the drip stand. He reached into the folds of Watanabe's bloodied kimono and withdrew a clip for the Shingen. Reloaded.

Two Asian men, their arms folded, were standing on the top stair leading up to the building. One of them spoke into a hand-held radio.

"Get back in the ambulance, John. Take them with you." Kennedy nodded towards the paramedics. "Watch them."

Lightholler glanced at the men on the stairs, then back at Kennedy. He said, "I've got your back."

Kennedy wheeled the gurney towards the stairs. He had a pistol in his holster. He had two dead friends on his conscience. He had a strange idea at the edge of his thoughts.

He said, "This is Yukio Watanabe. He represents Kobe of New York Prefecture."

The men looked at each other. One cracked open the door and spoke to someone within the shadows.

"He needs medical attention," Kennedy added.

The door opened wide and a man emerged. He scampered, crab-like, down the stairs. He wore faded surgical scrubs and his gloves were the colour of rust. He approached the ambulance.

The paramedic leaned out and said, "Abdo wound, single bullet. Might be the spleen, might be the stomach." He rattled off the details. "BP stable, second flask of saline running now."

"Saline?" the doctor muttered.

"We're out of colloid."

The doctor peeled off the gloves. Turning to the men on the stairs, he said, "Bring him inside."

One of them stepped lithely down and seized the gurney. Kennedy grabbed the other end. Its wheels clacked loudly on the quiet street as they heaved it up the stairs and into the doorway.

Kennedy stepped back down as Watanabe's body vanished within.

The lights went out one by one.

The doctor glanced at him appraisingly, turned and said, "Yoshikawa?"

The other man guarding the stair, having secured the door, came down to join him.

"This is no good." The doctor crumpled the stained gloves in his hands, looking from Kennedy to the battle-scarred ambulance and back. "You being here is not good at all."

Kennedy looked across at the bodyguard. He was low and wide and built for sumo.

"We were never here," Kennedy said softly.

"No one ever is," the doctor replied. "But it's something we need to be certain of."

The accumulation of threats and danger coupled with Kennedy's instincts to form a new level of appreciation. Nashville was in flames.

And they think I'm behind this.

He saw bronze and orange leaves spiral onto an untouched chessboard pregnant with a thousand possibilities. A place where a threat was as good as an assault.

The doctor appeared confused, perhaps by Kennedy's poise. He frowned as a conclusion dawned upon him. "Yukio Watanabe, you say?"

"Yes."

"Then you are Joseph Kennedy?"

"Yes."

"Oh, dear." The doctor glanced away again, this time surveying the street. His gaze held expectancy. His watchful eyes searched the dark for vengeful shadows while the sumo wrestler shifted on nervous feet.

"Who are you affiliated with?" Kennedy demanded. "Kobe or Shimamura?"

"I am a doctor. My affiliation is with the injured."

"Of course it is. I see no reason to further disturb your work. I've been quite busy tonight myself."

The doctor looked up past the trees. Plumes of smoke rose over the skyline. A helicopter flitted among the clouds. He looked back at Kennedy and read a terrible promise in his eyes.

"You have my word that no one will hear of this place," Kennedy said. "Is that good enough for you? Good enough for your Family?"

"Dear gods, yes."

Kennedy turned his back on them. He walked back to the ambulance. His legs felt hollow, his chest shuddered with each heartbeat. He looked back over his shoulder. They were gone.

Lightholler had the ambulance door open. He leaned out towards Kennedy and said, "Remind me never to play poker with you."

XI

April 26, 2012
Nashville, Tennessee

Cramped between Reid and the cold curved buttress of the Raptor's passenger cabin, Malcolm managed to snatch two hours of fitful sleep. The tac agent and a medic played cards while the prisoner moaned through his own dark dreams.

There was a turbulent descent through dense cloud, followed by a brisk run across the rain-spattered tarmac, a brush with local airport security, and a cab ride through Hades.

Nashville field office, 2 a.m. Triple shifts. A map-covered wall. Red pins marked the skeletal remains of burnt-out city blocks. Blue for the various roadblocks and military depots. A trail of black pins made their way along First Avenue, trailed the Cumberland River and doubled back onto Sixth. It broke off westwards, towards the city limits.

The phones rang and the doors swung back and forth as police, agents and soldiers filed in and out of the command post. A cloud of cigarette smoke dodged the air-conditioning. Malcolm found herself a vacant room. There was a lounge chair, a coffee table, a sink, a phone and a television. She had the shakes. *Too little sleep and too much caffeine.* She missed her sister, she missed her apartment, she missed her cat. An advertisement on the television caught her eye. Someone calling someone long distance, a dog bounding through fields of long grass, homewards bound. She missed her life.

She felt her eyelids tearing up and bit her lip. She laughed quietly at herself.

Too little sleep.

They had the prisoner locked up in the infirmary. When she'd last checked, he was still sleeping. His bandages had been changed, a fresh spool of white cotton for his head and legs, but a rucksack served for his pillow, a coat for his blanket.

They had the ambulance downstairs. Prints had been sent to the lab, panels to ballistics, seeking to confirm the paramedic's wild account. Other witnesses, an assortment of police, medics, soldiers, gangsters and hotel guests—nearly forty in total—were sequestered amongst the cubicles of the office's top floor. Reid and the local outfit were going over their stories.

Preliminaries: five downtown hotels are attacked over the course of an hour. The Baymont, Embassy Suites, Vanderbilt, Wyndham and Bismarck. Joseph Kennedy, John Lightholler and an unnamed Japanese associate—recent occupants of the Bismarck—rescue a hotel floor of terrified civilians. They are seen exchanging gunfire with a number of Asian men by at least four witnesses.

The Japanese embassy is fire-bombed in what appears to be one of many reciprocal actions. Meanwhile, Kennedy bluffs his way past two lines of security: police and military. He steals an ambulance. Two paramedics attached to said ambulance state that they transferred his wounded accomplice to a private residence on Sixth Avenue. They don't know the address. They state they were left trussed and blindfolded in their vehicle while Kennedy and Lightholler set out on foot.

From there the story became sketchier; a haze. Reports of break and entries, stolen vehicles—possibly rioters, possibly Kennedy's crew.

Had there been a falling out amongst Joseph's men? Were the gangsters in any way affiliated with his project, or a spanner in the works? And where was Joseph's secret army?

She flashed back to a cubicle on the office's top floor. Agent Reid, a lit cigarette in the ashtray, another at his fingertips, smiling half-heartedly over a mouthful of coffee and saying, "Everyone lies, Agent. We just need to know if they're lying more than usual..."

She rose from her chair and splashed water over her face. She thanked God there wasn't a mirror in sight. Her notes were in a bag on the coffee table. She had the Raptor on standby for the flight to Arkansas. Joseph had four hours to slip loose of the net that had closed down over Nashville. It was time for her to get back on track.

She abandoned the quiet of the room for the chaos outside and passed the tac agent in a corridor. She skirted the infirmary.

Was there some way of extracting the prisoner from Reid's grasp? Instinct and a rooftop in Savannah told her that he might still be of some value in her pursuit.

She found Reid dozing at one of the cubicles. He had his feet on the desk and a magazine propped over his eyes. There were drool stains on his collar. He jumped when she touched his shoulder.

"I'm heading out, Agent Reid."

He nodded. The last of his exuberance had been spent asking the same questions to an assortment of indifferent, exhausted and frightened faces over the last few hours.

"How did it go?" she asked. "Any news flashes?"

"Nope," he muttered, still half-asleep.

She took a breath and braced herself for the request.

Reid rubbed his eyes vigorously. He rolled his head on his neck, stretching out the kinks. When he looked back at her, there was a knowing twinkle in his eyes. He said, "Spill it, Agent."

"I want to take the prisoner with me."

His face took on a reflective quality. "What *did* you find back at the lab?"

"Nothing."

"And the database?"

"The database was helpful."

"Go on."

"I think I know where he's headed."

Reid glanced across the crowded room and his gaze fixed on the map. He followed the thinning trail of black pins, headed west. He said, "Arkansas?"

"That's right."

"Want to tell me why?"

"Call it a substantiated hunch."

"Right." Reid lit a cigarette. He pulled up a chair and said, "Take a seat."

Malcolm sighed, and dropped into the chair next to him.

"I've got men combing Sixth Avenue. They're looking for the place where Kennedy dumped his buddy." He leaned forwards. "I'm wasting their time. I know those paramedics are holding back, but I'm fucked if I can figure out why. I'm fucked if I can figure what hold Kennedy has over them."

"They're terrified that he can still harm them."

"With what? Those slants we pulled out of military aren't talking, but pounds to peanuts they were *after* Kennedy, not with him. I'm thinking he soured his deal with the japs somehow. See, I've got this feeling that there's something else going on with Kennedy. Something the director can't—or won't— discuss with us. And I have to tell you, I'm tired of blundering around in the dark."

Malcolm shrugged.

"*Especially* when I'm thinking my partner's holding back on me too."

She smiled sweetly. "I'll tell you what. You keep the prisoner and I'll get out of your hair."

"No, you don't." He reached across and grabbed her arm.

She kept quite still and held his gaze.

He released her slowly. "Sorry."

She felt the reply at her lips but was speaking before she could stop herself. *Too little sleep, and too late in the show for old secrets.*

"Those hoops Director Webster had me jumping through... Well, let's just say my connection with Joseph Kennedy goes back a ways before Camelot."

Reid chuckled. "And to think I had you pegged for screwing the boss."

Malcolm flushed at the accusation. She dug her nails into her palms. "I have better taste, Agent Reid," she said, and moved to rise from her chair.

He reached out for her again, gently this time. "You don't get it. I'm talking about my fuck-up, back in Savannah. I *knew* you couldn't have climbed so high in the Bureau on merit alone. That's CBI politics and we both know it. What I'm trying to say is that it didn't take me too long to realise that you didn't get there on your back either." He smiled wearily.

She looked back at him, puzzled now. "Remind me, which finishing school did you attend?"

"I should have known you had something on Kennedy."

"If this is turning into an apology, you're taking your sweet time."

"You're good, Agent Malcolm. You're already on par with a lot of agents I've worked with."

"Let's not get too cosy, Agent Reid. I'd convinced myself I got this job because of my abilities, maybe because of my *professional* relationship with the major. Now I know it was to satisfy one of the director's darker whims. I've been played for a fool."

She wanted to say it all. Tell him the things that linked Webster to Kennedy in a ten-year-old mesh of duplicity. Instead, she fell silent.

"I don't give a fuck how it happened, I'm just glad you're here," he replied.

She examined his face for a hint of mockery, but his expression held no trace of humour. She asked, "Do I get to take the prisoner?"

"Does he know where Kennedy's headed?"

"We both know he's held back on us. I just think that by the time you've beaten it out of him, Kennedy will be long gone."

Reid snorted. "There's madness to my method."

She arched an eyebrow. "Quite."

"What backup have you organised in Arkansas?"

"None. I've been chasing your tail for the last eighteen hours."

"Nice. What time's your flight?"

"Whenever I'm ready."

Reid surveyed the room, then ashed his cigarette. "You know *exactly* where he's headed?"

"I know of four possible locations."

"You're going to need some help."

The arrogance was gone, at least for the moment. The curtain had fallen on his Nashville production and she had four counties to cover: Garland, Greene, Phillips and Searcy. She could always lose him in Arkansas, if push came to shove.

"Okay," she said. "But from here on in, we're a committee."

"Committee?" Reid replied. "I thought you were the boss."

"Don't get too excited. Tell me, can you get the prisoner back down to the airport?"

"Shouldn't be a problem. I'll delegate this to one of the locals and give the director a buzz."

"You don't call the director till you have everything. Words to live by." She tried not to sound too earnest.

"Fine." Reid winked. "There'll be time enough in Arkansas. I'll meet you downstairs in thirty."

XII

April 26, 2012
Shiloh, Tennessee

They'd crossed the Tennessee River at Savannah and that was when Lightholler had first really noticed it. Kennedy staring over the low sidings of the narrow wooden bridge at the sluggish waters below; his head then craning back at the view as they crossed once more onto land.

Not that Kennedy'd had that much to say before. Hot-wiring the sedan, stolen just outside Nashville, had produced the gem, "Product of a misspent youth". And the long drive through the night, south and then west, had been supplemented by only the odd brief offerings of conversation. Pulled up to one side of the highway while a convoy of trucks rumbled north towards the city, he'd mentioned that his gun could do with some cleaning.

"The Shingen or the Mauser?"

"Both."

Finally, snaking along the bypasses, switching back through the small towns that dotted southern Tennessee, Kennedy had talked about a number of things. His amazement at the fact that two weeks ago he could have made his way across the Confederacy in any manner he chose. His wonder that they had spent yesterday in a rat's nest, at the mercy of a host of enemies and looking to a gangster for survival. He talked of New York and the roads they had travelled since.

But since the bridge and the river and the little township of Savannah, Tennessee, a new form of stillness had ensued. They drove through Pittsburg Landing in silence, Kennedy navigating with gestures and nods, and Lightholler gave up asking questions.

The windows were cracked open for air but the sedan still reeked of gunpowder and fear-caked sweat. He thought he could taste metal in his mouth.

Shiloh was a gas station, a church, a general store and a souvenir stand. A nailed-up wooden board with fresh black paint advertising bait for sale. There were no cars on the road. Long stretches of trees crowded out of the darkness, broken by the occasional scar of chain-linked fencing or barbed wire.

"What time is it?" Kennedy didn't bother glancing down at his wrist.

Lightholler checked the dash. "Quarter to four."

"Good."

"That's 4 a.m."

Kennedy gave a half-hearted smile. "Good."

The road was winding back alongside the Tennessee River. Kennedy pointed and said, "Make a right along here."

Lightholler made the turn. The road pulled away from the river through a tunnel of high tree branches. It widened into a courtyard. A single lamp, suspended between two thick black posts, threw a dim circle of light on a small hut at the courtyard's edge and faded into a broken expanse of long grass.

"Where are we?"

"Shiloh." Kennedy had a hand up to his brow. He brought it away with a smear of blood on his fingers.

"Told you that needed stitches."

"Suture kit." Kennedy patted a paper-wrapped package by his side.

"It's still swollen." Lightholler peered at Kennedy's forehead. "What did you do with the ice pack?"

Kennedy shrugged.

"I can try to fix it for you now. Here, or under that lamp post?"

Kennedy switched on the interior light. The pale yellow luminescence barely lit the sedan. "The lamp post," he said.

Lightholler opened his door and leaned against the car. He took a cigarette from his pocket and lit up. Glancing at his feet, he saw the ground littered with cigarette butts. There were some crumpled paper wrappers and a couple of crushed beer cans. He kicked one away.

"What is this place?"

Kennedy was looking at the light. The lamp was a translucent globe, suspended between the bores of two large cannons. They were propped against each other on a wide cement base, linked by a bronze plaque. The grassy field beyond was heaped up at regular intervals. Lightholler took a few steps forwards. The field was bordered by a row of cannon pieces.

He almost tripped over the first headstone.

"Shiloh National Military Park." Kennedy's voice was close to a whisper. "The battle fought here was the South's best chance of keeping Grant out of the Western Confederacy."

"How'd they make out?"

Kennedy indicated the graveyard with a nod. After a moment he said, "Places like this, I get this sense. This feeling that it's still happening somewhere. The battle, I mean."

"According to you, it is."

"I guess so. I didn't really mean it that way. I'm talking about some kind of resonance, like an echo."

Lightholler had been to Flanders. He'd walked the barricades of Paris and stood among the ruins of the De Gaulle Line, where the preserved monuments of French and German tanks still faced each other across the Seine. Was there a patch of earth that *hadn't* been contested in the history of the world?

"Let's get you fixed up. We have a lot of ground to cover."

Kennedy sat cross-legged on the gravel while Lightholler crouched down before him to examine the wound.

"Wait a second." Kennedy scrambled to his feet. He walked over to the sedan and returned carrying a cloth bag. He rummaged around inside and produced a bottle.

Lightholler checked the label. Sour mash. "Antiseptic," he said. "Good idea."

Kennedy reached into the bag again and withdrew two cups. He winked and said, "Anaesthetic."

"*Not* a good idea."

Kennedy poured a small amount in each cup. He offered one to Lightholler. He raised his own and held Lightholler's gaze. "To absent friends."

Lightholler nodded and downed the shot.

Kennedy refilled their glasses.

"We don't know for sure," Lightholler offered gently.

"They ain't here," Kennedy said mournfully. "Enemies of the state."

He gave a dry laugh. “Dead in defence of the South. This stinks to high heaven. Stinks of Webster.”

Lightholler gave him a perplexed look.

Kennedy took another mouthful before placing his cup next to Lightholler’s. “The director of the CBI, Glen Webster. It’s his style. Maybe they’re dead, maybe they’re not, but either way, he got them. And that story about dying for the South. Redemption? That’s just him twisting the knife.”

“Why?”

“It’s clever. It shows results for the Bureau, and it pisses me off, big time.” Kennedy shook his head. “There’s been no love lost between us, as far back as I can remember, but this…”

“You’ve betrayed every ideal you ever stood for. What were you expecting?”

Kennedy frowned. “You don’t know what you’re talking about.”

“As far as they’re concerned,” Lightholler added hastily, “that’s *exactly* what you’ve done.” He made a sweeping gesture with his hands. “They all think you sold them out. You told me so yourself.”

“Maybe, but all of this … the accusations, the murder charges. That’s been in the works for a while. It’s proactive—almost as if Webster had just been waiting for the right opportunity to bring me down again.”

“Again?”

Kennedy picked up his cup and swished the liquor, watching the dark fluid swirl. He made a low sound in his throat. “He’s always been small time.”

Lightholler dribbled some of the liquor onto his sleeve and pressed it against the wound. Kennedy growled but didn’t move. Positioning himself to keep out of his own shadow, Lightholler picked up the kit and locked a suture into a clamp.

“Might need four or five stitches.”

“Great.”

He chose a pair of forceps and focused on the injury, seeking where the tissue was puckered up.

Kennedy said, “Those guys…”

Lightholler pulled back.

Kennedy’s eyes shone brightly. His smile was enigmatic. “Morgan. Hardas.”

"I never really got to know them," Lightholler murmured.

"You weren't exactly catching them at their best."

"We can do this later, if you want."

"Let's get it over with. I'd hate to think we wasted all that liquor."

Lightholler began working on the wound. Kennedy winced each time the needle broke skin, but kept still enough to permit a reasonable closure.

"Didn't know my own strength," Lightholler muttered at one stage, but Kennedy was someplace else. There was the occasional snatch of birdsong from the adjacent woods and a light wind was rising. The sky's edge went from pearl grey to a fine pink haze.

"There," Lightholler said finally. "It's done."

Kennedy brought his fingers up to touch the repair. Lightholler brushed the hand away.

"Later," he said. "Give it some time."

"Is it worthy of Michelangelo?"

Lightholler twisted his head as if inspecting a painting. "More like Picasso, but it'll have to do."

He helped Kennedy to his feet and they walked over to the sedan. Lightholler drove.

Kennedy's dark mood appeared to have passed for the moment. Lightholler tried to picture Hardas and Morgan, but there wasn't much he could dredge up to endear either of them to him. Hardas had played the thug for the majority of their brief acquaintance—drawing a gun on him at the Lone Star hadn't helped matters. As for Morgan, he was just a fearful intellectual who enjoyed the sound of his voice a little too much; someone who'd bitten off more than he could chew.

Lightholler had called it back in New York City: they were amateurs. Yet he wondered how much they might have seen and endured since hooking up with the major's holy cause. The answer came with a bludgeoning finality.

They died for it.

Kennedy had talked about travelling through time. The journal spoke of secret installations and of a black and silver orb, a metal crab in a coiled lair of tubes and wiring. Another world where great wars spanned the globe and rockets journeyed to the Moon and Mars and beyond. A world where a Kennedy *had* become president—yet he still died in Dallas in '63.

So much different and so much the same. Lost in his musing, he hadn't realised he had spoken his question aloud.

"How do we know what?" Kennedy replied. He reached for his brow but stopped short, catching Lightholler's glare.

"How do we know things will be any better if we succeed?"

"How do you mean?"

"Assuming everything you've told me is true," he said, "what makes you so sure that the other world—Wells' world—is any better, or more justified in existing, than our own?"

"There's no guarantee, John, but there's one thing I'm sure of. In his journal he states that he operated on a man from his future. Our world, real or not, will be gone within the year."

"Gone." The entire weight of the word sank down on him. "Because of this war?"

"Most likely."

Lightholler couldn't help himself. *One man may start a war; it takes a few good men to stop one.* "And this war started because…?"

Perhaps Kennedy hadn't noticed the provocation. His reply was distant and softly voiced. "I've wondered about that myself." But when he turned to look at Lightholler, his expression revealed a doleful acquiescence. "What's done is done."

"We wouldn't be going to Nevada in the first place if you really believed that."

"You're right." Kennedy nodded slowly. "Thing is, I don't know how to fix this. I wouldn't know where to start. Maybe the future's not carved in stone, but it's out there. Do we go back a week and stop the Brandenburgs? Two years, and destroy the journal? Three, and stall Camelot? I don't know. Go back a hundred years and deal with Wells. Nip it in the bud. Clean the slate. That's all that makes sense to me."

"I've read most of the journal, Joseph. Wells might have been misguided and he might have been insane. He might have contemplated murder, but that doesn't make him a criminal."

"Do you think Stalin thought of himself as a criminal, or Sorel, or Attila the Hun for that matter? Judge his actions and their consequences—not his intentions—the way you've judged mine. This is all wrong. I know it and you know it. Otherwise *you* wouldn't be here."

Was that why he had stuck by Kennedy's side? He glanced up at his reflection in the rear-view mirror and rapidly looked away without quite understanding what had perturbed him.

"Something got stuck here," Kennedy continued. "A record-player needle in the final groove, going round and round in circles, but never moving on. *There*, they had what we've only just discovered. That and much more. *They* had their final conflict more than fifty years ago and it ended in atomics. We chose to *start* ours with them. *They* moved forward. The journal is patchy, it's the work of a madman, it describes some dark, dark times, but it's still progress."

"Is that sort of progress a good thing?"

"It sure beats oblivion."

"If it was so good, why did Wells do what he did? Why did he seek to destroy *his* future?"

"Your guess is as good as mine. Why bother questioning his motives when we don't know his methods? We just have to stop him."

"You don't know what he did?"

"You've read the journal, John." Kennedy's reply was matter of fact.

"Most of it. I've read most of it."

"The journal ends on the day of the sinking. It ends with a one-word entry. He never mentions how he actually planned to intervene. He had long-term plans for the world. The *Titanic* was just the first phase. He was just flexing his muscles."

Lightholler hit the brakes. He swung the sedan off the road and let it idle. He looked over at Kennedy and started laughing without amusement.

"*Jesus*, Joseph, how do you expect us to stop him then?"

"I have a few ideas."

"You know, this cryptic shit of yours is starting to wear a little thin at the edges."

"I'm hoping we get the luxury of arguing the finer points of our mission, but for now, how about we get to Nevada first?"

"I always thought we were going to try and stop Wells on the ship. Isn't that why you dragged me into all of this?"

Kennedy's look was one of laboured patience, the sort he might give a child. Then he read something in Lightholler's eyes. "John, the ship is our *last* chance. We were—" He caught himself. "We *are* going to try and intercept him in the desert. But the accuracy of the machine may be unpredictable, especially on a complete insertion."

"A what?"

"Doc will explain that to you. For now all you need to know is that the

Titanic has always been a contingency plan. Wells lay low after arriving in 1911. If we don't catch him in the desert, we can be sure of finding him on the ship."

"So I'm just part of your contingency plan."

"No, you're my last hope," Kennedy replied solemnly.

"But why *me*?" He was surprised at the plaintive tone of his question. "There must be lots of guys who fit the bill."

"You were on the shortlist of suitable candidates."

"Suitable for *what*? Killing yakuza? Providing first aid? Hijacking an ocean liner?"

"Something along those lines," Kennedy replied. He was smiling.

"I just don't get it."

"I had five guys in mind, John, all reasonably experienced, reasonably talented … qualified in one way or another. They just weren't *hungry* enough."

"Hungry?"

Kennedy shot him a piercing look. "You've been waiting to do something like this your whole life."

"When did you become the psychologist?"

"Tell me I'm wrong, John."

"You're more than that. You're completely insane."

"And you're an empty, dissatisfied shit trying to escape your ancestor's coat-tails."

"I think you're describing yourself," Lightholler murmured.

"So, you finally get it then?"

"I get it."

Lightholler looked away. He put the sedan in gear and brought them back onto the road. All he had seen and done … for the sake of contingency. For the sake of friendship?

He asked, "How am I doing so far?"

"I'll keep you posted."

Lightholler heard the gentle laughter in Kennedy's voice and kept his eyes on the highway.

They crossed the Mississippi some time after dawn and abandoned the sedan by a watering hole near the aptly named town of Mud Lake. They washed in a frigid stream. Kennedy stood in the water beating his arms against his chest for warmth while Lightholler's sturdy, pale body cut through the sparkling blue.

Surfacing for a lungful of air, Lightholler said, "Tell me, which one of us is Tom Sawyer?"

They retrieved their clothing and the satchel from the sedan, then walked back into town, arguing briefly along the way over which car to steal. Lightholler favoured a battered black Austin; Kennedy suggested a lighter colour, saying it would be less conspicuous and better protection against the heat of the day. They settled on a cream-coloured Blitzen with Louisiana plates.

They switched plates at the next town and drove west.

Arkansas unfolded in hills and valleys, in forests of oak and pine, laced by the languorous tresses of the slow, wide river. They ate in a diner across the road from a train station and watched as negroes rolled crates along the platform and loaded them into the long grey freight car of a Confed Pacific.

Kennedy thumbed through a discarded newspaper, held the headline up for Lightholler to read. **Nashville Redoubt. Japanese Assault Halted.**

The kicker called it a "Night of Infamy". President Clancy was convening Congress that afternoon. Kennedy scanned the paper for his name and found nothing. He interpreted the mild euphoria he felt as a result of poor sleep, but that assumption took little away from his satisfaction.

They got back into the car and headed west again. He nodded off mid-afternoon and woke to find they were just outside Little Rock. He offered to take the wheel at the next gas station, but Lightholler shrugged off the suggestion.

The Ozarks grew out of the horizon, a purple fringe, gold-tinged in the early afternoon sun. They switched at Benton after he told Lightholler they were about an hour from Morning Star. Lightholler was asleep before they hit the highway.

He turned on the radio and trawled for a local station. Between the evangelists and easy listening he caught a traffic report. A trailer truck had jackknifed on Route 70. There was oil on the road and a trapped passenger. Delays were expected.

He reached for Lightholler's cigarettes and lit one, drew a breath and tossed it. He flicked the dial and came up with some classical music. He turned up the volume, keeping an eye on Lightholler's closed lids. He let the music carry him.

His mind drifted. Considering the music's perfection, he began to question his own delusion. The scheme he'd formulated so many months ago had lapsed into chaos. It had fallen prey to powers as inexorable as gravity. Lightholler was right to question his role in the great disaster ahead.

A wind in the road brought them up to a crest. An oncoming coupé winked its lights at them. He slowed down. He made out the flash of emergency vehicles and the outline of the road train spread in a heat haze across the blacktop. There was a fire engine, an ambulance and two black-and-whites. A line of traffic had built up ahead.

He nudged Lightholler awake and explained the situation. Lightholler urged him to pull over.

A black van had broken down on the shoulder just ahead of them. Someone was working on a flat tyre while a woman stood by the roadside. She had her hair tied up in a scarf and, despite the heat, she had a shawl wrapped tightly around her body. Turning, she waved at them.

"I guess we'll need to double back. Find another approach," Lightholler said as they rolled to a stop.

Kennedy nodded.

Lightholler stared at the approaching woman. "All these people, why does she choose *us* to play Good Samaritan?"

Kennedy slipped the car into gear. The woman had reached his window. She motioned him to unwind it. He looked over at Lightholler, shrugged and shifted back to park. He rolled down the window.

Lightholler tapped his shoulder and pointed at the windshield.

Kennedy looked up. Two men were approaching from the van. He turned to look at the woman. She had wisps of black hair that curled from beneath her scarf. She wore a pair of heavily tinted sunglasses. Her shawl had fallen open. She had a nine-millimetre Dillinger in her hand.

Kennedy only had time for one word.

"Patricia?"

A GAME OF CHESS V

The Kennedy Defence

These are primarily weapons for those with patience, stubbornness and resourcefulness. Not for the faint at heart, the Kennedy Defence begins with a violation of principle and rapidly proceeds to parts unknown. Even in the hands of a seasoned player it outfolds more like a work in progress rather than a fully formed strategy. The encouragement of White's unimpeded advance to the centre, and the unfavourable early exchange of a pawn, finds little favour with today's masters. Most believe that the defence is too cramped and requires meticulous handling. The intriguing manipulation of the White's own pieces into a barrier against further development, however, may occasionally bear rich fruit.

Black's best chance is that the opponent will overplay his hand.

Excerpt from Modern Chess Openings
Leon Browarnik

I

April 26, 2012
Houston, Texas

It always started off blurry, out of focus. Nothing more than peach fuzz. Shifting pink shapes against a pastel backdrop.

Webster marvelled at the convenient design of hotel rooms. If the mirror wasn't exactly opposite the bed, it was damn well close enough.

The image sharpened and the sound cut off abruptly. That was where Agent Birch stepped on the audio cable while trying to adjust the lens. By the time the agents realised their error it was all over. She was in the shower and he was lying on the bed staring at the ceiling, so all that was heard was the steady stream of water in the background.

Webster didn't need the sound. He'd seen the footage maybe thirty times by now. The film canister was propped on the table beside him. It was labelled: "Desert Inn, March, 2007. Room 12. Subjects: Caucasian male, 45; Caucasian female, 27".

He selected a purple pill. No-Som. Chased it down with a mouthful of water. He'd started taking them soon after the quacks had told him that the only way they could remove the pain was to remove his sight. He'd been popping them since New York had fallen. He hadn't slept in three days. He had two bottles: purple for up, pink for down. He'd save the pink for the flight out west, mixing and matching pharmaceuticals. Pastel City.

Purples gave him that buzz. That pop, pop, pop. Watching Malcolm's pert ass pop-pop-popping up and down. Peach fuzz. He'd popped an eye at Mazatlan thanks to that turd Kennedy.

He squinted watching her slide slow, up and down. A writhe that was part passion and part show, if he read her right. He watched as Kennedy's hands worked their way up from her waist to her breasts.

He took inventory.

He had his bag packed.

He had the Kennedy files on his desk next to the canister. The stuff Malcolm didn't get to see. The pathology report from late 2007—her miscarriage, scraped and scoped under a different kind of lens. What would Kennedy make of that?

He had Kennedy pumping up and down while the lab rat squirmed.

He had a thousand men, sequestered throughout the South and ready to roll.

He had a flight booked for Phoenix, as per President Clancy's request. A connect to take him to Vegas, and from there a scout to the *Patton*.

He was going to get to see the closing shot, up close and personal.

No-Som gave him that buzz, kept him up and running; his red eye skittering across maps and documents; dry mouth spitting out the orders and commands. Thoughts racing. Hot-wired.

Clancy convenes Congress. Kiboshes the Kennedy Crusade and calls on Clan and Country.

He liked the sounds the words made in his head.

She'd twisted around now to face the mirror but Kennedy was still holding on to her tits for dear life. Her hair was in her face, masking the eyes, but her lips were pursed in a rictus of desire.

Webster couldn't see her eyes but he could see what he thought were rivulets of sweat.

He had a nursery rhyme going round and round in his head. Maybe the last purple was a bad idea. Flight was in four hours.

Pop goes the weasel.

II

April 26, 2012

In transit: Houston, Texas / Phoenix, Arizona

He'd taken his first sedative over an hour ago, and coming down felt like breathing out *real* slow. It felt like something was emptying.

Buzz became headache and a dull weight on his eyelids.

The Raptor's cabin was empty. A bright seam was visible under the cockpit entrance. Through the windows, the flash of wingtip navigation lights and the flicker of distant stars. All else was darkness. Webster thought about the other Raptors—sleek black darts winging their way across the country towards their shared destination.

President Clancy had called him at 0600 hours, and Webster had told him that Nashville was a bust. No Kennedy, no Camelot operatives. They'd worked the story till they'd turned failure into success. They played down the Kennedy angle and juggled the kill-ratio until they were left with a whole bunch of dead nips and a reasonable number of martyrs.

Webster told him about the next phase of Avalon, the set-up in Arkansas. Clancy told him to kill the Kennedy angle. Webster explained that he had evidence pointing to a third *secret* camp, under Kennedy's command. Clancy had told him to *kill* the Kennedy angle.

Then the President filled him in. He confirmed that the Kaiser was alive and well and running the German show from Danzig. The Germans were concentrating on the East Coast, hell bent on relieving their New York beachhead. To that effect, they were routing all of their troops east of the Mississippi. Paratroopers held Richmond, and were working their way towards Washington. Brandenburg squads had already disabled most of the major choke points in a three-hundred mile radius of the beleaguered capital city, while the 5th Fleet controlled the waters from Maine down to Key West. Additionally, a joint British and Canadian force had blasted corridors through Pennsylvania and New York State and were digging in outside of Pittsburgh and Albany.

While the Japanese appeared stymied by the well-coordinated Anglo–German assault on the Union, they'd met with a series of successes in their ongoing Russian and Indian campaigns. Heavy counterattacks were expected as the Japanese shifted the bulk of their army from the American West Coast, but for the moment the Far East appeared contained.

The Confederacy was expected to stave off any move from the south. To date, that had meant isolated firefights with Mexican forces in southern Texas. Large troop concentrations, however, had been reported by high-altitude recon flights across the border. It appeared as though the Mexicans were waiting for more conclusive results on the part of their Asian allies before making any real commitment.

That left the west.

Confederate forces were scant along the Nevada–Arizona border. Clancy had told him he'd been assured by the War Office that the japs weren't going to try anything across the desert. That they weren't going to cross the Black Rock, the Smoke Creek, or the Mojave. "If they come, they'll come from the north," he'd been told confidently.

Clancy had marched across enough deserts in his time. He told Webster he didn't buy it. Hence the need to set up an Advanced Command Post on the *Patton*. Hence the need to send nine senior military staff out west.

Webster had taken it all in. It was no surprise that Clancy had relegated Kennedy to the bottom of the shit list.

When the conversation turned to the *Patton*, Clancy told him the airship was packing atomics. He had mentioned a fleet of *six* German stratolites sighted over the Arctic, and they'd pondered the significance of such a flotilla.

Webster protested that he had things to do in Houston, but the President would not be swayed. He rang off at seven. Webster was back in his office by eight.

He went through a list of Bureau operatives currently stationed aboard the Confederate stratolite. He assigned a separate detachment of tactical agents for bodyguard duty. They would arrive on the *Patton* within the next six hours. He went through his files on the other men who'd be joining the post. All capable, all reliable. He had dirt on five of them, a reasonable majority.

He ran the Desert Inn footage a couple more times. It helped fuel his purple-driven thoughts.

He'd boarded the Raptor at sunset. He was thinking he could snatch a few Zs before Phoenix, maybe a couple more on the shuttle. He was thinking about Kennedy. Clancy might well claim he was no longer important, but Kennedy or his cohorts had been sighted at *two* different flashpoints that had escalated the conflict: Nashville and Savannah. And nearly half of Kennedy's men still roamed Nevada.

Kennedy appeared guilty of a crime that put Webster's paltry frame-up to shame. Imagine that? Imagine promising away a continent that wasn't his to give. Webster found the whole idea utterly fascinating—so marvellous and beyond belief that he simply couldn't put it to rest. What could Kennedy have been thinking? And who was his paymaster? Japan or Germany?

The age of conquest was long gone, but everyone was still going through the motions, offering first aid to a rotting carcass. Populations might be moved, languages and beliefs could be banned, but in China, Afrika, Australia—so many places—revolt was merely a question of *when*. The Union danced to Japan's tune, while thrice-conquered Paris champed at the worn German bit. Amusing … terrifying … pitiful.

He thought about the two Emperors, Ryuichi and Wilhelm. Of their personal injuries. Two sons dead: one by design, the other by default. It had all the trappings of a feudal skirmish, and all the charm of vendetta … and emperors rarely suffered alone. These two had America laid out between them.

"Two eunuchs disputing a whore," he said, wondering which outcome he despised the least.

From Camelot to Avalon.

Camelot was like the grail itself. Once so close within his grasp and now forever lost. And like the grail—like any holy or unholy artefact—it reflected the desires of its observer. For Kennedy, it was the means to some unknown yet predictable end. Unknown in that his masters remained a mystery—though it now occurred to Webster that he had most likely been hedging his bets. Predictable in that he would certainly have secured himself a position of power in the new world order.

Webster knew what he himself wanted. *One America, united and free.* He was just uncertain about the asking price.

Drowsiness washed over him. He rubbed at his eye socket and adjusted the thin cotton sheet that passed for a blanket. He tried to concentrate on some image that might ease him into pleasant dreams. He pictured one of his secretaries, the thin one with the large tits. He put her in a bikini. He put her in a spa. He gave her Malcolm's face.

Delicious.

III

April 27, 2012

In transit: Las Vegas, Nevada / *CSS Patton*

He'd changed planes at Vegas. From there, the *Patton* was an hour away, tucked beneath the horizon's rim.

To either side of his scout, two more flew in loose formation. Generals Cathcart and Mayhew had shaken hands with him briefly on the tarmac before they'd boarded their respective craft. The rest of the command post personnel were on their way. At the limit of his vision, glints coursing amongst the stars, Webster could make out their military escort: a wing of Corsairs.

Dawn presented him with two sunrises.

The sun was a ruby haze at the world's edge. Above it, the glowing golden orb of the *Patton* basked in its reflected light. She grew with each passing moment. A speck, a smudge, a sphere, until finally she hung up there occluding half of the sky. A vast hornets' nest of plastic and iron, surrounded by a horde of scouts.

He'd been present for the stratolite's launch three years ago, but the object that greeted his eye now was barely recognisable. The ballonet system was almost completely concealed by metal plating. The under surface was densely packed with all manner of appendages: living quarters, hangars, cargo holds and weapon platforms. Silver stalactites of communication towers hung inverted beside the downwards mast, where a radar dish swung in slow arcs.

They circled the *Patton* for twenty minutes awaiting clearance to land. Two decks were currently active, and the stratolite was holding zero airspeed to facilitate the stream of arrivals. His pilot brought them in a wide approach towards one of the flight decks. They skirted the massive spherical domes of the ballonets, flying just above an array of long tubular structures that plucked at the sky like Medusa's mane.

When they finally got the green light, Webster found himself with another pink under his tongue. He held on to the harness, both arms tight across his chest. The pilot killed the jets as the deck's maw beckoned, a thin stretch of flickering lights that seemed too transient to be of any guidance. It vanished as the pilot brought the scout into a steep angle of attack.

The wide frame of the *Patton*'s bow loomed impossibly close now. The jets kicked back in and the scout pitched forwards and up. Flame-scored walls, seemingly too narrow for their scout's wingtips, lurched into view. He felt the tugs as the arrester gear hit wire after wire, a pummel of blows to his gut.

As the scout rolled to a halt, two crewmen ran up to the plane's sides. They wore fur-lined oversuits and their faces were completely concealed behind elaborate oxygen masks. He watched as they secured the bay doors. They gave the thumbs up and the pilot hit the canopy release. Webster inhaled great gulps of the fresh air. He felt light-headed and nauseated, on the brink of vomiting. His heart was a jackhammer in his chest.

He would have to do this again.

Admiral Illingworth greeted him outside the pressure doors. The admiral wore a white dress uniform. The relics of a frown carved his swarthy face. He made polite enquiries about the flight while they waited for the two generals to disembark. Then he gave them the tour.

He led them down a spiral stairway that traversed four floors of hangars. Each wide expanse stretched unfeasibly into distant darkness. Each held the capacity for forty scout planes, and perhaps a thousand crewmen moved between the levels, attending their duties. Illingworth pointed out the flight director's station with a casual wave as they left the air fleet.

He told them that while the *Patton* spent most of her time well above forty k, all habitats were pressurised to eight thousand feet. He further explained that despite the gargantuan mass of the great vessel, only five per cent of her volume was occupied space. The remaining ninety-five was devoted to helium. The inert gas was stored in the multitude of cells that comprised each ballonet.

The admiral showed them the dining rooms and the library, the observatory and the lab. From the rear-viewing chamber, amid a bristling array of anti-aircraft weapons, he showed them the row of self-rotating propellers. The blades extended well beyond the reach of their vision. He showed them the greenhouse, the heat pumps, and the energy storage batteries—huge carbon towers arranged like the magazine of a giant's gun. And at Webster's insistence, he showed them the Kaiser's gift—a gift that had eased the way for the war games in Arkansas and the increased German deployment in the Confederacy. A gift that had inexorably bound the fates of the two nations. He showed them the atomics.

The tour ended in the Eye, a glass-walled sphere that hung suspended beneath the lowermost habitat of the stratolite. Patrolling scouts winged back and forth across the sky below them where the Earth was a murky brown smudge. They drank scotches.

The pink was kicking in and Webster made his excuses. A few more hours' sleep would get him back on track. He followed his bodyguard along the narrow connecting passage tubes, his tired mind pleased with the fact that both he and the *Patton* shared the distinction of possessing a single yet all-seeing eye.

A red light was flashing on the console by the desk in his quarters. He had a message from Houston. It was coded, and revealed that an Avalon operative had made contact from Arkansas. Webster rued the scotches and the pills and the long flight. He washed his face and moistened the socket. He placed a call to the Houston office, selecting a frequency and activating his personal scrambler.

The operative called back within ten minutes.

Webster wasn't surprised to hear a male voice on the speaker. Malcolm, playing the cards close to her chest, was true to form. He was very surprised to hear what the operative had to say.

"Can you confirm that, Black Knight?" Webster said.

"Yes, sir. Guinevere secured Pendragon late yesterday afternoon. He's in custody, along with one accomplice."

Webster felt a momentary spell of giddiness. He put it down to the pink. He said, "Details, please."

"Pendragon was approaching Morning Star in Garland County. As you know from my prior reports, Guinevere tried to arrange watchposts around the four towns called Morning Star in Arkansas. Looks like we were in the right place at the right time, sir."

"Brevity, Black Knight."

"Sorry, sir. Pendragon was intercepted by our unit outside an engineered crash site. He came quietly. He's currently being held, along with the accomplice and our previous prisoner, in a lockup in Hot Springs."

"How many agents in your unit?"

"Four, sir."

"She's an insidious creature to have kept quiet about this, and you took your sweet time in sharing your knowledge."

"This was my first chance to contact you without arousing suspicion."

"Were there any official plans to notify me?" Webster's voice was ice scraping ice.

"She said she was going to contact you following a preliminary interrogation of Pendragon."

"Prevarication. She's an apt pupil, though foolhardy. When is the interrogation scheduled to take place?"

"Some time this morning, sir. She's just waiting on final results from the evidence lab in Savannah."

"What more evidence could she possibly require?"

"Some latent prints taken from our first prisoner."

"Fair enough. Your assessment of her current behaviour, Black Knight?"

"Frankly, sir, with Guinevere it appears to go beyond not seeing the forest for the trees. She wants to count every fucking branch."

Webster smiled thinly. "That would be consistent. For my own part, I've always found napalm to be a fitting remedy for troublesome forests." He paused to allow the agent a brief, simpering chuckle.

"There was one other thing, sir. Guinevere spoke briefly to Pendragon and his accomplice this morning."

"A preamble to her interrogation. How quaint. Any sign of collusion?"

"Not at all, sir. Guinevere appears clean, Pendragon seems very surprised to find himself in his current predicament."

"Have you secured a recording of their exchange?"

"I have, sir. Where would you like it sent?"

"Hold on to it for the moment, Black Knight. Just give me the gist of it."

"She confronted him about some camps, sir, clearly pertaining to Camelot. She questioned him about the location of a third camp, in addition to the Nevada and Louisiana installations. He sounded distinctly shocked by the accusation, then… offered to show her the site himself.

She terminated the interview without replying."

Webster felt his pulse quicken. How could Malcolm possibly know about the third camp?

How could Kennedy?

Apart from his own hinting at its possibility to Clancy yesterday, its existence was a complete secret. As long as Malcolm tied it to Kennedy, everything would be alright. If she took it a step further, she would require silencing and that would be such a pity.

"Are you still monitoring their conversation?"

"Of course, sir. So far Pendragon and his accomplice haven't said anything of any interest. I suspect they know they're being tapped."

"No matter," Webster said. "Call in your location to the Arkansas field office, it's time to end this little farce. Request a squad of tac agents. No soldiers, no police. Once they've arrived, you may act in my name..." His voice trailed away.

And do what?

He couldn't leave the *Patton* at present, and there was no way he was bringing Kennedy onto the stratolite. Alpha camp lay somewhere in the sands below. The thought of taking him *there* was a pleasant irony, considering that was where he'd been heading anyway. Pleasant, yes, but it held the melodrama of a penny dreadful. Clancy wanted the Kennedy angle killed. Perhaps a literal response, then, was required. Kennedy could always be linked to the third camp—Webster's brain child—posthumously.

"Take over the Hot Springs installation and hold it with your men till I give you further orders. I don't need to remind you to take every precaution when dealing with Pendragon."

"Hardly, sir. What about Guinevere?"

"Secure her as well. I'm curious to know where her suspicions stem from. She may appear clean, so treat her thus, but watch her."

"Yes, sir."

Webster replaced the headset clumsily.

Patricia Malcolm. Who'd have thought it?

The third camp had been covertly constructed on Texan soil. It held a thousand men, compared to the four thousand that had been scattered in Kennedy's camps. Men skilled in tasks as vulgar as rape and mass murder, as delicate as sabotage and assassination. Men who made Kennedy's trainees look like blushing debutantes, whose actions would tarnish Kennedy's reputation beyond any hope of redemption. Whose actions would bury Kennedy with them in the bloody dénouement and reprisals of Webster's vision of Camelot.

How could she know?

How can Kennedy be shocked, and then offer to show her the camp himself?

He needed to sleep on it but he couldn't get the question out of his head. He kicked off his shoes and drew the blinds. He threw himself onto the bed and stared at the ceiling. He wanted to know if he could have Kennedy killed and still survive himself without knowing which nightmares had driven that asshole down the path he'd chosen.

It was a tough call.

He popped another pink.

IV

April 27, 2012
Hot Springs, Arkansas

The cell was a standard ten feet by twelve. There was a bunk bed, a washbasin, a chair and a toilet. A discoloured brick wall separated them from the other prisoner.

Lightholler lay stretched out on the lower bunk, his head propped up on his folded jacket.

Kennedy sat across from him on the chair. He had his elbows on his knees, his hands supporting his chin as he leaned forwards. His face held a look of despondency, and only the slightest sideways flicker of his eyes betrayed any interest in the tactical agent on the other side of the bars.

The tactical agent had his feet on the edge of a desk as he thumbed through a paperback. Kennedy watched the ash mount on the end of his untouched cigarette. He watched as the residue fell away in little grey slabs into the ashtray. The agent looked up at Kennedy and winked before returning to his reading.

Kennedy looked back at Lightholler. His eyes were closed, his face relaxed in slumber. The words were so faint he thought he'd imagined them. He leaned closer.

"What now?" Lightholler repeated. He saw that he had Kennedy's attention and added, "She seemed … informed."

"I don't know." Kennedy looked away. The agent seemed immersed in his book. "To be honest, I'm not sure why we're still alive."

"Comforting," Lightholler murmured.

Kennedy got up and went to join him. Lightholler moved his legs aside and Kennedy perched on the edge of the bunk. He continued in a low undertone. "They can't have moved us too far. I think the flight was a feint, I can't see any other reason for blindfolding us for the trip. If we were back in Texas, the director would have paid us a visit by now."

Lightholler nodded.

"And look at the walls," Kennedy said. "It's a recent paint job. This is no Bureau cell."

"We're still in Arkansas."

"And we're still alive."

"*And* we have company." Lightholler signalled towards the brick wall with a subtle gesture. He gazed back at Kennedy with a spark of his old self. "What do you make of it?"

"They didn't even put us in separate cells, John."

"Perhaps they mistook us for allies."

Kennedy almost smiled. "They lack the personnel or the floor space. They're more worried about one of us communicating with the other prisoner. Either way, this is a rogue op. It's small time." His voice was now barely audible. "And as for the other thing…"

Lightholler stared at him questioningly.

The floor was dusty. Kennedy etched the outline of a circle in the dust and started to sketch a series of spokes coming out from beneath it. His crude rendition of the carapace. Lightholler stopped him at the seventh line. He nodded. Kennedy swept the image away. Lightholler mouthed, "Red Rock".

Kennedy smiled. His voice was the softest whisper. "They don't know."

He rose from the bunk, stretching. He let out a yawn and saw the agent looking at him. He winked back.

How had Patricia been dragged into this? She'd worked Evidence Response, sorted through forensics and surveillance photography. She'd worked the cold crime scenes where tapered yellow ribbon announced "Police line" and "Do not cross". She didn't pound sidewalks. She didn't carry a weapon. So what was she doing here?

It might have been a year since he'd last seen her. Her purposeful, hurried steps had taken her away from the Houston Bureau offices. He'd wanted to call out to her, but had instead remained silent, craning his neck to prolong the vision.

And this morning, seeing her in the cell, he'd felt the same thing that he'd felt then. That swift movement in his chest, a sense of something being snared and released, and then just a dull grey ache that slowly faded to less than nothing. He wondered what was worse: her involvement, or the fact that her presence evoked a world he'd long thought lost.

She knew he had a third camp, but she didn't know why.

He'd had to stop himself from commenting, from reaching out a hand to touch the side of her face.

Yesterday, emerging from the ambush site, Agent Reid had said, "Aren't you at least going to tell her she's looking good?"

Kennedy had said, "You're looking good, Patricia."

Then Reid had slapped on the cuffs and secured the blindfold. Kennedy's last vision had been of a rueful smile playing across her face.

They were bundled into the back of the van and driven for what might have been half an hour. From there they had been transferred to an aircraft. They'd taken off and landed and been shifted to another vehicle. It had been done reasonably well. They'd been driven around for another hour or so before being led down a series of corridors to this cell.

Another prisoner had accompanied them for the last leg of the journey. He was now being held in the adjacent cell. Kennedy had whispered the name Shine, but received no response. Now all he could hear was the occasional sound of movement from next door.

The tactical agent rose from his chair. He sauntered over to the cell till his face was an inch away from the thick black bars. He eyed Kennedy casually and said, "Mazatlan, huh?"

"Among other things."

"So I've heard."

Kennedy smiled with the lower half of his face.

The agent reached through. He grabbed Kennedy's shirt and forced him up against the bars, hard. Kennedy's wound peeled open at the edge. The agent bared his teeth. "This is as pleasant as it's going to be from now on, *Major*."

"Hey." Reid's voice was a shout from the other end of the room. "*Hey*."

The agent released him and Kennedy fell back with a stumble. The agent wiped a bloodstained hand against his trousers and walked back to his desk.

"You'll have to excuse him, Major Kennedy." Reid stepped up to the bars. "You killed his brother in New York."

Kennedy went to the basin and ran the water. He checked his wound in the mirror and wiped at it with a damp towel. He said, "I haven't killed anyone in weeks."

"What about Nashville?"

Kennedy stared back at him vacantly. "Nashville?"

Reid snorted. He said, "This is going to be fun."

Lightholler was out of his bunk. "When do I get to see an attorney?"

"Attorney?" Reid laughed outright. "Who'd represent you? The best deal you're going to get is a blindfold to go with your bullet."

Kennedy said, "What are you waiting for, Reid? What's holding you back?"

Reid walked past the bars, his fingers a staccato caress against the metal. He moved out of view to stand before the adjacent cell. There was no sound from the other prisoner.

He reappeared after a moment and said, "I'm pacing myself." He gave them both a mock salute before leaving the room.

Kennedy turned to Lightholler triumphantly. "They don't know a thing."

Lightholler's face was drawn and pale. He said, "Where's the journal?"

V

A rudimentary search of the room yielded no obvious recording device. She'd expected as much from the small prison, but the last few days had taught her that there was no such thing as "undue" caution.

There was a table and three chairs. A curtain was drawn over the two-way, and someone had left a magazine open on the table, but neither gesture convinced her that this was anything other than another interrogation room. She tried to picture Joseph seated across from her, one hand cuffed to the table, and her thoughts swept back to their earlier encounter in the cell. He was unshaven, wounded, he'd dyed his hair. He reeked of a variety of unpleasant odours. What had he become?

I'll show you, Patricia.

What, Joseph? What could you possibly show me that might justify all of this?

He looked vulnerable. Mortal.

Captain Lightholler had undergone a startling metamorphosis himself. He'd shaved his head and looked more gaunt than any photograph had suggested. Aristocrat to thug in the space of a week.

These two men were the bane of the Confederacy?

She pulled the folder from her bag. As she placed it on the table, her eyes caught the various accessories she'd brought with her from city to city. Her fingers brushed the purse spray and the lipstick, the nail file and her house keys. She picked up her compact and examined it curiously, as if it were some artefact recovered from an archaeological dig. She flipped it open and looked at her reflection, angling the image this way and that.

She closed it, closed the bag and placed it on an adjacent chair. She opened the folder and sat down.

Here were the notes she had made back in Houston, the punch cards and the documents she had taken from her office. Her notes on Morning Star and the ENIAC print-outs. Here was her new life.

She thought about Joseph and the look on his face; about Reid agitating for her to make the call to Houston while the tac agent stood in a far corner of the room, smoking. She shook her head, wishing it all away.

Reid's now-familiar step coursed down the hallway. She hastily slid her notes into the folder and placed it closed upon the table. She was already standing when the door flew open. She composed her face and said, "What is it, Agent?"

"Kennedy knows we haven't told the director."

"He can't know that."

"He knows."

Reid scanned the room. His glance took in the two-way, the table, her folder; a stern expression crossed his face. He softened it and made his tone placatory as he continued. "You did great in Morning Star, Agent Malcolm, but this is going way too far."

"I want a decent shot at him, and I want it without that tac agent breathing down my neck."

"There's only so much protocol I'm prepared to ignore. No more unsupervised communication with the prisoners." Reid began pacing the room. "What the hell were you thinking anyway?"

"I'm close."

"You're too damn close. This ain't your field and you know it. I call Webster and we have specialised interrogators down here in two hours. Hell, I should be doing it myself."

"You wouldn't know what to ask."

She returned to her seat without looking back at him and reached for the folder.

"And just what the fuck is *that* supposed to mean?"

"That there's something else going on here. Something that runs deeper than Camelot."

"I've been saying that all along." Reid's face was a twisted scowl. "What I don't want are any more unscheduled interviews. Tell me what you've got. I've held off calling the director, but my balls are on the line here."

"You paint a pretty picture."

Reid's smile was a polite curl of the lips. "You're *not* interviewing him alone. He'll run rings around you. If you don't want the tac agent, you're stuck with me, and if you're stuck with me I need to have some idea of what we're looking for."

"Fine." She opened the folder and removed her notes. She began sorting through them, shuffling them like a deck of cards. He watched hungrily. She asked, "Did you ever hear anything about Director Webster's involvement in Kennedy's presidential campaign?"

"Just rumours, never proven."

She tapped an envelope that lay on the desk beside her folder.

His eyes widened marginally. He shrugged it off and said, "Ancient history. What does it have to do with Camelot?"

"Motive."

She handed him the files. She watched as he scanned the top page, a frown forming on his face.

"Are you sure about this?" he asked finally.

"As sure as I can be," she replied. "There's a third camp."

Reid replaced her notes on the desk. He slid into a vacant chair. "Okay, so there's a third camp."

She eyed him incredulously.

"What?"

"A *third camp*, Reid. You went to Bravo, Carter's at Alpha—why weren't we told about the third one?"

"It might have been Kennedy's deal on the side. Black ops. We've got Kennedy now, so we can deal with it."

"These are from the director's files. *He* authorised the transactions, not Joseph. An ancillary payroll index, but the names correspond to the codes from Camelot's database."

"Give me those." Reid snatched back the notes.

She said, "A sample list of the personnel is on page six."

"Arson, armed robbery, manslaughter, rape, murder one. Nice."

"A thousand of them. They all rotated through 4th Mech-Cav, but none of them appear to have received any Special Forces training."

"You went through all the records?" he asked coldly.

"I couldn't check them all," she replied. "I didn't want to leave an obvious trail on the ENIAC." She'd made herself as clear as she dared. The only person authorised to observe her computer search was the director himself. “Back in Savannah you told me, and I quote, ‘Those Alpha boys are a scary bunch of fuckers.’”

Reid smiled.

“What the hell do you call these guys then?” she asked.

“All of the instincts with none of the refinement,” Reid mused. His eyes, still on the list, narrowed. “They ain’t choirboys.”

“The camp was established within six months of Alpha and Bravo. No mention of any location. No memorandum issued from any office. All I have are the names and the numbers.”

“What did Kennedy say when you confronted him?”

“The allegation took him completely by surprise. Then … he offered to take me to the site.”

“What more do you need? They were in it together.”

Malcolm thought she noticed the slightest tremor as he reached for his cigarettes. She said, “Here’s how I see it. Alpha and Bravo were training saboteurs and assassins. The third camp, let’s call it Omega, trains killers.”

“Semantics,” Reid replied, lighting up.

“Perhaps, but at first I thought the same as you, that Omega was an ace in the hole created by the director and Major Kennedy. I couldn’t determine their agenda, but I suspected that they were the only ones in the hierarchy who knew about it. When the major turned rogue, its existence became a liability justifying the director’s obsession with hunting him down. So the director builds a case against him on one side, assigns Wetworks on the other.”

“I can see how that might work.”

“That’s why I didn’t want the director to know we had him. Not yet at least.”

Reid’s curious expression soured under her gaze. “You didn’t want Kennedy to suffer an ‘accident’ before coming to trial.”

“That’s what would happen, isn’t it?”

“It’s in the cards,” he replied. “But every moment you keep this from Webster, you drag us down with Kennedy, and I can’t have that. So I’m going to ask you again: what the hell were you thinking?”

Half a minute earlier and she wouldn’t have been able to reply. It was a question she’d been asking herself all morning, fostered by the new intelligence that Joseph had unknowingly given her.

"I wanted the final print matches from Savannah. I wanted the major's story." Her words seemed to come from some other source, as if channelled. "Then I was going to contact the President's Office, the Executive Department. Let *them* deal with the Bureau's recent activities."

Reid gave a low whistle. "Every time I come close to thinking I've got your number, you pull the rug out from under me..." His voice faded into thoughtful reflection. He drew deeply on the cigarette and said, "At first you thought the same as me. What did you mean by that?"

"I thought they were both in it together."

"Aren't they?"

"Major Kennedy doesn't know about Omega."

"Didn't you just tell me that he offered to show you the site. What am I missing here?"

"I know him well enough to know that he had no idea what I was talking about. Whatever he's up to, it has nothing to do with a camp of hired killers."

"What was he offering to show you then?"

She thought about the desperate look on her prisoners' faces. She thought about the money Joseph had skimmed and siphoned into a number of disparate charities. Call it guilt, call it blood money, call it insurance. She thought about Berlin and said, "I don't dare imagine."

Reid flicked his cigarette to the floor. "We have reasonable evidence that Kennedy was working with the japs, we have circumstantial evidence linking him to the Germans, and we have his own admission of the existence of a secret installation. We also have ballistics and prints placing him at the location of at least two murders in Osakatown. If you're right about this—and, let's face it, all we have here are a few names and your instincts—but if you *are* right, Omega camp is Webster's baby and *both* of them have been running black ops. We're screwed."

Hearing him echo her fears gave them horrifying substance. She took the notes from his yielding fingers. "We never had this conversation."

She felt ill. She'd hoped that sharing her burden might have brought some comfort, an end to her dread. Perhaps she had counted on some startling refutation, a lucid analysis that would have rendered all her theories useless. Instead, Reid had his face in his hands.

"Make your call," she said. "Let's just finish this."

"Ballistics placed Kennedy at the two murders," Reid repeated, looking up at her slowly. "Right?"

Malcolm nodded distractedly.

"Where are the rest of your notes? Where's your stuff on Osakatown?"

"I've got that here." Perplexed now, she reached for her folder and passed him the relevant pages. "I'm still waiting on the prints though," she added, trying to muster some enthusiasm.

"I know." He examined the documents carefully, running a fingernail down the scrawled lines. He asked, "Where's your inventory on what we seized in Morning Star?"

"It's all in lockup."

"Not the stuff," Reid replied gruffly. "The paperwork. Kennedy and Lightholler had two guns on them, didn't they?"

"A Mauser and a Shingen."

"Not a common handgun, the Mauser," he murmured.

"Major Kennedy seems to favour them."

"He does, doesn't he." Reid was becoming more animated. "Where did you record the serial numbers?"

She walked over to his side of the table, leafed through her notes, and pointed to where she'd documented her findings. He placed the page next to the Osakatown ballistics report. The serial numbers were identical. She looked back at him and said, "That's impossible."

"Could you have copied one from the other by mistake?" he asked.

She checked the dates. "No way. This is the first time I've looked at these notes in days. Maybe..." Her voice failed her.

"Jesus." Reid shook his head. "Anyone who found Kennedy was screwed." He chuckled softly. "It's been a set-up from the word go. We never had a chance."

"How could I not have seen this?"

"*No one's* supposed to see it. The frame-up's too obvious. There aren't too many people who could engrave an existing serial number onto a new gun and plant it at a major crime scene."

"Joseph never murdered anyone."

"Not in Osakatown, at any rate," Reid muttered.

Malcolm felt something shift deep within her; a growing sense of horror at the enormity of the director's crime, counterbalanced by some new shred of relief. In this matter, at least, Joseph's hands were clean.

Still, she couldn't bring herself to speak Webster's name. "*He* ordered the deaths of eight agents, just to make certain the major was put away?"

"It's starting to look that way." Reid's burst of vigour ebbed rapidly. "I wonder if he'd lose sleep over a couple more?"

She rested her hands on the table, leaning forwards next to him. "What can we do now?"

Reid pressed his palms together and put the fingertips to his lips. "I see three options." He turned so he could see her face. "Hear me out. I'm just thinking out loud, okay?"

"Okay."

"First option: we kill all three prisoners and deny ever finding the weapon. Come up with some sort of cover story."

She told herself Reid was being pragmatic. She formulated a response and the coldness of her words astonished her. "The tac agents know what really happened here. We would never be able to sustain the story."

"I know," he replied. "Second option: inform the director and buy into his conspiracy. Hope for clemency."

She resisted the urge to move away from him but remained silent.

"Third option: go with your plan. Brace Kennedy and the others, and tell them about the frame-up. They might have thought that they were safe for the moment. They might have thought that Webster was still in the dark. This little twist might make them more cooperative. Then we approach the Executive Department." He lit another cigarette. "What do you think?"

Malcolm walked slowly back to her seat. She said, "I'll have the tac agents alert the Raptor, let them know we're planning on flying to Houston. That should appease them. In the meantime, we interview all three prisoners, separately and together."

"Sounds good," Reid replied. "But *I'll* take care of the Raptor. I want you to find the nearest ENIAC and trace every last fuck on this list, so we can account for everyone who's ever trained at *Omega*. Any *one* of them will be able to give us the location."

He caught a look in her eyes. "What's the matter?"

She was thinking back to the memorandum she'd brought with her from Houston. "I was just wondering what happens if it turns out that the President is already involved."

Reid's expression darkened. "Then," he said, "we might as well get ourselves fitted for shrouds."

VI

April 27, 2012
Hot Springs, Arkansas

Lightholler stood numbly with his hands behind his back while the tactical agent snapped on the cuffs. There simply hadn't been enough time. No time to evaluate the consequences of the journal's loss. No time to devise a new strategy to deal with their captors. Not nearly enough time to—

"Just a few questions." Reid was watching them from the other side of the bars. His eyes flicked from Kennedy to Lightholler and back. "No blindfolds or bullets."

Kennedy stepped up to the bars and said, "I'll tell you what you want to know."

"I know that, Major," Reid purred. "We've dealt with the appetiser and we're working our way through the main course. Think of yourself as dessert."

Lightholler checked Kennedy for a signal. He had no idea what form the gesture might take or what his response would be. The cuffs had his wrists pinned close to his spine. A tug on the bracelet and he tottered a step towards the door. Kennedy fixed him with a resolute stare.

Lightholler said, "Be seeing you, Joseph."

They led him past the adjacent cell. It was empty now. There was a pile of soiled bandages coiled on the floor. The tactical agent directed him towards a corridor that had been concealed from the vantage of his cell. Occasional pale squares and bare nails on the yellow walls marked where a poster or calendar may have hung. There were no clocks and no windows.

The corridor opened into an area that had been divided into several workspaces. Government-issue metal desks competed with filing cabinets for floor space. It had the look of a station house rather than a governmental office. The windows had all been sealed over; the little bands of light that crept into the room were skewed columns of dancing dust. Judging from the angle of the light, the day was almost done.

Reid directed him past a coffee recess where an urn simmered. He felt a sudden pang of hunger.

"After you, Captain." Reid indicated a small room that lay beyond the recess.

The tactical agent gave him a nudge. The room was sparsely furnished. There was a table and four chairs, a phone and an ashtray. The mirror on the far wall had to be a two-way. Lightholler gave it a brief self-conscious glance. There was a faintly unpleasant tinge to the air that hinted at putrescence. The agent undid one of the cuffs and clasped it to a metal link embedded in the desk. Then he and Reid left the room.

Lightholler kept his eyes on the table. He felt as if his face might betray every wild thought that flashed through his mind. Hadn't he driven through the streets of New York anticipating just this moment, this escape from madness? His own words returned derisively.

When we do get hauled in, I'll be sure to remind them to add abduction to the charges of conspiracy and treason.

He'd accused Kennedy's crew of improvising in New York, and they'd continued to do so across half of America: commandeered an airship and a bullet-ridden scout, ridden freight trains and stolen cars. Gangsters had guided them, and intrigues had formed and clung about them, and somewhere along the line he had begun to believe.

Kennedy had little to say about their captors, but there was something between him and the girl. That much was certain.

He could tell his captors now. Tell them how he'd been taken at gunpoint. Tell them about the deals Kennedy had brokered, selling out his country many times over, all for a madman's crazed delusion. They'd believe it. All those roads travelled and all those deaths. The children's faces pressed against cracked window panes on the streets of Nashville. His opportunity stood before him. It was a doorway, a linchpin—it was a beam of the purest light. A simple turn of phrase and he might never see Kennedy again.

A simple turn of phrase and he might never see anyone again.

A truck stop in Pleasant Valley, Tennessee. Dishwater eyes and flapjacks. "I think that a couple of days from now, none of this will matter."

"I can't afford to tell you. If we get captured..."

"They'll just put us both in an asylum, if we're not hung for treason."

He realised he was straining his cuffed hand against the bracelet.

Damn you, Joseph, just when did "you" become "we"?

There was movement from beyond the room. Lightholler raised his eyes slowly to the door. Reid held it open for Malcolm. Her hair was tousled and lines creased the edges of her dark eyes. She sat across from him and placed a folder on the table. Reid lingered at the door for a moment, arms crossed, as if forming a mental picture of the tableau. He moved to the table and pushed the ashtray towards Lightholler and offered him his old brand. He gave an easy smile as he lit their cigarettes.

She asked all the questions.

"When were you first approached by Kennedy's men?"

"Who was your contact?"

"Are you aware that Rear-Admiral Lloyd is dead?"

She rehashed conspiracy.

"What was your role with the Brandenburgs?"

"Why did you leave New York?"

She talked frame-up, planted guns and false accusations. She showed him the paperwork: matching serial numbers, one retrieved from Kennedy's Mauser and the other from the Osakatown murders. She asked him about Camelot. Dates. Numbers. Locations.

He said, "I received a letter from the British War Ministry. It asked me to cooperate with Major Kennedy and the CBI. I had nothing to do with the Germans."

Reid said, "*We're* CBI—so why aren't you cooperating?"

Malcolm said, "Where is the letter now?"

Lightholler shrugged. Kennedy had suggested that this was a rogue operation, down-scaled and outside of the director's sphere of influence. Malcolm was implying corruption from the top down.

"I'm a British citizen with diplomatic immunity," he replied.

"Your immunity ran dry round about the time you decided to shoot up Nashville."

Reid smoked and paced. Malcolm needled and probed. Lightholler waited for the offer.

Reid agitated. He swept piles of paper off the desk and crumpled the cigarettes in a meaty fist.

"This isn't what you were asked to do," Malcolm cajoled. "This has nothing to do with the War Ministry. You're as much a victim as these guys were."

She spread photos on the table, from Osakatown. She pursed her lips thoughtfully and removed another batch of photos from her folder—the Queens Midtown Tunnel. She caught him off guard.

She said, "You were there."

Lightholler blinked but said nothing.

"He was there, Reid."

Reid pounced. He made the offer.

"Frame-up or not, we'll place you at the Tunnel. Conspiracy or not, we'll place you at Nashville, Osakatown and every fucking homicide between here and New York City. Give us Kennedy and we'll give you complete amnesty. Give us Kennedy and we'll give you back your life."

Lightholler noted Malcolm's flinch.

"Tempting." He smiled feebly. "I need to use the rest room."

Reid looked at his watch and then back at Malcolm. "Let's bring him in." He picked up the phone and dialled a number. "We're ready now."

"Rest room?"

"It can wait, Captain."

The tactical agent opened the door. He led his prisoner to the chair by Lightholler's side. *There* was the source of the putrefaction, the decay. The prisoner's head was wrapped in a bandage that extended down to obscure half of his face. He walked with a limp.

"I believe you and Mr Newcombe are acquainted," Reid said with a wry grin.

Lightholler cast the prisoner a fleeting glance. The prisoner nodded back with a pained expression. Recognition came as a thunderbolt. Lightholler wondered if anything could surprise him after this.

The photographs were still on the table. Osakatown and the Midtown Tunnel. The cold-blooded murders of that terrible afternoon in New York.

Amnesty and a life returned? What life?

They'd said nothing about the journal.

Tell me, Joseph, what will we do with your time machine?

VII

The tac agent fumbled with the prisoner's wrist. The desk only held a lock for one pair of cuffs. Malcolm gazed at Newcombe with a tinge of remorse; the man needed further medical attention.

"Leave it," she said.

The agent shot Reid a look. He nodded and dismissed him. She decided to let it go.

The prisoner was broken—damaged goods well before he'd been scooped out of the Atlantic—but he served as a caution to Captain Lightholler. *Look*, she thought, *this is what we can achieve just by mere neglect.*

Reid kept looking at his watch. The other tac agent would be back from the airport any time now and Lightholler wasn't giving them anything. Was it time to move on to Joseph, or pursue the Tunnel angle? She gave Reid what she hoped was a veiled look of entreaty.

He took the cue.

"Well, Captain," Reid said, "what's it going to be?"

"Don't know. I can't think straight," Lightholler replied, and he was clearly troubled. The prisoner's arrival had prised something loose. "I need to eat something. I need to take a piss."

"Captain. Please." Reid had seen it too. He gave Malcolm a look of mock horror.

"Captain," she said gently, "if you would just—"

The phone's sharp peal startled her. She glanced up at Reid, who responded with a shrug. She picked up the phone.

Reid moved to the door. He was beckoning the tac agent, saying, "Piss break."

The agent made a show of weary indifference as he released Lightholler from the table. He clamped the free bracelet around Lightholler's other wrist and led him out.

"Make sure he washes his hands," Reid called out after them. He looked back at Malcolm with a smirk.

She gazed at him questioningly. Why had he cut Lightholler loose? Why had he broken their rhythm?

"This is Evidence in Savannah," a voice was saying over the line.

"Sorry. Agent Malcolm here. What have you got?" She snatched a scrap of paper from her notes.

"The print matches you requested are back."

She cupped the mouthpiece and said to Reid, "Prints are back."

"'Bout fucking time," Reid replied. He was still standing by the door, watchfully.

"Go ahead," she said to the lab technician, and he gave her the details. She asked if he was certain, and he confirmed it was a verified match. She looked over at the prisoner. Her hands were shaking.

The technician was still talking, saying something about a partial print. He paused, mid-sentence, and said, "I'm sorry, did you say you were *Agent* Malcolm?"

She wondered what was taking Captain Lightholler so long, wondered how to play this out, and here was another asshole struggling to come to terms with a female operative. She said, "Yes, this is *Agent* Patricia Malcolm."

"Are there any other agents there with you? I'll need to talk with one of them."

She held the phone away from her for a moment, fuming, and caught Reid's eye.

"What?" he said.

She rolled her eyes and handed him the phone. She looked across at the prisoner and shook her head. "What *were* you thinking?"

There was a sudden brisk movement at the corner of her eye. Why was Reid holding his pistol?

"You fucking bitch."

"Reid?"

"You fucking conniving *bitch*." Reid held the gun centred on her chest. He closed the door and walked back to the table. He perched on its edge.

"Evidence control just came through with the partial print off Kennedy's gun, honey, and it's yours." His voice was a snarled rasp.

"Are you insane? Of course my prints are on it. I'm the one who disarmed him."

He lashed out at her chair with an abrupt kick. She landed on the floor, her legs twisted beneath her. He was standing over her with the pistol in her face. He kicked her again. His boot smashed into her hip, sending a searing jolt of pain down her leg and up her spine.

"I'm talking about the gun from New York. The gun from Osakatown."

Hot tears streamed down her face. "That's impossible. You *know* that's impossible."

"Is it?" He reached for the phone again, his eyes never leaving her.

"I'm being set up." She tasted tears and blood in her mouth and she was crying and she was furious with herself and terrified beyond any previous concept of the sensation. "Framed like Joseph."

"Your precious, fucking *Joseph. You* copied the serial numbers, *you* faked the whole fucking thing." He dialled a number and spoke into the mouthpiece. "Bring your men in now. This shindig is over."

He slammed down the phone. He groaned and dropped to the floor.

The prisoner was standing above him. He had Reid's pistol in one hand and the ashtray in the other. The ashtray had a clump of blood-tangled hair on its scored edge. He looked down at Malcolm and said, "Are you okay, miss?"

She looked over at Reid. His face was pressed against the floor, a trickle of blood was pooling near his mouth. An ugly bruise was forming over the base of his skull. His chest moved with shallow gasps.

She looked back at the prisoner; he was swaying a little in the tide of his exertion. He kept the gun aimed at a point just beyond her.

He said, "Are you alright?"

She wiped at her face with the back of her hand. Her leg ached and there was a dull throb where Reid's boot had connected. She wanted to vomit. "I'm okay."

"I'll need your gun."

She patted herself down awkwardly. Her skirt was heaped up above her knees and she had to struggle to remove her jacket. She said, "It's in the outer office."

Reid was starting to move, his fingers scrabbling at the cement floor.

The man who had been her prisoner reached for Reid's cuffs. With one eye still on her, he twisted Reid's wrists up and locked them behind his back. Reid groaned.

She looked up and said, "What are you going to do now, Mr Morgan?"

VIII

The tac agent rapped on the interrogation room door. The door swung open.

Lightholler hesitated at the entrance and a shove from behind propelled him into the room.

Agent Reid was gagged and cuffed to the desk. The lower part of his face, caked with fresh blood, was bound by a roll of bandages. Agent Malcolm was on her knees.

Morgan, unfettered, held a gun at the back of her neck. Reid saw them and let out a stifled howl.

Lightholler stepped back. The tac was right behind him, reaching for his weapon.

"Hold it right there." Morgan's voice was gravel.

Reid bellowed, kicking at the desk.

"Easy, bud. Relax." The tac had his hand on the holster.

Lightholler slammed a heel where the tac's shin should have been, overshot and tumbled. The tac glanced down at him and drew his pistol.

The room shuddered explosively. Lightholler was deafened. He saw Morgan's lips move. "Drop it."

The request was redundant. The tac agent's forearm was torn flesh and bone. He was staring at it incredulously. He said, "Shit," as his pistol clattered on the floor.

Lightholler booted it to the far corner of the room.

Reid fell silent.

"Oh, *fuck*." The tac agent was bent over, nursing his arm.

"Get those off." Morgan was pointing at Lightholler's wrists.

"*Jesus Christ*," the tac agent howled.

"Captain?" Morgan urged.

Lightholler struggled to his knees and reached for the agent's key chain. The agent, in an oddly obliging manoeuvre, shifted his wounded elbow to facilitate the exchange. Lightholler removed the keys. The question roared in his brain. *What the hell happened to Morgan?*

The historian's pale eyes were still watery blue but they fixed towards some undefinable distance. His face was lined and carved from steel. Possessed.

"Can you manage, Captain?" Morgan asked in his new voice.

Lightholler nodded. He fumbled with the key, slipping it into the lock. A twist and he was free. He rubbed at his wrists, still dazed.

"Captain?"

Lightholler looked up. He was remembering the last time he'd seen Morgan, in the *Shenandoah*'s hangar. What had happened since? Where was Hardas?

"Would you mind cuffing the agent?"

The tac had his injured arm pressed close to his chest. Lightholler hesitated, read Morgan's glance, and proceeded to apply the cuffs. The agent growled his anguish.

Lightholler got to his feet and retrieved the other pistol.

"We have to get out of here," Morgan said. "This piece of shit," he gestured towards Reid with a nod, "just called in some backup."

Despite a thousand questions, Lightholler shifted the tac agent to one of the chairs while Morgan attended to Agent Malcolm.

"I'm sorry about that." Morgan was extending an arm towards her. She waved him away angrily and rose to her feet. "Take a seat." His gun was now trained back on her.

She dropped into one of the chairs.

Reid was making feral noises at the back of his throat while the tac moaned a low keening lament. Blood pooled on the dirty floor. Morgan tugged the bandages away from Reid's mouth.

Reid tried to spit.

"Who's coming?" Morgan asked.

"Girl scouts." Reid's saliva was more formed, it splattered against Morgan's shoes.

Morgan turned. "Any ideas, Captain?"

Lightholler stared back wordlessly.

Morgan's eyes narrowed. He looked over at Malcolm, who now sat with her hands under her thighs, rocking gently. "She can get us airborne."

"Don't you do a *fucking* thing for them," Reid said through gritted teeth.

Morgan advanced on him with the back of his hand raised. He turned to Malcolm, as if seeking her approval. She looked away. He dropped his hand and replaced the crude gag. He reached for the phone and ripped it from its socket. He grabbed the back of the tac agent's chair and pushed it up against Reid's. He tied their wrists together with the bandages and the phone cord. He examined the tac's wound and bound the skin above it with a spare strip.

Gesturing towards Malcolm with the gun, he said, "This way, if you will, miss."

She rose unsteadily, avoiding the wild fury of Reid's eyes. Lightholler took her arm and this time she didn't resist. They followed Morgan out of the interrogation room.

IX

The sounds registered indistinctly at first, faint and far away—the muffled slam of a door, the furtive scurry of running feet—but the gunshot's echo rang clearly in Kennedy's ears.

His thoughts pounded inchoate; murderous and feral, plotting impossible retributions. A part of him realised that it had been small arm's fire, loud and abrasive, rather than the softer crack of a rifle. He felt the raw graze of his throat but couldn't recall shouting. Only the gripped steel bars of his cell were real. Those, and the gunshot's proclamation: no companions, no journal and no hope.

The running footsteps drew nearer, quickened, and a part of him realised that it would all be over soon.

His eyes fixed on the gun first. He only had a vague impression of the forms that stood beyond the bars. They blurred into the aspect of Lightholler and Morgan. He'd sought to save a world by snatching it from fire. He'd only served to fan the flames. Morgan's spectre, the charred evidence of his crime, shambled to one side. He wondered where Hardas's ghost hovered and it was all he could do not to mouth a muted apology.

"Major, are you okay?" the spectre rasped.

Time jerked forwards. The gun didn't fire, the shapes didn't resolve into his enemies. He stared at Morgan thickly for a moment, trying to make sense of it all.

"Joseph?" Lightholler advanced. He had a set of keys in his hand.

Kennedy stepped back from the cell door. Lightholler wore a spray of dried blood on his shirt. Morgan, scarred by older wounds, had a smear of fresh blood on his sleeve. Blood on the keys.

"We're alright," Lightholler said.

"Whose blood?"

"A bit of everyone's, Joseph."

Only then did he notice Patricia. She was standing across the room from him, watching their reunion with silent censure. She stood awkwardly, favouring her left leg. Her clothing was rumpled but there was no apparent sign of injury.

"What happened?" Kennedy asked.

"I'm not entirely sure." Lightholler entered the cell and rummaged around, grabbing his jacket. He gave the bunks a quick inspection and said, "Let's go."

"What about Reid? Where's Hardas? What's going on?"

"It's good to see you again, Major." Morgan spoke softly, but swiftly. "Hardas is dead." He held Kennedy's gaze, didn't shy away or blink. "Reid and another agent have been secured. Agent Malcolm says that the other tac is at the airfield with the Raptor. That's where we're going."

Kennedy looked at Patricia. She remained silent.

"Reid called in backup," Morgan added. He motioned Kennedy towards the doorway. "Backup he isn't supposed to have."

Patricia nodded briskly.

The details could come later. Kennedy walked out of the cell and inspected the surroundings. He took in the adjacent cell—the one Morgan had occupied—the blinded windows and the corridor that must have led down to the interrogation room.

"This is a field office," he said.

"County Sheriff's," Patricia replied.

"And we're still in Arkansas, right?"

"We're just outside of Hot Springs," she answered wearily.

He turned to Lightholler and said, "The journal?"

"Downstairs in the safe." Lightholler offered a wicked smile. He rattled the keyring. "Nothing's been touched."

Kennedy shook his head and muttered, "Evidence Response." He gazed at Patricia with relief. Anybody else would have turned that manuscript inside out by now.

He followed the others towards an exit that had been obscured from view.

Morgan was alive. They had the journal. They had a plane.

Nothing was impossible just because it was improbable.

X

April 28, 2012
CSS Patton

Webster stood at an unfiltered view port. At sixty thousand feet, dawn was a swift transition. Cloudscape flashed pink at the world's edge and moments later day was upon him.

The stratolite's Eye pulsed with activity. Intel techs pored over the latest maps. Meteorologists jostled with navigators for the scopes that ringed the glass-walled sphere. Surveillance officers peered at the various monitors and compared notes. Command and control.

A table had been cleared among the work stations and a young officer stood before it, propelling coloured markers back and forth across a map of the West Coast with each new intelligence he received.

Webster took meticulous note of the general conversation that flowed around him. He glanced at various screens, taking memory snaps of their contents for later analysis. A deputation from the German Expeditionary Forces was due aboard the *Patton* at 0900 hours. That left little time to finalise his dossier in preparation for their parley.

The fossil of a smile creased his face. He'd forgotten how good all this tasted.

Recent years had brought him an accumulation of paperwork, of other people's projects to be ratified or vetoed. Conferences were attended and hands were shaken, but the last decent thing he'd sunk his teeth into was Camelot, and look where *that* had led. He put the thought aside.

Clancy had told him to kill the Kennedy angle, and amazingly enough he had been able to do just that. It was only forty-eight hours since the matter had been discussed, but apart from the exchange with Reid, he had given Kennedy scant thought. His smile broadened. All those long months of suppositions and counter schemes and all it took was an atomic detonation, a civil war and the threat of world-spanning conflict to place everything into perspective.

He put together a sketch of the latest reports. There had been delays in the relief of New York. A Canadian recon party had turned up a pair of Luftwaffe pilots thought lost in an earlier sortie. They hung from makeshift crosses in a cotton field outside of Scranton. An uprising by the surviving enclave of New York's Japanese residents had been brutally suppressed.

British marines had arrived on the outskirts of the city to be greeted by scenes of misery and terror; lean-faced Brandenburg troopers with empty eyes escorting convoys of the civilian dead out of the ruins.

German paratroops had skirmished with a detachment of Union regulars at Fredericksburg, and there had been reports of entanglements between Union and Confederate forces all along the Mason-Dixon Line. The conflict was thus far confined to firefights and artillery exchanges, but there was little hope of averting full hostilities between the two Americas.

At the southern border, a column of Mexican tanks had crossed the Rio Grande. There had been heavy fighting outside of Laredo, but no further advances had been noted. The most recent scout sweep suggested that the Mexicans were entrenching within sight of the border, and it was only with a small amount of resentment that Webster wondered if memories of Kennedy's last campaign in Mexico had curbed their enthusiasm for a rapid advance.

At sea, the new German submersibles had exceeded all expectations, tearing through the Japanese shipping and disrupting commerce between the West Coast and the Japanese Isles. The 5th Fleet dominated the waters.

Further afield, the reports were less reliable. A widely cast net gathered more rumour and hearsay than facts. Espionage agents in India provided reasonable evidence of an insurrection in Delhi, following the Japanese encirclement of Lahore. The Japanese were apparently being welcomed as liberators as they pushed into the subcontinent.

Less convincing was the report of an entire Russian army group's surrender following a tactical atomic blast in Kazakhstan. To Webster's mind, it was more likely the result of a maladroit attempt to destroy supplies as the Russians fell back on their proven strategy of "scorched earth".

He included it all in his appraisal, highlighting the information he felt could be endorsed by credible sources. He noted that offers had been made by Ryuichi to the reigning families of the Saudi Peninsula. Another fortnight of similar successes in East Russia would bring the Japanese to the foothills of the Caucasus Mountains. The Japanese were, in a vast pincer movement, closing on two-thirds of the planet's known petroleum reserves.

He didn't plan on saying anything at all about the German stratolite fleet.

President Clancy had told him two days ago that a flotilla of six stratolites had been observed above a Russian weather station at the polar ice cap. The most recent account, garnered from a Bureau agent aboard a Norwegian whaler off the coast of Sakhalin, placed them six hundred miles from the Hokkaido shores. They could strike at any time.

Whilst the military applications of stratolites had yet to be officially demonstrated, Webster had read reports of colonial disputes where rebellious towns and cities had mysteriously burnt to the ground under mysteriously clear skies. And he'd seen the stockpile aboard the *Patton*. Three ugly cylinders, snub-nosed and fin-tailed, arrayed beyond the standard ordnance of high-yield conventional explosives. They comprised fifty per cent of the Confederate atomic stockpile, and they were all at his fingertips.

If the Germans hadn't seen fit to inform their Confederate allies of their intentions above the Japanese Home Islands, it was of no immediate concern to him. The knowledge might provide useful leverage in the months to come, though, when dealing with the victors of this war, whomever they might be.

Webster moved away from the view port. One of Clancy's three-star generals was examining the central map. He gave Webster a cursory nod and vanished swiftly.

Yesterday, at a meeting with senior staff, the same general had chided him for offering input into the military aspects of the campaign and Webster had smiled thinly. The general had gone on to remind him that his role was merely one of intelligence rather than the formulation of strategy. Webster had taken the general outside and reminded him that screwing a fifteen-year-old schoolboy in a room of the Tucson Holiday Inn was an interesting combination of statutory rape and sodomy. The general, pale and trembling, had agreed that Webster's point of view might well be of some value in the coming meeting with the Germans. Webster had assured him that he would leave the big decisions to the experts.

He scanned the dispositions of the Japanese forces on the central map. So much for not trying anything in the desert. The japs weren't supposed to cross the Black Rock, the Smoke Creek or the Mojave deserts. They were supposed to come from the north—that was the projection. So what were they doing in Yuma? What were they doing in Reno? There were two divisions massed at the edge of the Demilitarised Zone, an unhealthy mix of Union regiments among them. They had to have been airlifting troops since Berlin to have mobilised so rapidly.

The Confederacy had one reinforced division dug in along the Grand Canyon. Between them and the Japanese forces were three regiments, hastily brought across from southern Texas following the Mexican encroachment; that was all.

The Germans had promised reinforcements, but the Confederacy's western defences appeared bleak. Still, he felt certain he'd be able to wring a few extra battalions from the thinly stretched German Expeditionary Forces. And, at the end of the day, there were always the atomics.

The Eye was filling rapidly as the morning staff arrived to relieve the previous shift. Webster elbowed his way across the crowded chamber and made for the lift. It rose slowly towards the underside of the *Patton*'s massive hull. A throwback to gentler times, its clear walls had been designed to offer a spectacle to the newly arrived. It gave one the impression of floating upwards, past the inverted spars of antennae and the spiralling tubules of water-capture devices, into the belly of an immense creature of the air. He only half-seriously considered taking a purple.

Back in his quarters, he found himself thinking again about the map. Military strategy was hardly his strong suit, though he'd found over the past few days that his suggestions had been met with more than polite acceptance. He wondered if it might be more useful to utilise some of Kennedy's men, after all. They *were* trained in sabotage and demolition work. Why ship them down to Alamogordo when they might be of more use interfering with Japanese supply lines?

He smoked a cigar. He was thinking about Kennedy again. He changed tack and, like a reformed addict, prided himself with another example of abstinence while berating the craving. He told himself he would check in with Reid after the meeting.

There was a knock at his door. A smooth-cheeked military police officer stood at attention outside the cabin.

"You're wanted on the bridge, sir."

Webster followed the young officer down one of the long corridors that spanned the stratolite. There seemed to be more traffic than usual for the hour. Depending on proximity, most of the transport aboard the *Patton* was provided by motorcar or mini-rail. Now, however, squads of crewmen and sailors were marching in both directions along the causeway. The pilots were suited up in thermals and flight jackets.

He became aware of a strange sensation in his stomach, and realised what was happening.

"Why are we climbing?"

The MP pulled up and replied, "We've just got report of two jap strats on a long-range scout sweep."

They were now rapidly ascending. Fire crews moved to their stations, while scout crews mustered for launch. The fact that no alarms had been raised did not alter Webster's preliminary assessment. The *Patton* was preparing for battle.

He was ushered onto the bridge and led to where Admiral Illingworth stood with his senior staff. He picked up snatches of conversation as he moved across the deck.

A pilot was examining a series of silhouettes in a large bound folder and pointing to two of the images. "That one and that one," he said.

An observer remarked, "The *Hiryu* and the *Soryu*. They're supposed to be over the Pacific."

"Well, they're here now," the pilot replied grimly.

Nearby, a navigator and his radar techs were bent over a scope. The navigator reached for a chart and said, "See? They caught a mid-strength jet stream at forty-five thou. They don't want to be flying any lower than that with the draught they're carrying. If they hold to current, they can make up to one-seventy miles an hour and still maintain a scout swarm. We need to be at sixty-five ourselves and running silent if we want to slip their radar."

"We need to be at seventy if we want to avoid their scouts," one of the techs commented.

"We hit them now," the other tech muttered, "and we go through them like shit through a goose." He lowered his voice at Webster's passing.

The mammoth stratolites, under their own power, could barely exceed velocities of fifty miles an hour in a calm. With a jet stream behind them, however, they could reach speeds of up to one-seventy. Any faster and structural damage became a genuine risk.

As for the scout swarm, scouts were the only aircraft that could match altitude with a stratolite. Anti-aircraft fire balked at eighteen thousand feet and surface-to-air missiles scattered at thirty-five. The latest prototype jet fighters maxed out at fifty-five, so the only thing that could touch a stratolite was one of the small gnat-like planes. Webster pictured the anti-aircraft weaponry he'd seen on his first tour of the *Patton*. There had also been some larger-bored weapons amongst the bristle of turrets. At the time he hadn't really considered their implementation, but he had to wonder now what uses they might be put to in the hours to come.

Illingworth welcomed him with a gruff nod. He gave a brief update. The two Japanese strats had been sighted over the DMZ and were bearing due east. All evidence suggested that they had no knowledge of the *Patton*'s current position. The Germans were now aboard but the meeting would have to be delayed. He would be much obliged if the director began a pre-emptive discussion with the envoys.

Illingworth's staff moved over to the foredeck's large view port. The sky was filling with scouts. Some hung in the air, as if suspended by invisible wires, while others swooped past in practised ellipses that orbited the vast stratolite. The bridge's buzz was rising to fever pitch as more of the staff assembled.

Webster made his way to the exit.

The German delegates were being debriefed on the operations deck. Webster decided to take a detour via his cabin. He was due for his eye drops and wanted to see if he had any updates on the file concerning the Japanese air fleet. He found some comfort in the fact that two jap strats over Nevada meant two less to trouble the German flotilla over the Sea of Japan. Their deployment struck him as a curious misuse of resources.

He'd almost gained his deck when he felt a tug at his sleeve.

"Beg pardon, sir. Urgent dispatch from CINTEX." The communications officer had a sheaf of print-outs in his hand. He thrust one forwards to Webster and stood rocking from side to side, awaiting a response. Webster dismissed him with a severe look and resumed his step.

He examined the page as he walked and got as far as the second paragraph before stumbling to a halt. Crewmen shouldered their way past him as he scanned the rest of the report.

Reid had never called in. Webster's team had arrived at the station house to find no trace of Kennedy or his captors. Malcolm's Raptor had logged a departure time of 1700 hours from Hot Springs. The flight plan, registered with the Little Rock field office, anticipated a Houston landing. The Raptor had never arrived.

He read the next few lines in astounded disbelief.

How was he supposed to chair a meeting with the Germans when one of his Raptors had crashed three hundred miles off course in the Louisiana wetlands? How could he be sure that Kennedy was dead when the crash site was fried beyond all recognition? And how could he have any hope of wading forwards when the blood-steeped past dragged at his heels with all the promise of the abyss?

XI

April 28, 2012
Outskirts of Las Vegas, Nevada

Shine removed a strip from the torn fringe of his shirt and wrapped it around his head. He tied it back and wiped the torrent of sweat from his brow.

He'd waited two nights for the major to show. He'd listened in to the police band as the township of Morning Star was being shut down. There was no point waiting any longer. He'd walked into town and stolen aboard a freight car and watched the limestone bluffs of the Ouachita Mountains give way to Oklahoma's gently rolling plains.

He'd hitched a ride at the border and spent the night lying on a flat-bed, under cold, slow-moving stars. They'd been forced off the road at dawn, somewhere in Nevada. Within moments a rolling cloud of sand heralded the arrival of a panzer division. He'd availed himself of the confusion to slip away and spent the early hours perched on a sand dune a few hundred yards away from the procession.

All that remained before him was the broken expanse of what had once been the I-15. The tanks had been rubber-shod, but thirty of them had managed to reduce the highway to a stretch of rubble. The little township of Las Vegas lay ahead. Another sixty miles north and west lay Red Rock.

He began the slow trudge into town and paid no mind to the odd rig that rattled along the shattered highway. He passed easily for one of the dispossessed, drifting east and west with the tides of war and loss, so when a truck pulled to a halt before him it took some moments to react. There were already two tac agents on the roadside before he grasped what was happening.

"Don't even think about it, boy," one of the agents snarled. He had a submachine-gun cradled in his arms.

Shine looked up at the truck. Its rear had been converted into a holding cage. He spied a group of prisoners through the torn, stretched canopy. The majority of them were indian. He thought he could make out a couple of blacks amongst the men.

"Looks like we bagged ourselves the runt of the litter. Might as well toss him in with the others."

They ordered him to the ground. They removed the knife along with his boots. They tore off his bandana and ripped open his shirt and ran rough hands over him. The driver emerged from the cab and unlocked the back of the truck while the other agents trained their weapons on the crowd. He mounted the platform under watchful stares. He felt the crowd part as the cage door clanged shut behind him and found himself propelled towards the front of the platform. He caught looks of curiosity or faint surprise. He recognised a few of them from the camps and met their glances with a nod. The truck lurched forwards with a crunch of gears and a spray of loose asphalt.

"I knew you were coming, Martin."

He turned to address the familiar voice and his father gazed back at him with rheumy eyes and a warm, steady smile.

"Are you alright? What's happening, Pa?"

"We got the order, son. We're fading in." His father reached up to squeeze his son's bare shoulder and said, "The major's on his way."

XII

April 28, 2012
Alamo, Nevada

The voice told him to relax. It told him that the major knew what he was doing. Morgan shook his head, thinking, *That's all well and good, Hardas, but you're dead, so what the hell would you know?*

The voice cackled harshly, the way he used to laugh, but with a touch of genuine amusement. *Damn straight. Cold and dead, but you're going to be alright, so just relax.*

Morgan dispelled Hardas's voice with another shake of his head. He saw the major looking at him curiously and made himself smile back. *It should have been me.* Peering outside, past the grimed glass, he focused on the slow drift of distant clouds.

"This is it," Kennedy said, finally. "Check your restraints. It's going to get a little bumpy from here on in."

"What about the others?" Agent Malcolm asked. She'd seated herself as far away from them as the small cabin of the cargo plane would permit. She spoke without looking at him.

"They're secure," Kennedy replied evenly. He made a quick final survey of the cabin and checked his watch. He caught Morgan's look and said, "We're going to be okay, Darren."

"I'm not worried, Major. Just surprised."

Kennedy cocked an eyebrow.

"Things seems to be going our way for a change."

Lightholler laughed. Kennedy winked at him and turned his attention to the cabin's window.

They were coming in to Alamo low and fast.

Kennedy and Lightholler had been walking on eggshells around him ever since Hot Springs. Lightholler must have told the major what had happened in the interrogation room. Perhaps when things got quiet enough, someone might care to explain it to him as well. He'd heard the shot go off, but was as surprised as anyone else to realise it was he who'd fired the gun.

They'd only asked him about Hardas after they were airborne. After they'd collected the journal from the safe, mopped up the blood from the cell floor, and transferred Reid and the others from the station house to the hijacked Raptor. After Kennedy had wired Tecumseh and ordered the fade-in, had given the Raptor's pilot his new coordinates, and had Reid and the others—all except Agent Malcolm—bound and stowed in the Raptor's cargo hold.

Morgan had been sitting in a quiet internal discourse with Hardas when the major had turned to him and asked, "What happened, Darren?"

And he had asked himself, *What do I tell them?*

And Hardas's voice, channelled by Morgan's grief and configured by his subconscious, had replied, *Tell them everything*. So he told them about the German carrier group and the battles at sea and the *Parzifal* and the attack on the trawler and Newcombe's fuddled attempt at betrayal and Hardas's last stand. He told them how the smugglers' ship had vanished in a vast plume of smoke and flame, and how he'd found Hardas sprawled, his jacket a honeycomb of bullet holes and his face a bloodied, broken wreck.

He told them how he'd found Newcombe still talking on the radio when the *Parzifal* herself had been rocked by an explosion. How he and Newcombe, lying side by side on the burning deck, had fought over the heated barrel of Hardas's pistol and how he'd put a bullet between Newcombe's wide, frenzied eyes. He told them how he got the idea of stealing Newcombe's identity while watching the corpse simmer.

He never mentioned the fact that as he was co-opting the identity of one companion, he believed he was absorbing that of the other. That a part of Hardas had somehow seemed to fuse with him while everything else around him burned on the tossing waters.

Catching Kennedy's careful look, however, Morgan wondered if the major entertained some insight into his peculiar new condition. Hardas's voice had sustained him through two terrifying days of deprivation and pain and he wasn't about to let it go.

He stole a glance out the window. On cue, he observed a sputter of sparks stream back from the far propeller. A wreath of smoke enveloped the engine. They were going to be cutting it fine.

Alamo's landing field was a long stretch of dirt that ran five thousand feet before dissolving into scrub and barren soil. Kennedy had had men working at the field since 2010, when the base at Red Rock had gone up, but he'd insisted on making this look good. That was why there was a line of fire engines on what passed for the tarmac. That was why the starboard engines were on fire.

The plane was a Hughes T-7. One of three planes that had been waiting for them at Louisiana when their Raptor had touched down. It was an old four-prop, slow but sturdy. Kennedy had assured them it would make it down on two engines. That would be confirmed or denied shortly.

Morgan forced himself to keep his eyes on the steadily approaching ground. He had a brief flash of his escape from the *Shenandoah* in what might have been another life, and heard the voice inside say, *Keep it together*. He saw his face twisted in a savage grin in the window's reflection. The craft convulsed as a metal plate on the far engine peeled back slowly, and then vanished in a blue stream of flame. Morgan fixed on the horizon's rising shimmer.

The landing gear rattled into position. He felt the vibration as the air brakes kicked in. The wind screamed. The Hughes crunched strip and leapt skywards, struck earth again and skidded momentarily, sending a shower of dirt into the air.

He was thrown against his restraints. The wail of sirens became plainly audible over the plane's protesting roar. Out the window—now a barely transparent smear of brown—he saw two fire trucks racing alongside.

Morgan felt faint. His eyes raked the cabin.

Kennedy was already out of his seat and working his way over to Malcolm as the plane continued its smoke-encased careen. She had her head hunched down as she struggled with her belt. He dropped down beside her, grabbing her chair for support. She seemed to fall into him, then sat back abruptly as he loosened the restraint.

He said, "John, Darren, I want you ready when we blow the doors."

Morgan was on his feet, swaying. The plane was slowing down.

Lightholler had the satchel. He was laughing. Kennedy bustled them to the rear of the plane, using headrests for handholds. The Hughes lurched to a halt. Kennedy twisted the emergency release. The door burst open with a wave of pure heat and strong hands emerged through the thick haze to sweep them from the cabin.

Firecrew and paramedics shuffled them towards a waiting ambulance pulled up alongside the plane while two men played a hose of water and foam across its steaming fuselage. Morgan recognised Tecumseh's swarthy, sweat-drenched face amongst the emergency crew.

Tecumseh flashed him a smile before turning to Kennedy. "Cargo secured. We're good to go."

"Where's Doc?" Kennedy called back to him.

"Making ready."

"And Shine?"

"Hasn't shown."

A billow of dust at the far end of the strip declared the arrival of the legitimate emergency team. Kennedy, glancing nonchalantly across the field, said, "Get this crate off the strip and torch it. We'd better roll."

The back of the ambulance had been cleared of beds and two iron benches had been welded in their place. Despite the lack of equipment it was crowded. Two of the emergency crew had squeezed in next to Lightholler as the vehicle pitched forwards and ran a loop around the wounded plane.

One of them said, "What do you do for an encore, sir?" The other nudged him and gave Kennedy an embarrassed grin.

Kennedy seemed about to reply when he spied the expression on Malcolm's face. He returned the crewman's smile, but said nothing.

The Hughes was away from the runway now and lumbering unevenly over a patch of dry grass. Tecumseh's crew had remounted and their motorcade was racing away from the craft in the ambulance's trail. Morgan saw two men leap from the Hughes' cabin and within seconds the plane was consumed in a ball of blue-white flame. He watched as the second emergency team, drawing towards the wreck on a tangent path, slowed to a halt.

"Man, oh, man," the first crewman said.

"What is it?" Kennedy asked.

"Next time I pick you up from the airport, sir, I'll be damn sure to bring along some marshmallows."

"Great," Malcolm muttered. "Dinner and a show."

Instinctively the others looked to Kennedy, as if seeking permission before bursting into laughter.

"Where's Agent Reid?" Malcolm asked. "Where are the others?"

"They're in that ambulance back there," Kennedy replied soberly, pointing out the rear window.

"And what are you going to do with us?"

"Us?"

Her reply was stern silence.

His face hardened. "You'll know when I know, Patricia." He glanced at their surroundings, gave Lightholler a knowing look and said, "Déjà vu."

The two men's communications had been minimal but Morgan had noted a new cadence and rhythm to their talk. An undercurrent of understanding through tacit exchange. He envied them.

The ambulance halted at a series of sheds by a barbed-wire fence. Three trucks were arrayed before them. They were a shabby, hyphenated collection of six-wheelers: olive-drab, ex-army and nondescript. The crewmen unsealed the bay door and they all piled out. At the far end of the airfield the Hughes belched plumes of dark grey smoke. A small crowd was forming a perimeter around the smouldering wreck.

"We don't have much time," Kennedy said.

Morgan nodded. Red Rock lay approximately forty miles north and west from here. He'd made the trip from Alamo once before, and even then, with no demand for haste or urgency, it hadn't been a pleasure. Highway 93, a ramshackle scar of blacktop at the best of times, was out of the question. It would be off-road from here.

Tecumseh and another crewman were approaching one of the emergency vehicles. They unlocked the back of the ambulance and began hauling out the prisoners. All three were bound at the wrists and ankles. They all had cloth bags over their heads. Morgan saw the makeshift bandages on the tac agent's arm and winced with an abrupt fusion of pain and pity. Then he recalled his own transient experience as Reid's prisoner and muttered, "Fuck them."

Tecumseh marched them to one of the trucks. A bag slipped back and Reid's face, blinking and furious, scanned the group and turned on Kennedy.

"What the—"

Tecumseh had the bag back in place and Reid's question became a garbled rant.

"Bring them along, Chief?" Tecumseh asked, carefully.

Kennedy didn't look over at Malcolm. He said, "For now."

Tecumseh nodded sagely and led them up a ramp into the back of the truck.

Other crewmen were carrying Malcolm's bag and a few of their belongings to another of the vehicles.

"What about you, Tecumseh? You coming with us?" Kennedy asked.

Tecumseh smiled broadly and pulled at his collar, revealing a sky blue ghost-dancer shirt beneath his uniform. "You know I wouldn't miss this for the world."

He turned away from Kennedy and gave some instructions to his men, speaking in a lilting sing-song dialect, a variation of the Sioux tongue that Morgan couldn't place. A group of his crew returned to the emergency vehicles. They farewelled Tecumseh with solemn gestures. Four of Tecumseh's remaining crew climbed in with the prisoners, another three joined him at the second truck, leaving four with Kennedy.

Kennedy was watching as the emergency vehicles coursed back towards the crash site. The remaining crew stood by his side, following his gaze. The look on Malcolm's face suggested that she'd seen enough.

Lightholler edged up to Morgan and asked, "What was that?"

"I think it was a traditional send-off," Morgan replied.

"It seemed to take a while."

"I don't think Tecumseh expects to see them again."

They made their way to the last truck.

XIII

April 28, 2012
Pahranagat Mountain Range, Nevada

Thirty miles out of Red Rock

There had been a short stretch of road leading away from the airfield. They hit the checkpoint at the edge of the small township where the phantom of a river gasped feebly beneath an iron bridge. The few vehicles that crawled the streets were military and everyone they passed was in uniform.

Tecumseh hung out of the leading truck's cab to exchange words with the guard and Malcolm watched in dismay as the two men shared easy laughter. It looked like Joseph had his fingers in any number of pies. The guard waved them over, but only after exchanging a similar, albeit briefer, form of the ritual she had seen at the airstrip.

She recalled Tecumseh from the files she'd gone through in Houston. He was supposed to be a medicine man. That meant more than just a religious figure. The bulk of Joseph's men at Alpha were supposed to be indians too. What were they doing meeting him at the landing field? Wasn't Alpha supposed to have been locked down? Director Webster had indicated that they'd found the camp undermanned and Reid had said the same.

They slowed down and the prison truck snaked into view in their trail. Two armed men were stationed on the roof, swaying with the truck's uneven motion. They had removed their emergency gear, perhaps because of the heat, and now wore bright blue shirts stamped with a series of designs she couldn't make out with the dust and distance.

She thought about Reid and the other agents, bound and blindfolded since Hot Springs, while she'd been kept close by Joseph's side. He hadn't questioned her. He hadn't laid a finger on her. Was she even his prisoner?

She had never seen this side of him. Whatever goal he'd pursued seemed to be drawing near. Its imminence displayed itself in the singularity of his pursuit.

Someone had tried to frame her. Someone had placed her prints on Joseph's gun. And so Reid had turned on her. She might have been able to reason away his actions in the face of the set-up. She found it impossible to accept the fact that he'd brought another team along; that he had been bound to betray her. *And what if Morgan hadn't intervened?*

She shook uncontrollably, despite the heat.

"Patricia?" Joseph eyed her with concern.

"I'm okay."

Kennedy worked his way up to the truck's cab. There was a tremor as the vehicle resumed its stuttering pace. A moment later he clambered back towards them. "A long-range confed patrol came through the checkpoint before us. Jap patrols have been sighted in the area."

"This far east?" Morgan exclaimed.

Kennedy shrugged. "The main Confederate defences are being set up along the Grand Canyon. This region's up for grabs."

He spoke about the Confederacy in an abstract fashion, as if it was something he could be no part of. Wherever his allegiances lay struck Malcolm as a cold and distant place.

"What about the Rock?" Morgan asked.

"Clear," Kennedy replied, guardedly. "We just have to take it slow. We may run into some hot spots." He searched Lightholler's and Morgan's faces. They both appeared to take his news with worn resignation. "I'm setting up a corridor between here and the Rock. We'll be okay."

Lightholler grunted a response.

She found herself giving Joseph a supportive look and wondered what the hell was wrong with her.

Despite her boots, she had sand between her toes and her feet ached. She had sand on her face, in her hair, and grit lined the corners of her eyes. The air in the truck's hold was stale and dry and hot, yet she saw with some disbelief that Lightholler and Morgan were nodding off. She spied the pistol on Lightholler's belt, just out of reach. His eyelids fluttered. He caught the quick movement of her eyes, and the look he gave her was one of almost disdainful challenge. *Go on,* it seemed to say, *let's make this trip a little more interesting.*

Really, she thought, *I just want to go home.*

It was hard to imagine she had ever had one; harder yet to imagine ever finding her way back.

They'd been travelling for almost two hours before they heard the first bursts of artillery; soft crumps that scarcely made themselves heard over the truck's incessant rattle. No one commented at first, as if such an observation might be impolite. She flinched with each muffled blast.

Joseph was unmoved. "Mortar fire," he finally growled. "Eighty-one millimetre."

"Yep, heavy weapons," Lightholler murmured. "They're outgoing."

There was the deep whistling decrescendo of more shells.

"Incoming," Morgan corrected. He looked over at Kennedy.

Kennedy scurried up to the cab. Scurried back. "They're incoming."

"What did I just say?" Morgan scowled.

The truck heaved sideways and rolled onto rougher terrain. Kennedy, braced against a chair, reached an arm out to Malcolm before she could be thrown from her seat. The truck groaned to a halt in a thick swirl of sand.

"Everybody out," he commanded.

They poured out onto a shallow sand-drift thrown up by the truck's passage. His men had already formed a semicircle around the vehicles, crouched low. They unrolled three sheets of dirt-brown canvas and threw them over the trucks, securing the edges with a piton here, a pile of rocks there. They gathered her together with Lightholler and Morgan and motioned them towards a furrow between the trucks that lay under camouflage.

They dispersed, moving fast and low out over the sand, establishing a perimeter. At a hand signal one of them went to check on the other prisoners. He appeared at the back of the truck with a thumbs up gesture before dropping to the ground close by. The men were disciplined, they kept close order. They operated with a cohesion she hadn't expected.

These aren't terror troops, she told herself. *They're veterans.* Veterans of the 4th Mechanized Cavalry. They might have been without their tanks and banners but they were the men who'd marched into Mazatlan.

Tecumseh scrambled towards them and offered Kennedy his field glasses. Malcolm saw him peer in the direction of a coil of black smoke under the lowering sun. After a few moments scanning the horizon he said, "Can't see shit for sand."

"I'll have an update any time now," Tecumseh said.

Joseph nodded and Tecumseh disappeared. He was back in a few moments.

“We’re picking up a lot of local radio chatter, jap and confed. Looks like a couple of recon patrols bumped noses up ahead.”

The artillery fire grew more sporadic. Some of the men had reappeared and one was talking to Joseph. He came into the trench and emptied the contents of his backpack onto the ground. Military rations. She gave Morgan a confused look.

“Sleep when you can, miss,” Morgan said. He wiped his hand against his shirt, broke open a ration and tore off a strip of dried beef. He handed it to her with a surprising amount of grace.

“Eat when you can,” Lightholler concluded.

The beef tasted like sand. She tried to look grateful.

The barrage lasted forty-five minutes.

XIV

April 28, 2012
Alpha Camp, Nevada

And still the men were singing. It was a dark melody they took up in turn, their throaty voices wringing subtle tones from the prayer. Occasional snatches were reprised. *Wicahcala kin heya pe lo maka kin…*

They had skirted Las Vegas and found the I-15 intact further west where the panzers must have gone cross-country. Earlier, the truck had pulled over onto the side of the interstate and one of the agents had emerged with his gun and instructed them to stop singing. The tune was maintained, a low whispered harmony, and one of the indians had asked, "Will you shoot us if we continue?"

The agent had looked at their faces and looked at his feet and then stared out at the mountain range that never seemed to move and said, "No, but keep it down," and the men had resumed their expectant hymn.

The song was transforming. Shine might be the prisoner of white men, but somehow the melody dispelled the taint of slavery and replaced it with a spark of hope.

The turn-off to Alpha, once little more than a faint flattening of the desert floor, was now well advertised with an assortment of tyre markings that indicated the passage of cycles, trucks and armour. They followed it into the afternoon sun.

Alpha had the air of abandonment. The motor pool bristled with an array of tracked vehicles and the guard towers were manned, but there was a new desolation about the place. The truck was waved through the gates and motored on past the training grounds and field hospital to the barracks. They were intercepted by a squad of tactical agents and directed to Block C.

His father told him that half the barracks had been converted into a temporary prison; the rest were being used by the agents and rotating long-range recon patrols. He said that there were approximately forty agents, three platoons of recon and a detachment of Texan armour watching thirteen-hundred corralled men. The rest of the crew were still out in the desert but had been giving themselves up or taking up new positions.

When Shine asked him how he could know all this, his father leaned in close and replied, “We know about the *other place*. We know it’s close by.”

Shine didn’t let his face betray his knowledge.

“Some of us are in contact with Tecumseh. He told us the major is coming and bringing the end of days.” He sounded like one of the ghost dancers. That was their creed: that the major would bring about some great and cataclysmic change.

Shine made to speak but his father hushed him with a gesture.

“I don’t need to know no more than that, and I know it ain’t that simple, but Tecumseh says the japs are closing in. He says we may need to buy them some time. This is the best way we know how.”

Shine’s glance took in the rest of the prisoners. “How many of them are ghost dancers?”

A negro, tall and rangy, who’d squatted alongside Shine earlier, spoke while picking at his teeth. “Enough, my brother. Won’t be too long now.”

“They got to know they fucked up,” one of the indians said. “Can see it in their eyes.”

“Big time,” another added, and there was a chorus of low chuckles.

“They wanted to send us south to fight the Mexicans. They talk about sending us out west now to fight the japs, but they just talking. Fact is, they too scared to give us back our guns.” His father laughed until it became a hacking cough.

The tall negro sucked at his teeth dismissively. “Got the japs on their doorstep and they shitting their pants.”

His father spoke again, softer now. “They don’t know we don’t need guns.”

An agent came round and told them to shut up. He unlocked the cage and the men were marshalled into a cordoned area in front of the blockhouse.

“You going to process them now?” the agent asked one of the guards stationed there.

The guard sniffed the air. "I ain't doing jack till these redskins been scrubbed down."

"Not my problem," the agent said and walked off with a leer. "Get it done, bud."

The guard ran his eyes over the prisoners, making a show of his displeasure. He counted them off, "Redskin, coon, coon, redskin, redskin," marking a list he carried with him. He rapped against the blockhouse door and two more men came out of the building.

"Redskins to the showers, coons to processing." His eyes sought Shine among the knot of men and he added, "Watch that one, he's a killer."

The two men shared cold laughter and began dividing up the prisoners.

XV

April 28, 2012
Pahranagat Mountain Range, Nevada

Twenty miles out of Red Rock

It had been thirty minutes since the last round had detonated. They were perched in a narrow gorge just beyond the encampment. Lightholler had watched as Kennedy tracked the spurt of sand with his field glasses.

Kennedy'd said, "Stray shell," and kept his eyes on the distant ridge.

Tecumseh worked his way back to their position with a radio operator in tow. Lightholler shifted to give them some room. The operator squatted down and passed his headset to Kennedy. "What do you make of it, sir?"

Kennedy listened intently, fussed with the frequency and listened again. "I make at least two platoons of jap recon."

The operator nodded.

"They've taken heavy losses. They're pulling out," Kennedy said. "The confeds sound like Rangers but there's a lot of chatter."

"Rookies?" Lightholler ventured.

"Green enough," Kennedy replied. "But they dislodged those japs." He paused for a moment, as if weighing his options, then said, "Let's move out."

The men broke camp swiftly. One moment Kennedy was giving the order and the next the crew were rolling down the camo and loading up the vehicles. Everything was taped down or tied with thick rope to diminish movement.

Lightholler watched as one of the crew affixed a rake to the back of the prisoners' truck. It was a wide, low structure. Anyone following would have difficulty determining their number. Another crewman was working his way around their trench, gathering the remains of their rations.

Kennedy inspected the rake and then climbed into the back of the prisoners' truck. He spent a few minutes inside and returned in deep conversation with one of his crew.

He drew Lightholler aside and said, "I'm thinking if we're in a pinch we arm the prisoners."

"Needs to be a tight fucking pinch."

"I know it, but we have no real idea what's up ahead, and this is the only way through to the Rock."

"What if we're facing Confederate forces?"

Kennedy cast an eye over his men. Tecumseh's truck was grinding its way back onto the trail.

"Would you fire on them, Joseph?" Lightholler pressed.

"We're twenty miles out of Red Rock." Kennedy clapped Lightholler on the back. "*Twenty*. Hell, John, this close, I reckon I'd fire on *you*."

Lightholler nodded, slowly. "I do believe you would." He followed Kennedy back to their truck.

Morgan and Malcolm were already seated and secured. There were four of Kennedy's men with them, carrying assault rifles; scuffed and non-reflective. Decked out with magazine cartridges and two grenades apiece. They had their goggles slung around their necks and wore combat fatigues so that their cobalt blue shirts were only a glimpse at the lapels. Each carried a tomahawk secured to his belt. Their face camouflage was composed of thin black streaks and their dark features looked as though they'd been raked by shadows.

Kennedy made a rapid gesture with his hand and they rose as one and approached the tailgate. Two took positions at the back of the truck, and Lightholler could hear the scrabble of boots on metal as the others clambered up the ribbing into position on top. Kennedy took a seat next to Malcolm. Rather than her customary recoil she seemed almost relieved to see him.

The truck's engine shuddered to life. They would be tracing a wilder tract of desert floor now, skirting the gulch beyond the faint path they'd been following.

Kennedy began to speak in measured tones. He explained that they had to move slower now; that the afternoon sun threw long shadows but nightfall would leave them just as exposed. He told them they would all have to suit up: fatigues, camo, the works. They were about to pass through a battlefield. He unlocked a canister battened to the truck's platform and removed two rifles.

"You have to be out of your fucking mind, Joseph," Malcolm said.

He told them that while he was sure it wouldn't come to that, he wasn't taking any chances.

He made no mention of the fact that the soldiers they might encounter had a reasonable chance of being Confederate.

He opened the breech, revealing the swollen maggot of a five-fifty-six round, and showed them how to change the magazine for reloading; explained the importance of squeezing the trigger rather than pulling it. He replaced the guns in the canister and left it unlocked.

"What about a pistol?" Morgan asked, eyeing the rifles with distaste.

"If you're close enough to use a pistol, you're too damn close. Without the right training, you're less than useless and more of a liability."

"He can handle a pistol well enough," Malcolm added icily.

"How are you with desert camo?" Kennedy asked Lightholler.

"I'll manage."

"You do Darren. I'll take care of Patricia."

Kennedy removed a stack of combat fatigues from an adjacent cache. He sorted through the pile and selected a set for himself and passed a uniform to each of them. Malcolm gave him an empty look and began to unbutton her shirt. Morgan and Lightholler grabbed their equipment and hurriedly shifted away from her towards the rear of the truck. The two crewmen fixed their eyes on the desert.

Lightholler stole a glance. She had replaced her blouse with the uniform shirt and was leaning forwards. Her legs were outstretched, her trousers at her ankles, and she was inspecting the mottled edge of a bruise on her thigh. She ran her palms along her thighs, brushing away the grains of ubiquitous sand. He turned back to find Kennedy's eyes on him.

"You and her, huh?" he mumbled softly.

Kennedy ignored him.

Malcolm was trying to tuck in the folds of her shirt. The uniform was at least two sizes too large for her.

"Sorry about the fit."

She shrugged.

When they were done, Kennedy checked their bandoliers and adjusted the straps on Morgan's emergency belt. The belt's pouches, empty for the moment, would accommodate anything from a knife to an anti-personnel mine.

Kennedy knelt down before Malcolm and bade Morgan and Lightholler take a seat. He withdrew the camouflage kits from the cache and handed one to Lightholler. He opened his tin of cream and set it aside, inspecting Malcolm's features. He reached out and brushed back her hair, looking for earrings, adjusting her collar to check for a necklace. Any bright or potentially reflective surface had to be removed, he explained.

He took her hands, making sure she wore no rings or watch. He stopped short of examining the pale band where an engagement ring might have once sat.

"What happened to your face?" she asked him.

"John hit me," he replied.

She looked across at Lightholler, and he said, "He had it coming."

She gave a short laugh and Kennedy told her to keep still but he barely contained a smile. He was smearing a two-shade combination of burnt cork over her cheekbones.

"We have to break up the strong structure lines," he said, perhaps more for Morgan's benefit, perhaps just for the sake of talking. "We need to break up the contours along the cheeks, the nose and chin."

"Joseph."

"Keep still."

"This place you're taking us to…" Her voice trailed off, and Kennedy put the cream aside. He'd been etching a pair of scratch-thin streaks along her neck. "Do you have atomics there?"

"No."

"Hand on your heart?"

"Hand on my heart." He reached up to continue applying the mask.

She brushed the hand aside, firmly. "If you have *anything* there—poison gas or biological weapons—anything that's going to bring great harm to anyone, American or Japanese, just leave me here now." Her voice was soft and strangely compelling. "Please."

Lightholler wanted to say, *Tell her*. Suddenly embarrassed, he returned to working on Morgan's camouflage.

"I swear, I have nothing like that at Red Rock."

"If you're lying, Joseph, I promise you, I'll kill you myself."

He leaned closer, placing the finishing touches on her cheeks, and said,

"Then we have nothing to worry about."

She looked across at Lightholler and Morgan. Lightholler found her face, broken up by the blotches and streaks of cream, savagely beautiful. His nod of approval was awkward.

After completing Morgan's face he began to work on his own. The kit mirror was thankfully tarnished. It felt better not having a clear view of his own visage. It was somehow simpler, applying the camouflage to the indistinct reflection in the glass.

It took them twenty minutes to reach the fringe of the battlefield. Their procession ground to a halt following a signal from the first truck. They dropped the tailgate and Kennedy told Malcolm and Morgan to sit tight. Lightholler reached into the weapons canister and withdrew a holstered Mauser. Malcolm suggested, matter-of-factly, that he take another gun.

"There are more than enough spent Mauser casings lying around without you making any further contributions."

He gave her an odd look and she added. "We're in enough trouble as it is."

She said "We"... How do you do that, Kennedy?

He replaced the Mauser and selected a Browning.

Kennedy nodded, saying, "We're sticking to confed ordnance all the way from here. Shoddy, but serviceable."

He ordered two of his men to stay with Malcolm and Morgan, and led Lightholler away from the vehicles.

There was the faint sound of a low breeze and the cooling creak of the trucks as they settled. Kennedy dropped down and fastened a paper-like covering over his boots. He indicated to Lightholler to lift his feet and slipped on similar covers.

They moved across the desert floor in silence. He followed Kennedy towards the sloping edge of a bluff that rose away from the trucks. Looking back, he saw that he'd left no clear prints in the sand. He could taste gunpowder on the air—and something else. A subtle, biting scent.

"Stay close by me," Kennedy whispered. "I want to hear your assessment."

Lightholler, slightly bewildered, closed the gap between them. He crested the bluff, stooping low by Kennedy's side. The scent became a stench.

He could make out the rest of Kennedy's crew, fanned out and working their way down to the smoking ruin below them. Kennedy had the binoculars out again. He passed them over.

Lightholler scanned the carnage. He made out the silhouettes of seven vehicles, charred and smoking, amid fresh shallow craters of blackened sand. One appeared to be a personnel carrier, the other six were jeeps. The burnt-out frame of a mortar weapon, poised amidst the vehicles, was surrounded by a pile of Japanese bodies.

There were more bodies spread out over the mesa, splayed in the graceless posture of violent death. Lightholler counted forty. Kennedy's men moved among the dead. A dust devil swirled on the furthest ridge, a gloating dervish of sand and smoke. He handed the binoculars back.

Kennedy did a quick once-over before pouching the glasses. One of his crew waved them over, before crouching back down to examine something by the mortar.

Lightholler followed Kennedy's steps down onto the plain. He tried to keep his eyes on the ground, while tracking the movement of Kennedy's men. They scampered from body to body, inspecting uniforms and shoes, checking dog tags, ammunition and supply cases. They left little indication of where they had passed but he saw many boot prints: light where men had run; deeper where they had dragged heavy munitions. He saw cigarette butts and crushed ration containers.

He reached into his pocket and pulled out a deck of Texas Teas. Made to light one when Kennedy extinguished the flame with a swift movement.

"Not till we reach the Rock."

He stopped and stood there, his head tilted slightly back as he gave the horrifying tableau a slow three-sixty.

Tecumseh rose from the wreckage of a jeep and gave the all clear. Kennedy signed to one of his men. The crewman vanished back up the broad face of the bluff and returned shortly with Malcolm, Morgan and their escort in tow.

Without a word, Kennedy's men positioned themselves in a loose circle around the gathering. They stood facing outwards, their rifles and submachine-guns at waist height, bringing to mind Lightholler's encounter with the Brandenburgs in New York City all those days ago.

Malcolm stood by Kennedy's side. She had a handkerchief over the lower part of her face and her eyes were wide, pale holes in her camo-darkened face. Morgan was looking at a corpse that lay crumpled a few yards away. He fingered his rifle nervously.

"What do you think, John?" Kennedy asked.

For a moment it felt as if he was back at Sandhurst.

"This was a heavy platoon." Lightholler pointed at the mortar. "That's what we heard coming in. Eighty-one mil." He pointed to the personnel carrier. "That's the command car, and that's a medic's jeep. They had a doctor here as well as the usual medics. Sharpshooters, snipers, radio gear. Judging by the set-up, I'd say they sighted the Rangers first but were overwhelmed by heavier firepower." Lightholler pointed northwards. "Tyre tracks suggest they were retreating in that direction."

"Not bad," Kennedy said. "Not bad at all."

Tecumseh smiled through pressed lips.

"It was a heavy platoon, alright," Kennedy continued. "One of three that was bringing up the rear. That puts us right between the other two, so I'll make this brief. This is reconnaissance in force. They set up first but they were surprised here. The action was all local: sniper fire taking out the mortar team, grenade-launchers for the jeeps. Most of the kills are clean; one to two shots apiece, the occasional knife wound where it couldn't be helped."

"I don't see any Confederates," Malcolm ventured in a small voice.

"There were never any Confederates here."

"What about the cigarettes and the rations?" Lightholler said. "Those are confed."

"False trail," Kennedy replied. "Just like those tyre markings you pointed out. The crew that passed through here marked the real trail. Only two jeeps made it out of here, four japs on foot, and they were dragging one of their wounded."

"They didn't get too far either," Tecumseh added.

"Okay," Kennedy said gruffly. "Let's get out of here." He brought his fingers to his mouth and gave a long shrill whistle.

Suddenly there was movement all around them. The ground broke open where mounds of earth had been. Fallen foliage parted and fell to one side as more of Kennedy's men emerged from the wasteland. Lightholler counted twelve of them.

Twelve of his men took down a platoon?

Kennedy communicated with the sign language Lightholler had

observed earlier—a rapid exchange before the soldiers drifted back to their places of concealment. As a final coda, Kennedy summoned Tecumseh. "We need to place anti-personnel mines here and up along the false trail."

Tecumseh nodded gravely.

Clearly Kennedy had no problem with burning his bridges. He said, "From here on in, it's a clear route to the Rock." He turned and began trudging back up towards the trucks.

"Why did you bring me out here?" Malcolm asked, falling into step beside him. She cut an unlikely figure walking in his shadow, conjuring up the image of a youth marching off to war.

"I don't want you kept in the dark any longer, Patricia."

"The first time I met Webster," she said, gasping with the exertion of their ascent, "he asked us what we thought an army of your men—scattered through the Union and Confederacy—might be capable of doing."

"And?"

"With all the information at his fingertips, and all the resources at his command, I still don't think he has a damned clue what he's up against."

"Webster's not my enemy," Kennedy said softly. "I see that now."

Observing her difficulty with the climb, he held out a hand.

She clasped it and said, "What's going on, Joseph?"

"It won't be long now, I promise. Just stay with me."

She fell silent and let him guide her back along the trail. He left her standing with Morgan and Lightholler while he went to inspect the prisoners' vehicle. He returned after a few moments and said, "They're okay."

She thanked him and walked to their waiting truck.

Kennedy said, "We'll be at the Rock within an hour."

Lightholler gave a low whistle through his teeth. "Hard to believe we made it this far."

Morgan's look became suddenly earnest. "What about Shine?"

"I don't know." Kennedy frowned.

"We might have to take one of Tecumseh's men with us instead."

"I can't see anyone convincing a ghost dancer to board the carapace." The frown deepened.

Some new thought manifested itself in the flash of Kennedy's eyes. His face took on a less serious aspect as he continued in sonorous tones, "One thing I can't abide among my men is low morale." He checked the pouches at his belt and withdrew a pack of cigarettes and tossed it to them.

Lightholler snatched it out of the air with deft fingers. He checked the pack. Crumpled and worn, it bore the lettering of a popular Japanese brand.

"Exhale that way," Kennedy said, pointing eastwards, in the direction they had come.

"You've got to be kidding me."

"Trackers'll catch that scent from half a mile in this wind."

"Over *this* stench?"

Kennedy nodded. He turned back to the truck.

Lightholler lit up and was surprised to see Morgan's hungry look. "You smoke now?"

"A little."

Lightholler flipped the pack. Morgan shook it and brought a cigarette to his lips. He lit up and cupped the cigarette between his hands as he inhaled.

"We talked about war a while back, you and I," he said, drawing a deep lungful of smoke. "Had you asked me then what I thought about war, I'd have told you that it describes a situation where two nations, unable to achieve their goals by diplomacy, come to believe that they each have the means of imposing their will by violence. I'd have said that it was a tool used to define the balance of power among adversaries."

"And now?"

Morgan ditched the cigarette. "Now I think it's just an absolute fuck-up. Go ask that dead Jap back there if he cares who wins or loses this fight."

"Even if we manage to go back and fix things," Lightholler said carefully, "we won't take any of this away. There'll always be war. Let's just hope we only get to fight the right ones."

Morgan looked down at the crushed butt and remembered where he was. He pocketed the refuse and said, "Let's just hope no one has to fight any of them at all."

XVI

April 28, 2012
Alpha Camp, Nevada

Shine and his father had been assigned to the commissary. Most of the tables had been disassembled. The remainder were pushed together in the centre of the room to form a single counter. Shine watched as a group of agents streamed into the building and made themselves comfortable. They wore their uniforms open and a number of them had their boots propped up on the tables. They looked exhausted and restless at the same time but there was the occasional burst of strained laughter.

He caught the tail end of a joke, followed by a harsh cackle of amusement. The speaker drew his eye. He was hatchet-faced under a mop of unruly thick hair. The butt of his pistol swung loosely in his shoulder holster.

"Alright, alright, alright. What do you call a coon in a limo?"

"The chauffeur?" someone ventured across the table.

"Nah." He guffawed loudly and slapped his thigh. "A thief."

Shine slowed his steps. He felt his father grab his shirt-sleeve.

"You eyeballing me, boy?"

"Don't…" his father murmured

"Be the last thing you'll ever do."

His father propelled him through the kitchen door. There were seven other people in the room. Three leather-faced indians, stooped by age and injury, worked over a large vat that bubbled and oozed a warm savoury scent. A tactical agent sat in a corner of the room. His eyes flicked briefly across Shine and his companions before being drawn back to the steaming stew.

"We'll get started on the vegetables." Shine's father moved slowly towards a rack of shelves where bowls of tomatoes and potatoes had been laid out.

There was a large window set in the wall beyond the shelving. It faced the north end of the compound where the land began to rise up into the low mountains that surrounded distant Groom Lake. Somewhere out there, beyond the pale purple hills, the major was working his way towards Red Rock. His father had told him so.

Tecumseh, the medicine man of the ghost dancers, had contacted them from the *other place* to announce that his arrival was at hand, that he was bringing the culmination of all their prayers for a world's restitution.

While Bravo camp had its mixture of indians and negroes, its faithful and its atheists, most of the men who'd trained at Alpha were ghost dancers, members of a religion that had been outlawed by the United States over a hundred years ago. The major had never discouraged their ideology. In fact, it could be argued that he'd promoted its practice. Shine had overheard their whispered conjectures in the barracks that afternoon and, listening to their words, he'd begun to appreciate the harvest sown by Kennedy's tolerance.

One of the prisoners had claimed to have visited the *other place*, saying that it lay in the heart of the Demilitarised Zone between the Japanese and Confederate factions.

Another said that the place was in the Arctic Circle and contained a weapon that shrivelled man and machine alike, that reduced atomics to dust.

One of the elders, a companion of Tecumseh who'd led a company at Mazatlan, described a spirit-dream he'd entered, just the previous night. He'd seen the major and Tecumseh crossing the Central Plains at the head of an army of all the indian dead. None of the others spoke after this pronouncement.

It had occurred to Shine that, occasionally, a man may become something more than a man. He may become the vessel for the aspirations of many. And under such circumstances, what boundaries or limitations could hold him back?

He stared out into the deepening shadows and held his hand against the glass. He heard his father's voice calling him back and stood blinking for a moment as he regained his bearings. He saw his father struggling to peel the jacket of a potato with a bread knife and asked, "Where are the regular knives?"

The tac agent chuckled. "Like we're going to leave knives around a bunch of redskins." His laughter grew with appreciation of his own joke and then ceased with a sudden spluttering cough.

"Hush, now." One of the old indians was standing close by him and something flashed, bright and cruel, at his fingertips.

A shallow red line appeared across the pale cords of the agent's neck.

Other men crossed the floor with a swiftness that belied their age. Their fingertips formed dazzling patinas, courtesy of the razored metal shards they extruded from callused pads.

The agent stared at Shine in astonishment.

Shine's father replaced the half-peeled potato on the shelving. He approached the agent with a broad smile. The agent made the slightest movement towards his gun holster, then thought better of it. He'd opened his mouth to speak when a sputtering sound burst from his belt radio.

"Go on," Shine's father said. "Answer it."

The agent gingerly reached for the receiver and brought it to his ear. He made a strange sound in his throat and said, "It's for you."

Shine's father took the receiver and listened for a few moments. He placed it on his own belt and held out his hand. The agent handed over his Dillinger.

He transferred the pistol to Shine and said, "We're to wait here a spell."

"Want me to do anything?" Shine asked.

"Maybe later."

There was an explosion of noise in the commissary. The sound of tables being turned and shattering glass. Three pistol shots rang out and echoed and then there were just the low moans of the injured. Distant gunfire sounded like the crackle of cheap fireworks.

The door swung open. Two ghost dancers stood at the entrance. Behind them lay broken furniture, cracked plates and three agents sprawled in a communal spatter of dark blood.

The remaining agents, unarmed, were on their knees. Shine's father led their prisoner in and dropped him on the floor by his comrades. One of the agents, his hatchet face now pale and blood-streaked, met Shine's eyes in abject fear.

"Tell me," Shine asked. "What do you call a coon with a gun?"

XVII

April 28, 2012

CSS Patton

"Sir."

Webster barely glanced up. He'd set up office at one of the spare consoles in the communications room. His needs were immediate and the rate-limiting step in his intelligence gathering was the journey from communications to his cabin five decks below. That was too long.

"This just in for you."

He accepted the post from the com officer with a curt nod. It was an encrypted dispatch from CINTEX. He ran it through the decoder. It was sketchy; shoddy work someone would have to answer for. He decided that somewhere out there, a village yearned for its lost idiot. He made a note of the person's name and read on, filling in the blanks.

Malcolm's Raptor had refuelled at Barksdale air force base, Louisiana, prior to its final flight. Evidence Response personnel were still working the crash site but Webster was willing to bet his last dollar that no trace of Kennedy or his crew would ever be found. Two abandoned parachutes had been retrieved ten miles from the wreck.

The parachutes were bait and Webster wasn't biting.

He took a shot in the dark, rifled through the files on his desk, and pulled the notes on Hughes Aeronautics. Thirty flights in the Louisiana region, and three had departed Barksdale within half an hour of the Raptor. One bound for Houston, one for Nevada, and one that accompanied the Raptor over the Louisiana wetlands. Promising.

He penned a belated order grounding all Hughes Aeronautics planes pending further review.

He requested a trace on the three out-going flights. It returned within minutes, and confirmed his suspicions. There was no word on the Houston or Louisiana flights, but the Nevada-bound plane had crashed near a town called Alamo. He ran a scenario through his head and tacked an addendum to his order: "Check for other plane crashes—nationwide—in the last twenty-four hours. Check for survivors. Dispatch three tac squads to Alamo."

He summoned the com officer and sent the revised order off to Dallas.

He skimmed though the intelligence reports. Local recon placed at least twelve patrols—friend and foe—between Alamo and Alpha. *Is that where Kennedy's headed?* Perhaps he was making for the Demilitarised Zone and the Japanese border beyond. San Francisco or Fresno. *But if he wanted to join up with the Japanese, why not just stay in New York?* Unless, of course, he'd had prior knowledge of the German assault.

The permutations were staggering; they fucked his weary brain.

Illingworth had called an emergency briefing for 1500 hours, which left him just under an hour.

Webster poured himself a coffee and sorted through arriving reports, separating data from detritus. Apparently the German delegates were making good on their assurances from the morning's summit, in the form of panzers and planes. It sounded like the Germans had committed more forces to the region than anyone had hitherto expected. Why was that?

The information he'd requested came back within twenty minutes. There had been four crashes all told. One light aircraft lost in the Mississippi Delta, two transport planes brought down by Japanese fighters over New Mexico, and the Hughes at Alamo.

Alamo… Four to six survivors, whisked away by paramedics whose arrival on the scene—as described by one eyewitness—was almost prescient. And they were surprisingly well organised for a bunch of coloureds.

Obvious. *Careless.*

Webster allowed himself a grim chuckle. He had to wonder, what would Kennedy run out of first—planes or pilots? Had to wonder what the *hell* had drawn him back to Nevada.

He glanced at his watch and prepared a final order, this one to send to Alpha: "Ship Kennedy's men west without delay and torch the camp."

He left it with the courier and made his way to the operations deck. Arriving early for the briefing, he took a seat near the back of the room and let his eye fall casually on the crowd of officers as they filed into the large chamber. All the services were represented, including flight, security, military police and repair teams. Thirty men had seated themselves by the time Illingworth made his entrance. Four of Webster's own covert agents, all senior officers aboard the stratolite, arranged themselves in chairs close by and did nothing to acknowledge him.

Illingworth began with aerial photographs and an outline of the recent troop dispositions. The subject rapidly turned to the two Japanese stratolites, targets too sweet to be ignored. Their presence, in addition to the two army divisions advancing across the desert, represented a significant effort. He outlined their various options. These ranged from an all-out attack, coordinated and led by the *Patton*, to a strategic withdrawal to the Arizona state border. He played his cards close to his chest.

Right here, over Alpha and close to Kennedy, was where Webster wanted to be. He skimmed his notes and decided to divorce himself early from the thrust of his own intentions. He leaned forwards and tapped Paterson—the flight director—on the shoulder and murmured in his ear that observation posts were best suited for observation, so perhaps a withdrawal *was* in order. He made sure he was overheard, and was pleased to find his view received with respectful evasion.

The German delegates were present for the briefing, and as more facts came to light the discussion burgeoned into a full-blown war council. Before long, calls were made and President Clancy and Kaiser Wilhelm were patched through via secured shortwave link-ups.

The German delegates recommended that they maintain a conservative approach till more of their forces could arrive. A dispute over authority threatened to bog down the talks in a mire of bureaucracy. Webster had his opportunity, he just needed a mouthpiece.

He spied his three-star acquaintance from the other day, General Boyfucker, on the other side of the room. Quietly leaving his seat, he approached the man and took him aside. Before long the general's look of apprehension transformed into one of appreciation.

They returned to the proceedings and, when given the opportunity to speak, the general echoed Webster's words with an unexpected eloquence that singled him out for future use. With an obtuse reference to the intelligence at hand, he stated that—in view of Japanese military conduct in the Union north—he strongly suggested a strong defensive stance.

"Perhaps they never had any intention of risking unreliable Union forces against the South," he announced. "Perhaps they were merely conducting a holding action, tying up German–Allied forces around New York. Perhaps the push is happening right here. Right now."

Little argument was offered.

The German delegates confirmed that their panzers had crossed the state line as promised and were digging in west of Las Vegas. Three squadrons of Luftwaffe fighter-bombers and two more of Confederate scouts were en route. Additional regiments of Texan Rangers and standard Confederate units could be rapidly mustered.

Clancy took his cue. After Berlin, he said, no Japanese airship—stratolite or otherwise—would see the outer reaches of *any* Allied settlement. He stated, in sonorous tones, that it was better to decide the Confederacy's fate *here* than on the outskirts of Dallas. He thanked the Kaiser for placing German forces at the Confederacy's disposal at this key juncture.

It was a *fait accompli*. The Kaiser acquiesced; Webster smiled. The *Patton* was going to war.

Command of the mission was handed over to Admiral Illingworth. He summoned his squadron leaders, arranging a squadron briefing to be held at the flight director's station.

The meeting ended and the deck cleared. It was almost five o'clock and Webster hadn't eaten since dawn. The attack wouldn't be launched for another few hours. That gave him ample time to peruse any new reports. He'd suck down a cigar and have a meal brought to him.

Out in the passageway, Steiner—the Abwehr's envoy to the German delegation—stood waiting by Webster's motorcart. He struck a casual pose but his expression was guarded.

"Do you have a moment, Director Webster?"

Webster's bodyguards, invariable in their presence, subtle in their distribution, were mixing with some of the bridge crew. A senior agent lurked further down the passage. There were others present whom Webster didn't recognise; possibly crew, more likely German operatives. There were probably more covert agents than soldiers in the immediate vicinity. It was a vaguely amusing notion.

"I'm on my way to communications, Mr Steiner," Webster replied.

"That suits me."

Webster gestured towards the passenger seat with a sweep of his arm and took the wheel. Steiner climbed in. There was a faint scuffle in the background as the various operatives clambered into adjacent vehicles and the unlikely motorcade made its way along the conduit.

"That was... interesting," Steiner ventured after a few moments.

Webster shot him a sidelong glance, but remained silent.

"Why are you doing this, Webster?"

"Why do I do anything?"

"*That* is a question that sends my agents scurrying through the alleys in their overcoats and slouch hats," Steiner commented wryly.

Webster smiled. A crinkle at the corner of his mouth.

Steiner gave his nails a cursory examination. "I can only imagine what you discussed with your general, prior to his performance."

Webster narrowed his eye and shook his head with a slow, dismissive air.

"They will be flying non-essential personnel off-ship," Steiner continued. "I was to be included, but declined to leave. How about you, Mr Webster? Do you plan on being around when the shit hits the fan?"

The provocation was oafish, the cliché stale. Hardly the German's style. Webster said, "I'll stick around to hold your hand."

Steiner chuckled. "That's a gratifying thought."

"And what do *you* want, Mr Steiner?"

"I want our panzers to regroup at your installation north of Las Vegas."

"What installation?"

Steiner gave him a facile smirk. The profile pegged Steiner as deep German intelligence. The request to use Alpha nailed him as one of the few German agents privy to Camelot.

Our panzers. The rest just stood to reason.

"How many regiments of your tank division are composed of Brandenburg Special Forces?" Webster enquired, gently.

The smirk faded, replaced by a look of cunning recognition. "All of them."

"Your men in New York should have stayed aboard the *Titanic*."

"You should have kept a tighter leash on Kennedy."

Dark urges slithered within him. Webster kept the seethe to a slow burn. He pondered Steiner's request, broodingly. The presence of German elite armour and the unexpected presence of so many Japanese troops in the region provoked a number of difficult questions. Nevada was but one of the routes that led into the Confederacy and it was an unforgiving path at that. Why this sudden attention on the region by ally and enemy alike? And why was he so certain that it all boiled down to Kennedy?

Webster said, "There's no installation north of Vegas, at least not any longer. It's been razed to the ground. So you're free to use whatever's left of the site."

They were pulling up to the communications foyer. Webster killed the motor.

Steiner climbed out of the cart slowly. "I suggest you have a word with your men on the ground. Last thing I heard, your base was still up and running."

Webster eyed him curiously, but didn't reply.

Steiner's expression was sombre. "That was ten minutes ago."

The convoy of attendant carts eased to a halt and the men poured out. Three of them followed Steiner towards the elevator vestibule. The rest stood a little distance away from Webster's vehicle.

He gave a meaningful look at the nearest agent, then entered communications with his retinue of five. They had a German tag-along, decked out in maintenance kit, who hung back from the crowd with moderate discretion. Webster tossed him a snarl. The German slipped back further and faded into the scenery.

Communications held a subdued air. All the stations were manned but the usual drone of the radio network was absent. There were intermittent bursts of coded relay but none of the usual white noise. All eyes were on the monitors.

He spied the courier across the room and strode over.

"My dispatches."

The courier directed him back to one of the operators. He had his head down like the others, tracking a series of green blips across a darkened screen.

"My dispatches," Webster repeated.

The man glanced up and pointed at a stack of sheets in his out-tray. He returned his attention to the monitor. Webster picked up the sheets and began to rifle through them.

He found the order to burn Alpha, stamped as sent. He said, "I need immediate confirmation on this."

"No can do, sir," the operator replied. "We've been running silent since 1630 hours."

"What are you talking about?" Webster growled.

One of his men stepped up. "Admiral Illingworth shut down all off-strat communications following the briefing."

"Good for him." Webster leaned forwards over the console. "Nevertheless, son, I need that confirmation, *right now*."

The operator squirmed in his seat. He glanced at a co-worker for support.

"Better call the chief," his companion suggested, without looking up from his own screen.

The operator backed out of his seat and selected one of the handsets that peppered the walls of the com room. His companion, noting the baleful attention of Webster's murky eye, attempted to describe the task at hand. He pointed to the screen and said, "We're patched into the navigation frame. Passive radar reception. That's our first wing, scouts and fighters, deploying now."

Webster grunted.

"No one's ever done anything like this before."

Webster turned to watch the operator at the handset. "Call me old-fashioned," he said. "I was never one for precedent." He turned to his agent. "This isn't happening fast enough."

The agent slid away, and Webster reverted his attention to the co-worker with the penchant for idle chat. He jotted some numbers on the back of his dispatch. "Can you get me a visual on these coordinates?"

The operator scanned Webster's scrawl. "Over the horizon. No line of sight."

Webster retrieved the document swiftly and folded it into his pocket.

The agent returned with the operator in tow.

"Sir, the chief is getting the admiral on the line. That's the best I can do for you."

"Thank you." Webster approached the handset. He paused, turned back to the agent and said, "Secure the other operator."

The co-worker gave a faint cry of protest that faded to nothing at the agent's approach. The rest of his team signalled their support by shifting either side to facilitate his departure.

Webster took the phone.

“Please make this fast.” Illingworth’s tone was frostily polite.

“I need a verification from my ground team.”

“What do you need to know?”

“I need to know if something is on fire.”

There was a thoughtful pause on the line, then Illingworth said, “I can spare a scout for reconnoitre. No communications after launch. It’s all direct lines and face to face from here.”

“I’ll send along one of my men.”

“Give me a sec.” Illingworth returned after a few moments. “Okay. Have him report to flight deck three.”

“By the way, I’ve co-opted one of your staff, Peter. He saw too much.”

“How do you sleep at night, Glen?”

“With one eye open.”

Webster rang off. He selected one of his entourage and gave careful instructions. He led his procession from the communication room. He told the German operative to fuck off. He took the radio operator aside and said, “No good deed goes unpunished,” and sent him down to the Eye under escort.

He climbed into the cart, accompanied by the last of his guard, gunned the motor and began the tedious drive back to his cabin. Grey walls flashed past, corridor after corridor of curved metal. Clusters of motorcarts slid by as air crew and sailors attended their posts.

His meal was waiting for him. He left his guard at the door and brought the food inside himself. The porthole admitted the wan glow of looming dusk. He removed the patch. He put on a sweater. He lit a cigar and watched the blue smoke seep into the ceiling vents. He sucked the coating off a pink and spat out the core. He dozed, fitfully.

He was splashing cold water on his face when there was a brisk rap at the cabin door. Stepping over, he jerked it open. The young officer almost spilled into the room. He made an effort to compose himself.

“The raid, sir.” He barely flinched when he saw the ruined aspect of Webster’s unveiled eye. “They’re about to commence their primary run.” He quickly retreated, to wait outside the door.

Webster towelled off and replaced the patch. He cast a glance at the porthole where pinholes of starlight flickered faintly. The sky was a purple bruise. A trio of scouts wheeled in the distance. He followed the officer into the corridor. His guard joined them at the cart.

There was no traffic now. The pilots were on the flight decks or aloft, arrayed at the rendezvous points. The sailors were at their stations and the combat teams were at their gun-mounts. All non-essentials were long gone, evacuated to Flagstaff and points east.

The cart raced down the empty passageway.

Webster asked for a rundown and the officer sketched out the tacticals.

The *Patton* had been able to put ninety scouts—almost two-thirds of her complement—into the air. The stratolite was holding at forty-five thousand feet, pitched above a swift easterly. They could make a ready descent into the jet stream and be back over the Grand Canyon in about an hour. Alternatively, they could climb to sixty-five, sit back and watch the fireworks.

The guard gave a whistle of admiration. The young officer warmed to his subject. Webster sifted through the account.

Different altitudes demanded different strategies. Their current height facilitated a rapid launch sequence. Mass retrieval of returning scouts was practicable, but there was the threat of standard enemy fighters. The best defence was afforded by a dense fighter screen, supported by the *Patton*'s own anti-air turrets. Resembling an aircraft carrier, the stratolite behaved primarily as a platform for the delivery of aircraft. Her metal-plated, multiple-ballonet structure was sturdy enough, but it would only take limited fire. She could tolerate the loss of a third of her ballonets, though, and remain aloft. The helium would never ignite.

Sustained enemy action, however, would bring her down.

Above sixty thousand feet it was a different story. Maintaining a scout swarm was hazardous at that altitude. The strat was safe from generic aircraft. Hostile scouts were vulnerable to friendlies and, failing that, anti-aircraft fire due to their diminished manoeuvrability at such heights. Above sixty thousand, the *Patton* was more than just a transport service. She could make deliveries of her own. Standard ordnance, dropped from those heights, redefined the term "devastating".

Webster considered the German stratolite fleet perched over the Sea of Japan, and said, "This is all theoretical, isn't it?"

"Mostly."

"No one has ever attacked a stratolite before, have they?"

The officer bristled. "Director, the japs enjoy air superiority close to the DMZ. Their FS-Zs and Ronins will be watching the desert, the airfields.

We're sending in six squadrons of rocket-armed scouts from on high. They won't be expecting an attack from above."

"We'll find out soon enough, I suppose," Webster purred.

XVIII

Operations stank of nicotine. Glowed twilight, radar-screen emerald and battle-alert red. Hummed with expectation. Silent running, darkened ship. Two of the walls to either side of the forwards view port were manned by an array of radio operators. A quorum of senior officers crowded the main radar screen observing the pastiche of readings gathered from advanced reconnaissance. A relief map to its left, layered in shades of sapphire and jade, displayed red circles indicating the last known positions of the two Japanese strats. Crosses marked enemy landing fields at the edge of the DMZ; crimson wedges for recent bandit sightings. The *Patton* was an isolated blue circle on the near edge of the map.

A series of wedges, blue and white, were the scout rocket squadrons and their attendant fighter cover. Webster peered closer and realised that the raised swirls—curved across the map in streaks of cobalt and sky blue—represented the jet streams; shaded for altitude and velocity. There was a horrendous beauty to it all.

He made his way forwards and was intercepted by one of his people.

"Director." The agent extended a slip of paper. "Recon scout's back. He couldn't get clearance to land but we got a message across."

"How did you manage that?"

"Morse code, encrypted and flashed between the Eye and the scout."

"Good work." He examined the note: "Alpha in flames. Two outgoing convoys. Smaller: eastbound, trucks. Larger: northbound, tanks, trucks, horses. German column due south and closing."

Why northbound? He'd ordered Kennedy's men to be shipped west. Tanks meant someone's long-range recon were involved. They were too far north for Germans, even if they were Brandenburgs. Steiner must have intervened. But how? He searched the deck, scanning for the German, without success. *Horses?*

"Find Delegate Steiner. Ask him to meet me in my cabin."

Admiral Illingworth and Flight Director Paterson held court by the view port. Webster pressed his way towards them. There was motion across the starboard side wall. Chinese whispers along the console till the chief radio operator approached the radar array, addressed the flight director and said, "We're go."

Paterson sought Illingworth's consent before giving the order. He said, "Let's hear it."

The operator relayed the command and the speakers sputtered to life.

"*Diving into the clouds for a closer look.*"

"*Roger that, Red Fox 5.*"

"*Wolf leader from Red Fox 4. Nothing out here but empty sky.*"

"For Christ's sake," Illingworth bellowed across the room, "filter it. Squadron leaders only."

There was an agitated buzz among the officers. The speakers hissed and snapped.

"*Red Fox leader from Wolf leader. Thick as soup out here, no cloud-churn, no strat-sign. Take your scouts down to thirty k.*"

The officers focused on the radar composite with hopeful, willing eyes.

Stillness stretched out; a low murmur of prayer and curses.

"*Wolf leader from Red Fox leader. Two jap strats sighted. No scout swarm, no fighter screen. Repeat, no fighter screen. Course and speed to follow.*"

A muted cheer echoed within the chamber.

The coordinates came through. A crewman made the relevant adjustments on the skymap.

"They're on our doorstep," Illingworth glowered. "They're at thirty-five k and they'll have fighters, so where the hell are they?"

"Might be on a wide sweep, scouting ahead." Paterson approached the console. "Have Knight and Bishop squadrons keep watch for returning flights."

"They could be aboard the strats, refuelling," an air officer suggested.

"We're talking standard fighter cover. FS-Zs, not scouts, at that altitude," Paterson replied gruffly.

"They're skimming real low for stratolites," Illingworth said. "Probably looking to catch a stream." He viewed the skymap and pointed at two of the darker blue curves. "There, or there, I'll wager. They're making for Phoenix."

"They want to hook up with the Mexicans," Webster offered.

Paterson nodded his agreement.

"We need to find those jap fighters," Illingworth said. "If they're not out there flying escort, they're incoming till proven otherwise."

"Then we should call general quarters," Paterson replied. "I'll put up a swarm."

"Not good enough." Illingworth shook his head. "Unless you find me those jap fighters, we're taking her up."

"Give me five minutes, Peter."

"You've got three." Illingworth disengaged himself from the flight director and summoned his first officer. He inclined his head skywards and said, "Make ready for ascent."

"Aye, sir."

Webster studied the flash of Paterson's glare. The officer who'd escorted him earlier leaned in and whispered, "Supposed to be Paterson's show while we're in combat."

Webster nodded.

"Paterson wants more planes in the sky," the officer continued. "Wants to be able to exploit any initial attack with a second wave. The admiral wants us high and clear. Moment we hit those strats they'll open up their active radar. We'll light up like a Christmas tree."

"We're out of their line of sight," Webster said, glancing at the skymap.

"Depends on who's looking at us."

All eyes were on the radar screen. All ears strained to catch the next burst of radio transmissions.

"*Wolf leader to White Rabbit. We're in position.*"

"I'll show you those jap fighters, Admiral." Paterson cleared his throat. "Divisions two, four and six hit the *Hiryu*. One, three, five, hit the *Soryu*. Bishop, Knight, Castle squadrons escort odds. Rest take evens. Stay in tight."

The chief keyed the orders. Webster hunched forwards. His companion was staring at the dull unblinking screen of the radar display. The skymap was running on a five-minute lag and the radar was motionless. It hadn't been updated since their arrival. The officer said, "Keep your eyes on the screen, sir. Any minute now we'll have active data coming in from the scouts."

Webster's hands were balled fists in his pockets. He fumbled for the pill container, rolling it back and forth, flicking the top open and shut. Data trickled in mumbles from the radio operators, in the low-key murmurs among the senior officers, the consternation etched on Paterson's brow. Illingworth and his first officer held a silent discourse of deliberate glances.

"*Jesus, switch to manual controls.*"

"*Red Fox leader to cubs, disable auto-release.*"

"*Wolf leader to White Rabbit. We got a proximity glitch with the strats. Half our ordnance's gone.*"

"*She's turning into the wind.*"

A chorus of angered dismay swept the chamber.

"What just happened?" Webster cast an eye on the screen. He tried to form some connection between the disembodied voices and the frozen display. The radar lit up.

"Rocket guidance must have been on auto-fire." His companion scanned the update. "This is all fucked up."

Paterson was at the starboard console, huddled with his men. He made his appraisal and snarled a string of directives to the chief.

"*The* Soryu*'s launching her scouts.*"

"*Hound leader, 020 bandits twelve o'clock.*"

"*Knight leader, 015 bandits three o'clock.*"

An airman shot Paterson a fretful look. "Pull them out?"

Paterson ignored him. "Identify aircraft and maintain contact," he barked. "Bring up the fighter escort." He turned to Illingworth. "Happy?"

"Don't sweat it," the admiral replied. "We're holding position."

Paterson seized the chief's microphone. "Wolf squadron, back off. Draw their fire. Hound, take out those flight decks. Red Fox target the ballonets."

The radar was a kaleidoscope of emerald and lime. Flashes of specks swirled mercurial around the two outsized jade markers. They seemed too small to be of any consequence, too trivial to bring any harm to the massive Japanese strats, each a minor city in its own right.

Scraps of radio broadcasts broke in on the fragments of heated discussion. Webster sorted through the babble, attempting to impose order on the rapid flow of information.

Knight squadron: fifteen pilots downed to a man.

A wing of jap fighters, sweeping wide as predicted by Paterson, mauled by Confederate interceptors.

Nearly a fifth of the rocket launches misfired due to computer error.

The *Soryu*'s central ballonet array in shreds.

A flight officer, close by, was giving Paterson his own evaluation. "Maybe fifty bandits all up—they managed to launch a squadron of scouts apiece. Our interceptors are all over them. Looks like we still managed to catch them napping."

Paterson signalled the radio chief. He handed back the phones. "Have them concentrate on the *Soryu*."

"*Close in Hound 7, follow me.*"

"*I've got a clean shot.*"

"*Look at that jap bastard climb.*"

"They're making a run for it," Webster's escort enthused.

Webster found the radar display unfathomable now. Scouts and fighters flickered back and forth, lost to contact or blown from the skies. From what he could see, the two strats were being driven apart. A wedge of scouts soared among them.

"The one to port's making rapid ascent," his escort continued. "Fuck knows what the other one's doing. There's another wave of jap interceptors coming in from the south. They'll have to get through our fighters first."

"*Think we nailed her.*"

"*Scratch one strat. We got them cold.*"

"*Bishop leader to White Rabbit. Confirming previous report. The* Hiryu*'s on fire. She's going down.*"

This time the cheer filled the room. Paterson was smiling now, nodding. He collared one of his men. "Let the fighters chase her down. I want all rocket squadrons on the *Soryu*."

"Aye, sir."

Illingworth interjected. "We bring the *Hiryu* down and I want all your crews making for those abandoned strips east of Vegas."

"My boys need refuelling. Some have taken hits."

"We can't launch and receive at the same time, and I don't want any fresh trails leading back to the *Patton*. We'll recover our boys soon enough."

A com officer approached the view port. "I have President Clancy on line one."

Paterson said, "He'll want a second strike."

"Let's finish the first one, shall we," Illingworth replied.

Paterson grinned.

Illingworth said. "I'll bring the *Patton* up to fifty-five. There's a juicy nor'westerly that can take us closer to the DMZ."

"Patch the President through on line four. I'll take it over here." Paterson cupped the mouthpiece and added to Illingworth, "Any chance of sending supply scouts with extra fuel to rendezvous at those strips?"

Illingworth relayed the command to his first officer.

Webster found the glut of information intoxicating. It would take a while to process. One strat was down, the other seemed ripe pickings. What was he missing?

He eyed the sullen dark of the view port. He envisioned the gnat-like scouts flittering among the stars. He tried to imagine how it felt aboard the *Soryu*, stalked by puny, venomous marauders.

There was a sudden bright tinge on the horizon's edge. Impossibly white, and just as soon spent, supplanted by a faint ochre glow. He had the impression of a ripple that snapped across the twilight's canvas.

"What the hell?" Paterson's voice rang out.

Webster swung back on the radar display. The screen was a green smudge.

The lights flickered.

Radio operators pulled back from their headsets clutching their ears, then checked their phones. The radar shimmered and died. The lights died. Voices cried out, shocked, fearful and angry.

The emergency lights kicked in, suffusing the chamber blood-red. He felt a slight shudder sweep across the deck.

Illingworth called general quarters and the order resounded through the speaker system. "All hands, man your battle stations."

Klaxons whined and sirens answered dimly from adjacent chambers. Technicians huddled around the radar display. Operators, back at their posts, worked their equipment furiously.

Webster's eye was drawn back to the view port. Strands of purple and teal snaked from the orange cloud perched on the world's edge. It brought to mind burning celluloid projected upon a screen. He thought the glass would be hot to touch, but didn't dare test his theory.

Illingworth was at his side.

"I suggest you run a damage report," Webster said quietly.

"I just did." Illingworth's reply was strained and feeble.

"Are all the electrics down?"

"Just the sensitives. We'll drift until the auxiliaries take effect. The radar array will take a while. We lost one of our recon scouts. It might have been fifteen miles closer to the blast than us." He found his voice. "Think it was deliberate?"

Webster shook his head. "Sacrifice two stratolites to take down our scouts and fighters? Hardly. That nuke was meant for Phoenix. Perhaps a target further east. Somewhere close by, though, otherwise they wouldn't have it armed."

Paterson joined them. His cheeks were wet beneath blood-shot eyes. His voice was steel. "What are we looking at?"

"Depends on which strat detonated. Depends on altitude and distance. I'll have to work the figures."

"My boys…" Paterson's voice trailed into nothing.

Illingworth said, "I'll clear operations and re-establish contact with the President."

Paterson nodded numbly.

Webster said, "You better send more recon scouts. Find out what *really* happened out there." He turned to Illingworth and added, "Now might be a good time to make for higher ground."

He held their stares and tried to put some emotion into his expression. He crinkled the folds of skin around his eye and made the edges of his mouth curl down at the sides. They shuffled away from him and began dispatching their commands. Long moments passed and behind him he sensed the beginnings of stability. He corrected himself. It was more a passing semblance, but the voices were hushed now, the communications more ordered. A few of the radiomen had their stations operative and the routine lighting resumed with a warm and steady glow.

He reached out to touch the pane of the view port and it was as cold as ice.

Pre-dawn, and the *Patton* was a lifeless husk pitched on uncaring seas. Suspended out over the Nevada–Arizona border, derelict and insensate, billions of dollars worth of steel and high–grade plastic listed within a swarm of bi-winged gnats.

Pinked to the gills, Webster lay face up on his bunk while renegade dreams buffeted him along narrow corridors, down, down, always down, towards that infinitely sharp barb that awaited the soft pulpy orb of his right eye.

A GAME OF CHESS VI

End Game

... Only
There is shadow under this red rock,
(Come in under the shadow of this red rock),
And I will show you something different from either
Your shadow at morning striding behind you
Or your shadow at evening rising to meet you;
I will show you fear in a handful of dust.

I

April 28, 2012
Indian Springs, Nevada

They'd been navigating by torchlight. When they struck a stretch of the old highway, the horsemen would lead at a rapid gallop. Where the 93 had crumbled to mortar and rock, they picked their way forwards carefully, looking to Shine for further guidance. He sat in the lead truck, squeezed between his father and the driver.

They were slowing down. The driver pumped the accelerator and crunched the gears savagely as they rolled to a halt. The headlights failed. Shine had a strange glimpse of his surroundings, highlighted by an unearthly illumination. The truck shook violently and settled.

Thunder rumbled, a sudden single crack, and the world became a cloud of roiling sand.

The face of a horseman loomed wildly into view, lit with a sickly amber hue that was promptly swallowed by the swirl. Shine clambered past his father and burst from the truck's cab.

The sand was thick. It filled his eyes, his mouth, his lungs. His body was racked by a violent spasm of coughing. He spat gobs of red paste. The heavens howled, rent by the cries of distressed horses. They fought their riders and pounded the earth.

A hand reached out and forced something into his grasp. He fumbled with the goggles, slipped them on, and pulled his shirt up over his mouth. The wind dropped abruptly, now keening with a sorrowful moan. The sand hung sluggishly in the air, drifting slow.

He reached out to the nearest man and shouted, "Where the hell did that come from?"

The ghost dancer grabbed his shoulder and turned him roughly to one side.

Shine stared in disbelief at the horizon.

Another figure emerged from the sand. He leaned forwards, bracing his palms on his haunches, and forced out a vigorous, hacking cough. He turned to Shine and said, "Are we too late, son?"

Shine gazed at the fireball that seethed and churned the night, and replied, "I don't know."

II

April 28, 2012
Naquinta Springs, Nevada

Ten miles out of Red Rock

The red dust was falling. It eddied and whirled with the occasional gust and dropped in a fine coating that gilded the trucks, the trail and the meagre outcroppings of sagebrush with an even layer of amber.

Morgan peered over the landscape, staring between interlaced fingers.

No one moved.

This was the way it would be forever; the trucks and the bodies, huddled under the protective rise of the bluff, preserved for all eternity. A snow globe of red flakes trembling beneath the malevolent glow of a new sun.

Get up.

Give me a sec.

Get up, you lame fuck.

Language, David.

Heh.

Morgan shifted in the dirt and raised himself slowly to his knees.

Lightholler looked across at him and said, "There may be more."

"I don't think so." Morgan brushed himself off and got to his feet.

The others stirred around him.

Kennedy gently disengaged himself from Malcolm's grasp and removed his goggles. "Get down, Darren."

Morgan dropped to the ground.

Kennedy crawled his way over to Tecumseh's side. "Have someone check the trucks, the radio gear."

Tecumseh gave him an empty look.

"Just do it."

Tecumseh signalled to his men. Two of them broke away from the group guarding the agents and inspected the vehicles. They emerged from the cabs with a brisk shake of their heads.

Tecumseh turned back to the major. "I need to be with my brothers now, sir."

"I understand."

Morgan made his way over to Kennedy. "We're only a few miles out."

Kennedy gazed at him with sudden intensity.

Ask me what happened, Morgan thought. *Ask me why I haven't had a drink in three days; why I haven't fallen apart at the seams.*

Kennedy broke off the look and nodded slowly. His eyes fell on Lightholler. "You okay?"

Lightholler was inspecting his forearm. He'd been sitting closest to the tailgate when the shock wave had sent their truck careening off the trail. There was a deep gash where the door had snared his arm.

"I'll live."

The sky was darkening again, reclaimed by the night. A faint nimbus remained amongst the clouded stars; an after-image etched into the fabric. Morgan could still read the expressions on his companions' faces in the dun light. They mirrored his own.

"Patricia?" Kennedy spoke softly.

Her face was a smudge of sand and camo cream. A fresh abrasion extended from her hairline to her jaw. She blinked slowly and worked a thin smile with some effort.

Kennedy let his hand fall on her shoulder. "Good soldier."

She put her hand on his and then let it slip away.

The men were chanting. Their voices, oddly melodic, were a low drone drifting over the bleak desolation. Occasionally a single voice would rise up, wrenching some unexpected note from the hidden skies, then fall back to nothing.

Lightholler appeared disturbed by their song. He peered warily at the ghost dancers, edged closer and whispered, "Are they praying to it?"

"No," Kennedy replied.

"They know what it is," Morgan added. "They're praying for the Earth."

Lightholler gave him a doubtful look. He'd clearly been ill prepared for his encounter with Tecumseh's ghost dancers. They sat in silence as the chant drew to a close.

Malcolm said, "I'm going to check on Agent Reid and the others."

Kennedy let her go.

They tracked her cautious movements over the alien landscape. The prisoners were grouped together beside the third truck, secured to one another by coils of thick rope. They were guarded by a couple of Tecumseh's men. The rest of the crew were still gathered around the medicine man, their heads bowed.

"You told me you saw Red Rock in ruins, a radioactive wasteland," Lightholler said to Kennedy. "That detonation was high altitude. Close, but not *that* close."

"There may be more." Morgan echoed Lightholler's earlier observation.

"A blast like that might have been meant to disrupt communications." Kennedy kept Malcolm in sight as he spoke. "I can't come up with any other explanation, and if that's the case we can expect company soon."

"We're in no condition to deal with any threat," Lightholler commented darkly.

"I think we can still do this," Morgan said. "I think there's still time."

Lightholler said, "You'll tell me what you've done with the real Darren Morgan when we're finished here, won't you?"

Morgan laughed nervously.

"Frankly, I don't want to know," Kennedy said. Then he added, "Grab some winks. Have a smoke. We march in ten." He went over to check on the prisoners.

"So much for our pep talk." Lightholler sighed. "Once more into the breach." Returning his attention to his wound, he added, "Last thing I need's a bloody infection."

Morgan nodded absently. He felt the desert's chill begin to work its way through him. He'd be warm again soon enough once they started marching. He just hoped his leg would stand up to the ordeal. He considered smoking a cigarette but was dissuaded by the burning taste of murky air that already filled his lungs.

Lightholler removed the canteen from his belt and poured a measure of water over his forearm. He worked the accumulated grit away from the wound's edge with the bunched-up hem of his shirt and said, "I got to read some more of the journal."

"What did the major tell you?"

"Everything."

"What do you think?" Morgan asked.

"Eloquent, articulate, insane."

"You're talking about the journal, right?"

Lightholler snorted and left the question dangling.

"Do you believe it?"

"I'm here, aren't I?" Lightholler lurched to his feet. "I'm going to raid the medical supplies."

"Bring me back some morphine. Make it a double."

Lightholler chuckled. "I'll see what I can do."

Morgan thought about the ghost dancers. What would they make of all this? They knew that the nuclear explosion wasn't of the world beyond the senses. It bore the scent of Man. No, it wasn't of the world beyond the senses, but it would be felt there. *That* was why they were praying.

So.

So.

I was never the class clown.

I had you pegged as the school bully.

You'll never know.

You're not even here, Hardas.

Neither are you.

Morgan leaned back and closed his eyes, an uncertain frown forming on his face.

III

April 28, 2012
Indian Springs, Nevada

They'd been arguing for a while now. Shine watched them from his vantage point, a cleft in the rock face that marked the westernmost portion of their dog-legged route. His best reckoning put them twenty miles from the Rock. On foot, by night, under the blood-red cloud, it might take him seven hours. What was he waiting for?

His father had asked him to sit there till the parley was over.

He recognised some of the chieftains: Michael Iron Horse, Jimmy Crow God, Cole Thomas, Charlie Wilson and Jackie Red Thunder. They represented the Sioux descendants of the last warriors lost at Wounded Knee. They represented the Objiwa peoples who'd wandered far from their native lands to band with their ancient Lakota enemies. They represented the local tribesmen of the Shoshone and Washoe nations. They also spoke for the blacks whose tribes had been left on some far and unremembered shore. In more peaceful times, their gathering would have called for a response from the National Guard.

They had guessed that he journeyed to Major Kennedy's secret domain—that *other place*. They knew that the government agents had been ordered to torch the camp, and they knew that a detachment of German tanks was nearby and closing in, but they had no real comprehension of what lay ahead—only a determination that their time had come. And they made none but the most severe of requests: they asked to accompany him north.

What had begun as an honour guard rapidly swelled to an escort of twelve-hundred men as they bled in from the fade-out. These were the soldiers who'd sworn fealty to the major. The latest incarnation of the ghost dancers, a cohort of the major's trainees whose beliefs had shaped—and in turn been shaped by—the mysteries of Red Rock. Sieved from the major's old unit, salvaged from the privation, disease and squalor of the labour camps, they'd found succour in the banned religion of Wovoka.

The original tenets of that faith had stated that the ghost dance ceremony would return the indian nations to their homes. That the Earth would be covered with dust and a new world would come upon the old. All the long dead would come back, all the whites would disappear.

More than a hundred years ago they wore their ghost shirts of sky blue; cotton cloth, brightly painted with thunderbirds, bows and arrows, suns, moons and stars. They believed these shirts would protect them from the white men's bullets. They bore no weapons save for defence. The dance was the message and the harbinger of a redemption that would never come. They were massacred at Wounded Knee Creek. One-hundred-and-twenty men, two-hundred-and-thirty women and children.

The practice, prohibited by death, was buried along with its practitioners, only to rise again in small clandestine movements during the intervening century. The major had contravened military law by turning a blind eye to its observation. When had he decided to mine the common vein of their desires?

Shine coughed and wrapped himself tighter in the thin blanket. There seemed dust enough to satisfy the direst of prophecies, but the blast had triggered discord amongst them. Now there were questions, or so it seemed. He looked up at the menacing sky and wondered if he could honestly blame them.

They talked amongst themselves another hour before finally approaching him. Shine's father was among their number.

"Thanks for waiting, son."

"We've made our choices," Iron Horse said. "It's just a matter of ratifying it with our brethren."

"I understand," Shine said. "I know this is more than you bargained for."

"This?" Iron Horse let out a mighty laugh. He was joined by the other chieftains, until the night was filled with the sound. "*This?*" His sweeping gesture seemed to include everything. "We recall a time when the Moon was brighter in the sky, when Venus was not yet a star in the heavens, and the Sun came up in the west. This is merely a trifle."

Shine listened to the reply, dumbfounded. "Then what were you fighting over?"

"The right of passage," Crow God said. "Most of the tanks and trucks have been disabled by the electromagnetic pulse. We could only recover fifty-three horses. We had to decide who gets to ride with you and who must suffer to follow behind on foot."

Shine understood that the suffering was in the delayed arrival, not in the fact they'd be walking.

"You're coming with me?"

"Who else can lead us?" His father said. "You'll have to leave a trail so the rest of us can follow on."

"You can't walk those miles."

"I can't take a warrior's horse either. The strongest of us will force-march overnight. We should only be a few hours behind you."

"Pa…"

"Yes?" His father drew out the word playfully, as he had when teasing him as a child. It was sadly absurd and strangely comforting.

"I'll see you up north."

The chieftains began to work their way back through the stalled procession to where their men had encamped. They stood among the kneeling figures, making their selections with cold deliberation. Iron Horse remained close by.

Shine's father extended a hand. "I'm hoping that by the time I get there you'll be long gone, son."

Shine's hand fell away from his father's grasp. *How long have you known about the carapace?*

Iron Horse said, "The old men say the Earth only endures…"

Shine, both astonished and relieved by his father's complicity, simply nodded.

Iron Horse offered a hopeful smile. "See that it does."

IV

April 28, 2012
Red Rock, Nevada

To Malcolm's credit she wasn't slowing them down. If anything, it was Morgan's stride, restricted by his injured leg, that set the pace.

They marched with the bulk of Kennedy's men, arranged in two files further back along the trail, the prisoners kept between them. Three soldiers scouted ahead, their figures emerging through the haze from time to time. Tecumseh dropped back to apprise Kennedy of their progress.

The Rock lay beyond the next rise.

They had been on a steady incline for a while now. Their path snaked between low hillsides that rose slowly to enfold them, while to either side the crests of two mountain ranges marched under the crimson skies of false dawn. If the camp truly lay ahead, Lightholler could find some solace. By default or design, Kennedy had built his base within a natural fortress of shale and stone.

Malcolm watched until Tecumseh disappeared ahead before speaking. "Ghost dancers? Is that what all this has been about?"

"There's no such thing as ghost dancers," Kennedy replied. "That's a tale used to frighten little children."

"Your association with them alone merits a death sentence. Does Webster know?"

"It's the least of my crimes. As for Webster," Kennedy shrugged. "He wouldn't care if I was training cannibals, provided his work got done."

"Who do you serve now, if not Webster? If not the Confederacy?"

Lightholler had posed a variation of this question himself, but now they felt like another man's words, spoken lightly in a place far removed.

Kennedy said, "You've come this far. Your answer's almost in sight."

Malcolm shook her head and murmured, "It had better be good, Joseph."

Her path wandered slightly away from them now, an unconscious expression of the gulf that widened and narrowed between her and Kennedy with each new revelation and mystery.

Fresh sounds reached them: the clang of a hammer ringing somewhere against rock, the stutter of an engine struggling to come to life. Voices chanting an unknown hymn, the words manifesting seemingly out of the desert sand itself.

The singers, a group of men in bright shirts of blue, appeared out of the night. They stood to either side of the trail, which widened into the dry bed of a vanished lake. They beamed smiles at Kennedy, and nodded greetings to the rest of the party without missing a note.

A man stepped out from their ranks. He was slender by comparison with the indians. A mop of thick, curly black hair hung over his brow. He surveyed the party with an easy smile and said, "Welcome back, Major." Spying Lightholler, he extended a hand. "You must be the good captain."

Lightholler met the stranger's grip evenly.

"Folks around here call me Doc."

Seeing Malcolm, he made what amounted to a clumsy bow. He greeted Morgan with a wave.

So this is the much vaunted Doc, the medico turned physicist, recruited by Kennedy to fix his time machine. Either that or the elaborate charade was drawing to a close, Lightholler mused. Standing amongst the ghost dancers and the rest of Kennedy's motley band, Lightholler was willing to hedge his bets. At this moment in time, he'd give the arrival of the men in white coats or the blessed advent of the time machine itself even odds.

His wounded arm throbbed beneath his tightened bandages to remind him that there was more to misery than just plain old hunger and exhaustion.

The sands stretched far and wide. He made out the low shapes of buildings in the distance, the mountains beyond; everything was a sundry shade of red. He had yet to see the goddamned rock that gave this goddamned wasteland its name. He looked across at the prisoners and felt a moment's kinship that was swiftly dispelled by the expressions of bitter hatred stamped upon their faces.

I'm allowed this, Lightholler thought. *I'm allowed my doubts. Stranger in a strange land, welcome to Red Rock.*

V

They were given warm clothing, and a medic tended to Lightholler's arm. He offered to examine Malcolm's face but she waved him away.

Once she had scrubbed off the filthy blend of camouflage and grime, there wasn't much left to treat. She ran a finger gingerly along the line of her wound. It might scar, but then again it might not.

Joseph told them he had to confine the other agents, and to debrief a squad of ghost dancers who'd skirmished with a Japanese patrol on the western outskirts of the base. He noted that forwards elements of a mechanised division had been sighted not fifteen miles away, their tanks and trucks disabled by the blast, bogged down in the sandstorm's wake.

He said he had to talk to Doc.

He left them seated around an oil heater in one of the prefabs that ringed the camp grounds.

She'd never seen him so shaken. Not even at Morning Star.

Morgan and Lightholler seemed untroubled by—or beyond reacting to—Joseph's words. Lightholler was assembling a cigarette from the loose tobacco leaves in a spent packet, rolling it carefully. He licked the edge to secure it and lit up. He drew back and passed it across to Morgan.

There were no windows. The smoke, thin and fetid, curled its way towards a narrow outlet in the walls.

A ghost dancer, leaning against a wall by the entrance, followed their movements impassively. He appeared to reserve the lion's share of his attention for her. Perhaps she was under guard; perhaps he thought she was Big Chief Joseph's squaw. It really didn't matter.

Lightholler broke the silence. "What are we waiting for?"

Morgan shook his head dolefully. "Got a bad feeling that the blast threw a spanner in the works."

She'd noticed that the base was poorly lit and had ascribed it to secrecy. "Trouble in paradise?" she ventured.

Morgan's look was scornful. Lightholler just rolled his eyes.

"It's not too late to turn back," she said.

Their looks turned incredulous. Morgan said, "Lady, you haven't got a clue."

"Then why don't you enlighten me." Her tone was acid.

The historian appeared oddly uncomfortable. Lightholler's look was roguish. *Boys caught out of their depth.* Morgan reached for the makeshift cigarette and smoked it to the stub. He coughed.

"Fine," she said.

She got to her feet and began to pace the room. There were ten bunk beds, their mattresses stacked at intervals between them along the walls. A row of lockers covered the far wall. There were no posters or pictures to remind anyone of anywhere else. There was a rustic heater in the centre of the room; a doorway opened into a bathroom and shower cubicle.

"This is where the rotating trainees would stay," Morgan said after a while, his tone placatory.

"Rotating from where?" she said shortly. "Alpha? Bravo? The Moon?"

Lightholler chuckled.

"We never knew where we were," the ghost dancer said, his voice low and surprisingly reverent.

They all looked across at him.

"We knew in our hearts, of course. But up here…" He tapped his temple and shrugged.

"So where *are* we?" she probed gently.

Morgan opened his mouth to speak but something stopped him. Lightholler stared with unconcealed interest.

"This is the *other* place." The indian's smile was enigmatic. He wasn't being facetious. His look suggested that his answer was complete.

"What happens here?" She cast a swift challenging look at her companions. They held their silence.

If the indian was surprised by her ignorance he kept it well hidden. "Change," he said. He nodded sagely but offered nothing more.

Lightholler's face registered total surprise. "They know?" he blurted to

Morgan in disbelief. "All of them?"

"They don't know," Morgan replied wearily. He looked over to the indian. "They believe. It's an entirely different thing."

"I don't get it."

"How else are you going to keep a secret this big?"

The handle turning in the door gave her a sudden start. Joseph stood at the entrance.

"Let's go," he said grimly. "There's something I want to show you."

"It's about time," Lightholler said.

They rose to their feet.

VI

They headed towards an isolated structure that stood at a distance from the shadows of the main compound. The stars above twinkled faintly through the russet penumbra of falling sand. It fell softly, insidious, announcing itself at the palm's crease, the lip's crust, the eyelid's edge. *This*, Morgan thought, *is what comes of sundering eternal bonds. The inexorable meets the unyielding and actuality is found wanting.*

He peered ahead. Kennedy and Malcolm had almost reached the building's entrance. They walked in close conversation. Was he her Virgil or she his Beatrice? Morgan's own guide pricked his thoughts with a sharp reprimand. *Save that shit for later, pal.*

A torch sputtered nearby; a sentry watching the hazy perimeter. Other ghost dancers were scattered near and far across the grounds. He felt every eye inspecting their staggered march.

Doc's oasis glimmered feebly where a guard smoked a cigarette under the pale glow of his lantern. The encrusted water was a still membrane of red sand; the palms, leaning at odd angles, a gateway fallen to ruin.

"Nice set-up you have here," Lightholler remarked offhandedly.

Morgan replied, "We run a kids' camp here each summer."

Lightholler sniggered. It was another example of the churlish attitude he'd displayed at the Lone Star, but there was a twist; some fresh warp in his weave that wasn't anger and wasn't fear but something altogether less wholesome. When planning his recruitment, they'd envisioned an ally sworn to their task. Now Morgan couldn't picture the man beside him commanding an ocean liner, much less the fate of the world.

They were only a few feet away from the entrance now.

Lightholler, perhaps reading something in Morgan's expression, said, "Your trail of breadcrumbs … back on my ship. You were tossing them from the stern."

Faced with the memory, Morgan reddened.

Lightholler laughed with surprising warmth. "I'd give anything to retrace those steps."

"That's why we're here, Captain."

Kennedy and Malcolm stood at the entrance. He held a ghost dancer's torch, unlit, before him. Her silhouette traced the lines that nature had generously sculpted there, while hiding the scars of recent travails. Confederate Gothic. She offered Morgan a look that bordered on apologetic. She'd never know what those days of captivity had done to him.

His answering smile was a worn mask. "I guess it's time to go down to the dragon's lair."

VII

Kennedy gave the darkened base a final sweep. Torches dotted the terrain. The rock formation that gave its name to the installation seemed a reprimand to the heavens.

Lightholler cocked an ear at a strange sound and, tracing it to his feet, examined the sparkling sheets of molten sand. "Well, how do you like that?" He cast a sceptical eye over the small building but made no further comment.

Shafts had been excavated and caverns hollowed out and the adobe had been finally replaced by this unobtrusive lean-to, but this was where Hardas, Morgan, Shine and Kennedy had listened to Doc's lessons. Here they'd puzzled out the workings of the time machine, and journeyed forwards and witnessed the fruits of their labour: sand-picked bones floating on a radioactive tide. It may have been Patricia's unforeseen presence, or a phenomenon born of the scarlet glow—faint now in the western skies—but Kennedy was struck by how much the view recalled his vision from the carapace. Not so much the sights, but the attendant feeling of perfect despair.

I'm not going to make it.

He hid the dread behind the rampart of his face.

"We'll skip the fanfare," he said, and knocked sharply on the door.

It swung open on sturdy hinges to reveal the soot-grimed features of Hayes, a ghost dancer, his sweat-stained blue shirt open to the navel. Wisps of smoke escaped from behind him and wafted into the night air. He gave Kennedy's entourage the once-over and stepped aside. They descended the stairs. Doc may have forewarned him, but hearing was one thing and seeing another. The antechamber was filled with fumes. Torches tilted at odd angles, hung from improvised receptacles on the chamber's walls. A single lantern hung suspended above the elevator. Two technicians studied a tangle of cables by the elevator doors as they attempted to wire the system to a battery array.

"I've been using the service duct," Hayes said.

Avoiding their eyes, Kennedy directed his companions to a circular iron door near the room's hub. From without, the structure might have passed for a derelict shack, tacked on to the main installation as an afterthought. Within, however, concrete slab walls curved inwards to an arced dome whose apex fused with the central elevator shaft. The walls themselves were scored with an incongruous blend of computer monitors and indian glyphs. The monitor readouts were blank or sizzled white-grey in silence. The ancient symbols, thrown into relief by the torchlight, were an arcane prelude to the possibilities that dwelt below.

Kennedy approached the duct. The technicians stole furtive glances, their awed faces cowed by Hayes' stern reproach. The indian helped him raise the thick casing of the service door. Tendrils of black smoke curled around the raised edges and spewed out in a noxious cloud as the door clanged open.

"We're working on the ventilation," Hayes offered contritely.

Kennedy nodded in faint acknowledgment. The duct was lit by lanterns, fixed at regular intervals along the ladder's rungs. "Will you be okay getting down?" he asked Morgan.

"Should be fine." The historian's face was bright with anticipation, in stark contrast to the others who eyed the shaft dubiously.

Lightholler spoke up. "After you," he said, and bowed to Kennedy with mock deference.

"Let them know we're coming down," Kennedy called across to Hayes.

Hayes picked up a hammer and tapped a lead pipe that accompanied the duct, giving the signal. Kennedy grasped the top rung and lowered himself into the opening. He'd negotiated twenty feet before glancing up to check the others' progress. Little light made its way down the shaft. Below, a weak red glow flickered. He had to squint against the rising vapours.

Patricia was a few feet above him. He continued the descent. The rungs chimed with their steps, the duct echoed their ragged breaths, and indistinct murmurs floated up from below. The encouraging thrum of the auxiliary generator rose steadily. He dropped the last few feet to the metal floor below.

A red lantern swung by the ladder on the unnatural draughts that swept the chamber. An elaborate blanket flapped over the entrance that led to the cavern beyond. A map of the night skies had been worked into the weaving. Its filigree of cerulean and emerald luminaries rippled portentously.

He reached out a hand to support Patricia's waist and helped her gain the ground. He watched, slightly bemused, as she fussed with the oversized uniform she'd been given earlier.

"I need a shower," she said. Her tone was almost an accusation.

"You look fine."

Lightholler dropped to the ground between them. He landed lightly and began making a rapid survey of the room. Kennedy followed his eyes as they scanned across the walls. There were fewer markings here. The glyphs, where present, were subtle arrangements. Rather than the miscellany of workmanship found above, they clearly demonstrated the craft of a single hand: Tecumseh's guidelines for that other world.

Carve the dream here; forge the reality there.

Lightholler approached the blanket and laid a hand against the coarse fabric. "Through here?"

"Uh-huh."

Morgan eased himself to the floor with a grimace. He eyed the cavern and said, "Looks different with the power out. Looks more like what it is."

"And what is that?" Malcolm asked softly.

"A gateway," Morgan replied.

Kennedy parted the blanket's folds.

Morgan stared.

Unpowered, the carapace was faithful to its name, more shell than device. It was as if the force that nestled within the baroque exterior had been extinguished.

She's dead in the water, bud.

No, not extinguished. Something still pulsed within the dense black-silver canopy. The ozone was a faint presence within the smoky haze, and it was colder here. Nothing obvious, just the slightest prickle of his skin against his clothes.

The major will get her going, Morgan thought. *We'll get there, Hardas.*

Sure we will.

* * *

Malcolm fell forwards, clutching her abdomen. She heard a voice—Joseph's —swearing, and felt arms grab her, cradling her slow pirouette.

The floor heaved. She closed her eyes. Bile burned the back of her mouth and it took every effort to hold back the contents of her engorged throat. Blood whipped within her veins, steel-tipped lashes of ice.

"It's alright," a voice said. "Slow breaths. Deep breaths. Don't fight it." Strong arms embraced her. A strange scent that was the loamy earth, but also smouldering coals, enfolded her in a secure cocoon.

"It can't be," she said in a small voice.

"Of course not."

She looked up into the deep brown of Tecumseh's eyes. He held her tightly. She fought the urge to flinch away from the medicine man. Joseph observed their exchange, pale-faced. The others remained standing, their eyes fixed on the machine.

"It *can't* be," she repeated.

Tecumseh's voice was warm and persuasive. "Accept that realisation and look upon it again."

She glanced up, hesitantly, trying to glimpse it from a safe angle—if such a thing was possible. Joseph was watching her anxiously. Tecumseh crooned the words of an unknown tongue in her ear.

The wounded beast crouched on twelve metal segments in a nest of its own matted cable.

Tecumseh's song wound its course, soothing her mind as his arms supported her body.

An intelligence seemed to lurk behind the mirrored casement of its sculpted shell. She came to realise that it was only a reflection of the onlookers.

Tecumseh's song faded into a sigh.

She turned to him and said, "Thank you."

The medicine man nodded slowly.

"How did you know what would help me?" she murmured.

"This is what happens when any of my brothers first view the device. You see what we have seen. Your sense of being here before will fade."

"You should have warned me," she whispered to Joseph.

"What would have sufficed?"

He was a prick and a bastard and absolutely correct.

Tecumseh shot her a mischievous grin and said, "You should see it when it's powered up."

She gave a nervous laugh and rose to her feet, trembling. She crossed to Joseph's side and cast Tecumseh a final discomforted look of thanks. He bowed and stepped back into the shadows.

Lightholler gazed in absolute wonder.

It was a spider; silvery-black, frozen in a web that was the distal extensions of its own limbs. Ornate cowling veiled a sleeping power that pledged an infinity of promises. He had to blink a number of times to put the machine into perspective.

Doc and another man were checking an assortment of cords that wound into a Medusa's knot at the carapace's underbelly. Lightholler traced the cords to a freestanding generator that was in turn plugged into a fitting in the cement-rendered wall.

He shifted his gaze to take in the entire cavern. The carapace occupied the bulk of the hollow. Computer monitors perched idle on wide unmanned consoles; a wall of shelves was crammed with documents and maps. A gantry, secured to the ceiling, could be rotated to offer access to the vehicle. There was only one etching adorning the thick walls here: a solitary buffalo, painted in fine strokes of red and white, defiantly facing the hunched machine. A bunk bed, up against the far wall, seemed out of place. There was a small night table adjacent to it, crowded with books and a crude model of the carapace that had been broken into two segments. Above the bed was a pale patch of wall where something had once hung.

Malcolm was back on her feet. He'd seen her drop to the ground, yet had been unable to move from his place, held as frozen as the inert machine. She gave him a look that wasn't reproachful but kept her glance away from the carapace.

Kennedy spoke. "We don't know how the interface works. We don't know where the atoms slip up against each other, or how it is that the carapace slides through. We don't know how here and now becomes there and then."

Lightholler said, "Thank you, Joseph."

It was okay now. Everything was okay. He understood Morgan and Hardas and Shine and Kennedy and the ghost dancers. He understood Wells.

He believed.

VIII

Morgan remained transfixed. It was Doc who broke the spell.

He approached them as they stood staring at the machine and led them to one of the consoles. He outlined the situation. Despite its altitude, the atomic blast's discharge had battered the installation. Waves of gamma radiation had white-capped a sea of ionised particles in a brief, sudden pulse that had assaulted every operational electronic device in the region. There was no way of knowing the radius of the effects, since communications were down.

The radar was down.

The carapace was down.

Some of the damage was superficial and some was permanent. The carapace could be restored to full function but the programming necessary to configure their destinations was lost. Entire sub-routines needed to be recalculated from scratch, and with all the computers disabled that process in itself would take long hours. It might not be possible.

To make matters worse, the machine required an external catalyst for its first jump. The generator that was meant to effect that leap was a burnt-out casing lying by one of the carapace's supports. A makeshift generator was charging from an external source linked to Alpha but the juice was trickling in slowly. By Doc's estimate they were looking at another fifteen hours before the carapace was powered up for complete extraction.

Doc turned to join a technician by one of the monitors. The major filled them in on the rest.

He began with a précis for Malcolm's benefit, covering the journal—how they'd found it and where it had led them. She snuck cautious glances at the machine while the major summarised the manuscript's contents. Her initial bewilderment turned to horror as Kennedy outlined the results of his first voyage in the carapace.

She asked her questions. They suggested a keen mind and supported Morgan's theories about her prior relationship to the major. He reflected that their parting couldn't have been acrimonious nor had it been conclusive. They completed each other's sentences, used gestures for phrases and glances for affirmation; but nothing could soften the blow. Sometime in the imminent future, there would be no detectable human life on the planet.

Malcolm excused herself and wandered over to the bunk bed, where she sat by the night stand toying with the model of the carapace. Tecumseh joined her. They shared quiet words.

Kennedy wrapped things up. He said his ghost dancers were already encountering Japanese soldiers at various points north and west of the Rock but there was only so much that could be achieved by the two hundred men under his command. He needed to go over the latest intelligence. He needed to get out there and brief his platoon leaders. He needed to blunt the Japanese advance.

"What you need to do is catch some sleep," Lightholler told him.

Kennedy shrugged it off.

Malcolm returned. She seemed more at peace. Stepping alongside Kennedy, she said, "We need to talk."

He shot Morgan and Lightholler an ambiguous look and said, "I'll catch up with you. Get some rest yourselves."

"Is there anything we can do to help here?" Lightholler asked.

Kennedy shook his head slowly. "I don't think so."

"You'll tell us when you need us," Lightholler insisted. "Won't you?"

Kennedy gave him a threadbare smile. "Have you ever known me to hold back?"

Morgan put his hand on Lightholler's shoulder and said, "Let's scrounge up another cigarette and grab some shut-eye."

Lightholler let himself be led back through the folds of the blanket. Morgan directed him towards the ladder but Lightholler, slipping out of his grip, drifted over to one of the walls and stared at the markings.

Morgan had been expecting this. "Captain?" he said. "John?"

But Lightholler just worked his way around the small chamber. His expression changed in the lantern's ruby glow, adopting an intensity that was lent an edge of malice. He stopped for long moments before an illustration that depicted a flooded valley where a bird wheeled and soared above the waters. On its back, between vast wings, rode the figures of a multitude of indians. He grunted something between a chuckle and a sigh.

He's just beheld a machine whose existence challenges every rational belief he's ever held, Morgan thought. *A dormant god that, when woken, was the threshold to anywhen.*

The carapace screamed madness to the observer. Thrust a medicine man back to his myths in the search for vindication, until he scribed the answers on cavern walls. So who could blame a young woman—who'd just made the shaky transition from jailor to collaborator—for doubling over in pain? Or even a ship's captain—who'd staked everything on a stranger's promise, and found every fear and hope realised in a hole in the ground in the desert— for wandering aimlessly around a chamber staring at modern petroglyphs, reassessing all of his convictions?

"That's a flood legend," Lightholler muttered, pointing at the final sketch, articulating the conclusion of his tangled thoughts.

"It's a prophecy, actually," Morgan replied.

"Really?" It wasn't the condescending tone he'd used earlier.

"The medicine man who began the ghost dance religion foretold of a great flood that would wipe the land clean of white settlers. But just before the deluge, gigantic thunderbirds would drop from the storm clouds to retrieve the worthy. When the waters finally receded, the indians would be returned and the lands restored as they were."

Lightholler examined the image again, curiously.

Morgan continued, "It's unusual to see a solitary thunderbird. They were usually depicted in flocks, often accompanied by lesser bird spirits like falcons or eagles." He pointed to the massive outstretched pinions. "The beating of its wings was thought to bring the rolling thunder. The beak snapped lightning."

Lightholler shook his head as if to clear away disturbing thoughts. He walked to the exit, grasped the ladder's rungs, and began to climb. Morgan waited a few moments and steeled himself for the shooting pain in his leg, then followed.

Topside, Hayes and one of the technicians were still working on the elevator. As Morgan emerged, Hayes indicated Lightholler's silhouette beyond the entrance. Morgan joined him.

"Okay," Lightholler said, "here's the thing I can't get my head around."

"What's that?"

"The ghost dancers know, or at least they suspect, or believe, that Kennedy has the means of going back into the past. That he can in some way restore things. Right?"

"Those who know—Tecumseh and Hayes and some of the engineers—know exactly what he has in mind."

"But why are they satisfied with that?" Lightholler asked. "If they want the land clear of white men, why help Kennedy go back to 1911? Why not take the machine for themselves? There's enough of them. Go to 1492 and stop Columbus in his tracks; make a pit stop in South America and dump Cortez and his conquistadors in a shallow grave?" His voice held a mixture of mistrust and dread.

"I asked Tecumseh something like that myself, once," Morgan replied. "He didn't even bat an eyelid. He said, 'Stop those fools and others would arrive in their place.' Arm the indians with machine-guns to halt the Spanish muskets and all you do is replace the white authority with a native one that would be equally deplorable. He said, 'Had the white man not come, what lessons would we have learned?'"

"He'd given it some thought then," Lightholler said.

"Wouldn't you?"

Lightholler nodded.

"Does his point of view surprise you?"

"It's a little too noble for my tastes," Lightholler said dryly.

"You really weren't ready for this."

"For an elite army of negro and indian fanatics? No. I was too busy dealing with Kennedy's personal insanity." He gave Morgan a gauging look.

"Well, I suggest that you put your thoughts of 'noble savages' aside," Morgan said. "Try to dispel a lifetime of fear and platitudes."

"They don't scare me," Lightholler said.

"I'd like to believe you, but we're the odd ones out here. A few of the ghost dancers—Tecumseh in particular—seem able to sense, on some plane, an injury that's been dealt by the carapace. An injury to the world, to existence itself, that requires healing. I figure that if they had a hell, it would be at the bottom of the Atlantic; and if they feared a devil, he would be white and look an awful lot like Doctor Wells. So whatever their long-term beliefs are, regarding the ghost dance and the restoration of their lands, their peoples, their immediate priority is still going to be to right Wells' wrong."

Lightholler shivered. "Makes you feel kind of insignificant, doesn't it?"

Morgan heeled the butt of his cigarette. "Yeah, I've had the same feelings myself, on and off, ever since this whole thing started." He tapped the cold sand over the smouldering ash. "I call it perspective."

Lightholler laughed and said, "Let's get out of here."

Back in the prefab they arranged two mattresses on the floor. Lightholler fashioned some pillows from rucksacks and linen he'd found in one of the open lockers. They lay staring at the ceiling.

Morgan glanced at his watch from time to time. The minutes crept past midnight with reluctance.

The occasional volley of gunfire, the odd crump of light artillery, broke up the silence.

Lightholler asked, "How the hell does he expect us to rest?"

Morgan formulated a reply but it was hard to put the words together. His thoughts were a jumble, notions jostled for attention. Hardas pressed his consciousness, sweet-talking him with offers of sudden bright bursts of bravery that all ended, cold and still, on the *Parzifal*'s shattered deck. He finally opened his mouth to speak and found Lightholler asleep.

He picked up an old magazine and lay on his side, squinting to read the print in the half light. The text blurred, each ponderous word slipping in and out of focus. There was a photograph of a woman. Blonde, pale, frosty. Teutonic chic. *Come to Berlin*, she said. *You'll never want to leave.*

He only meant to rest his eyes for a moment. To let closed lids soothe chaotic thoughts; after all, the major might return any time now. Sleep had been a dull weight nudging at his brain for long days on end; so when the magazine slid to the floor it took him with the subtlety and breadth of nightfall. It was like opening a door.

IX

April 29, 2012
Red Rock, Nevada

Kennedy brought Patricia to his quarters, a sparsely appointed collection of rooms for which he'd rarely found use.

Fatigue had overtaken her. First contact with the carapace had left her barely conscious. He coaxed her towards the shower and sorted through his belongings for a fresh set of clothes. He grabbed some fresh shirts, socks and a pair of boxer shorts from his wardrobe and laid them out by the shower recess.

He'd given her kitbag a cursory run-through at Morning Star, retrieving his Mauser and her Dillinger but leaving her notes untouched. As if to say, nothing you discovered could possibly interest me now. Nothing you imagined verges on the truth.

He examined them now.

There was an assortment of punch cards, useless without an ENIAC. There was an Atlas print-out with nine international listings for Morning Star. There were photographs: graphic forensic shots from the Queens Midtown Tunnel and Osakatown. The crimes that had been laid at his doorstep. *She really should have known better.*

A separate folder contained the names of trainees, allegedly associated with Camelot's third camp. The accusation she'd thrown in his face back in the prison cell. She'd scrawled a series of notations along the margins. There were additional scraps, copied from financial transactions and police charge sheets. The name *Webster*, underlined, had been etched deeper into the paper by someone else's hand.

Pieced together, they suggested a scheme designed to poison the tip of Camelot's blade. To set bloodier and more definitive endpoints for the project's completion and mire Kennedy in the grisly aftermath, when governments, both North and South, might be scrambling for a scapegoat. He read on, tracing her leaps of faith and intuition, from faked serial numbers on his pistol to a document implicating Webster in the abortive election campaign of '98.

It was an impressive body of work.

He had to admire the crude simplicity of Webster's snare. Spanning the rapidly hatched frame-up to the carefully crafted insertion of a third source of trainees, his vision had sustained what appeared to be almost a decade and a half of ill-masked hatred. Longer, if you went back to Mazatlan.

For want of an eye…

Kennedy wondered at his own detachment and replaced the papers.

She emerged from the recess wearing a T-shirt and the boxers. She held the elastic of the shorts bunched in a fist at her side, hitching them to her waist. The shorts ended midway down her thigh, where a purple discoloration marred the pale alabaster of her skin. Her hair, damp and tangled, framed her face. The scar was a vivid weal across her cheek.

"You might want to put another shirt on. It gets cold out here."

She nodded. Her eyes flicked across to her files.

"How did you find me?" he said. "How did you know to look in Morning Star?"

"Something you used to say, every once in a while, pointed me in the right direction."

"Uh-huh." He watched her move across the room.

She thumbed through the pages of her notes before replacing them on the bed. "I worked so hard to catch you, Joseph. I wanted to find you first. Find you alive. Bring you in."

"You *did* find me first," he offered.

"All I managed to do was ensure that you ended up exactly where you wanted to be."

He took a step towards her. She turned to face him with her hands on her hips.

"What does that tell you?" he asked.

"That you have more luck than brains, and all of it's bad."

"Maybe it says that I couldn't have done this without you."

"You've caused enough mayhem without my help, Joseph." Her tone was indecipherable.

"I'm saying, maybe it's supposed to be this way."

"And I'm thinking you've spent too much time with your ghost dancers. Don't you dare try to reckon me into this madness of yours. I'll be no part of it."

He gave her a questioning look.

"For God's sake, Joseph, do you know what you've got down there in that cavern?"

"I know better than anyone else. I think."

"Well, *I* don't think so." She frowned. "If you had any real understanding, you'd have destroyed the thing the moment you found it."

He held back his reply. She needed rest, not goading. She needed to stop talking and get some sleep. But she wasn't finished.

"Joseph..." Her look was almost imploring. "Can't you see what's been happening here?"

He listened to her words with a slender notion of dread. She was about to say something extremely important. How could he possibly know that? Somehow his time away from the carapace had left him unprepared for this: the unpleasant sense of premonition associated with exposure to the machine.

"Think back to when you were first given the journal," she urged. "To when you found the machine. Camelot was in development and you were the project's golden boy. You had a three-year mandate to reunite the states.

"Don't look so goddamned stunned, Joseph, I was given complete access to all your files. *Three nations* looked to you as the redeemer. And now, barely two years on, they curse you. Your director slaps together a frame-up, wants you dead. You're an enemy of the German *and* Japanese empires. And right in the middle of established peace talks, we're all plunged into ... into *this*."

"You're not thinking straight," he said.

"Don't give me that. I've never been so sure of anything in my life." She grasped his shoulders, sat him down on the bed, and stood before him. "The world you saw in the future is the world *you* made, Joseph."

"That's not true, Patricia."

"And what's worse," she said, ignoring his defence, "the absolute, total *fucking* horror of it all, is that you've known it the whole damn time."

"That's not true."

She sat down next to him and spoke softly. “You’ve known it the whole time, Joseph. What else would have driven you all those months and all those miles?”

He felt unwell; a sickness that had coiled latent in his heart now seeped through every vessel, coursed through artery and vein. “I’m not responsible for all this,” he said. “I want to *stop* all this.”

“You *have* to stop it. You’ve left yourself no choice.”

He nodded—mostly to himself—and asked the question that had preyed on his mind since Morning Star. “Will you come with me?”

“I don’t know.”

X

Tecumseh's going to tell me that the radio's working.

More and more, Kennedy was becoming convinced that control of events was illusory, self-mastery an exertion, and free will just a poor and dirty joke.

He despised himself for asking Patricia to accompany him on his journey. After she'd drifted off to sleep, he wandered the compound in a dream, his steps strangely sluggish, his mind struggling for the password at each sentry's challenge.

He's going to say that the Japanese are coming from the west and the north.

He's going to apologise.

He found the medicine man at the western watchtower. The tag was a misnomer. A culvert, burrowed into the western face of a low-lying ridge, sufficed for the observation post. Tecumseh sat alone, poring over a series of maps. He managed a grin at Kennedy's entrance.

"Hey, Major, we got a radio working. There's a lot of interference out there, though. Hayes is trying to put together a picture for us."

"What have you got so far?"

"Mixed tidings. Shine was picked up and brought to Alpha late yesterday."

Kennedy smiled. "Is he okay?"

"Some of our crew managed to leave the camp before the atomics went off. He was with them, but there's been no radio contact—not even smoke signals—since then."

"How many got away?"

"Near fifteen-hundred."

Shine played it by the book. Yet instructed to make his way to the ranch, he'd somehow managed to end up at Alpha.

"We need him. We need those men."

"I've sent ten runners south." He read the need on Kennedy's face and added, "It was all I could spare."

"I'm going to assume that was the good news. What do we know about the blast?"

"It was a jap strat, somewhere out west."

"What was the target?"

"No target, at least not as far as we can tell."

Kennedy stared.

"The whole *strat* detonated. Somewhere out over the Mojave. No one's sure if it was deliberate or not. And no one can tell where it was supposed to be headed."

"That bullshit didn't wash with Berlin. Why should it be any more convincing now?"

"Before it went up, it was hit by a wave of Confederate scouts, early last night. Latest intel's talking about an accidental trigger."

Kennedy gave it some thought. "They might have intended to blanket the ionosphere. Damage communications, radar, transportation."

"Don't think so, Major. Hayes figures there's two jap divisions due west of us, and a third further off to the north. That blast would have given them a world of hurt too."

"Any friendlies in the region?"

"The odd long-range patrol, a couple of regiments of Rangers by the state border, and that column of German tanks north of Vegas. Nothing particularly close by."

"Are the German tanks workable?"

Tecumseh scanned a report. "Maybe thirty per cent."

"Tell me more about those jap divisions."

"If they're the same guys that crossed the Demilitarised Zone two days ago, they're the 2nd Imperial Tank Army. We're looking at one armoured and one mechanised division, plus a regiment of Union artillery. Last word had them steering north of us, but their main body's about twenty miles out… and mobile."

"*Union* troops?"

"I'm as surprised as you are to see them out here."

"They were probably holding them back in reserve. If the pulse hit the japs' own artillery, they're stuck with the Yankees. But why here?" Kennedy added, muttering. "And why now?"

"I reckon we might've aroused their interest, creating that corridor from Alamo. We've also been operating some hit and runs on any patrols that wandered too close to home."

"So they could still pass us by."

"They just might." Tecumseh shifted uneasily.

"Tell me what you're thinking."

"I'm sorry, chief. I'm thinking that maybe one of my Braves suffered too much from pride, and talked when he should have walked. I worry that someone might have given our legends too much credit, and been a little too vocal about it."

"No one knows what we have here," Kennedy said.

"Maybe… or maybe someone suspects that we have something worth hiding, worth protecting. The path through Red Rock is as good a road as any into Texas."

Kennedy checked his Einstein. A fine crack now cut across its face. Dawn was six hours away. Another eight hours, nine to be safe, might see them through.

He said, "We need to keep drawing the japs south. If we're lucky enough, they'll bump heads with the German armour and we can leave them to duke it out."

"I've got a platoon engaging Japanese patrols out past the lake bed. You want me to throw more men south? I've got three fresh squads between here and Alamo I can bring down."

Kennedy inspected the map. Tecumseh pointed to the positions of the Japanese patrols and the locations of the squads.

"Bring them down but skirt them along the edge of the base," Kennedy said. "Don't let them strike. The japs might know we're out here but they don't know where. Their intel's as screwed as ours. We've been hitting them from the east and south; we throw in a force from the north and they'll come straight through here. We have to concentrate our attacks south and draw them away."

"You want to give the appearance of an ordered retreat?"

"No," Kennedy said.

Tecumseh's expression grew more intense. The medicine man's fears had sparked new possibilities. Kennedy chewed them over.

"You think the Japanese are coming through here for a specific reason..."

"Maybe," Tecumseh said.

"Then let's give them what they want." Kennedy selected another map from the pile and let his hand drift across the chart to a point south of the Rock.

Tecumseh's concern gave way to fiendish satisfaction. He said, "It might work."

"In the meantime I want snipers and knife-men on their officers. I want their fuel, water and ammunition depots extirpated. Leave the Union forces untouched for the moment."

"Untouched?"

"Go easy on them." Kennedy stared out beyond the culvert to where the ridges fell away into an expanse of low dunes. The night's storm had swept across the mounds leaving its signature in hollowed-out banks and heaped knolls of sand. He gazed to the west.

I crawl in the sand out there. I die out there.

"Major?"

"What is it, Tec?"

The medicine man's eyes were hooded in shadow. "We can hold them."

"Let's hope so."

XI

Morgan woke with the taste of ash in his mouth. His world lurched vertiginously.

He rubbed at his eyes and temples and made out Lightholler's outline amongst the shadows. He remembered where he was and fumbled for his watch. Quarter to two and the major hadn't showed.

He needed to take a leak. His fatigues clung to him and chafed. Now that he was awake he might as well cough his way through another of Lightholler's musty cigarettes. He staggered to the toilet and relieved himself. Ran the faucet, splashing cold brown water over his face and hands. He returned and reached for the packet by Lightholler's side, slipped it into his shirt pocket. Lightholler didn't stir.

Outside, his damp face tingled bitter cold. Exhaled vapour mocked his nicotine cravings. He groped for the packet in the dark. Three bent twigs remained of Lightholler's supply. He puckered one and set out towards the distant glow of a sentry's torch.

"Darren." A voice called to him from a clutter of stacked crates beyond the prefabs.

Morgan squinted into the darkness, half-expecting Hardas's ghost to slide out of the recesses. Kennedy was stooped on an overturned crate near the edge of the grounds.

"Major?"

Kennedy rose from his perch and began searching his pockets. He produced a butane lighter, slender and familiar. He flicked the wheel and its tip glowed bright and furious. Morgan leaned forwards and dipped his cigarette in the radiance, then stepped back, his eyes still on the lighter.

"It was his spare," Kennedy said. "I took to carrying it around. Here, it's yours." He handed the lighter to Morgan.

"He would have been pleased with the way you're turning out," Kennedy added after a while. "Surprised as hell, but pleased."

"He wasn't so bad, Major."

"The guy was a sour fuck, Darren, but I loved him all the same."

Morgan curled the lighter in the palm of his hand and pocketed it. "Thanks."

"I was about to check in on you."

"We're fine," Lightholler said from the shadows. Wrapped in a blanket, he had emerged from the prefab, a couple more bundled under his good arm. "It just feels strange, sitting on our hands only an arm's reach away from your… machine." He dispensed the blankets and the three of them huddled like crones.

Morgan handed him a cigarette and the lighter.

"Navy issue," Lightholler said. "Nice." He lit up and handed the lighter back. "What's happening out there?"

"There's a Japanese force due west. We're luring them south." Kennedy's look was oddly placid.

"You've got, what, maybe a hundred-and-fifty soldiers here, right?" Lightholler said.

"Closer to two hundred."

"Casualties?"

"Acceptable so far. What are you smiling at, John?"

"I'm not smiling. You've got just on two companies staving off an army. I'm wondering at your definition of 'acceptable.'"

"Those're my boys out there." Kennedy's reply was a soft undertone.

"So what can we do to help?" Morgan asked earnestly.

"You can rest up." He turned, smiling, to Morgan. "You can conserve your energy."

"I'm not fond of having others fight my battles," Lightholler grumbled.

"Me neither," Morgan offered. Reading their glances, he continued, "Not any more."

One of the ghost dancers was approaching. His shadow covered the ground swiftly. "We need you in the south tower, sir. Sacagawea's platoon returned with sixty-three scalps."

"*Scalps?*" Morgan mouthed.

"Figure of speech," Kennedy said, unconvincingly. He turned back to the ghost dancer. "Go on."

"We've rigged up another transmitter. Tecumseh's taking it out now to the squads on the west ridge. We're going to use Morse code, phonetic Sioux, to track and report jap movements."

"Any news on those squads?"

"Don't expect to hear from them for a while yet, sir. They got no wheels, no radio and they're too close to the japs for smoke signals."

"What about the crew from Alpha?"

"Nada."

Kennedy nodded. "Okay, I'll be there in two."

The ghost dancer sprinted back into the night.

Lightholler asked, "Do they really believe their shirts will keep bullets away?"

Kennedy let the blanket slip away from his shoulders and undid the flaps of his jacket. Sometime during the night he'd managed to change into a fresh uniform. His shirt, sky blue and buttoned to the collar, was covered with the familiar symbols and talismans of his crew.

Lightholler smiled faintly. "You're shitting me."

Kennedy tapped his chest. There was a muted chime. Lightholler reached for the shirt and felt the bulky layer of material that lay beneath it. Kennedy lifted it to reveal a second thicker layer of moulded plastic and ceramics.

"They all remember what happened at Wounded Knee," Morgan said. "This time they're wearing armour."

"I'll make sure both of you are kept up to date." Kennedy caught Morgan's intense stare. "And I'll let you know if we need you." He handed Lightholler his blanket. "But the last thing I want to worry about is you two hobos running around my compound." He eyed them firmly. "Get back inside. Get some rest."

They stood in silence for a short moment before Kennedy added, "I *mean* it."

Lightholler raised his eyebrows.

Morgan shrugged.

They exchanged a look and began the short walk back to the prefab. Morgan looked back from the doorway to find the major still standing there, but he didn't appear to be watching them. His gaze was fixed on some distant object.

XII

Kennedy stood outside the prisoners' prefab, peering up at the night sky. Nothing remained of the recent turmoil save the fine drift of tumbling sand. He couldn't shake the notion that the nuclear blast and the pulse it had spawned demonstrated a greater scheme at work.

The bouts of foreboding had faded to mere inklings of gloom, easily explained away by situation and circumstance, but he was still here, waiting to see Reid.

He'd detoured by his quarters and peered through the window, pleased to find Patricia curled up and sleeping in bed. He'd examined the forwards areas and spoken to the men who guarded the night. He'd checked each machine-gun post and surveyed the freshly laid minefield, pointing out where the charges might have been too obvious. He'd walked a mile out into the desert and sat under the stars, examining his base with an enemy's eyes. Finally, he'd gone over the new plans with Tecumseh, yet some misgiving had drawn him here.

There was no further news on the men who'd left Alpha. Contact with the Japanese vanguard had been restricted to brief scuffles and short exchanges of rifle fire. The ghost dancers had carried out their pitiless tasks of assassination and sabotage, and left their traces in the night.

There was a vestige of smoke in the chill air. Dawn was less than four hours away, and more than likely it would bring enemy planes and armour and a resumption of the conventional face of war. Until then, the various sides would feint and probe in darkness.

He'd placed a work detail on the camouflage. What hadn't been torn away in the storm hung in tattered nets, yet the sand had done its own part to obscure traces of their presence. They'd have to rely on the reduced visibility of the storm's wash, along with whatever repairs might be effected between now and sun-up.

A sentry opened the door and told him that the prisoner was ready.

Reid was propped up in a chair in one of the hastily converted barracks rooms. He was unable to conceal his surprise at Kennedy's entrance.

Kennedy pulled up a chair and turned it backwards. He sat down, leaned over the back rest, and said, "Who were you expecting?"

"Don't know." Reid rubbed at his wrists. "It's 3 a.m., bud. Maybe your girlfriend."

"Well, you get the bonus plan tonight." Kennedy cracked his knuckles. "You get me." He rocked his chair forwards, putting him closer to Reid's face. "And I'll be glad to extend that little love-tap Morgan gave you, ear to ear, just to see the expression on your face. Are we clear, *bud*?" He rested the chair back on its four legs.

Reid gingerly reached for his injured scalp in an almost unconscious gesture. "We're clear." He placed his hands on the table and sat stoically.

After a moment of silence, Kennedy spoke. "What was your assignment?"

"I was told to secure you at Hot Springs, holding you there until I received further instructions."

"Who gave the order?"

Reid just stared.

"Why would Webster do that?" Kennedy asked. "You already had me in custody."

Silence.

Kennedy thought it over, and said, "That wasn't part of the original plan, was it?"

"No." Reid shook his head. "But it was the first he knew of your capture. Malcolm was holding back on him. She said she was waiting on further evidence."

"But you went ahead and contacted him anyway, didn't you," Kennedy said. "Even after she'd told you about the third camp."

"No," Reid said. "It was before that."

"Before?"

Reid nodded.

"So you were never really assigned to me. You were watchdogging Malcolm."

"Something like that," Reid replied. "Look, I was pulled away from duty at Bravo camp. Webster seemed to think Malcolm could draw you out."

Reid studied Kennedy's face and realisation dawned in his expression. "Christ, she *wasn't* on your payroll, was she?"

"Now why in the world would you think something like that?"

"Her prints were on the gun we retrieved from Osakatown... Your gun."

Kennedy patted the Mauser at his side. "This gun here?"

Reid shook his head, as if trying to jostle his thoughts into order. "*Damn*," he swore softly. "What a fuck-up."

"Sounds like you backed the wrong horse."

Kennedy rose, scraping the chair away from him, and made for the door.

Reid looked up at him, his face a mixture of emotions, and said, "You've got a bunch of redskin extremists. You've got the director shitting himself. What the hell's going on here?"

"You tell me."

"I've been doing a little research. Hughes Aeronautics hasn't made a dime in two years. And five of your top physicists are AWOL. Propulsion experts. So tell me, what the hell are you building out here?"

Kennedy glanced over at the sentry and said, "Make sure he and the others get a decent meal, cigarettes. Whatever they need."

"Hey," Reid called out. "*Hey*."

Kennedy was at the exit. "What is it?"

"You better get your boys praying to their sky spirit or whatever hooey they got going. Once the director finds this place, we're *all* gonna be toast."

"And how's he going to do that?"

"He's been a step right behind you the whole way," Reid said, "and now you've stopped moving. Don't worry. He'll find you."

"I've got one more place to go," Kennedy replied, "and he *sure* as hell ain't going to find me there."

Outside the building, Kennedy stood on trembling legs. He felt his body's revolt against the long hours of wakefulness and deprivation and willed his worn limbs to give him just a few more hours. Meaning to check out the progress at the motor pool, he found himself strolling back across the grounds, instinctively scanning the area.

From his position, the entrance to the carapace was lost in the Rock's misshapen silhouette. Then he saw it. A flicker of movement; a shift of shadows. He froze and made out a solitary figure hunched near the base of the formation. He strode towards it with a measure of renewed vigour.

"Hey," he said.

Doc rose from his haunches with a groan.

Kennedy's enquiring glance posed the question without words.

"We're getting there," Doc said, his voice strained. "But we've got a ways to go. I'm taking a breather."

"Out here?"

Doc shrugged. He looked uncomfortable.

Kennedy gazed past him, at the unmarked grave. Ninety years ago Wells had buried his friend Gershon here.

He asked, "What do you think *he'd* have wanted?"

Doc selected a pebble from the desert floor. He ran his thumb across the smooth edge before laying it before the grave's marker. "What he's got, I guess," he muttered. "Peace."

Something came together then for Kennedy. A connection forming between Reid's stale offerings and the night's events. He understood what he had to do.

He returned to the makeshift lockup and gathered the prisoners in a group. They stared at him suspiciously, but their expressions turned to astonishment when he spoke.

"I've got a job for you," he said.

XIII

"You hear that?" Lightholler nudged Morgan.

Morgan shifted and moaned.

Lightholler strained his ears for the sound, then rolled over and looked at his watch. He'd slept for two hours. Knotted muscles, cold and strained, protested as he performed a series of stretches. His arm ached dully. He gave the wound a quick inspection and went to wash his face. When he returned, Morgan was pulling on his boots. Looking up he said, "What is it now?"

"I thought I heard a plane." Lightholler crossed the room and opened the door slowly.

A blush of soft rosy light suffused the camp, an unreal, pre-dawn glimmer of hideous splendour. The horizon was a tawny haze. The base seemed smaller in this half-light. A horseshoe of squat buildings hunkered under patches of cowled netting and a blanket of crimson grit. Where they curved around the opposite edge of the grounds, they blended readily with the rolling mounds of sand and stony outcroppings.

There were no ghost dancers in sight, but recent experience had taught him that he couldn't trust his eyes where they were concerned. He peered out to the distant mountain ranges that ringed the installation and realised that even now his instincts cried out for some form of escape. He let out a short, contemptuous laugh.

Morgan checked his watch. "The major never called us. What are we supposed to do?"

Lightholler stepped outside.

Morgan said, "I think we better wait."

"For what?" The air bore a faint scent of cinders. To the far west the low cloud cover was augmented by a thin pillar of tarry grey smoke, but there were no sounds of battle. He decided that he was looking at consequences. "Kennedy may be caught up."

Morgan joined him by the doorway. "Hayes will know where the major is." His eyes drifted towards the smoke. "Looks kind of close, doesn't it?"

"Yeah, it does."

They threaded the doubled row of prefabs that comprised the north barracks and ducked under a series of ropes securing the camouflage, finally emerging into an open area. Their course took them towards the obelisk of red rock. Lightholler hadn't been able to make it out last night, yet it stood less than fifty yards beyond the shack that marked the entry shaft to the carapace. As they approached, he noticed the colours shifting along the formation. Some trick of the light perhaps. This was the rock Wells had mentioned in his journal, the landmark that had guided Kennedy in his search for the carapace. He wondered how that moment of revelation must have felt.

Morgan stopped.

Lightholler turned to see what had caught his attention. A ghost dancer had materialised on the path behind them.

"We're looking for the major," Morgan called out to him.

"He's looking for you," the dancer replied severely. "Follow me." He turned sharply and began leading them back towards the western edge of the compound.

"What's happening out there?" Morgan asked the dancer tentatively.

The soldier made no reply but quickened his step. He led them past a block of buildings and through the motor pool where several trucks were lined up by a gas pump. The trucks, like everything else in the compound, lay under canvas and netting. Lightholler spied a small gathering of men by a storehouse, remote from the rest of the western façade.

"That's the armoury," Morgan murmured.

Kennedy was standing amongst a number of ghost dancers. He acknowledged Morgan and Lightholler with a weary nod. The dancers parted to give them space.

Two of them climbed into a jeep parked near the building's entrance. It spluttered to life and tore across the pebbled surface of the motor pool towards the desert. The others made their way to the trucks. More men emerged from the armoury bearing heavy-looking olive-coloured canisters between them. They began loading the equipment onto the vehicles.

Lightholler said, "I thought nothing was working."

"We got a few of the trucks operational." Kennedy turned his attention back to the dancers. He pointed to a growing pile of gear next to one of the trucks. "Less of those and more medi-kits," he called out to one of the dancers.

"Anything else?" Morgan queried.

Kennedy gave him a blank look.

"Anything else *operational*?"

Kennedy shook his head. He was squinting against the rising sun and his expression was unreadable. He didn't offer anything more.

"You wanted to see us?" Lightholler prompted after a few moments.

"Yeah." Kennedy's eyes fell on their uniforms. He saw the blue shirts beneath their jackets and a smile applied itself to his worn features, but his voice remained distant and removed. "You guys wanted to help out."

"That's right." Lightholler's reply was guarded. "If we can."

"What's going on, Major?" Morgan was looking out past the white caliche of the desert floor, his eyes drawn back to the column of smoke, which was now a tapering grey spiral in the distance.

Kennedy reached out, gently grasping both men by the shoulder. "Come with me."

He walked them back towards the main cluster of buildings, halting at a smaller prefab. A body of ghost dancers, led by Tecumseh, were approaching across the grounds.

Lightholler followed Kennedy's gaze as it swept the compound and came to rest on the outlying formation of Red Rock itself. He experienced a moment of clarity and said, "Where are you going, Joseph?"

Morgan's puzzled gaze shifted between the two men.

"Shine's guiding a platoon of my men over from Alpha. They're on horseback. Only a few miles away now."

"Shine's coming here?" Morgan said, elated.

"There's another fifteen-hundred men held up at Indian Springs," Kennedy continued. "They've got trucks, tanks, weapons. They were hit hard by the pulse."

"Where's Indian Springs?" Lightholler asked.

"About fifteen miles south of here, give or take."

"We're going to Indian Springs?" Morgan asked.

"No."

Tecumseh's band was almost upon them. They halted at the edge of the grounds.

"What's in the trucks?" Lightholler asked.

"Fuel, distributor caps, fuses, circuit-breakers, wiring, tape and a shitload of ammo."

Clarity sludged as Lightholler tried to recap last night's events. Everything seemed a muddled footnote to his vision of the carapace. His initiation. "Eight hours," he said. "That's all Doc said we'd need."

"Doc wasn't giving any guarantees, John."

"But we're camouflaged," Morgan said. "They'll have a hard time finding us."

"No guarantees."

Lightholler composed his thoughts. "Your men have been drawing the Japanese south all night. There's bound to be enemy units between here and Indian Springs. Can *you* guarantee that you'll get there? That you'll be able to lead those men back here in time?"

"No, but I can assure you that I'll be best able to put those men to good use." There was a disturbing finality to his answer.

Morgan wrung his hands with slow, deliberate movements. His return to form was vaguely unnerving. Tecumseh remained just out of earshot.

"Darren," Lightholler said, "could you excuse us for a moment?"

Morgan's pale eyes blinked slowly. He backed away, shifting to where the dancers were loading the last of the trucks.

Lightholler turned to Kennedy. "Alright, Joseph," he said. "what's going on?"

"The journal's in my office, along with my files," Kennedy said. "Over there." He pointed to the smaller prefab just ahead of them. "Tecumseh will run the base's defence. I have complete faith in him. And Morgan will be alright—he knows what he has to do. Shine will want to go out on patrol. Don't let him leave the base. You're going to need him later on."

"For Wells?"

"For Wells."

Lightholler nodded slowly. "What makes you think you won't be here?"

"Nothing that I can explain to you right now."

"We still have secrets?" He didn't try to disguise the irony in his voice.

"Just the one."

"Fair enough, but tell me, Joseph, why do I have the sneaking suspicion that you're leaving me in charge?"

"Think of it as holding the fort." Kennedy flashed him the slightest smile. "Doc will have you and the rest of the crew primed for launch."

"Does he know that he's Gershon?" Lightholler asked softly.

Kennedy appeared only mildly surprised. "That's not entirely accurate, John."

"Does he know that he's *our* Gershon?" Lightholler probed evenly.

"He found out last year."

"I bet he was pleased as punch." Lightholler pressed it home. "I just wanted to be sure I knew how big a bastard you are."

"I think you've got the general idea." Kennedy cleared his throat. "I brought you all together. Shine, Doc, Morgan and you."

"And Hardas."

"And Hardas. The others have all the information you need to see this through."

"Of course they do." A part of Lightholler had suspected that it was always going to end this way. Even back in New York, in his hotel room, he'd had some sense of the burdens he'd be shouldering. He smoothed the bitterness from his face and asked, "Have you told Malcolm?"

Kennedy bit at his lower lip. "I wouldn't know what to say."

"Now *that* would be a first."

Kennedy chuckled hollowly.

"Is she coming with us?"

"I'd be happier if she did."

"I'll do what I can."

"Thanks, John. It's been … interesting." Kennedy offered his hand.

Lightholler let it hang there for a moment as he framed the thought. "Why me?" he asked.

Kennedy turned the palm of his hand so that the gesture became one of entreaty. "Because if the worst happens, you'll have the best chance of doing what's right."

"How do you reckon that?"

"Explosive charges have been placed all around the carapace. You've spent the least time here. You'll find it easiest to do what's necessary."

"Is that the way it works?"

Kennedy gave him a look. "So it would seem."

"It won't come to that." Lightholler reached for Kennedy's hand and gripped it with a surge of melancholy. "Be seeing you soon, Joseph. Okay?"

"Sure." Kennedy squeezed back.

Tecumseh's band had recommenced their approach. The medicine man came to within a short distance of them before stopping. He dropped to one knee and selected a granule of sand from the dust at his feet. He resumed his stance and examined the particle. "More's the pity that you don't get to see our dance."

Kennedy placed a hand on his chest. "I'll know it here."

Tecumseh inclined his head forwards slightly and began the ritual of leave-taking.

XIV

Kennedy's convoy departed before dawn. Five trucks, a personnel carrier and two jeeps. The rest of the compound's vehicles had been scavenged for parts that might facilitate repairs at Indian Springs. Three had been spared for Tecumseh's use.

The transfer of command had been seamless but held an unreal quality. Tecumseh kept Lightholler appraised of the morning's events, more as a matter of politeness than policy. Hayes came by the office to report that progress was being made, and even Doc made an appearance. Every illusion was in place to suggest that the carapace's successful departure was a *fait accompli.*

Lightholler browsed the files.

The final team would include Doc, Morgan, Shine and Lightholler. Hardas's seat would be offered to Malcolm. Kennedy's would be saved in anticipation of his return.

Lightholler conducted a quick inventory of their equipment, which included three contemporary White Star Line officer uniforms. There were Mausers and weapons of more antique and dubious quality; identification papers and carry belts adorned with gold. Doc briefed him on a number of scenarios Kennedy had devised for their mission; they ran the gamut from a subtle snatch-and-grab to seizing control of the *Titanic.*

Lightholler found himself staring at the scientist. Doctor Dean Gershon, Kennedy's trump card. The physician-physicist who'd mastered control of the carapace. He'd pilot the machine through a series of insertions back to 1911, there to bear witness to Wells' capture in the desert, or play avatar to Kennedy's final mind-fuck aboard the *Titanic.*

Either way, it was going to be entertaining.

Morgan and Shine were sitting outside the office. Lightholler could hear their murmurings through the door. Any joy at their reunion had been tempered by the major's sudden abdication. Yet neither of them seemed surprised—or dismayed—at Lightholler's sudden promotion. Token gesture or not, he wondered who could envy the burden of his particular station.

He called them in.

Shine was wearing a ghost dancer uniform, his blue shirt open so that the darker material of body armour showed at his throat. He and Morgan drew chairs away from the walls and joined him at the desk.

"Sorry to keep you," Lightholler began. He felt faintly ridiculous. "I've just been going over Tecumseh's report."

"They get the decoy up, Captain?" Shine asked.

The fifty ghost dancers who'd accompanied Shine had been assigned to help with the rapid construction of a counterfeit base, five miles south of the Rock. Stripping the unused prefabs that ringed the grounds, they'd been shipping the parts to the new site all morning.

"It's almost operational," Lightholler replied. "Tecumseh asked me if I wanted to ride down and inspect the site but the notion struck me as unnecessary."

"The major had his reasons for leaving you with the reins."

"Did he say anything else to you when you saw him? Did he give you any indication…" Lightholler let the question fade away to nothing. Behind the cool veneer of his expression, he craved an answer. *What the hell does he expect me to do?*

"He wanted to know how many ghost dancers were marching up from Indian Springs," Shine replied. "He told us to go on ahead. He said that you now spoke for him."

"*Damn.* He lets the prisoners go—no one here knows the why or wherefore—and then he goes running off on some fool mission to rally a motorised column that has no wheels."

Morgan averted his eyes, making a show of inspecting the walls of the office. "How much more time do we need?" he asked.

"Doc says six to seven hours."

"Was eight hours at dawn. At this rate we won't be moving out till sundown."

"Have you found Malcolm?"

"She's over by the prison, sifting through the stuff that Reid and the others left behind. Looking for answers, I guess."

"Aren't we all? She coming with us?"

"She told me she'd let the major know her answer."

Shine seemed heartened by the avowal, but Morgan's face told the whole sorry story. No one really thought Kennedy would get through to the column, much less return in time for their departure.

"So what do you want us to do?" Morgan asked.

It was the same question Lightholler had thrown at Kennedy and, for his sins, he'd been given command of yet *another* doomed ship. Now, though, he felt as if some answer was finally due.

"I'd like you to keep an eye on Malcolm. See if you can help her. We find out why those prisoners are gone and we might get a handle on what the major is up to."

Morgan seemed satisfied with that. Shine gazed at Lightholler expectantly.

"You've been on the go all night. You could probably do with a break," Lightholler said.

"I'm fine, Captain."

Lightholler nodded. "Perhaps you could join Doc down in the cavern, then, and see if he needs a hand. He had to send his engineers to assist with the decoy."

"I have other skills, you know."

"You have other duties too."

"Yes, sir."

Morgan lingered by the door. "You okay with this, Captain?"

Lightholler felt a tiny twitch in his eyelid. Any sign of weakness now would be the ultimate betrayal. He said, "I'm almost enjoying myself."

"Just wanted to say, I'm glad you came aboard with us."

"Well, I'm glad *one* of us is." Lightholler folded away the files and followed them out of the room.

XV

The plane was small, with wide, slender wings. Morgan peered up at it through the fine slit of the camouflage. It seemed to hover, slow and careless over the base.

"Scout plane," one of the ghost dancers muttered. He dropped the binoculars and returned his attention to the transmitter, his movements becoming feverish. All he produced, however, was a series of high-pitched whines.

"Doesn't *look* like a scout," Morgan offered.

The ghost dancer glanced sideways at him. "It ain't one of ours."

"Getting anything?" his companion asked.

"Nope."

They all looked up. The plane had completed a turn and was winging its way back westwards.

The radio operator delivered a sharp clout to the side of the transmitter. He made a final attempt to locate the plane's frequency before shutting the machine off with a shower of curses.

"Think they made us?" Morgan asked.

"We'll know soon enough."

Besides a few rounds of artillery fire, discharged earlier that morning, this was the first real sign of interest from the outside world.

Word was that another patrol of Japanese recon had been ambushed, out by the decoy site. Tecumseh's men had waited long enough for the patrol to sight the buildings and send out a report, before putting the hapless soldiers into the ground.

The radio operator turned to Morgan. "We're due at the west tower.

Did the captain want you coming out that far?"

The truth was that Morgan had no idea what Lightholler wanted. He'd joined Malcolm at the prisoner barracks, as requested, only to be told to stay out of her damned way as she combed the rooms. After an hour of watching her stare at furniture arrangements and sift through ashtrays, he'd made his excuses and left.

He'd wandered for a while until he was co-opted into a labour team, refreshing the camo over the skeletonised remnants of the south barracks. It was there that he'd happened upon the two ghost dancers. They'd all huddled down at the first sound of the approaching aircraft.

The labour team, their work completed, were heading back to the armoury.

Idle hands do the devil's work, bud.

Morgan responded to the voice inside his head, saying, "He didn't tell me *not* to."

The radio operator shot him an odd look. "What's that?"

"I'll help you with the shortwave."

The ghost dancers took it for an answer. He slung the transmitter over his shoulder and followed them away from the concealment. He stumbled across the pitted remains of the grounds. Dug up overnight, they would present an uneven plain to eyes in the sky.

At the west tower he let the transmitter ease to the floor with a sigh of relief, and listened as the men gave their report. He felt like slinking away. He wanted a drink, badly. He wanted to wheedle a cigarette. His ears pricked up at the news that the decoy had come under further attack. Lightholler was somewhere out there.

Watching him, a ghost dancer said, "Didn't think you could turn any whiter, man."

"Leave him be, Everett," the radio operator said.

"Don't you worry 'bout him, Frost," the dancer said. He turned on Morgan. "Soon you'll be on your merry way." His laughter was brief.

Morgan had an idea of the incongruous image he struck. His recent wounds were a mantle, and word had already circulated about his role in the escape from Hot Springs. Now Hardas kicked in, wresting Morgan's tenuous control.

"What have you got for me?" he demanded.

"I'm headed out to relieve the watch on the ridge. Thought you might want to see what we trying to hide from."

"Ain't nothing he needs to see," the operator said. "Thanks for the assist, Mr Morgan. Now you better go on back to the office and wait it out."

"I'd like to take a look, if that's alright."

The radio operator addressed Everett directly, saying, "You don't bring him back, you don't bother coming back yourself." He stared at Morgan again, bleakly, and added, "Shit, I better tag along."

White sand lapped at bare knuckles of broken rock. Sunlight glanced off the low ridge that braced the western horizon. Morgan glanced back at the culvert. The radio operator put his binoculars to his face and did a rapid scan. He gave the all clear and they stepped out onto the sands, then began to work their way from dune to dune. He instructed Morgan to stick close to their trail.

"Minefields," he offered, by way of explanation.

Morgan observed their movements—the light steps, half-sliding, that left little trace in the sand. His approximations were laboured and clumsy and he gave up after the pain in his leg mounted to a steady throb.

Everett, observing his attempts, gave a wide smile and said, "Don't worry. We'll clean that shit up on the way back."

Morgan nodded back thickly.

Ten minutes' march brought them to the foot of the ridge. He wiped the beaded sweat from his forehead and looked back again, cheered to see that the base was lost from sight. The cliff presented a moderately difficult climb and that was good too. The ridge was part of a rocky wall that encircled two-thirds of the base. It wouldn't be any easier for Japanese troops to descend this face—especially under fire—and there were dancer gun emplacements trained in this direction.

Morgan ascended to where the others were already perched. Everett was calling across to two sentries spread flat across the summit. They signalled back and one began crawling towards them along the ridge's brow.

"Gee, but they sure glad to see me." Everett turned to the radio operator and said, "Slip Mr Morgan the 'scope, Frost."

The radio operator unslung the binoculars and handed them across.

Morgan skimmed the horizon. An undulating profile of purple blue greeted him, untenanted and bare, melting into cinnamon skies. Strangely disappointed, he made to hand them back.

"Pan down," Frost suggested.

He returned the viewer to his eyes. There was an area of grey and brown that could have been scrubland at the edge of his field of vision. He panned across and adjusted the focus.

"Don't forget to breathe, man." The ghost dancer's voice was a whisper in his ear.

Morgan let the binoculars slip. "Has to be hundreds of them out there."

"Thousands," Frost grunted. "But they're right where we want them to be." He took back the binoculars and slid them into their case.

Morgan tried to catalogue the vision. A tent city stretched out to the west and south. Tanks and trucks, clearly operational, arrayed in loose formation. Smaller figures of men milled back and forth in large knots between dark pavilions that may have housed more vehicles or munitions.

"Been gathering together since dawn," Everett said. "*Pre*-dawn. That's how they deal with what we bring them. Draw their supplies together under one central picket. Keep their command local and covered. They stopped our lightning strikes cold, but they all in the one place."

"Look where that column's headed," Frost said.

Everett studied the movements with his own set of binoculars.

"They're making to assault the decoy."

Frost said, "Won't be pretty."

The sentry had reached them and was scrambling down next to Everett. "Going to be damn ugly, if you're asking me."

Everett handed him a fresh canteen and said, "I'm thinking you're a glass half-empty kind of guy. Tecumseh's got the decoy covered."

The sentry took a swig and replied, "I'm the guy what's leaving you up here on this hilltop while I'll be taking a dip in Doc's old pool."

The ghost dancers all laughed.

Morgan smiled weakly.

"Anything else you'd like to see?" Frost asked him.

Everett had already begun snaking his way over to the sentry post.

Morgan said, "Think I might be done here."

"Then let's move the fuck out."

Frost led them back down the slope.

XVI

"Martin, can you work that equation for me again, incorporating the new variables?"

Shine gave Doc a questioning look.

Doc slumped heavily at his desk, his forehead supported on an outstretched palm. He removed his reading glasses and said, "Re-enter those coordinates I just gave you and try them against the location data set."

Shine typed in the numbers as requested. The computer, patched together from salvaged terminals, was barely serviceable. He instructed it to operate the stats parcel and hit the *enable* key. Its components, narrowly compatible, seemed to shudder within the machine's metal casing.

"Sorry, Doc. I'm never sure what you mean by the variables."

"That's okay, Martin, they … vary." Doc rose from his slouch and approached the printer. "Whenever we select a point of view, whether it be time, location or the insertion angle, whatever's left varies. But as long as the resultant equation equals Pickover's Constant, it's workable."

They both stared at the paper tray, waiting for the results to come in.

"We need to get this right," Doc continued. "The two staging runs between here and 1911 *have* to correlate. The first stage has to be a small jump—real short, like a couple of hours back. It's a pilot study, a test run, calibrating the relatively minute changes between the new time–space location and the point we started from. Then we can proceed further with a second-stage jump. But this second insertion has to be placed in exponential series between our baseline and destination."

"Two weeks, right?" Shine said.

The printer began hammering away. A curl of paper wound its way through the machine.

"Give or take," Doc said. "That's why I have you doing calculation after calculation."

He snatched the results sheet from the reel. His eyes raced across the spreadsheet and he pored over the graphs.

"How's it looking?" Shine asked.

"Grim." Doc crushed the paper in his hands and tossed it onto the floor.

Shine glanced down. Paper scraps were scattered everywhere.

Doc went over to the keyboard. He fussed with the insertion angle and retyped the question. "All the equipment is already stowed aboard. We'll be fully charged in just over two hours, but without the math, what we've got here is a strapless slingshot."

"What about all that stuff? Want me to pack it while we're waiting on the next print-out?"

Doc followed Shine's eyes to the grey canisters that lay arranged around the carapace's struts. "Trust me, you don't want to go anywhere *near* that shit."

The printer began to rattle again. Shine tore his eyes away from the canisters and examined the results sheet. Doc stood at his shoulder.

"Any better?" Shine asked the question with little expectation.

"Could be worse," Doc said.

It was with some relief then that Shine watched him strip the sheet delicately away from the spool and take it back to his station.

"Okay, let's try bringing the first stage a little closer."

XVII

Malcolm had gone over the prison barracks with a fine-toothed comb. Studied the composition of the rooms, noting with interest that in one of the larger cubicles three chairs had been arranged against a wall. She had pictured Joseph, then, standing before the three prisoners. Pacing back and forth. But had he been interrogating them?

There was no overt indication of violence. No scratches, scrapes or bloodstains. Just the ash that might have fallen from Reid's cigarette, ground into the floor.

What could he *possibly* want to know that she couldn't tell him? Why would he violate a basic tenet of information-gathering by having all three prisoners present at the one time? The room's set-up brought to mind her meetings back in Houston.

This was no Box, she reasoned. This was a briefing room.

What terms had he arrived at that justified his releasing them?

Malcolm trod another circuit of her own room. Joseph's office, empty now, lay across the hall. All of his files—all the documentation pertaining to the whole sordid affair—were hers for the reading.

She didn't know what else to do. Walking past her bed to the door, she felt reprimanded by the disarray of her bedsheets. *I'm not coming back here*, she told herself, smiling sadly. She straightened the sheets, but only found the letter after arranging the pillow.

The paper, a leaf torn from her notebook, shook in her hands.

She read his letter with dazed wonder, and heard again last night's earnest request. "Will you come with me?"

You've consigned us all to hell, Joseph, and you're *not going anywhere.*

What choice does that leave me?

She went out to find Lightholler.

XVIII

April 29, 2012
Echo Site, Nevada

Lightholler handed the field glasses back to Tecumseh. "That's impressive for a morning's work."

"We've had practice. This was going to be the original location of the installation."

Lightholler gave the expanse a general once-over. The prefabs had been thrown up on a level plain, ensconced within moderately high shelves of rock. A trail wove its way into the ravine from the southwest. The plain itself was just a wide digression in the path. It squeezed back to a narrow stretch of desert, and continued to wind its way to the northeast. Following it would bring you up behind Red Rock, but between the trail and the base rose high cairns of broken stone, impenetrable to any mechanised vehicle.

"This would have been the place to build it," Lightholler said.

The carcasses of gutted trucks and jeeps had been made to appear outfitted in the semblance of a motor pool. Heat demons shimmered along the trail so that the distant prefabs looked as though they might have been etched upon water. "Echo" was as apt a name as any for the decoy; this *Fata Morgana* of Kennedy's hidden place.

"I've had word. Shouldn't be too long now." Tecumseh was using the field glasses again. He studied the bodies of the Japanese patrol he'd eradicated, spread haphazardly where the path broke through the western cliffs.

The ghost dancers were dug into the earth approximately fifteen yards away from the trail, concealed in a similar fashion to the men Lightholler had encountered on the previous afternoon. Thirty men comprised the team. Ten more, occupying Echo site itself, had taken up posts throughout the installation. Lightholler considered the fact that this particular venture was going to expose almost a third of Red Rock's total complement.

If it failed, the Rock would be left wide open.

Delay and electronic detonation mines had been positioned to either flank of the two-hundred-and-fifty yard region Tecumseh had designated as the kill zone. Heavy machine-gun teams had been placed between and behind the line of explosives. A few nested in select breaches, higher up along the rock wall. An assault squad, located just in front of Tecumseh's surveillance post, lay in wait for deployment, while two-man security teams covered the escape routes where barbed wire had been impractical.

"How's this going to play out?" Lightholler asked, his voice a whisper.

"They know where we are," Tecumseh said. "Way the major wanted to run this relies on the assumption that the japs want to take this place, not destroy it."

"Why is Red Rock turning into the world's worst-kept secret?" Lightholler asked.

"That's the nature of secrets, Captain. Revelation is only ever a matter of time." Seeing Lightholler's frown he added, "They probably know about Alpha camp. But if they *really* knew what was going on here, they'd have more than two divisions on site, believe me."

"True enough."

"They'll use artillery to soften us up. Fire wide, if they can help it. They don't want to demolish the only way in, and they don't want to wipe the place out."

"Are we going to be safe here?" Lightholler asked. The trail was only a stone's throw away.

"If they aim straight we'll be alright."

Lightholler didn't find that entirely reassuring.

There were less than six hours to go, by Doc's last estimate. They might have done nothing, Lightholler reasoned. Left off building decoys and marshalling defences, let the minutes slip by until the carapace was fully functional. The Japanese might have held off on any further advance.

The ongoing delays in Doc's progress made that course look more and more like a long shot.

Tecumseh was nudging his shoulder. Lightholler looked over at him. The medicine man had a hand cupped to his ear. Lightholler strained, but all he heard were the soft sighs of dry desert breeze.

There.

The distant drone rose rapidly. Tecumseh pointed upwards as a recon plane soared briefly into view.

"Secure your goggles and keep your head down," he said.

The first shell smashed into the rock face across the way, not a hundred-and-fifty yards from their position. Striking midway up, it sent showers of stone and sand down onto the trail. The Japanese guns found their range, dropping shell after shell across the plain. Fountains spewed sand and debris high into the air as a block of prefabs embered cinder-red on Echo's edge.

Five minutes of heavy fire, then everything faded to silence. Smoke and ash lay thick on the ground, cloying at Lightholler's lungs, clouding his vision. He suppressed a cough and adjusted the goggles.

The smoke thinned, seceding to grey vapour. A low, intermittent rumble manifested at the threshold of perception, intensifying his unease. He placed the palm of his hand on the wall of their concealment and felt the earth tremble.

The clank of tracked wheels became distinct.

Other sounds carried: the voices of men. Tones of command, bawled in unfamiliar speech.

Lightholler peered carefully out of their burrow. A few samurai moved in and out of the unsettled dust close by. They crouched down, taking bearings, searching the sides of the trail and the way ahead. Clued in now, perhaps, to the mysterious apparition of enemy soldiers who seemed to manifest and melt away as readily as their namesakes. They scoured the terrain and then moved on, towards burning Echo.

The crack of rifle fire rolled suddenly through the ravine, muted, and one of the figures dropped. The rest scattered along the trail and began answering with suppressing bursts of machine-gun fire. The rifle fire, episodic and short-lived, was choreographed to suggest a limited number of men and munitions. The Japanese vanguard might suspect that they were dealing with assassins and saboteurs; brothers to the men that had been sniping their officers and burning their fuel depots these last long hours. Then again, they might smell a trap.

The invading vanguard lay longer bursts, spraying the prefab walls, advancing again into the face of diminishing replies from Echo. The rifle fire was confined to intermittent shots. Lightholler watched the figures disappear into the smoke-shrouded construction. He glanced at Tecumseh.

The medicine man had his eyes fixed on the trail's western extremity. He raised an arm, penetrating the roof of their shelter. Any casual onlooker might suppose that a grave was unwillingly releasing its tenant. Vigilant eyes, however, would recognise the first signal.

Heavy machine-gun fire chattered within Echo, answering the summons. Lightholler tried to imagine the thoughts flitting through the minds of the Japanese officers. There was clearly more here than met the eye. Pull back and bombard, or press on?

Do it, Lightholler urged. *Bring what you have.*

Scampering feet answered his plea. More figures rushed along the trail before the unseen armour resumed its fearful clatter.

The burrow shuddered. Grains of sand began sliding down the walls in widening streams. Spears of light penetrated the burrow's cover, spotlighting dancing motes of dust.

Steadying himself, Lightholler looked out along the trail. Tanks rumbled by slowly in two columns. Men advanced in file beside them. There were no Union uniforms included in the mix. Long crimson-snouted Dragon tanks rode beside stub-nosed light battle armour. Track-churned sand raised thick clouds of dust. Lightholler counted twenty-five vehicles in all.

"They're packed in pretty tight," he said through gritted teeth.

Tecumseh nodded. His eyes narrowed decisively. He punched a closed fist through the roof. Phase two. Echo's occupants had thirty seconds to evacuate.

Lightholler was forced to his knees as the blast rocked the narrow chasm, its energy funnelled along the trail. The den began collapsing around them in earnest. Cries filled the air, a confusion of commands and curses, all in Japanese.

Tecumseh called across to him, "Be ready." He had his submachine-gun tucked under his right arm.

The fifteen-second delay between the charges at Echo and the flanking mines seemed to stretch into an indefinite period that found Lightholler flailing for balance on unsteady ground. He secured his weapon and scrambled up the burrow's buckled edge.

The mines detonated in sequence, catching both edges of the convoy in a ripple of destruction.

Heavy machine-gun fire slashed out from the dancer emplacements, raking the sides of the convoy in a devastating broad fire that sought the vehicles with automatic weapons and poured on the hapless soldiers.

Tecumseh was up and out of the burrow, perched on its crest and ululating a fearsome war cry. His gun coughed bright death, selecting choice targets among the chaotic mass. Lightholler painfully clawed his way up and dropped to one knee by Tecumseh's side. He trained the muzzle of his weapon across the mass, but held his fire. He was superfluous.

He watched the withering fire move across corpses that only responded reflexively to the scorching metal. Incendiaries and anti-tank weapons ranged along the arrested armour. The tanks popped and sizzled. Peeled like overripe fruit, revealing the pulpy contents of bodies mixed in metal.

Return fire was clumsy, striking where the dancers weren't. A Dragon tank sent a shaft of red flame along the rocks, catching a machine-gun nest before bursting into flames itself. Three light tanks were working their way towards Lightholler's position when the second line of mines ignited.

They settled into their craters on ruptured bellies. Caught between the inferno that had been Echo and the assault team, the Japanese soldiers were carved to a man.

Tecumseh gave a new signal and the assault team descended into the kill zone. They moved rapidly among the dead and dying, searching for officers and couriers. Rifling through the blood-crusted uniforms for documents and maps that might yield further knowledge of the enemy.

Lightholler let his gun slide down to his side. He hadn't loosed a single round.

Probing fire from the western boundary of the trail, light at first, heralded enemy reinforcements. Encountering one end of the ambush, the fresh soldiers began to dig in. Lightholler turned to alert Tecumseh but the medicine man was already calling for extraction.

The assault team dispersed, working their way back from the trail and siphoning towards the various escape routes that led out of this place. Heavy machine-gunners dismantled their weapons and withdrew in good order, pulling back in teams of two and three. Security teams provided covering fire.

Within moments, only Lightholler and Tecumseh crouched by the kill zone. Tecumseh gave the ground a last contemptuous look before leading Lightholler up to the first checkpoint.

The Japanese reinforcements, perhaps emboldened by the sudden stillness, began infiltrating the lines of broken armour. Hitting the checkpoint, Tecumseh gave the final command and all along the perimeter of the kill zone and further back up along the trail the last of the mines detonated. From Lightholler's vantage the ravine was a river of flames. The pungent odour of unspeakable death flayed at his senses.

Tecumseh said, "This will give them food for thought."

"Let's get back to the Rock," Lightholler said.

XIX

April 29, 2012
Red Rock, Nevada

Malcolm barely got as far as the communications centre before she was intercepted. The sentry began herding her towards the carapace's enclosure.

"But I have to see Captain Lightholler," she pleaded before the shack's entrance.

He didn't reply, but his eyes flicked to the south. She followed the movement and saw another trail of smoky haze rising there, seeking to join the murky helix that now almost encircled the base.

"There's no seeing him now," the sentry replied.

The sky flamed—a brief, bright flare. She sought the sentry's eyes for an explanation and found herself reaching out to him as the ground pitched beneath her. He caught her clumsy movement and swung her around, propelling her back towards the shack. Hayes, the large engineer, filled the doorway.

She shot the sentry a last glowering look. "If the captain doesn't get my message, we're all dead."

"Doesn't matter. The dance has begun, ma'am." He nodded in the direction of the latest inferno.

Somehow, between the horror of Joseph's letter and the aftershock of distant explosions, there was time for new dismay. "Where in all your teachings did you learn to welcome death?"

"It's not death I welcome—it's rebirth. If I come across the captain, what should I tell him?"

She didn't have an answer.

Joseph seemed content enough to forfeit his own life. Content enough to bargain with the devil himself, if it might bring his dream a little closer. She understood now that she loved him more—and less—than she'd ever realised in the past. His letter had been meant for her alone. It was rationale, apology and, most definitively, goodbye.

"Are there any underground shelters here, apart from this one?" she asked.

The sentry shook his head.

"Then tell Captain Lightholler that everything the major and Commander Hardas saw here will come to pass. He can deal with it accordingly."

The sentry made ready to go.

She heard Tecumseh's healing song again, a whisper in her ear, and called out softly, "May your dance bring good cloud, soldier."

"Thank you ma'am. *Pilamaya. Wankantanka nici un.*"

Hayes was smiling as she turned to enter the building.

"What did he say?" she asked.

"He thanked you for your words, and asked the Great Spirit to watch over your journey."

"Journey?"

Hayes drew her into the antechamber.

XX

Doc was testing the virtual model of the machine against the latest algorithms. Shine divided his time between entering the occasional data sequence and monitoring the carapace's restoration.

It hummed. It glittered. In the sporadic flicker of generator light, he could swear it was moving. The cables twisted around its struts seemed to stir. Stare long enough and there was the sense of falling inwards, as the carriage shifted silver to black and back again: mercurial. He could almost convince himself that he was observing a physical manifestation of the machine's peculiar influence, as if time itself might be fraying at the carapace's edges.

He wondered how Doc dealt with protracted exposure to the machine; how he managed to skate along the perception-shifts while trying to remain rational and restore its function.

"You'll give yourself a headache."

Shine broke free of the enchantment and looked over to see Morgan's dour expression.

"Seems like you're almost done here," the historian added.

Shine nodded slowly. "It's almost charged. Doc's finalising the equations. Where's Captain Lightholler?"

"Working his way back from the ambush." Morgan gazed at the pile of grey canisters stationed by the carapace. "Please tell me that those are extra supplies."

"I think they're Joseph's insurance policy." Malcolm stood between the parted folds of the star-adorned blanket. She entered the room unsteadily, her eyes carefully directed away from the machine.

"Any luck with your investigation?" Morgan asked.

She shook her head. "I have no idea where the prisoners went." Her face wore a vexed expression. She turned her attention to Doc. "May I interrupt your work for a moment?"

He swivelled in his chair and offered her an ambiguous smile.

"How long would it take you to restart the machine if you disabled the generator?"

The smile faded. "At full charge, ten to fifteen minutes. What's on your mind?"

"I was wondering what precautions have been taken to avoid a repeat of last night's performance," she said. "If there's another pulse, then that's it. We're finished."

"That EMP was the result of an accidental detonation."

"Who's to say there won't be more accidents?"

"We all know what's coming." Doc spun away from her, and returned to his computations.

After a few moments he stirred in his seat, the chair making little movements as he fumbled for a pen. He swung back to her and said, "Guarantee me a fifteen-minute window and I can have the carapace operational. But you best be damned sure that those minutes don't coincide with another 'accident'. Can you guarantee that?"

"No."

"And if I disable the generator, right this moment, can you give me a safe time to reactivate it?"

"Of course I can't."

"No..." Doc drew a deep breath. "You can't. No one can, but at least someone has the presence of mind to recognise our predicament."

"We're in a room full of explosives, surrounded by the Japanese army, and the clock is ticking," Morgan said. "I think we *all* see our predicament."

"When the carapace has a decent charge, I plan on shutting the generator down," Doc said, more gently now. "Once we have our crew assembled, I'll re-engage the power. But if anything happens during those fifteen minutes, if there's another pulse..." He made a hopeless gesture with his hands. He returned to his work.

For long moments there was just the low whine of the generator.

"So," Morgan said, turning to Malcolm, "does that mean you're coming with us?"

She stole a glance at the carapace. "I'm not sure. I don't know what purpose it will serve, but I think I owe it to Joseph to accept his invitation. *If* you all agree." Her voice had lowered to a raw whisper.

"Well, we can't leave you here," Doc said. "Besides, Tecumseh told me you were coming. I've already arranged for your essentials to be sent across."

"Tecumseh said so?" She walked in a daze to the bunk bed and sat heavily on the mattress.

The printer recommenced its loud stutter. Doc turned swiftly back to snatch the results. Morgan joined him at his station.

She was staring at the carapace now. The intensity of her gaze suggested that this was no easy task. Shine, unsure of what drove him, approached her.

"I remember you now," Malcolm said. "You must have been fifteen at the time."

"Sixteen."

"You were working for the major back then?"

"A little. I was helping my father."

"We didn't think to look for you when we were hunting Joseph."

"You wouldn't have found me."

"You became a ghost dancer," she said.

"Ghost dancer trained, but I'm something else." For no reason he could comprehend, he added, "I'm supposed to kill Wells."

She mustered an odd smile. "I remember you as a schoolboy, Martin."

"I'm not supposed to be like this." A lump shaped itself in his throat. He looked away from the carapace. "That damn machine is muddling my thoughts."

"It's clearing them, Martin. That's part of what it does."

"My father's somewhere out there. He's marching up from Indian Springs." He composed himself. "This used to feel like the most important thing in the world. Now it just feels like running away. But how can we stay?" He felt caught up in the immensity of the idea but pressed on. "This place. I can't know for sure, but I don't think it lasts."

"I don't think it's meant to." Her eyes glittered a brilliant ebony lustre. "I don't think it's meant to at all. It's just that I can't imagine the alternative."

Distant sounds—ones that could only be the muffled import of explosions travelling down the service shaft—murmured ruin. They grew louder.

The carapace had almost slaked its thirst. Its energy reservoir hovered at ninety-five per cent, but it remained without direction and therefore was without use. Shine watched as Doc pushed back his seat and walked over to the generator. He pulled the plug and said, "We pick up the last five per cent when we reactivate."

"The data sets are almost complete. Once they're through, I'll have to run them all simultaneously against the model. If they're a match-up, we're good to go. I'm thinking another four hours."

Seeing the incredulous look on Malcolm's face, he added, "It took me six months to develop the calculations for our first prospective insertion. Another three to develop this one. I've been reworking the damn thing for eleven hours straight now, so please, cut me some slack."

The carapace dozed in fresh shadows. Shine had to look twice. The cavern's smooth walls, the machine's hushed purr. He felt as though he was seeing the machine as Wells might have seen it for the first time, through fearful, haunted eyes.

The ubiquitous whine of the generator dwindled to silence.

XXI

Lightholler rapidly crossed the broken ground, heading towards the shack. His security team fanned out to either side.

The rest of the base, partly dismantled on Echo's behalf, approximated Wells' Waste Land more with each passing moment. Ahead, eclipsing the shack in afternoon shadow, the rude stump of Red Rock cleaved the sky.

The escort closed up. One checked his headset and triggered a swift reply on his Morse key.

"Captain, the japs are trying to dig in at the foot of the west watch. We can expect an artillery barrage at any time."

"How long can we hold them, Davies?"

The security man fired off another message. They waited for a reply, crouched by the shack's low entrance. Moments later, the receiver let loose a furious staccato.

"Hard to say, sir. They're being more cautious. Sounds like they're bringing a tank battalion around the western ridge. And a battery of eighty-eights, Union guns, are being set up northwest of the tower."

"What do we have out there?"

"Two squads of tank busters, four machine-gun teams and a batch of snipers. Sixty men all up."

"Where's Tecumseh?"

"Holed up behind enemy lines. He got pinned down behind their first rush of berserkers."

In his mind's eye, Lightholler saw them again. Line upon line of crazed infantry, charging across the field of mushrooming flame and glazed, boiling sand. He shuddered inwardly and said, "I need to go back out there."

"Captain, you need to be right here." Davies' face contorted darkly. "Besides, we have more squads concealed around the base."

Lightholler didn't bother scanning the landscape. He had about as much chance of identifying their hidden positions as the Japanese.

"We're more likely to run out of ammunition than we are to run out of soldiers," Davies added.

An ear-piercing shriek tore the sky. A spout of sand and earth erupted not twenty yards from the shack. As soon as the debris had settled, Davies sprang into action.

"We're taking you inside, Captain."

They guided him into the small building. Hayes was waiting inside.

The air was cooler within the antechamber. Dazzling light glowed from a strip of fluoros along the wall. A monitor screen, split four ways, displayed mottled images of the desert beyond. The elevator doors were slightly parted and a tangle of free wiring suggested that the device remained out of commission.

The team arranged themselves around the circular entrance that led to the service shaft.

Hayes pointed to a small black box that hadn't been there during Lightholler's inspection. Two thin wires connected it to a length of lead piping that spanned the building's height and penetrated the floor.

"That's the detonator."

Lightholler recalled Kennedy's words: *You'll find it easiest to do what's necessary*. He would have spat if he'd had any saliva in his mouth.

The look in Hayes' eyes, so resolute in beliefs he could never comprehend, filled him with a sense of self-loathing. He hadn't earned this role. He'd fought Kennedy tooth and nail the entire time. He glanced down at his shirt. Sweat-stained and dirty, it still bore patches of the brightest blue. He didn't deserve to wear it.

He looked at Hayes and said, "I'll go on down. You don't have to wait here."

"We wait till the major returns or you depart. You'll need me to start you on your journey." Hayes lifted the heavy entrance to the shaft.

Another explosion, further out, rattled the shack walls.

Lightholler began his descent.

XXII

Standing at the cavern's entrance, Lightholler made a quick survey, taking in the explosives, the quiescent generator. "How much longer?"

"Three hours, to get it right," Doc replied irritably.

An exceptionally thunderous blast rocked the cavern. They all looked up to see a fine seam open in the high smooth vault of the ceiling. A sprinkle of dirt cascaded down to form a small mound on Doc's desk.

"Less, at a pinch," he added hastily.

Unruffled, Lightholler said, "I've seen what the ghost dancers are capable of. We'll get those hours, with time to spare."

"And if we don't," Morgan said, "you'll make sure there's nothing left here but dust and ash."

Lightholler eyed the canisters unrepentantly. "If it comes to that."

They watched Doc work in silence.

It was some time before Morgan realised that the shelling had ceased. He turned to Lightholler and said, "They've stopped."

Lightholler nodded.

"Is that a good thing?"

"Not likely."

There was a clatter of footsteps on the ladder. Davies brushed the blanket aside carefully and entered with downcast eyes. "The enemy is in the camp." He seemed more subdued by his proximity to the carapace than by the statement he'd just uttered.

"How many?"

"At least a battalion. They're advancing with flamethrowers. They're razing the site, inch by inch."

Lightholler shot Doc a look and then searched the others for their expressions.

Morgan said, "Go up, Captain. Man your station."

Malcolm rose from the bed purposefully and walked over to where the others were standing by Doc's desk.

Doc hadn't shifted, nor had he slowed down. He kept running his equations. "I'll enable the generator."

"Wait for my signal," Lightholler said.

"I'll need fifteen minutes and the first insertion stage is still labile. I'll have to wing it."

"Just find us a dry spot to land, Doc. We'll give you your fifteen minutes." He turned to Shine. "Martin, you're with me."

Morgan gave Lightholler a look. He nodded back. Davies took point and they ascended the rungs in darkness, a red glow shining beneath them, a halo of bright light above. Davies pushed the door aside and they broke into the brightly lit antechamber of the shack.

There were four ghost dancers there, packed tightly with Hayes in the small domed room. They had two radios barking a cacophony of foreign speech. Morgan watched as Lightholler crouched low by the black casing of the detonator. He turned his eyes away to scan the monitor.

The first shaky image, shifting black and white, was taken up by the bulk of the Red Rock formation. Scanning the other three windows on the screen, he saw images north, south and east of their position. It was an alien landscape of pits and craters. The prefabs were aflame. Grey on grey, the pictures seemed unreal. They had the feel of old documentary footage. The shape of a body, writhing half-seen among the dunes, brought it home to him. He didn't need a colour image to know that the soldier's shirt, torn and muddied, had once been a vivid blue.

A platoon of Japanese soldiers were working their way forwards on the north screen, shrouded in a grainy haze. Behind them, the remains of Doc's oasis blazed fitfully. Grey liquid fire spewed from their weapons. They were almost on the camera when the earth beneath them broke open. Charred ghost dancers danced among them. A brief sparkle of filtered sunlight flashed on an exposed blade. It buried itself in astonished flesh. A soldier's face, mouth and eyes wide black holes, pitched and flopped in front of the screen. The burnt shadows vanished, leaving a pile of corpses. The image died as a flamethrower's flask ignited.

To the south there was no movement, but to the east three Dragon tanks lurched among the debris. A company of Japanese soldiers picked their way past the buildings that had once housed Major Kennedy's office. Morgan watched as two figures detached themselves from the skeletal frame of a prefab. They hung upside-down, suspended from the smouldering rafters. In seconds the ground beneath them became a hollow pit, brimming with dead and wounded. The company dispersed riotously. Grenades deployed, the dancers were reaching for their guns when Dragon fire whipped over them. Their flaming bodies dropped into the fresh pit below.

The company resumed their approach.

"Captain," Shine said softly, "the generator."

"There's no time, Martin, and nowhere to go." Lightholler's hand strayed over the detonator. He closed his eyes.

"*Captain.*"

There was a sudden burst from one of the radios. Davies cocked an ear.

Then both radios emitted a chorus of anguished cries. Morgan didn't need to speak Japanese to appreciate their meaning.

On screen, the soldiers had stopped moving. The tanks had settled into their clouds of dust and the soldiers hunkered down low to the ground among them.

Lightholler's voice was a low growl. "What are they saying?"

"Tanks..." Davies was stooped by the nearest radio. He twisted the dial, catching a new thread of agitated dialogue. His dark face accentuated bright bared teeth. "There's a column of tanks."

Lightholler watched as the Dragons started up again. They were turning around.

Shapes flitted across the screen. Another tank veered into view. It bore unusual markings: two broad, vivid diagonal stripes. Handprints were smeared along its side. It shook violently, firing off a round. The explosion pummelled the walls of their enclosure before coming to a halt. It sprayed a salvo of machine-gun fire on the evaporating line of fleeing men. Japanese soldiers began running, headlong, away from the shack.

A second tank pulled up alongside the first. A head emerged from the commander's hatch, leonine and bearing a full war bonnet of notched, wind-blown feathers over long braided hair. He turned towards the camera. Two buffalo horns adorned the wild ruffle of his headdress.

"It's him," Hayes murmured.

"Him?" Lightholler asked. "Who's *he*?"

"Michael Iron Horse," Shine whispered. "He led the left flank at Mazatlan."

"Well, I'll be damned." Lightholler's face gleamed in the monitor glare and twisted in dark delight. "The cavalry's arrived and bless me if they aren't indians."

XXIII

April 29, 2012

Groom Mine, Nevada

"The Japanese are pulling back, sir, rallying this side of the west tower."

Kennedy acknowledged the captain's words with a forbidding smile. He surveyed the escarpment. Twenty-two functioning heavy Jackson tanks had been recovered from Indian Springs; spoils taken from Alpha's occupying force. Fourteen of them were now arrayed before him. The remainder had been dispatched—along with a portion of the men—to Red Rock, under Iron Horse's command.

Ghost dancers, riding the armoured side-skirting, had managed to decorate the vehicles while they were in transit. Bold black stripes of war paint now adorned each side. The bloody red hand of Lakota war parties, not seen in well over a hundred years, branded the turret of each vehicle. Besides the tanks, there were a number of trucks and an armoured car. The car, liberated from a platoon of long-range recon, brandished its new pennant—a red hand on a field of white.

Beyond, stretched out along the incline, his men were grouped into their various companies. They'd run all night, initially following Shine's path, and then trailing the refurbished convoy. They were still running in now, massing as they arrived at the foot of the slope.

Nearly a thousand men.

"Everyone in position?" Kennedy asked.

"Almost, sir."

"Looks like we won't be missing Tecumseh's dance after all."

A low rumble of laughter emanated from the ghost dancers nearby and died out swiftly to silence. A few stood at attention. The majority leaned forwards, hands on thighs, or sat hunched over, catching their breath.

Some refreshed themselves from canteens or chewed on rations.

"Get them ready, Captain. Three-up formation."

"No reserves?"

"We only get one shot at this. No reserves. I want a tank spearhead and mortar cover all the way down the slope."

"Yes, sir."

"Why are you smiling, Captain?"

"My uncle was with you at Mazatlan, sir. This formation sounds a little familiar."

Kennedy smiled. "Leave off on the sniper deployment for the moment."

"Very good, sir." He moved off towards the first company. His orders were conveyed in a silent exchange of hand signals.

Kennedy scrambled up to the escarpment's edge and lay flat next to his scouts. He was handed a pair of binoculars. Below, where the rock fell away to rolling desert, a settlement of plastic and steel had grown overnight. It shimmered into the distance. He made a systematic appraisal of the enemy.

Perhaps as many as two brigades, and more than two hundred tanks, stood among the rows of tents. There was no telling how badly they'd been affected by the electromagnetic pulse. They were attended by enough mechanics and crewmen, however, to offer a modicum of hope. Infantry mingled with engineers and camp followers seeking shade from the unremitting Nevada sun. Each officer walked with two samurai guards in tow, their katanas sheathed but rifles at the ready in response to last night's brutal culling. Apart from the members of the elite Hachiman Brigade, he identified Imperial Watchmen among the grenadiers of the 2nd Imperial Tank Army. His best guess: twelve thousand troops.

The earlier reports from the west watchtower were accurate. The Japanese command had dealt with the night's guerrilla warfare by gathering their supplies at a central depot. Fuel tanks sat side by side with water drums and ammunition caches, all contained within an extensive picket line.

A large detachment of mixed infantry was beginning to make its way forwards. A company of tanks advanced alongside them. The attendant dust cloud made it impossible to estimate their number, but their destination was clear. They were bound for Red Rock.

He searched westwards, beyond their march, to where the desert flats rose up into the ridge that guarded his installation. So close, and yet so impossibly far away.

Moses never entered the Holy Land, he told himself. *You had your chance, Joseph.*

His roving eyes settled on the artillery regiment, a mixture of self-propelled eighty-eights and one-twenties. He managed to smile, however, when he recognised their insignia. Union troops. He let the idea gestate.

Patting the adjacent scout on the back, he withdrew from the escarpment's edge. His captains approached him, wearing their feathered war bonnets and shirts of tanned hide and buckskin over the body armour. The designs, blue-green, were inlaid with fine metal strips and beads. Their faces, starkly daubed with red and white streaks, were fearsome masks.

Kennedy said, "I want the snipers on those far ridges to the west and further down beyond this one. Have them target the Hachimans. I don't want my boys going hand-to-hand with samurai."

"They can take them," a captain offered.

Kennedy leered. "I want my men to have a straightforwards action, Captain Red Thunder, not an entertaining one."

"Understood, sir."

It took five minutes to finalise the deployment. The Japanese reinforcements had yet to move off. Iron Horse morsed in to announce that the Red Rock installation was under heavy fire, but holding. The cavern was secure.

Hayes informed him that two hours might see them through.

Kennedy approached his command car and retrieved his satchel. The journal was in safe hands with Lightholler for the moment and the remaining contents were secure. He eyed the sturdy antennae array mounted on the back of the vehicle. In Tecumseh's absence, any of the captains might have led the ghost dance ritual. He looked among the men, making his selection.

He called over Jimmy Crow God.

Reaching into the satchel, Kennedy withdrew the drawstring pouch. It contained a sample he'd obtained on first finding the carapace, when he and Hardas had scoured the amazing artefact for clues to its origins. It was sand he'd swept from the floor of the machine. Sand from that other world, that *true* world, from a time before Wells had spun it on its new, darker axis.

He gave the bag a final squeeze and handed it over to Crow God.

The sun, just past its zenith, glared balefully. It was almost time.

Last night he'd struck a bargain with the devil but the relief he'd sought had not arrived. A final inspection of his troops, however, found no faults. His men had reclaimed Alpha and run through fire under atomic cloud. They stood ready to run again … one more time.

If there was one thing he truly desired, it was this. That the true world this day might reclaim could acknowledge the brave souls whose blood had been shed in its rebirth. Friend and foe alike.

No. There was one other thing. He thought about Patricia and felt the grit aggravate the corner of his eyes. He wiped away the moisture.

A radio transmitter, close by, bleated its request for a response. The signal came from the Japanese watchpost they'd encountered on first approaching this ridge. It hadn't been cleared yet. Two dancers hastily approached the post and worked their way among the bloodstained sandbags, carting away the dead. One of them secured the transmitter and donned an earpiece. He listened in.

"It's their ops centre, sir, requesting an update."

"Perfect," Kennedy said. Donning his helmet, a simple, unadorned metal bonnet, he cleared his throat and seized the microphone.

The bulk of the enemy artillery were Union conscripts—members of the 82nd, a division that had once prided itself on including representatives from all forty-eight members of the former federation of American states. He found the notion inspiring. Perhaps it was time to serve up his own particular interpretation of Camelot.

He turned to Crow God. "Bring my command car and all of the Jacksons up to the ridge's edge, all turrets on lowest elevation. Minimise their exposure. Have them target the depot but under *no* circumstances is anyone to fire on the Union artillery. Fire on my command."

"We'll be within range of their one-twenties," Crow God said.

"I know. Let's hope they pay us close attention. There's a flag in my satchel. On my signal I want you to run it up the car's antenna. I want them to see it clearly."

It had hung in his office since Camelot's inception. On a whim he'd brought it with him to New York and it had followed him through every step of his journey. Until recently, the journal had been wrapped in its folds.

He addressed one of his radio operators. “Have us patched through on all known Japanese frequencies. I want them to know who they’ve been dealing with. Besides, our friends at Red Rock will be listening.”

“Sir, yes, sir.”

As one the tanks surged forwards, the sound of their advance thankfully lost to the teeming multitude below. Tossed sand rolled forwards in a brown mist to shower down over the escarpment’s drop. Crow God had the command car verging on the edge of the steep parapet. Kennedy shouldered the radio pack and mounted its running board. He worked his way up to the bonnet and looked down through falling dust.

Another burst of Japanese, more insistent, shattered the silence.

He keyed the transmitter.

“This is General Joseph Robard Kennedy. You are currently surrounded by elements of the 1st Rangers Armoured Division, *United States* Armed Forces.” He turned to Crow God and quietly murmured, “Fire.”

The twelve powerful one-oh-five-millimetre cannons discharged as one. The tanks roared and the ridge itself seemed to quake. The air howled around him, while below the depot belched thick black smoke. Smaller explosions rippled among the ammunition dumps, toppled dominoes of bright red flame.

He glared down at the Japanese host, rekeyed the transmitter, and announced, “I respectfully await to discuss the terms of your surrender.”

The smoke cleared slowly. The radio twittered static. Nothing more.

He raised the binoculars to his eyes. The Union batteries had drawn a bead on them. A single one-twenty hurled its formidable reply. The shot flew wide, tearing at the earth half a mile from their position. Two more cannon opened up, their shells remaining strangely clear of the ghost dancers’ formation.

Kennedy said, “Show them the flag.”

“This symbol has rarely been kind to our people,” Crow God replied.

Another blast, less wide, rocked the ridge.

“We’ll try to give it a new meaning in the world to come,” Kennedy murmured.

Crow God scuttled over to the antenna and began to run up the banner. It rose, limply to the apex where it draped heavily against the antenna mast. Hot air whipped around the Jacksons. It rose lashing the standard around its mast. The flag, unseen for eighty years, unfurled in magnificent splendour. Forty-eight stars on a banner of red and white stripes.

Kennedy removed his helmet. "This is General Kennedy of the United States Armed Forces." His voice shook slightly.

Veterans among the Union forces might have remembered a younger Kennedy's call in the aftermath of the last Ranger War. Senior officers might have recalled yet another Kennedy, riding through the streets of Dallas.

"On behalf of the provisional government of the United States of America, we hail our northern brothers of the All-American Fighting 82nd. Please lower your sights and await further instructions."

Another shell whistled overhead. It opened a crater just beyond the assembled companies of ghost dancers. Kennedy cast an eye back over his men. None had fallen, none had flinched.

"Fire."

The Jacksons launched a second volley. Their sabot rounds ripped the earth. The depot was obscured by a foul cloud of sooty debris.

"Officers of the Imperial forces of Japan, come forward under a flag of truce and your men will be spared. You have two minutes to comply."

The Union guns ceased.

Crow God leaned back in the driver's seat, his face struck with wonder. He had the small bag in his outstretched palm. He handed it over to Kennedy. "This one's yours, sir. Today these men would gladly march with you into the Hunting Grounds and beyond."

"I just need them to follow me down this hill."

"Give the order."

Kennedy scanned the plain. The 82nd, spread out to the west of the blazing depot, was in disarray. Most of their guns had been turned away from the escarpment. A few were now trained on the dormant lines of the Japanese tanks. A task force of Hachiman samurai, distinctive in their black leather sachimono, elbowed their way towards them through the disordered crowd of scattered soldiers.

More disciplined units rallied at the foot of the slope. They divided into two columns and began working their way along the lower mounds of the escarpment. A sudden disturbance, sand banks billowing in long, low waves, heralded the first movements of the Japanese armour.

"Major," Crow God said, "what are we waiting for?"

Kennedy replaced his helmet and tightened the strap. One of his sergeants, a black ghost dancer, approached him carrying a small pail of red paint. Kennedy bowed his head forwards and felt the gentle pressure of the dancer's coated palm against his headpiece.

"Good cloud, sir," the dancer mumbled.

"Good cloud, sergeant, and give 'em hell."

The dancer retreated, smiling.

Kennedy sealed the mouthpiece of his air filter and looked over at Crow God. The indian's goggles illustrated his warped reflection: a leering death's head under the emblem of a bloody red hand. He gripped the pouch tightly, then loosened the drawstring and raised his clenched fist high into the air where every dancer's eye would see.

"Captain Crow God, prepare to have our snipers take out those samurai, then redirect them onto the officers. Captain Red Thunder, cover the hillside in smoke; I want a three-up formation on my mark, straight down the hill. Captain Wilson, bring up the Jacksons. Carve us a path toward those eighty-eights. Our new Union 'allies' will need a little inspiration."

They acknowledged his commands.

He looked out east, to where his men lay under siege, and pictured the tortured golden-brown outline of Red Rock as it would appear under this bright late-noon sun.

"*Ate Wankantanka, Mitawa ki.*" He opened his fist. "*Wicahcala kin heya pe lo maka kin.*"

He let the handful of otherworldly dust slip through his fingers. "*Wicahcala kin heya pe lo maka kin.*"

An answering bellow tore itself from a thousand throats.

"*WICAHCALA KIN HEYA PE LO MAKA KIN.*"

The Jacksons kicked forwards, the mortars coughed lethal fire and the ghost dancers swarmed. They swept down the hill like a curse.

XXIV

April 29, 2012
Red Rock, Nevada

Lightholler emerged from the shack and stepped into an abattoir. He thankfully accepted a gas mask from one of the ghost dancers. At the very least, he thought, it would conceal his sickened expression.

Shine, a radio in hand, was by his side. Morgan and Hayes stood back by the entrance. Malcolm was at their elbows, straining to get past them. She froze, taking in the scene that had first met his eyes.

The sea of bodies spread as far as the eye could see: tangled among the smoking residue of shredded armour, huddled in newly formed ditches, twisted and pinned where they'd fallen. There was no movement.

The saviours of Red Rock had swept through in the wake of Iron Horse's armour. Every Japanese soldier had been impaled to confirm the kill. The ghost dancers had collected their wounded, but their dead remained among the enemy. Time permitted the salvage of men who might still fight, but the dead had danced their last.

"Tell Doc not to bother coming up," Lightholler said. "His former occupation won't be of much use at present."

"What about Joseph?" she said. "Where *is* he?"

Lightholler pointed westwards. The horizon was lost in dismal grey fog. He ushered her back into the shack, his hand maintaining a firm grip on her arm.

Shine's radio crackled abruptly. "*Wicahcala kin heya pe lo maka kin.*" Kennedy's voice, distorted and broken in transmission, was an unfamiliar snarl.

"What's *happening* out there?" she asked.

"A massacre. But it's bought us some time. Tell Doc to wrap up the equations as soon as he can." Lightholler gave the grounds another cheerless inspection. "They'll be back."

Hayes said, "I'll fire up the generator."

"Don't," Lightholler said. "We don't know what the japs have behind those two divisions. I don't want the carapace primed until Doc has the coordinates locked in."

He stepped back out onto the grounds. His escort had shifted away, regarding him with watchful eyes. Morgan and Shine were talking quietly by the radio. Dust whirled to the south of the compound's ashes.

Lightholler felt the thunder in the soles of his feet well before he saw the horses break through the eddying smoke and dust. The posse pounded across the grounds and halted before him in a storm of flying sand. There were four riders in all.

Tecumseh dismounted awkwardly. His right leg was a seared fusion of flesh and uniform. His face bore a ragged cut that ran red across his brow. He gripped a tomahawk in his gnarled fist. Lightholler had supposed it to be ceremonial, but Tecumseh's weapon was dulled with black gore. His eyes peered at Lightholler from darkened sockets. "How long?" His voice was a hoarse croak.

"Two hours. Maybe less. Where's Captain Iron Horse?"

"He's reclaimed the western defences and holds them now." The medicine man grunted. "I leave these men to you." He indicated his companions with a wave.

They dismounted and stood at attention, each offering a brisk nod. Their war bonnets were adorned with fresh red symbols among the feathers. According to Shine, each distinctive marker represented a kill.

Tecumseh's bonnet was a spray of scarlet.

He grabbed the reins of his horse, a dappled Appaloosa, and remounted with barely a wince. He gazed down at Lightholler. "*Wankantanka nici un.*"

"Where are you headed?" Shine looked up from his radio.

"The major's attacking their main supply dump. He's turned the Union guns against them but the fighting is fierce. He's five miles out. With your leave, Captain, I'll ride out to join him."

Morgan said, "You'll never make it through their lines."

Lightholler wasn't sure at which point they'd all come to realise that Kennedy was lost to them, but it was their silent, bitter accord. He said,

"You won't get past their guns."

Tecumseh struck the fabric of his shirt. "The prairie is so big and wild, there is so much space for bullets to spend themselves. I will be spared."

Looking up at Tecumseh now, Lightholler marvelled at the hope that had brought him through so many terrors and obstacles. Who could have ever truly believed that this task would be an easy one? This final battle, waged not so much between good and evil as between ignorance and insight, smacked of Armageddon.

He grabbed one of the horses and mounted up before anyone could protest. His selection, a white sorrel, was robust at seventeen hands high. It gave a slight whinny and stamped at the pebbled earth.

Tecumseh shot him a dark look.

Lightholler said, "Two hours to ride in, find the major, and ride out. Piece of cake."

Tecumseh said, "You are not coming with me, Captain."

"We have seven of your best warriors watching the cavern. Iron Horse holds the western ridge. As you say, the prairie is so big and wild." Lightholler pointed at his chest. "We'll be spared."

Shine looked up at him, pleadingly.

He said, "We're going to need a radio, Martin."

Shine shouldered the radio pack eagerly and approached the horses. He mounted up.

Morgan eyed the three riders pensively, focusing on the savage aspect of Tecumseh and Lightholler's own visage, alien behind the gas mask. He shrugged, grabbed a pair of reins, and struggled onto a chestnut stallion. Glancing over at Lightholler's white steed he asked, "Does this make me Pestilence or Famine?"

Lightholler snapped his reins and the charger wheeled westwards on a cloud of white powder. He threw Morgan a look over his shoulder and said, "Take your pick."

XXV

April 29, 2012

Groom Mine, Nevada

Kennedy's command car careened wildly, its course a rowdy sideways slide down the rocky decline. The driver was using all his skills just keeping the vehicle upright.

Halfway down the slope and the enemy guns would find their range. Kennedy called a halt and the car skidded into a trough of flung shale. He adjusted his goggles and surveyed the attack.

The escarpment was a knuckled promontory in a sea of smoke. A V of Jacksons ploughed forwards, their shells directed at the wide picket of enemy supplies. Heavy machine-guns sputtered ruin among the climbing formations of Japanese infantry. Within moments, the tanks had entered their thinning ranks. Ghost dancer mortars chased the rolling armour, creating a region of whirling shrapnel and sudden death.

The first wave of dancers whooped and leapt, a surging blue crest of bared bayonets and metal-lashing gunfire. They broke upon the Japanese ranks and punched through. Serried cobalt arrowheads drove onwards, piercing the chaotic grey columns of enemy infantry.

The deformed shell of a Jackson was a blackened, corpse-ridden husk. A second Jackson, the target of multiple bazooka rounds, surfed a swell of pebbled sand. Its crew, with their chainmail face plates and exposed body armour, rode its skirting like knights of old. They leapt off as the tank fireballed, a landborne comet that detonated at the foot of the slope.

The next wave of dancers struck little resistance, their movement a grim ballet among the fleeing soldiers, but along the hillside an intolerable number of blue-shirted bodies writhed, or lay too still.

Kennedy looked out to the Union guns. The glint of flashing metal through flame-tinged fog told him that too many samurai had evaded his snipers. The Japanese infantry was re-forming on the plain; a wide, deep cordon of men, taking up defensive positions around the depot. A few eighty-eights, in enemy hands or under their instruction, still pounded the hillside, grinding man and machinery into gristle.

He said to his radio operator, "We can't let them dig in." He indicated a transient gap in the enemy line that was filling with sapphire-robed members of the Imperial Watch. They had mortars, heavy machine-guns and rocket-launchers among their kit. "Tell Wilson to bring up armour through there, mortar cover all the way. Have Crow God's shooters pick away at their tank busters, fire at will. Red Thunder needs to split his dancers. Three companies engaging the picket lines, four intercepting those reinforcements making for the Rock."

"Yes, sir. What about the last two companies?"

"Have them follow us."

His driver glanced back at him while the operator dispatched the orders. "Follow us where, Major?"

He gave his driver's shoulder a squeeze and pointed towards the growing barricade of bristling iron. "Through there. We're going in with the tanks."

The driver grinned, turned to peer through the windshield, and floored the accelerator. Kennedy renewed his white-knuckle grip and the command car resumed its stormy route.

Striking the plain, they bounced along the fissured stone through a hail of flying metal. Bullets rang against the plating, snagged the snapping fabric of the flag. He felt a glancing blow strike his helmet. The radio operator's grip on his shoulder drove him further beneath the command car's cover. The ear-pummelling clank of steel tracks on splitting rock told him his armour was nearby. A choking bank of dust and filth obscured the clash in swollen tiers of glowing cloud. Shells shrilled by. Mortar fire rutted the dunes, sending showers of thick ochre spray into the already grime-filled air.

"*Pull up.*"

The driver braked hard. Two Jacksons surged out of a bulwark of sand and pulled ahead. Trucks, their frames seething with clinging dancers, listed into view. They set upon the Watch's position. Dancers sprang from the sides of each truck and filed between the advancing Jacksons. A squad formed beside the settling command car.

Kennedy tossed their leader a fleeting look.

"Red Thunder says we're with you."

Kennedy shrugged. He jumped the side rail and dropped onto the sand. He called out to the driver. "Grab the flag, leave the car."

The driver bundled the flag and joined him on the ground, along with his radio man. They all crept forwards, the squad fanning out to flank them. A shell, striking the side of the motionless car, rocked it in place. Another smashed through the rear deck. As the fuel tank erupted, Kennedy thrust himself forwards. The heat of the explosion washed over him. A metal wheel sliced the sand where he'd crouched.

He thrust himself forwards again.

The ground to all sides was a fractured hellscape. Frantic, afflicted cries completed the abyss. Shapes shifted in the haze ahead, multiplying as he advanced. They moved like men in fear. Lacking the dancer's way, gracelessly stirring the shapes of ungainly packs and setting up weapons in plain sight, they perished under the rapid machine-gun fire of Kennedy's squad.

He forgot the cavern and the journal and Patricia's scent. The universe tottered on every gained inch of ground.

They came across a pile of watchmen. Their blue robes, parted and torn, revealed body armour not dissimilar to his own. Each soldier exhibited ghost dancer handiwork in the slashes, thick and deep, applied to their throats. A dancer lay moaning with his hands over his groin. Black skin puckered around the rude entry site of a fifty-calibre round. His clamped fingers barely staunched the flow of bright blood.

"Company of Imperial Watch," he called out to Kennedy. "Setting up machine-guns, launchers. Twenty feet ahead."

Kennedy signed to his squad leader. Six dancers began snaking forwards low over the sand and vanished into the smog. He told his radio man to call the tanks to cover.

Short bursts of gunfire were answered with wild shrieks, then silence, then a low keening whistle.

He sent the tanks onwards.

"Please," the dying man whispered.

Kennedy had a brackish taste in his mouth. He signed to his squad leader. The leader crossed to the man and brought a pistol up beneath his jaw.

"Thank you, Major."

The man had his gaze fixed on Kennedy. Kennedy held it firm. The Colt fired. His head fell back in swift release.

They pushed forwards.

They found their first samurai face down in the blood-crusted sand, a neat hole beneath his ebony plait. Another two bore the mark of Crow God's snipers. The ground ahead presented a particularly choice piece of earthwork. He signalled Wilson's tanks.

Eight of the original fourteen had made it this deep into the camp. They found partial cover in newly fashioned hollows. Nose up, turrets depressed, each presented a limited target to their exposed foe. Ghost dancers dropped in the dirt beside the sunken vehicles.

The watchmen, augmented by standard infantry and samurai sharpshooters, had sought cover among the casings of dead armour. Not far behind them, the artillery barrels of the Union 82nd pierced the sky, uselessly. The samurai had done their work.

The Jacksons spat sabot rounds and machine-gun fire. The dancers saturated the Imperial line with mortar fire, yet the Japanese held their ground.

The column of enemy reinforcements would soon be out of range, bound for Red Rock. He couldn't raise Iron Horse on the radio. He couldn't raise Hayes.

A Jackson stewed in the blast of a rocket's detonation before breaking up in an expanding ball of white flame. Scathing heavy-weapons fire nailed his men down. Incoming rounds sprayed dirt across his goggles and mouthpiece.

There was a length of metal piping thrown wide of the shattered tank. Kennedy reached for it and felt the iron burn his fingertips. A bullet skimmed its curvature with a clang, sending a tremor up his arm. He ran the tattered remnant of the flag along its searing length and rose to his feet. He sent the tanks forwards.

The air sang with bullets. He managed to brandish the banner in one mighty arc, two, before a blistering explosion in his right shoulder sent him back down to his knees.

His vision blotched. His fingers fumbled in the dirt for the pipe.

He was about to rise again when a one-twenty whipped the air overhead with a deafening wail. Then a salvo of blasts rent the air.

Ahead, the Union guns, now lowered, were hammering the rear of the Japanese line. Stray shells slammed into the ground behind the pinned dancers.

He rose to his feet again, slipping on slick earth. Dancers gripped him under each arm as they surged into the swirl of sand. He still had the flag. Figures lurched ahead and fell away. A samurai whirled out of the storm, katana raised. A tomahawk, its ribboned haft still quivering, cleft his face into crimsoned halves. Another's swinging blade encountered the crossed staves of two dancer axes. Okinawa steel met Sioux iron in a shower of sparks. The dancer thrust the samurai to the ground and dropped the point of his knee on the Hachiman's throat. Kennedy heard the cartilage crack, distinctly and clean.

He'd somehow exchanged his flag for a watchman's machine-gun.

He squeezed the trigger. His body vibrated, synched to the weapon. He sprayed the enemy line. The barrel glowed red, then white. He held the trigger taut. His vision swam. The barrel melted. He cast aside the gun and reached for his Mauser.

Blasted from behind and ravaged from the fore, the line of Imperials fell apart.

A Jackson swayed past. Then Kennedy's hand was on the side grip and he was riding the skirt. The tank was plastered with ghost dancers. An adjacent rider cast him a wild grin. The tank rose and fell on the crushed Japanese defences to enter the Union perimeter.

Dead samurai lay twisted among the Union slain, but too many had been undone. The guns were undermanned. Turned outwards and low, the one-twenties and eighty-eights were arranged in a ring.

Seeing the arrangement of the Union redoubt, Kennedy laughed, but the sound that emerged from his shielded mouth was a dry cackle. Circled wagons awaiting indian saviours redefined irony.

His radio man planted the flag on a mound of cracked earth.

Kennedy approached the nearest gun.

XXVI

April 29, 2012
Red Rock, Nevada

Malcolm had kept silent about Joseph's letter. She hadn't warned the others of his chosen doom. Lightholler, Morgan and Shine might be headstrong—or at the very worst naïve—but she'd never pegged them for lunatics.

So much for that.

She couldn't use the radio for fear of alerting the enemy. Standing before Doc Gershon, afraid to disrupt his efforts, she pondered her choices.

He misread her silence and said, "You couldn't have known they'd go out there. You couldn't have known they'd try to find him."

She shot him a quizzical look.

"I know about the major's arrangement, Miss Malcolm."

Confusion gave way to astonishment.

"I've been down here the whole time," he explained. "I saw everything."

"Why didn't you *say* something?" Her voice rose in abject fury. "Why didn't you stop him?"

"It was his choice to make." Doc returned his attention to the terminal.

But that wasn't enough. She leaned on the desk looming above him. "And here we are, with everyone off on some futile attempt to rescue someone who won't *allow* himself to be rescued, and the Japanese are hammering at the door. Meanwhile, you're still struggling with the jump points and Joseph's sacrifice was for *nothing*."

"The major's diversion bought us some time. His bargain will take care of the rest."

"What about Lightholler and the others?"

"They're with Tecumseh. He'll get them back in time."

"How can you be so *calm* about it all?" she demanded, exasperated beyond belief. "Where is your heart, Doctor?"

"It was buried in the sand a century ago, by Wells," he replied evenly.

He returned to his calculations.

XXVII

Lightholler's band swept through the relic of Red Rock, covering the devastation on swift hooves. The ghost-dancer horses had received a training no less rigorous than the men themselves. Sure-footed, the mounts found purchase among the smoking pits as easily as on the infrequent stretch of untrammelled desert sand.

The marks of the incursion were written on the scorched ruins of the prefabs. The armoury was a Stonehenge of skewed pylons, the grounds were littered with the Japanese dead. Deep tank tracks in the scored earth plotted the path of Iron Horse's havoc.

The kills grew fresher, until the occasional wounded soldier glanced up from a broken body with uncomprehending eyes. Morgan watched as an infantryman, piled among corpses, struggled to bring his rifle to bear on them. The soldier dragged his gun's stock in the earth like a crutch. Shine caught the clumsy movement. The rifle barrel wavered in their direction. Shine, seeking the soldier's eye, shook his head slowly. The soldier dropped his rifle and slumped back into his comrades.

Under an orange sun their path was criss-crossed by wayward black smoke.

Tecumseh trotted his mount to Shine's side and tapped out a question on the transmitter. The reply took long moments. Tecumseh grunted the translation. "There's no road west to the major. The bulk of a mechanised division lies between us. It's one thing holding them off, another thing entirely traversing their ranks."

"So what now?" Morgan asked.

"You return to the cavern and await your departure. You ensure some meaning to the destruction by fulfilling your part in all this."

"By sitting underground and listening to you all die? By leaving the major out there?" Lightholler's sorrel, in tune with his rider, snorted hot gusts of defiance.

"At what point in your instructions did the major ask you to hold out hope for him?"

"When he stood outside my hotel suite in New York and asked me for a few moments of my time," Lightholler replied. "I plan on giving them to him now."

"Your loyalty is only exceeded by your stupidity," Tecumseh muttered. "We'll take the southern path, skirt Echo, and try to come up behind the old Groom ore seam. There are mines and other snares out there, so follow my trail well."

Tecumseh picked a path through the rocks that guarded the southern entry to the base. Low hills rose into sharp banks of bare stone that cut the sky. Red Rock dropped behind them. From their vantage point, the installation—once so well concealed—was a blackened stain on the desert floor.

Fifteen minutes of riding gained them little ground across the harsh terrain. Morgan glanced at his watch often. His heart had soared at the thought of finding the major, but the possibility that they would run out of time was becoming all too real. What would Doc and Agent Malcolm hope to achieve alone in Wells' world?

Tecumseh had his binoculars out. He surveyed the western skyline. There was nothing to see in the distant haze but a shimmer of broken horizon.

"*Ceta'n*," he muttered.

"I beg your pardon?" Lightholler said.

"Hawk," Tecumseh replied. He handed the binoculars to Lightholler.

Morgan looked up. A solitary bird, its crown a dappled black, its tail white-banded and broad, soared among the thermals. Wings beat rapidly, then fixed to a languid glide.

Tecumseh's ravaged face was a portrait of bereavement. Did he suddenly mourn the passing of this damaged world? "*Ceta'n ote*," he added, qualifying his assessment. He directed Lightholler to a point beyond Morgan's vision. "Many hawks."

Lightholler shifted his point of view and handed the binoculars distractedly to Morgan. Morgan adjusted the focus. The bird was long gone. There was a stipple of black smudges in the far distance. He played with the focus and they resolved. He handed the binoculars on to Shine.

"They have Mitsubishi FS-Zs among those bombers," Lightholler said. "Where the hell are they coming from?"

"They might have repaired some of the captured airfields on the border," Tecumseh suggested.

"Even so, those interceptors will be running on fumes."

"It hardly matters. We have no anti-air defences."

Morgan could see them without the binoculars now. Wing upon wing of heavy bombers, low and to the west.

Many hawks.

XXVIII

April 29, 2012
Groom Mine, Nevada

It was a place Kennedy had frequented only in his dreams these last ten years. This was where Cambyses' Persian army, fifty-thousand strong, had vanished without a trace. Where Carthage was lost and the Crusaders fought and died. Here was where Napoleon had sought to destroy an empire, and Prussia carved a new one. This might have been the Sahara or the Gobi, the Simpson or the Mojave, but one simple act could turn them all into the same dark place.

This was the churning whirlpool of war in the sand.

A crew of Union gunners manned the nearest one-twenty. The vehicle, partially dug into the sand, had its gun almost resting on the dunes. Kennedy worked his way towards them. He hunkered down with them, his hands over his ears to blunt the crashing bellow of its blast.

"Who's in charge here?"

The commander seemed unfazed by Kennedy's squad. He eyed them cursorily before saying, "Thought you were, General." His salute was an airy gesture as he turned back to his spotter. "Hit 'em again."

The loaders secured the ungainly bulk of the round and the one-twenty roared flame.

"Where's your commanding officer?"

The commander gestured to a point behind him with a toss of his head. "Captain Hobbes."

Tracer fire illuminated the smoke and danced across the notched plating of the gun's armour.

"Hit 'em again."

Kennedy detailed two of his men to cover the gun and negotiated the cleft landscape of the Union enclave. He found the captain standing by the slashed remains of a tent. His staff, two lieutenants and a warrant officer, stood with him by a radio set.

Hobbes was a heavily built man. The broad features of his face were lost in the ambiguity of caked dirt. He snapped a salute and said to Kennedy, "Aren't you supposed to be dead?"

"I'm working on it, Captain." Kennedy returned the salute. He felt something catch in his shoulder, only now recalling the recent wound. Their exchange was yelled over the pandemonium of the artillery barrage.

"Clearly. When did you get promoted?"

"About five minutes ago."

The captain's face contorted into an ugly scowl. "And the provisional government?"

"You're looking at it."

"Lousy son of a…" The captain punched his meaty palm. He turned away from Kennedy, but as he took in the faces of his staff his look of disgust swiftly melted into something else. "You had the japs going for a while," he said. "The colonel was considering a parley."

"A colonel is in command of this army?" Kennedy asked.

"Your snipers took out a Japanese general and lieutenant general last night. They lost a lot of momentum dealing with your supply raids, and your decoy took out an entire battalion. There isn't supposed to be any confed resistance out here, and I haven't seen anything like your uniforms before."

A battalion? Kennedy's bared teeth were thankfully concealed behind his mask. "We're Special Forces."

"I'll say," the warrant officer volunteered.

"What changed the colonel's mind?" Kennedy asked.

"Full-strength reserves are only ten miles back, and they called in an air strike three hours ago."

Kennedy's men had taken up position within the Union defences. Ghost dancers helped man the understaffed guns or took defensive positions to cover the Union crews. The redoubt was a vortex of dust and burning wreckage.

"So why did you throw in with me?"

"You're Joseph fucking Kennedy. I thought you might have had something up your sleeve."

"I did," Kennedy replied. "You."

"Christ, what were you expecting *us* to do?"

"I was expecting you to butt out of this while my men took out the enemy supplies. You were a bit more enthusiastic than I expected."

"Hell of a nice flag you had waving on that hilltop, sir. We just got carried away. Well, now that we're stuck in this situation, what do you want us to do? Visibility is down to shit. We just been aiming low and hitting anything that moves."

"I have spotters up on the escarpment. I want your guns to prevent that brigade of tanks from deploying, and take out the column of reinforcements that are making for my base."

"Piece o' cake. Anything else?"

"You can tell me more about that air strike, Captain."

XXIX

April 29, 2012
Red Rock, Nevada

"All I'm saying is that we can't stay on open ground." Morgan's comment was directed more to himself than his companions.

Shine, intent on Tecumseh's radio transmissions, nodded his accord. Even the horses seemed edgy. They scraped at the plateau's pebbled surface. Reined in on the narrow shelf of bare rock, the three horsemen drew their mounts closer to Tecumseh, as if that might afford protection from the incoming fighters.

"This fast becomes a fool's errand," Tecumseh murmured.

The battlefields were spread out below them. Dispersing vapours roofed the gorge that had housed Echo. A thicker black cloud extended over Red Rock's west reach and a pall of filthy, flame-edged smoke burgeoned in the far distance where Major Kennedy had struck. Elsewhere, seared patches of earth documented slaughter and devastation. The extent of the Japanese camp, beyond Kennedy's attack, stretched towards the western horizon.

"Okay," Tecumseh said, finally, "those fighters will only be able to make a few runs before they have to turn back. The bombers are another problem entirely. Iron Horse has gone to ground, and the cliffs around the west tower will afford his men some cover. The major's men, however, are dangerously exposed." He turned to Lightholler. "Your cavern will withstand a limited raid from the air, but after the bombers leave, the ground assault will resume.

"Will you see reason now?" He peered intently at the three men.

"Did you speak to the major?" Shine asked.

Tecumseh shook his head.

"Could you get us to him if I asked you to?" Lightholler asked.

"Maybe, but once there, I can't see us returning in any reasonable length of time."

"I can't see him ditching his men," Morgan offered glumly.

"*We're* his men," Lightholler said.

"No," Tecumseh said. "You're his weapon, fashioned to undo changes that were wrongly made."

Lightholler looked at him for a long time. The expressionless cast of his mask did little to conceal the regret of his reply.

He said, "Take us back."

XXX

April 29, 2012
Groom Mine, Nevada

Atop the escarpment, Tom Shine had made short work of directing the Union guns. His last transmission had assured Kennedy that the column of Japanese reinforcements was mired in the detritus of their own shattered armour. Of the four companies Kennedy had dispatched in their pursuit, however, barely two hundred men remained. Red Thunder, warned of the impending air strike, had been instructed to disperse them. They would have to find their shelter somewhere on the open plains between the Japanese camp and the environs of Red Rock.

Little appeared to remain of the Japanese depot. Kennedy's men, scattered and bereft of any specific orders, had taken to following their own dark itinerary. Death, random and swift, struck from the shifting sand.

If not for the fact of the inbound bombers, he might have called this victory. Modest, Pyrrhic, but victory all the same. The Japanese camp was a turmoil of disordered ranks. There was no evidence of leadership among the confusion. If triumph was determined by the moral collapse of the enemy, it was prefigured in the fleeing shapes that loomed and vanished in the sandstorm.

But still the bombers were inbound.

Only one company of men and seven of his Jacksons remained to augment the thin blue line of Yankee regulars. If Hayes' last estimate was correct, he only needed ninety minutes.

The Japanese guns fell quiet. The Union forces, deprived of targets, stared out into the retreating haze. The attacks ceased and the silence of their adversary screamed his intentions. Even the infantrymen had halted their appalling suicidal rushes against the ghost dancer lines.

A band of samurai broke through the perimeter. Hurdling the piles of their dead, they emptied their machine-guns; ornate, pearl-handled weapons that gleamed in their hands. They leapt from cannon to cannon. A flash of sharp silver skewered a gunner here, a dancer there, before the concerted efforts of Kennedy's band finally stretched them in the dust. The glittering edge of a shuriken still protruded from the side of an eighty-eight where it had missed its mark.

"They're coming."

There was nothing to do but seek cover beneath the armoured hem of the artillery.

Shadows, long and dark, swept over them. Machine-gun fire ploughed narrow channels, raking the ground. Dust, freshly settled, flurried in clotted droves, plastering his goggles.

The bombers began to drop their payloads. Time and again he was heaved bodily against the underside of the tank as the landscape reformed around him in tectonic mockery of some act of creation. The clamour was a vice, compressing his skull.

Ninety minutes…

If the cavern was being targeted, they would barely last nine.

Kennedy pictured the vaulted ceiling crumbling beneath the barrage. The carapace, sundered and sinking beneath its own weight. Cracks splitting through the framework of Tecumseh's mysterious art as the walls themselves gave way. And Patricia, grey and silent and broken within the mausoleum he had constructed.

There was Hobbes' radio set, tilted crazily near the frayed pennant of his command tent. A globe, pale red, flickered still on its console.

He dived across the sand and rolled between the criss-cross path of strafing fire. He latched onto the set and dialled up a prearranged frequency with bloodied fingers.

The signal was there, loud and clear.

He brought the mouthpiece close to his lips and shouted his question above the din of falling doom.

"*Where the fuck are you?*"

One last gesture of defiance.

One last grab for the ring.

A blast tossed him onto his back. His shoulder exploded in a callous burst of agony.

Looking up, he saw a fighter swoop down through a break in the cloud. He saw the wingtips flare brightly and felt the rapid thud of bullets as they danced towards him along the desert floor. The fighter bobbed wildly, as if already preparing for a victory roll, then rolled over completely in a nebula of red flame, disintegrating.

Behind it, soaring past the wreckage, two Confederate biplanes veered back up into the clouds.

A voice, muffled by static, crackled over the radio set. "On my way, Joseph. We should arrive at your soirée any time now."

Kennedy crawled back to the transmitter. "You sure took your damn time." He coughed into the mouthpiece.

Despite the interference, Webster's reply still managed to seethe some secret satisfaction.

"You have no idea how difficult it is to hijack a stratolite. I suggest you and your men find yourself a deep, deep hole. I'm in foul spirits."

XXXI

April 29, 2012
Red Rock, Nevada

They galloped four abreast. Calamity dogged their heels, a rolling wave of destruction that lashed the tortured earth with jubilant abandon.

The Rock loomed wildly with every juddering stride as the foam-flecked horses bore them across the burning plain. The shack, cloven to reveal the domed cement entrance to the cavern, was less than a hundred yards away.

Lightholler fixed his eyes on the quaking hoof-tossed earth. He cringed at each fleeting shadow that heralded another plane's strafing run. They entered a vast darkness too thick for cloud and when he emerged he found that he was galloping alone.

He reined in hard, twisting his stallion in a tight turn that brought him to rest a short distance from the dome's entrance. Tecumseh and the others, just feet away, had also stopped, and they had their heads tilted skywards. He lifted his eyes to join theirs and a vertiginous shudder racked his body.

"Jesus fucking *Christ*." Morgan, bent back in his saddle, was in danger of losing his seat.

Shine was trying to settle his mount.

Tecumseh just stared in awed wonder. Perhaps he was thinking about his thunderbird, perched above the deluge, snapping lightning and bringing thunder. For above their heads, impossibly large and impossibly near, hung the *Patton*.

XXXII

April 29, 2012
CSS Patton

Webster, standing at the stratolite's Eye, gazed down upon the wastes of Kennedy's realm.

Pre-dawn, the *Patton* had been a lifeless husk pitched on uncaring seas. Suspended out over the Nevada–Arizona border, derelict and insensate, millions of dollars worth of steel and high-grade plastic listed within a swarm of bi-winged gnats.

Pinked to the gills, Webster lay face up on his bunk while renegade dreams buffeted him along narrow corridors, down, down, always down, towards that infinitely sharp barb that awaited the soft pulpy orb of his right eye. The pounding of his heart resolved into the steady thud of a fist against his door.

With heavy, cloddish movements he lurched towards the cabin entrance.

"Director." The agent's voice broke through the syrupy miasma of pharmaceutical enfoldings. "Radio. Inbound. Urgent." Words forced their way through ramparts of delirium. "Black Knight."

That did it.

Webster's eye throbbed syncopal as he clawed his way out of stupefaction.

By the time he'd traversed the five decks to communications, his head had almost cleared. His desk was as he'd left it. A light flashed, agitatedly, on the receiver.

He heard Agent Reid's voice, tremulous, saying, "Who could have imagined?"

Who indeed?

And then, inconceivably, Kennedy was on the line with his proposal.

The offer: information, the only currency worth dealing in, and the negotiation was to be held face to face in Kennedy's own lair.

"What's in it for you, Joseph?"

"I'll let you decide that."

"Surely we'd be more comfortable up here."

"I want to show you what's behind the curtain, Director. But you only have sixty seconds left to triangulate my whereabouts and I'll be done in thirty. Bring enough security to make yourself comfortable. Your pilot only gets the coordinates in the air. If your plane is escorted, we blow you all out of the sky. I'll call back in three for your answer."

Then Agent Reid's voice. "Director, you *really* need to see this."

Then static.

He'd assembled his best men, blustered his way past Illingworth's feeble protest, and was airborne in fifteen minutes. No escort. Reid's tone, chilling and awed, had left no doubt.

He'd be entering his enemy's camp, outnumbered and outgunned, yet this bore no scent of a trap. Behind Kennedy's bid, he'd sensed a desperate need. He knew—beyond any shadow of a doubt—that this would end with Joseph on his knees.

Reid had greeted him on the runway, a desolate stretch of recently smoothed sand. Will-o'-the-wisps flitted among an uneven tract of low mounds, suggesting some ancient, troubled burial ground. The entire plain lay cupped between the crenellated ridges of craggy rock. Reid led him past the rounded knolls—squat, prefabricated buildings, meshed under cowled netting, blending into the desert. Phosphorescent glows purposefully followed his every movement. They coalesced into a body of figures that converged on his destination: a twisted clot of red rock.

Kennedy met him at the door of the shabby profile of a dilapidated cabin. He'd greeted Webster's security team—three seasoned tactical agents—by name. He was unshaven, his brow disfigured by a poorly sutured gash, and was wearing a garish shirt of blue, partially concealed beneath Confederate fatigues. Thinner, paler, dishevelled, he had a haunted look.

Webster didn't dare mistake him for a cornered prey.

The shack was more smoke and mirrors. Within, a grey dome enclosed an elevator shaft. The walls were a mishmash of primitive paintings and damaged electronic equipment.

"From here on in, Director," Kennedy had said, "it's just you and me."

Webster had offered a brilliant smile. "That strikes me as an unwise course."

"Your men stay up here. This isn't something you want to share."

Webster cast Reid a dissecting look. The man had suffered some injuries, but that wasn't what ailed him. Some new knowledge had stamped itself behind the agent's eyes. The vacancy of his stare sought some crucial misplaced item. Webster decided it was hope.

"Don't take anyone down with you, sir," Reid said.

This was getting interesting. Webster said, "After you, Joseph."

They descended the ladder. Blank screens and exposed wires; the noxious scented tresses of torchlight confirmed that the same pulse that had struck the *Patton* had wrought its wrath here. It also explained his presence within these strange walls.

Kennedy's penchant for melodrama had been evident from the hovel's entrance to the ruby-lit chamber at the foot of the shaft. A blanket, embroidered with a map of the stars, iced the cake.

"Through there?"

"Through there."

There might have been someone operating a computer terminal. He didn't recall. The cavern was large, its roof cathedralled into darkness beyond the flicker of torches. He stared at the machine. Form, alien and inexplicable, somehow revealed function.

"Well..." he said after long moments.

"Yes?" Kennedy murmured.

"My eye." Webster turned to Kennedy. "It doesn't hurt."

The smile Kennedy had returned was oddly warm, though it didn't sit well on his harried features.

"You didn't build this."

"No. I found it."

"And it's broken."

"Not quite."

Webster removed his patch and ran a finger around the numbed ridge of the socket. "This explains a lot, Joseph." Part of him was working the odds. Reid plus three tac agents against Kennedy's little army. There was the *Patton*, he supposed.

He took a step towards the machine. There was…

His thoughts muddled, reshuffling. Ideas became kaleidoscoping colours. It tasted like a purple flashback.

Kennedy's expression was bemused.

Webster smiled at him. "I had to consider it," he said.

"I'd expect nothing less."

"So. Why am I here, Joseph? Gloating doesn't feature heavily among your flaws."

"I need your help."

"You should have come to me earlier."

Kennedy gave a scornful laugh. "The thought of you and this, together, has kept me awake for long hours."

"And yet, here we are."

Kennedy's face had resumed its haggard mien. He'd explained how he'd discovered the machine; shed from a world where America had never blinked, never splintered, never faltered at the first trembling step. He described the attempts to determine the machine's function, and the nuclear holocaust he'd witnessed, unveiled by its first and only journey. He outlined the objectives of his mission and the make-up of his team.

The Lightholler scenario fell into place. The manipulation of governments, the movement of funds, a push here and a shove there, revealed the deft touch of Kennedy's hand.

It would appear that the reckless act of a madman had undone the world; a slow, lingering death a century in the making. Solutions lay in prevention, Kennedy argued. An incisive intervention to excise the cancer that was Wells.

It had sounded rather simplistic. It sounded no less reckless than Wells' own performance. Yet voiced in the presence of the machine's aura, it had the cold ring of truth. Webster reasoned that he might have even considered such a solution himself. Perhaps.

And still his eye did not hurt.

Then Kennedy told him what he already knew. What he had seen from the air as he'd descended into this lost valley. That an army was poised on their borders, led by men who might have some inkling of the treasure buried nearby. That the machine, struck hard by the pulse, required long hours of restorative work. Hours he didn't have.

Webster asked, "What happens to this world after you leave?"

"I don't know."

"Is it destroyed? Lost?"

"That's what happens if I fail," Kennedy replied.

Webster's throat was as dry as his socket now. He rasped, "And if you succeed?"

"I don't know. Never coming into being, maybe this place just fades away."

"I find that very disturbing. I have no intention of just fading away. It doesn't suit my temperament." There was the low drone of a generator humming at the machine's base. "I'm going with you."

Kennedy didn't appear surprised. He said, "It's a lifeline, Webster. Not a lifeboat."

"Have you told that to Miss Malcolm?"

Kennedy's jaw worked beneath the stubble of his chin, but he made no reply.

Webster said, "So I suspected. Joseph, I don't see you bargaining from a position of strength here."

"She comes with us," Kennedy said.

"Fine," Webster replied. "Fine. Then I'll take your berth."

"I can't let you do that, Glen. I can't unleash you on that world."

It was as gracious a compliment as Webster had ever received. He asked, "What did you want from me, exactly?"

"You're on the *Patton*. I need planes. I need you to gain me those hours."

"And in return, I get the satisfaction of a job well done?"

"No. In return, you get the satisfaction of knowing that I face the same fate as you. I'll stay behind. I'm supposed to die here, anyhow."

"I believe you."

Webster took a final look at the machine. Black and silver, shimmering with hope and expectation and the promise of horrors undone and worlds remade. *Deus ex machina*. He thought about what he might do with such a beast and looked back at Kennedy.

"Martyrdom suits you, Joseph." He thought about what he might do. He said, "How much time do you need?"

At 0730 hours he'd briefed his tactical agents aboard the *Patton*. By 0800 they were stationed throughout the stratolite. At 0815 he'd convened an emergency meeting with five other members of the Advanced Command Post.

He had his files with him. He showed them what he had on them. By 0930 he'd secured control of the *Patton*. He informed Houston of the regrettable loss of the stratolite, with all hands, over the Arizona state border, before shutting down all external communications.

He put forty-five scouts in the air. Twenty-five functioning turrets were mounted with one-oh-five millimetre cannons along the broad waist of the massive airship, and three atom bombs were nestled among the standard ordnance of the bomb bays.

The *Patton*, licking its wounds, swung westwards…

And now, riding low at twenty thousand feet, the stratolite—Webster's reluctant mistress—taunted the Japanese guns. She poured contemptuous fire upon the crushed lines of armour and infantry. Her scouts darted among the formations of bombers, bringing them down upon the shattered units. The Japanese fighters, caught off guard and wedged between the first wave of Confederate air and the brutal metal of the *Patton*'s anti-aircraft cannon, broke off contact.

Webster strode from scope to scope. A few of the operational cameras delivered detailed images of the carnage below. One featured the rock formation he'd spied by dawn's light that morning. Though the shack was rubble, the dome shield itself appeared intact. Other cameras focused on the main body of the Japanese divisions, showing smudged abstracts of black and grey and red, a twirling rondo of smoke and flame. Distant images, transmitted from lenses on the ballonet array, showed the Japanese fighters reforming far to the north. Close at hand a lone fighter, soaring too close to the *Patton*'s guns, played Icarus.

He dropped half a purple. This was no mistress he rode. This buxom steel wench, corpulent and grotesque, was the Whore of Babylon, grinding the desert flat. He stretched a hand out before him, lining up his naked eye view of the devastated installation beneath his palm. Squeezing and thinking, *Crush you all.*

Here are your hours... Here are the minutes you craved. Dished up by your foe on the piled bodies of your rivals. So tell me, Joseph, is this what it feels like to be you?

XXXIII

April 29, 2012
Groom Mine, Nevada

Kennedy worked his way back along the path his men had shred through the Japanese ranks. Beyond the line of eighty-eights, abandoned and silent, he traversed a tormented terrain on elbows and knees. He sought the higher ground where some of his men remained gathered; there, to watch the world unfold.

The bodies were thick at the foot of the escarpment. They formed battlements. The occasional afflicted face of a ghost dancer turned to him in passing, and to each he croaked the same reply. Strengthened, each turned on his back and gazed at the sky in expectation.

Good cloud was coming.

He scaled the incline with a firmer grip, rising to his feet as the sounds of diving planes and answering fire rose and fell. The crest of the escarpment gave way to the wide ledge of rock where not so long ago his men had deployed. It was barren now, save for a small party within the conquered Japanese watchpost. There was no movement among the sandbags. His men sat at odd angles.

He heard sounds, stifled and crackly, issue from the radio he'd employed earlier. A slumped body moved slightly, shoulders heaving as it voiced a reply. It coughed harshly. Kennedy advanced with softer tread. Tom Shine was saying goodbye to his son.

He turned to face Kennedy. Disbelief gashed a smile across his anguished face. Sorrow and pleasure played there. The radio crackled again. He spoke into the mouthpiece and then said to Kennedy, "Take it. I'm done."

Kennedy stared stupidly at him for a moment.

As if offering the simplest of explanations, he said, "I can't move, Major."

"You did real good, Tom." Kennedy gently removed the mouthpiece from Shine's wavering grasp. He removed his air filter and said, "Kennedy here."

There was a riot of responses. He thought he heard Patricia's voice in the background.

The air was filled with distant explosions as some resumption of fighting took place beyond the edge of the ridge.

"How much longer?" he asked. His voice was brittle in his ears.

"An hour, maybe less." It was Lightholler.

"Is everyone safe?"

Lightholler's reply was lost in a screeching howl of distortion.

Another voice broke into the conversation.

"I think they're fine, Joseph. I must say, though, that I'm surprised you're not huddled down there with them." Webster's voice sounded slurred. His words ran together in a monotone drawl.

"Couldn't get there if I wanted to, Glen, and besides, we had a deal."

"I can't imagine what I was thinking."

Indistinct noises vied with the static. He thought he might have heard Lightholler calling to him again.

"From my vantage," Webster continued, "the fighters seem more intent on bringing me down than causing your base any more damage. More jap interceptors are inbound. Looks like I'm going to be the main event now. How do you like that?"

Kennedy, eyes still on Tom Shine, nodded absently. His comrade's face had slackened. Something within the old soldier was receding.

"If you tell me where you are," Webster continued, "I might be able to plot you a safe course back to the Rock."

"Now why would you want to do something like that?"

"It's something I'd like you to live with."

Shine was moving his lips. Kennedy drew closer, bringing his ear to the old man's mouth. He did so with dread, fearful of receiving some brutal explanation of why so many men now lay broken.

Shine whispered the coordinates and closed his eyes.

Kennedy quoted the numbers back over the radio, curious to see how this might all play out.

Static ebbed and flowed as the moments drew themselves out. He adjusted the amplitude slightly, unable to raise the cavern or Webster. An approaching rumble might have been one of Webster's scouts, dispatched to deliver the *coup de grâce*.

He spied the drawstring pouch lying in the dust. Were there some grains of that *other* world, paler, purer, mixed among the white powdered sand? He'd been awaiting revelation so long now that he was undeterred when some final spark of the carapace effect ignited itself in his brain.

There *was* no other world. There was to be no exchange taking place here; no fading away or destruction. The ghost dance begins in fire and ends with a whimper but not all tears speak of sorrow. He should have paid more attention to Tecumseh… what he was about to witness was renewal.

"Dragon." Tom Shine's eyes had fluttered open.

Fire licked at the earth around him, swept by wild winds. He turned on his knees to see the flaming snout of the Dragon tank bearing down on him. He heard a voice crash through the static and then, somehow, echo from close by.

He pitched forwards into oblivion.

XXXIV

April 29, 2012
Red Rock, Nevada

"What the *hell* just happened?"

Lightholler made sure that Morgan had copied the coordinates. He'd heard every word of the major's transaction with Webster, but was unable to break back into the communication. Absorbed now in recalibrating the transmitter, he ignored Doc's cry.

"You saw that, didn't you?" Doc was talking to Morgan.

Lightholler suppressed an urge to call for quiet and concentrated on his task.

A bright glow suffused the room...

Everything slipped...

"You saw that, didn't you?" Doc was talking to Morgan.

Lightholler suppressed an urge to call for quiet and concentrated on his task.

A bright glow suffused the room. He swiftly turned towards the source but the carapace had reclaimed its shadows.

Doc was staring, open-mouthed, at the energy reservoir. "You *saw* that, right?"

Morgan said, "I saw it."

Only Malcolm wasn't looking. She still gazed with mute despair at the now silent radio.

"What happened?" Lightholler demanded.

Doc stammered in his haste. "The carapace reservoir just exceeded one hundred per cent. That's *impossible*."

"Why is that impossible?"

"Because I haven't re-engaged the generator yet."

Malcolm was tugging at Lightholler's sleeve. "Please," she urged. "Get him back."

"Is it reading right now?"

"Yes."

"Please, find him."

"I'm trying." Lightholler tore his eyes from Malcolm's pleading face. "And what the hell was that light, Doc?"

"I don't know."

The cavern shuddered again. Fresh silt deposited itself on the growing stalagmites of spilt earth.

"Brilliant." The carapace, verging on full power, flexed unknown muscles. "Will it still work?"

"There's a slight problem with the proximity of the first staging point. We're looking at forty-five minutes."

"Brilliant."

Doc went back to his numbers. Lightholler returned to the shortwave. The others hemmed him in, forming a tight circle around the radio.

"Major, are you there? Please respond, over."

The radio yielded white noise.

XXXV

April 29, 2012
CSS Patton

The Eye was a seething mass. Agents and intel techs strove for his attention. He'd stopped giving orders five minutes ago. He stared at the radio's console with mounting frustration. Kennedy's silence was becoming wearisome.

Its balloon array in tatters, the stratolite hung well west of the cavern's entrance. Confined to the lower airs, it limped on, drawing the Japanese planes back over the scattered remains of their anti-aircraft cover.

Webster glanced at one of the screens. Nothing moved within the waste land of Red Rock. Beyond the monitors, the sky was a tapestry of grey tracer-laced pom-poms. Tufts of smoke bloomed, tiny fists catching and crushing the occasional interceptor. There was no need for fire discipline, no need for the *Patton*'s gunners to be circumspect in their targeting. All the scouts were long gone. Only the recon flights remained aloft. They'd called in, one by one, sustaining the litany of approaching enemy planes.

He peered down at the coordinates he'd received. A camera, trained on the site, displayed a swirling black maelstrom.

"I don't think I can help you now, Joseph," he murmured. He turned off the transmitter.

He cleared the Eye of all but his senior agents. The remaining men, covert operatives placed among the stratolite's crew when she'd first been cast to the winds, represented all the *Patton*'s services. He listened to their appraisals.

There were at least eight Japanese squadrons inbound. A flight of rocket scouts had been spotted among their formations. There'd been some external attempts, from Dallas and Houston, to contact the *Patton*.

All had been ignored, as per his orders.

One communiqué piqued his interest. The flotilla of German stratolites secreted above the Japanese Home Islands had delivered their atomic stockpiles over Tokyo, Hiroshima and Nagasaki.

He reviewed his options. Their scarcity alleviated his task.

More than a hundred Japanese planes were on their way. The *Patton* wouldn't live out the hour.

He gave orders to make west at full speed. All unnecessaries were to be jettisoned in order to gain the highest altitude. He dismissed the men, telling them that he was not to be disturbed. He shook their hands at the elevator vestibule and sealed the Eye's entrance at their departure.

He had everything he needed right here.

He returned to the transmitter and dialled up the frequency that had earlier cut into Kennedy's conversation.

A voice, unexpectedly soft, unexpectedly sorrowful, answered his transmission.

He ignored Malcolm's wasted supplication. Joseph Kennedy was long gone.

He spoke over her protests, saying, "Please listen to me very carefully. You need to ensure that all your electrical equipment is deactivated for the next thirty minutes. After that, you will be free to do as you will. Good luck, Malcolm."

She started to reply but something in her voice set the pain coursing through the parched void of his socket. He cut the broadcast.

He reached for the remote and primed the atomics, setting the timer for twenty minutes. He removed two bottles from a flap pocket of his jacket and eyed them judiciously. He selected a handful of purps and downed them dry. He wished he'd thought to bring along a cigar.

XXXVI

April 29, 2012
Red Rock, Nevada

"For God's sake." She flew across the cavern floor towards the generator. "Don't touch a damned thing."

Doc fell away from the machine.

"Unplug it and make sure those damned explosives don't have a dead man's switch."

"Where is he?" Lightholler was asking. Fixed on the problem of Doc's first insertion point, compass in hand, he was poring over a series of maps.

"That wasn't Joseph."

Lightholler looked up. Morgan left Shine's side and approached them.

"That was Webster."

The crash of stray blasts, the steady rattle of the cavern's cracked walls, formed an eerie counterpoint to her words. *Kennedy and Webster.* The shock of their unholy alliance still hadn't had time to sink in.

"What did he want?" It was Doc who spoke. Witness to their dark pact, his voice trembled with rage.

"It was a warning."

"A warning?" They were the first words Shine had uttered since talking to his father.

"Heaven help us." She shook her head, disbelievingly. "He's going to use his atomics."

XXXVII

April 29, 2012
CSS Patton

The timer read three minutes.

Webster stood before the glass enclosure with his hands pressed against the frame.

The stratolite was listing to port. One of the Eye's scaffolding beams had been snagged. It dangled beneath the *Patton*, twisting slow, presenting Webster with a dazzling view.

The Japanese air force could not be accused of tardiness.

He removed the patch and held it between thumb and forefinger before letting it fall to the floor. The purple bottle, empty, rolled away from his feet to rest against the wall, then back again, making little chiming noises.

The timer read two minutes.

He had a nursery rhyme going round and round in his head and it went, *gun mouth trigger*.

The pistol was cold to the touch. He placed the barrel against his forehead, enjoying the momentary relief of the chilled metal against his brow. He shifted the pistol with the intention of cooling the arid chasm of his mouth. That was nice. The floor lurched beneath him as another rocket detonated somewhere within the stricken stratolite's bowels, so rather than a clean furrow through his brainstem the bullet shattered his palate to lodge under his frontal bone.

His head hurt.

He was on the floor and there was something in his eye. Something was dribbling into his socket. He wiped it away in futility and all the while the white and grey and red matter slid down his forehead into his eye.

He glanced at the clock but it had to be all wrong because it was running backwards.

He glanced at the gun in his hand and said, "Oh."

It was hard to gather his thoughts. It felt like there was a hole in his head and all of his thoughts were billowing through the hole in his head and sliding down the front of his face into his mouth. He spat into his palm and examined the contents, brain, blood and slivers of cartilage, and said, "Crap."

He giggled and drooled, "The enemy of my Kenemy is my fiend."

That brought the smile back to his face.

Outside the window, shiny silver pixies danced and the cloudscape streamed fast-purple-slow.

Malcolm was riding him, looking down upon his beaming face.

There you are. He smiled.

He had a nursery rhyme gurgling at the top of his skull, spiralling out of the hole in his head, and it went, *pop goes the weasel.*

XXXVIII

April 29, 2012
Red Rock, Nevada

The hush that followed that great final quake was thick and heavy.

The carapace, grimed and dull beneath a pall of dust, hummed softly at full charge. Tecumseh and Hayes stood with Shine beside one of the machine's struts. Tecumseh, eyes closed, had a hand resting against the machine. His lips were moving and Malcolm was unsure as to whether he was offering consolation or prayer.

For her own part, it was all she could do just to breathe. Each inhalation seemed to come at the bequest of some hidden authority that had to remind her, cajole her, to draw the next shuddering breath. Each became a drawn-out sigh, but there were no tears.

Doc Gershon had explained to her that the first staging point—that initial skip before the long leap back in time—placed them within a small radius of their current position. Lightholler, Morgan and Gershon were at the maps now, searching the adjacent vicinity, slicked red with blood in both space and time, for that dry spot to land.

She didn't imagine for a moment that this little ark would be encountering any doves.

They were rolling up the maps. Gershon cleared his desk. He removed the spool from the printer and turned off the computer. Lightholler had a large trunk with him; he lugged it heavily towards the underside of the carapace. Shine had to help him lift it through the circular hatch.

They adjusted the soiled garments of their uniforms, buttoning up shirts and securing the straps of their helmets. Gershon put on a helmet. It looked like dry land wasn't in the offing.

Tecumseh and Hayes moved to another console next to the generator.

Lightholler approached her. "Are you ready, Patricia?"

She nodded numbly.

He led her beneath the carapace's shell.

She felt the ghost dancer's eyes upon her with each tentative step. Firm arms hauled her into the belly of the machine. The sterile sweep of its white curving bulwarks was a stark contrast to the cavern that had been her world for such an interminable time. Six seats were arranged, two before and four behind the hatch, on a raised dais. There were sealed lockers arranged along the walls and a console that occupied a full third of the cabin. A single keyboard was embedded within. The paucity of equipment was slightly disturbing.

Above the keyboard, through glass unseen from without, she saw Tecumseh staring up at the machine. The air had a metallic tang to it. She tasted the electricity's dance. Part of the view screen was devoted to a computer readout, but the numbers that flashed emerald across the screen meant nothing to her.

Lightholler directed her to one of the four seats at the carapace's hindquarters. He secured her with a thin strap of black leather and took the adjacent seat for himself. Morgan and Shine silently took their places alongside.

Beside her, a smaller console had been etched into the metal. Two palm-sized discs lay beneath a sheath of clear plastic. One was green, the other a dull shade of red. Some design, a subtle twirl, was carved into the surface of the green disc. If the disc could spin, she would see a whirling vortex with no centre. She decided that it was a rebus; an enigmatical representation, to any seated here, of the journey to come.

Doctor Gershon took a seat at the lower tier. The chair next to him remained empty.

Her glance shifted from the seat to Tecumseh's expectant gaze below.

Gershon was awaiting some signal from the medicine man. He grasped a lever protruding from his console and inched it forwards. The discs in his console began to pulse slowly.

She turned to Lightholler, afraid for a moment to speak aloud in this place.

His look, eager and hopeful, was an invitation.

She said, "Wouldn't Joseph want us to take Tecumseh in his place?"

Lightholler's face broke into a dark smile. "Why don't you ask him yourself?"

She looked out to Tecumseh, across an expanding gulf of space and time. The medicine man appeared to meet her gaze firmly and she knew. To each, it seemed as though the other had gone entirely from the world.

THE FIRE SERMON

I

Stage 1

Doc had talked about winging the first stage, saying that the labile state of the chronogeography in the region made insertion a risky prospect. Pressed to speak English, he told Lightholler that a radius of the last two hours and ten miles was likely to pitch them into the centre of a battlefield. That's what had given Lightholler the idea.

He thought only he had heard the delicate sound, faint and distant, of an eggshell cracking. His companions' eyes told him it was no delusion. Yet the screen still showed the cavern's interior: Tecumseh, a frozen effigy before the screen.

Doc called out, "Get ready, I'm blowing the hatch. This is only for calibration, so you'll have sixty seconds, max."

Nothing changed.

According to Doc, the brain compensated for the abrupt shift in time and space by filling in the gaps with old information.

There was the slightest sensation of rocking. It was hard to believe that they had moved at all.

"*Get* ready."

Lightholler was at the locker. He pulled the trunk heavily onto the floor.

Shine and Morgan were reaching for weapons. Their hands fumbled among the ordnance.

Lightholler's weapon was a thick and bulky cylinder in his arms. Morgan shot him an incredulous look before lifting his own choice from the stockpile, a ghost-dancer assault rifle.

Shine cradled a machine-gun.

Lightholler caught one glimpse of Malcolm's bewildered expression. Behind her, on the screen, the cavern was melting. Veiled sunlight and a stony stretch of desert superimposed itself in a bizarre double exposure.

He dropped through the hatch.

Shine and Morgan were beside him on the ground. His vision swam as nausea contended with dizziness to see which might incapacitate him first. Shine's father had come through with the coordinates but Doc's timing could have been a little kinder. They'd been pitched into an inferno. Roasting wind whipped frenzied flames as a Dragon tank crested the ridge.

Major Kennedy faced the monstrosity on bended knees.

Shine fired short bursts to no avail. Morgan's rifle chattered uselessly against the tank's ribbed underbelly. Lightholler hadn't fired a weapon since Nashville. He put the rocket-launcher to his shoulder and took the shot.

The Dragon, perched on the ridge's edge, seemed to crumple inwards as if clenching the missile. It slid back over the escarpment with a roar.

They dragged Kennedy's prone form to the hatch. With Malcolm's fervent hands clutching at his face and chest, they hauled him through the opening. Lightholler boosted Morgan through the threshold and reached across to Shine.

Shine bent to kiss to his dead father's brow before accepting Lightholler's hand.

Doc's voice was a strident bellow from within, urging him back.

Lightholler gripped the hatch's sides. Hands reached under his arms, dragging him up. His feet clear of the hatchway, he heard a voice—quite clear and strangely familiar—issue from a radio nearby.

"Major, are you there? Please respond, over."

II

Stage 2

"Why here?" Kennedy was nursing the scalded weal of his right shoulder.

Malcolm was still staring at him with wide eyes. He turned, catching her look, and his face softened.

Shine was smiling too.

On screen, the desert liquefied to a verdant sea of shifting green.

"I had to do the calculations from scratch," Doc said. "The only maps I had were the ones you'd left in your office. This was the only region I could get a fix on."

Outside, shades of green and brown resolved into rich, leafy woodland.

"Where are we?" Malcolm asked.

"New York." Kennedy turned to hide his evident dismay.

Malcolm peered at the forming image on the screen, as if half-expecting to find a squad of Brandenburg shock troopers bursting through the tree line at any moment. "*When* are we?" she asked fearfully.

Doc scrutinised his monitor, then turned to face them. "Near as I can tell, we've jumped two hundred hours, give or take."

Morgan struggled with the maths. This sudden roller-coaster, tacked onto the end of long days of terror, hardship and loss, left his mind numbed.

"Nine days," Shine said. "I thought stage two was a fortnight."

Doc said, "Next time, *you* plot the fucking insertion."

Lightholler chuckled faintly.

Kennedy's eyes shifted across the group with faint amusement. He addressed them all. "Thank you." The quiver in his voice told of his own sufferings.

"I've never been to New York," Malcolm said, "but I don't recall it being known for its greenery."

"We're in Central Park," Lightholler said. "Again." He shot Kennedy a pointed look.

Morgan said, "We had a shit of a time getting out of here in the first place."

"Well, you can relax then," Doc said. "Final insertion's in three."

"Three minutes here's about all I could stand," Morgan said.

"Did *anyone* pay attention to my explanations?" Doc asked. His lighter tone failed to undermine the reproach.

Kennedy sighed wearily. "That's three *hours*, Darren."

Malcolm said, "Let me take a look at that shoulder."

III

Lightholler emerged from the hatch to give the surroundings a cursory glance. Fortune had placed the carapace on a small grassy sward enclosed by a thick clutch of elms. He could make out the occasional worn stump of stonework through gaps in the foliage. Here and there, a rusted twist of fencing was apparent. This was the zoo. They were at the south end of the park.

Only certain regions of Central Park had been preserved by the Eastern masters of the city. The rest had been allowed to surrender to the whims of nature. Straying from the overgrown pathways into the wilder portions of the park wasn't recommended. The zoo's former denizens had borne progeny, and encounters weren't unheard of.

It was late morning.

He wanted to sprawl in the grass. A cool breeze played among the leaves. A bird flew overhead where clouds gathered, disappeared above the tree tops, and then repeated the exact same manoeuvre.

He moved away from the carapace, away from where time hissed and spat like boiling fat.

Three hours would return him to the Waste Land. Finesse on Doc's part might permit the strangest encounter yet. An appointment with Doctor Wells in the desert. Would he be sitting there picking the brains of a dying man, or would they catch him in the act of burial? Either way, Shine would put him in the ground.

Secret hope urged a late arrival. This should be decided at sea, Lightholler mused, with ice as the sole witness. Concluded in the safe harbour of New York, with the original *Titanic*'s silhouette a welcome addition to the city's skyline.

There was the sound of soft footfall and he looked up. Morgan and Kennedy were standing by the carapace. Morgan had a long grey coat over his uniform.

Kennedy said, "Let it go. It's too risky."

Morgan's reply conveyed infinite sadness. "I can't, Major. He's out there somewhere. We can't just abandon him."

Kennedy said, "He's lost."

"So were you."

Kennedy placed a hand on Morgan's shoulder. "Darren, listen to reason. He left with us on the *Shenandoah*. He sailed with you on the Atlantic. He never disappeared in New York."

Lightholler approached them. There was a strange discordant buzzing in his head. He realised what day this was.

Morgan persisted. "And on April 15, 1912, the *Titanic* was lost, taking with it two-thousand-four-hundred souls, so what the *fuck* are we trying to do here? Why are we bothering? If we're here to make a difference, let's start now. And if we have to end a life in order to fix the future, then let's save one as well."

"John?" Kennedy turned to Lightholler. The look on his face, the whole twisted expression of his body, was a plea.

"It's going to rain." The bloodlust still curdled at the base of Lightholler's brain. "What exactly did you have in mind, Darren?"

IV

Morgan could still picture their faces. Doc and Malcolm openly appalled; their expressions conceding his hopes, but seemingly unable to forgive his intentions. Lightholler offering an oddly impassive smile.

He'd told them that he simply had no choice in the matter.

When the major reached for his own coat, there'd been mutinous protest. He'd turned matter-of-factly to Doc, saying, "We'll be back, with or without him, in two hours. Martin will stand watch."

Malcolm had said, "Don't go out there," but there'd been no force behind the words. As if the deed itself was an accomplished fact.

"We leave in just under three," was Doc's last cold pronouncement. "With or without you."

They stood on 59th with the crumbling wall of the park behind them. A light drizzle pattered the street.

"First thing I want to do is slap some sense into Morgan." The words were out before Morgan realised their import.

Kennedy gazed at him, saying nothing.

Morgan hesitated before continuing. He found it difficult to curb his anticipation. "I know," he said, "the plan is to stay out of sight."

Kennedy fixed him with a cheerless look. "There is no plan, Darren."

They were both similarly garbed; heavy coats concealing their stained uniforms. The tilted brims of fedoras covered fugitive brows. Morgan felt the bulk of the pistol, an awkward lump, in his armpit.

The occasional car slid up 59th. A Japanese couple, pushing a baby carriage, scurried past. Morgan found himself tipping his hat.

It felt like the weekend.

Kennedy stepped into the street. Morgan, surprised, hurried after him.

A blue Yamamoto braked to a halt before the major's stern figure. Kennedy walked around to the driver's seat.

"What day is it today?"

The driver, a middle-aged man with hawkish features, peered curiously back at Kennedy. "Sunday." His tone held the indulgence one might offer a slow learner.

Kennedy leaned into the vehicle. "And the time?"

The driver, more alarmed, said, "It's just after ten." He started to wind up the window.

"Wallet and keys." Kennedy inserted his Mauser into the remaining small gap. "Now."

The driver was fumbling for his effects.

Kennedy turned to Morgan, who was struggling with his own gun.

"Leave that," Kennedy growled. "He's at Kobe's."

Kennedy muscled the driver out of his car and examined the licence. He handed the pistol to Morgan and withdrew five sturdy bars of gold from a pouch at his waist. He handed them over to the terrified man. Casting the Yamamoto an appraising glance, he said, "Next time, buy American."

Kennedy drove. Morgan felt sick. His hands shook, he needed to go to the bathroom. Strange wheels were in motion. "What are we going to do?"

"I don't know."

V

Lightholler ran down Second Avenue. The rain, heavier now, had cleared the street.

He'd donned a coat and some equipment and left Malcolm, Doc and Shine at the carapace. They couldn't have stopped him if they'd tried. Somewhere out there, three grey men in grey suits were driving him to Queens, to a dark appointment with the dread Agent Cooper. Somewhere out there, a killer, cold and heartless, lurked in shadows.

He was looking for a Hotspur with one headlight.

He was looking for answers to a question that everyone else had forgotten.

He was looking to meet his saviour.

Kennedy figured they had a ten-minute window. That was a rough estimate of the time it would take Hardas to complete the journey from Kobe's to the Lone Star on foot.

It was hard to keep his thoughts lucid. He found himself considering the disposition of his men and had to remind himself that his ghost dancers were nine days and many miles behind … ahead … one or the other...

When had he last slept?

The windshield wipers beat an inviting rhythm before his exhausted eyes.

They passed Stuyvesant Square and he was already scanning the streets, looking to see how much detail he could distinguish through the driving rain. Damp lanterns, unlit and forlorn, dangled from the telephone lines, announcing their arrival in Osakatown. Then it was 12th Street and Kobe's was coming up on the right.

I'm in the desert, dying.

He turned on to 12th.

I'm in the Lone Star, waiting for Lightholler.

Morgan, beside him, was hunched forwards and leaning on the dashboard. They rolled towards Third Avenue slowly, windows down, the rain a refreshing tingle against his face.

A carriage horse stamped on the corner opposite Kobe's joint. The windows, veiled beneath a wide awning, reflected the dreary street darkly. Kennedy pulled up beside a phone booth and peered into the storefront.

"He's not in there."

Morgan said, "He might be further back inside."

"Never." Kennedy slipped the Yamamoto into first gear. "He'd be watching the street."

They turned down Third and doubled back along 11th Street. A white Ford was parked opposite the squalid rear entrance to Kobe's. It had two occupants. The street was otherwise empty.

"Which way would he have gone?" Morgan's voice had a hysterical edge to it.

"Best bet is to make for the Lone Star. Catch him before he goes in."

"What if he's already there?"

"Then it's over."

Morgan gave him a pleading look.

"For God's sake, Darren..." Kennedy was studying the street. "The Lone Star was full of people that day. How do you think *we*—not to mention everyone else in there—are going to handle our arrival?"

"Who *gives* a shit? That's not our problem," Morgan replied. "The question is, how badly do you want him back?"

Kennedy gave the rear-view a swift glance. He tried to imagine the confrontation.

The Lone Star was six blocks away. He floored it and dodged through sparse traffic. The rain-swept streets were barren. Just over a block away he spied a figure closing in on the café's entrance. Hardas.

A white Ford pulled in ahead of him, sending a spray of muddied water onto the windshield. He slammed the horn.

Morgan was already on the street and running.

The white Ford.

Kennedy was out of the car.

Two grey suits spilled out of the Ford. Bureau agents.

Morgan was halfway down the block.

The agents broke into a run.

Hardas gained the café's entrance and was lost from sight.

Kennedy called out to Morgan, who skidded to a halt and turned back to face him, his expression lost in the rain. The agents were almost upon him. Probably figured they'd deal with Hardas and the others after taking him down. That was Cooper's crew for you. That was Wetworks.

There'd be no confrontation in the Lone Star. No paradox to deal with. Kennedy had the Mauser in his hand. He drew a bead. He felt sickened. He pictured Patricia and told himself, *I have to remember to drop the piece when I'm done here.*

He squeezed the trigger.

The lights were out. The tunnel stank of automobile fumes and horse manure. Wet tyre tracks, lit by the bright cones of passing headlights, left runes on the asphalt.

Lightholler raised the collar of his coat against the cold and fastened his air filter mask. He tasted sand and felt his face twist into a peculiar smile.

He stood behind a pylon and waited.

Kennedy and Morgan were on their way to Kobe's to rescue Hardas. They were also waiting for him at the Lone Star.

He stood in the shadowed twilight of a tunnel.

He sat squeezed in the back of a Hotspur.

He was due back at the carapace.

This dark knowledge he pursued was insane.

He turned to leave, and had gone twenty yards when a red light, somewhere overhead, began to flash, casting the tunnel in hellish hues of scarlet. He looked back to gaze down the vacant, shit-strewn lane of aristocrats. In the distance, the single headlight of a white Hotspur bobbed into view.

He pulled up behind a pylon, his heart in his mouth. The last thing he needed was to be seen by the guard or his younger, foolish self, for that matter.

The Hotspur slowed down. He tried to remember how it had felt. The fear, the impotence of it all. That vague spark of hope when they were slowing down. Agent Collins would have his cash out.

Where was his saviour?

The Hotspur rolled to a halt.

This dark knowledge...

Lightholler stepped out into the beam of its headlight.

VI

Kennedy swung the Yamamoto onto Lafayette and hooked left onto Bond. He took another left at the Bowery and then cut back along 14th. No one was following.

Morgan said, “You left the gun?”

“Of course I left the gun. How the hell else is Patricia going to think I was framed.”

“How long do we have?”

“Three-quarters of an hour.” He tossed Morgan a look. “We’ll make it.”

The rain fell in sheets. One of the sedan’s wiper blades was faulty. It scraped its remorse on the scored windshield.

He turned up Fifth Avenue. It was a straight run to the park from here.

“Are you okay, Major?”

“I think so.”

They covered the next few blocks in silence. Morgan fiddled with the radio briefly. He strummed the dash.

“What do you think would have happened if we’d walked on in there?”

“Let’s not play that game, Darren.”

“You think Hardas would have come with us?”

Hardas’s loss was a yawning pit in his gut. This wasn’t helping.

Kennedy said, “There might have been more agents in the area. They were Wetworks. We’d be in body bags right about now.”

“I’m just saying, what do you think would have happened? Would Hardas have come with us?”

All Morgan needed was the right answer.

“I think so,” Kennedy replied. “I just don’t know how I could have left any of them behind."

Morgan nodded dolefully.

"Except for you, of course."

"Huh?" Morgan was examining his face.

Kennedy permitted a curl at the edge of his lips.

"Come to think of it," Morgan said, "two of you is more than I could handle."

Kennedy laughed outright. The park appeared ahead.

"I'm sorry, Darren. About Hardas."

"I know."

They left the sedan on 58th and walked the block to the park. They scaled the brittle brickwork and began working their way through the undergrowth to the glade.

"What are you going to tell Patricia?"

"You saw the look on her face when we were leaving." Kennedy slowed his steps. "I think she already knew."

"Does this mean we're going to fail?" Morgan asked.

"If there's anything the last few days have taught me, it's this." Kennedy reached over and squeezed Morgan's shoulder. "*Nothing* is set in stone."

They pressed on through thickening brushwood. Kennedy, somehow attuned, felt the carapace's presence before sighting its alien bulk crouched amid the dripping green. Patricia and Shine sat on a spread of canvas beneath its squat carriage. Doc was examining one of the struts. Kennedy could see that the surface of the machine was scorched black in places, perhaps caught in the backwash of Lightholler's rocket-launcher.

It was fifteen minutes till extraction.

Malcolm gazed up at him with mournful eyes. "Are you okay, Joseph?"

Kennedy nodded. "You aren't surprised?"

She blinked slowly. "No."

He couldn't repress the next question. It left him bare and raw. "Do you hate me?"

She shook her head but her lips were pursed in anguish.

He cast about the gathering, adrift. "Where's Lightholler?"

Malcolm said, "Think about it."

"Jesus *Christ*."

"What?" Morgan swept the group with his eyes. "Oh, crap—the tunnel."

"Why would he want to go back there?" Shine asked.

"To find the shooter," Morgan said. "To see who intervened."

"Don't you get it?" Kennedy spun on him. "He *is* the shooter."

"I think I've heard enough."

Someone was crashing through the bushes.

"John?" Kennedy turned, trying to form the words of consolation. He stepped towards the trees.

"No, not John." The figure gripped two Dillingers in his gloved hands. He tilted his head back to reveal narrowed eyes beneath the brim of his rain-soaked fedora. His delicate features, otherwise composed, might have brought to mind a painter or a musician. He stepped into the sward.

"Fancy meeting you here, Agent Malcolm."

She hissed her reply.

He looked to Kennedy and said, "Don't even think about it."

Kennedy's Mauser lay on the streets of Osakatown. He let his hands fall to his sides.

"All of you. I want you over there." He indicated a clearing to one side of the carapace.

They moved like the dead. He eyed the carapace and said, "Cute. What does it do?" He stepped closer and said, "Oh, sweet Jesus." His eyes flicked from Kennedy to the carapace and back. "You sneaky little shit."

Kennedy couldn't muster a reply.

"Webster wanted it dry, but what you just pulled in Osakatown wrote me a blank cheque, Major Kennedy."

Kennedy edged towards Malcolm.

"Any way you like it, lovebirds."

The Dillingers barked twice.

Shine toppled to the ground.

"So much for the scariest man in New York." He turned back to Kennedy. "That was the best you had to offer?"

"Yes." Kennedy was smiling now.

"What's so fucking funny?"

"You have a knife blade sticking out of your chest."

Cooper glanced down at the sliver of metal embedded between his ribs. "Fuck."

He glanced across the clearing. An empty handle sat in Shine's lifeless hand. "Fuck."

He coughed up blood, staggered forwards and said to Kennedy,

"You're coming with me."

Kennedy was hurled to the ground by the blast, his chest a searing explosion of agony. He raised his head from the muck to eye his killer.

"You're coming with me." The assassin dropped to his knees as if relishing this final exchange. There was another blast and he pitched forwards into the mud.

Lightholler stood behind him.

"You took a shot to the chest, Joseph. I'm hoping that blue shirt of yours lived up to its name."

Kennedy clutched at his chest. The armour had held. He felt the puckered gap where the material had torn. The skin below was a raised, mottled area of darkest blue.

He turned to look at Shine. He looked away.

Lightholler rolled the Confederate's body over with his toe. It made sucking movements as the mud relinquished its hold. "Who's this?" he asked. He'd pocketed the Mauser and stood with his arms folded over his stomach, as if suddenly cold.

"That," Patricia spat hatefully, "was Agent Cooper."

"Strange. I had an appointment with him tonight in Queens."

Kennedy gaped at him with wonder.

"I've put Lightholler in a cab. He should be catching up with you at the Lone Star any time now." Lightholler coughed. Blood spilled between his lips. "I told him he's a marked man."

Kennedy's wonder turned to horror. He stumbled towards Lightholler.

"Never occurred to me," Lightholler rasped, "that one of those agents might have got off a lucky shot." His hands parted, revealing a darker stain on his shirt. "The prairie might be big and wild, but that tunnel didn't leave me much room to manoeuvre." He reached for Kennedy. His hands groped at the torn blue armour. "Wish to hell I was still wearing mine."

He went slack in Kennedy's arms.

VII
Insertion

The screen was a patina of burnished green and bronze.

Shine was dead. Lightholler was fading fast. Kennedy turned to face Malcolm with empty eyes. She placed her hand on Lightholler's wrist. She looked back at him, shaking her head.

"Doc?"

Gershon was making some adjustments on his keyboard. His reply was laced with grief. "Give me a minute. If I don't stabilise our insertion, no one is going anywhere." He typed rapidly as he spoke. "Get him out of the chair. Lay him flat. Darren, get my medi-pack out."

They all scurried about the cabin, as if haste might serve as a cure.

Malcolm eased Lightholler out of the chair. He slid to the floor heavily. A sticky pool of blood had formed beneath his seat. Morgan had the pack open. They emptied it hurriedly, littering the floor with rolls of bandages and syringe sets. Kennedy, out of his seat, cradled Lightholler's head.

Doc, at his console, grunted his frustration.

Lightholler's eyes opened. He said, "Are we in the desert?"

Morgan, bleak, replied, "Almost, John. Why?"

"'Cause I'm fucking freezing." Lightholler let out a blood-flecked chuckle. He looked up at Kennedy's eyes, which were dark beneath quivering lids. "Whole time I was running around with you I was dying."

"You're not dying," Kennedy said.

Lightholler winced. "I'm so fucking cold."

"*Doc.*"

He was at their side. "Major," he spoke through gritted teeth, "we have to get out of here right now. I can't get a decent fix. The carapace is going to slingshot out of here, and I can't stop it."

"Slingshot where?" Kennedy's gaze was fixed on Lightholler.

"Nowhere we'll find." His voice dropped. "And not in any condition we'll recognise."

"Are we here?" Morgan asked.

"Briefly." Doc's eyes flitted from Lightholler to Kennedy, then he was up. "We have to move *now*." He had the hatch open and was already flinging their bags onto the sand below.

Kennedy said, "Doc, take his feet. Morgan and I can support his shoulders."

"No." Lightholler struggled weakly in their grip.

Kennedy repositioned himself, grabbing his armpits.

"No," Lightholler protested weakly. "You're not burying me in the desert with Martin." He looked up, pleading with Kennedy. His eyes searched for Doc. "Please."

Doc eyed the readout. The screen beyond showed rolling dunes, crowned by the now terrible aspect of Red Rock itself. He said, "Ninety seconds."

Lightholler reached out to touch Malcolm's arm. His fluttering fingers were ice. "It's okay," he told her. "It doesn't hurt."

Kennedy lurched with Lightholler in his arms, making for the hatch.

Lightholler's hand fell away from her. His voice was a sigh. "It's 1911. No one can help me here. *Go*."

"Sixty seconds."

Kennedy's face was a contorted knot.

"Get my ship to safe harbour, Joseph."

"He doesn't want to be here," Doc said. "He doesn't want to rest here."

Kennedy turned to Morgan. "You heard the man. Help Doc with Martin."

Morgan reached out, touching Lightholler's arm.

Lightholler's face rippled a weak smile.

Doc mumbled something under his breath. Lightholler nodded back feebly. Then Doc helped Morgan shift Shine's body out of the hatch.

Kennedy leaned close now. "I can carry you. Across the fucking desert if needs be."

"There's a cigarette in my pocket. Pop it in my mouth and get the fuck out of here."

Kennedy fumbled with the flap before retrieving the cigarette. He slipped it between Lightholler's pale lips and lit the tip.

Lightholler drew a shallow breath. He smiled and looked up at Kennedy. "You still here?"

Kennedy ran a hand over the stubble of Lightholler's head. "God speed you, John."

Lightholler nodded, still smiling.

Kennedy drew Patricia to the hatch's mouth. Hands reached up from below, guiding her down to the soft sand. They all stood up, staring at the murky underbelly of the carapace. Kennedy landed on the ground beside them. Soft plates of fused sand cracked beneath his feet.

The hatch closed. Doc was leading them away, back from the machine's struts.

Something gathered beneath the carapace. The struts became translucent. It floated on a cushion of swirling sand as all around them a sudden wind rose. Licks of ruby-tinged flame danced beneath the machine. Vapours, twining where the struts had stood, were tangible moments of time laid bare. He was sure of it. Kennedy took a step towards the machine.

The roaring gust climaxed in a great implosion, as if nature itself sought recompense for this outrageous intrusion. Then the carapace was gone.

Her hand reached out and found his. He returned her gentle squeeze. No one said a word.

VIII

March 11, 1911
Red Rock, Nevada

They buried Shine beside Gershon's fresh grave.

They made camp on the far side of the rock, well away from the burial site. Wells' footprints, at least three days old by Kennedy's reckoning, were a faint trace that died two miles out of the camp, where they'd struck stone.

The sun was waning beyond distant purple-topped hills.

Morgan laid out the meal. There were slices of cold meat, crumbling rolls of bread and a container of vegetables. He reached for the container, removed the tomatoes and started to slice them. He cored out the stem and applied the blade to the centre, dividing the tomato first before working from the edges. He bit his lower lip. A cool breeze swept the sands.

"I keep thinking I'm going to wake up."

"I keep *wishing* I would," Doc replied.

"Hell of a thing." Morgan grabbed another tomato. He fashioned a windbreak, using the container, to keep the sand off the slices.

Doc said, "I couldn't hold the carapace in place."

"You got us here."

"We missed Wells."

"We'll take him on the boat."

"Without Lightholler?"

"We might find him before then," Morgan offered. "She doesn't sail for a year."

"Without Shine? Needle in a fucking haystack."

"We have the journal. We know where he goes."

"He hasn't written yet. What if things play out differently?" Doc was staring beyond the rock.

"That's not you buried out there," Morgan said softly.

"I know."

"And maybe Martin gets another chance in this world."

"Or maybe he ain't born at all." Doc caught Morgan's expression. "Who knows?"

"Hell of a thing."

IX

"Do you prefer sunrise or sunset?"

Kennedy held the middle distance in his vacant eyes. He mightn't have heard her.

They sat closer now, almost touching. A chill had taken the air, seeming to issue from the desert floor below them rather than the darkening skies above.

After a while he said, "You've asked me that before, Patricia."

"I know. I remember. Things change."

"What did Tecumseh say to you? Why did you decide to come?"

She recalled the medicine man's pronouncement. *Your sense of being here before will fade.*

"Everyone saw something different in that thing," she replied. "You knew that, didn't you."

Kennedy nodded.

"Tecumseh told me that for some reason, I'd shared the same experience as some of the ghost dancers."

"Does that bother you?" His question was distant but not indifferent.

"Not for the reasons you might have suspected."

His smile flitted across his face, like it had business elsewhere.

"This is your last chance," she said. She realised she might have been talking about any number of things.

"I know that." His reply suggested a similar understanding, but she was pretty sure he was missing the point.

"Joseph, you've done this before. You've … been here before."

"Down this road? I'm tired, Patricia, so very tired."

"You've sat here before."

He turned to her now, his face wounded beyond any physical injury.

"Sometimes Lightholler is with you, sometimes it's Hardas. Once, I think, Tecumseh. That's what he told me anyway."

He was staring.

"This is my first time. You always left me back there."

"How many times?" His words were breathed rather than uttered. "How many times have I done this?"

"You can't measure something like this. It's too big." She grappled with the concepts. "Our world, our reality, has swung round and round in this loop, back and forth, bouncing between you and Wells. He sends it skewing off kilter, you make it right again, and then he bounces on back. Over and over and over. He's not the problem, Joseph, you *both* are, and Tecumseh believes that reality won't tolerate another joyride."

"But you're here now," he said. He spoke like a child.

"I'm the messenger." She reached out to touch his cold face.

He kept still, letting her hand complete the caress.

"Is it because I forget everything?" he asked. "Like Wells? Is that why I get it wrong?"

"I don't know."

"I'll keep a journal myself. I won't forget any of them. Martin, John, David." His look was intense. A fire had returned to those damaged eyes.

She said nothing.

"I like this part of the day," he said after a time. "The sky changing colour with each passing moment. It's all just fluid. Look up, look away, look up again and it's a whole new world."

She brought her lips to his and imparted a soft kiss. He looked confused. She ran a hand through the thick knots of his hair and said, "That's a sunset, Joseph."

DEATH BY WATER

I

April 10, 1912, 1300 hours
RMS Titanic, out of Southampton

"Patricia will be alright, Joseph. It'll only be a couple of weeks."

"I know," Kennedy replied. "I've booked return passage from New York. We plan on staying in London for a while when this is over."

London was grey, cold and dirty. More like the squalid descendant of the city Morgan had known, rather than its ancestor. He nodded in what he hoped was a heartening manner.

Kennedy was no longer paying attention anyway. He was already out of his chair and pacing. Passing the porthole, he tossed an appraising glance at the white froth of the Channel's waters. Three hours would bring them to Cherbourg. They'd make Queenstown by tomorrow morning. After that, it was all open seas and it looked like he was already counting the hours.

"That was Wells, wasn't it?" Doc said. He'd removed his necktie and collar and wore his shirt open, but still looked ill at ease. He squirmed in his chair, finding no comfort in its plush grandeur.

Kennedy said, "I'm pretty sure of it."

"He walked straight past us."

"What did you want me to do, Dean?" Kennedy asked. "Shove him overboard?"

They'd taken to abandoning the titles and ranks they'd been so familiar with. Morgan was still coming to grips with the false intimacy that step entailed. Standing idly by as Wells had boarded ship had been a good deal more difficult. A year's interaction with this era had affected them all.

Their non-intervention pact, designed to avoid causing the *smallest* ripple in their contact with the world, had left them handicapped.

Diminished. Left to each other's company, they'd managed to retain strong memories of the world they'd left behind, but the price had been their friendships. Too many secrets had been shared, too much darkness revealed. Their closeness had conceived something worse than the contempt of familiarity. Looking into each other, they'd found themselves.

Morgan was still able to feel some sympathy for the man who'd brought him here. Poor Joseph. He gave Patricia and Kennedy two months at the most. After that, they'd be at each other's throats.

"My gut told me to stab him there and then," Doc said.

"That's why we're listening to our heads," Kennedy said. "Whatever happens out here happens at sea. Whatever happens only takes place after we're sure Wells hasn't already acted."

"You may be comfortable with this, Joseph," Doc replied, "but I'm having a hard time playing it by ear. He's not on any passenger list."

"He isn't the only voyager travelling under an assumed name."

Lightholler's absence had left a greater void than Morgan could have imagined. Without him there'd be no storming of the bridge. No attempt to subvert the *Titanic*'s course, nor deal with the actions of her senior crew. Their best course had confined them to locating Wells before he boarded ship.

They'd failed.

His trail ran cold in Nevada. The manuscript, more preoccupied with the order of his thoughts than the details of his journey, was of little use. They'd spent weeks scouring the frontier towns, their investigation stymied by the closed faces of a people wary of strangers asking too many questions.

In New York, they'd checked the hotels from Times Square to the Bowery. Combed the beaches from Brooklyn to the Jersey shore. They held vigil at Coney Island on the day Wells had devoted to memorialising Gershon and he'd passed them unseen, a ghost moving through the new century.

Morgan thought out loud. "It's like he knew we were here. Like he was *expecting* us. From the time he arrived at the pier, he made sure there were people around him."

"Cagey fuck," Doc said. His task of winning Wells over was going to be a Herculean effort. He'd exchanged his Hippocratic oath for one of vengeance, taking Kennedy's vitriol to new heights.

"Can you blame him?" Kennedy asked.

Doc's scowl was his reply.

"He's in first or second class," Kennedy continued. "We know he never signed on as crew, that he ingratiated himself with the ship's elite, and that he had the freedom of the ship. We'll find him. We brace him right after we leave Queenstown."

He looked over at Morgan. "You're being quiet."

Morgan said, "I'm thinking."

II

April 10, 1912, 1640 hours
RMS Titanic, Cherbourg

Kennedy stood on the forecastle. The *Nomadic* and *Traffic*, two purpose-built White Star tenders, had completed their exchange. Twenty-two passengers had made the ship their cross-channel ferry. Many more had come aboard.

The tenders bobbed below, toys at the *Titanic*'s hem. He followed the pale luminescence of their wash to the darkened Normandy coast. The fortifications of Cherbourg were glittering gems set in ebony.

Couples roamed the deck, savouring a first night at sea. He watched them. The women in their gloves and long coats. Their hats trailing long scarfs, wrapped close against the cold. Their faces concealed, harem-like, from his curious eyes.

Patricia would be back at the hotel by now. Would she be sitting by the fire, reading? Perhaps by the window, looking out past the gaslights at this night?

Would she forgive him?

Up until the last minute she'd insisted on sailing with them, going so far as to purchase her own ticket. The arguments she'd offered were all sound and delivered with her usual flair for reason. He'd evaded each one of them, saying, 'You were never here, Patricia. You told me so yourself. Stay in London. Be safe.' Her farewell kiss had been a chill waft against his cheek, far colder than the breeze that now played upon the deck. Her face, lifted up to his, had borne the thinnest scar.

Their physical wounds had mostly healed. They needed no journals. The permanent lines that etched their bodies were the caustic reminders of crueller days. Hardas was dead. Shine was dead. Lightholler was lost to them.

A man entered the deck alone. He wore a hat over thick black hair. His skin was unusually pale, even for this climate. He wore no gloves. Kennedy nodded to him without knowing why. Wells nodded back, a cursory, veiled gesture.

What seeds had the doctor already planted?

Kill him now and dispose of the body. Would the disaster be staunched?

Leave the body to be found. The cruise would almost certainly be delayed, but what repercussions might follow?

There was an abrupt whirring, the clank of metal links against metal. He started at the unexpected sound. Spun suddenly, looking for the telltale tongues of flame erupting from a Dragon tank.

He felt a hand on his shoulder. "Just the windlass, friend. Just the anchor being drawn."

For the shortest moment he believed that everything had been illusion. A last boon, granted by his dying brain in the desert. He turned with the greatest relief.

Wells said, "Are you alright?"

Kennedy nodded.

"First time out, huh?"

The man was only inches away from him. The deck, quite empty now. Kennedy nodded.

"You'll get used to it."

Bells pealed from the bridge, ordering steam, and three sharp whistles issued from above.

Wells was already walking away. Two crewmen, crossing past one of the capstans, momentarily obscured Kennedy's view. By the time they'd passed, he was lost to sight.

Kennedy, astonished, reconsidered his options.

III

"So, how does it compare?"

Doc's question, coolly delivered, reflected the methodical mind at work. It allowed no space for the opulence of their environs.

Morgan had led him on a brief tour. They'd explored the first-class reception and saloon; the smoking room, panelled in finest mahogany and inlaid with mother-of-pearl. They visited the lounge where they discovered a realm of green velvet and polished oak. Desiring no food, they'd bypassed the restaurant to end up in the reading room. A marble fireplace, unlit, took up the far wall. Deep soft chairs nestled in the old rose hue of the rich carpet.

Morgan said, "The truth of it is that this seems less real."

"They used the same materials on Lightholler's boat, though, didn't they?"

"Except for the lower decks."

Doc let out a hollow laugh.

A curtained window looked out to sea. They might have been in any parlour save for the view of dark ocean set against darker skies. The *Titanic* ploughed her course with steady grace.

Morgan continued. "I had a right to be on that ship."

"You paid passage for this one," Doc replied.

"I'm not saying that I'm not supposed to be here. Just that I don't belong."

Doc's smile was rapier thin and just as deadly. "When was the last time you felt like you belonged anywhere?"

Why don't you go ahead and tell him?

Morgan ignored the voice. A year in the company of Hardas's spectre had made him no more comfortable with the phenomenon. So strange that while he could no longer picture the commander's face, his voice still rang true. Hardas wouldn't be cooling his heels in any reading room. He'd have his hands around the good doctor's neck right about now.

"What's so funny?"

Morgan's grin broadened and he said, "I just can't believe we're here."

Doc nodded slowly.

"We don't need to kill him, you know," Morgan added, after a while.

"I know that." Doc's reply was even. "Thing is, you didn't need to see it, night after night. Month after month."

"That wasn't you. You've said so yourself often enough. That wasn't your grave."

"Saying is one thing, Darren. Believing is very much another. I don't care to see another death, not anyone's, but I care *less* to see this old dame go under, or the world that follows."

There was a movement at the doorway. Two couples in evening wear swept into the room. The women took seats at a table by one of the windows, and immediately drew writing implements out of a cloth carry-all. The men, positioning themselves by a vase, fell into a conversation. They looked too amicable for Morgan's liking.

It was time to move on.

They met up with Kennedy on the first-class promenade. A wind had risen—almost a gale. It rattled lightly against the enclosing glass of the covered deck. Kennedy led them down to their cabin in silence.

IV

April 11, 1912, 1135 hours
RMS Titanic, Queenstown

They mounted the boat deck soon after breakfast. Morgan, having heard that they were entering St Georges Channel, insisted that they view the arrival. He'd boarded Lightholler's ship at Queenstown for the centenary cruise.

Today's dawn had been clear. The ship described a gentle arc as they approached the Daunt Light Vessel perched outside the harbour. Stopping to take on a pilot, they continued past the opening at Roches Point. It was just shy of midday. A three-master was slowly pulling past them. Riding light, it rolled dramatically in the North Atlantic swell while the *Titanic* registered the waves with only the slightest bob.

They dropped anchor two miles off the coast while two more tenders ferried over the last of the passengers. A lively tune, played on Irish pipes, travelled across the water.

Wells was nowhere to be seen.

A gentleman standing to one side of Kennedy's group was observing the new arrivals closely. These passengers, primarily steerage, were being conducted along the third-class promenade. He said, "At least this lot speaks English."

Kennedy produced his darkest smile and the man moved away.

Catching Morgan's look he asked, "I'm supposed to agree with him?"

Morgan muttered, "You're supposed to fit in." He doffed his hat at the departing man.

"This isn't so different from the place we left," Kennedy growled.

"You can resume your eccentricities when we reach New York." There was gentle laughter behind Morgan's chastisement.

"I saw Wells last night."

Doc and Morgan eyed him intently.

"He was out here, on the forecastle deck. As far away from me as you are now."

"Why didn't you say anything earlier?" Doc asked.

"I don't know."

"What happened?"

"Nothing, Darren."

"Did you talk?"

"No. There were crewmen milling about."

They fell silent. The sound of the anchor being drawn up was more indistinct from this height. It evoked no fears or memory save for Wells' face, cloaked in shadow.

The mighty ship whistled its departure and then turned once more past Roches Point. The southern Irish coast, a postcard of low hills and verdant fields, slipped to starboard. Long years ago his ancestors had worked similar fields not too far east of here, in Wexford, until driven away by famine. He'd visited the county once, when touring the British dominions. Now as then, nothing called to him from those gentle slopes.

Someone below decks played "Erin's Lament" on the pipes, but it was Morgan's nudging invitation that summoned him away from the railing to lunch. The selection was varied, their choices spartan. Wells didn't show.

"He's keeping to his quarters," Doc suggested at one point. "That, or going on about his work."

"We'll comb the ship then."

They separated after the meal. He sent Morgan down to F deck to search the squash court, pool and Turkish baths. Doc took D, checking the first- and second-class dining saloons as well as first-class reception. Kennedy had a coffee in the Café Parisien. He cased the Grand Staircase, the first-class lounge and the smoking room, then perused a bookcase in the library and spent a brief time in the gymnasium. Mostly he kept to the deck, doing a round of the promenades.

Families sat together, the women in clusters of deckchairs with blankets drawn to their waists, or strolling arm in arm with their partners. Men stood smoking by the lifeboat davits while children played at cards or dominoes or dashed across the deck in their sport.

Truly, Wells had gone to ground.

Kennedy kept sight of the vanishing Irish shore till sunset.

V

April 11, 1912, 2000 hours
RMS Titanic, out of Queenstown

They took their dinner in the saloon. Their table offered an excellent view of proceedings. At table six, Captain Smith entertained the Astors and the Wideners. Ebullient conversation rose and fell with the arrival of each sumptuous course.

Morgan searched the room, logging the attendees and their seating arrangements. There was Thomas Andrews, the ship's builder, and there was William Stead, editor of the *Review of Reviews*. Sometime mystic and author, he'd penned a novel in 1892 titled *From the Old World to the New*. Interestingly, it described the loss of an ocean liner at sea; interestingly, she'd struck an iceberg in the North Atlantic.

He spied the Carters and the Thayers. The Strauses and Bruce Ismay, chairman of the White Star Line. Benjamin Guggenheim was in the company of a young woman who could only be Madame Aubert, his latest mistress. *Bully for him*, Morgan thought.

This inventory of the dead only served to reinforce his feelings of detachment. The year of 1912 had known a number of disasters. The *Príncipe de Asturias*, sailing out from Spain, was lost with five hundred hands. Towards the year's end, the *Kiche Maru*, caught in a storm off the coast of Japan, would disappear with a thousand souls. Come August, typhoons would batter the coasts of China, causing devastation on a previously unseen scale. The death count would exceed fifty thousand.

What was so unutterably important about *this* ship then?

He cast back to the question he'd posed to Lightholler over a year ago. *What shapes history, Captain? Events or personalities?*

As if on cue, Colonel Astor turned from his seat to regard Morgan with cool eyes. He had his hair slicked and parted in the middle. A generous moustache countered the angular severity of his face. Someone muttered a quip and he returned to his meal.

You, Morgan thought. *Scandalised in a new marriage, seeking escape from the spotlight in Europe, and now returning home. You're the only survivor of Wells' list of the damned. You spoke for your dead brethren. The ripples of your agitation swelled to cause a major rift between America and England.* A rift that might have been avoided with the *Titanic*'s safe arrival in New York. Was this the heart of the matter then? A united America and England might have altered the direction of the Great War.

It was impossible to fathom the motives behind Wells' intervention without a clearer understanding of the world he'd known. One thing was certain, however. This ship was the nexus point. He realised that when it came to the muddy conundrum of events versus personalities, one important factor had to be kept in mind. Even the heaviest door may pivot on the smallest of hinges.

He turned to Kennedy, eager to discuss the possibilities surrounding Astor.

Kennedy, silent the entire meal, said, "Gentlemen, I think it's time we took this to the next level."

VI

"I do hope you've been availing yourself of our amenities," the steward said.

"I've taken a tour of the ship, Crawford," Wells replied. "That was more than enough for me."

"Very good, sir. I'm sure you'll have some marvellous adventures to relate when we arrive at New York. At the very least, you'll be able to offer a detailed description of your stateroom."

"I'm not one for long journeys, I'm afraid. I'll be more than pleased if that *is* the highlight of my voyage."

"I take it, then, that you'll be dining here in your cabin again tomorrow. Dinner for one?"

Wells granted a smile. "Perhaps. I'll let you know. I may be dining with a lady friend."

Crawford cocked an eyebrow. "Indeed, sir, here's hoping. Good night, sir." He had the dinner plates balanced evenly on an outstretched hand. He backed out of the cabin with a grin.

Wells poured himself a shot of whisky and downed it. He had his journal open to the last entry. He wondered how he was going to run it.

Sometime in the next two days, Ismay would begin his fruitless quest to break the company's transatlantic crossing record, held by the *Titanic*'s sister ship, the *Olympic*. By nine o'clock Sunday morning, the first ice warning would arrive. Should he approach Andrews in an attempt to avoid the excess speed or wait for that fateful day?

Sunday, April 14, 1912. He wrote the date down. Topped up his glass and drained it. Should he leave it to the lookouts or stand ready by the bridge? The binoculars were in his trunk in the baggage compartment.

He was doodling. He looked down at the sheet and read the name he'd written with a smile. Marie. Underlined, and with exclamation marks. She was attractive in an unusual way. Smart, a little older than he liked. Perhaps a recent widow, which would explain her condition and allow him to entertain any number of short-term possibilities in this era. Significantly, she wasn't on any passenger list he could recall. Dinner for two was becoming an interesting alternative.

He poured himself another measure.

VII

April 12, 1912, 0900 hours

RMS Titanic, North Atlantic

The captain's vessel inspection would take place sometime after ten, if the previous day was anything to go by. It would take in the corridors and public rooms of all the classes. The kitchens, the pantries, saloons and shops would all be toured. The Captain's extensive entourage would include Thomas Andrews, the chief engineer, the pursers, the surgeon, the chief steward and the department heads. Morgan, donning one of Lightholler's uniforms, modified for his build, would have little trouble joining the procession.

Doc, a size too large to be considered for the task, was attired in the livery of a bedroom steward. He had the unenviable mission of searching through the cabins in first and second class. Kennedy, wearing an engineer's uniform, would take the lower decks.

Morgan met up with the captain's staff on the enclosed first-class promenade. Their march took in the majority of the ship, examining and noting the cleanliness and condition of the pristine equipment. Andrews and the captain spoke often; Andrews suggesting that perhaps the wicker furniture on the starboard side be stained a shade of green, or that one of the reading rooms, less popular than expected, would make an excellent stateroom. He appeared to take in every detail, at one point stating that a sirocco fan in the engine room could do with replacing.

Of interest: a fire in bunker ten, one that had started over a week ago while the ship was in Belfast, still raged. Morgan wondered at its significance.

He encountered Doc backing out of a stateroom on B deck. Morgan nodded. Doc shot him a disgruntled look and shook his head. Morgan muttered, "Back to work then, lad."

Making certain that only Morgan could see him, Doc offered a two-fingered salute.

Andrews seemed approachable. He was quite happy to answer enquiries from other members of the assembly. Morgan, catching his attention as they ascended the staircase to A deck, said, "I was supposed to meet up with a Jonathan Wells this afternoon, but he's nowhere to be found. Do you know him?"

"Elusive chap, that one," Andrews said. "One of JP's mob." He touched a finger to his nose and smiled. "Had a brief chat with him this morning." He inspected Morgan's uniform.

"Dawkins, sir." Morgan spoke hastily, giving the name of a crewman known to have signed on but never sailed upon the ship. "Transferred over from the *Olympic*."

"Well, Dawkins, he booked passage under the name of Ryers, for what it's worth. C deck. Keeps to himself mostly. American, like yourself." Andrews seemed to be fishing for information.

Morgan thanked him. Before Andrews could voice a question he was interrupted by a passenger descending the stairs. Morgan slipped back into the crowd. The entourage was dismissed at the entrance to G deck. From here the captain would proceed to the engine rooms with only the chief engineer in attendance.

Morgan doubled back to B. Doc must have been in one of the staterooms or moved on. He checked the passenger list at the purser's office on C deck. Ryers' cabin was down the port-side corridor, across from the barber's shop. From where he stood, he caught a glimpse of the safe, beyond the thick glass window. He stood there for a moment and tried to imagine how it must have looked to Hardas, locked below the icy depths of the Atlantic. He felt a chill and cheered himself with the thought that *this* deck would never see any more water than the daub of a soaped mop.

He went to find Kennedy.

VIII

They met in the smoking room.

Most of the passengers were still finishing their lunches. A few couples idled in the Verandah Café next door. They were left to themselves. The Georgian splendour of the empty chamber dwarfed them. They stood by the fireplace while Kennedy inspected the day's postings. They'd made three-hundred-and-eighty-six miles in the twenty-four hours. Morgan told him that they had lit more boilers overnight. He said that they'd make five-hundred-and-nineteen today and increase the speed to five-forty-six on Saturday.

Doc asked if that would crack the record for the crossing and Morgan told him that the *Mauretania*, a Cunard liner, easily held the record at a pace of twenty-six knots an hour. Kennedy gazed at him, impressed.

Morgan said, "That's why you pay me the big bucks."

Kennedy chuckled briefly at the remark before sobering at his own news. "I had no luck below."

Doc said, "My back's killing me. These guys have packed more luggage for a week's cruise than I've worn in ten years."

Morgan said, "It shows. Did you check out cabin eighty-six on C deck?"

Kennedy started to smile. No wonder Morgan was in good humour.

Doc checked a slip of paper from his wallet. "The steward was in there, name of Crawford. I didn't get a chance to check it out."

Morgan said, "He's our guy."

Kennedy's response was a cold decree. "We take him tonight."

IX

Wells was reading a novel he'd removed from the library on the first day of the voyage. Jerome K Jerome's *Three Men in a Boat*. He leafed carefully through the cut pages to the front. 1889. A first edition. Timeless when he'd first read it as a youth, Jerome's experiences on the Thames were something he could now readily identify with.

He acknowledged Crawford's gentle knock at the door and bade him enter.

The steward smiled as Wells presented the spine of the novel to his enquiring look. He said, "I see you have been keeping yourself amused at least, sir. How was dinner?"

"Fine."

"Our chef hangs on your every word, sir. I'm certain he'll be delighted with your appraisal. I must say that I'm sorry to find you dining alone."

"If you must know, Crawford, I took a turn on the deck earlier. With my friend."

"Indeed? Same time tomorrow?"

"Thank you."

Crawford bowed and left.

Wells went to his valise and removed the journal. Since arriving on the ship he'd made no entry of any consequence. Merely dates and names, a form of shorthand detailing his scattered thoughts. He turned to an earlier entry and wondered at the state of mind of the author. He looked at his wrist. Only a fine seam of raised tissue remained of his attempt at surgery. *Knives*. He snorted at the thought.

He poured himself a glass of whisky, and pledged he would allow himself two tonight. He reached for the ink and a pen, and began sketching, the nib tracing an irregular sigmoid curve. He went over the peaks, making them sharper, and completed the drawing with a flourish.

"Not this time," he murmured.

There was another knock at the door. Without thinking, Wells said, "It's open."

He slid the journal aside, waiting for the ink to dry. He had the whisky to his lips when the door opened. He glanced up and the glass dropped to the carpet with a soft thud.

"*Gershon?*"

"Yes. And no."

The man had a gun in his hand but that was the last thing that Wells noticed. The stranger was a dead ringer for Gershon. Older, heavier, with tinges of grey at the sides of his thick curly hair. The voice was the same.

Wells rose unsteadily from his seat, reaching out to the apparition, already mouthing an apology.

"Don't you take a fucking step."

Wells froze.

Two more men entered the room, flanking the doppelganger. One of them also carried a gun. Unlike the contemporary piece the first man bore, it was a Colt automatic, its barrel extended by the black cylinder of a silencer. The man locked the door behind them and said, "Hello again, friend." It was the person he'd spoken to on the first night, out on the forecastle.

The steward's bell was out of reach, by the bed. All Wells had at his disposal was the pen. He swayed uncertainly. "Who are you?"

Gershon's twin said, "Back up against the porthole. Keep still. Mind you, if you decide to leap outside, I won't be fussed."

Wells backed up as instructed. The other two men approached his desk.

Wells' eyes flitted to the journal and back. "Did *he* send you? Did Jenkins send you?" The accusation was a whisper.

"Didn't I explain to you that Jenkins isn't coming?" The lookalike's voice rose to a pitch of anger that Gershon had never shown. "Didn't I tell you that the night before you buried me?"

"Doc," the second gunman said. His quiet tone was admonishing.

"Jesus Christ. This isn't happening."

The double's gun was aimed firmly at his chest. "Didn't I warn you that your presence in this time changed everything?"

"*Who are you?*"

The second gunman placed the Colt in his coat pocket. His companion reached for the journal, placing his fingertips on the fresh pages. The inked outline of the iceberg smudged beneath his thumb. The second gunman withdrew another manuscript from beneath his coat. It was old, water-damaged; the pages coated in modern plastic. He began to flick through it rapidly. The coating snapped against his fingers. He said, "My version's not smeared."

The other man said, "What does that mean?"

"We need to check both versions for discrepancies."

The other nodded.

Wells thought he was going to faint.

The gunman said, "My name is Joseph Kennedy. This is Darren Morgan. You knew Doctor Gershon."

Wells nodded stupidly. Gershon was dead.

Kennedy said, "It's best you take a seat, Doctor Wells, we really need to talk."

X

They sat around the table with the two journals between them. The clock chimed eleven on the mantle.

Morgan explained that they were the descendants of the world Wells had created. A world consumed by atomic fire.

Wells may have had the hollowed look of the fanatic, but there was nothing of the extremist in him. He sat quietly while Morgan summarised the events that followed the wreck of the *Titanic.*

His history—like any child's primer—focused on the wars, disasters and sweeping social movements that had slashed across the twentieth century; the contest between socialism and monarchy, despotism and freedom. He touched briefly on the advances. Mentioning the stratolites, though, he felt a shudder run through his body, recalling what those great behemoths had wrought. Despite the presence of Doc's gun, cradled in his lap, the occasion exhibited all the civility of a college tutorial.

Kennedy, Doc and Wells remained silent throughout the dissertation.

Kennedy spoke up now, saying, "Why don't you tell us the way things are supposed to be, Doctor Wells, and why you set about changing them?"

Wells had polished off two glasses of whisky during the discourse and his reply was marred by a slight slur. "Joseph Robard Kennedy," he said, trialling the name. "Who was your father?"

"Richard Fitzgerald Kennedy."

"And his father?"

"Joseph Patrick Kennedy."

"Which one?" Wells sounded agitated now.

Kennedy replied, "I know that a John F Kennedy died in your world. In this world. Was he running for president?"

Wells said, "He *was* the president. He was assassinated at Dealey Plaza."

"In 1963?"

Wells nodded.

"That would be my great-uncle."

"I never heard of any Joseph Robard Kennedy in my world," Wells said.

Kennedy said, "My grandfather was John F Kennedy's older brother."

"Ah. Your grandfather was part of a bomber crew. He died childless over Germany during the war. What else would you like to know?"

"He's lying," Gershon said. "I say we just get this over with and kill him now."

Wells said, "It's no lie."

Morgan felt the truth of his words. Kennedy's face, set in despair, mirrored the sentiment.

"How did you find that?" Wells asked. He pointed at the sea-soiled journal without touching it.

"We found it here," Kennedy said. His voice had become a cold monotone. He was cutting to the chase. "Where you left it, in the rotting corpse of this ship."

Morgan watched Doc finger the pistol's grip.

"Why did you do that, Doctor Wells?" Kennedy asked. "Why did you sink the ship and then leave the record of your crime in its belly? Do you make a habit of tempting fate?"

"I sank the ship?" Wells seemed incredulous now.

"This is the *Titanic*," Morgan said. "With a length of eight-hundred-and-eighty-two feet and a displacement of sixty-six thousand tons, she is the grandest creation of mankind to date. Her captain is renowned world-wide. She is described as being virtually unsinkable, yet she strikes an iceberg on her maiden voyage with a loss of two thousand lives. Thing is, she's been visited by a time traveller. A time traveller with an agenda that includes the date of the assassination of the archduke of the Austro–Hungarian empire. Tell me, Doctor, what are we supposed to think? That you came here for a joyride?"

Wells stared at him, aghast.

"As a consequence of your actions, a bitter falling-out between America and England circumvents an alliance which might have won the Great War. The rest is a nightmare."

Kennedy said, "What we'd like to know is how you did it."

"This is a nightmare." Wells' mouth was open, his eyes two pools of dread.

"Frankly, I don't give a shit." Doc raised the pistol.

Kennedy placed a hand on the barrel, guiding it gently away. Morgan wondered if sometime in the afternoon they'd arranged this little game of good cop, bad cop.

"One thing about you is familiar," Wells said to Doc.

Doc eyed him curiously.

"I don't know how or why you got involved in all this, but you're as trapped by Kennedy as you ever were by Jenkins. You were my friend and it breaks my fucking heart, so why don't you just do it. Pull the fucking trigger."

Doc gave Kennedy a look and put the pistol under his coat.

Kennedy turned and said, "How and why, Doctor?"

Wells glanced at the clock. It was eleven-thirty. "In my world, in forty-eight hours and ten minutes, we strike an iceberg. It's a glancing blow along the starboard side. A gash, three hundred feet long, is carved, taking out the first four compartments and the forward boiler room. She takes on fifteen feet of water in the first ten minutes. She's under by two-twenty."

Kennedy and Doc turned to Morgan.

Morgan said, "She strikes at 3 a.m. Monday morning. Port side."

"Is it so unthinkable?" Wells asked. "She was travelling fast through an ice field. There was no moon, no wind, and no fucking binoculars in the crow's nest. The wonder is that she didn't strike anything sooner." He drained the remains of his glass and slammed it on the table. "I'm here to avert all that. If there's any truth to your words, the only thing you can accuse me of is failing at my task."

"What about Sarajevo?" Kennedy asked. "What about your lists?"

"I'm a surgeon, damn it, not a butcher."

Morgan looked at Kennedy. "What do we do now, Major?"

XI

April 13, 1912, 0200 hours
RMS *Titanic*, North Atlantic

Most of the running lights had been turned off for the night. The ship cast a dim glimmer on the black waters. It was after two o'clock in the morning.

If there was anything to Wells' account, two days would see her foundering right about now. He'd outlined the fate of the ship, his story scattered with anecdotes that had a haunting resonance with the tale Kennedy had known. The Strauses leaving together for one final embrace. Ben Guggenheim and his valet standing on the deck in evening wear. Ismay fleeing in an undermanned lifeboat, and Hartley's band playing till the last.

Resigned to his captivity, Wells had finally retired to a bedroom.

Kennedy, Doc and Morgan faced one another across the sitting room.

"What do you make of it?" Kennedy asked softly.

Morgan said, "The journal could be interpreted to support Wells' claim."

Doc spoke for the first time since putting away his gun. "No decent criminal ever views his act as a crime. Take a look around you." His gesture included the cabin and everything beyond. The whole ship was held in his embrace. "She has more lookouts than any other vessel currently at sea. She's built like a brick shit-house. I don't see it playing out that way. I just don't buy it."

"A lot of people won't," Morgan said solemnly. "Even with the last of the lifeboats putting out to sea."

Every passing moment lent more truth to Wells' assertion. Kennedy found it increasingly difficult to reconcile the broken figure of the surgeon with the mastermind his thoughts had crafted from the journal. Had the *Titanic* made it to New York, her arrival would barely rate a postscript to the events preceding the Great War. The sheer wealth of information at Wells' fingertips, the disposition of the ships in the region, the list of passengers, dead or alive, spoke of some great calamity befalling the ship. That, or the entire journal was a tissue of lies, the fabrication of a maniac, hidden behind Wells' dull eyes.

But Wells wasn't Webster. He wasn't Kennedy. His scheme, slapdash and half-formed, would be the reaction to a crisis in progress. It lacked the refinement of the chess master or the statesman. It was the slash of the knife rather than the cool calculation of prevention. And Kennedy had misread it all.

Had he ever been so blind?

Morgan said, "Astor is the problem."

"I was thinking along those lines myself," Kennedy replied. "Let's take Wells at his word for the moment. According to him, none of the lifeboats went down with the ship, and it was the *Carpathia*, rather than the *Californian*, that arrived first. There were more survivors too. Astor's wife makes it, and he isn't around to antagonise the tribunals."

"Where are you going with this, Major?" Doc asked.

"I'm not sure. We need to know what he plans on doing."

"So you believe him?" Morgan asked.

Kennedy nodded slowly.

"We know he hasn't intervened yet," Doc said. "Whatever he plans on doing is just a half-assed measure if it only buys the ship three hours." He looked over at the bedroom entrance. "We just need to keep him holed up here for the next two days and it's a moot point."

"Followed by a mad rush to the lifeboats," Morgan added dully.

"As opposed to?" Kennedy ventured.

"There are *three* of us here now," Morgan said. "Maybe we can get it right this time."

"Getting it right," Kennedy said pointedly, "entails letting history take its course."

Morgan shook his head. "I know what Patricia told you, Joseph, and I appreciate your faith in Tecumseh, but they didn't know that Wells was trying to *save* the ship. We can make a difference here."

"Difference is what condemned our world, Darren. We're not here to judge the form of Wells' intervention. We're here to stop it cold."

"But we're already intervening," Morgan said. "Look at the divergence in the journals."

"I can't explain that. I don't know if it points to our success or failure. But you were happy enough to stop Wells when you thought he was the villain."

"That was when we were trying to save two thousand people, not consign them to the bottom of the Atlantic."

"We're not here to save a ship, Darren. We're here to correct an imbalance. I agree with Doc. We hold Wells under house arrest till midnight of the fourteenth."

"I need to think about this," Morgan said.

Doc said, "I'm just hoping that we read it right all along. I'm hoping we get to joke about this on Monday morning."

Kennedy tried to mask the bleakness in his reply. "Here's your chance to think up some one-liners. You're on first watch." He rose from his seat with a sigh and beckoned to Morgan. They both made for the door. He turned to Doc and said, "Please, try not to shoot him."

XII

The *Titanic* was a catacomb. They crept along the passageway as if heavier steps might set the great ship downwards in its first spiral into the depths. Kennedy ignored Morgan's hushed protests all the way back to the cabin.

Morgan cornered him in the suite. "Joseph, I can't believe that all this has to pass when we have the power to stop it."

"You're thinking like Wells now," Kennedy replied shortly. "We might have the power, but we don't have the right."

"You couldn't have known," Morgan pressed. "None of us did. You were surrounded by conspirators from go to woe. You couldn't have suspected that Wells' motives were any purer than anyone else we'd dealt with."

"This isn't about me, Darren."

"There are women here. Children. Would you consign them to a death sentence? What gives you *that* right?"

Kennedy emptied his pockets. He placed the Colt and the journal on the mantle and removed his coat. "I didn't tell you everything Patricia told me."

Morgan eyed him darkly and said, "Go on."

"We've been here before. Done all this before."

"Done this how?"

"Time and again, we've journeyed back here, over and over, and each time we've stopped him. There are subtle variations, but the consequences remain unchanged."

"How can you know this?"

"Tecumseh knows this. He told Patricia."

"You can't believe that."

"I do. I believe it now more than ever. We stop him. Maybe we kill him, maybe we dissuade him, but each time we get it wrong and reality doubles back on itself. A double-stranded helix, stretched tight between our intrusions. And it's old, Darren, old beyond its years. It won't endure another playback. It's going to give.

"That's the knowledge my ghost dancers died for. Those experiences with the carapace, the ones we dared not share with each other, weren't delusions. They weren't premonitions. They were scraps of memory, drawn from our previous attempts. They were warnings."

"No," Morgan said. "I don't believe you."

"Doc tells me that sometimes he hears Lightholler talking to him. He thinks it's guilt. He thinks he could have saved him in the desert. I haven't the heart to tell him that he's talking to an echo. You see, sometimes Lightholler *is* here with us." Kennedy threw him a penetrating look. "Sometimes it's David. Never Patricia, not till now."

"What does she have to do with this?"

"I don't know. She told me she was the messenger."

"Some fucking message. How are we supposed to get it right?"

"By holding Wells back; by not joining his foolish crusade."

"*Jesus*, Joseph, I don't know if I can just stand back and watch this."

"I get the feeling that's always our problem. You're a historian, Darren. Standing back and watching is what you do best. If I entertain any doubts about your ability to perform that role…" His voice faded to nothing. He began to unbutton his shirt. "I'm turning in. We'll talk about it in the morning." He walked into the bedroom.

Morgan crossed over to the table. A decanter sat by three empty glasses. He hadn't had a drink since arriving in the desert. He poured himself a finger of bourbon, walked over to the mantle and placed it next to the journal. He stared at the Colt, shivering. The night had grown colder.

If they stopped the *Titanic* from sinking, Wells would have no reason to come back here. The Edwardian decline, instead of gasping with the ship, might be preserved a little longer. The world might follow its path to a war that found its causes in the century's birth, but without any of the acrimony between America and England. Was that so bad?

Yet the *Titanic*'s loss—in both worlds—had changed maritime rules forever. Patrols would be established to watch the sea lanes for ice. Wireless communications would be maintained at the highest available standards. Hubris, battered by Nemesis, would herald a new era and there would be a lifeboat for everyone, forever more. Was that worth fifteen hundred souls?

He took the glass and knocked on Kennedy's door. It swung open to reveal him sitting upright on the bed. He had a gun in his hand.

"Is it loaded?" Morgan asked. He glanced down at his glass and added, "'Cause I'm starting to wish that I was."

Kennedy dropped the gun beside him. "I didn't know which way you were going to go."

"Me neither." Morgan entered the room and leaned against the wall. "Patricia will think we failed."

"We'll tell her otherwise," Kennedy replied, "The lifeboats won't be full, we know that. We won't be taking anyone's place." His voice, distant and chill, was empty of promise.

"We're going to need Wells' help once the normal timeline is re-established. My facts won't be worth a damn."

Kennedy nodded thoughtfully.

"I've been fascinated by the *Titanic* for as long as I can remember," Morgan said. "I could never get my head around it. All so important and all so senseless at the same time. It was our first modern fable. A cautionary tale that belonged to everyone. It was our century's fall. Our departure from the Eden of the Industrial Age. Our casting into the wilderness. Boys who'd read about it, seizing newspapers from street vendors, lay buried in mud two years later on the fields of France.

"In 1991, I interviewed some of the *Titanic*'s survivors and members of their families. There was this one woman: she hadn't sailed, but her father and uncle were lost that night. She told me that a few days after the disaster, they'd been seated around the table for breakfast. Her mother had held a newspaper in front of her and said, 'Your father won't be coming home, dears.'

"The survivor list hadn't been printed yet, so the girl had asked, 'How do you know, mother?'" Morgan's mouth was dry. He wet his lips with the bourbon and continued, hoarsely, "Her mother told her, 'This morning's paper says that some children were lost. Your father would never leave a child behind, no matter what happened.'"

Kennedy gazed at him with shining eyes.

Morgan said, "It's strange. Here we are, with complete knowledge of what will happen in two days' time, and we're the ones at a disadvantage."

"How do you figure that?"

"Everyone else aboard will act in accordance with their own sense of pride, or honour, of hope, desire, fear, despair … Some will be lucky, some will be practical. Some will be downright evil. Most will suffer briefly but terribly." Morgan shrugged. "We're trapped by legend. We've entered mythology and it's a strange place. It bears only the smallest resemblance to actual events."

"Meaning?"

"Meaning, you're the natural heir to the Astors and the Guggenheims, the Wideners and the Thayers, Joseph. I don't see you climbing into any lifeboat, empty or otherwise."

XIII

"You came here by misadventure. We came through fire, only to find ourselves facing a fool rather than an enemy. You should have sat quietly somewhere and stuck to your investments. Left the big decisions to the guys who can handle them. Get back in your room, the sight of you sickens me," Gershon hissed.

"I'm here because you asked for my help." Wells' voice was a croaky rasp. "You called me down to the Waste Land."

"That wasn't me, Wells." Gershon's snarl was unfocused. It took in everything. It was aimed at the world.

"Why did Kennedy pick you, of all people?"

Gershon's smile was appalling. "I think I was supposed to elicit some spark of humanity in your soul. I think I was supposed to dissuade you from your path of destruction. I think," he let out a terrible laugh, "I was supposed to become your friend."

"Looks like he read you wrong."

"Nobody's perfect." Gershon stepped towards the porthole. Dawn's wound opened along the horizon. The ocean was flat and calm. "Get back in your room."

Wells retreated to his bedroom and closed the door. Gershon's disdain was a chisel, chipping away at his resolve. He could accept that the ship had sunk in their world. Could imagine how it might have played out. He considered Morgan's sketch of a hundred years gone wrong. The ship might have been lost, but the antiquated ideas of the late 1800s had somehow persevered. Kennedy's world had missed the glancing iceberg of Hitler's Germany and the Holocaust that had ensued. It had missed seven years of the worst bloodshed the world had known; its own conflicts spread thin across the years in disturbing parallels on the fields of Europe, in the jungles of Vietnam and on the bloodied streets of Dallas. Missing the horrors, it had missed the messages. Monarchs ruled vast kingdoms and colonies. No one yearned for the stars that lay beyond the smelter-borne smoke of sprawling cities. No one sought for rights among the disenfranchised. Instead of taking one great leap forwards, Kennedy's world had huddled in the footprints of the previous century. Technology, cowed by the loss of man's grandest venture, had been vaster than the empires, but much too slow.

Stultified, they had stumbled, unready, upon armaments that could shatter worlds, and then proceeded to use them. Kennedy and his men weren't soldiers or agents or missionaries; they were refugees from a dying world.

The only thing you can accuse me of is failing at my task.

He could see how they might have misread his attempt. He could even empathise with their desire to let matters follow their own murky course. He just couldn't accept standing by and letting the disease that was the *Titanic*'s destruction follow its own natural history. Not when he could still intervene.

He glanced out the porthole, plotting escape. It opened onto the hull, offering no practical pathway. There was no chance he could work his way aft to the second-class promenade, and the forwards shelter deck was well beyond reach. Dropping into the ocean, in the hope of being spotted by a lookout, was a less appetising prospect. He looked down at the water. Daybreak's golden gleam made it no more inviting.

He had to get away from Gershon or the early hours of the fifteenth would find him out there, regardless.

The thought of trying to overpower the doppelganger made him sneer. He pictured the two of them squabbling over the pistol. Neither was a man of action. It would end in blood, stupidity and tears.

He stripped the sheets from his bed, knotting the ends. He could leave the fashioned rope dangling out of the window and conceal himself in the wardrobe or under the bed. Gershon's confusion might buy him precious moments. He tested the sheets for strength and the knot unravelled. He tied it with a double hitch. There was barely enough bedding to make it out the window. He needed to rip the curtains from the four-poster bed. He needed to do it quietly.

There was a muted sound from without. He bunched the sheets in a disarray on the bed as Gershon entered the bedroom.

Behind him there was a gentle knock on the cabin door. Gershon cocked an ear and motioned Wells to silence. His face betrayed his anxiety.

The knock was repeated with some insistence. Kennedy wouldn't have bothered with the nicety, it had to be Crawford with his breakfast.

Gershon edged back towards the cabin's entrance. He had his pistol up and close to his chest. There was the rattle of a set of keys being retrieved, the creak of a body leaning up against the door.

"Get rid of him," Gershon mouthed.

Wells remained silent.

Gershon returned his attention to the latch. Wells lunged forwards instinctively.

Gershon turned towards him, pistol raised. He staggered, struck from behind by the cabin door.

Wells caught a glimpse of Crawford, framed in the entrance. He crashed into Gershon's legs, sending him sprawling to the floor. The steward, his tray's contents smeared over his uniform, tottered into the room. Gershon's roar was an incoherent howl of pain and fury over the sound of shattering plates.

Wells gained his feet and burst past Crawford into the passageway.

Cabin doors began opening up and down the corridor. He pushed past an elderly man in a dressing gown and sprinted into the second-class promenade. He raced past startled onlookers, down the aft stairway and through the second-class accommodation, panting along the corridor. The second-class dining saloon was being prepared for breakfast. He tore past bustling stewards to gain the next stairwell, took the stairs in twos and threes, and stumbled onto E deck.

There was no sound of pursuit.

Leaning up against the warm bulkhead of the engine casing, he caught his breath. The walls emitted a steady throb that massaged the knotted muscles of his back.

He couldn't stay here and he couldn't return to his cabin. His options were dwindling rapidly.

There was no approaching Andrews or any other members of the senior crew. Only God knew what explanation Gershon was concocting for Crawford's benefit.

The binoculars were in the baggage compartment on the orlop deck below G. He had thirty hours to get them to one of the lookouts. After that, after they'd negotiated the ice field, he'd return to the society of the ship and see what cards were dealt to him.

He made his way down to Scotland Road.

XIV

Kennedy settled Chief Steward Latimer's concerns by presenting false identification and a contribution to the stewards club. He explained that Mr Wells had swindled a certain American building magnate out of a good deal of money. He and his companions were charged with securing the criminal and bringing him to justice. He apologised for the untowards commotion that had taken place earlier on C deck.

Latimer accepted the details with a show of understanding. It appeared that Wells wasn't the only gambler who'd signed on under another name. Latimer assured Kennedy that while more than one card shark had secured passage on the *Titanic*, hoping to ply his grift, the staff of the White Star Line had everything in good order.

They both agreed that the maiden voyage was hardly the setting for an all-out manhunt. Kennedy and his men would be permitted the run of the ship, but discretion would be greatly appreciated.

Only Crawford—the steward who'd been attending to Wells—seemed unconvinced by the tale. Notwithstanding his subtle display of misgivings, he acquiesced to Latimer's order. Wells' cabin would be sealed off after a thorough search.

They found nothing of interest. A careful examination of the two journals revealed no other difference besides the smudged line drawing of the iceberg. Wells hadn't bothered to make any further entries in Doc's presence, despite having been left with the manuscript.

It was late afternoon. Splitting up again, they scoured the ship. Doc, infuriated and miserable, was assigned the upper decks and first-class accommodations. Morgan took second-class and the crews' quarters along Scotland Road. Kennedy searched the lower decks. It was one thing seeking a stranger on a ship of this size, quite another looking for someone who didn't want to be found.

Warnings were posted at all the dining rooms—after all, Wells had to eat sometime. These warnings, like every other aspect of this interference, had to be discreet. No record could be left of their activities. Tomorrow night, the White Star Line's staff would have other problems to concern themselves with.

They had decided to reunite on the boat deck. Kennedy arrived first, and stood outside the gymnasium, leaning on the railings between the lifeboat davits. More than once he reached out to touch the brightly painted wood of lifeboat seven. It felt sturdy enough.

A cool breeze had shifted most of the other passengers indoors. A few remained, reading or writing letters while wrapped in the blanketed cocoons of their deckchairs. He spied Morgan and Doc as they emerged through the first-class entrance. Their disappointed faces relayed the news.

They exchanged the results of their vain expeditions.

"You're sure he didn't give you any hint? Any idea what he had in mind?" Kennedy probed.

Doc shook his head. "He was more interested in why you'd recruited me."

"I'm wishing now that I'd let you shoot him. I've got a strange feeling that's how this is usually resolved."

That morning, Kennedy had shared the same appalling revelation with Doc that he'd related earlier to Morgan. Doc had nodded glumly, as if his worse fears had been substantiated. He'd seemed almost relieved. His recent close proximity to the carapace had provided sinister visions that he'd chosen to disclose only in the aftermath of Kennedy's account. Murky dreams of cold black water.

He said, "I couldn't even look him in the eye, Major, much less shoot him."

Kennedy made himself nod understandingly. He wondered what difference Hardas or Lightholler might have made. He couldn't picture it. The alternatives were sealing themselves off.

He thought about the watertight doors he'd seen below deck.

"We have to stop him," Morgan said. It was muttered quietly, the conclusion to some internal monologue.

"You've been up all night, Doc," Kennedy said. "You need to get some rest. Darren and I will continue searching. I've managed to enlist some of the stokers and firemen. They're watching the engine rooms. He won't get past them. Whatever he's going to try has to involve the bridge or the wheelhouse. He doesn't dare approach Andrews, Ismay or the captain."

"If his cabin's clean, we need to go through any items he may have stored with the purser or down in baggage," Morgan suggested.

"Ship's staff have already gone through his belongings," Doc replied.

"They wouldn't know what to look for."

Kennedy agreed. "I've been down there before. I'll take baggage, you brace the purser."

He rode the elevator down to E deck, then took Scotland Road past the boiler casings, working his way forwards. Baggage was stored on G and the orlop deck. He found another set of stairs and negotiated the labyrinthine passages towards the squash court. No one was playing. He entered the first-class baggage compartment, pistol drawn, and began to search.

XV

Wells tore a bite from the roll he'd pilfered outside the third-class dining saloon. He had an apple someone had discarded and another roll in his pocket. He had the binoculars safely strapped under his shirt. Their metal casing nudged painfully against his ribs as he shifted to find a position of comfort. The mailroom, dimly lit, was heaped with the shadows of mail sacks. They passed easily for body bags in the gloom.

This was one of the first places that had flooded—would flood. One of the officers, perhaps Boxhall, would come down here after the collision to find the room awash. The mailmen would spend a short time trying to shift the sacks out of the water before realising the futility of their task. None of them would survive the sinking.

He checked his watch: 6 p.m. He wound the mechanism. The last thing he needed was to lose track of the time. It would be thirty hours, give or take, till they struck.

He stared through the darkness at the curving wall of the starboard bulkhead; daring it to buckle, open a seam, finger-wide, and admit the icy waters of the Atlantic. He heard some movement from the opposite wall. Someone was trying to gain entry through the baggage hold. He inched his way back along the floor and worked his way towards the bulkhead. He burrowed deeper under the piled bags of mail.

A crack of light widened into brightness. He heard breathing, ragged, coming from the doorway, and then a voice—Kennedy's—calling out to him.

"Mr Wells, I have the master-at-arms with me and I fear his patience is drawing to a close. I've assured him that you would come peacefully, but

I can't vouch for his frame of mind. He makes our mutual friend seem perfectly charming by comparison."

Kennedy, trying to match the patois of the era, was laying it on thick. He'd plainly spent too little time among the people of this world. *Our mutual friend.* Wells pictured the master-at-arms as some Dickensian throwback, with mutton-chop sideburns and red, spider-veined cheeks. He had to suppress a hysterical urge to laugh, and tried to slow down his breathing.

"Come, come, Mr Wells. You'll miss your supper."

There was a desperate edge to Kennedy's invitation. They were moving through the room. It was hard to gauge the number of footsteps. Then came the sound of more men tramping down the stairs from the post office above.

It was over.

Voices issued from the stairs, one saying, "This should be the last of it for today."

Another replied, "With all the Marconigrams going out to Cape Race, you'd think no one had the time for writing letters."

"You would at that."

With the approach of the newcomers, the footsteps on the mailroom floor scuttled away into silence. He heard the door to the baggage hold close.

"Did you hear something, Smithee?"

"Might have been the door to the outer office. I've been meaning to pass a message on to Mr Andrews about that."

The postal clerks gained the mailroom floor. He felt the sacks shift above him as more were added to the hoard. They continued their work in silence, the only sound the labour of their task, as bag was piled upon bag.

Finally they departed. He waited for ten minutes before stealing up the metal stairs to the post office. It was deserted. He waited a little longer before exiting the room and climbing the stairs to the third-class cabins on E deck. He found a lavatory and stood relieving himself, wanting to cry, wanting to vomit, but only producing a dry, retching gag in his throat. His clothes, damp through with perspiration, clung to him with a heady stench of fear.

Someone was taking a shower. They'd left a pile of fresh clothes by one of the water closets. He grabbed a shirt and trousers and escaped back down to G deck. He removed his shoes and traversed the narrow corridors with an ear out for any sound of movement. A cabin door was open.

He peered in to see a young man lying on one of the bunks. He had a thick comb of blond hair and tawny skin but his background was unplaceable. The man took in his appearance and ogled him curiously.

"Do you speak English?" Wells asked hesitantly, turning an eye back to the corridor.

There were three other bunks in the bare room. Two of them showed signs of occupancy but one remained untouched. The man narrowed his eyes, saying nothing.

Wells reached for his wallet and emptied its contents onto the bed.

The man examined the pound notes and returned to Wells with a newly appreciative gaze. "Been a bad boy, have we?" His accent hinted at the lilting tones of England's north.

"I've had my moments," Wells replied with a measure of relief. "Can I stay here a while?"

"This lot would buy you a berth above with change. I like your watch, though. Did you pilfer that too?"

Wells had his shoes tucked under his arm. He glanced down at his watch, thankful that the binoculars remained well concealed behind the bundle of stolen clothing. "The watch is mine. Yours tomorrow night if you let me stay. But no one must know." He felt a twist in his abdomen and added, "I'll need food too."

"Mum's the word then." The man swept up Wells' money with all the deftness of a croupier. He drew a small trunk from below his bed and shovelled the booty inside. He glanced back up at Wells with a leer and said, "Welcome to steerage, mate."

XVI

It's out there, Morgan thought.

The evening was cool. He stood by the ship's stern on the poop deck. The last of the sun was a pink sheen at the ocean's edge. They were sailing into darkness.

He peered at his watch. Doc was due on deck any time now.

Out there and waiting for us.

You're just an echo. The major told me so.

I'm barely that.

Morgan closed his eyes, banishing his dead companion. He reviewed the afternoon's events.

The purser's office held no items belonging to either Wells or his alias. Kennedy had found Wells' trunk in the first-class baggage compartment. It showed signs of being ransacked, and recently. None of the adjacent bags had been touched. Whatever he intended on using was small enough, light enough, to be transferred in a small carry-all.

A gun would serve little purpose. If he planned on using explosive charges, in order to disable the propellers, he'd have to get past Kennedy's guards outside the engine rooms. He might try to drop anchor. He might even try to warn Captain Smith directly, or first officer Murdoch.

He would have felt safe with me, bud.

Morgan started a thin-lipped smile. "He would have at that, Commander."

Doc's figure emerged from the shadows ahead. They acknowledged each other wearily.

Morgan said, "Good, you brought a coat. Joseph will be up to relieve you at midnight."

"What are you going to do?"

"Catch a bite at the saloon, check out the lounges and the smoking room, and then turn in early. My watch starts at five."

"Three of us," Doc shook his head miserably. "Searching the largest ship in the world for one man."

Morgan couldn't think of a response. Someone had once said, "History repeats itself. The first time as tragedy, the second time as farce." It certainly seemed true enough this cold, black night. Surely, he mused, by the time you had gone through the motions of uncountable revolutions, returning and returning and always getting it wrong, you were left with something far worse than that.

Kennedy had said this would be their last chance. The next step was oblivion.

They shook hands.

"Good luck, Doc. I'll see you in the morning."

He traversed the second-class promenade and took the aft stairs down to C deck. He walked the port-side corridor, stopping outside Wells' cabin just to give the door handle a cursory twist. It was still locked. He reached the Grand Staircase and descended to the first-class reception room.

Kennedy was waiting for him by the elevators. "See anything?" The question was voiced with little expectation.

"Nothing."

"We need to eat."

Morgan followed him into the saloon. They took a corner table by one of the colonnades. Arched windows, sealed against the night, reflected the room's glow. Kennedy ordered the lamb. Morgan ordered the beef.

"Who's that?"

Morgan turned to follow Kennedy's gaze. A thin gentleman, with brown hair and a thriving beard, was observing them over a pair of narrow glasses. He held their stare for a moment too long before turning away.

"That's Stead."

"The mystic?"

"The very same." Morgan prodded some vegetables, chasing them around his plate.

"Considering his choice in ocean liners, he's no Nostradamus."

Morgan laughed briefly. Stead was on Wells' list. So were Andrews, Smith, Murdoch, Wilde.

Astor.

"Joseph, whatever Wells plans on doing is subtle."

Kennedy gave him a look.

"I know that must sound crazy in light of these last few days, but look at his list. The guy's a catastrophic thinker. He wants to save the ship, but he only communes with the people he knew had died. Maybe he's superstitious. Maybe he's overly cautious. I don't know."

"Subtle." Kennedy seemed to be testing the word.

"Whatever he has in mind has to take place with the barest of notice. Nothing drastic. He won't sabotage the engines or brace the crew, nothing like that. He's the same as us. We're all creeping through history like it's hallowed ground, because we know that's exactly what it is. He's only looking to cause the shallowest ripple."

"Using something he had in his trunk."

"Something that might have been lacking on the ship."

"You mean apart from enough lifeboats."

Morgan mustered a tight smile. "Apart from that."

"Something that might make the smallest, yet most pertinent of differences."

"But nothing too reliable. Remember, the ship struck an iceberg in our world too."

"Three hours later."

"Which reminds me," Morgan said, "you have to relieve Doc at midnight."

Kennedy shook his head.

"You're not going?"

"The lookouts. This ship has the most lookouts of any vessel at sea. They're on a rotating watch."

"But there were no functioning binoculars in the crow's nest. That came out at the tribunals. A damaged pair had been lost by Fleet earlier in the evening. They'd supposedly been the latest design."

They were both smiling now.

Kennedy said, "That stupid little shit. Whatever he gave Fleet didn't last the night."

"Think he'll try again?"

"He didn't have us to contend with last time, but I wouldn't put it past him."

"What do you want to do?"

"Nothing tonight, we need to conserve our energy. We should go get Doc and bring him in out of the cold. Tomorrow, one of us watches the crow's nest and forecastle, another watches the bridge and wheelhouse. We'll do it in overlapping shifts to avoid fatigue and suspicion."

"Looks like we're going to have ringside seats."

Kennedy nodded dolefully.

"And what happens after midnight? What happens after we strike the ice?"

"It's women and children first, I guess."

XVII

April 14, 1912, 2230 hours
RMS Titanic, North Atlantic

Wells had washed his old clothes in the sink and left them to dry overnight. They could have done with ironing but they'd pass muster. All he needed was a few moments on the boat deck. Just long enough to pass on his message.

After that he would try to conceal himself in one of the lifeboats. He'd be quite safe there. No drills would be held today. Captain Smith, entertaining little desire to distress the sensibilities of his passengers, would cancel them.

It was ten-thirty. Most of the first- and second-class passengers would be at Sunday service, along with the senior staff. Their hymns would include prayers for the safety of those travelling at sea. He might not have shared their faith but he had every intention of seeing their prayers answered.

Wells reread the communication he had penned. It was cryptic enough to endure a rudimentary scan by the wireless staff without attracting too much attention. The recipient wouldn't know what to make of it at first. It wouldn't prevent any collisions but it should guarantee the timely rescue of everyone aboard.

He thought of it as his insurance policy.

He made his way to the third-class promenade on C deck. He wore an old black coat over his shirt and trousers. The brim of his cap was pulled low over his forehead. The binoculars were strapped to his waist.

There was an electric crane by the entrance to the second-class promenade. He stepped behind it, removed the coat and smoothed the creases from his shirt. He pulled back his cap and adjusted the ragged mop of his fringe. A metal gate, guarding access to second class, was unlocked.

He swore to himself that there would be no need to bolt it shut tonight. Climbing the aft stairwell to B deck, he spotted the picture of himself outside the second-class smoking room. It was a line drawing that had been pinned beneath a warning posted by the entrance. The warning informed the reader that certain unscrupulous gentlemen had boarded the ship. It cautioned against playing at cards or gambling with unfamiliar persons. It identified him as Jonathan Wells. Anyone sighting him should notify the master-at-arms at once.

Wells almost smiled. Kennedy certainly was a piece of work. Thankfully, the deck was bare. There might still be time to reach the Marconi Room, two decks above. Dealing with the wireless operators, possibly forewarned of his arrival, would be another problem altogether.

Head down, he ascended to A deck. He didn't see her till they collided at the top of the stair.

"I'm so sorry." He crouched to the floor and retrieved the book she'd dropped. It was a volume of psalms.

"Mr Wells," Marie said, "it appears as though clumsiness is the *least* of your transgressions."

He flinched, but her smile softened the censure.

"Really, I may just have to turn you in and have you charged with neglect."

He gave her a questioning look.

"You were supposed to join me for a stroll along the ship, sir. I even recall the promise of a shared meal." Her eyes flashed. "*If* you can spare the time from fleecing the innocent rich."

His initial impulse to elude her was replaced by a new strategy. Her dark, secretive eyes offered new hope.

He said, "I assure you, my transgressions are entirely manufactured. My name will cleared by morning, Marie. And when that happens, I'm hoping that a pleasant lunch might follow."

"Indeed, and how do you hope to clean the ledger of your misdeeds?" Her tone was somewhat playful.

"With this." He held up the letter. "The thing is, I need to have this sent off ship." He made his face a mask of discouragement. "And, unfortunately, I'm not certain how to accomplish that."

"That *would* seem to be a dilemma. I see that you have no stamps, and you will have a hard time finding a postal box before we reach New York."

"The wireless room, Marie. I intend to have this sent as a Marconigram, but I don't know how to deliver it safely."

She crossed her arms and lowered her head, presenting him with the wide brim of her hat. "If you are suggesting what I think you are suggesting, I assure you that I am no accomplice to criminals, sir."

"Of course not," he protested. "I envisioned you more as a saviour." He didn't need to work at the sincerity of his declaration.

"It all hinges on this then?" she asked, glancing at the letter. Her look became almost eager.

"You can't imagine how much so."

"Who is it to be sent to?"

He pointed to the destination. The message itself was concealed beneath a fold of paper.

"Why, this is intended for another ship."

"I have friends aboard her. Friends who may be able to assist me in clearing the record."

"I see," she responded. "There is much more to you than meets the eye, Mr Wells."

He offered a mock bow. His relief was a spring of the purest joy welling up within him. "I try, ma'am."

She snatched the letter from his hand and placed it within the pages of her book. "Where are you going now?"

"I need to … lie low, as they say." Catching her look, he added, "Until this message has been acknowledged and acted upon."

She smiled, glanced at his clothing, and said, "I *do* hope that you are better attired for our luncheon."

"Marie, if you deliver this successfully, I assure you that I'll greet you in white tie and tails."

"I shall hardly recognise you."

The sound of returning passengers filtering into the Palm Court brought back all his fears. "Tomorrow then," he said quickly, doffing his cap.

She smiled. "Perhaps even earlier. Good day, sir. I have an appointment to keep in the wireless room."

She vanished up the stairs.

People began to file past, and he was already receiving some curious looks from the attendants in the Palm Court. There would be little chance of gaining one of the lifeboats undetected now. He descended to third class with hasty steps. The memory of an earlier incident had sparked an idea.

XVIII

Kennedy inspected himself in the mirror. His figure cut an incongruous image within the splendour of the stateroom. By starlight he would have no trouble navigating the decks.

He removed the uniform and selected a suit from his wardrobe, then packed a few items in his trunk. Patricia's photograph lay on top of a stack of folded clothes. He placed it in his shirt pocket.

It was late afternoon and the Atlantic had already assumed the flat and smooth aspect of a lake. Morgan had assured him that the only commotion the ocean would see tonight would be the ship's death throes. He'd expanded on the subject, detailing the bodies in the water. Their cries, ignored by those in the lifeboats, would remain to echo throughout eternity. It was Morgan's last attempt to play devil's advocate. A half-hearted attempt to test their resolve.

Kennedy had been unable to picture it. All he saw were his ghost dancers, silent among the sands. All he considered were the accounts of those who'd facilitated his journey back. If they were right, eternity itself might be numbered in hours.

He left the cabin and went to join the others in the first-class smoking room. He checked the day's postings. As Morgan had predicted, they'd made five-hundred-and-forty-six miles in the last day. He stood for a while among the gathering passengers, impatient for the gleanings of post-luncheon hearsay. All talk centred around the pace the ship had set. Some spoke about the meal, some complained about the weather. They had no fucking idea.

Morgan and Doc arrived together. They wore heavy coats over their attire. They were due to start their watch at sixteen-hundred hours. He led them out to the promenade deck. It may have already grown colder.

"I tried to inspect the lifeboats," Morgan said. "No go. Wells would have a hard time concealing himself up on the boat deck. Those boats are sealed up tight."

"I did a round of the lounges," Doc said. "I checked with the pantries and all the restaurant staff I could find. No food has gone missing."

"Good," Morgan said. "He'll be hungry and tired. He won't be thinking straight."

"No, by now he'll have found a berth in second class or steerage," Kennedy said. "He'll have a full stomach and have slept like a baby. This guy thinks he's on a righteous crusade."

"But he doesn't know what we know, and there'll be no convincing him," Doc said. He sounded a little mournful.

"Well, would you take a look at that." Morgan was peering towards the bow of the ship.

Ismay was there, conversing with a young couple. They all watched as Captain Smith made his way aft and stopped to talk to the small group. Smith handed Ismay a folded sheet of paper. Ismay pocketed it with barely a glance.

Morgan snorted.

"What?" Doc asked.

"Looks like we get to watch while Wells misses his last golden opportunity. That was an ice warning, from the *Amerika* or the *Baltic*, I'm not sure which. Ismay is going to keep that little message all to himself. One more nail in the coffin."

Smith had continued his progress, and was making his way towards them. He might have been heading for the well deck. They stood aside, and Kennedy averted his glance. He caught Morgan eye-fucking the captain.

He gave him a sharp nudge in the ribs and whispered, "Behave, Darren. He's dead in twelve hours."

Morgan snarled back through gritted teeth, "Maybe so, Major, but I'm not too pleased about being dragged along for the ride."

Smith gave them an absent nod and disappeared beyond the Palm Court.

Kennedy said, "Gentlemen, you know the plan. I'll be back on deck at seven. I want one of you snatching some rest at all times. We need to be as fresh as possible for tonight." He put a hand on the railing. "And try to find yourselves somewhere warm."

He went below to check in with the firemen standing watch over the engine rooms. Morgan had urged that Wells would be subtle, that sabotage was out of the question, but *nothing* was impossible just because it was improbable.

Besides, he could always put some of the crewmen to better uses.

XIX

It was colder than Wells could have imagined. The aft funnel had been designed as a ventilator shaft rather than a smokestack; erected more for show than function. The gusts that drifted up from below provided only the barest warmth. He was perched on a ladder just beneath the lip of its opening. He watched the stars sail past the lids of its metal eye, measuring the moments until he could act.

He'd lifted the idea from a stoker who'd given more than a few people a scare back at Queenstown. The crewman had surfaced, coal-smeared, from the funnel's brim and waved at the passengers. His sour joke, once recalled as an ill portent for the journey, would hopefully be recast as a humorous anecdote once they had safely arrived in New York.

The *Californian* must have received his warning long hours ago. Should the worst occur, they wouldn't shut down their wireless set at eleven-thirty-five, thus missing word of the disaster. They wouldn't confuse the distress rockets with a celebration. And they *would* arrive with ample time to take on all the passengers.

Should the worst occur.

He brought the binoculars to his eyes and stared up at the night sky. He went through all the settings. The stars glittered back at him, clearer; resonating his own sparkle of anticipation.

He'd never dreamt that his desires would be so hard won. That he'd be contending with men from another time, content to see the ship doomed. It made the struggle all the more worthwhile. After all, nothing worth having was ever gained simply. He'd be back and warm in his third-class bunk by midnight.

He bided his time, filling the hours with his own studied recollection of the events. White-tie dinner served in the first-class saloon, fresh daffodils on white linen, while Wallace Hartley and his band provided the entertainment. He pictured the decks, clearing one by one as passengers sought the warmth of their cabins and lounges. The ocean, calm and black, and only barely disturbed by the ship's passage.

The iceberg would be seen long minutes before it posed any danger. The wireless warnings would be reviewed and the *Titanic* would follow a safer, more reasonable course; through the ice and beyond.

Finally, he climbed down, prised open the metal plate, gaping slightly where the stoker had loosened it, and emerged from the funnel's ash ejector onto the boat deck at nine-thirty. The lookouts would soon be due to change shift. He needed to intercept Lee or Fleet, the two crewmen assigned to the ten o'clock shift. They'd be standing close by the gantry of the crow's nest.

He crossed the engineers' promenade, hugging the boiler casing of number two funnel. He concealed himself within the deckchair storage area as a crewman ambled by. He waited for long moments before dashing across the length of the first-class promenade, skirting the lifeboats.

No one was in sight.

He raced down the two flights of stairs to the forecastle. Two men stood beneath the lofty rigging of the foremast. He examined them carefully. Most of the lights had been turned down to aid the lookouts. There was no moon and the stars offered little ambience to the chilly night. In the distance, they strode the horizon.

Nothing moved over the empty expanse of the deck.

One of the crewmen had sighted him, and both appeared to be gazing in his direction. Mustering his excuses, he fought the urge to flee. They lost interest, turning away to complete some exchange before separating. Wells gave the deck a final survey. Kennedy and his men had to be close by. It was a matter of acting now or finding himself a seat in one of the lifeboats.

He drew a deep breath and approached the crow's nest.

"Mr Fleet?"

The crewman nodded, stamping his feet.

"A cold night."

"Aye, sir. And it's going to get colder."

"I believe it's your watch."

Fleet nursed a steaming mug of coffee. He nodded between mouthfuls.

Wells withdrew the binoculars from beneath his shirt. "I've been asked by Mr Andrews to supply you with these."

Fleet's eyes widened at the shipbuilder's name. Since leaving Southampton four days ago, Thomas Andrews had busied himself about the vessel, attending to minor design flaws and overseeing last-minute repairs. Wells hoped that the delivery of these binoculars would be seen as merely another example of Andrews' attention to detail.

The crewman turned them over in his hands, studying them in admiration. The binoculars were remarkably compact and extremely light by comparison with the standard issue.

Drop them, Wells thought, *and I drop you over the side, fucker.*

His pulse was racing now. He realised he was holding his breath. He exhaled slowly. "They're German," he said.

Fleet seemed to find the explanation satisfactory. Wells detailed the function of each mechanism, and watched closely as the crewman put the binoculars to his eyes, making sure that the device had been mastered.

"Worth a pretty price, these," Fleet marvelled.

Wells had made enough transactions in the past few hours. "Just keep a sharp watch, Mr Fleet. Good night."

The other crewman was returning.

Wells thought he caught a stir of movement among the capstans. He withdrew from the forecastle with hasty steps. It was now only a question of selecting his vantage. He wanted to catch a glimpse of the iceberg as they passed. Someone had to bear witness to Fate's defeat and it would make a peaceful coda to the evening.

He had two hours to kill. He needed to stay out of sight until then.

He worked his way aft to the second-class promenade. A shadow, lurking by the Café Parisien, might have been Gershon. Wells stole into the second-class smoking room and secured himself in the lavatory. He locked the door. Catching his reflection in the mirror, he began to chuckle. It had come to this.

Occasionally someone would knock on the door. He murmured his excuses and kept an eye on his watch. The lounges would be clearing shortly. The stewards would turn down the lights in the public rooms, hoping to encourage their patrons to retire for the night. The ship would sail on, undaunted, into a new dawn.

His thoughts returned to the girl.

Unescorted women crossing the ocean to visit family and friends were frequently given protection by gentlemen sharing the expedition. Marie had asked him for just that on the first night of the voyage. His acceptance, tempered by his incomplete knowledge of her place on the list, had been desultory. He could make up for that now.

Today she'd accused him of neglect. She would never know the extent of his protection. He had taken all of the passengers into his keeping. All of the crew. If Kennedy and his men slept safe this night, they would have no one else to thank.

It was cold.

He hugged his coat to himself and stepped out into the darkened room. He climbed back up to A deck and approached the starboard railing. His hair lay damp against his beaded brow. His reddened eyes blinked and watered in the frigid air. The strains of a Strauss waltz rose from somewhere behind him, a low, soft melody that was swiftly surrendered to the night.

I'm entering uncharted waters, he thought. *Hic sunt dracones.*

The magnitude of his undertaking began to dawn upon him. Tentatively he placed both hands on the ship's rail. It was one final test of reality, one final test of faith. Cold steel retaliated with teeth of ice. He held his grip till the burn of it receded to numbness.

He glanced towards the ship's stern and watched as a young couple emerged from the aft stairwell, their burst of laughter cut short by the sudden cold. They huddled together and after a brief exchange returned to the warmth within.

Wells allowed himself a moment's pride. They'd never know how cold this night could get.

Resuming his vigil, he was startled by the brittle clang of the ship's bell. Three sharp reports issued from the darkness above. The final peal still rang over the waters as he reached for his watch.

Half eleven. Nodding slowly to himself, he replaced the timepiece. His hands shook violently.

"Steady," he murmured.

His hands were still shaking.

Everything shook. A tremble rose from the deck to rack his body.

How fast had they been going before the order had been given to change course? Somewhere, orders had been given and received. Calloused hands were straining against levers.

"Steady..."

He was almost certain he could sense the change. The flutter of butterfly wings that would herald a brighter, better world. He looked out to the flat, calm ocean, the moonless night. Beyond the ship's illumination the dark waters rose up so that he felt as if he and the ship lay at the centre of a vast opaque bowl. Nearby, a mist had risen. Light, caught in some peculiar manifestation, twinkled like a chandelier suspended from the heavens.

He scanned the distance. Nothing broke the flat horizon. His eyes were drawn towards the stern of the ship.

It was close, very close. Two irregular peaks gliding black against the black night sky. He noted the smaller sheets of ice, mirror shards on the ocean's counterpane. They drifted into the darkness.

The air glistened with shaved ice, a gentle flurry in the iceberg's wake.

He was running now.

He sprinted back down to the second-class promenade, heedless of the few crewmen and passengers who were assembling on deck. He gained the aft railing. Beyond, the third-class promenade was spattered in ice. A few men gathered by his side to survey the scene.

The iceberg was lost to view.

Some of the steerage passengers had ventured out onto the rimed deck below, their subdued voices muttering uncertainties. A couple of them began to kick frozen blocks along the wooden floor. Their laughter rang false in the wintry night. There was an odd stillness to it all and he suddenly realised that the engines had stopped.

They were dead in the water.

He turned to the crewman beside him. "How?" he mumbled uselessly. "Why?"

Kennedy, masquerading in a White Star Line uniform, looked back at him sombrely. Gershon and Morgan stood alongside him, similarly garbed. Wells didn't register any surprise. They all looked at him with the strangest sorrow, as if to suggest that he'd somehow let them down as well.

Kennedy said, "I kept Mr Fleet busy in the crewmen's mess. You gave the binoculars to one of the firemen in his place. He gave them to me. No one will ever know."

Wells watched the man's lips move, but couldn't grasp the words.

"They didn't see the iceberg till it was too late, Doctor Wells," Morgan said. "They're not supposed to."

"So that was your play," Kennedy said. "What else have you got?"

Wells made a fist and jabbed Kennedy hard, just below the right eye. Kennedy slipped on the icy deck and caught himself against the railing. He straightened up and held his stance. Wells punched him again, catching his jaw. There was a slight cracking sound. Kennedy fell back against the rail and regained his footing shakily.

Morgan and Gershon kept still.

Wells looked at his hand. Two of his knuckles were distended. He was weeping, but voiced no sobs. Kennedy was bleeding from a gash above his cheek.

"You've drowned us all."

"Destiny drowns us, Doctor." Kennedy's words stumbled over his swollen lips. "I'm just the middle man."

Wells raised his bloodied fist.

Morgan stepped forwards.

Someone cried, "What's going on here?"

Wells reeled towards the voice. He wiped his face. His hands dropped to his sides.

Marie repeated the question. "What's going on here?" She wore a coat and shawl over her evening dress, and had a lifebelt under her arm. The promenade was otherwise empty now. Kennedy and the others said nothing, gazing at her unexpected intrusion with astonishment.

Wells started to laugh. In his anguish, he'd somehow forgotten all about the Marconigram. He turned on Kennedy and snarled, "I hope it's just the loss of the ship that suits you, asshole. The *Californian* is on its way. No one dies tonight, fucker."

"Mr Wells?" Marie's voice was strained. She looked wretched.

Kennedy and his men stared at her. Faced with this first outwards sign of the disaster, he supposed, they might have been suffering their first feelings of remorse.

"Mr *Wells*," she pressed.

He pulled away from Kennedy, triumphantly "I'm sorry, Marie. My language. It's just that—" He was stopped short by her expression.

"Marie is my middle name."

"I beg your pardon?"

"My name is Patricia Marie Kennedy, and here is your Marconigram." She let the document flutter to the damp deck. "I'd also appreciate it if you'd stop hitting my husband. He's had a very difficult day."

Wells stared at the slip of paper. Moisture spread across its cream-coloured surface like a stain.

Kennedy stepped forwards and placed an arm around her shoulders.

"You're his..." Wells gazed at her uncomprehendingly. "You didn't send it?" He felt his legs giving way beneath him.

Suddenly Morgan and Gershon were by his side. Supporting him. Restraining him. They seemed as stunned as he was by her disclosure.

"You used your *wife* to bait me?"

Kennedy had both his arms on Marie's ... on Patricia's shoulders. He was staring into her eyes. "No," he murmured. "I had no idea she was aboard."

She said, "You told me not to come aboard because I was never with you on all those other attempts. But that was all the more reason for me to be here." Her cheeks were slick with tears.

Other attempts?

"It doesn't matter now." Kennedy's voice was coaxing. "We have to get you off this ship." He turned to Morgan and Gershon, who indicated their assent. Wells found himself agreeing with them.

"I'm so sorry, Joseph." She was shaking in his arms. "I only realised that the boat was *supposed* to sink today. After he had given me the wireless message." She cast Wells a grief-stricken look. "You understand now, though, don't you?"

He was back outside the Flamingo's lobby, peering at the black Oldsmobile.

He was in the desert, following Gershon into the sandy depths.

He was face to face with the carapace in the heart of the Waste Land.

Other attempts? The images merged into some fractional offering of meaning, but there was nothing here to understand, save the imminent loss of fifteen-hundred lives. He gazed past her to Kennedy, and saw Jenkins' eyes staring back at him.

It was over. Kennedy's expression told him so. He didn't bother to struggle as they led him down to D deck. Their cabin was on the starboard side of the ship, just beyond the corridor's entrance.

Three decks below, the mailroom would be filling with water.

Kennedy opened the door and nudged him into the room, a small suite. The movement was gentle. There was no attempt to pay him back for the swings he'd taken. Kennedy offered him a drink. He declined. Kennedy indicated a chair and he sat down heavily.

His eyes strayed to the carpet. It was completely dry. A journal, the water-damaged alternative of his musings, was opened on a table. The fresh account of his memories lay closed beneath it.

Patricia and Kennedy sat on a lounge. Gershon took another chair and Morgan leaned up against the wall between Wells and the entrance. They spoke amongst themselves as if he wasn't there.

No one knew she'd stolen aboard. Neither Gershon nor Morgan had known that she and Kennedy had eloped two weeks earlier. Once embarked, she'd secured a berth on C deck and pursued her own agenda, keeping watch over Wells. She explained that they'd shared a common steward.

Crawford must have found her as charming as he had. The steward had supplied her with an accounting of Wells' movements up to his escape on the previous day.

She asked Kennedy, "When did you realise that the ship was supposed to sink?"

"Two nights ago," he replied.

"So why did it have to come to this?" She was inspecting Kennedy's injuries. She finally turned her attention back to Wells. "Why didn't you let him convince himself?"

"We tried talking to him," Morgan said.

"You held me prisoner in my own room," Wells protested.

"We were having trouble dealing with the news ourselves." Gershon spoke with surprising civility.

Wells looked at him and nodded slowly. He turned to Patricia and said, "How was I supposed to convince myself?"

"The last entry in your journal made no sense. Less than the rest of it, in any case. But something occurred to me after you gave me the letter." Her voice assumed a contrite tone, as if only now realising that she was discussing the private entries of his personal diary.

"What was the last entry?"

Morgan spoke up without needing to examine the text. "It's a single word, written in the margin on the last page. It says, 'Santayana.'"

Patricia rose from the lounge and approached the journal. She turned it to the last page and pointed to the word. "You pressed the pen harder here. You might have been resting the journal against your hand, or up against a wall. You were in a hurry."

"Santayana." He repeated the word.

"I think you wrote this after you realised that you'd failed, the last time you were here. I think you wrote it as a reprimand to yourself."

"What does it mean?" Kennedy asked. "Is it a place?"

"It's a person. He was a philosopher," Wells explained.

Gershon asked, "Why him? Is he aboard?"

Wells shook his head dismissively. There was only one strong association he could make with that name. Only one reference he could attribute to the thinker. He quoted, "Those who do not remember the past are condemned to relive it."

As he spoke, Patricia studied his expression. She must have read something there. An odd look of comprehension crossed her face. "Those were Santayana's words?"

"Yes."

The last time you were here.

"Not a reprimand then," she said. "A warning. A warning to yourself."

"I don't understand," he replied, but that wasn't entirely true. For all his bluster, he'd hardly bother to make an entry like that—not just for the sake of scolding himself. Not once he was aware that he'd failed.

"I asked you, Doctor, when we met, why you sank the ship and then left the record of your crime behind," Kennedy said. "I accused you of tempting fate, but I was wrong. You were appealing to it."

"Now do you understand, Doctor Wells?" Patricia spoke slowly and forcefully.

"We have to get out of here," Wells said. "We don't belong."

Kennedy eyed him sadly. "I think he gets it."

XX

April 15, 1912
RMS Titanic, North Atlantic

Doc slipped back into his civvies. Morgan dragged a sweater over his shirt. Their uniforms formed a small heap on the bed.

Morgan surveyed his trunk. There was nothing there he'd miss. He kicked it shut.

Kennedy and Patricia stepped out into the corridor to play catch-up while irate passengers flurried past them.

They returned to the sitting room to confer with Wells. Journal in hand, subjugated by his own discovery, he'd said nothing more to the group. He was talking now though, and Morgan heard the exchange of low voices through the thin partition of the separating wall.

"I never really thought this far ahead." Doc was looking out the porthole.

It was hard to say if they were sitting any lower in the water.

Morgan said, "The first few lifeboats will be undermanned." He remembered Kennedy's words. "We won't be taking anyone's place."

"I was just thinking about Ismay and those other men; those who managed to escape early in a lifeboat. I don't want to be tarred with that brush."

"No one's going to know."

"We'll know."

"We've lived with worse."

"That doesn't make it any easier."

Morgan nodded. He returned his attention to the wall.

"Patricia and the major," he said, after a moment.

"Go figure."

"It's shaping up to be quite the honeymoon for them."

Doc loosed harsh laughter.

The door opened.

Kennedy had a hoard of lifebelts under his arm. He said, "We're set to go."

They forged their way through the entrance to the first-class reception. A crowd was forming by the elevator doors, near the Grand Staircase. Wells hesitated at the vestibule.

Kennedy looked at him and said sharply, "Everything *we* know about the ship from here on in is fiction. We need you to guide us, based on your own knowledge of the *Titanic*. You need to stay focused, Doctor Wells. Can you do that?"

"Sure."

"We don't change a thing, and we don't interfere."

Wells nodded dully.

"It's twelve-ten. What's happening?"

"The crew will be mustering on the boat deck, standing ready to uncover the lifeboats. The first distress call goes out any minute now." He turned to Patricia. "There won't be any trouble getting you away at this time." There was an urgency behind his words. He seemed quite accepting of her new status as Kennedy's wife. "They won't separate newlyweds this early on," he added.

"We'll part for now," Kennedy said. "Is that okay, Patricia?"

Her nod was demure. She made no protest. A far cry from the woman who had snuck aboard ship at Southampton. Some dynamic seemed to have changed. What had transpired between them? Morgan tossed Doc a questioning look. Doc shrugged it off and returned his attention to Wells.

There was the slightest slant to the carpeted floor.

Wells said, "We need to get off this level. We need to be on the boat deck."

They skirted the crowd by the elevator and began to ascend the stairs. Each of them carried a lifebelt by their side. Each wore a heavy coat. Kennedy had both copies of the journal folded in a pocket of his jacket. Morgan had also seen him slip the Colt into a holster on his belt.

Wells spoke softly, explaining as they climbed. "The first few lifeboats will be half-full. You may be out there for hours before the *Carpathia* shows up. There'll only be a few blankets and provisions."

"I'll be warm enough." Patricia wore one of Kennedy's coats over her own. "I'll be fine."

On C deck a line had formed outside the purser's office. Stewards bustled among the passengers, chiding their tardy patrons. There was no sign of panic. Had Wells stood here, journal in hand, in his twisted variation of this night?

He wasn't looking at the queue now; his eyes were on the domed skylight. It soared above them to crown the stairwell. They continued upwards. More than once Morgan misjudged his step. He let his hand guide him along the wainscoting. There was no obvious list but he found his senses no more reliable than the stewards who worked their way past with reassuring smiles.

They encountered Crawford on the A deck landing. He gave them a quick once-over, smiling at Wells and lingering over Kennedy's injury. He didn't appear surprised at the company they kept. He directed a curious eye towards Patricia.

"Four guardians tonight, Miss Marie. I believe you may have set a new record for the Line."

Catastrophe had reset her pale features in a new cast. Some inner glow burned there, fuelled by hope or despair. She returned his smile, bitter-sweet.

Hartley's band had already assembled in the lounge. They played a lively ragtime tune. People stood around in various states of dress. Haphazard combinations of nightshirts and dinner jackets, evening gowns and robes; each outfit reflecting the individual's level of alarm or credulity. Morgan wandered past the quick and the dead, the saved and the lost, ticking off their names in his head. One woman wore a thin cotton dress. Her stockinged feet were bare. He couldn't place her.

Wells led them up to the boat-deck foyer. The linoleum floor was tracked with wet prints. The mirrored walls reflected a cheerful glow from the cut-glass light fixtures. Everything was a lie.

They went out into the darkness.

Only a hardy few had chosen to brave the cold. They huddled far from the railing, smoking and watching the crew at their work. There was little wind but the air itself was a barrier of ice. The quiet was torn by a fearsome howl as somewhere below the boilers vented excess steam. Kennedy shouted something that was lost in the roar. He gestured and they quickly entered the gymnasium.

People were clustered in small groups around the equipment. Protests vied with ridicule as they tried to make sense of it all. Morgan was thinking about those who were below decks. Too few would have the luxury of debating their alternatives. The occasional couple broke away, returning to the misleading warmth of the decks below. He had to resist the urge to try and stop them at the door.

A young man approached, eager to compare notes. "You seem prepared for an adventure," he said, eyeing their outfits. He wore a light jacket over his night clothes.

They looked to Wells. He made a soft gurgling sound in Kennedy's ear. Kennedy frowned.

The man's smile faded. He stammered an excuse and returned to another knot of passengers who were sharing some joke.

Wells said, "Do you mind if I have a few words with your wife in private?"

Kennedy shook his head. He took Morgan and Doc aside, saying, "According to Wells, Murdoch will permit men into the boats. He's loading the starboard side." He spoke as if continuing a prior conversation.

"We're getting off now?" Morgan tried to make the query sound casual. He didn't know *what* he wanted.

"We can if we choose to." Kennedy answered as if in a dream, as if he was already under water. With one utterance he finally relinquished command. "We're finished here."

"You could have chosen another turn of phrase," Doc observed.

Kennedy didn't smile. "If we divide up, it'll be easier for us."

Morgan asked, "What did you have in mind?"

"You and Patricia first." He was talking to Doc.

"You got any reason for that particular combination?" Doc asked.

"Wells insisted that we get you both off the ship as soon as possible."

"Why me?"

"He calls it payback."

"And if I refuse?"

"You have to do it."

"That's not your decision to make."

"Why are we listening to Wells?" Morgan asked.

"Because he's the only one here who knows how this ends."

"I'm getting a fair idea of that myself," Doc said. "How did he convince Patricia to leave?"

"He made the correct… diagnosis."

Morgan looked across at Patricia and Wells. They were standing before a large map of the world, crossed by the shipping routes of the White Star Line. It covered the far wall. He was talking to her quietly.

"What's wrong with Patricia?" Doc was staring at her now. His expression changed. He turned back to Kennedy and said, "Oh, Jesus."

XXI

The first lifeboat was already in the water. Caught in the brilliance of the distress rocket, it was bared in a brief flash of light.

"See," Wells said to Patricia. "Plenty of room."

Its lantern had yet to be lit. Abandoning the penumbra of the *Titanic*'s glow, it faded from sight. She peered after it.

Wells examined his watch. It was ten to one. "Lifeboat five's next, I think." He urged the group towards the davits.

"It's too soon," Patricia said, hanging back. "You told me one of the lifeboats returns to the scene after the sinking. I'll board that one."

"That's lifeboat fourteen. It's one of the last to leave the ship, and only saves one person from the water."

Patricia said, "One person is enough."

Kennedy took her arm gently. "You're going in this one. Doc will be right by your side."

Wells caught Gershon's look of dismay. He clearly took no pleasure in the arrangement. Wells had expected nothing less.

"The next few boats won't be full," Morgan said. "We'll have plenty of time."

Kennedy nodded firmly in agreement.

An officer prepared the boat. Passengers stood well away, eyeing the manoeuvres warily. Ismay stepped forwards and began berating the officer. The officer broke away from his activities to enter the bridge.

Wells said, "This won't take too long. Smith will tell him to follow Ismay's orders."

Within moments the officer had returned. The lifeboat was swung out over the side and made ready for boarding. He called out, “Come along, ladies.”

Patricia turned to Wells and said, “How does it feel, knowing all this?”

“It’s like the closing night of a play I’ve seen all too many times.”

Couples strayed forwards. A small number overcame their reluctance and stepped aboard. Kennedy led Patricia towards the lifeboat. He beckoned to Gershon.

Gershon extended a hand to Morgan.

Morgan refused it. “I’ll be seeing you soon.”

Wells said, “So long, Dean.”

Gershon ignored him.

Kennedy and Patricia embraced. He whispered something in her ear. Gershon hung back beside Ismay, who was coercing a party of seven into the boat. Ismay called out, “Are there any more women before this boat goes?” He looked over at Patricia. “Any more women?”

She stepped forwards uncertainly. She was still holding Kennedy’s hand, dragging him forwards.

He brushed her cheek with a last kiss and said, “Remember.”

“I won’t need to,” she replied. “You’ll be there to take care of it.”

He helped her into the boat.

“Any more women?” Ismay spied a young girl standing among the crowd. “Come along, jump in.”

“I am only a stewardess.”

Wells told her, “Never mind that. You’re a woman, take your place.” He glanced at Morgan and said, “Does that count as interference?”

Ismay was already ushering her towards the boat.

Morgan said, “I’ll let it slide. I suspect it was a done deal.”

Gershon stood awkwardly by the lifeboat. He threw Kennedy an uncomfortable look. The officer herded him into the boat. He took the place by Patricia’s side.

Murdoch emerged from the bridge and called out to the officer, “You go in charge of this boat. Stand by to come alongside the aft gangway when hailed.” They shook hands. Murdoch said, “Goodbye. Good luck.” His face was impassive. He would have known that this was farewell.

He signalled the crewmen to lower away and the lifeboat began its descent.

Wells and Morgan made their way to the railing to join Kennedy. By the time they'd reached him the lifeboat hung suspended halfway down the steep hull. Patricia had removed one of her coats. It was draped over the stewardess's shoulders. She looked up past Wells to catch Kennedy's eye. She brought her fingertips to her lips and blew him a kiss before returning her attention to the stewardess. Gershon had his eyes directed to the water below. He didn't look back.

"Nothing happens to the lifeboats," Kennedy said to Wells.

"Nothing."

"Good." He stepped back from the davits and cast a glance towards the ship's stern.

Wells followed his gaze. Hartley's band had come up from the lounge. Further along the deck more people were lined up outside the raised roof of the first-class smoking room. He observed a woman standing slightly apart from the others. She wore a white shawl tightly about her head and neck. A fringe of auburn hair trailed her lined brow. He hadn't spoken to her throughout the journey but there was a disquieting familiarity about her now.

He approached her with a sense of dread. Kennedy and Morgan were watching him closely. They didn't try to stop him.

"Virginia?" He ventured the name as a hopeless whisper, praying he was wrong.

"Yes?" She looked up him expectantly. "Do I know you, sir?"

He felt hollow, a stand-in at his own performance, but there was no one else around to utter the lines. He asked, "Where is your lifebelt?"

"What is the urgency? Mr Murdoch told us that everything would be alright." She stared up into his eyes. "Everything is going to be alright, isn't it?"

"I don't know," he replied. "I don't think so. Take this." He handed her his lifebelt. "Get in the next boat."

"Won't you need it?"

Wells was already walking away.

"Was that in the script?" Kennedy asked him.

The question chilled him to the bone. He nodded his reply with horrifying certainty.

"There's a few more things I need to ask you," Kennedy said.

"I thought we were done here."

"We are."

"Then save it for the lifeboat."

"That won't work for me."

"Really?" Wells liked the desperation in Kennedy's eyes. It went some way towards assuaging his own fears. He asked, "Do I have anything to gain by this?"

"Probably not."

He examined his watch. "Then you've got ten minutes."

"The smoking room is close by," Kennedy said. "We can talk there."

Another lifeboat had been drawn out over the side. Officers were calling out to the passengers, cajoling them. No one moved forwards. Morgan's attention was fixed on the proceedings. He turned back to find them moving away and stared with a mystified look. "We're going back inside?"

"*We* are." Kennedy indicated Wells with a nod. "You're not."

"I don't get it."

"Patricia and Doc are gone, Darren. Now it's your turn. You've manned your post to the last, but that's the way it goes. I told you, we leave the ship in stages."

Morgan stared back at him blankly. "What about you?"

"I'll see you on the *Carpathia*." Kennedy made to walk away. Morgan caught his sleeve. Kennedy looked slightly surprised. "Don't let this ship drag you down with it, Darren. Get into one of the boats. Go. I release you."

Morgan's eyes were imploring.

Kennedy placed a hand on his shoulder and squeezed gently. "I release you."

It was an incantation, a charm. The revocation of a spell that didn't come lightly.

"Thank you." Morgan's reply was the softest whisper. He turned and walked with heavy steps towards the officers' promenade. The lifeboat, half-full, swayed at the *Titanic*'s side.

Kennedy strode the other way without a backwards glance. Wells hesitated before following him down the aft stairwell and into the smoking room beyond.

XXII

There were no more women around. No children in sight. Murdoch ordered some crewmen into the lifeboat. Fifteen of them piled in. There were at least twenty places to spare.

Murdoch levelled Morgan an impatient glare.

His legs betrayed him. He was walking towards the side of the ship, stepping over the railing and into the swinging boat. Other men had approached the barrier and were now climbing aboard. Morgan shifted aside.

Hey.

Morgan raised his downcast eyes.

Hey, bud. You brought me here, just like you promised.

The voice had always come from within, but there was no mistaking it. He told himself it was the cold, his maddening fright, that had congealed into some tangible mass, yet there was Hardas's shifting eidolon, huddled among the occupants of the lifeboat. It seemed to gaze at Morgan broodingly. No one else gave it any notice.

You need to get out of this boat.

Morgan closed his eyes. *Leave me alone.*

All in good time.

Murdoch was calling for more passengers. A brief wail of venting steam drowned out his entreaty. Softer murmurs rose around Morgan. Prayers and curses, dovetailed with the dying screech of the boilers.

You're condemning me to death.

There are things worse than drowning. Stay here and you'll kill yourself within the year.

He knew it was delusion but there was no denying the impact of the words.

He released us from our duty, bud. Not our honour. He ain't leaving the ship, and you know it. So how can you?

The morning's paper had said that some children were lost. And your father would never leave a child behind, no matter what happened.

He had told Kennedy the wrong story.

"Excuse me." Morgan rose from his seat. The other passengers stared at him in wonder.

He worked his way back to the lifeboat's side, ignoring the hands that reached for him. Murdoch was signalling the crew to lower away. The lifeboat lurched and dropped a few feet.

Morgan leapt, gaining the railing. Murdoch reached a hand across and dragged him over the barrier. His expression was incredulous.

Morgan muttered, "I left something on the ship."

"I fear it's going to cost you."

"You have no idea."

Murdoch shook his head and walked away. Most of the remaining passengers had filed down to the aft lifeboats. The deck was bare.

Morgan looked down at the water. Hardas's shade was dispersing in wisps. It might have been a cloud of escaping steam or the clotted respiration of the saved.

So long, bud.

Morgan turned away.

XXIII

Four men sat playing cards at one of the tables. Cigar smoke coiled thickly above their heads. A few other men stood by the bar drinking. Everyone should have been in bed. Everyone should have been safe.

A silver-haired man seated nearby absently waved at some bottles that sat opened near several upturned glasses. Kennedy filled two glasses from a bottle of whisky. The alcohol splattered down the sides of the glasses and spilled onto the bar's polished surface. The silver-haired man gave him a dark look.

Wells said, "Put it on my tab."

The man took his drink and strode away.

There was a wooden box on a shelf behind the bar. Wells worked his way around the mahogany expanse of the counter and fished out two cigars. He bit off the tips of them both, and handed one across to Kennedy.

Kennedy said, "I don't smoke."

Wells produced an ornate lighter from below the bar. Kennedy cocked his head in puzzlement.

Wells raised his glass. "To fatherhood."

Kennedy touched Wells' glass with his own. He brought the cigar to his lips while Wells lit it carefully.

Wells lit his own, then said, "I made sure Patricia got aboard, and you helped clean the slate between me and Gershon. I'd say we're even, so make it fast."

Kennedy didn't miss a beat. "What happens to Astor?"

Astor. When it came to the *Titanic*, the man's fate was an invariable feature of most accounts. He was credited with enough acts of bravery, wit and style to fill any number of disasters. Wells somehow found the thought disturbing. He gave Kennedy the short version, between rapid puffs.

"Is that it?" Kennedy asked.

"That's it. They found him in the water days later, decayed, his head staved in. They only recognised him by his shirt. His initials were stitched into the collar."

"He goes down into the cargo hold in my world, as well," Kennedy said. His expression was pensive.

"I guess he liked animals."

"You were with him."

"I was there?"

Kennedy nodded.

"Looks like I get around. What's so important about Astor?"

"He's the linchpin. His survival is what sent my world to its doom."

"Forget about it. He dies."

"I need to be certain of that."

"He *dies*." Wells ashed the cigar. "All the American millionaires die tonight." He was in strange spirits now. He added, "How much are *you* worth, Kennedy?"

Kennedy snorted.

Wells said, "I've got no idea what you have in mind, but I'll tell you something for free. There are twenty lifeboats on this ship, four are already gone. The rest are going to fill fast. When this ship goes ass up, fifteen-hundred people will end up in the water. Only fifteen of those will get taken into the boats. We're talking a one per cent return here.

"Now, you're in reasonable shape—better condition than most of the passengers—so I'll be generous. I'm going to give you a one in twenty chance of clawing your way out of the water. Thing is, you're also a sentimental bastard. I have no idea how you made it as far as you did. Taking that into account puts you back squarely behind the eight ball. I suggest you put aside any crazy notion you've got fermenting in there and get into a lifeboat. That's your only way out of here. That's where you'll find me." He glanced at the clock perched behind the bar and stubbed out his cigar. "Adios."

Someone was standing beside them. He'd approached silently and was regarding them over a pair of oval glasses.

The blood drained from Kennedy's face.

Wells felt a slight shudder sweep his body, feet lightly tripping over his grave. Things were going to take a little longer than he'd expected. He said, "Hello, William."

Stead smiled back. "Good morning, Jonathan."

Wells continued, impelled by some unknown power. He said, "This is Joseph Kennedy. Major Kennedy."

"I know."

"Of course you do." Kennedy extended a hand.

Stead shook it politely. "So many times," he said, "but never like this. Never like this. Only two of you, but two will suffice. Where is the girl?"

"She's safe," Kennedy replied.

Wells reached for his drink and held it with unsteady hands.

Stead indicated the fireplace with a nod. "Take your time, gentlemen. We'll talk because we always talk."

Wells glanced at Kennedy.

Kennedy placed the stub of his cigar on the counter.

"We can leave right now," Wells said. "We'll take the next lifeboat. We don't need to hear this."

"Really?" Kennedy was miles away. Years, perhaps.

"We don't need to hear this again," Wells said stridently. His outburst seemed to have come from somewhere else. He didn't dare utter another word, for fear of what might be loosed.

Kennedy reached for his drink and rose from his seat.

Wells gazed at him despairingly. He drained his glass and made for the exit. Each step was a momentous endeavour against the imperious force of Stead's announcement.

We'll talk because we always talk.

He was drawn back in a decaying orbit to where Kennedy had placed a third chair by the hearth. The fire was a low flicker dancing on the wood. He took his place.

"Usually this is an exchange of information," Stead began. "Understanding for wisdom. But not tonight. Am I mistaken?"

Patricia Marie Kennedy might be safe and gone, but her words still haunted Wells.

Other attempts.

Spurred by the catalyst of Stead's arrival, they tripped a switch in his head. A curtain parted somewhere for him. Suddenly he was in the wings and looking on, and he saw it all for what it was. The faded backdrop, the dusty set, and all the actors weary beyond measure.

The horrors mounted upon themselves, vertiginous; burgeoning in the mystic's presence. They crashed over him—not as revived memories, but as previous encounters, here, on the ship. They stretched out before him now, diverging into two strains. One found him in a pool of his own blood, lying at Gershon's feet; the other found him in the water. They alternated, twining about themselves, but always knotting at the end—in his death. It was as immutable and assured as the loss of the ship itself.

He understood that the notion was completely insane, just as he recognised it as being the absolute truth. This was closing night.

"You're not mistaken," Wells said.

Kennedy's expression hinted at his own insights. He said, "An infinite number of possibilities. The revision of a thousand decisions."

It sounded like a recitation to Wells. The litany of all of Kennedy's nights, spent chasing him throughout eternity.

"One way or another," Stead said, "it ends tonight."

"Till the next time," Wells replied wearily.

"I know that you're seeing this tragedy in a new light, Jonathan, now that you find yourself backstage. But you've been watching the cast and the props with no consideration for the theatre itself. Joseph didn't say anything to you about this, because he can scarcely credit it himself. Yet it's the fear of it that spurs him on."

Kennedy said, "There *is* no next time, Doctor Wells."

"That can't be true."

"Jonathan, there are things that even the experience of a thousand lifetimes won't teach you, and you've had many more than that. The seams are already showing. The cracks are there. The device that sent the two of you back and forth is at odds with reality. In its own way, it is the greater force of the two. It is set to prevail."

"Nothing is carved in stone," Kennedy said.

"True enough," Stead replied. "And what follows the dawn is closed to me. The night, however, may be plainly read."

"What happens?" Wells asked.

"I feel like Sisyphus and this rock has grown too heavy." Stead was looking at the fire.

"*What happens?*"

"The same thing that always happens, Jonathan. Death by water."

"I wasn't meant to make old bones." Kennedy's voice was a murmur of acceptance.

Stead threw him a piercing glance. "You, sir, weren't meant to exist at all." He rose from his seat. "There are dreams that lie fathoms below our waking thoughts. I once wrote a book wherein an ocean liner struck an iceberg in the Atlantic. There was so much loss, so much terror. I entertained the thought that by consigning the story to paper, I might keep it bound there. The arrogance of that deed binds me to this night. I don't dare imagine the retribution your earlier acts might warrant." He tendered a slight bow. "If it is any consolation, you should know that this is where you belong, gentlemen. Good night."

He retrieved his glass, rinsed it out, and returned it to the bar. He left the smoking room in silence.

"It's not carved in stone." Wells was staring at the embers. "It's writ on water. There are a few lifeboats left. We can leave any time we like."

Kennedy nodded, absently.

"I'm usually dead by now. Gershon usually kills me in this timeline."

"He shoots you in your cabin," Kennedy replied.

"We're never here, talking like this."

Kennedy remained silent.

"There's a man travelling in second class by the name of Lawrence Beesley," Wells said. "He gets on a lifeboat within the hour and lives to write an account of the sinking."

Kennedy turned to regard him.

"In the fifties, there's a resurgence of interest in the *Titanic*," Wells continued. "They make a movie about it and Beesley is one of a few survivors called upon as a consultant. But he only knows the end of the story through hearsay. Only by what he saw from the safety of his lifeboat. When they begin filming the actual sinking, he forges an actor's union card and slips onto the set."

"He gets on the ship?" Kennedy had a strange smile on his face.

"He gets on the ship. Stays while all the lifeboats are filling. Thing is, the director spots him just at the last moment and tells him to leave."

"He gets a second chance and chooses the water," Kennedy mused.

Wells asked, "What is it about this place?"

"I'm not sure," Kennedy replied.

Wells reached for a poker and stirred the coal. The fire hissed and the cinders danced. He said, "I think I know why this kept happening to us."

Kennedy nodded slowly. "It's what Stead was trying to tell us."

"We have to get off the ship right now."

"It's okay, it'll be taken care of," Kennedy replied. "I already knew. I told Patricia."

"Will she be able to handle it?"

"She took care of you, didn't she?"

Wells smiled. "I wonder if we got it right this time?"

"*We?*" Kennedy gazed at him for long moments. He said, "I think it's as close as we've ever been."

Wells considered the experiences of his untold nights on this ship. It didn't *have* to end in the water, but he'd be damned if he left the *Titanic* before Beesley, or Ismay.

There would still be time.

He said, "Officer Lightholler is only loading women and children on the port side. It's not going to be a popular decision, no matter what the storybooks will say. That's where we'll be the most use."

Kennedy stirred at the officer's name. He patted his coat pocket. The edge of the journal was just visible at the brim. He said, "We have to get rid of these first."

Wells felt a sudden pang. The sensation passed swiftly. His eyes wandered up towards a painting that hung above the fireplace. It was titled *The Approach of the New World*.

Kennedy continued, "They can't ever be found. This is where we break the circle."

He removed the documents and tossed them into the fire. The journals flared briefly. The plastic coating dripped to cover both manuscripts in splashes of coloured flame and they burned as one.

XXIV

There was a glow on the horizon. It seemed to flicker.

"It's a masthead light," Wells explained to Kennedy. "Captain Smith has ordered a few of the lifeboats to row out to her. Some will try. It's a safer bet than hanging around here, waiting to be swamped after we hit the water. All the accounts will say that she seemed to recede from their approach. Some will argue that she's a whaler, trespassing and unwilling to reveal her presence. Most will decide that she's the *Californian*. Personally, I could give a damn." He turned away from the view. "She never comes to our aid."

An officer stood nearby, operating a Morse lamp. He was repeatedly signalling to the far-flung light. Another rocket split the skies, raining shooting stars of bright white fire.

"Someone on the *Californian* does report seeing this, however." Wells sneered contemptuously at the pyrotechnics. "They're going to think we're having a party on board."

Kennedy was staring at the empty davits. "Which one's next?"

"Lifeboat four."

They descended to the enclosed promenade on A deck. The boat dangled tantalisingly out of reach beyond the thick glass windows. Crewmen worked at their seams, trying to pry them open. The deck's list was more pronounced, keeling forwards and to port.

All illusions of rescue had been rapidly dispelled. Cries rose from the steerage passengers on the well deck, their fury hardly abated by the distance. Kennedy and Wells, loading the lifeboats, had already witnessed an attempt by some men to force their way through. The charge was held at bay by pistol fire. Kennedy himself had stood with gun drawn beneath his coat. Wells, catching the glint of the barrel, forced the Colt back out of sight.

After the brief mêlée they'd both watched as Ismay had slunk into the lifeboat. Wells had offered the Line's chairman a parting gesture that Kennedy didn't recognise, but couldn't possibly be mistaken for "Bon Voyage". Ismay had averted his eyes.

The gathering on A deck was small; a who's who of America's and Europe's elite by Wells' report.

Within minutes the windows had been cranked open. Glacial draughts seeped into the promenade. Kennedy organised the male passengers into a protective ring while Wells helped a woman adjust her lifebelt. Lightholler began loading the next boat. Astor was close by his side.

Kennedy stared at the two men, merging them into the apotheosis that had been his friend. He wondered how John might have handled the revelations this journey had brought.

Better than most, I suspect.

A frail-looking woman had just stepped into the boat. Lightholler was involved in a heated discussion with Astor as to whether her son should be permitted to join her. Astor snatched a bonnet from another woman and pressed it firmly on the young boy's head. "There," he pronounced firmly. "He's a girl now. Put him aboard."

Lightholler surrendered.

There was a faint irony in the fact that John's character seemed closer to the ancestor he'd scorned rather than the one he'd cherished.

Kennedy glared at Lightholler and muttered, "The man's a fool."

"He's following the only code he knows," Wells said. "He doesn't trust the lifeboat's strength. He doesn't know that only one of them will return after the sinking. He'll refuse to leave the *Titanic*, given every opportunity to do so. Saved by blind luck, he's going to be the last man to board the *Carpathia.*"

Kennedy softened his face and said, "I knew his great-grandson."

"What was he like?"

"Chip off the old block."

Astor was helping his own wife into the lifeboat. There was little evidence of her condition. The boat was now two-thirds full. Astor spoke to Lightholler again, but in gentler tones. It was to no avail. Lightholler wasn't going to permit him to board, despite his wife's delicate state.

Kennedy's eyes played over the lifeboat's occupants, settling on Astor's wife, as well as the children who sat clasped to their mother's chests. There were no men.

Lightholler ordered two of his crew into the boat. He issued the command to lower away.

This was where Astor would bid his bride farewell before descending to the cargo hold on F deck. He would be seen again briefly with his beloved Airedale. He'd be found in a few days with the side of his head caved in.

A snatch of rhyme returned to trouble Kennedy.

Full fathom five thy father lies
Of his bones are coral made
Those are pearls that were his eyes
Nothing of him that doth fade
But doth suffer a sea-change
Into something rich and strange.

"What are you thinking?" Wells asked.

"I'm thinking about the path to hell, and how well it's paved."

"Be that as it may, it's time we made our move."

Yet Kennedy's attention remained fixed on Astor. He said, "You go on ahead. I'll be up in a moment."

He felt someone brush against him. An alarmingly familiar voice said, "There you are."

Kennedy spun around to face Morgan. "What the hell are you doing here?"

"I couldn't find a lifeboat that was to my taste," Morgan replied, shakily. His gaze slipped away from Kennedy's pained eyes.

"Jesus, Darren."

Wells said, "The pickings are getting slim."

Lifeboat four, creaking down towards the water, seemed to punctuate his assessment.

The ocean's stealthy advance loitered by the *Titanic*'s bow. Lightholler had departed for the boat deck and the remaining men were milling about the opened windows. One suggested a hand of bridge and four of them began trudging slowly towards the stairwell.

Astor remained with his valet by the railing. He was smoking a cigarette.

Morgan had thrown away his last real chance of escape. His beaten stance called for some meaning to it all. There wasn't much on offer.

Kennedy said, "Looks like you're just in time, Darren."

Morgan gave the scene a swift review. His eyes came to rest on Astor. "Has he been down to the kennels yet?"

"Perhaps all he needs is a little push in the right direction."

Wells placed a hand on Kennedy's arm. "There's one lifeboat left. Collapsible D. It's just above us, on the boat deck." He checked his watch. "We can still make it."

Morgan said, "There are two more lifeboats."

"They don't get released till after she goes down. It's going to be a shit fight climbing aboard. You don't want that."

"Can I get down to the kennels and be back in time?" Kennedy asked.

"She founders in twenty-five minutes, and I doubt you'll make it back by then," Wells said. "Below decks will be awash."

"Astor made it."

"That's just a story," Wells said. "We don't really know what happens."

Kennedy bared his teeth. "Not knowing what happens will be a pleasant change."

"For God's sake, man, you're going to be a father." Wells leaned in close. "You've got a family now."

"And I know they're safe. That's a better hand than most people have been dealt tonight."

"Let it go. I told you—Astor *dies*."

"I need to see for myself."

Wells shrugged and turned to Morgan. "Can't you make him see reason?"

Morgan laughed darkly. "Nothing's less likely."

"If you come to your senses, I'll be on the boat deck." Wells' face was a pall of hopelessness. "Don't be too long. I'll try to hold them off launching the lifeboat."

"Don't interfere," Kennedy said firmly.

"Speak for yourself." Wells reached out a hand to grasp Kennedy's. "I'll see you topside."

Kennedy nodded. He approached the railing with Morgan in tow.

Astor had his hand in his coat pocket, and he pulled out a packet of cigarettes. He turned at Kennedy's advance and said, "Well, and what now, I wonder?"

"You've seen to your wife, Colonel?"

Astor nodded glumly.

"As have I mine." Kennedy offered his hand. "Major Joseph Kennedy." He watched Astor wince in his grasp. "Tell me, Colonel, didn't you bring your dog along for the voyage?"

XXV

Above the Grand Staircase, the chandelier hung askew.

They descended level after level in Morgan's wake. A few stewards stood along the stair, holding lifebelts before them as if presenting arms.

The ship groaned around them, offering preternatural grumblings as she vainly dealt with the Atlantic's piecemeal intrusion. Morgan was thinking about a book he'd once read. Like Stead's portentous novel, it dealt with an ocean liner lost at sea after colliding with an iceberg. Similarly, it had been published in the previous century, its dire message unheeded. It had been titled *Futility*.

Futility, from the Latin *futilis*, as in leaky or related to pouring.

He tried to dismiss the image of crumpled bulkheads and surging waters.

They were back on D deck, their cabin only yards away down the corridor. They had stood here, long ages ago, with Wells saying, "We need to get off this level. We need to be on the boat deck." He was up there now, perhaps boarding the last lifeboat.

Morgan led them down a smaller staircase and out along Scotland Road. The corridor, so accustomed to the tramp of crewmen, was empty. It leaned crazily towards the bow. They worked their way against the gradient towards a wrought-iron gate by the engine casing. The enclosing walls of the great turbines below were cool and silent now. He twisted the latch and held the gate open for his companions, and suppressed the impulse to run back down the passageway.

The gate slammed after them with disconcerting finality.

"I hope you remember the way back," Astor whispered.

Morgan gave him a strange look. He was thinking about breadcrumbs. The Astor he remembered was an elderly man who'd led his country through turbulent years. That country would never come into being, and this man would be dead within the hour. Morgan nodded to him reassuringly.

A wooden block was set in the wall above the doorway ahead. "Crew Quarters" was carved into it. Morgan reached the door and tried the latch.

He gazed back at Kennedy, his expression empty. "It's locked."

Kennedy shoved him aside and tried the latch. He pulled back and threw himself against the door. It held firm.

"Is there another way?" Astor ventured.

Kennedy slammed against the door again. It creaked its objection. Something was propped up behind it.

Morgan couldn't think straight. They would have to back up. Traverse the aft corridors and return below, somewhere rear of the quarters.

Kennedy took a few steps back, his head tucked down and his shoulder forwards as he prepared for another charge.

There was a snapping sound from beyond and the door fell away on its hinges. Wells was standing there, within the small landing. He was wearing a lifebelt. His clothes were wet. He held an axe at his side.

Kennedy straightened up.

"Turns out the collapsible wasn't to my taste either." Wells smiled at Morgan. He nodded a greeting to Astor and added, "Down here."

They took the winding metal stair down to F deck. They twisted their way between the boiler casings along a dimly lit passage. The carpet was damp in patches but there was no sign of water. The walls were dry. The kennels lay ahead.

Astor pointed up. A stain stretched across the ceiling.

"The compartments above us are flooded," Wells said. "We'll have to leave by the way you came."

The door to the hold was secured by a heavy lock. It split at Wells' third attempt. He left the axe quivering in the wooden panelling.

The entry opened into an expansive, high-roofed compartment lit by a series of naked bulbs that dangled away from them to cast wild outlines on the walls. A foul stench assailed Morgan, disorienting him further. The howls of distraught animals tortured his ears.

He eyed the caged animals. They pressed against metal, hackles raised, ears folded back. He watched Astor make his way to a larger stall at the far end of the hold. Stood transfixed as Kennedy followed him, the axe in hand. He had the weapon reversed, the haft upright.

Astor was calling for his dog in muted tones. A sharp yapping reply was echoed by the other animals. Morgan couldn't stir from his place. Kennedy had the weapon raised. There was a swift movement and a dull clatter as it struck the floor. Wells was close by Kennedy. They struggled silently while Astor, preoccupied, worked the stall gate.

Morgan regained his motility. He raced up to them.

"He's seen on deck with the dog, damn it." Wells' voice was a growled whisper.

"It's just a story," Kennedy replied, just as softly. He reached for the holster at his belt.

Wells had his hands locked around Kennedy's wrist. "A bullet wound will be much worse."

Kennedy stopped thrashing. He could have taken Wells any number of ways. "That's why you came down here?"

"We don't change a thing, and we *don't* interfere."

"How do we know this isn't how it's supposed to play out?"

"You didn't murder me. You don't kill him."

"Why do you think I came down here?"

"The same reason you haven't left on a lifeboat. To bear witness. To pay penance."

Morgan took in the scene bitterly. *It's going to cost us*, he thought.

Astor returned, smiling triumphantly. Behind him padded a small wiry dog, its coat dappled in gold and black. The terrier jumped repeatedly at the back of his thigh. He leaned over to scratch behind her cocked ears. "We should probably get going."

"What about the other dogs?" Wells said. "What shall we do?"

"Rules of the sea, old boy." Astor laughed. "Every man—and dog—for himself."

Hurriedly, they moved among the cages, opening them. Within moments the cargo hold was transformed into a menagerie of animals that ran furiously around the room, snatching at portions of food and menacing one another.

They made for the doorway. They had difficulty avoiding the animals underfoot. Astor had his dog tucked up under an arm, the terrier licking excitedly at his face and chin. Morgan held the doorway open and Astor scurried through, pursued by a small horde that raced, barking, into the damp passageway.

Morgan heard a faint mewling sound. Wells stood before him, a small cat in his arms.

"Hurry up," Astor shouted from up the hallway.

Morgan said, "You're out of your mind. Leave it."

Wells shook his head decisively.

"Kill it."

"Gentlemen, I urge you to hurry." Astor's voice was more distant.

Kennedy was nowhere in sight. He still had the gun.

They ran out into the passageway.

Kennedy stood beside Astor at the foot of the winding stair. Water was spilling down in a cascade of icy spray. The dogs, directionless, were milling around their feet.

"Let's go," Astor cried, and began climbing the stairs.

They followed at his heels. The dogs pursued them up the watery stair. At the top they found Astor staring. The crew's quarters were flooded. A wave frothed towards the landing. Beyond, the water surged out towards the corridor's roof. Underlit, it seemed to course with a malign intelligence.

They sloshed their way hurriedly past the iron gate, calf-deep in the freezing water. They forded a path through the swirling debris to the next stairway. The dogs thronged at their knees.

On D deck, the reception area was saturated. A tide of water lapping at the vestibule coaxed wicker furniture down into its maw.

A middle-aged man in a corner of the room was hunched over an open suitcase, picking at the scraps that floated away from his overturned valise. Kennedy called out to him and the man answered with a feral growl. Wells advanced and the man swiped him away with a poorly thrown punch. One of the dogs, a greyhound, bounded forwards and tore at his jacket with snapping jaws. His eyes flashed primordial understanding. He threw the bag aside and ran for the Grand Staircase. They all dashed after him.

Morgan slipped on the stairs, slamming his jaw against hard oak. He scrambled to his feet, with Kennedy dragging him up by the collar. The ship seemed to heave beneath them, shifting violently. He couldn't catch his breath. A knot of muscle in his chest clenched tightly. Springing up onto A deck, he was granted a view of the stairwell below. It wound down into the briny water.

The first-class entrance had been abandoned, save for two men. Guggenheim and his valet. Neither wore a lifebelt. Guggenheim turned to Astor and said, "Goodbye, John." He knelt down to pat the terrier, and offered the rest of them a cursory nod.

Soft music greeted them on the boat deck. Hartley's group had abandoned their spirited ragtime in favour of a waltz. The pack of dogs dispersed along the slanting floor, their yelps only compounding the surreal aspect of the night. The shrieks from distant decks might have been the wind but there was no movement over the ship. The air was a frigid mantle.

Astor turned to face them and said, "My gratitude to you all." He continued to Kennedy, "I believe you would have made it quick, and I'm thankful for that, but I so wanted one more moment with Madeleine, even if it's shared across the water." He drew the terrier into his arms and left them, returning to the railing.

Kennedy's jaw hung slack.

Wells said, "He must have seen you."

There were no lifeboats in sight. Passengers stood quietly in small groups. A few glanced back at them with quick, furtive movements.

Kennedy said. "He's as tied to this as we are."

Wells reached into his pocket and withdrew the scrawny mass of the cat. He presented it to Morgan.

Morgan glanced at Kennedy.

"Patricia likes cats." Kennedy's tone was remote.

Some undertow had already taken hold of them. It curled about in a manifest coda to all their dark nights on this ship. It promised an end, at last, to misery.

Morgan felt it reaching a tendril towards him. He found himself taking a step back.

"Do any cats survive the sinking?" he asked softly.

"It can be our secret," Wells replied.

Morgan reached out and drew the cat away from their dark current. It stirred, warm in his palms.

XXVI

The band fell silent.

In the ensuing stillness Morgan heard voices joined in prayer. A small gathering on the second-class promenade began singing a hymn.

The stern decks were crammed with steerage passengers and crew. Ahead, the *Titanic*'s bow had yielded to the black ocean. Her rigging jutted out of the rising water, isolated and forfeit. Much further out, the lifeboats coasted beneath the flicker of lantern light; lost stars spread out across the water.

The singers wavered. Individual voices struggled to carry the melody, faltering, until the deep tones of a cello swelled beneath them, bracing their song. The rest of Hartley's band joined in.

"Is that what I think it is?" Kennedy asked.

"Nearer, My God, to Thee," Wells intoned. "That's last call, gentlemen."

Some crewmen were gathered around the officers' quarters. Oars had been arranged beneath the collapsible lifeboats. It looked like they planned on sliding them down onto the deck. Within moments, collapsible A was loose. It crashed down to entrench itself in a portion of the splintered floorboards. Collapsible B dropped next and landed upside down on the port side of the deck.

Wells looked at them and said, "They're going to be our best bet."

"It's going to be a shit fight," Morgan replied.

Captain Smith emerged from the wheelhouse. He had a megaphone pressed to his lips. "Do your best for the women and children, and look out for yourselves." He moved across the deck, repeating the message at regular intervals.

"If you miss out on the lifeboats, get into the water fast," Wells said. "You don't want to be caught on the stern. The crowds will drag you down, if the ship's suction doesn't." He was bent forwards, hands on his knees, as if preparing for a sprint. "The ship's baker has thrown most of the deckchairs overboard. Gather a few together. Stay as dry as you can. It's the cold that will get you, not the water." He turned to them and said, "Good luck."

Kennedy tightened his lifebelt.

Morgan's eyes strayed to the bulge of his holster.

Kennedy caught the movement and said, "Do you want me to shoot you?"

"I'll take my chances, Major. See you on the lifeboat."

Kennedy crouched down too, more for balance, as the bow dipped further towards the water.

"Joseph?"

"What is it?" Kennedy's eyes, hooded in shadow, revealed nothing.

There was a sudden gurgling noise as the ocean began boiling over the forwards railings. It swept towards the bridge.

"May your dance bring good cloud."

Kennedy gave him the broadest smile. "Good cloud, Darren."

The ship lurched suddenly. Then Kennedy was running, Wells at his side, towards the upright lifeboat. Morgan, stumbling, gave chase.

Someone had cut the falls of the collapsible and it was sliding forwards. Passengers and crew pitched themselves desperately into the retreating boat. A crest of water crashed over the boat deck, spilling most of the collapsible's occupants. It careened into a davit and began drifting against the forwards funnel. The bridge slipped beneath the water.

Smith had cast aside the megaphone. Morgan caught a last glimpse of him diving over the ship's side.

Kennedy and Wells were lost to sight.

The lifeboat slipped by, yards away. Morgan felt the cat scratching wildly within his coat. He scanned for a deckchair or a barrel, seeking a dry way to safety. A crowd of people poured from the first-class entrance. They dashed aft at the sight of the oncoming water, only to find themselves blocked by the promenade railing. They swarmed over the barrier or climbed to the irrational safety of the quarters' roof. The air was rent by their screams.

A woman tore past him, the woollen bundle of a child pressed to her chest. Two men fought over a lifebelt. It split, sending them both off balance and skittering along the deck.

The ship tilted forwards in preparation for her plunge.

Morgan reached for the side railing. Bodies slammed past him, hurled to the waves below. He dragged the hem of his coat as high as the lifebelt permitted, bringing his burden up to his neck. He gave the sloping deck a final search for Kennedy. The collapsible bobbed amid a throng of black bodies.

All along the ship the lights flickered and went out as one.

Morgan leapt out into the void.

XXVII

Kennedy flailed. A thousand blades pierced him.

He rose only to be drawn down again. The cold pinioned him. He twisted and turned—each frantic movement a paroxysmal spasm.

He broke the surface yards away from the collapsible. He searched for Wells and Morgan. A plank struck the side of his head and he was thrown into the arms of another passenger. Hands scraped his face, hooking under his belt. He lashed out viciously and reached into the darkness. His fingers scrabbled over the edge of a deckchair, tearing at the material.

He tumbled with his prize, seeking balance. The ocean foamed.

The *Titanic* was an impossible shuddering cliff face towering above him. It loomed there, casting an avalanche of bodies and debris. Gutted and torn from within, it trumpeted the Apocalypse; an unearthly, ear-splitting clamour that drowned out the cries of those in the water. It hung there, tottering for long moments, while overhead the vast black finger of her funnel clawed at the sky.

His breath came as rapid stabs. He kicked out towards the collapsible. One chance in twenty. Thrashing bodies churned the ocean in fierce eddies. Astor's face, a haggard knot of terror, flashed into view. Slipped past. He reached out and his hands closed around a gnarled end of rope. Benumbed, he began pulling himself along its length, only sure of his grasp by the sight of his own frozen fingers shifting along its twining cable.

A crescendo of noise threatened to crack open his skull. He twisted, staring up. The funnel had curved forwards on itself as if seeking severance from the ship. It broke from its mooring, plummeting, filling the night.

The collapsible was a body's length away.

His hand clutched its side, fingernails tearing at the wood. One in—

The sky fell in an explosion that flung him bodily into a cloud of ash as the funnel struck water inches away. He was spinning, borne on a soot-capped wave, turned over and over.

He gasped for air, swallowing brackish water.

His chest was caught within a vice of frost-tipped jaws.

He knew nothing save this ice-clad, endless, wave-tossed existence.

He broke the surface.

He spun, searching the waters for a lifeboat. The *Titanic* towered within an expanding circle of her waste. Her stern reared back, slapping the ocean in harsh, futile protest. The wave reached him, a swell that lifted him high above the devastation for a brief moment.

He sought the ruins for a boat. He found the staves of a barrel and propped himself partially out of the water, snatching at the frigid air for sustenance. The cold worked its way through his bones. Despite the pain, his eyes were drawn back to the ship. Her stern rose again: majestic, terrible. Silently she began to glide, forwards and down, in a final approximation of her earlier grace.

The waters closed over her. Bodies, near and far, jerked among the fragments. Their cries were one long dirge. He lent his own cracked voice to the proceedings without knowing it.

Arms closed around him. Sluggish, pulling him away from the barrel and down. His own reflexive retaliation was lethargic; shrugging and twisting slow. A fist connected weakly with his jaw. An open hand tugged at his belt. He kicked, swinging broad sidewinders. Grabbed a handful of thick hair, yanking Wells' pale face into view.

He released him.

Wells hurled himself back, treading water and staring at Kennedy.

Kennedy panted, floundering. Other bodies, still, glided between them.

"Easy," Wells mouthed, spluttering water. "Slow it down."

Kennedy couldn't catch his breath. He reached for one of the staves.

"Easy. Easy. Don't wear yourself out." Wells gripped a splinter of wood.

Kennedy's lungs were raw. He tried to speak.

Wells was making slow movements, paddling towards him. Further out, others remained locked in intimate embraces. Their short-lived meetings, a flurry of dying reflexes; slow-dancing amid the wreckage.

"She's gone." Kennedy's racked mind couldn't distinguish the subject of his loss. He mourned everything.

"She'll be okay."

"Yeah."

"Yeah."

They kept the remains of the barrel between them. Their faces were separated only by the haze of their laboured breaths.

"I almost made it," Kennedy wheezed.

Wells was nodding. "Same."

"Lifeboat. Where?"

Wells shook his head.

"One in twenty."

"Was being generous." Wells coughed out the words.

The cold snaked its way through Kennedy. It coated veins and nerves. He looked down. Wells had him grasped firmly by the sleeve. He tried to cover Wells' hand with his own. His fingers fumbled, feeling nothing.

A body passed by them, face down, drifting slowly. It made a languid turn, as if performing some elaborate routine. The rictus of Astor's smile was interrupted by a shattered corolla of split skin and bone. Some last kiss, imparted in the ship's departure. His face returned to the water.

It was growing quiet again. The ocean was a flat calm. Tranquil.

Kennedy felt himself slipping on the wood.

"Easy," Wells said.

Kennedy nodded. He had never been so tired.

"*Carpathia*. One hour."

Kennedy nodded.

"Keep your head up."

Kennedy nodded. He wiped his face against his sleeve, trying to dislodge the frozen moisture that crusted beneath his eyes. "Patricia."

"You're a father in December."

Kennedy nodded.

An hour. He looked at his wrist. His Einstein was frozen at two-twenty. He fumbled with the clasp. The pulp of his fingers tore open. The watch slipped off his wrist and into the water. He reached down.

It wasn't so cold now. He tugged at his holster, releasing it.

He turned back to Wells. He tried to talk. His lips were strips of skin flapping uselessly.

Wells' face was a blue-tinged mask of repose.

"Wells," Kennedy croaked.

He made no reply.

"Jonathan?"

There was no reply. No thin wisps of respiration.

A mist must have risen elsewhere, because it was getting harder to distinguish any shapes in the water. Something nudged against him, nestling against the crook of his arm. He tried to turn but the attempt barely elicited a ripple.

The echo of a thousand, thousand days and nights pressed themselves upon him. He followed them to where they coalesced and saw a multifaceted jewel, each edge a petrified moment. An infinite number of possibilities, awaiting his decision. Light flashed a brilliant rose red across its surface, drawing him in.

He made his selection, choosing here and there among the dazzling hues.

Is everything okay?

Everything's okay.

They sat closer now, almost touching.

I had the worst nightmare, Patricia.

Just a dream, Joseph.

I killed them all.

You imagined the whole thing.

John. David. Martin. Wells.

Dreams…

A chill had taken the air, seeming to issue from the desert floor below them rather than the darkening skies above.

Do you prefer sunrise or sunset?

His sense—of being here before—faded.

His sense of being faded.

I'm tired, Patricia, so very tired. But you're here now.

There was the soft promise of life beneath the swell of her abdomen, tight against her shirt. She kept still, letting his hand complete the caress.

Is it because I forget everything?

Forgetting will be a good thing, don't you think, Joseph?

Shifting hues, bronze and orange, spiralled above the chequerboard sand, darkening.

I like this part of the day. The sky changing colour with each passing moment.

It's all just fluid. Look up, look away, look up again and it's a whole new world.

There was the soft touch of something penetrating his insensate shroud. Some last quiver of her salved his broken lips.

That's a sunset, Joseph.

WHAT THE THUNDER SAID

... And what you thought you came for
Is only a shell, a husk of meaning
From which the purpose breaks only when it is fulfilled
If at all...

And the end of all our exploring
Will be to arrive where we started
And know the place for the first time.

I

April 15, 1947
New York City, New York

The harbour waters were a murky green where they lapped against the stone barrier of the park. Further out they slipped to a sullen grey under the sky's low cloud. Four or five ships drifted on the horizon, the ocean's traffic bare this afternoon.

A woman stood along the barrier. She wore a fur coat over her dark burgundy suit. A parasol was perched over her shoulder as she gazed out to sea. Otherwise, Battery Park was quite empty. The rain had dwindled to a light spatter that she seemed to ignore.

Morgan limped over to one of the park benches and sat down. His knee always ached with the season's change, and this tardy spring had summoned the aftertaste of every injury that had ever plagued him.

And I only am escaped alone to tell thee…

The morning's edition of the *Times* had reported that the *Queen Elizabeth* had run aground just outside of Southampton. The photographs of that dour town showed him that little had changed over the years. A later edition proclaimed that the liner had been refloated and was being towed for repairs. The image of the ship, listing among a wreath of tugboats, called out to him. The first time as tragedy, the next as farce.

It struck him as a fittingly trivial echo of this forlorn anniversary.

As always on this day, the recollections paraded behind his weary eyes. His balancing act on collapsible B, under Officer Lightholler's strained instructions. The soft splash of water as body after exhausted body toppled over the side of the upturned lifeboat. The thin smear of mist over the *Titanic*'s grave. Dawn had revealed the *Carpathia* and an unbroken field of ice to the west. A solitary berg towered among the growlers, its hem decorated by a broad scrape of red and black paint. Lipstick on its collar.

The days that followed had relegated the world he'd known to the substance of fantasy and each passing year had only strayed further from his memory.

There had been no erring to Wells' inventory, however. Over the years, Morgan had discovered new depths in man's inhumanity. The Great War had bled continents dry. Most recently, he'd learned what a disgruntled Austrian painter could do, given the might of a rebuilt Germany for his brush and the worn palimpsest of Europe for a canvas. He'd discovered what happened when scientists were given unlimited resources and a mandate for victory—at any cost.

Here, all the suffering his own world had known had been compacted into a few short years; a brief, violent foray on the borders of hell. While some might argue that a new hope had been kindled in the wake of these terrors, Morgan recognised it for what it was: the brutish variation on a time-worn theme.

Only one consolation remained to him, but it blazed brightly enough. The stagnant world he'd left behind had blundered into oblivion. This place had seen its darkest hour and survived to view the dawn. That had to count for something.

Wells' journal had warned of the cold days that would follow this dark centrepiece of the twentieth century. Not all the criminals would be brought to justice, nor all the victors know true freedom. It spoke of further conflicts and shadows, but it also spoke of expectation. The weapons of horror, tested so thoroughly, would be put aside. The Nazi experiments in social reconstruction, only now coming to light, would determine the yardstick of humanity's depravity.

Those depths would never be explored on such a scale again. In far-flung colonies, the browbeaten indigenous would flex hidden muscles against their distant masters. At home, the downtrodden would begin to find their own voices and their cries would grow to resound throughout the years.

The changes would be slow and hard-fought, but there were no quick fixes. He'd learned that under the crimson skies of Red Rock, and the lesson had been enforced in freezing water, while the corpses glided by. The future was to be gained moment by moment. A leap from the shoulders of giants, or a stumbled climb from the deepest pits of iniquity, but always forwards.

The past was to be regarded with a steady eye and never a thought for the "what if" or "might have been".

Untrammelled by the footprints of travellers from the future, this world was no paradise. It was not, by any stretch of the imagination, the best of all possible worlds. It was the only *possible* world, and it had been granted a reprieve.

Today he would pay tribute to the friends and adversary who'd paid for that acquittal in the dearest coin.

Morgan approached the barrier. Standing before the water, cold and miserable, he decided this would be the last time. Half of his life had been a cenotaph to his years in Kennedy's service. It was time to move on.

The drizzle had ceased. The sun broke through the clouds and a dim rainbow stretched out in the distance, arching from ocean into nothingness. The young woman was watching him with unveiled interest. He wondered what fascination he might engender, an old man tossing crumbs into the ocean. She approached with a curious smile at her lips, only to stop a few feet away from him.

Morgan reached into the paper sack and grabbed another handful of crumbs. Gulls swooped low over the water now, crying out in anticipation. She followed his movements, watching the crumbs arc over the water, the birds lunge forwards to snatch them before they struck.

"Excuse me," the woman said. "I'm sorry to interrupt you."

Morgan ignored her. This ritual, performed for the last time, would not be profaned by an inquisitive bystander, attractive or otherwise.

She seemed unfazed. She simply waited until he'd emptied the bag before speaking again. "Mr Morgan?"

She had his complete attention now.

"I hate to disturb you, and I realise that this is late notice, but my mother is staying in town tonight. She was hoping you might be able to join us for dinner."

Morgan stared, dumbfounded.

"My name's Josephine Kennedy. I've heard so much about you."

II

Morgan emerged from the cab and gazed up at the hotel's façade with a sigh. Patricia's choice in accommodation, by default or design, only stirred more memories. The Waldorf remained one of the few places unaltered by the vagaries of time and change. He shuffled across Park Avenue and entered the lobby. She was staying in the Astoria Lounge.

Of course.

A bellboy directed him along the corridor, but after thirty-six years he still recalled the way. Passing the door that had opened into Lightholler's suite, he trod softly, fearful of disturbing old ghosts.

The door to Patricia's suite was ajar. Muted voices issued from within. He waited long moments before rapping lightly on the frame. Josephine greeted him. She had changed into a light-coloured satin dress and wore her hair down.

"It's good that you came. Mother will be so pleased."

Morgan nodded timidly. She had Kennedy's eyes.

He felt shabby in his threadbare suit. He removed his fedora and followed her down the corridor into a drawing room. Patricia was seated by a wide table that had been set for four. She turned to look upon Morgan, and welcomed him with a warm smile. Her skin, always pallid, was translucent over the fine bones of her face. She wore a long black dress, but her look wasn't one of mourning.

"Are those for me?" Her laughter tripped lightly, a gentle frisson to her voice.

He held the bouquet of lilies in the meat of his fists, shifting uncertainly from one foot to the other.

She rose from her chair and glided towards him. She gave his arm a gentle squeeze and kissed him on the cheek. "It's so good to see you, Darren. It's been too long."

He found her affection a strange bounty after all these years. He followed her to his seat as in a dream. The opulence of his surroundings, the gentle patter of rain against the oak-framed windows, the company he'd never thought to share again, transported him to some other realm. Josephine took her seat and Morgan looked over at the empty setting. On a night such as this, anyone might walk in to complete their circle.

Patricia placed the flowers in a vase.

Two waiters entered with their meals. The banquet was served and consumed in silence. Their only words had been in answer to Patricia's toast. *Absent friends.*

Throughout the feast, Morgan's stare returned time and again to the vacant seat. His gaze occasionally fell upon Josephine, cataloguing her features. Patricia's pale colouring and dark hair, Joseph's eyes. Some amalgam around the fullness of her lips. The rest, a throwback to some distant ancestors.

A waiter, returning to collect their plates, served sherry from a bottle on a polished salver.

"I hope that was to your satisfaction." Patricia took a delicate sip from her glass. She regarded her company amiably.

He murmured his assent.

She said, "Let's sit in the lounge where we can be more comfortable," and led him into a smaller room.

The chairs had been arranged in a circle by a large window fronting Park Avenue. The rain, relentless now, strummed the glass. An occasional flash of lightning basked the view in a distant glow, too far away for thunder. A ginger cat was stretched out on the sill. It paid the inclement weather no regard.

Catching Morgan's glance, Patricia said, "He keeps me company when Josephine goes off on her little adventures."

"Adventures?"

"My daughter has spent a considerable time abroad these last few years."

Josephine withstood Morgan's appraising stare with a steady gaze. He blinked away, his rheumy eyes flashing sudden unease.

"Are you pressed for time, Darren?" Patricia asked.

"Yes." He viewed them both now with trepidation.

He spied a framed photograph on the mantle. Joseph and Patricia at Coney Island. It had been taken the day they'd gone there in search of Wells. It was washed out, the white sands leeching the colour out of the late afternoon sky. Skeletal roller-coasters back-boned a prehistoric backdrop. They stood in the foreground, hands clasped. The fine details of their faces lost in the poor translation of light to film.

"No."

Patricia said, "That's the only picture I have of us." She turned to face him. "Is there somewhere else you have to be right now? I appreciate that this is all rather last minute."

Morgan wondered if she already knew the answer. If she knew how he spent his nights, reading by lamplight or listening to the wireless. Typing manuscripts that would never see the light of day.

"Why am I here, Patricia? Why tonight of all nights?"

"Please, Darren, sit down."

He surrendered. Josephine remained standing, her hands resting on the back of her mother's chair.

"We made no provisions," Patricia began. "We gave no consideration to what might follow. Those long months chasing Wells' faint trail across America didn't permit such thoughts. Those nights at sea were too fraught with unpleasant revelations." She paused for a moment, as if composing herself, though her countenance betrayed no emotion.

"Doctor Gershon resumed his medical studies. He has a successful practice out on Long Island. He had no interest in being here tonight." She shrugged. A slight, delicate movement at her shoulders. "As for the rest of us... we never strayed far from where we touched land. You in the Village. Myself… close by." She let the sentence die, as if reticent to divulge further details.

"We sought no further journeys. We lived our quiet lives watching the disparities grow between what we knew and what we saw unfold. We were told this was our last chance to right the wrongs of untold cycles. But there were no guidelines, no protocols to follow. Our arguments were garnered from sensations gathered at the foot of an abomination."

Morgan glanced at Josephine nervously. Her expression was unreadable.

"Our proofs lay in the words of a shaman and a spiritualist. Wondering if we succeeded, we greet each new dawn as a stay of execution, each evening with a touch of apprehension. Am I wrong?"

Morgan shook his head wistfully. He felt bared before her.

"There was no denouement," she said. "I don't know what I'd been expecting, what sign I looked for in the clear skies of that last cold night. Before I stepped out into the lifeboat, they had both taken me aside, our quarry and my husband. The former shared with me one final, horrifying notion. The latter, my dear Joseph, entrusted me with one final task. I knew then that was to be our parting."

Her daughter gave her shoulder a squeeze. Patricia raised a hand and left it on Josephine's.

The wind rattled the panes. Flashes of lightning seared the night in blazing forks, but still no sound heralded their fire. Morgan longed for his reading room and the low crackle of his fire. Patricia topped up her glass. Josephine brought the decanter around to him.

Patricia continued, "In all of Doctor Wells' protracted ramblings, one consideration had never been voiced. I suppose he had never paused to give it wonder, but that last night opened all our eyes. So I put it to you now, dear friend. Why was the carapace programmed to arrive in the Nevada desert in 1911?"

Morgan recoiled at the machine's naming.

Josephine's eyes glittered with anticipation.

"Because that's when he'd arrived." He stated the observation carefully, as if he might still skirt the issue.

"I'm talking about the original journey that Wells made. The *first* one."

Morgan was confused. He said, "The machine had no fixed destination. He was on the run. It was a random event."

Patricia asked, "Has anything in our lives been truly random?"

Morgan drained his glass. The alcohol fuzzed his wild thoughts.

"Wells always believed that the machine he'd escaped in had been cobbled from some other device," she continued. "A device that had been flung—backward or forward—from some distant time. A device that had been tested with disastrous flights into the future. And perhaps that is where the masters of the carapace first travelled, curious to its origins. Can you imagine how Jenkins must have felt when he realised that the machine had actually arrived from his own past? From 1911, to be precise."

“That’s not possible,” Morgan said.

“They called it a carapace, Darren. They called the device a shell because they’d come to understand it for what it was. One device, constantly changing its husk as it cycled through the aeons.”

“Wells saw two of them,” Morgan offered, his voice small in the quiet room.

“Wells saw the machine and its old, shed crust,” she replied. “The heart of it remained elsewhere, shifted to another casing. But there has only ever been one conduit. One machine. Jenkins was planning an expedition that was bound for failure. The machine he hunted was the one that we arrived in.”

“Impossible.”

“Surely your experiences have taught you the emptiness of that word.”

“Then where did it come from in the first place?”

“I don’t know. How can we ever know. Some tear in the cloth of our reality. Some Promethean fire never meant for us. Does it matter?”

“Of course it matters.”

Patricia sighed.

“You’ve known this all this time?”

“Yes.”

“Never sharing it.”

“You were left with enough on your plate.”

“Then why share it now?” There was a hint of indignation to his tone. The hour was getting late.

“I’ve been judicious with the money Joseph left me, making careful investments over the years, putting everything in place. In three months we get to finish what Joseph started thirty-five years ago.”

“Three months?”

“Josephine has organised everything,” Patricia said. “I just thought you might appreciate coming along for the ride.”

Kennedy’s daughter smiled at him with all of her father’s cunning.

Morgan straightened in his chair. He said, “I’m an old man, damn it. What do you want from me?”

She rose from her seat and approached him with supple grace. “I don’t want anything from you. I just thought that this might ease your nights and give new promise to your days.”

Morgan nodded slowly, his eyes moistening. “Where are we going?”

There was a rumble in the distance now, but it was low and gentle. *Datta, dayadhvam, damyata*: give, sympathise, control. The thunder was nothing but a warning of the storm to come.

"We're going back to the desert, Darren. We're going to Roswell."

III

June 30, 1947
Roswell, New Mexico

In the pre-dawn hours the great trucks grumbled along the interstate. Some contained dairy products and some contained munitions. Some contained livestock and some cigarettes. Some were empty, returning along familiar stretches to familiar storehouses, there to restock.

And some were not.

Their convoy was made up of five trucks. Morgan rode in the first one, between Josephine and the driver, Alan.

Seeing her dressed in a black shirt and trousers of a military cut under her heavy coat, it was still difficult to imagine her among that rough band. Over the last few weeks Morgan had pressed her for her story. Her responses had been guarded. Recruited by the Strategic Services, she had cut her teeth in some delicate activities prior to the Allied landings in Normandy. She'd supervised the destruction of vital German rail lines and raided supply depots. She spoke perfect French, Italian, Russian and German.

Two nights ago, seated around the coals of a dying fire, he'd watched her field strip and reassemble an Enfield rifle, blindfolded. The men had cheered her on. Patricia's disapproving stare had been unconvincing. Daddy's little girl.

Morgan glanced at Josephine's hand on the armrest. No ring had ever girded those deft fingers. She would be thirty-five this December, but the term spinster seemed at odds with her form. She was more like a nun. The bride of her father's dark vision.

The turn-off wound past the barbed mesh of cattle fences. The occasional farmhouse peered through stretches of long, thin grass in the moonlight. There were no telegraph lines here, no ostensible connections with the outside world.

Their own temporary residence was a ranch on the outskirts of Six-Mile Hill, just outside Roswell. Patricia had obtained a two-year lease on the farm. She was taking no chances. Some of Josephine's men had been out here for months already, mixing with the locals and setting up surveillance posts.

Wells hadn't been specific in his details. Sometime in the next thirty-one days the carapace would complete its sinister rendezvous. The authorities would arrive the following morning. That gave them less than twenty-four hours to act.

None of the men had been given any more information than was necessary. Their particular brand of fanaticism was a far cry from the major's ghost dancers. They required no causes. Their allegiance had been bankrolled on the interest of Kennedy's gold, and their previous experience with Strategic Services ensured they would be quite comfortable with the arrangement.

They reached the farm at sunrise.

Morgan sat beside Patricia as the trucks were unloaded. The men worked briskly, untroubled by inquisitive eyes. He was daunted by them. Age and infirmity made him feel like prey. He feared that a prolonged glance might earn him a confrontation. Hardas wouldn't have blinked twice, but Hardas was long gone. Morgan rubbed his eyes and wheezed in the cool morning air.

IV

July 7, 1947
Roswell, New Mexico

Patricia had never remarried. There'd been no shortage of suitors, of course. She was wealthy and single. The lines that had engraved her face thirty-five years ago had left a melancholy splendour that could still be seen now, beyond the opaque wall of her proud exterior. She simply had never found his equal.

Over the last few nights she had willingly shared the narrative of her life with Morgan, yet she remained closed to him. Each chronicle had been related with distance, as if she was interpreting another's tale. The ghost writer of her own memoirs.

She had borne him no ill will. He realised that now. She'd simply thought it better to spare him her own designs; designs she could never have concealed from him. Constrained by the hand she'd been dealt, raising a daughter and building an empire, she could never have understood his lonely years.

Joseph Patrick Kennedy, the man who would have been Josephine's great-grandfather, had died childless over enemy skies. His sibling, John Fitzgerald Kennedy, was a hero of the South Pacific, and already taking a few small steps towards his destiny. Sundered from her family by a wild shift of paradigm and fate, Josephine struck Morgan as the final casualty of the major's crusade. Patricia had forged her into a weapon, her skills honed in secret schools and dark deeds abroad. Her willingness in this scheme hardly justified her involvement.

We made no provisions, Patricia had said. *No consideration to what might follow*. Morgan hoped that she'd at least given her daughter's future due consideration.

It was morning. Josephine's men, distributed throughout the town, were returning in shifts. She remained in the field surveying the watchposts.

Morgan was frying up some bacon and eggs. Alan and another veteran had joined them in the kitchen for breakfast. Patricia served up some coffee. She seemed to enjoy the company of her daughter's crew. She fussed over them, buttering the toasts that Morgan brought to the table. They, in turn, seemed moderated by her presence—returned to some earlier, pre-martial state. It felt like the commissary at Red Rock.

The radio crackled quietly in the background. Morgan had grown used to its low drone. The occasional short transmission, detailing an alteration of shifts or the request for more supplies, had become ubiquitous. The sudden burst of static now didn't jar him. He was reaching for a slice of bread when the others pitched out of their seats, scattering their plates.

He gave Patricia an enquiring look.

She removed her apron with slow, precise movements and arranged it over one of the chairs.

"What's going on?" he asked.

"It's here," Patricia said softly. "It's time."

V

After all the toil he'd endured, after every turbulent step he'd taken—first from New York to Savannah, and then across that lost America to Red Rock, each stride blunted by blood and violence—he was astonished by the ease of it all.

The ranch owner and his wife stood before the remains of their stable. The carapace projected from its side at an odd angle. Two of the struts had been sheared off, the rest were lost from view within the wreckage. The black and silver sheen of its carriage was obscured by a coating of dust and ash. Coils of smoke drifted from damp wood where a fire had been extinguished.

Josephine wore a black suit without insignia. She stood with one of her men, who was similarly clothed, deep in conversation with the distraught couple. She had a clipboard in her hand. She appeared to be making copious notes as they spoke. All the while, her squad moved around the machine. They worked in teams of three, dismantling the remaining supports. They seemed untroubled by the machine's distorting aura.

Morgan stood a short distance from the debris. Patricia was watching from afar.

A vehicle pulled up beyond the rise. Morgan assumed it was another of Josephine's retinue. He called Patricia over. She approached with hesitant steps. Of all of them, she'd fared worst in the carapace's proximity.

Arriving at his side, she offered Morgan a curious look.

"This is new," she said. "I'm not getting any resonance."

"Me neither," Morgan ventured. "I'm fine."

They neared the ruins. Josephine had interrupted her discourse to cast a watchful eye over her mother. They kept walking until they stood scant feet away from the machine.

"Nothing," Patricia said. "I don't feel a thing."

The carapace was lifeless. There was a glaze to the sand by the imprint of its struts, but Morgan could sense no energy lurking beneath the darkened canopy.

"What do you think it means?" he asked.

"I think it means that we haven't been here before. That we're finally making fresh tracks." She gave his arm a brittle squeeze. "I think we've finally got it *right*." She leaned against his shoulder, momentarily overcome by the revelation.

There was a movement from beneath the carriage.

One of Josephine's men emerged from the stable and rushed straight past them towards her. He spoke loudly, disrupting her exchange with the ranchers. "Josephine, you got to see this."

She seemed unsurprised by the outburst. She signalled to one of her operatives, who stood on a low hill beyond the ranch house, and he waved back. She offered an apology to the couple, excusing herself, and broke away from them. Her offsider was beckoning them away from the scene.

Some men Morgan hadn't encountered before were racing over the hill towards the carapace. They wore white coats over their uniforms.

Josephine disappeared beneath the curve of the machine. Morgan took tentative steps in her trail. Other men converged. They wore hard hats and dark coveralls. Josephine began handing out orders, getting the men to clear a path beneath the wreckage.

Three of the white coats arrived, bearing a crate between them. A fourth hovered behind, his face concealed behind a filter mask designed to protect against the fumes. They opened the box and began to dole out the equipment: bandages, tourniquets and a long arrangement of poles and canvas that opened up into a stretcher.

The masked man reached down to retrieve a worn satchel. He turned to the others and said, "Bring him out slow. We'll get IV access as soon as he's clear. The opiates will still be working so I want a full fluid resus. He'll be as dry as the desert." Seemingly satisfied with the instructions, he pulled down the mask and turned to Morgan. "Long time no see."

Morgan felt a thrill of exhilaration. He said, "Hey, Doc."

Gershon pulled on some gloves. He moved with a litheness that suggested a much younger man. He said, “Be with you in a moment. Had a hell of a time getting down here,” and advanced in the wake of the other medics.

They emerged a few moments later with Lightholler. He lay still on the stretcher, pale, his arms crossed over his chest. They placed the stretcher on the ground and began working on him. One placed an oxygen mask over his face while the others cut away at his clothing.

“I’ve got a pulse,” one of them muttered.

Another inserted a metal cannula and began pumping blood from a hand-set.

Gershon bent over Lightholler’s abdomen, inspecting the wound, Josephine by his side.

The medics communicated in low murmurs as long moments passed.

Lightholler’s eyes flickered open. He tried to swipe at the mask. Josephine replaced his arm by his side.

“Patricia?”

Josephine offered a fragile smile and hushed him.

Patricia took a step forwards. Morgan was pressed close behind her.

Lightholler’s glazed eyes came to rest on each of them in turn. He blinked his bewilderment. He gazed at Josephine again in confusion, before settling on Gershon. “Doc?”

“Keep still, Captain.” Gershon turned to one of his medics and said, “Start the antibiotics. Make sure facilities are prepped and ready for us. We’ll be doing a hemicolectomy and proceeding from there.”

“Darren, Patricia…” His pained expression smoothed itself into understanding. His voice was frail. “You did it?”

They all nodded solemnly.

Lightholler’s face cracked a weak smile. “Where’s Joseph?”

Gershon was concentrating on the wound. He stepped away, avoiding eye contact, and said, “Get him out of here.”

The medics heaved the stretcher off the ground and began marching back up the hill towards the waiting ambulance.

Gershon removed his gloves. He rolled them up and placed them in his pocket. “He’ll be alright, Patricia.”

“Thank you, Dean.”

Josephine’s men were hauling the carapace’s struts back to the trucks. It now resembled a broad convex disc. Some men were working at removing the outer plating. The couple who'd found the wreckage were nowhere in sight.

Morgan examined Gershon's face. The thick coils of his dark hair had receded to a white patina. There were heavy lines around his eyes and mouth. He was considerably thinner.

He said, "Nice work, Doctor Gershon."

Doc smiled. He turned to Patricia. "What are we doing with this?" He indicated the carapace with a nod.

"We're stripping it bare. All we're leaving is the husk. They can make of it what they will."

Morgan dropped to his haunches. He held a thin shard of polished sand in his hands. It crumbled to dust between his fingers. "Are we done here?"

He surveyed the prospect. Josephine was standing on a low mound, overseeing the clean-up. Gershon was collecting the leftovers from the resuscitation and storing them back in the crate. The morning sun, slung in a hammock of cloud, poured its light through the trees. It was already growing warmer.

Patricia said, "We're done."

VI

July 10, 1947
Roswell, New Mexico

Josephine left the ranchers with more than enough money to rebuild and expand their damaged property. A trust account, established in their names, would ensure a healthy income for their children's children.

The small town was still reeling with excitement. A local afternoon rag had run the headline: *Roswell Army Air Field Captures Flying Saucer on Ranch in Roswell Region. No Details of Flying Disk are Revealed.* A day later the *New York Times* had issued its own refutation. *"Disc" near Bomb Test Site Is Just a Weather Balloon. "Flying Saucer" Tales Pour in from Round the World.*

That afternoon they received word that Lightholler was recovering well from his surgery. Gershon assured them that he would be fit for discharge within a week.

Patricia owned a property in Canada. That was where Lightholler would be sent to complete his convalescence. Morgan was to report there by September. Patricia assured him that if he had not arrived by then, she'd dispatch Josephine's men to round him up.

"John's going to need some help readjusting," she said. "You're welcome to stay as long as you like. Unless, of course, you have other plans."

She explained that the property was in St John's, located on the Avalon Peninsula in Newfoundland. Overlooking the Grand Banks and cresting the continental shelf, it was nestled on the easternmost tip of North America. Nothing else needed to be said. She'd made her home as close to Kennedy's final resting place as was humanly possible. There was no refusing the offer.

The following morning Josephine set out early. She left by moonlight to finalise some arrangements with her crew. They'd been dispersing over the last few days, until only a few remained to man the convoy. Morgan would get the chance to catch up with her soon.

He was already planning his journey north and away from New York. It was time to move on.

It was still dark when he climbed into the truck's cab beside Alan. The vehicles had been loaded with the machine's carcass. Once across the Arizona border they would separate, distributing its remains across the breadth of the country. Morgan planned on bearing witness to its destruction. He could already picture the undecipherable beacons of smoking pyres. World without end.

Patricia stood outside the front of the ranch house, wearing a dressing gown. She waved him farewell, her figure spectral in the dim porch light.

Alan fired up the engine and they shipped out.

Sleep came rolling over Morgan in waves but no whimper escaped his lips. He slept knowing that the future was out there, unknowable but pristine. He rode the highway, rising and falling with the truck's rocky motion, following the path towards a single, impervious destiny, and nothing disturbed his slumber.

In the pre-dawn hours the great trucks grumbled along the interstate. Some contained dairy products and some contained munitions. Some contained livestock and some cigarettes. Some were empty, returning along familiar stretches to familiar storehouses, there to restock.

And some were not.

CODA

I

February 26, 1999
Las Vegas, Nevada

Wells was due to meet up with Mary at the Beef Barron in twenty minutes and he still had to give the paper another read through. The raw findings of his research, consigning his preferred operation to the scrap heap, would require a brave face.

So why had he left the hotel room? Why was he here?

He watched the dealer lay out another hand. The house pulled a five. The marks should have all sat on their cards and watched him bust, but they were marks. So one by one they made their suicide plays. Someone doubled, someone drew, someone split Kings to sit on fifteen and twelve.

He suppressed a snort. He'd done enough time behind the green felt. He watched as the dealer pulled twenty-one and turned away from the table.

There, but for the grace of God, go I.

It was almost four o'clock. The restaurant was on the next level. It was simply a matter of walking down one of the hallways to the lobby and beyond.

His head was aching.

It might have been the ceaseless chime of the one-armed bandits, or the tedious hum of the muzak. He decided to get an aspirin before the meal and found himself standing at the glazed doors of the Flamingo's entrance. Filtered sunlight spilled an unhealthy ochre stain on the carpet. He thought the fresh air might be soothing. He stepped outside, and his head roared dully with the sounds of the street.

Other surgeons would be arriving for the conference. He cast about, hoping for a friendly face, and his eyes were drawn to an Oldsmobile, parked just beyond a small roundabout. He could just make out two figures behind the car's tinted windshield.

They were staring at him.

He approached, wondering what drove him forwards. The driver's window slowly slid down and a pale hand in a black sleeve emerged from the darkness, offering a slight wave. He peered into the car, expecting one of his associates. He was faced with an elderly couple.

They smiled at him amiably. He couldn't place them.

"Doctor Wells?" the man asked.

"Yes." He returned the man's grin, feeling somewhat foolish. "I'm sorry, but do I know you?"

"Not as such," the man replied.

"You knew my mother," the woman added after a moment.

She was well past her seventies. There must have been some mistake, yet something about the pair made him strangely comfortable.

His headache was gone.

"What's her name?" He couched the question carefully.

"Her name was Patricia Marie Kennedy. You helped her out once."

"I'm sorry, but I don't remember her."

The man must have read the doubt in his voice. He said, "We'd better not keep you, Doctor." He began to wind up the window. "It was good finally meeting you."

Wells stood bewildered. "You too."

The car had pulled away from the kerb before he identified the cause of his confusion.

How had they recognised him?

Then he glanced down at his jacket, saw the name badge peering over the edge of his pocket, and laughed.

The Strip was filling with people. Parents urged errant children past gaudy displays. Couples strolled by, waiting for sunset and the city's fluorescent resurrection.

Some insight told him that there were worse encounters to be had on this street.

He felt profoundly relieved.

The Olds pulled up at a set of lights across the street. He threw the couple a final wave before turning back into the hotel.

ACKNOWLEDGEMENTS

In the middle of 1997 I sat down with a note pad and began writing. What began as a short story evolved into the monolith you have before you. I hold the following people responsible: Natan Kowalski, Darren Rose and Rani Gerszonovicz. This book would not exist in any recognizable form without their support, indulgence, encouragement and advice. Virginia Lloyd's commitment to this work, both as editorial consultant, and dear friend, was unwavering. I'd like to take this opportunity to express my gratitude to her for her tireless efforts.

I also want to thank Cath Trechman, Nick Landau, Vivian Cheung, Katy Wild, Tim Whale, Lizzie Bennett, and Martin Still; the Titan's crew, for their enthusiasm and support in launching this book. Steve Saffel, my best friend I've never met, was there from the first edit to the last. He steered my manuscript to safe waters.

Finally I would like to thank Lisa who quite simply, on a day-to-day basis, makes the improbable possible.

ABOUT THE AUTHOR

David J. Kowalski is an obstetrician and gynaecologist practicing in Sydney, Australia. He has been published in professional journals but this is his first work of fiction. *The Company of the Dead* is the winner of two prestigious Aurealis Awards for Best Science Fiction Novel and Best Novel. He is currently working on his second novel.

www.thecompanyofthedead.com
www.djkowalski.com